THE FALL LINE

A Tale of Old Jamestown

by

Errol Burland

DORRANCE PUBLISHING CO., INC.
PITTSBURGH, PENNSYLVANIA 15222

ISBN-10: 0-8059-7193-9
ISBN-13: 978-0-8059-7193-4

Printed in the United States of America

First Printing

For more information or to order additional books, please contact:
Dorrance Publishing Co., Inc.
701 Smithfield Street
Third Floor
Pittsburgh, Pennsylvania 15222-3906
U.S.A.
1-800-788-7654
www.dorrancebookstore.com

Certainly virtue is like precious odors,
most fragrant when they are incensed or crushed:
for prosperity doth best discover vice,
but adversity doth best discover virtue.

Sir Francis Bacon, *Of Adversity*

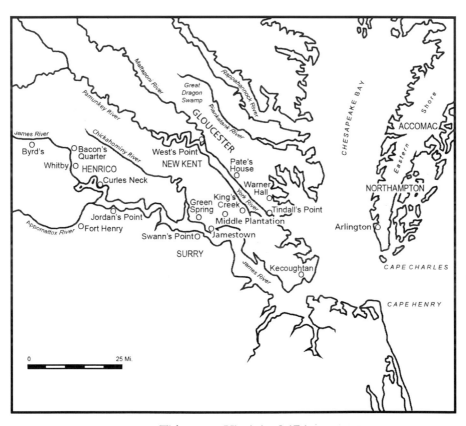

Tidewater, Virginia, 1676

Dramatis Personae

(Historical characters are in regular type; fictional characters are in italic type).

England

The Bacons of Friston Hall

Squire Thomas Bacon, ("The Squire")
Elizabeth Brooke Bacon, his wife, (deceased)
Elizabeth Bacon, their daughter, ("Bess")
Nathaniel Bacon, their son, ("Nat")

The Dukes of Benhall Lodge

Sir Edward Duke
Lady Catherine Holland Duke, his first wife, (deceased)
Jane Duke Wyatt, their oldest daughter
John Duke, their only son and heir
Alathea Duke, their youngest daughter
Lady Elinor Panton Duke, Sir Edward's second wife
Elizabeth Duke, their daughter, ("Lyn")

Others

Sir John Berkeley, Baron Stratton, brother of Sir William Berkeley
Sir John Berry, a sea captain and Royal Commissioner
Henry Bokenham, a wastrel
Robert Brooke, an attorney
Farley, the tenant of Hinton Hall Farm

John Grey, an attorney
Herbert Jeffries, Lieutenant Governor of Virginia and Royal Commissioner
Offley Jenney, a Suffolk gentleman of ancient lineage
Francis Moryson, a Virginia planter, diplomat and Royal Commissioner
John Ray, a clergyman and botanist; tutor to Nat Bacon
Samuel Wiseman, secretary to the Royal Commissioners
Henry Wyatt, a gentleman, married to Jane Duke

Servants

Jemmy, Squire Bacon's hostler
Job, son of Sir Edward Duke's housekeeper Rose
Martin, Lyn's governess
Preston, Squire Bacon's major domo
Rose, Sir Edward Duke's housekeeper
Rosie, Rose's daughter, a Benhall village cottager

Virginia

Sir William Berkeley, Royal Governor of Virginia
Lady Frances Culpeper Berkeley, his wife
Thomas Ludwell, a gentleman and planter; Secretary of State of Virginia
Philip Ludwell, his brother; a gentleman and planter; Deputy Secretary of
    State of Virginia

Council of State

Colonel Nathaniel Bacon of King's Creek, York County; a gentleman and
    planter; first cousin to Squire Thomas Bacon of Friston Hall
Elizabeth Kingsmill Bacon, his wife
Thomas Ballard of James City County, a gentleman and planter
Ann Ballard, his wife
James Bray of James City County, a gentleman and planter
Joseph Bridger of Whitemarsh, Isle of Wight County, a gentleman and
    planter
Sir Henry Chicheley of Rosegill, Lancaster County, a knight and planter
William Cole of Baltrope, Warwick County, a gentleman and planter
John Page of James City County, a gentleman and planter
Alice Page, his wife
John Pate of Gloucester County, a gentleman and planter
Thomas Swann of Swann's Point, Surry County, a gentleman and planter
Augustine Warner of Warner Hall, Gloucester County, a gentleman and
    planter

House of Burgesses

Thomas Godwin, Speaker of the House
Thomas Mathew of Cherry Point, Northumberland County, a merchant
    and planter
Dorothy Mathew, his wife

Planters, Settlers, Soldiers and Others

Anthony Arnold, a Captain in Bacon's Army
Major Robert Beverley, a planter and soldier
Giles Bland of Westover, Charles City County; Commissioner of Customs
William Byrd, Henrico County, a gentleman, planter and Indian trader
Mary Horsmandan Byrd, his wife
William Byrd II, their infant son
James Crewes of Turkey Island, Henrico County, a planter and Captain in
    Bacon's Army
John Custis of Arlington, Accomac County, a merchant and planter of the
    Eastern Shore
William Drummond of James City County, a merchant and planter; former
    Governor of Albemarle County, Carolina
Sarah Drummond, his wife
Billy and Johnny Drummond, their sons
George Farlow, a Captain in Bacon's Army
John Goode of Whitby, Henrico County, a planter
Thomas Hansford, a Captain in Bacon's Army
Robert Hen, Thomas Mathew's swineherd
Robbie Hen, his son
Ingram, a soldier of fortune
Henry Isham of Doggams, Charles City County, a planter
Thomas Jervis of Fairview, Elizabeth City County, a planter, merchant and
    sea captain
Agatha Jervis, his wife (deceased)
Richard Lawrence of James City County, an innkeeper
Pierce of Stafford County, Thomas Mathew's overseer
Rachel Pierce, his wife
Samuel Swann of Swann's Point, Surry County, son of Councilor Thomas
    Swann
Sarah Drummond Swann, his wife

Servants and Slaves

Abraham and Hannah, house slaves at Curles Neck

Clarissa, maid at *The Unicorn*
Jacob Hartwell, overseer at Bacon's Quarter
Martha Hartwell, his wife
Jake Hartwell, his son
Pitts, caretaker of the Jamestown Statehouse and jailer

Sea Captains

Captain William Carver, retired
Captain Gardiner of the *Adam and Eve*
Captain Grantham of the *Concord*
Captain Larrimore of the *Rebecca*, later the *Loyall Rebecca*
Captain Morris of the *Young Prince*
Captain Prinne of the *Richard and Elizabeth*

Indians

Cockacoeske, Queen of the Pamunkeys
One Ear, an Occaneechee brave, nephew to Rossechy
Rossechy, King of the Occaneechees
Squirrel, nephew to Cockacoeske

Horses

Blue, the Hartwells' blue roan
Coke, John Grey's chestnut gelding
Fancy, Lady Elinor Duke's chestnut mare
Folly, Nat Bacon's black war horse (Virginia)
Lark, Lyn's bay pony
Mignon, Lyn's dappled gray mare
Prince Rupert, Nat Bacon's black stallion (England)

CHAPTER 1

JULY 1660

She knew it was a sin, but venial, not mortal, and therefore surely worth the risk. The sun rode high, pushing back the jutting brow of Benhall Lodge to the east and the gloom of Dod's Wood to the north. Silverlace Green danced before her – she could almost swim in its verdure. With quivering nostrils she absorbed the grass scent as a bee sucks nectar. She circled and circled on the greensward, her arms outstretched and her cotton smock puffed out like a kite. Eyes tight shut, she turned until a love ly dizziness seized her and she had no sense of up or down or even whether she was still bound to earth. Perhaps she had become a small, free-floating moon. She let herself go, wholly, and fell with ardor to the grass, pressing her cheek gratefully to the springing blades which still held a hint of dawn's freshness. Her eyes still closed, she inhaled the green scent of summer and then, wasted, rolled over and lay supine, stricken with joy.

As the dizziness passed, she slitted her eyes and admitted the blue of the noon sky. Slowly, slowly she opened her eyes wide and let the great Suffolk cloudscape become a part of her. A lark called from the north field and her heart turned over. The world stopped and the moment was set in her memory like a jewel in a monstrance.

Stone crushed stone as footsteps trod the gravel walk. The child turned her head slightly and glanced from the corner of her eye, her heart beating fast. Would she pay for her ecstasy? The steps were too light for Father or John, but too heavy for Mother who was, in any event, in childbed. Pray God it was one of Rose's maids come to call her to dinner. Pray God it was not Alathea. The crunch of gravel became a snake hiss as the walker reached the grass. The child opened her eyes wider. Now she could see the familiar ugly thickness of the soles of her sister's boots and the swinging hem of the yellow cotton gown the older girl had worn at breakfast. A shadow fell across the child's face and she reluctantly pulled herself up and tucked her skirts around her knees and squinted up at the newcomer's stolid form and pale, expressionless face. The deep set eyes were lightless, like currants in dough. They were her father's eyes. Father and Alathea, formed in the same thick mold, the male obverse and the female reverse of the same coin. The lark trilled again but the magic was gone and the bird's song went disregarded. Slowly the child rose to her feet and brushed her frock. She stared at Alathea. Silence lay thick as congealed blood as the swords of their several wills clashed. Finally the larger girl laughed coldly and spoke.

"What a slut it is, lying in the grass like a toad. Did you show everything you have to the villagers as you twirled about like a mad thing? You know Father can see you from his library. You court it, do you not, just like your mother, even though you are not yet a woman. How many times has the Welsh witch coaxed Father to fill her up? But God has intervened ... you're the only one she's carried to term. The Devil must drive her. She's insatiable ... she won't stop. Or at least she won't stop until she produces a boy. Perhaps then she'll leave Father alone and slake herself with other midnight lovers." Alathea backed slowly from the child, laughing. "Succubus, succubus, succubus." The large girl liquefied the word indecently. She adjusted her shoulders and, both hands on the small of her back, thrust out her capacious breasts. "Father says come to dinner. Now." Turning, the girl stomped back to the Lodge, rolling her hips in derision.

"Fat cow," muttered the child. This was a sharper attack than usual. Normally she passed beneath the notice of Sir Edward Duke and his second, and favorite, daughter, but ever since her mother had taken to her bed earlier in the week Alathea had sought every means to make her life miserable. The child straightened her hem and peered over her shoulder, hoping that no telltale grass stains marred the fabric. She pulled up her stockings and ran a moist palm over the toes of her boots and, as soon as she heard the slam of the great oak door, followed Alathea up the path, lost in thought.

John says to ignore her ... she's jealous of Mother and the new baby. John the peacemaker. He said he'd ride with me all the way to Snape Priory this afternoon, if it was not too hot. Perhaps I can ask him what a "succubus" is. It doesn't sound very pleasant. Mother calls him ... what? A "sycophant." Is that like a "succubus"?

As she followed the sun-warmed gravel path to the lodge, the child wondered if, as her mother claimed, her half-brother was a fair weather friend. Still, beggars could not be choosers. Of her three half-siblings he alone had stood by her, shielding her on the one hand from the icy gusts of Jane's superiority and on the other hand from the smoldering lava of Alathea's malice. A little king, Sir Edward Duke ruled his household with a rod of iron and John was Sir Edward's crown prince and must be obeyed. It was the natural order of things. But perhaps, in his case, he had earned his youngest sister's fealty.

2

John was waiting for the child in the great hall. As her eyes adjusted to the interior gloom she glanced up at his bland face with trepidation. John had the Dukes' pale, waxy coloring, but his hair was lighter than Sir Edward's and Alathea's mud brown and now, in full summer, it was streaked with straw color. Try though he might, he could never get it to curl and today, as usual, it fell straight to his shoulders like a flight of arrows. Like Jane, he had the first Lady Duke's light blue eyes, pale as a spring sky. Normally his face was guarded and expressionless, but the child knew that, away from the shadow of Benhall Lodge, he could bubble with laughter like a springing fountain. Away from Father, his face could flood with color and his charm could float to the surface like a speckled trout from the depths of a murky pond.

Perhaps, thought the child, she could coax the hidden John to the surface today. In a flood of warmth, she rushed at him and hugged him close. Stilling a smile, John frowned his disapproval at his half-sister's disheveled condition and ordered her upstairs to wash, double time, while he waited on Sir Edward. Having given the child her instructions, the Duke son and heir wheeled and left the cool darkness of the old hall for the new southern cross-wing where the modest Elizabethan solar had been converted into a great staircase which led to the expansive modern bedchambers above. Turning right at the stairwell, he crossed the passage, paused at the stout oak door of Sir Edward's library, and raised his hand to knock. It was his father's custom to ride out every morning to survey his acres and instruct the laborers and cottagers. Upon his return he retired to his library and, almost without exception, John visited him there at half past noon to discuss business before dinner. The meeting was as much a part of John's day as morning and evening prayers. God owned his thoughts upon waking and upon retiring, but at all other times he belonged to his father. Indeed, the young squire would have been hard pressed to distinguish Sir Edward Duke from his divine Maker, so closely were the two aligned in his unconscious mind. Without noticing that the child had remained in the old hall, John simultaneously knocked on the oak with his right hand and lifted the latch with his left in a gesture so familiar that he performed it without thinking.

The child paused by the great fireplace, quite alone. She heard kitchen sounds from behind the screen hall to the north, but the great oak table had not yet been set. She judged that she had as much as half an hour before dinner and, as she could wash and change in five minutes and nobody but her mother would know the difference, she had some leisure to look about her. Slipping off her boots, she clambered onto one of the fireside settles and peered closely at the pargeting over the mantel. She never ceased to wonder at the delicate plaster tracery which, wordlessly, set forth her family history. Edward Duke, her great-grandfather, had built the house during the reign of the mighty Elizabeth. In his pride he had caused to be placed, on the left, the Duke arms, and on the right, the arms of his lady, Dorothy Jermyn, daughter of a knight of Rushbrook. The child's grandfather Ambrose, (whom she had never known), had wed an Elizabeth, (for whom the child was named), and left children, of whom the oldest and mightiest and richest and most favored was her own father, Sir Edward Duke. When Sir Edward inherited, (when? she could never remember), he had made all those changes to the house which her mother despised, but he had left the coats of arms intact. Indeed, they had been recently painted and looked as fresh as they might have when they were created almost a century ago. Although she was learning history and heraldry at her mother's knee, she had not mastered the Jermyn part, and she could not recall the meaning of the blazons and emblems on their shield. But how she loved the Duke coat of arms: a bright blue field, slashed with a chevron, on which were placed three charming brents with silver beaks and red feet. If she stretched to her utmost she could reach the red feet of the nearest brent and she touched it quickly and then shrank back, for she was absolutely forbidden to play about the mantel piece. She thought she could remember the list of sea fowl from John's book. She clambered down from the settle and, seeing herself still unobserved, took a few turns on the hearth and then, standing solemnly before the fireplace, hands behind her back, addressed the three red-footed brents.

"*Seapies, coots, pewits, curlews, teal, widgeon, brents, duck, mallard, wild goose, heron, crane, and barnacle.* There you are, my dears. You are named among the sea fowl and I love you. Now goodbye, I must run upstairs." And she turned and did just that.

The child reached the broad landing and, glancing left, found with relief that the door to Alathea's suite was closed fast. A quick look west showed her the open door of Jane's chambers which stood always in readiness for Sir Edward's oldest daughter who had brought such honor to the family by that fine, if unexpected, marriage to Henry Wyatt of Kent. Jane rarely visited Suffolk, but nobody was permitted to use her elegant rooms, which were cleaned and aired as regularly as though she lived there. As always, the child admired the soft blue of the bed hangings which were embroidered with summer flowers, from the humble daisy to the soft pink rose. Although Jane had done much of the needlework, Lady Duke herself had done most of it. The child knew, instinctively, that her mother took her role as stepmother to Jane, John and Alathea as seriously as she took her role of mother. But she also knew, in her heart, that Lady Duke saved her best love for her own child. She moved quickly down the west facing passage which paralleled the great bed chamber suite of Sir Edward and Lady Duke. One of the casements had swung open and she glimpsed the emerald sheen of Silverlace Green winking in the noon sun. She longed to knock upon her mother's door to ask after her health, but now she had surely used

4

up all her time and she must hurry to her room. Yet as she passed the great oak door it swung open and Elinor Duke stood there, a hand on each jamb supporting the huge weight of her pendant belly. The beloved face was gaunt and creased with pain, but the gentle lips smiled as they always did on this beloved only child.

"Mother, mother! Did I wake you? I am so sorry; I was running to my room because I am late to change for dinner."

The child rushed to her mother and threw her arms around that cherished being and the babe that lay within. She was supposed to love this little brother, (it was not allowed to be a sister), but she had never found it in herself to do so. In her secret heart she thought the babe-to-be an enemy who, like a thief, was stealing her mother's health and happiness.

Lady Duke stroked the child's wild curls and leaned down and kissed the top of her head. "You did not wake me, Lyn. It is rare now that I really sleep, nor will I until the babe is born. But please God that will be soon and all will be more normal and pleasant. I wanted to catch you before dinner to tell you that I will not be down. What little I can stomach they will bring me on a tray. You must know that the midwife arrives this evening and after she comes I will not leave my room until the happy event is over. I need to spend a little time with you after dinner to tell you some things. And after that John has promised to take you for a ride; isn't that splendid of him?"

The child responded to the unspoken message in Lady Duke's words, the plea for normalcy. She swept her growing apprehension about her mother under a false brightness, like dust under a rug, and hugged Elinor anew.

"I shall come up right after dinner. But now I must run or I will be late and Father will be furious. If we have cherries I'll bring you some."

Elinor smiled. "Yes, Lyn, bring me some cherries," she said softly and watched the girl run down the hall, black curls dancing on her slight shoulders. A great fear gripped Lady Duke as if a mighty hand had seized and wrung her heart and she pushed the old oak door until the lock clicked sharply and turned to her bed where she dropped like a stone.

Even her father's presence at dinner could not dampen the child's spirits. The midwife was coming this very day and surely her mother's health would improve then. Once this annoying baby arrived Elinor would be as light afoot as she had always been. Mother and daughter could resume their rides, Lady Duke on Fancy, the bright chestnut mare with mane and tail the color of sunlight, and the child on her new pony, Lark, a dark bay that looked as though it had been toasted too well around the edges.

The child pushed her duck under her French beans and smiled to herself. Lyn and Lark: it was one of the secrets she shared with her mother. She had been christened Elizabeth for her grandmother, Ambrose's wife; and also, she was told, for the great queen during whose reign the foundation of the Duke fortune had been laid. Sir Edward had insisted on the name, and he always used it, in its full resonant glory. But as a stream finds its way around a boulder and follows its own willful course, Elinor Panton Duke, a Welsh heiress sold into a loveless marriage, circumvented her husband in this, as in many things. From the moment that she saw her own violet eyes mirrored in the pool of her daughter's timeless blue gaze she named her babe Lyn, or "lovely lake," and claimed her for her own. The battle of the child's name had been joined in November of 1650 and continued now, almost ten years later. To the Dukes and the rest of the Suffolk gentry the child was "Elizabeth." To Elinor Panton, the Welsh witch, and to most of the servants and cottagers, she was "Lyn." When the pony arrived, mother and daughter compounded the crime. Only they knew that the name "Lark" derived, not from the songbird, but from the Suffolk river which, with the Linnet, flowed into the Alde which bordered the Duke holdings. "Linnet and Lark" … "Lyn and Lark." Dear Mother. She had bound the names with a spell; a little magic would survive in Suffolk. Thus, Elinor had whispered to her daughter, did the Welsh trick their English overlords. There was more than one road to mastery.

Lyn crumbled her bread and glanced at her father, relieved to find that he was in close conversation with Alathea and had not noticed her daydreaming. She felt John's right elbow in her left side. With only four of them at table – Sir Edward at the head, John to his right, Lyn to John's right, and Alathea across from them, there was no room for error. She must sit up straight, pay attention to her father, not speak unless spoken to, and eat everything on her plate. The prospect was daunting. Sir Edward paid no heed to climate, whether natural or familial. Hot or cold, summer or winter, in sickness or in health Dukes ate three courses for dinner unless they lay abed under a physician's orders. Anything less showed an unseemly weakness. Dukes were not weak; they prevailed in all things. But, Welsh minx that she was, Lyn had found her way into the hearts of the serving maids and it took only a tip of the head or a wink to instruct them to give her more or less of any item, so that, at least in this way, she controlled her father's rule. Today her stomach churned with anxiety for her mother and anticipation over her ride with John. The healthy appetite she had felt on Silverlace Green had fled and she poked desperately at her viands, hoping they would disappear. With Sir Edward still locked in conversation with Alathea, John quickly took Lyn's plate, slid the contents onto his, and dispatched them instantly. Lyn smiled in appreciation and brought a keener appetite to the dessert course of fruit and cheese, so that when Sir Edward addressed her she was sitting up properly and doing her duty by her meal and was able to attend as a true Duke should.

"I have given Alathea permission to rest this afternoon, in this unpleasant heat. What are your plans, Elizabeth? Will you practice on your harp or work on your drawing?"

"If you please, sir, my mother has requested my attendance after dinner and then I believe that John is going to take me riding."

The ever present furrows in the creamy brow deepened.

"How is this? When did you speak to your mother? You know she is not well."

"Yes, sir, but on my way to change for dinner she stopped me in the hall and told me that she had some things to say before I rode out and before the midwife came."

There was a cold silence. Sir Edward could not gainsay his Lady's request to talk with her own child; but he was not pleased.

"Well, see that you do not tire her. Her time has come. It is true that the midwife arrives this evening from Brampton and soon I hope that you will be able to greet your little brother. Lady Duke's wishes must be complied with. But what is this about riding with John? Is this a proper day for such frivolity?"

Lyn steeled herself for a stout reply, but fortunately John intervened, with his soothing tenor which honeyed all discord.

"The suggestion came neither from Elizabeth nor from me, sir. Lady Duke requested my attendance this morning and, after a careful inquiry about your health, asked if I had the time to exercise her mare and give Elizabeth another lesson on Lark. It has been a month since either animal has been farther than the pasture and she felt badly that the child's riding had been interrupted so soon after the creature arrived." John cleared his throat. "I believe she also had in mind that it would be a kindness to distract my sister, given the circumstances. She was concerned that the child not fret herself about the coming blessed event."

Alathea snorted, but then caught herself as her father's cold eye wandered her way. The creamy brow creased further and the silence was prolonged. Sir Edward raised his goblet and finished his wine and carefully aligned the vessel with the pewter dishes and the soft silver utensils which glowed in the dim light.

"Today Lady Duke's wishes shall be followed in every respect. But it would have been more seemly for you to have brought these issues to me for my disposition. When I get a moment I will cast up a schedule of Elizabeth's activities and I will certainly include her riding. It will likely be some months before Lady Duke will be able to instruct her daughter again."

Sir Edward rose, as did his three children. Bowing slightly to them, he left the old hall and sought the quiet of his library. Alathea followed on his footsteps and made her way up the great staircase to her chamber. John looked down at a somber Lyn and smiled and winked.

"There, Lyn, that was not so bad, was it? Father has a stern way about him but he is always just. Run up to visit your mother and then meet me at the stables at three o'clock sharp. I will have Lark and Fancy ready to go. Run along now."

Lyn threw her arms around John's slim waist and leaped up the stairs like a deer to the comfort of her mother's arms.

The great oak door was slightly ajar and the child slipped through it and pushed hard with her back until she heard the snick of the lock. The east-facing room was dim as the sun was past the meridian. The casements had been thrown open to catch the gentle breeze which stirred the creamy muslin summer curtains and the pale green bed hangings with their embroidered latticework of vines and fruit. Elinor lay propped up on the great bolsters, her face as pale as the linen. She smiled and signaled Lyn to climb upon the bed and snuggle down beside her. The two lay in blissful silence for a few minutes as Lady Duke stroked her daughter's hair. She pondered how to say what she had to say without unduly alarming the child. Before she could order her thoughts Lyn sat up straight, her hand to her mouth.

"Oh, mother, we had cherries and I forgot to bring you some. I am so careless."

"Nay, love, do not be distressed. I want nothing to eat, but I have an endless thirst. Bring me a glass of water and then I must tell you some things which I have been shamelessly deferring."

Lyn approached the set of Venetian glassware with trepidation and ever so carefully poured a goblet full of crystal well-water from the stately ewer. Holding it with both hands, she placed it on her mother's bedside table and resumed her position against the soft linen of the bolsters. Lady Duke drank gratefully and began to speak.

"Lyn, you are old enough to know something of how children come into the world. When I knew that I was going to bear this child I told you all that I thought was fitting and you showed a good understanding. Do you have any questions for me now?"

"Oh no, mother. I have seen the ewes swell and the lambs come in the spring. And I remember when Fancy gave birth to the colt which died, and you said she should not be forced to bear another. You said that the fattening and the babes – it was God's way of providing for us and that later I would learn more, when it was time to marry, but I think I understand everything."

Lady Duke smiled at Lyn's naiveté. Would that her child could always remain so innocent, but life did not permit that, even to those who fled to the cloister. They were not more holy; they were just hiding their faces behind their hands. She continued.

"I am glad you remember Fancy and the colt, as you can see that God does not always want the babe to be born, but sometimes calls it home before it spends any time on earth. It is for God's greater glory, but it brings terrible pain to the mother. Now you need to know that what happened to Fancy happened also to me."

Lyn sat up and looked alarmed but Elinor went steadily on. "As you know I married your father in 1647, two years after Catherine Holland passed on following Alathea's birth. You also know full well that you were born in 1650 (and have been my treasure for almost ten years now). But what you do not know is that before you came I might have had another babe, a little son." Elinor's gaze shifted to the casements, seeking the light. "We had not decided whether to call him Edward for his father or Ambrose for his grandfather when he slipped away. He did not live two days and, though it is twelve years ago, I feel the pain still."

Lyn was silent, her mouth an "O." She could not believe that there had been a forerunner — a child who could have been as loved as she by Elinor.

Her mother continued. "There is more, my linnet. After we were blessed with you, twice more I might have given Sir Edward a son and you a brother, and yet two more babes slipped through my fingers and were called to God. If you look back you may remember my sometime 'illnesses' and put those memories together with what I am telling you now and much will become clear."

Indeed the pieces of the mosaic fell into place for Lyn and the design became clear. She particularly remembered her mother's strange illness two years ago, and the unusual hush surrounding it. She had taken her one and only trip to London then, spending several months in the Wyatts' elegantly uncomfortable town house, sandwiched between the twin plagues of Jane and Alathea. John had stayed at Benhall and when the family was together again all seemed as before, except that the furrows on Sir Edward's brow were deeper and the Lodge seemed darker and wholly empty of joy.

Elinor scrutinized the heart-shaped face with the broad brow, the deep blue eyes lushly fringed with black lashes, the perfect nose and the delicate chin surmounted by lips so soft that they might have been bruised by the wind. It was her own face – her Welsh face. This child had not only been a part of her for nine long months but was a part of her still and would ever be so as long as they both drew breath.

"You see it, don't you, Lyn? Now go to my dressing table and bring me the silver box you are always asking about." The child did so. "Open the box." Lyn carefully lifted the soft, glossy silver lid and saw within a piece of fine lace and some rose petals for scent. "Now open the lace." With trembling hand, the child obeyed. "See those three locks of hair? All dark, like yours, though none so beautiful. That is all that remains on earth of my little boys; they are waiting for me in heaven."

Lyn stroked the fine down gently. Each lock was bound with a blue ribbon. And amazingly each tiny memento was a different shade of black, though, it was true, none so dark as her own mane, which shone with blue lights. She was still speechless. She might have had three brothers, had God willed it so. And immediately she wondered if it had been so, would the furrows on Sir Edward's brow have been less marked and the ice in his voice less piercing?

Elinor smiled. "Do not cry, Lyn. It is the way of the world, and it has nothing to do with you, except that you would have loved your brothers as much as I. Just as Fancy still carries me gaily though she lost her colt, I too have much to live for, and perhaps this time a little brother will care to stay awhile and keep us company."

Lyn's face smoothed as she thought of the future. It was true; the three little boys were angels in heaven, but the fourth might be a playmate for years to come.

"Now, my dear, put away the box for I fear that I have more to tell you. You should know that it sometimes happens that not only the babe declines to stay in the world, but that the mother is too weary to linger as well." Elinor's face seemed to shrink as she said those words. Lyn's heart jumped in her breast. What was coming next?

"After your birth, each time I bred it seemed to go increasingly harder with me. I was very ill the last time; that is why you had to stay in London so long. And this babe has not sat well with me, though I have striven not to show it." Elinor sighed and turned her head to the windows again, seeking the breeze, but the afternoon lay still as glass. "My child, you are not to be alarmed for I trust in a few days we will be blessed with a brother for you and renewed health for me, but still there is a chance that either or both of us will be called to go, and that I will not be here to see you become a woman."

Lyn could sustain her silence no longer. The growing flood of feelings burst out and she flung herself upon her mother and let the tears flow. Great gulps and sobs broke from her as the gentle hands stroked her again and again and the gentle voice fell like rain to sooth her anguish.

"My child, it is as I feared. You are too young and tender for this. I should have laid the groundwork slowly, but in truth I did not have the courage to wound you. Now I have put this great load upon you and it is too much to bear. I fault myself; 'tis a grievous error."

Lyn's grief subsided somewhat and she clung to her mother as the quiet of the afternoon once more enveloped them. Elinor continued.

"Now, child, I have more to say, and you must grow up in leaps and bounds to hear this and to pay heed. I am now talking to a great girl, to a real lady. Should God take me to join my little boys you must know that at all times I will be looking down on you with love. You will always have a part of me to guide you on your path to womanhood. But that path will be stony, as it is for all mankind. It is a poor gift, but I am going to try and give you some signposts to assist you on your way. Now listen closely, for I am at the end of my strength and I will not be able to repeat these words. First, you must know the honest truth that there has never been a proper love between your father and me – sometimes a sort of regard, but often not always that.

You have felt and known this, I am sure. Such things cannot be hidden. If I go your care will fall to Sir Edward and for that reason I charge you here and now to do as I say. Obey him in all things small, for if you oppose him he will crush you like the corn between the stones. But in all great things, above all in your choice of a husband, follow your own heart even if you must defy his will. I am living proof that when a woman is given away like chattel it is the death of her soul." Elinor sat up and took Lyn by the shoulders. "Look at me Lyn, and swear. Remember my words. You need not swear on the good book, but take your oath on the love that is between us, for it is the strongest thing I know. Say after me that you will be obedient to your father in the small things, but in the great things you will be your own woman."

Lyn stared into those eyes which were mirrors of her own, and the oath was taken.

Elinor sat back, exhausted. "Now, child, I have only a few more things to say. To my sorrow I have no family to which you could turn in trouble. As you know I was the only child of parents who died when I was small and who placed me with a guardian who shed his duty as soon as the opportunity arose. Nor is there anyone in the Duke family to whom I could gladly entrust you. But among your three siblings there is some hope. Remember my words. Despite her proud demeanor, Jane will do her duty by you, and that is more than I can say of most. John will be your friend, but only in fair weather; he does not have the strength to stand up to his father. And Alathea is, without doubt, your enemy. Never trust her and always watch her." Elinor leaned back and touched her daughter's cheek. "Pray God that your path is sunny and that you can store these words like old garments in a chest and never bring them out for use. But should things go badly let your heart be your guide."

Lyn leaned forward and stroked her mother's brow.

"I swear it mother. I will not forget."

Lady Duke gasped and reached once more for the Venetian goblet. Lyn slipped from the bed and ran to help her.

"I would that I had not had to place this burden on you, Lyn, but it is a mother's duty. Now go out into the sunshine and ride for me as well as for yourself. With John on Fancy and with you on Lark it will be almost as though we are together. I know he has a secret planned for you, so go with joy and put what we have said behind you. Always know that my love will never leave you."

Silently, Lyn kissed the soft cheek and turned to the door.

John idled in the stable yard, secretly pleased to be alone in the summer sun, with no greater duty calling than escorting his little sister on a pony ride. The tiniest breeze caressed his cheek and the doves in the cote above the great stable door bobbed and cooed in tender conversation. The straw which littered the yard shone like gold and a sweet-spicy scent wafted over the stone wall from the herb garden which lay to the east of the house, next to what remained of Lady Duke's lawns, parterres and borders. She had been ailing since winter and the gardens had languished, as she was the only one who gave them any thought and care. John heard the jingle of harnesses as the stable lads prepared Fancy and Lark for their ride. He pried a pebble from the wall and tossed it from hand to hand, gazing at the unkempt lawn. A lizard eyed him with a cold, reptilian gaze, flicked its tongue, and scurried between the rough-hewn stones. His thoughts stayed with Elinor Duke. A gentle lady, and one who had been ever kind to him, but she had a depth of reserve which prevented her, for as long as he could remember, from being wholly present to any but her own child, Lyn. John mentally bit his tongue. "Lyn" always came to mind and he had to force "Elizabeth." Really, if you thought about it, the little push and pull about the child's name summed up his father's second marriage, a most imperfect union. Sir Edward's domination of his family was, to all appearances, complete, but there was a certain subterranean quality about Elinor and Lyn which seemed to take them beyond his power, not by prevailing in conflict, but by avoiding conflict altogether. He thought of his own mother, who had died when he was just a lad, but whose image he carried intact. She had been a matched pair with Sir Edward: strong, forceful and proud. The present Lady Duke suffered the yoke of marriage like the rack. He wondered where it would all end.

John tossed his pebble into the rosemary bushes, kicked the straw and frowned at the back of the house where the Lady lay, behind those casement windows, awaiting her fate. He was a more than competent draftsman, and his artist's eye took in the entire façade and, as usual, refashioned it. Sir Edward had poured Elinor's entire fortune into renovating the Tudor hall and although the changes provided the required space for a growing family the character of the old building had been destroyed. The crosswings, where the young Dukes had their suites, Jane and Alathea in the south and he and Lyn in the north, could be tolerated. But the reduction of the great hall to half its former glorious height in order to accommodate the sweep of the Lord's and Lady's chambers was as brutal as a beheading. Instead of rising nobly above its hillside site the lodge squatted and lowered as though angry at the indignity inflicted upon it. John sighed. Compared to the elegance of Glenham Park or to the comely symmetry of Friston Hall, Benhall Lodge was an oddity. Moreover, its situation was poor. It brooded over the river, but there was no river view, just an ugly steep rise from Benhall Street which brought you unceremoniously to the front door. The back, or eastern, façade was wholly undistinguished, marred by the stables and kennels and with a garden such as could be found at the meanest Suffolk farm. The northern prospect was cut off by the dank reaches of Dod's Wood and although the southern view had promise it had not been developed – the casements gave onto a humble mix of pasture and field bordered by ragged trees.

Now when he was master of Benhall…. John killed the thought before it had life. How wicked to let his mind wander to a time when his father would be no more. The young man mentally chastised himself and strode inside the stable to see if the horses were ready. As he entered the building's pleasant dimness the stable clock struck three. The lads were surprised when Mister John's honey voice had a bite to it – what had ruffled the young master?

Lyn fled to Lark as though she had hounds at her heels. Astonished, John lifted her up and settled her properly on her little side saddle. Trails of tears marked her face and John saw that he had his work cut out for him to bring joy to this afternoon. He supposed the child had been corrected by Lady Duke, which was all to the good. The tears would quickly dry in the glow of this perfect summer day; they needs must start soon.

The chestnut and the bay stood in companionable silence, heads down, in the vast skeleton of Snape Priory barn. The heat of the day had long passed and it was the magic hour between day and night when the earth rested, pausing briefly before donning the deep blue and silver of its evening garb. Seated by John, backs against an ancient pillar, Lyn sighed in perfect happiness. She counted the wonders of the afternoon. First they had seen the yellowlegs in the curve of the Alde, a bird whom she had not seen all spring and had supposed would not return to its nest. Then the family of water rats which she had watched growing to maturity had made a showing for John, shoving off from the muddy shore, a silver V trailing in the river water behind each sleek head. Then John had let her explore the ancient barn to her heart's content and had told her the whole history of Henry's dissolution of the religious houses and how Snape Priory had been burned to the ground long ago and the Black Monks left homeless and destitute. Nobody knew how the barn had escaped the King's wrath, but here it stood today, a timber skeleton as much, John said, as half a thousand years old. And finally, just as the westering sun dipped beneath the horizon, turning the Alde to gold, she had found the cunning squirrel's nest in the eastern-most wooden pillar of the barn and had carefully removed the soft down where the babies had lain in the spring before venturing into the forest. Now, as she and John sat together on the bare earth, backs to warm wood, she stroked the downy nest and thought of her mother. The new babe should have just such a home as this … she would see to it.

As the last rays of sun disappeared John's face was blanketed with shadow. He opened his eyes, stretched hugely and smiled down at Lyn. *What a charming companion his little sister had been*, he thought. *Clever in nature lore; still biddable, but very much her own person; and she promised to be as fair as Elinor Duke whose beauty his father had purchased as though choosing a precious stone.* But the pleasures of the afternoon had made him careless. Night had fallen and he would have to borrow a lantern from a cottager or they would be hard pressed to reach Benhall Lodge safely, even if they followed the familiar gentle curve of the river road.

John rose to his feet and pulled Lyn up with him. "Come, sweeting. Tuck the nest in Lark's saddlebag and let us start back. We'll beg a light at Tolliver's and be home for a very late supper. I daresay I'll have to answer to Father for not getting you back sooner, but we'll jump that hurdle when we reach it. Come along, up you go."

Lyn leaned down from Lark's saddle and kissed her brother's forehead. "This has been one of the best day's ever. Thank you, John."

"It has been my pleasure. Now, do we have everything? Follow me and we'll soon have a lantern to see us home."

They retraced their steps in the gloaming, Fancy and Lark pushing the pace as they sensed that their stable lay ahead. A ride of an hour and a quarter brought brother and sister to the junction where the Lodge's drive left Benhall Street and mounted steeply to the right. A three-quarter moon ensilvered the mansion's western front and the quarrels of the gallery casements sparkled in the cold light like jewels. The house frowned at them and John thought it odd that Sir Edward had failed to have the cressets lit. The great chimney stacks rose black against a sky of midnight blue; they too seemed lifeless. Perhaps Lady Duke had been brought to bed of the much-wanted son ... it was possible. If that were the case then even the Duke household might have lost its rudder, if only for a moment. It was a happy thought.

"Come child, there's nary a servant to help us with the horses, nor a light in the window. Let's take the stable lane. We'll act as our own grooms and then as our own kitchen maids. My stomach is cleaving to my backbone, it has been so long since dinner. As for you, I seem to remember eating your dinner as well as mine. You must be famished."

Nodding with fatigue, Lyn trailed John as he turned left towards Dod's Wood and then right onto the lane which skirted the Lodge's north cross-wing. Tolliver's lantern shone like a star and Fancy's bright tail caught the light and acted as a beacon. The stable lay as quiet as a tomb in the moon-light. John's heart caught. It was most odd that nobody was about; the silver silence was uncanny. He and Lyn entered the gaping mouth of the stable and he hung the lantern on a peg. Within seconds the riders had slipped saddles and bridles from their mounts and had led them to their loose boxes, unbrushed. The boxes were tidy, with water in the buckets and corn in the mangers. Suddenly, across from Lark's box, a pale head loomed like a death mask and a strange horse nickered, causing Lyn to jump.

"What's that beast, John? I've never seen it before."

"Why it must be the midwife's. I have heard that she rides about the country like a man, with nary an escort. Still, the women swear by her. Do you suppose...?"

"Oh John," Lyn cried. "Do you suppose the baby has come?"

Care sat on John's shoulder like a corbie. If the babe had arrived, why was Benhall Lodge shrouded in silence? Fires should be blazing, voices should be raised in song, servants should be gathered to welcome John and Lyn home. Latching the boxes, he seized Lyn by the shoulder and hustled her towards the kitchen wing, muttering "we'll soon find out."

Impatient with suspense, John shoved the kitchen door open without ceremony, Lyn behind him like a shadow. No fire blazed on the huge hearth; food and drink sat unattended on the sideboards, as though a ghostly hand had stilled the cook and the kitchen maids in mid-task. The housemaids, who should have been tidying the great hall and preparing the bedrooms for the night, were gathered together at one end of the massive trestle table where the housekeeper, Rose, sat like a hen with her chicks. The cook and the kitchen maids were huddled opposite and between the two groups sat a miscellany of stable lads and gardeners, heads bowed and expressions glum. The silence was profound.

John substituted anger for his true feeling, fear. "Rose, whatever are your people doing? Here we are, hot, tired, dusty and hungry from a long ride, and I find that we must light our own way, groom our own horses, and now, I suppose, find water to wash in and prepare our own supper."

The soft, full face of the housekeeper looked blankly back at him and then her eyes fell to her lap. The others cast their gazes down as well, as though at a church service. John cleared his throat to speak, but Lyn was before him.

"It's mother – is it my mother? Has something happened?"

Rose looked up, her face creased with care. She glanced at the other servants, but got no help from them.

"Master John, and little Mistress, didn't anybody tell you? Haven't you seen Sir Edward or your sister?"

John lashed out. "Would I be asking you these questions if we had? What has happened? Answer me or you'll be the worse for it?"

Rose nodded slowly and pushed the cane-bottomed chair back from the table. The scraping sound tore at Lyn's nerves. The housekeeper made her way to Lyn's side and looked down at her with sorrow.

"I regret being the one to tell you, Mistress Lyn, but the baby started this afternoon, and it did not go well. The midwife arrived an hour ago, too late to help. Just now Sir Edward called us together and told us that the Lady and the babe are no more. It would have been a little boy. God bless you, child, and God bless Lady Duke and the little one."

15

The world spun in a great gyre of flame and Lyn sank to the floor and her mind fled from the terrible words to darkness.

CHAPTER 2

AUGUST 1661

An honest sunbeam pierced the rose colored hangings and ruthlessly exposed the down on Alathea's upper lip. The girl frowned in annoyance and moved the looking glass into the shadow. Gazing steadily at her image, she adjusted, first her cap, and then the lace which she had tucked around the deep neckline of her bodice in order to soften the effect. She stroked the delicate white stuff and then let her hands slide downwards to the twin mounds below. Smiling, she traced each breast with a caressing finger and thought of her father.

True, she had initially been furious to be excluded from the trip to Whitehall to witness King Charles award Sir Edward the baronetcy which was the fruit of the Dukes' staunch support of the Stuarts in the late troubles. Jane, so well-connected and so mannerly, would be there with Henry and a whole passel of Wyatts. And John, the son and heir, would of course be front and center; there was talk of his securing a minor post with the Duke of York and the opportunity was too good to be missed. But she, of all the Dukes, was ordered to stay home. Well, naturally Elizabeth would remain in Suffolk as well, but that hardly counted. Alathea had not been assuaged in the least by Sir Edward's claim that he needed her at Benhall to keep the household in order and to prepare the great celebratory fete. But when the budding baronet had pressed the keys of the Lodge into her hands and whispered that his real motive in keeping her in Suffolk was to keep his most precious daughter from London eyes, her fury died. That she believed: that Sir Edward chose to keep his treasure locked up at home. In any event, it was not every sixteen year old girl who was entrusted with running a great house and she intended to make the most of it.

And had she not reaped a fine reward for her obedience? Within a week after Sir Edward and John left for London a cart had arrived bearing two lengths of silk and a length of velvet for her alone, together with the Flemish lace which lay under her hand at this very moment. Ten days after that a wagon had brought a treasure of food and drink: bottles of Bordeaux and sherry wine, great rounds of Dutch cheese, crystallized fruit from beyond the Alps, jars of cinnamon and mace, and fragrant Virginia tobacco in soft pouches of deerskin. And just yesterday the glorious painting had arrived, the one which, even now, hung in her anteroom. Alathea rose and moved swiftly across the bedchamber and into the little room which opened off the landing where she kept her prayer stool and her writing table.

There, in pride of place, was the lustrous oil which Sir Edward had bought from Master Lely himself. It had caught his eye, he wrote, during the first sitting for his own portrait and he had not been able to resist its purchase. Alathea drew her father's letter from the drawer of her writing table and caressed it, searching for one stirring sentence. There it was.... "If you set modesty aside, my dear," the baronet wrote, "you will see yourself in the central figure." The girl replaced the letter and, mesmerized, approached the painting and, with her finger-tip, slowly traced the outline of the glorious female nude who showed the world a luxurious expanse of back and hip and thigh as she reclined in a shower of gold. The woman's head was depicted in rapturously up-lifted profile, her dark, liquid eye fixated on a fall of gold coins which arced from an airy window to the cunning center of the work, the mysterious, hidden triangle which Venus called her own. Unthinking, Alathea stroked her own waist and hips. It was very like, even to the dark eye. But there was a difference. The luscious cone of Danae's breast was tipped with tender pink, whereas Alathea's twin mounds ended in dark bosses like miniature shields. Stirred, the big girl stepped away from the painting and slid her hand twixt bodice and skin. Drawing her neck back and casting her eyes down, she assessed her treasures. Yes, there she differed from the rapturous woman in whose lap tumbled an eternal fall of gold. Her breasts were not like the lips of kittens but like weapons, and she would use them so. In all other respects she agreed with her father: she and the Danae were one.

Hearing a heavy tread on the staircase, Alathea started and readjusted her lace. She walked boldly from her anteroom onto the landing and confronted Rose.

"Oh, bless me, Mistress! There you are," the housekeeper cried. "The cart is all packed and ready. They didn't know whether you were going to ride part of the way or be driven. Shall I tell them to saddle your horse nor not?"

"I'll take the cart. Give me five minutes and I'll gather my last things. Are you sure I shall be in Ipswich by noon tomorrow? I must be there when Father and the Wyatts arrive. Oh, and did you pack the preserved strawberries? You know that Jane loves them above all things."

"Yes and yes, Mistress. You won't be late and I have sent Lady Jane more berries than she will know what to with. Now, you'll spend the night in Ipswich and be here two days hence?"

"Yes, Rose, we'll be here Friday – Father, Jane, Henry and I. John decided at the last minute that he dare not risk offending the Duke by asking for leave so soon after getting his appointment. A pity he won't be here for the fete, but Father thinks he made the right decision. Now, everything is set for Saturday. Just follow my list and the whole thing will go like clockwork. Oh, and keep an eye on Elizabeth. I'm sure the child would find a way to disgrace us if she could."

Lyn's heart lifted as the rumble of Alathea's cart and the calls of her outriders disappeared in the distance. In all her ten years she had never been at Benhall Lodge without her family and the freedom was intoxicating. She reentered the great hall, grateful for its cool dimness, and hurried upstairs to shed her gown and slip into the comfortable, loose frock in which she did her gardening. In the year since her mother's death she had gradually claimed Elinor Panton's garden as her own, and thus far she had been given a free hand in this, her living memorial to her mother. Alathea threatened great changes when the mighty Jane arrived to, among other duties, advise Sir Edward on Lyn's education. But she had not been idle in the past year, not a bit of it. John had continued to instruct her in drawing and French and she loved her harp well enough to practice on her own, but change was in the air and she must make good use of her days of freedom.

Hurriedly Lyn shed her good skirt and bodice and donned her gardening smock, peeled off her silk stockings and replaced them with old cotton things which bagged around her slim legs, and stuffed her feet into her comfortable boots. She raced down the backstairs, stopped briefly in the kitchen to grab a fruit knife, crossed the flags of the little yard where the well stood, and gazed, with a critical eye, at Elinor's parterres. Sadly, all the roses had perished of neglect and she had had the bushes removed, for there was no bringing them back. In their stead she had planted hollyhock and gillyflower and bright star-like feverfew and all the humble things which the cottagers would give her. Against the north wall, which bordered the stable lane, she had improved on her mother's herb garden, and here she had her greatest triumph. In the sun trap formed by the rosy bricks marjoram, rue, rosemary and thyme grew in abundance; and in the shady corner near the well green mint flavored the air with its sweet spice. Hands on hips, Lyn eyed the bright profusion of her garden and chose the feverfew as the best gift for her mother. Fetching a twist of embroidery silk from her pocket, she culled four of her best blooms with the fruit knife and bound them together in a happy, informal bouquet. She dashed back to the kitchen to replace the knife and before Rose could interdict her, called out that she was riding Lark to Benhall St. Mary's and would be back for dinner.

The sun rode high as Lyn crossed the lane and she lingered briefly in the cool, aromatic stable before catching a hackamore from its peg and leaving through the north door. She climbed the bank to the pasture where Lark stood in a shady corner, rhythmically switching his tail to keep off the flies. He looked sullen at his mistress' approach, but made no effort to avoid her as she slipped the harness over his dark head and swung up on his broad back, flowers in hand. The village was quiet as Lyn and Lark traversed it; the men were still in the fields and the women were inside, starting to prepare dinner.

Five minutes later the girl and the pony had left the last cottage behind and reached the top of the rise which gave onto a sweeping vista of field and farm as far as the eye could see. To the right the Alde curved gently as far as Snape Bridge where its clean line became smudged in the broad expanse of the estuary. A stand of old oak marked the Priory barn, though its ancient skeleton was shrouded in green and not visible. Lyn thought of her fateful ride with John and unconsciously tightened her grip on the flowers which emitted that astringent scent which she thought of as "green." To the east the patchwork of Benhall's fields spilled down the slope and ended at the edge of an unexpected and uncharacteristic wilderness. They said that Squire Bacon kept his fields fallow so that his boy could hunt right in his backyard. Young Bacon ... the wild one who looked so like his mother. In the far distance Suffolk sea and Suffolk sky melded in a gray-blue haze. And beyond that were worlds unknown, worlds where doubtless she would never set foot.

Lyn sighed and collected her thoughts. Kicking Lark's stout sides, she urged the pony downhill, to the right, where Benhall St. Mary's nestled in a green cup of land, its flint walls taking form and direction from a squat Norman tower. Beyond the church, on the southern slope, the graveyard lay, and in it her mother and the four little boys who had chosen life in heaven over life on earth. Lark knew the path well and within minutes he brought his mistress to the shade of the familiar oak which marked the south-east corner of the churchyard. Cloud-galleons sailed the high Suffolk sky, their pure white forms edged with silver and gray. Lyn sniffed the air; tonight it would rain. She slipped from Lark's back and hopped over the low stone wall to the modest row of four headstones which was all that remained of Elinor Panton and her hopes and dreams. Catherine Holland had a great sepulcher in the church itself, but Sir Edward Duke's second lady had given him neither obedience nor a son; she could lie outside for eternity. Lyn smiled coldly. It was better so. Her mother would have preferred this disposition over all others. The girl glanced at the angle of the sun. It must be noon, time to leave her offering and return to the Lodge. Slipping the thread from the flowers, Lyn gave each blossom a kiss and laid a single flower on each grave, sending her thoughts heavenward as she did so. She turned to leave but then, torn, she retraced her steps to her mother's grave and pressed her lips to the warm stone. The marble was already stained by the weather and stealthy lichens had claimed a foothold. Lyn wept to see that nature was covering the traces of her mother's days on earth and vowed that, in her memory at least, Elinor Panton would remain unstained and unchanged. Eyes blurred, the child untethered Lark and climbed onto his broad, warm back. As though witting of her pain, the pony rolled his great eyes and retraced his steps to Benhall Lodge with as much care as a figure in a pavane.

Friday arrived and with it the newly minted baronet, proud Jane Wyatt and her complaisant husband Henry, and triumphant Alathea, a gift of pearls clasped on her thick wrist. Sir Edward and his family had passed the night at Ufford and arrived home rested, fresh and eager for dinner. Within half an hour of their arrival all but the Wyatts had gathered in the great hall where the woodwork shone with beeswax and each quarrel of each casement glinted like a jewel. Sir Edward, in a new suit of tobacco brown with gold buttons, stood before the empty fireplace and rocked back and forth in his stiff boots, eyeing his domain. Alathea sat in Elinor Duke's chair, which she had made her own, smoothing the folds of her rose colored gown and adjusting her lace. The silky fabric and the pallid skin of the girl's neck and shoulders might be interchangeable, Lyn thought unkindly, but for the fact that the lace caught the sun and Alathea's flesh did not. Lyn began to fix the sops-of-wine which she had slipped into her sash but, frozen as usual in her father's presence, she abandoned the task and sat motionless on the fireside settle. She glanced surreptitiously at her cream colored frock which she had trimmed with brilliant green ribbons and hoped that it was grand enough for Jane. The new blue silk must be saved for tomorrow's fete and this was the best she could do, though the waist felt too high and the hem showed more stocking than it should. She must have grown a good bit in the two years since Elinor had made the gown; she had no other.

Suddenly the world came alive. A summer breeze wafted in from the garden and Jane Wyatt descended the great staircase in a striped confection, Henry behind her, brave in burgundy. Rose, who had been eagerly watching from the screen passage, bustled in with glasses of sherry followed by a maid with savories.

"My goodness, Rose, only think, you don't look a day older!" cried Lady Wyatt as she swept into the hall. "Come Henry, where are you? Don't dawdle; the whole family is waiting for you. Goodness, Father, you look somber. I hope you have something brighter to wear tomorrow. Alathea, stand up love, and let me look at you. You *will* wear rose, but it isn't your color – you need more contrast with that white skin. My crimson would suit you better. And who is this? Elinor's child? Why Elizabeth, you are quite the lady, quite grown. Charming frock, dear, but the cut is already out of date and it is too small, we'll need to have it altered. But, yes, the green and the flowers – that is very well done. With those eyes and that hair you don't need much else, nor did I at your age. Well, I am amazed. Five years and more since I have stood in this hall. To think I have not been back since

Father's coach bore me to London and to Henry. Of course I would have visited, but three children in five years, well you cannot imagine. At least I kept my figure, did I not Henry? And now to return and find Elinor gone. Only think, man proposes but God disposes."

Lyn stood stunned under the torrent of Jane's effusions. The glacial, ever proper Lady Wyatt she remembered from those months in London had, like Pygmalion, come to life. Thankful to be included in the warmth of Jane's all-inclusive chatter, she even forgave her sister for the heartless reference to her mother. Sir Edward unbent, kissed Jane's cheek, and handed her glass of sherry, and ten minutes later the family was at table. The baronet sat at the head, facing the fireplace, with Alathea at the foot. Jane had pride of place on Sir Edward's right, and Lyn sat next to her, happily shielded from her father. Henry Wyatt, facing his wife to the baronet's left, not too subtly cast an appraising eye over the china and silver and Lyn had to cover her mouth so that he would not see her smile. Jane, Lyn thought, was like a good east wind, scouring all before it. She remembered her mother's words and her heart lifted: however formidable this sister might be, Elinor had said, she would do her duty.

"Henry, the bottle stands by you, is it not time to toast the baronet in his hall?" Jane cried.

Wyatt leapt to his feet and, to Sir Edward's discomfiture, personally made the rounds, filling each glass with the white Bordeaux his father-in-law had sent from London against the coming celebration. Lyn looked inquiringly at her father and received his nod of approbation to drink this one glass of wine, unwatered. If Jane could effect these changes, what would follow?

"To Sir Edward Duke, baronet, long may he and his line flourish," piped Henry in his reedy tenor, and his voice was soon overtaken by the family's echo, "long may he and his line flourish."

Jane's attention was already elsewhere. "Why Alathea, do you always sit at the foot?" she exclaimed.

Before the younger girl could reply Sir Edward interjected, "Of course, Jane. With Lady Duke's death the honor passed to her. And she has graced my table."

Jane flashed a quick look which suggested that "graced" was not the word she would have chosen to describe Alathea's stolid presence, but she held up her glass in her sister's direction and offered her a silent toast before looking about her again.

"My, Father, you do look elegant. How many suits did you have made up in London?"

"This and the ivory, trimmed with Duke blue, which I will wear tomorrow. Do you like the new mode, with the slimmer trouser, the vest and the matching coat? They say that once King Charles started the fashion it caught on with a vengeance."

22

"I like it very well, if a man has a good figure like you and Henry. John looked positively killing. I shall be amazed if he does not attract an heiress within six months."

Jane eyed Lyn. "Why, I do believe that gown is made from the cloth I gave you in London! If it is still good, we'll have it altered for you. It needs a different sleeve and the bodice is too plain. Unless you have other plans I'll come up to your room after dinner and we can look at your wardrobe."

Lyn blushed and looked at her father. Although she feared her sister's critical eye, it would be a pleasure to engage in some light talk about dress. Nobody had given her clothes a second thought since her mother died except for the quick fashioning of the hated mourning gowns and, more recently, Alathea's command to have the blue silk dress made up for the fete.

The baronet helped Jane to some gravy and answered for Lyn.

"It is a kind thought, but I beg you to defer the pleasure. If it is agreeable to you, after you have supervised the disposition of your belongings, I should like to discuss Martin with you and Henry."

Jane patted her lips with the soft damask napkin, nodding as she did so.

"La, yes, of course. First things first. Forgive me Father. Of course I can review Elizabeth's wardrobe later; we'll be here a good two weeks. Unless she has had a mishap Martin should be here by mid-afternoon with the rest of the trunks and you can see for yourself whether she will suit. Business first, then pleasure. Now, Henry, do have some more of Rose's wonderful peas and then let's see how the Duke strawberries have done this year!"

Lyn's heart sank. Who was Martin? Had she something to do with the fete or with Lyn's own future? Her hands grew cold and goose bumps of anxiety marred the smooth white flesh of her arms as her plate was removed and the promised strawberries were placed in the center of the table, glowing like rubies in a great Venetian glass bowl.

After dinner Lyn, left to her own devices, changed into her gardening smock and made a pretense of working in the herb garden. She saw Henry cross the yard to the stable where, doubtless, he was settling his horses. Within minutes he had returned to the house and the lawns and parterres lay empty under the ruthless sun. The heat was intense and nobody was outside who could find a reason to be inside. A movement from the upper south crosswing caught Lyn's eye: Alathea pulling her drapes against the heat. The big girl was doubtless going to lie down after dinner, as she normally did. Glancing around and seeing no one, Lyn slipped across the parched lawn to the south side of the Lodge and, hugging the wall, made her way to her father's library, unseen. As she expected, the casements were open to catch what breaths of air could be coaxed indoors on this sultry afternoon and she heard her father's voice clearly. She settled herself in the ragged border, back against the wall, fully intending to know who "Martin" was and what impact, if any, the woman would have on her life.

The baronet's voice rang out. "Come in, Henry! Come in and join us. You might close the door behind you. I am not particularly interested in the entire staff knowing our business."

"Why, 'tis just about Martin, is it not?"

"Well yes, but it goes somewhat beyond that. I am working on a plan for the girl's education and I want to discuss her character as well as her learning. That is not matter for the servants' long ears."

"No indeed, sir, I take your point."

"Good. And Henry, as I've asked you before, please call me Father. There is no need to stand on ceremony."

"Why, thank you. I am honored. I hardly knew my own, so it will warm my heart to call you so."

"And a good man he was, Henry, as you have often told me. Twice Governor of Virginia and a staunch friend of the first Charles. Perhaps it was a kind providence which let him pass on before the blessed martyr was sacrificed to the mob."

"You may be right, though I would that he had lived to see more of his children and to see his grandchildren born. He had a hard life. I can never think well of Virginia; it brought him to an early grave. For myself, I hope to live and die at Boxley Abbey."

"Yet I understand that Virginia now prospers under Sir William Berkeley and that a man can do worse than to plant there."

"All men say that Sir William has acted credibly since he succeeded my father in forty-one. He only acknowledged Cromwell when the sword was, quite literally, at his breast and now, happily, he has been reinstated. Did you know that he had just arrived in London when we were there? They say he carries a brief from the colony to defeat or somehow alter the Navigation Acts which, the colonists claim, hamper trade by forbidding the use of foreign shipping. He will have an automatic entree to Whitehall due to Sir John's standing with the King, but I doubt that his suit will prevail; the London merchants will not countenance it."

"Sir John Berkeley, Baron Stratton ... is he senior to Sir William or junior?"

"The baron is the youngest of the Somerset Berkeleys, but the greatest. Few are closer to the King and the Duke."

"Well, well perhaps you and Jane will have a chance to meet these grandees when you pass through London on your way to Kent. The Wyatt planet travels near the sun, does it not, Henry? We are honored by the connection. I doubt that John would have succeeded with the Duke of York without your intervention. You have my deepest gratitude. But come, let us discuss the child. I want to be prepared when Martin arrives."

Jane's sharp voice was heard. "Yes, enough of the Berkeleys, Henry. A tedious, grasping family. Do let's deal with Martin and Elizabeth. The child is well-looking and deserves some attention."

"Now Jane, don't be impatient," countered the baronet. "Sit down, sit down. I cannot stand your fidgeting. You never used to fidget – you were always as cool as ice."

"Well, now I am married and the mother of three, and I therefore have four reasons to fidget, where I had none before."

Henry laughed tolerantly. "Sit down, love, and tell Father what he needs to know about Martin."

"The woman is of unimpeachable character, though she is as prickly as a hedgehog. I have never known anyone to take a slight like she. However, her French is perfect, (her mother being from Paris), she is proficient on the harpsichord, and her needlework is astonishing, if I do say so myself. We would certainly have kept her on when she finished with Henry's niece Lucy, but she would never do for my three boys. If I could think of any other role for her at the Abbey I would keep her, but the woman was put on earth to shape young girls and it would be a pity to thwart her destiny."

"Well, Jane, I believe I have her character in a nutshell. She's a bit of a tartar and she won't bear any slackness, but the result is worth the pain, is that it?"

"Precisely, Father. Elizabeth has her mother's charm, but I already sense a wilfulness I would not care to see in a daughter of mine."

Although Lyn could not see her father's face she knew, to a hair, what his expression would be. Even as the afternoon sun beat down upon her as she crouched in the dry border below the casement she gave a little shiver. What would he say now?

"It is the exact word, Jane. Wilfulness. Her mother had it, as you well know. Elinor could go through the day in seeming compliance with my wishes, but underneath there boiled a very devil's brew of rebellion. And just as this child bears her mother's face and form, so she bears her spirit. If it is not checked now, it will grow rank and unseemly. She has had a year to run wild and I now intend to keep her on a very short leash."

Lyn heard Henry pipe up. "Oh, I say, Father, is that not a bit harsh? Why I thought the child was delightful. And not overly diffident – she spoke up nicely. And pretty as a picture."

Lyn imagined the looks which must be passing between Jane and the baronet. Jane got the first word in.

"Henry, I do declare, you have outdone yourself. Of course the minx is charming – so was the second Lady Duke. But underneath that soft demeanor there is a will of iron. And Martin is just the one to deal with it."

Sir Edward intervened. "Well, I need to hear no more. If I like her after interviewing her this afternoon I will take her on for a year on the same terms that you had her and then we shall see how it goes. The child is musical and draws well and loves to read whatever falls her way. If she learns French and keeps up with her harp and her drawing, and we add needlework, in five or six years I will have her off my hands on such terms as will benefit the entire family. In the meantime I will see that haughty spirit tamed and a sore which has been rubbed raw this past year will be assuaged. 'Tis a good plan and I thank you for your help."

Lyn heard chairs scraping on the old oak floors and she fled to the garden and raced across the lane to the stable where she sought her usual refuge, Lark's capacious box. The pony was in the pasture, so she could not pour out her heart to him. She flung herself upon the straw and angrily plucked at the golden reeds in her agitation. So she had a will of iron and it was rubbing her father the wrong way? Well and good. And "Martin" was going to fix the problem. Time would tell. She could stomach the French and the music and even, possibly, the needlework but nobody was going to own her soul. In all great things she would be her own woman.

The day of the fete dawned cloudless and sultry. As the sun's great globe began its ascent Lyn leaned from her casement and watched the laborers file down the lane from the village, each carrying a bucket. They had been directed to draw water from the horse pond and to freshen the lawns and gardens without turning the dry Suffolk soil to mud. Lyn feared for her gillyflowers and sops-in-wine and for the bed of forget-me-nots which she had coaxed to bloom, but today she was no longer mistress of the garden and all her greenery lay at the mercy of the villagers. She had been forbidden to "play the fool" outdoors and was confined to her room where she was to spend the morning preparing herself for the great event. Restless, the little casuist decided to define "morning" as the time between breakfast and noon, when the guests were expected. Since it was well before breakfast, she convinced herself, her sentence had not yet begun and she could pay a quick visit to Lark without violating her father's order. She slipped down the back stairs, grabbed two apples from the kitchen, and crossed the lane, waving to the laborers as she skirted the stable and made for the pasture. Lark pricked up his ears and trotted eagerly to the fence where he nuzzled her shoulder and lipped up the apple, snorting happily. She felt badly that she had not brought a gift for Fancy, so she gave her mother's mare her own apple and rubbed her soft nose in apology. With a quick pat for both animals, Lyn retraced her steps, sure that she had not been seen.

As she entered the kitchen there before her, like a monument, stood Alathea. Lyn gasped. Here was trouble. The strong hands gripped her shoulders and the cold monotone tolled her doom.

"Well, Elizabeth, just as I expected, you took no time in defying Father's wishes. What did I see upon rising? You, running across the garden in those filthy rags for all the village to see. Father thinks Martin is going to change things, but you are too deep for her, too deep for Jane, too deep for John, too deep even for Father. Only I see the devil that sits on your shoulder. Little witch! Father will learn of your disobedience as soon as I can catch his ear."

The older girl pinched Lyn savagely high on her shoulders, where the cupped sleeves of the blue silk gown would cover any marks, and pushed her towards the kitchen stairs. "Get up to your room and do not let me see you until the guests arrive."

Lyn raced up stairs, through her antechamber, and flung herself on the bed, stifling her sobs. Her shoulders throbbed and she knew they would bear ugly bruises for days. She turned on her back and kicked off her scuffed boots, sending first one and then the other sailing across the room. Finally she sat up, cross-legged, and scrutinized her conscience. In truth, she had only herself to blame for this contretemps. She may have complied with the letter of her father's command but certainly not with the spirit. She had defined "morning" to suit her own whim and now she was paying the price. And for such a small thing! Her mother would be disappointed that Lyn had exercised such poor judgment in choosing her battles. The child sighed and rose and began pulling off her ragged frock and her dirty stockings. Her path lay bleak before her. Without her mother, how would she know when to comply and when to defy? She must trust her heart. Somewhat calmed, Elinor's daughter dried her tears and rang the handbell for her breakfast and her bath.

Lyn's renewed vow of obedience was sorely tested as the morning progressed. No sooner had the maids removed her bath when she heard a brisk, authoritative knock. Cracking the thick, oak door, much to her astonishment she saw Martin. Yesterday the vinegary spinster had kept in the background, arranging the Wyatts' belongings, eating supper in the kitchen, and sleeping in Jane's anteroom. Yesterday they had not exchanged two words. Now here she was on the landing, upright as a church steeple, enveloped in an apron which crackled with authority.

"Good morning, Miss." The words themselves seemed to leap to attention as they left Martin's thin lips. "Lady Wyatt sent me to dress your hair and help you with your stays and gown. She said you had never worn stays before and I should make sure that all was in order."

Lyn opened the door wider, her mouth an appalled "O." Stays! Nobody had mentioned those constricting garments. And hair-dressing! She always wore her hair the same way and since it had a strong natural wave it was easy to create the few curls which fashion dictated must fall from each temple. Now, it seemed, her locks must be tortured into a new, modish coiffure. Well, she had vowed to obey, so obey she would. Lyn straightened her back, forced a smile upon the rosy lips which had been burgeoning in a pout, and flung the door wide open to her torturer. Two hours later a different Lyn appeared on the threshold: a little starched miss whose natural beauty had been constricted into as close a likeness as possible to poor Queen Catherine whose only claim to charm was her impeccable *toilette*. Try as she might a cloud remained on her brow and for those who knew her well it was not hard to see that a storm was brewing.

The fete began well. Summoned for noon, all had arrived by half past twelve and the housekeeper Rose, her daughter Rosie, her son Job, and the other recruits from the village circulated through the great hall offering claret cup in goblets of silver or crystal. Sir Edward moved slowly among the Suffolk gentry like a frigate among herring busses, acknowledging the obeisance of the Glenhams, the Thorpes, the Tyrrels and the Jenneys. Alathea sailed in his wake, sloop-like, while Sir Henry and Lady Wyatt exchanged greetings and small talk with the guests, bringing the tide of the Dukes' glory to its high water mark with the glamorous aura of Kent and London high life.

Feeling constricted in her stays and wholly unnatural beneath her stiff, artificial curls, Lyn retreated to the east wall and positioned herself on a settee under the casements where a breath of garden air eased the stifling atmosphere. She did her best to smile and bob and speak appropriately when spoken to and wondered how she could possibly survive the pending dinner and the long, dreary afternoon. Her heart sank as Pansy Clement, the rector's wife, dropped into the too-narrow space between Lyn and Squire Thorpe, her sheep's face painted with modest rapture. It was not every day that the Clements mingled with the Suffolk great. Pansy's diary entry for this day would be a lengthy one.

As the dinner hour approached Sir Edward made his way to the great fireplace and stood on the hearth facing his guests, below the Duke brents. The crowd turned, as if orchestrated, and the buzz of conversation ceased. Sir Francis Glenham stepped forward with purpose to lead the guests in a toast to England's newest baronet. Pansy Clement rose eagerly, glass in hand, and as she did so a great ripping sound reverberated throughout the hall as her skirt parted from her bodice. Regrettably Squire Thorpe's large right buttock had settled squarely on the little woman's skirt and Squire Thorpe's large right foot had found a place squarely on the little woman's hem so that when the rector's wife rose the threads of her cherished apricot silk ensemble parted like a spider web and Lyn saw more stays in one day than she had ever seen in her life. Poor Pansy gasped and seized her skirt and fled to the kitchen to hide her shame but not before Lyn burst into peals of uncontrollable laughter. Choking in her tightly-laced blue silk, her mirth nonetheless rose up like bubbles in champagne and her face turned pink with the effort to suppress it. Pansy Clement, with her aquiline features, had looked just like an ewe at shearing, profoundly startled at the world's seeing what it was never intended to. Lyn clapped her hands over her mouth and darted a glance at her father and the laughter died in her. But before the baronet could move a hair's-breadth Alathea swam into her vision, seized her arm and frog-marched her after Pansy. When the sisters reached the well of the kitchen stairs Alathea banished Lyn from the fete and told her to keep her room until Sunday when her transgressions of the morning and the afternoon would be dealt with by Sir Edward himself.

Lyn lay on her bed suffocating in despair. What a day of woe! Not only had she begun by violating her father's command but worse, far worse, she had now wounded his dignity. And that, she had good reason to know, was a mortal sin. The day was crossed by an evil star. Why had Alathea, always a late sleeper, risen so early and opened her casement at just the wrong moment? What evil fate had caused sheeplike Pansy Clement to sit next to hulking Robert Thorpe? Fortune's wheel was plunging down at an alarming rate, with Lyn bound fast to its rim.

Lyn turned on her side and winced as the stays cut into her ribs. Well, if she was banished from the fete, she certainly did not need to wear this wretched costume. She rose and with a great effort managed to reach the laces in the back and release herself from the blue silk which fell about her feet like water. She saw the shears which Martin had left on her dressing table after using them to trim her rich black locks. What was Rose's expression? "In over shoes, in over boots." It was true. Her situation could hardly be worse: the stays could be sacrificed. Grabbing the shears, she reached cautiously behind her and snipped at the constricting laces until the bone cage fell away, leaving her free to breathe. In a trice she was out of her petticoats and fine stockings and satin slippers and she stood thankfully in her linen pantaloons and chemise. She carefully folded the gown and petticoats and placed them in her trunk, with the damaged stays hidden underneath. Now to do something about her hair. Lyn perched on the stool before the looking glass and stuck out her tongue at the image she saw. This was not she – it was some strange London girl. It would not take a minute to recreate herself. She carefully removed the silk flowers and ribbons which Martin had bound in her locks and then pulled pin after pin from her hair, feeling her scalp spring back to life as she did so. She stood up, seized her hair brush and, leaning almost in half, vigorously stroked the shiny blue-black mass until it fell free, curling of its own will, not in obedience to pins and combs. Lyn felt so much better that she almost forgot her disgrace until the distant sounds and scents of the grand dinner floated up the staircase and penetrated her chambers.

It was only one o'clock. The guests would be at table for hours, then they would tour the grounds or settle at cards, and finally they would have a light supper before leaving in the gloaming. The hours stretched ahead interminably and Lyn did not think she could bear to wait in her room with nothing to do, until nightfall. Her books had all been read many times; they would not hold her attention now. Her harp and her needlework and her drawing required a calm concentration which was wholly beyond her. She glanced out the window to the gloom of Dod's Wood. Really, if you thought about it, it was highly unlikely that anybody would notice if she left her room. Both family and staff were inexorably yoked to their guests and would be for hours. If she left the Lodge now and was back by dark nobody would know the difference. In over shoes, in over boots: why not spend the afternoon with Lark and Fancy?

Lyn donned her gardening clothes, pulled the anteroom door snugly shut and stole along the west gallery to the great staircase. It was risky, but because of the frenetic activity in the kitchen and buttery, there was in fact less chance of being seen on the main stairs than on the kitchen stairs. All she had to do was descend unseen, slip through the new parlor to the garden, circle the lawn behind the screen of beeches and oaks and hazel, enter the stable from the north, and she would be home free.

Ten minutes later Lyn slid into the soft dusk with its familiar odors of acrid horse sweat and musty straw. The doves cooed and strutted in the loft and Sir Edward's stallion jerked his head and snorted. The Duke carriage horses – matched bays – rolled their great eyes but soon settled back to nuzzling their corn when they recognized the intruder. After assuring herself that she was alone with the horses, Lyn walked quietly to Lark's box which lay in the north-east corner of the stable. The rumps of the bays arched nobly above the stall doors and the silken swish of their tails mingled with the liquid gurgle of the doves. Already calmer, Lyn noted that both Fancy and Alathea's mare were absent. Likely on such a fine day they had been turned out to pasture and Lark with them. She reached the pony's loose box and slipped the latch, ready to settle down in the dim quiet and dream the afternoon away. It was then that she screamed.

She was looking into the proud face of a thin, nervy, coal black animal which looked as though it too would scream if it were human. The strange horse, which was untethered, danced back into the corner showing the whites of its eyes. Lyn stood frozen in astonishment, not knowing whether to advance or retreat. She composed herself and advanced a cautious hand to gentle the beast, wondering why this animal in particular, of all the guests' cattle, had been admitted to her father's stable. The black bobbed his head apprehensively and she approached it slowly, cooing to it like the doves. Carefully she reached out and stroked the Roman nose. The beast had quieted. Doubtless it had been as surprised as she to meet a stranger.

"Hush, hush, black one," crooned Lyn. "You are finely bred, I can tell, so tall and slim. But I think you are not much more than a baby, just a young lad. You have a long way to go before you are grown up."

The animal lowered its head and nuzzled her hand, wholly quiet.

"You are pure black, rare! I don't see a white hair on you! Were you put here because you are too fine to be with the others?"

30

The horse snorted and bobbed its head. A black shadow rose from the straw in the far corner and Lyn caught her breath. What was fate bringing her way now?

"Nay, Miss. Prince Rupert is a fine steed, but not too fine to be with the others. It is just that I am desperately late and I have hidden from my father's certain wrath until I decide what to do next."

Lyn was speechless. Who was this youth with the fine black horse? Before she could find her tongue, a stripling of fourteen years or so stepped out of the gloom and into a shaft of sunlight which streamed from above, through the open loft window. The chestnut highlights of his dusky hair flamed and the golden light caught the gold in his eyes. *He has eyes like a hawk,* thought Lyn, *barred gold and black, and they do not blink.* He stood before her, as slim and refined as his horse, his skin like gold and his features as hawk-like as his eyes.

"And who may you be?" came the imperious query.

Lyn's heart caught. "I am Elizabeth Duke, but my real name is Lyn."

The mysterious boy stepped forward and took Lyn's hand. "So I meet a Duke. Good afternoon. I am Nathaniel Bacon."

CHAPTER 3

AUGUST 1661

Lyn looked down at the slender hand which gripped her own with unexpected force.

It was not the hand of an artist, like her brother's, with its broad palm and flexible fingers. It was not the hand of a solider, like her father's, with its strong thumb and hard flesh. It was most like the hand of the King in the etching which John had brought back from London: seemingly as slim and delicate as that of a lady, but with a deceptive, imperious underlying strength which marked it for command.

The boy's grip relaxed and he stepped out of the shaft of sunlight and scrutinized Lyn. The hawk face unbent and the thin, well-defined lips smiled in delight.

"Why, you must be the youngest Duke, the one I have hardly ever seen." The boy stopped in mid-speech, gasped, and brought the fine hands to his mouth. "Oh, I am terribly sorry. That means you are the daughter of the lady who died last year. I truly regret your loss. Father spoke so highly of your mother and then she just ... disappeared as it were. We did not even hear of a service or a memorial of any kind."

Lyn looked up at the fierce face which was now kindled with kindness. The boy was a stranger, yet she felt that she could unburden her heart to him sooner than to her own family. In the five minutes they had been together he had spoken truer words of sympathy for the loss of her mother than any she had heard over the past year. Words tumbled from her lips, heedlessly.

"Oh yes, I am Elinor's daughter, her only child. Did you know that I might have had four brothers, but God called them all to Him soon after they were born? They are all in St. Mary's churchyard and my mother lies there too. You and your father are welcome to go there – don't you live just over the hill at Friston?"

Young Bacon stepped back and eyed Lyn, his face a perplexed mixture of surprise, superiority, curiosity and dismay. He laughed and then spoke.

"Why I believe the cat's got my tongue. Father says I am never at a loss for words ... quite the contrary. But you have stopped my mouth up quite neatly." The boy sighed. "It is all a little complicated; where should I begin? Well, I'll begin at the end, which is not logical, but it will get us where we need to go. Yes, I'm a Bacon from Friston Hall and, yes, we live just over the hill, past Snape, which makes us one of your nearest neighbors. But for reasons which are not completely clear to me, your family and mine do not get along, which explains why we only heard of Lady Duke's death in a roundabout way, not from your father. And which also explains why I am quite certain that we would not be welcome at Benhall St. Mary's, as much as I would like to honor your mother by visiting her grave. Come, be honest, has Sir Edward never said anything to you of Squire Thomas Bacon of Friston Hall and his daughter Bess, (that's my sister), and his son Nat, (that's me)?"

Lyn's looked up at her new friend, her eyes pools of violet. "Father has never said a word about the Bacons, and John and Alathea have just told me to make sure I do not walk or ride on your lands. But yesterday I heard Jane say that the Bacons are terrible Puritans and that they are 'laying low.' Is it true? Are you a terrible Puritan and are you 'laying low'?"

Bacon burst out laughing and escorted Lyn to the corner where the straw was piled high to form an aromatic, if prickly, divan. Bowing neatly, he seated her as elegantly as though they were at the royal court and then sat at her feet. The black colt had accepted their presence and paid them no heed, nuzzling greedily in Lark's manger for stray corn and bran. The stable settled into the somnolence of a hot summer afternoon, the silence punctuated only by the cooing of the doves, the silky swish of horse tails, and the shifting of great haunches as the beasts dozed in the pleasant dusk.

"Oh my, what a coil! Well, to make a long story short, and to make it fitting for little pitchers with big ears, it is true that the Bacons and the Dukes have not seen eye to eye about the church or, indeed, about much of anything for some time. We have been on opposite sides of the political fence these past decades, and more I will not say. You are too young and tender to know the reasons."

Lyn bristled immediately – here it was again, she was too young, too small, "just a girl" – why could she not be privy to those intriguing matters which adults spent endless hours discussing like dogs grumbling over bones? When Martin undertook her instruction would she be inducted into these mysteries? It was not for this boy to tell her what she should and should not know.

"I know what a Puritan is and what a Royalist is. You don't have to treat me like a baby."

Her retort only caused her new friend to burst into laughter once more as he threw himself on the straw beside her.

33

"Oh, it hurts, does it not? It is not long since I challenged my father with just those words and he told me that I should thank God for the innocence of childhood and that it would be all too soon that I would know more than I wanted to. Well, I have been at Cambridge this past year and I still want to know more, so I believe he is wrong on that score."

"Cambridge? That is the great university, is it not?"

"'Tis a university. And some may call it great, but I find St. Catherine's tiresome. (That's my college, you know.) I might as well have taken a papist's vows and entered a monastery, for all the freedom I have. You rise when they tell you, say prayers when they tell you, eat when they tell you, study, study, study all day long, and never a thought for a long walk in the country or a good brisk ride or raising a covey of pheasants. I was mad to get there, but between you and me it has been a great disappointment."

"Is that why you are home? Did you leave the university?"

The boy groaned and turned on his face and buried it in the straw.

"What a sharp one you are – you go right to the heart of the matter. The truth is I broke a few too may rules and overspent my allowance and father reached right out with his shepherd's crook and pulled his black sheep willy-nilly back into the family flock, with many a harsh word for my behavior. He thinks I need a little more instruction at home before I am prepared to 'honor the great halls of learning' with my presence. Pooh – I am not going to enter the church, why should I be a scholar?"

"I don't know, but I should love the chance to read all those great books. John wanted to go to Oxford, you know, but father would not let him. Said he was needed here at Benhall."

Bacon sat up. "Now if that is how your father thinks, I do believe I should get along with him! Your brother is going to inherit, as am I. We need to know how to rule, not how to split hairs with pedagogues. It all lies in the doing, not in the reading. Still, with my ancestry, I know I am fated for more years at Cambridge and then a term at Gray's Inn whether I like it or not."

"What do you mean, with your ancestry?"

"My goodness, it must be true that the Dukes do not discuss the Bacons. Do you really not know that I am plagued with being a descendant, however remote, of Sir Nicholas Bacon, Queen Elizabeth's Lord Keeper and, what is worse, of his son Francis, Lord Chancellor to old King James? Francis Bacon, first Baron Verulum and Viscount St. Albans. Not a day goes by but I am measured against him. Count yourself lucky that you have not been forced to read his essays and his high-flown ideas about education. When I am too hard pressed I remind Father that famous Francis ended his days in disgrace, but then he flies into a fury and it is bread and water for me. It is more politic to pretend that my illustrious ancestor was a saint, though the facts belie it."

Lyn hardly knew what to say. "I love reading, above all things. Do you think I could understand his books?"

Bacon turned on his back and howled with laughter. "Child, why would you ask for such a fate? You are blessed not to have the weight of history pushing you down. Leave well enough alone. Still," he added after a moment, "it is true that in their day, next to the princes, my ancestors were among the mightiest in the land. Perhaps some day ...." The boy rose to his feet and stretched. "But enough of that. The afternoon wears on and I must decide what to do." He glanced at Lyn again. "Speaking of which, why are you in that dirty frock and old boots when your family and the others are feasting like gluttons in their finery?"

It hit Lyn like a landslide. She had been banished for high crimes and misdemeanors and she was supposed to be in her bedroom-prison, her own personal Tower of London, awaiting her fate. Though she had briefly slipped through the bars, her cell awaited her. Fatigue and hunger and the excitement of meeting the hawk boy brought unexpected tears to her eyes and she lifted the back of a grubby hand to her cheek to staunch the flow. Quick as lightning, the boy whipped out a fine lawn handkerchief and dabbed Lyn's face. Mortified, she looked up and was astonished to see the golden eyes swimming with tears of their own. Why, the boy must have felt her pain as soon as she did! Lyn had never known such sympathy with another except, of course, with her mother – but mothers were a thing apart and hardly counted. She wiped her nose and smiled and rose to her feet beside her new friend.

"I am in terrible trouble. I went out this morning to see Lark against father's command and then I laughed at Mistress Clement just when they were going to toast father and now I have left my room again when I am under strict orders to stay there until I learn my punishment."

Young Bacon dashed the tears from his eyes and smiled. "Oh my, that is trouble indeed. It appears that we have both sinned against our fathers. Shall I tell you what I have done? It makes your crimes seem trivial."

The heart-shaped face looked up pleadingly at his and he made his confession.

"Well it all started when, against all house rules, I went to the Cambridge horse fair instead of attending study hall. I just wanted an outing, but instead I fell in love." Lyn looked at Bacon quizzically. "Not with a girl, silly. With Prince Rupert. No, not *that* Prince Rupert, the great warrior of the Rhine, but with this one here." The boy turned to the black horse, patted the beautiful arched neck, and stroked the fine head with the intelligent eyes. "As soon as I saw him I knew I had to have him. I had a good deal of money about me, as father is generous with my allowance and I had not had a chance to spend it. Of course it was not nearly enough to buy Prince, but I thought 'in over shoes, in over boots', why not offer part payment and see if I could convince the seller that father would pay the rest"

Lyn started at Bacon's use of the aphorism which had defined her day. Here was another link between the two of them. The youth continued.

"To my amazement they accepted the offer! Somebody at the fair, (I know not who), vouched for me as Squire Bacon's son and my coins, together with my father's reputation for honesty, made me the owner of a splendid half-broken colt before I knew what I was doing! Well, I walked him to the college on a lead and tried out my old cob's saddle and bridle, which fit well enough, and then I sent my servant home on the cob, with a note for father to forewarn him lest the bill fall due and he be taken by surprise. Well, *I* was the one taken by surprise! The very next day Father arrived in person, spent a few hours with the master, the bursar, my tutor and others, and the next day after *that* we were riding home with a huge black thundercloud, (metaphorically speaking), over my head." Bacon laughed wryly. "But at least I got to keep Prince Rupert. Father had to maintain his reputation so he paid up like a good one, as though he was the one who coveted the horse. And he *has* admitted that Prince was worth the price, though he is not fully grown and still needs schooling."

Lyn smiled. "I guess that describes you both."

Bacon tipped her face up with one fine hand and shook a finger at her with the other. "You are a sharp one, indeed. I begin to understand why you are in such trouble." Both children sighed and the youth continued.

"But that is only the beginning. Not long after I returned to Friston we received Sir Edward's invitation to this fete and father began muttering and stewing about whether to accept. After all, the two families had not spoken for decades, yours being Royalist and mine Roundhead. But you know? There is more to it than that. Father has never confided in me, but something bothered him with respect to how your father treated your mother." Bacon paused and Lyn's gaze never left his face. "I don't want to distress you, child, but to the extent that he knew her, Father thought the world of your mother, and something happened ... well, in any event, as long as I can remember Sir Edward Duke's name has not been a welcome one in Friston Hall. So the invitation presented a problem. Father clearly did not want to accept, but we had no ready excuse not to go and if we declined it would have published the families' discord far and wide and the Suffolk rumor mills would have turned the grist of gossip into more loaves than Our Lord ever made from fishes. Fortunately Bess was visiting the Hoveners at Bury St. Edmund's, so he told her to think of a reason to stay longer which, being a clever girl, she did. But he accepted on his own behalf and on mine, thinking, perhaps, that he could mend some fences.

"All our plans were made, everything was in train, we were dressed to the nines and they were just harnessing the grays to the chaise when Father

changed his mind and decided that if we rode we could get away more easily, particularly if we wanted to leave a little early, which was entirely possi
ble. Well, that was fine with me, because I wanted to show Prince Rupert to
the world and I thought my new gold silk would be perfectly set off by his
black hide, but Father would have none of it – he trusted neither me nor the
horse and he ordered me to take the cob. We had a great set-to and, to make
a long story short, I simply refused. He waited as long as he could and then
rode off in a great huff, ordering me to mount the cob and follow forthwith,
and on no account to be late. Of course as soon as Father turned the corner
I ordered Prince to be saddled rather than the cob, but some devil got into
the horse and we had a terrible time with him. It must have taken us half an
hour to get him under control and by that time it was too late. I gave it a
noble try – I galloped him cross-country and took every shortcut I knew,
but not being familiar with the lay of your land I got lost a couple of times
and by the time I reached Benhall Village I knew it was too late to present
myself to Sir Edward. The horse was in a lather so I took advantage of your
stable to cool him down while I thought what to do next – appear with some
feeble excuse, or just turn tail for home. And now, my child, you have solved
the problem for me. We have been talking this half hour and it is far too late
for me to meet your family – I have no choice but to ride back to Friston
and wait for a tongue-lashing."

Lyn was silent, amazed that this boy could be so wilful and yet so
debonair.

"So you see, Mistress Duke, we are both in for it. Tomorrow I will be
sore in places I do not even care to think about, unless I can bring the old
man around. And you may be confined to your room for a week."

"In over shoes, in over boots," said Lyn with a slow smile.

Bacon grinned. "Well, there is that, puss. What you are saying is: it can't
get worse than this, so why don't we have some fun? I like your spirit. What
do you have in mind?"

And that is when the madness began. Lyn could not bear to leave the
golden boy and the black horse – they were magic. How could she bind
them to her?

"If you are riding back to Friston, why could I not come with you? I
have a pony, but if Lark is too small I can ride Fancy, my mother's mare. I
want to see where you live. Imagine living so close and never having seen
Friston Hall."

Bacon seemed to take her seriously. "Now that is a thought, but the
problem is that I would never leave a lady to ride unattended, so I would
have to escort you home again, and it would end by our riding back and
forth between Benhall and Friston forever." They both laughed. "No, I
think we deserve an adventure. Why don't we saddle Prince Rupert and the
mare and take a real ride, a ride to the sea."

Lyn gasped. The sea lay a good seven or eight miles to the east, and she had no idea how to reach it, except by following the Alde. Bacon might as well have suggested sailing around the world. But the vision was enticing. She felt, somehow, that the ride to sea would cleave her from her family in a manner which could never be healed and that the wound, though painful, would give her her own identity. Without further thought she cried "Yes!"

The next moments were a blur. Fancy was enticed from the pasture and within minutes she and Prince Rupert were saddled and bridled. Fate seemed to be with the adventurers: not a soul stirred from the Lodge and not a single villager wandered down the stable lane. Bacon knew the country to the northeast of Benhall well, and it was not long before they had crossed her father's fields, paralleling the highroad, and reached the east-west way to the market town of Saxmundham. Turning east, they reached the outskirts of the town and then circled north to avoid notice. When they were well beyond Saxmundham they stopped at a cottage and, for a few pennies, persuaded an old woman to let them have some bread and cheese and fruit. The viands, together with the flask of wine and water that Bacon always carried, would serve for dinner and supper too, if need be. Once provisioned, they turned their backs on Duke land and Bacon land and rode towards the sea.

The riders crested the hill which sheltered Saxmundham from the fickle ocean wind and a whole new vista lay before Lyn. The ground sloped gently away, as if great earthen breakers were rolling east to meet the west-cresting waves of the North Sea. Scattered in the declivities were copses of oak and beech and hazel, still richly clad in summer green. Fields of grain rippled in the sea breeze and interspersed among them were sheep pastures with their wooly denizens mirroring the clouds above. The air felt more bracing than that of Benhall, tucked as it was in a river valley, and new odors wafted to Lyn's nose – the scents of gorse and broom and what she thought must be the faint tang of the sea. The landscape was open and exhilarating and she felt as though she could ride forever until she plunged into the shining expanse of the water which lay before them like cloth of silver.

Lyn turned to her companion. "It is wonderful, quite different from home. Shall we really ride as far as the ocean?"

"You can be sure of it. From here it is no farther than five miles, the way I am planning to go. We'll cut across some fields north of Knottishall, steer well away from the village and Red House Farm, and then go on to Leiston and from there it is an easy ride through the dunes to the water. There are cliffs, of course, but I know my way down to the beach. We should be there within the hour."

"Knottishall," said Lyn. "That is where the Jenneys live. They are at Benhall, right this minute!" Her mind wandered uneasily back to the Lodge and she shifted in her saddle and glanced at Bacon. He knew her thoughts.

38

"'Tis a noble old family. I believe they have been in these parts since the Conquest, but their fortunes have declined. Red House Farm is all but derelict. Well, I am glad they are not home, there is even less chance that anybody will recognize us. Come on, the faster we leave the faster we'll get there."

Bacon whipped up Prince Rupert who tossed his head and eagerly descended the hill, Fancy following with a good will. Using the farm roads, they passed north of Knottishall without incident and it was not long before they rode through the village of Leiston which was all but empty on this sunny afternoon. Bacon told Lyn that as many Leistoners made their living from the sea as from the land, and not always legally. She did not quite understand what he meant, but she was impressed with his knowledge. Soon after Leiston they left the fields and copses behind them and the ground leveled off and the soil became sandy, making easy riding. Now the vegetation was low and sparse, with thorny bushes bright with aromatic yellow flowers, and with dusty creeping plants which Lynn did not recognize. They came to a small stream and, after having let the horses drink to their content, they turned north and followed the stream bed as it wound down into a sandy gulch.

"This is the best way to reach the strand," said Bacon. "There are other routes, but this will be easiest on the horses. It takes us to a stretch of the coast where there is not a house or a cottage to be seen. I am not quite sure why, but I believe there is no safe harbor here, so the ships and boats avoid it. Once you come out onto the sand it seems like the rest of the world has disappeared."

The youth spoke truly. The horses made their way along the gulch, following the stream as it sought the ocean, and the cliffs rose higher and higher on both sides until Lyn felt as though they had entered a great church. And suddenly there, before them, was the chancel and the great east window which showed a pure blue sky above and a dancing silver sea below. A fresh breeze blew in their faces and Lyn clapped her hands for joy.

"Oh, 'tis rare, 'tis rare. I am so happy. This is the best day of my life." As soon as she spoke she bit her lip. She had used the same words to John at Snape Priory barn a year ago.

Bacon smiled and led the way splashing through the mouth of the stream where it broadened on the sand until they were well away from the cliffs and they could look up at the protective ramparts. Not a sign of human activity was to be seen: neither a farmer nor a herder above nor a sailor below. The gulls screamed against the steady beat of the surf and Lyn felt as though she was nearer the heart of the earth than she had ever been and that she could hear its steady pulse.

"I don't know about you, Mistress Duke, but I am famished. Shall we unsaddle the horses, tie them to that log and see what we can find for dinner?"

The thought of food made Lyn suddenly ravenous and she eagerly joined her companion in rummaging among the saddle bags, pulling out the Dutch cheese, the crusty rolls and the gold-green pears.

"Do you drink wine and water? I always carry a bottle with me. Here, you go first. Oh, and if you need to answer the call of nature, just tell me and go back there, to the base of the cliffs, and I'll look the other way. There is no sense in standing on ceremony or being uncomfortable."

This is a magic boy, thought Lyn. *He thinks of everything, and he makes everything seem right. It is natural to be with him and to do as he does. I wonder if I can keep him as my friend.*

As usual, Nathaniel Bacon answered her thoughts. "If we are to be friends I must know what to call you besides Mistress Duke. Didn't you say something about your 'real' name being Lyn?"

Between great bites of bread and cheese the girl explained the story of her two names and how she preferred the Welsh one to the English. Bacon listened intently and seemed fascinated.

"Names are important, are they not? More so, perhaps, than many think. Now let me tell you the story of another Elizabeth, for my family has a tale as well as yours, and it is a sad one.

My father married the daughter of a knight, Sir Robert Brooke of Cockfield Hall, Yoxford, and her name was Elizabeth. He is not shy to tell people that Elizabeth Brooke was the great love of his life and that he cherishes her name. When my sister was born in forty-five they naturally named her Elizabeth too. But here is the sad part: two years later, on the second of January, 1647, I was born and my mother died that very day. Even now it hurts father to use the name Elizabeth. So my poor sister is simply "Bess Bacon," at least at Friston Hall. For Squire Thomas there was only one Elizabeth and he has never yet met a woman who could take her place."

Lyn had stopped eating and gazed open-mouthed at young Bacon. It was clear that he was moved by the story of his mother's death and she saw that, once again, tears trembled in his golden eyes. He looked off to sea and blindly gathered pebbles in his fine hands and flung them idly at the white froth of the surf. Lyn rose from the sand and moved over to the ocean-bleached log on which he sat and quietly perched next to him.

"I did not know that you lost your mother, as I did. And you never knew her! At least I had mine for nine years. Her memory is so strong that I talk to her every day ... well, you know what I mean. But you..." Lyn let the sad thought speak for itself.

Bacon turned to her and smiled and patted her hand. "You are a sympathetic little soul, Lyn. Odd, I have never told the story of Elizabeth to anybody before now – and yet I have opened my heart to you, whom I met only this afternoon. You must work some magic on me."

Lyn gasped. There *was* magic – he felt it too.

Bacon continued, his voice low. "Father is the kindest person I know. He has given Bess and me everything. It would break his heart to know that I blame myself for murdering my mother ... but I do, and the stain will never be erased."

Lyn sprang to his defense. "Oh no, never think that, it is so wrong! How could you be guilty of anything, a newborn babe! Nobody thought that my tiny brother killed my mother; it was just God's plan. No, no please – it is a terrible thing to think."

Nat turned to her and then rose and looked once more to the sea. "What a balm you are, child. These are heavy thoughts for a perfect afternoon. But you make me feel better – truly you do. You are a cunning little magic charm, are you not? You bring me luck, I feel it in my bones."

Lyn laughed somewhat wildly. The sympathy between them was so perfect that it was painful. She felt the need to come back down to earth.

"But if I have magic it has not told me what to call you. You know that you must call me Lyn, but what is your true name?"

"My true name? Well, I was named Nathaniel for my grandfather, a man of conscience and a stout soldier, or so I am told. The Bacons are as full of Nathaniels as a nut is full of meat – you will find half a dozen in Suffolk. My father and Bess call me Natty still, though I am fourteen years of age and they should have stopped long ago. What would you like to call me, child?"

Suddenly shy, Lyn blushed. She would like to choose a name which belonged only to her – why not bind him with three simple letters and call him "Nat"? Before she could speak Bacon knelt down before her and placed a stick of driftwood in her hand, as thin and bleached as a bird's bone.

"Now Queen Lyn, you must place your royal sword first on one shoulder and then on the other and give me my knightly name. Come, don't hesitate, this does not bear deep thought, it must come naturally."

Proudly Lyn knighted the kneeling boy and dubbed him Nat, her special friend.

"Oh, that's a good choice," he cried. "My best friends at college call me that. 'Nathaniel' brings the whole train of Bacons with it, with their learning and their striving and their sense of duty. 'Natty' keeps me in the nursery. Only 'Nat' frees me to be myself. Well done, my queen. Let's face the world together as Lyn and Nat."

"Oh let's," cried the girl and, seizing his hand, the two of them walked to the sea.

The children wandered endlessly on the dark sand where the waves flirted with the shore, advancing and withdrawing in a timeless dance. As they walked, with only the shore birds for company, they exchanged further confidences and sealed their friendship. Nat told his fear that he, Squire Thomas' only son and heir, would stumble beneath the burden placed on him by his illustrious ancestors and disappoint the father he so dearly loved.

Lyn disclosed her abiding grief at her mother's death and her conviction that she would never gain her father's love and that, as her siblings' stars rose, hers would fade to nothing. That a stripling and a child should find such mutual sympathy seemed as natural to them as breathing. Each bore a burden that had never been shared and the opening of their hearts bound them close. The sun was westering above the cliff-tops and a band of purple shadow was creeping across the sand by the time they returned to the little delta where the stream debouched on the sand and the horses waited patiently.

As the afternoon waned the sea breeze died and a great peace lay on the water. The sky stretched limitlessly to the east, its blue mid-day brilliance fading to tranquil violets and purples. Below the expanse of sky the jeweled water flashed. A transient cloud-cover in the west passed and the rays of the setting sun shone in a last blaze of glory, tracing a path of gold upon the sea as far as the eye could reach. Entranced, Lyn strode into the water and began to follow the golden road as though she would pursue it until its end. Nat stood at the water's edge, stricken dumb. The sea had reached Lyn's waist before he could stir limb or tongue. He strode after the girl, the golden waves engirdling him, and called, mournful as a sea bird.

"Lyn, Lyn, do not go. Do not leave me."

Lyn turned in a glory of gold and jewel colors, the blue lights in her hair gleaming, her face radiant, her eyes amethyst.

"I will never leave you, Nat. I will always be with you."

The boy strode forward and encircled the girl with both arms. Her cheek was pressed against his breast and she could hear his heartbeat, the very essence of his being, as he held her close. The two stood locked together as the sun died in the west and its treasure of gold and gems was scattered profligately to the stars. There, for all time, the boy and the girl swore an oath of eternal friendship, never to be ended, not even by death. Profoundly weary, and profoundly satisfied, they made their way to the shore.

Lyn peeked south over the lime avenue from Bess Bacon's bedroom. The sun had not yet chased the moon from the sky and time hung in the balance between night and day, yet already Squire Thomas was booted and spurred and in the saddle. The rising sun caught the bright haunches of his chestnut as the animal disappeared into the dense leafy cavern, heading for Snape Bridge and the river road. Lyn swallowed and pulled Bess' nightgown closer about her. Within half an hour Nat's father would be at Benhall Lodge. And then? God forfend ... what then?

There was a tap on the door and before she could answer it she saw Nat's dusky head, his hair awry and his brow furrowed.

"You're up," the boy said. "May I come in? Or should you like to dress first?"

Lyn's world was turned upside down. Etiquette was the least of her worries. "Come in, if you like. Your father just left."

"I know. I saw them saddling the horse from my back window. I can't understand why Sir Edward did not respond more fully to last night's message, but Jemmy swore he was turned away with a few words from your sister to the effect that you should wait and return home today. Well, if anyone can smooth it over, it will be Father. He has a gentle way with him."

Lyn smiled wanly. "He does indeed. No wonder you love him so. I never saw anybody swallow his anger so quickly as he did last night when I all but fell from my horse." She looked around Bess' orderly bedchamber with its glowing fruitwood furniture and ivory hangings embroidered with strawberries. "I hope your sister does not mind sharing her bed and bath. As soon as I had washed I fell asleep like one dead. But now I wonder if we should have pushed on rather than just sending the message."

"Oh, as for Bess, she won't mind. She has a heart of gold. It's not her I'm worried about ... it's Father. He took you under his wing the minute he saw that you were dead with fatigue. But I? I'm going to reap the wrath of Jove, I assure you. I can tell when he's furious. First Prince Rupert and now this.... And he is worried about your reputation, a child of ten! It's quite a coil, Lyn."

"But it was worth it, wasn't it?" the child asked softly.

Gold eyes locked with violet. "Before God, it was." Nat smiled. "Better not let the servants see us *en deshabille*. When you have dressed knock on my door – I'm right across the hall – and we'll find some breakfast and await the verdict and the sentence."

Friston Hall nestled on a slope above where the Alde broadened into an estuary before joining the sea. The high-shouldered Jacobean manse was built in the form of a modified Greek cross and from its many windows one could see fields and woodlands to the north and west and the plain of the river to the south, while to the east the land declined gently to the ocean. Nowhere, thought Lyn, had she felt such repose as in the Hall's rosy brick walls. Squire Thomas had girdled his home with expansive lawns and gardens and at all times the sheltering trees crooned a lullaby as they were caressed by the breath of the river or the breath of the sea. Here was a place of healing, a place of peace.

As Nat and Lyn sat in the morning room, the exaltation of their ride, the weariness of their return and the distress of the morning receded. The two sat in companionable silence, waiting for the storm to break and hoping against hope that their transgressions would be forgiven.

Suddenly Nat stood. "I hear hooves. It must be Father. No ... stay there. He'll find us soon enough."

Lyn's heart beat a little faster as Squire Thomas Bacon entered the room. Nat's father was a man of medium height and coloring, with nothing distinguished about his face or figure except, perhaps, his eyes which were a piercing blue. Once again Lyn cast a quick glance at the portrait of Elizabeth Bacon which hung over the fireplace. Nat was the very image of his dark, imperious mother ... there was nothing of his father about him at all. Lyn scrutinized the Squire's kind face and swallowed painfully. He looked distressed.

"Well children, may I join you?" He touched Lyn's chin with a gentle hand and tilted her face towards his. "Did you sleep well, my dear? You look as fresh as a wood violet."

Nat spoke. "Yes sir, thanks to you. Lyn said she slept the night through and I did too, to my shame."

"And shame it is, Natty. You're almost a man and I hold you wholly responsible for yesterday's escapade. You certainly added to my gray hairs and I can tell you that Sir Edward Duke is not a happy man. You and I will talk later, but first I have a few things to say to Mistress Elizabeth and then I must see her home." He glanced at Lyn's attire. "I see that they washed and pressed your things as I asked."

Lyn blushed. Although her clothes and shoes were clean, she looked like a scullery maid. "Thank you, sir. You see, these are just my gardening clothes ..."

Squire Thomas smiled. "Do you love a garden, child? So do I. Now, let me tell you what I found out this morning at Benhall Lodge. It appears that last night's message never reached Sir Edward. He was busy putting the house in order after the fete and Jemmy delivered my note to Mistress Alathea, assuming it would be passed on. She told Jemmy to wait, which he did, and after a few minutes she returned and summarily told him that you could return tomorrow, (meaning today), and that was the end of it. Of course he believed that she had alerted the household."

Lyn frowned. "So my father did not know I was gone until they retired for the night and somebody looked in on me?"

Squire Thomas paused and sighed. "Elizabeth, nobody knew that you were gone at all ... nobody but Alathea. She told no one. I was the one who broke the news to your father and Lady Wyatt this very morning. They were astonished ... and not happy."

Two tears slid from the violet eyes. "Nobody looked for me last night ... and nobody looked this morning?"

"I fear that is so, child."

"'Tis scandalous," cried Nat. "They don't care a whit about her ... the most precious of all the Dukes and they discard her like chaff."

Squire Thomas whirled on his son. "Not a word out of you, boy! Your conduct does not bear scrutiny. Now, see that Mistress Elizabeth has all her things and order the chaise for me. I am going to drive her home as soon as she chooses to go."

Blindly, Lyn raised her sleeve to her face and dried her tears. "I don't choose to go home, sir," she said softly. "I want to stay here."

Now not only the violet eyes, but the gold and the blue were blurred.

"I do not have the power to keep you, child," Squire Thomas said. "Tell Natty when you are ready to go and I will see you home." And with those words the master of Friston Hall ascended to his library where neither Sir Francis Bacon nor any other wise man could tell him how it was that a parent could not love a child.

CHAPTER 4

JUNE 1666

Lyn stood in the gallery and watched Martin's black back as the cart jolted around Silverlace Green and dipped down the steep drive towards Benhall Street. The Alde was just visible through the screen of willows which framed the river's tranquil brow. It was a perfect morning but her heart was sore. She had parted badly with the stern woman who, for the past five years, had undertaken to form her. True to her oath, she had dutifully complied in all matters where her heart was not engaged. As a result her French was perfect, her drawing adequate, her music exceptional and her deportment beyond cavil. She had even submitted to the killing tedium of fine needlework. But nobody ruled her conscience, least of all Martin.

Having diligently completed the fifth year of her contract, the black-clad woman had declared herself satisfied that Mistress Elizabeth was finished to perfection and ready for the marriage market. She then asked leave to return to Boxley Abbey where Lady Jane Wyatt awaited her, eager to entrust to those competent hands the care of her fourth child, and only daughter. Just after breakfast this morning Sir Edward had tendered Martin his thanks, together with a little purse of gold coins, and had personally seen to the arrangement of her trunks and assisted her into the cart. Lyn had given her a cold hand and cold words, nothing more. It marked the end of an era.

Lyn turned restlessly from the casement and wandered downstairs into the hall. Everything was in perfect order. The wood shone as it had on the day of Sir Edward's great fete; the leaded glass gleamed; the air was redolent with the scent of the dried rose petals which she had preserved from the new bushes she had planted in Elinor's honor. Perfection was required, for Alathea would eat her last supper here tonight and would sleep in her maiden bed for the last time. Tomorrow morning, in the little church of Benhall St. Mary's, she was going to give her hand in marriage to Offley Jenney of Knottishall and she would spend her wedding night, and perhaps the remainder of her days, at Red House Farm.

Offley Jenney! They made such an odd pair, he so tall and thin, with carroty hair and skin like a girl; she so dark and ponderous with lightless eyes and a waxy complexion. Lyn shivered involuntarily. It was true that Alathea, at twenty-one, had never had another offer. And it was true that she brought Offley what, to the Jenneys, must seem a fortune: five thousand pounds and the complete renovation of Red House Farm! The modest brick manse which she and Nat had glimpsed on their ride to the sea was now double in size and each gable end bore, not the proper crow steps which adorned most Suffolk great houses, but the extravagant whorls and curves of the high Dutch fashion. It would not be surprising if the transformation of Red House Farm had cost her father as much again as Alathea's dowry. And what did Offley bring to the match? The *fact* of a husband, true. And a family history which, Nat said, went back to the Conquest. And a life estate in Red House Farm and its demesne. But there was no love ... not even the pretense of it. Alathea treated Offley like a servant and he, for his part, looked as though he was not even present when they were together, as if his mind and soul had fled elsewhere leaving only his body to go through the motions of the courtship ritual.

Yet Sir Edward seemed content. In fact he was the one who had initiated the contract and brought it to a head. Lyn surmised that he was driven by the desire to keep his favorite daughter nearby. It was hardly surprising, when you thought how shallow his relationship was with his other children. How odd her family was! Jane had not set foot in Benhall Lodge since the fete and John visited only once a year, at Christmas, and was always eager to leave promptly after Twelfth Night. And she? She was now the putative mistress of Benhall Lodge, but if she vanished tomorrow in a puff of smoke she doubted that her father would know the difference.

Lyn wandered downstairs and idly contemplated the three brents over the fireplace. She thought longingly of Friston Hall, in her mind a seat of peace and love. Since the morning Squire Thomas had returned her to Benhall Lodge she had been forbidden any communication with the family. The hand which Sir Edward had extended tentatively by inviting the Bacons to the fete had been withdrawn irrevocably. Lyn saw the Squire occasionally, and they always waved a greeting despite her father's interdiction, but she had never exchanged two words with Bess Bacon. As for Nat ... well, that was another story. How she cherished the memory of Friston Hall ... it was as though she had set foot in Eden, to be banished by the avenging angel just as she tasted paradise.

Lyn started and turned as she heard footsteps in the screen passage. "Why Rose, are you still here?" she asked as the housekeeper entered the hall.

"Yes, Miss. I'm just off to Rosie's, but I wanted to make sure that you didn't need anything before I left."

"I don't think so. The house is spotless. As long as the supper things are ready for tonight, there is nothing more to do. We are going to wait on ourselves this evening, you know. Father wanted you and your daughter to make an early start for Red House Farm tomorrow to prepare the wedding breakfast and if you spend the night in her cottage and take her cart you'll save a good half hour."

"It do seem odd not to be at Mistress Alathea's wedding, but she wanted the breakfast at her new home instead of here, and I can't be in two places at the same time."

"Well, most of us cannot, Rose, but perhaps you can."

The old woman blushed with pleasure. "Thank you, Miss. It will be a pleasure to work under you when Mistress Alathea is gone."

"I'm sure it was a pleasure to work for Mistress Alathea," remarked Sir Edward Duke as he entered the hall from the great stairwell.

Rose blanched. "Yes, sir. Leastways, I didn't mean ..."

"Of course you didn't. Now, off you go to Rosie's. We'll do very well by ourselves for one night. The wedding party will arrive at Red House Farm between noon and one. I want everything to be perfect."

The housekeeper dipped and bobbed and hurried to the kitchen, muttering to herself. Sir Edward took his usual place on the hearth and looked around him, finally focusing on his daughter.

"A lot of changes today, aren't there Elizabeth? Martin gone and Rose away for the night. The three of us will be alone tonight."

"Yes, sir," answered Lyn without expression.

"How does it feel to be the new mistress of Benhall Lodge?"

"I hope to please you, sir."

"I'm sure you shall ... I'm sure you shall. Does it bother you that I have turned off the servants except for Rose?"

"No, sir. With her living here and Rosie and Job coming in daily, I believe we can get along well enough. The villagers are always willing to help if we need more hands. After all, it will just be the two of us, most of the time."

"Exactly, Elizabeth. And I must economize, as I've told you. This wedding of Alathea's has been an expensive thing and it won't be long before I'll have to think of your marriage settlement."

The blood rushed to Lyn's face. "Oh, I hope not, sir," she cried.

Sir Edward frowned, his waxy brow creased with dark lines. "Jane married Henry at sixteen and your mother was not much older when she wed me. Do you have an aversion to marriage? Or ... have your affections been engaged without my knowledge?"

Could her father's dark eyes read her heart? If so, then he knew that her affections were indeed engaged, and had been these five years. "Oh, no sir. I didn't mean it that way. It is just ... well I shan't be sixteen until November and I hadn't really thought ..."

"Enough. I'm pleased to see that you are still innocent. Nonetheless, tomorrow's ceremony should give you something to think about. Now that Alathea is settled I shall start looking about on your behalf. Keep it in mind."

Lyn curtsied low so that Sir Edward could not read her face, which was pale with shock.

"Now," said the baronet, "as soon as Alathea is ready we are off to Red House Farm to supervise the last preparations. Before you join us this afternoon I want you to look over your things and your sister's so that all is in readiness for tomorrow. When you have done that, I want every room scrutinized, including the kitchen and the buttery. Then, when you have finished that, lock up tight and ride Fancy to Red House Farm to help your sister in whatever she requests. There is still a lot to be done."

Lyn curtsied again as Sir Edward turned and mounted the staircase and then she took the back stairs to her own rooms to avoid Alathea.

Lyn stared in the looking glass as she pulled the pins from her hair and ran her brush through it. There was no need to inspect the house ... it was in perfect order. She would look at her wedding costume and, once again, inspect her sister's things, but that was a matter of ten minutes. That meant that she had an hour, perhaps more, before she must set off for Knottishall ... a whole hour to peruse Nat's letters.

Her heart thudded beneath her linen bodice as she stroked her black mane, her thoughts far from Benhall Lodge. Nat! He was back in England after his three-year grand tour. His most recent letter had come from Dover, written just after landing from Calais. If he followed hard on its heels he might be at Friston Hall even now. Lyn shivered. Rosie would know ... she was a magnet for every scrap of gossip in and around Saxmundum, Benhall, Snape and Friston. She would see Rosie tomorrow at the wedding breakfast ... tomorrow she would know about Nat. And then she could plan how best to see him.

And when she did, what would he find? Their last interview – sweet forbidden fruit — had been at Snape Priory Barn when she was only twelve. Nat and his tutor, John Ray, were about to leave for Gravesend where they were to meet Ray's other charges, young Willoughby and Skippon, and take ship for The Netherlands to begin their grand tour. He had been desperate to make his adieux in person and, as always, she had leapt at the chance to see him. She had still been a child then, insouciant and flat-chested. That was not true now. She was still small, still had a profusion of dark curls, still had eyes which swirled with azure and violet, still had the same straight nose and tender lips, but now she was a woman. Would the innocent friendship of ten and fourteen be renewed at fifteen and nineteen? She would find a way to see Nat and, for better or for worse, get an answer soon.

Lyn moved impatiently from the glass. Would things really be so different now that they were grown? They had maintained their friendship for five long years, through half a dozen stolen meetings and more than thirty letters. Surely adulthood would not destroy the bond between them. Unconsciously seeking reassurance, she rose and moved to her armoire where, reaching behind her gowns, she removed a walnut box and carried it to her bed. Kicking off her slippers, she sat cross-legged in the center of the four-poster and removed a thick packet of letters from the box, each one limp with handling. The first were on the bottom and the latest on the top. Smiling, she reached for Nat's first letter ... it was, perhaps, her favorite. He had written in a bold, unformed hand on the very day that Squire Thomas had returned her, grieving, to Benhall Lodge ... the second day of their friendship. Clever Nat. Through a cousin of Rosie's who worked at Friston Hall, he had prevailed on the housekeeper's daughter to slip the letter to Lyn on the evening of her return. Even now, five years later, it burned with indignation. In fierce black letters he swore that nothing would destroy their friendship, and he had been true to his word.

Lyn smoothed the missive and returned it to the bottom of the pile. Bless Rosie! Nat had rewarded her with a gold coin for her first service to them and thereafter she had acted as their faithful postmistress. Maintaining the correspondence was easy for Lyn ... she simply had to walk to the village and drop by Rosie's cottage either to send or receive a letter. For Nat, away from Friston Hall, first at Cambridge and then in Europe, it was somewhat more difficult. He enclosed his notes under cover to Rosie herself and received Lyn's under the cottager's cover, so that there was a greater risk that the correspondence would go awry. However a benign providence must have guided them, for not a single letter miscarried in five years. Lyn had long suspected that Rose knew exactly what her daughter was up to, but if she did she kept silent. Lyn was certain that Sir Edward remained blissfully ignorant of his youngest daughter's secret.

Lyn pulled a letter at random from the middle of the pile. She smiled when she opened it. This one was dated April of 1663 and contained Nat's first report of his grand tour. He had been staying in Leiden, a university town, and he wrote about how boring it was to attend the botany lectures with Ray; he much preferred walking about the town, staring at the tall brick houses with their characteristic gables, seeing what the people ate and how they dressed. He had been entranced by the canals and he had drawn her a picture of one, with a little arched bridge over it, and a horse and cart on the bridge. In the background he had depicted one of the great Dutch mills and had written in the margin: "They truly look like this!"

Lyn quickly scanned the rest of the pile. She knew every word by heart: Nat's impressions of the cathedral at Cologne, his awe at the towering Swiss peaks, and his astonishment at the richness of Rome which he called a layer cake of history. Lyn returned her treasure trove to the box and, seizing the most recent letter, lay back on her bolster and placed it to her lips. This missive had come to her only last week – it was the one from Dover. A tear escaped her. The note brought her the first word that Nat had been ordered home early by Squire Thomas in order to complete his recovery from the scourge of smallpox. Lyn turned on her stomach and cradled her head in her arms. He had not even told her! He had been in the south of France when he was stricken, and she had not even known. Perhaps it was just as well; it might have killed her. In the event, the disease had been mild and he had survived without incident, not even with a blemish on his dear face. How the Squire must have suffered! As a convalescent, Nat was doubtless traveling slowly, but even so ... even so, he might be home. Tomorrow, she would know.

Lyn sat up suddenly. Time was passing. She must look over the wedding finery, change into her riding clothes, and order Fancy to be saddled. She smoothed Nat's letter and placed it with the others and then stored the box carefully in the corner of the armoire. She glanced quickly at the wicker form in the corner and determined that her maid-of-honor costume, in striped periwinkle and cream, was in order and that hat, gloves, stockings and slip pers were as they should be. Then, shoeless, she sped down the gallery to Alathea's chambers in the south crosswing. It felt odd to be alone in the house; the quiet was profound.

Lyn crossed her sister's antechamber quickly and entered the bedroom. The rose colored drapes were pulled against the sun and the light was dim, as usual. Alathea had always shunned the sunlight. The four-poster was freshly made up and the room looked as it should. The dress form was in the corner near a casement and Lyn pulled the drapes and let in the late morning light. She carefully examined the low-cut white silk gown studded with seed pearls, the petticoats, the slippers and stockings and the expanse of fine lace which Alathea would use for a veil. Drawing the drapes again, she turned to the dressing table and opened a silver box. There lay the lustrous pearl bracelet which Sir Edward had brought back from London on the occasion of his baronetcy and next to it was his most recent gift, a necklace of even finer pearls, perfectly matched and glowing like little moons in the dim light. All was in order here. Lyn grimaced. Tomorrow Alathea would be a vision in white, the very image of maidenhood. Why, she wondered, did she feel that the image was a travesty?

Her sister's French clock chimed noon and Lyn turned to go. As she reentered the antechamber something seemed amiss. In one corner stood the writing table. Lyn gave it a glance, collected some odd sheets of paper and put them in the drawer, and straightened the ink pots and quills and seals. Nothing was wrong there. In the other corner stood a prayer stool. Lyn ran a hand over the wood, testing for dust, and carefully closed the

Bible. Now everything was tidy, but the room still did not seem right. She glanced at the worn pink silk brocade wall-coverings. The wall between the antechamber and the bedroom was marred by a rectangle, head-high, colored a darker pink than the rest. Of course! The painting had been removed. Alathea's Danae. It was her greatest treasure. She would want it at Red House Farm and must have taken it already. Lyn thought it no great loss; to her eye Lely's work was vulgar and flamboyant and had no business in the room where Alathea said her prayers. The puzzle answered, Lyn hurried back to her room to change. If only the road to Red House Farm passed by Friston Hall ... but it did not.

Fancy picked her way cautiously up the gravel drive and Lyn had ample opportunity to study the ostentatious facade of her sister's new home. The brick work glared in the early afternoon sun and the fanciful curvilinear gables seemed to unfurl like flags although there was not a breath of air. She dismounted at the front door and handed the mare over to the boy who responded to her knock. The tiled front hall was pleasantly cool and she let her eyes adjust to the dimness and then ascended the right-hand arc of the graceful double staircase. When she reached the landing she turned right and followed a long hall which ended in richly carved double doors of burnished oak. She knocked and, receiving no answer, entered what she knew to be her sister's bedroom suite. She stopped, astonished. When she had last seen these rooms they were mere lath and plaster. Now the walls glowed with rich tapestries and thick carpets lay underfoot. The sconces, candelabra and other metal work was all gleaming brass, and the total effect was one of deep reds and blues pricked with gold. The furniture had been imported from France and its lines were light and full of movement, a far cry from the heavy, rectilinear Elizabethan pieces of Benhall Lodge. Lyn had to admit that the sitting room was stunning; but it had nothing of Alathea about it. She could see Jane in this grand setting, but not her stolid, slow, secretive sister.

Looking about her in awe, she crossed the sitting room to another set of double doors which gave onto the bedroom. The doors stood slightly ajar and she pushed them further open and entered. Alathea was standing by the huge four-poster bed, smoothing the coverlet of crimson silk, smiling. She looked up when she heard Lyn.

"You finally came. Better late than never, I suppose, but most of the work is done."

"It is truly beautiful, Alathea. I had no idea it was so grand."

The big girl sniffed. "Why shouldn't we have the best? I had the pink bedroom since I was ten. It was a child's room; this is a woman's."

Lyn removed her riding coat and placed it, and her reticule, on the fruitwood table which stood by the door. "The colors are wonderful. Did you choose them?"

"Father and I between us."

"Well, the effect is stunning. Now, what can I do to help? Are your clothes in order?"

"My dressing closet is there, through that door. I haven't had a chance to do much with it. Why don't you see what you can accomplish? I'll go find Father and have something to drink ... we have been working for hours." Alathea paused and asked reluctantly, "Shall I send you something?"

"Cider or perry would be welcome; I am parched from the ride."

"Very well," Alathea shrugged, and left the room.

Before retreating to the dressing closet, Lyn took a moment to look around her. The huge bed took pride of place, with its rich hangings of red and blue embroidered with fanciful animal shapes and strange oriental geometries. An elaborate dressing table stood under the southern window and on it were vials of scent and a set of silver-backed brushes. A great chest stood at the foot of the bed and Lyn could not refrain from opening it. A pile of soft woolen blankets was topped by a rug of silver fox, the pelts gleaming like opalescent pearls. Lyn carefully lowered the lid and hardly dared breathe. This room was fit for royalty and the cost must have been royal as well. She turned to look at the fireplace which stood opposite the bed and gasped. There, in pride of place over the marble mantel, hung the Danae, as though it were made for the room. And that was it ... that was the key. The Danae had not been made for the room, but the room was made for the Danae. The rich reds and somber blues and gleaming golds were all there, in Lely's extravagant brushwork. The entire suite took form and shape from the figure of the ecstatic woman in the fall of gold.

Several hours later Lyn had finished arranging her sister's extensive wardrobe, marveling at the gowns of all colors and weights, at the matching stockings and slippers, and at the drawers of fine under garments. The Jenneys were going to commence married life in a grand style. Evening was drawing in when she went downstairs, glad to find Sir Edward and Alathea sitting down to an informal tea set out in the breakfast room. She had eaten little that day and was famished.

As she poured herself a cup of tea and chose a piece of dark, rich, spice cake, she broke the silence which had entered the room with her.

"Everything is as perfect as I can make it, Alathea, just as I left your room at Benhall. But I saw no place for Offley's things. Have I missed something?"

Her sister darted a glance at Sir Edward and frowned. "What a puss you are, Elizabeth. Offley has his own suite and his own dressing room and his man has already arranged his effects. I would have had my maid handle my things, but this is her last day with Offley's mother. I won't have her services until tomorrow so it was as well that you could spare a few hours to help me."

Lyn looked confused, but was reluctant to say anything. Her father and mother had shared the big bedchamber at Benhall Lodge and surely most married folk did the same. Did Offley Jenney not plan to share Alathea's bed? And if not, what did that mean? Lyn felt a blush creep up her face. She knew that marriage entailed the union of mind, soul and body, but she was not clear on the details. It seemed wiser to drop the subject.

She finished her tea and poured another cup. "It was my pleasure," she lied dutifully. "Is there anything else I can do?"

"Nothing, thank you," interposed Sir Edward Duke, rising from the table. "When you have finished your meal it will be time for you to return to Benhall; I want you home before it is dark. Alathea and I have a few more things to do and then we will follow. I have a lantern if we are delayed for any reason."

Lyn rose and curtsied slightly and watched the ponderous pair leave the room. They were well matched, like animals from the ark. It had been a long day and she was glad to be left alone. She browsed among the breads and cakes, found a dish of strawberries, and helped herself lavishly to cream and sugar. If she spoiled her appetite for supper, so be it. She had just as soon ride home and retire to her bed, supperless. After half an hour, she sat back, replete and watched the dusk fall. She shivered a little as the light faded and remembered that she had left her coat and, more important, her reticule containing the house key in Alathea's room. What a coil if she arrived at the empty lodge and found herself locked out! Lyn took her tea things to the kitchen, thanked the serving maid and had her summon the boy whom she told to prepare Fancy for the ride home. Glancing with some apprehension at the dying light, she ran upstairs and pushed open the great oak doors into Alathea's sitting room. Strange ... she thought she would find her father and sister here, but the room was empty. She must have misunderstood their intentions. She remembered exactly where she had left her coat and bag – on the fruitwood table — and quickly crossed the thick carpets to her sister's bedroom. Light gleamed under the door. Could Alathea be here? She opened one of the doors slightly and was flooded with candlelight from the two great candelabra which stood, tree-like, one at each side of the bed. But it was not the candelabra which caught her attention, nor the rich bed-hangings. She was mesmerized by the crimson silk bed cover and the two white figures which disported upon it.

Alathea lay prone on the blood-red sheet, her face enraptured, like Danae's. Her father, nude, lay half across her, his legs splayed and his mouth and tongue busy in Venus' secret place. Alathea cried out and the baronet drew her under him, clawing her white flesh in his desire. He cleaved to her as a mollusk to its shell and the two became one.

Hardly knowing what she was doing, Lyn snatched her coat and reticule and fled. Now she knew what men and women did together. And now she knew why Offley Jenney and his bride had separate rooms and would keep them so.

Nat buried his face in Prince Rupert's mane and breathed the heady mix of horse sweat, wood smoke and Suffolk air. You could drop him down blindfolded at Friston and he would know where he was. It was the scent of home, and he was deeply glad to be here, with his father and Bess. The three years with Ray had been fascinating, and he would not have missed a minute – still *was* sorry he had missed the opportunity to see Marseilles, Nimes and Aix-en-Provence – but Suffolk was in his bones and blood and he supposed it always would be. He turned to Jemmy who was grinning from ear to ear.

"You've kept him beautifully, Jem. How he has filled out! I never thought he would have this height and this strength. How are his manners?"

"Oh, he's mannerly, sir, right mannerly. Why, he'll jump a stone wall without batting an eyelash. He's lost all his coltish ways – he loves to show his paces."

Nat stroked the glossy neck and heard a step on the gravel. Looking around, he saw his sister and it was his turn to smile.

"Why, good morning, Bess. I didn't expect to find you up, though it must be nearly noon. I kept you up unconscionably with my tales."

Bess Bacon looked lovingly at her brother. How fine he was on this glorious June day. He had gained a few inches in height while he was away – he was probably as tall as he would ever be, somewhat under the average. She wondered if that would bother him, as he liked to be best in all things. To her eye he was perfect: his proportions were exquisite, he had the look of a greyhound. She was glad he had kept his natural hair. She knew women who would give years of their lives for that profusion of black curls tinted with umber, but fashion was moving in the other direction and even the Squire was muttering about shearing his locks and buying a periwig. If he had any sense, Nat would keep his curls. The flawless gold skin was the same, unmarked by the smallpox, although his illness had made him a little paler than usual. The aquiline features were unchanged, unless they looked at the world even more fiercely than in the past. And those extraordinary eyes were still gold, barred with black. The eyes had changed – that was it. Nat was no longer a child. You could see experience, pain and even some cynicism in those hawk eyes. He must have had adventures abroad which he would never share with her – adventures that had made him a man.

"Oh, I got quite enough sleep, thank you. I could listen to your stories forever and Father could too. But he sent me to fetch you in to dinner."

The two walked back to the house companionably, arm in arm.

Bess glanced at Nat. "Were you paying attention last night when I told you that Alathea Duke is being wed to Offley Jenney this very day?"

"Of course! I can listen as well as talk. But you, of all people, know that I hear these things from Lyn. I've known the date for the past six months. I thought of arriving in mourning on behalf of Offley."

"Oh, Nat you are terrible. Alathea must have some redeeming qualities, we just haven't found them." She paused at the terrace and lowered her voice. "Shall you try and see Lyn?"

"Of course. I shall arrange it this very afternoon. She should be free after they settle Alathea in that excrescence which they call Red House Farm. I can hardly wait to see it. According to Father it's an embarrassment not only to the neighborhood but to the whole county."

"But how will you reach her?"

"Through Rosie, of course. She'll have my note this evening, I swear it. And then we'll meet wherever she says, whenever she can get away. Only think, Bess, it has been three years!"

"Natty, watch your step. In those three years you have become a man and Lyn has become a woman."

Nat removed his sister's hand petulantly and walked towards the house. "I'm not a fool, Bess. I know that things will be different." He stopped and turned. "And Father?"

"Oh, I'm sure he knows you are in contact with her, but we have never said a word. Least said, soonest mended."

Nat smiled and placed her hand on his arm again. "Wise words. Come, let's go inside."

Since Nat had arrived the previous evening Squire Thomas had not been able to stop smiling. His boy was home, safe and sound, after enough adventures to fill a library and after that dreadful smallpox scare. He would give the lad a few months at home and then it was off to Cambridge for his Master of Arts. After that, Gray's Inn, where all the Bacons had learned their law. The devil made work for idle hands and he would keep Nat's nose to the grindstone until he showed some sense of direction. John Ray had not been able to give him a very good report. The gist of it was that the boy was gifted, but impulsive. Well, he didn't need Ray to tell him that. Natty had been that way since he could walk.

Bess and Nat walked into the dining room and the Squire rose and kissed them both. "Your first dinner at home, Natty. Bess ordered all your favorite things – chicken with rosemary, tender new potatoes, French beans, that light cake that you like, drowned in cream.... Come, tell me what you think of this Rhenish."

An hour later the three pushed their plates back and moved to the terrace to take tea. The Squire's summer garden lay before them and the red brick of the stable block glowed through the shrubbery.

"So Mistress Alathea is now Mistress Jenney," mused the Squire. "And our little Lyn will be in charge of Benhall Lodge. Only think ... she's still just a bit of a thing."

Nat and Bess exchanged glances. "Have you ever talked to her, Father, since that day ...?"

The Squire frowned. "You know I have not, Natty. I can't come between a father and his child, however much I might wish to. But I see her often enough. She is as pretty as a picture. I think I would know if something were wrong. I suspect the baronet will find her a husband soon enough; he has never cared much for any of his children except Alathea, and that's a mystery to the whole neighborhood." He turned to Bess. "Come, child, pour me another cup of tea."

Nat looked across his father's flowerbeds and lawns. "What is that? Why it's Jemmy, running." He rose. "Something must have happened. I wonder if Prince Rupert ...?"

Before he could finish his thought the hostler burst upon the terrace, cap in hand. "Beg pardon, sir. Master Nat is wanted at the stable."

Squire Thomas rose, his face creased with perplexity. "What is wrong, Jemmy? Is it that black horse?"

"No, sir, not at all. It's little Miss Duke, the dark-haired one, come riding as though the hounds were after her, all trembling she is, and asking for Master Nat."

Bess cried out. "Lyn! Here? On Alathea's wedding day! Something terrible must have happened." She turned to her father. "Oh, let her be brought here at once."

The Squire nodded and Nat and Jemmy rushed across the lawn. Minutes later Lyn was seated on the terrace, still in her wedding finery, a glass of Rhenish in her hand. "I can't tell you, I can't tell you," she sobbed.

"Come, child," urged Squire Thomas. "Is it your father?"

"He is ... not injured."

"Well then, Alathea or Offley Jenney?"

"They are ... not hurt. They are all at Red House Farm, at the wedding breakfast."

"Has harm come to anyone?"

"Not in the way you mean ..."

"You are speaking in riddles, Lyn. How can we help you if you will not explain?"

Nat cried out indignantly. "Father, surely you can see that she is too distressed to speak." He kneeled before Lyn and took her by the shoulders. "Can you tell me, sweetheart?"

Her eyes full of tears, she nodded slowly. Nat looked up at his father. "Let me take her to the morning room and speak with her."

"All right, boy. I don't see any other way. We'll wait for you here."

Minutes later Nat and Lyn were seated where they had parted five years ago, Elizabeth Bacon looking down on them with her imperious smile. Unthinking, Nat held the girl close to his heart just as he had held her as a child. But she was not a child now. Her soft form molded to his and he soon unhanded her and settled her in a chair. Just as she had opened her heart to him long ago, so today the story of the Danae tumbled out incoherently, with a storm of tears. The most intuitive of men, the pieces of the puzzle came together for Nat in seconds and he knew that she spoke the truth. *That* was the shadow of Benhall Lodge that all Suffolk felt but could not name. *That* was the key to Sir Edward's secret and taciturn ways. *That* was why Jane lingered in Kent and John in London, leaving Lyn to face the horror. *That* was why Alathea smiled so coldly and so cruelly. And *that* was why Lyn must never return home.

Once again Lyn lay in Bess' bedroom watching the embroidered strawberries move on the creamy hangings, agitated by the evening breeze. The cold hand of dread squeezed her heart: her quest for help had failed. Nat believed her tale of horror; the magic between them was still there and they could communicate without words. Kind Bess would have stood by her as well, but Squire Thomas had forbidden his daughter to hear a word of the scandalous story. But the Squire, in whose hands her fate lay, the Squire did not believe her ... thought her tale the result of a fevered adolescent brain, turned by sibling jealousy. Sir Edward Duke was a knight and peer of the realm, he had said. No one of his rank would do what she claimed he had done; it was simply not possible. Lyn sighed and stirred. She would get no help here; it was time to go. The day was waning and her father would be returning to the Lodge soon from the wedding celebration. If it was her fate to share the same roof with him, as Squire Thomas had ordained, she must return home quickly and take to her bed, playing out the tale she had woven that morning. She had looked so ill at the wedding that Sir Edward had let her return to the Lodge right after the ceremony. He must never know that she had spent the afternoon at Friston Hall rather than in her own chambers. She must hurry away.

Lyn rose and sought her slippers just as Squire Thomas knocked on the door and asked leave to enter. She sat on the edge of Bess' bed and he took his daughter's armchair. They shared an awkward silence for some minutes and then the Squire spoke.

"Lyn, I think you know what I am going to say. Do not hold it against me. I have quizzed Nat and, to some extent Bess, and have cudgeled my own brains for any sign of ... this evil that you have related. Child, I can find nothing, no hard facts. I fear that, for whatever reason, you have invented a nightmare. Don't misunderstand me! The whole world knows that Sir Edward Duke has been a hard father, except to one child, and that one has been spoiled by over-indulgence. And the whole world knows that your mother's marriage was a bitter one. But you have taken these unpleasant realities and created a monster from them.

"I have no option but to ask you to return to Benhall Lodge and to not disclose this interview to anyone." Squire Thomas sighed. "I have my own work cut out for me persuading Natty that I have acted correctly ... he is furious. He made me promise to tell you this. If ever, God forfend, you find hard proof of ... the crime ... you must bring it directly to me and I will support you to the full extent of the law. But now, regrettably, there is nothing I can do for you."

Lyn leaned down and slid her feet into her slippers. She felt nothing ... she felt like stone.

Standing, she addressed the Squire. "I understand, sir. I am sorry I brought this mischief to your door just as Nat returned. You have been kinder to me than I deserve." Her heart moved within her and her eyes brimmed with tears. "Twice Fancy has brought me to Friston Hall in need. And twice you have given me refuge and advice. There is only one thing that I ask."

"What is it, child?" asked the Squire softly, his own blue eyes swimming with moisture.

"If Fancy brings me to Friston Hall once again, will you take me in a third time?"

Squire Thomas rose and drew Lyn to him. "Of course, my dear," he answered. "Of course."

CHAPTER 5

MAY 1670

Nat looked up from Coke's *Institutes* with a sigh. He crossed the study to the casements and threw them open to the sharp May wind. It might have been March, it was that cold. John Grey's papers flew up in a flurry and settled on the floor in chaos. Grey flung his quill into the cold, empty fireplace in exasperation and asked bitterly, "How will you ever learn the law of enfoeffment if you don't let me finish this summary!"

"To the devil with the law of enfoeffment!" Nat replied. "Why should I know what fools did with their land five hundred years ago?"

"Is that a serious question? Do you know what 'precedent' means? Our law is based on the wisdom of our forebears. Where have you been these past two years, Nat?"

"Oh, you're the scholar, John. I know enough if I know how to manage my father's lands, which I do already. I have no interest in how some feudal baron saw fit to do business."

John sighed. "Nat, if you are serious about the law you must learn it, root and branch."

Nat laughed and poured a glass of wine from the fine crystal carafe Bess had given him when he and Grey had set up these chambers together two years ago.

"You pride yourself on your logic, John. Don't you see the flaw in your reasoning? I *am not serious* about the law, so that nothing you say applies. Your what-do-you-call-it … major premise… is wrong, so the whole thing falls apart. Come, have a glass of wine while I put your papers to rights."

John smiled reluctantly and took the proffered glass. Since he and Bacon had met in the great hall of Gray's Inn on the first day of term all those months ago he had lain under the dark youth's spell, and today was no different. Just one glass, then back to Coke. When he finished this summary he would finally be satisfied with his digest of the law of real property and he would be ready for any examiner who cared to test him. As for Nat, without the summaries he would have received his walking papers long ago, despite his illustrious surname. As Bacon never cracked a book, the summaries were the sole means by which he learned what little he knew of English law. John tossed off his drink and smiled as the familiar image came to mind: the workhorse and the thoroughbred. He knew that some of his fellow students called him Bacon's whore. And it was true that he had the use of this spacious study, his very own bedroom, as much of Jemmy's time as was not devoted to his master, the use of his friend's second horse, and a thousand other benefits in exchange for a paltry tenth of their joint expenses. But, but, but ... did he not pay the rest of his moiety by showing the beauty of the common law to his friend and chamber mate? Who could put a price tag on learning? It was his own ability which had earned him the scholarship, however meager, which brought him to London; and it was his parents' example which had endowed him with a bottomless capacity for labor. His father had worked his way up from the Suffolk turnip fields to the magistrate's bench before death cut his life short, and his mother still maintained her cottage near Ipswich with the products of her own loom. Sharp mental tools and the discipline to use them: it was a better inheritance than gold and it had made his star shine bright at Gray's Inn. He might be a workhorse to Bacon's thoroughbred, but they were a matched pair which pulled well together. Whoredom did not enter into it.

Nat finished ordering John's papers and weighted them down with a glass orb. The two friends, moving as one, met at the window where the street noise was deafening as the day wound down to night. Shivering in the wind, which was half-winter, half-spring, they closed the casement and returned to the great table where they did their work. John scanned his summary while Nat busied himself at the fireplace. On the first of May, in a sudden spurt of economy, Nat had decreed that they would have no fires until November, but now he broke his oath, as he had so many, and was lavish with the last of the kindling and coal. John knew he should object, but when the cheery blaze danced high the spirits of both friends rose with it and they smiled at one another in pleasure.

Nat looked at John's fine, fresh face with its sea-gray eyes, wide mouth and curling lips, made for laughter. "Did you hear from your mother today?"

"Yes, my sole letter was from her. She is doing well, apart from the usual rheumatics, and she sends you her best. She has never forgotten your visit, Nat. You won her over wholly."

Nat blushed, a rarity. "Nonsense, why should I not pay homage to such a worthy dame? It was on my way home ... I hardly put myself out. I wanted to see where you were born, John. 'Tis as cunning a cottage as I have ever seen."

"Well, it's not Friston Hall, but it is home and I love it. And you? You had several letters. Were any of interest?"

61

"How politic you are. What you mean to ask is whether I heard from Lyn or whether my father has yet discovered that I have, once more, over-drawn my allowance."

John's face sobered. "And have you?"

Nat paced restlessly before the fire. "Yes to both. Lyn sent a bulletin ... and Father is furious. I expect I shall have to report home soon and account for my spendthrift ways and, as usual, be measured against you, the paragon of wisdom and industry." His tone was bitter and John flushed and averted his face.

"I am sorry to hear it. Perhaps if I went with you I could convince your father that my clay feet are fouler than yours by far."

"He would never believe it. And rightly so, as it is an arrant lie. No, Father is as enamored of you as your mother is of me." Nat lost his bitter tone and laughed. "It is the way of the world, is it not? Parents and children ... always that push and pull for supremacy. You made a great impression last Christmas ... I'll never catch up."

"You know you are first in your father's affections, Nat."

"I know it, John. That's where the rub is. Every time I err I strike a blow at him as well as at my own conscience and the pain is double."

"But what of Lyn? Still the same sad story? The train of unwanted and rejected suitors, the cold baronet, the ungodly alliance with the sister?"

Nat's face was filled with somber care. "Nothing has changed. Alathea's firstborn is the image of Sir Edward, but the neighborhood simply says 'la, how the child looks like his mother, nothing of Offley Jenney in him at all!' And you know she is carrying another child ... I believe it is due this month or the next, poor little monster."

"How can you be sure, Nat? All these years? If it is true someone besides Lyn must have seen something."

Nat turned on his friend like a cornered cat, spitting venom. "Never doubt her word, John, as you love me! Lyn is truth incarnate. What she says happened on the eve of Alathea's wedding is true, before God. Can you not see why Suffolk denies the obvious? The Jenneys have been pur-chased by the baronet; there is nothing they will not countenance to keep their new fortune. As for the servants, do you think for one moment that their eyewitness testimony, if it existed, would outweigh Sir Edward Duke's reputation? Nonsense. If they spoke out they would lose their places and never work again. No, father and daughter are too powerful and too clever by far. Man is helpless against them ... only God has the power to strike them down."

John was silent in the face of Nat's vehemence. What would come of his friend's strange intrigue with the child whom he compared to a wood vio-let, a sea sprite? For ten years the two had fostered a relationship built on a dream, yet it was the one thing to which Nat had been true. The girl Lyn was Bacon's lodestar. In all their discussions John had never asked the fateful question; perhaps it was time.

"And when Lyn is of age? What then?"

Nat had regained his composure. He looked surprised and almost amused. "In November of 1671 I shall wed her, of course!"

John swallowed hard. Well, he had started down this path, perhaps he had better continue. "Eighteen more months. I hope she can endure it. Does your father know your plan?"

"He does not need to ... I am already of age and can do what I like. The only question is whether Lyn can bear to wait out her time under that evil roof. Is it possible that she can remain unsullied? Ah, John, it is such a coil. I would remove her tomorrow, but the only place she could stay without the loss of her reputation would be Friston Hall and Father would never take her in ... not without absolute proof of the baronet's crime. Moreover, I am currently penniless, having drained my coffers at Meg's. You know that Father holds the purse strings and today's letter tells me that I will not have a sou until I return home and make an adequate accounting." Stirred up again, Nat paced the room in agitation, striking his forehead with the palm of his hand.

John sighed. "And Lyn's letter? Did it contain nothing hopeful?"

"Nothing. She did not say as much, but I suspect that the baronet handled her cruelly when she rejected the most recent offer from the earl's son. I shall see her when I go home and get the truth out of her."

"Do you still meet at Hazelwood?"

"When the weather is fine. It is in such poor repair that we cannot use it during the winter."

"Is that why you dared go to Benhall Lodge last Christmas?"

"Yes ... I have only done it a handful of times, the risk is so great. But I should die if I could not see her from time to time. Early on our letters were enough, but now ... now I must hold her in my arms when I can."

"You are playing with fire, Nat."

"I know it well. But you would understand if you had ever met her, John."

"Perhaps I will. Perhaps it will all come right."

Nat sighed at John's false optimism. The fire burned low and a weary silence fell in the great chamber. John was staring unthinkingly at his papers and Nat continued to pace when they heard a knock on the door.

"It's Jemmy, sure," said Nat, "coming to get our order for supper."

The door opened and the little hostler stepped inside, cap in hand. "Good evening, sir. Good evening Mister John. Mister Nat, sir, Mister Bokenham is right on my heels."

John rose in dismay. The last thing they needed on this unhappy evening was Nat's dissolute "cousin" to entice the young squire out on the town, spending money that he could ill afford on pursuits which he would be better off avoiding. A tall, gangly, swarthy fellow entered the room like Jemmy's shadow, showing his crooked, yellow teeth in a feral grin. He ignored John and clapped Bacon on the shoulders like a long lost brother.

"Natty, my lad, how goes it? I pried a few coins from my aunt's over-stuffed purse, hired the most God-awful nag you've ever laid eyes on, and left Brampton behind me yesterday for the lights of London. I would have been here long since if I had your black, but better late than never! You'll never send me away to entertain myself! It would be too heartless. Besides, I've already spoken for a room at Meg's ... that little redhead is still there, and pining for you, you may be sure. Come, the night is young and there are better things to do than waste those dark eyes on study!"

John bit his tongue and turned his back on Bokenham. Half the reason Nat's purse was always empty was this shambling rogue. He claimed some distant connection with Nat's mother's family and he turned up regularly, like a bad penny. Tonight, at least, Nat would surely say "no," penniless as he was and preoccupied with Lyn Duke. To his distress, he heard the manic tone in Nat's reply which always spelled trouble.

"I am without a shilling, but if you'll cover the cost, I'm your man. We'll sup at Merry Meg's and see what else she has to offer. Jemmy, fetch my hat and coat and stick. Once you've seen to John's needs you may have the night off."

John turned, hoping to shame his friend with a glance, but all he saw was a slim back disappearing in the direction of their bedchambers and he knew that all was lost. Within minutes the chambers were empty of all but himself. He wearily built up the fire and settled again to Coke, wondering idly if there had been a Meg in the great jurist's life. Sighing, he settled to work.

For hours John Grey wandered in the paths of the law, roads which were arid to some but alive with interest to him. The last log crumbled, sending a shower of sparks to the bed of embers below, and the student looked up, startled, at the mantel clock. It was an hour past midnight. Grey rose and stretched, his sinews cracking. Time to sleep; Nat would not be back before dawn, if then. As he ordered his papers he heard a firm knock on the door. It was not Bacon, who never knocked. It was not Jemmy, who always struck thrice in rapid succession. Probably a fellow student, desperate for some last-minute instruction. Before he could reach the door it was thrust open and, to his astonishment, he saw Squire Thomas Bacon, his visage uncharacteristically haggard.

John leapt forward as his friend's father staggered and reached for the back of a chair to steady himself. "Mister Bacon! So late! You look unwell!"

"Aye, John, I've been better."

"Let me take your coat. Sit down, sit down. I've some claret here on the sideboard ... here, don't say a word until you've had something to drink."

"Thank'ee, boy, thank'ee. That helps ... it is bitter cold for May. Is Nat about?"

"No, sir. He's ... well I'm not quite sure where he is. He left around six this afternoon and has not been back since."

"Was he by himself?"

John paused. There was no help for it. "In truth, sir, no. Henry Bokenham turned up and Nat decided to spend the evening with him."

The lines in the Squire's face deepened. "Worse and worse, John. If it were not for the Brooke blood in that leech's veins I would turn him over to the authorities for corrupting youth. He's a cardsharper and a scoundrel who preys on young fools like my son."

"Oh, sir, that's harsh."

"Harsh, but true. He draws out Nat's worst instincts. And tonight of all night's, for God's sake!"

"Do you bring Nat bad news, sir?"

"The worst," groaned the Squire.

"Is it ... is it Bess, sir?"

Squire Thomas looked up sharply. "Bess? Why no, lad, my daughter is fine." The older man took another swallow of wine. "John, what has Nat told you of our little neighbor, Elizabeth Duke?"

John paled. It was no time to hold anything back. "Virtually everything, sir. Her sad story, his fears and suspicions ... he has confided a great deal in me."

"Well, thank God for that. I won't have to start at the beginning. You have been a good friend to Natty, John, and a steadying influence. A pity that he has not outgrown his wild ways, but he is still young .... Well, I have come about young Lyn, as he and Bess call her. I'll tell you my tale and then we'll wait for my boy. We must return to Friston tomorrow ... or rather, today."

John cut to the heart of the matter. "Did Lyn finally bring her proof to you, sir?"

The Squire looked him squarely in the face, brilliant blue eyes fastened to those of sea-gray. "I should have believed her long ago, but I could not. I could not think so badly of a knight and peer. That such evil could reign so close to my home ... not possible. She came to Friston early this morning on her little mare, Fancy, her third such ride, just as she predicted. The housekeeper came with her ... Rose ... a fine woman ... been with the Dukes as long as I can remember."

"You are distressed, sir. Pray go on."

Squire Thomas propped his forehead in his hands as if in silent prayer. "The long and the short of it is that on the previous night the baronet, how shall I say it? *Approached* Lyn ... I cannot find the words. Made *overtures* to Lyn of a kind that no father should make to his daughter. The poor thing showed me the bruises on her shoulders where he had gripped her. He told her that since the other daughter, Alathea, was *unavailable* and since Lyn had showed her preference to remain at home, with him, by refusing four suitors, that he would take her at her word and make her his little wife until his first love was ready for him once again."

The men looked at one another, aghast. The Duke girl had lived with this nightmare for over four years and only now was she taken at her word.

"This ... *incident* ... took place in Lyn's bedchamber. By great good fortune Rose, who normally sleeps in a small closet off the kitchen, had spent the night in Master John's suite, as the kitchen wing was undergoing repairs. John Duke's and Lyn's chambers share the same landing. Rose was in John's antechamber, with the door half open, and she could hear every-thing in Lyn's rooms quite clearly. When Lyn screamed – yes, the poor thing cried aloud – the housekeeper rushed to her aid and saw the girl in her father's arms. The baronet was clad only in his nightshirt and he was obvi-ously ... *aroused*, no question about it. There was only one construction to be put on the scene – the man was about to ravish his daughter. Apparently he was so astonished at seeing Rose that he lost his wits long enough for her to hustle Lyn out before they could be stopped. The housekeeper grabbed a couple of cloaks on her way through the kitchen, wrapped one about the stunned girl and the other about herself, rushed to the stables, threw a bri-dle on Fancy and within minutes they were off to Rosie's cottage ... that's the daughter, who lives in Benhall village. They huddled in Rosie's kitchen until dawn broke when they planned to seek help from me. I would they had not waited for day, but so it was."

Speechless, John helped the Squire to another glass of wine and, paus-ing briefly, refilled his own glass.

"While they waited Rosie poured out such a tale about Red House Farm. Alathea's staff knows what is going on ... it is the source of black jokes among them. Offley Jenney spends most of his days at his mother's and when he comes to his wife's house he locks himself up in his own suite and only comes out for meals, which he takes with Alathea, with the utmost for-mality, each at the end of a long expanse of mahogany."

The Squire sighed deeply and drank. "When dawn broke they put Lyn on the mare and accompanied her on foot, Rose on her right and Rosie on her left, like an armed guard. I had just settled down in my library, with a pot of tea, to plan my day when my man brought the three women upstairs. The girl was as pale as a ghost. Bess is in Bury St. Edmunds, staying with her intended, and so, for the third time, I settled Lyn in my daughter's room. Poor thing, it has become her refuge. I spent the next hour interviewing the two serving women and when I had sent them on their way I talked with Lyn. The only positive thing that fell from her lips was the assurance that the baronet had never approached her before. Until that night she had sim-ply been overlooked, neglected, as she had been as a child. She could not say what prompted his advances, but Rosie told me that Sir Edward and Alathea had had a great falling out recently. Perhaps he hoped to strike back at the older girl by seducing the younger."

"Who can possibly say what goes on in a mind like his?" John paused. "All this happened only this morning?"

"I can't believe it myself. I left the girl – Lyn, I should call her – well-guarded. My man, Preston, is patrolling the grounds as though we were under siege and my own housekeeper has stationed herself right outside Bess' room and swears she won't move until I return. Lyn made me promise to keep her story a secret for now and she refused to consider any plan of action until she had seen Natty. Your heart would have bled, John. The only thing she would talk about was that Nat was the only one who had always believed her and that she could not decide anything until she had seen him. I thought of sending him a message, but I could not find the words, so I took horse and came myself, and here I am."

"You must have been in the saddle for twelve hours!"

"I suppose so … I really didn't notice. And now, to find Nat out with Bokenham … it grieves me deeply."

"He will pay the price when he hears your story. Look, it is already three in the morning. Let me show you to his bed, and I will lie down on mine, dressed as I am, and when he comes we'll be off to Friston whatever the hour. Sir, Lyn lies next to Nat's heart like a golden charm. When he learns her need the dross will be purged and you will see his true self."

Nat found her in his father's spring garden, standing on a verdant lawn rich with new growth. Late daffodils ran riot in the borders and the tulips were at their peak, their lustrous cups nodding as though overcome with delight. She looked smaller – almost shrunken – and her skin was pale and the thumbprints of sleepless nights lay under her violet eyes. He stood on the terrace, transfixed, and she ran to him and he enfolded her in his arms.

"You came," she murmured.

"Did you doubt it?" he responded with a half-smile, releasing her and stepping back a pace to get her measure.

"No," she gasped, and held him tight.

"Here she is," said another voice, and Squire Thomas stepped out upon the terrace. "Are you well, child? Did you rest at all?"

"Oh, yes, sir. They have taken good care of me, but they won't let me go farther than the garden. I did not expect you before tomorrow, if then."

"Well, we left London in a sorry state and had to spend one night on the road, but here we are, all four of us, reasonably fit. Come, its time to change for dinner. Then we'll have a talk this afternoon, when you feel up to it."

Nat and Lyn and the Squire crossed the flagstones to enter the hall. "All four of you, sir? Who else is there besides you and Nat?"

"Why Jemmy, of course, and Mister John from Gray's Inn. Surely you know who he is?"

Lyn looked up into Nat's golden eyes and smiled. "Nat's good angel, I am told."

The Squire looked startled. "Why, yes, my dear ... that may be. Now come inside and let's get some dinner into you."

John paced the dining room, waiting for the others. To the north the deep casements, which gave onto the terrace and the garden, had been thrown wide to catch the sweet scent of spring. The Squire's orange and lemon trees had been moved recently from the glass house to the terrace in their tubs, and John thought that he could see some white blossoms already and perhaps even catch a breath of their seductive odor. A movement caught his eye and he smiled to see that a butterfly had landed on one of the trees and was probing a bud for nectar. The lovely creature was a study in iridescent blue offset by black filaments as fine as embroidery threads. It moved its gauzy wings slowly, absorbing the sun, and then, thwarted by the unripe flower, caught a breeze and floated away. John's heart caught to think of the destiny which might await so fine a thing. He shook the image from his mind and turned from the bright garden to the cool room. There, not five steps from him, stood a woman with a pale, heart-shaped face beneath a mass of blue-black hair and eyes which contained all the shades of blue and violet which God had made.

"You must be John," Lyn said, and held out her hand.

Speechless, Grey accepted the soft offering and held it as though it were the body of Christ.

"And you must be Lyn," John answered.

The two stood in comfortable silence for a full half-minute when Squire Thomas and Nat strode into the room, arm in arm.

"And so, my dear," said the Squire, "I have made John Grey my man of business and sent him off this very morning on his first endeavor, to obtain your father's permission for you and Nat to wed."

The three of them were in the breakfast room: Nat and his father and Lyn. Lyn glanced at Nat who was studying his mother's portrait. The girl wondered if Elizabeth Brooke Bacon would have approved of the match; she knew that Squire Thomas did not. Not a word of reproval or disappointment had crossed his lips, but she knew full well that Squire Bacon's plans for his son did not include a marriage based on a childhood friendship, scandal and necessity. It was imperative that her father give his consent. That way, at least, the proprieties would be met whatever the gossip-mongers might think and might broadcast. And how could Sir Edward not agree, given the threat of exposure which they held as a secret weapon? He might well agree and he might settle on her the two thousand pounds which he had promised each of the four suitors whom she had sent packing. Surely that would ease Squire Thomas' concerns. The neighbors might hold up their hands in amazement, but there was nothing ignoble about the union of a Bacon and a Duke, sealed with a handsome dowry. She glanced at Nat again, willing him to look at her. He tore his eyes from the portrait, sought her own and smiled.

And Nat? Yesterday he had taken her in his arms on the sunny terrace and vowed to love and protect her forever, but what truly lay in his heart? She had worshipped him for half her life, but he? He was just coming into his manhood, testing various paths, rejecting some, choosing others, shaping his entire future. True, he disclaimed any interest in the law, the army, the church, or the court and swore that the life of a country squire was all he had ever wanted, but had he planned to take a bride so young, when he was barely twenty-three and when many men did not settle until thirty or older? Was there not an air of fantasy about their long-standing promise to wed when she reached her majority? Part of her had always doubted that it would happen. And today she was still full of doubts. Thrice she had come to Friston Hall begging, as it were, for a family. Her third request had been granted but she feared the consequences of the Bacons' kindness.

"What are you dreaming of, Lyn?" coaxed Nat. "We've gone over it many times. If your father is obstinate we can turn to your brother and bring some pressure to bear. It may take some months to sort it out, but in the meantime you will stay here, with no damage to your reputation."

"And your studies, Nat?"

Nat looked at his father and quickly looked away. "I know as much law as I ever shall, and as much as I shall ever need. John is the scholar. With him at hand, what more do we need?"

Squire Thomas grunted and rose and paced the room. "Speaking of John, it is getting on for noon; he should be back soon."

No sooner had he spoken when Preston entered with Grey on his heels. Nat and Lyn rose to their feet and three pairs of eyes sought John's face.

"I hope you will agree that half a loaf is better than none. Let me give you the result first, and then I'll give you the detail. Sir Edward has given his consent, but has withheld any settlement."

Nat and Lyn gasped and clung to one another. Squire Thomas smiled and frowned simultaneously.

"You have done well, lad. I am impressed. How did you come away with such a good result?"

John paused, seeking for the right words. He looked at Lyn sadly. "I fear that the consent was given in a mean spirit. The baronet said words to the effect that if Lyn chose to be disobedient, then he chose to have nothing more to do with her. In other words, she might do as she pleased but he would not subsidize her wilfullness."

Lyn's face fell but Nat spoke boldly. "What difference does it make why he agreed? All we need is his consent; we can do without his purse."

Squire Thomas looked at his son and shook his head. "Two thousand pounds is two thousand pounds, Natty. Ten years from now you'll not be so dismissive of such a little fortune. But you're right ... the main thing is the consent and the baronet won't go back on that for fear of the scandal we might spread. John, will you draw up the documents and tie this thing down? And find out about the special license ... we'll skip the banns and keep this a private affair." The Squire turned to Lyn and put his hand under her chin so that he could see her face clearly. "Are you sure you do not mind being wed here at the hall, with only a handful of guests? Most girls dream of something grander."

Lyn seized his hand and kissed it. "All I ask is to become a Bacon. How, I care not."

The Squire looked at the three young people. "Well then," he said. "We have a plan."

The lime avenue marched bravely downhill to where the Alde passed under Snape Bridge on its way to the sea. Lyn followed the brilliant green with a thoughtful eye and then turned to scrutinize the parlor once more. They had made a sort of altar in front of the fireplace by placing a small table there, covered in greenery, and bearing the family bible. She thought of Elizabeth Bacon's portrait, just beyond, in the morning room, and was glad that Nat's mother would not be present today, even in effigy. Most of the furniture had been pushed against the walls save for a dozen chairs which they had collected from the other rooms and arranged, pew-like, facing the fireplace. She stood, back to the altar, and counted the chairs: one for the Squire, who would walk her to the altar and then return to his seat; one for Bess Bacon, with whom she now shared the room with the strawberry hangings; one for John Duke, who had done far more than she ever imagined in fashioning a marriage settlement of sorts and in volunteering to represent the entire Duke family, which had otherwise disowned the baronet's youngest daughter; one for John Grey, without whom this day would not have been possible; one for John Ray, who had agreed to come from Black Notley to officiate at the marriage of his former student, he who was gifted but impulsive; one for Rose and another for Rosie, who had helped her in her hour of sorest need; one for Preston and one for Jemmy, who loved the Bacons, father and son, as they loved their own kindred; and three extras, just in case.

It would be a modest ceremony, but fitting. And now it was time to join Bess and don the simple cream-colored gown the two of them had fashioned over the past days. Lyn feared that it was too severe, but Bess had only smiled and last night she understood, for after dinner the Squire had presented her with Elizabeth Brooke Bacon's amethyst necklace and ear-drops, jewels which all but she had known were going to adorn her on this special day. What had Squire Thomas said? "They match your eyes and become you even more than they did her." It was a remarkable admission. Perhaps he had finally opened the last corner of his heart to her. She prayed that it was so and turned to go above to make her preparations to be Nat's bride.

Fancy nibbled at Prince's neck and the black snorted and tossed his head. Nat smiled down at Lyn and took her hand.

"I shall not shy away if you care to do the same to me," he said.

Lyn blushed. "Night has not fallen yet," she exclaimed.

"Must we wait for the dark? I love the twilight for its changing nature, neither day nor night, but with something of both. It is a stirring time ... a time for adventure."

Lyn's heart thudded in her chest. Did Nat not know that she was afraid ... that the image of those two white bodies on the blood red counterpane was seared in her memory?

"Shouldn't we see to the horses and check Rose's work? She only cleaned the kitchen and made up a bed in what was once the parlor, you know. I want to make sure she has not forgotten anything. Oh, Nat, how can you bear to honeymoon at Hazelwood, when it is all but a ruin! What have I asked of you?"

Nat slid from Prince and, circling behind both horses, pulled Lyn from her saddle. "Little witch, why are you buying time? Do you think I care under what roof we shall sleep tonight? I would take you under the bare sky with the racing moon to show me all your delights. Come, we'll see to the horses, but then you can put me off no longer. I feel as though I have waited ten years for this moment ... indeed, I have."

With Prince and Fancy content in Hazelwood's ramshackle stable, Nat led Lyn into the flint dwelling which was little more than a cottage tacked on to an old Norman watchtower. The tower itself was wholly ruined, but the cottage needed only minor repairs, and Rose had made the great kitchen warmly welcoming. Every surface shone clean, the flag floor was strewn with sweet-smelling rushes, and a thick bed of embers glowed in the huge fire-place. The parlor lay to the north, snugged between the kitchen and the tower. Although bare, it was spotless, its wood floor gleaming with beeswax. Someone had brought a huge old Tudor four-poster bed from upstairs and set it up here, where its white linen shone scarlet from the kitchen fire.

Lyn cried out with pleasure and began searching among the foodstuffs which Rose had left on the hutch. "Why she's thought of everything! Look Nat, here's fresh bread and honey ... a flitch of Friston bacon ... butter, salt ... table beer and six whole bottles of wine. And see, grapes from your father's glass house and some early strawberries. Here are fresh peas, and there some cheese. How could I have doubted her?"

She felt two hands on her shoulders and thought of the last time her father touched her, just so, just on the shoulders. Nat turned her around and cupped her chin and looked into her eyes. "There are appetites which do not call for food, Lyn. Gently, sweet, gently. Do you think I do not know what images you see when you think of earthly love? We shall go slowly, but before the night is out I shall show you the garden of love and teach you that it is a wholesome place. Eden remained pure after the offenders were driven from it and it is Eden that I will give you, if you trust me."

The violet eyes were dark pools in the dim light. They looked steadily into the golden eyes and then the pale lids closed in surrender. Lyn put her face on Nat's breast and listened to the beating of his heart. Ten years ago she had sworn an oath to stand by him, always, and she would keep that oath.

Twice Nat had risen in the night to build up the fire and now, at first dawn, it crackled merrily in the kitchen at Hazelwood. He drew the coverlet up around his bare shoulders and smiled down at his wife. Like a wild thing, she had burrowed among the bolsters and sheets and blankets until she had made a perfect nest where she now lay in absolute peace, breathing gently. But she had not breathed gently last night; far from it. Once assured that he knew and respected her fears, she had followed his amatory lead down every path of delight that he showed her and, when they had exhausted those, jointly they discovered new territory. It was a revelation. At heart she was a little pagan. He had always known it.

Hazelwood faced west and it was some time before the rising dawn thrust its fingers of light into the parlor and announced day. Lyn slept on, but Nat was restless. He rose again and slipped on his clothes. He would see to the horses and bring in a bucket of water. Perhaps he would start breakfast and that would catch his wife's attention. He was ravenous ... they had not stopped for supper last night. As he stepped into the unkempt yard with its tangle of hollyhocks and gillyflowers he was startled to see a horse approaching on the path from Friston Hall. It was his bay ... and on its back was John Grey. No one, least of all Grey, would have disturbed the newlyweds on the first morning of their honeymoon unless there was just cause. His thoughts leapt to his father ... something must have happened to the Squire. If it was Bess, his father would have come himself.

Dropping the bucket, Nat ran to the rickety garden gate and thrust it aside just as Grey dismounted and tied his reins to the fence.

"Is it Father?"

"Good God, no. Rest easy. Everyone is fine at Friston Hall."

The blood subsided from Nat's face and his heart slowed. "Then it is your mother? You must leave for Ipswich?"

"No, Nat. It's Lyn's father, it's the baronet."

72

Nat felt a renewed rush of blood. "What has the creature done now ... tried to revoke his consent? Reneged on John Duke's settlement?"

John put his hand on Nat's shoulder and led him to a wooden bench from which the paint had long since been stripped by the sun, leaving a dove-gray seat overgrown with honeysuckle. The friends sat down together, the one tall and blond and steady, the other small and dark and eager.

After a brief pause John spoke. "Jenney's man arrived an hour ago from Red House Farm. He knew that Lyn was staying at Friston Hall and he thought she was still there ... didn't know about the wedding or about Hazelwood."

"He came for Lyn? With a message from Alathea? That is a riddle."

"He came for Lyn, but with no message. He came with some news. Last night, sometime during the small hours, the staff was awakened by Alathea who had fled from her chambers, in disarray, clad only in her nightclothes. She, who never loses her composure, was like a mad thing. Jenney was not present, of course, so in desperation she called for the servants. They could make no sense of her ramblings, so they followed her to her bedchamber and there ..."

"My God ... there, they found the baronet. She decided to unmask him."

"No, Nat, not quite. There they found the baronet, stone dead. He lay among her sheets, nude, his heart stopped. It was clear what he had been doing ... in her panic she did not even try to conceal the crime. The messenger told me that she acted as she would have if her husband had died in her bed. And, I suppose, from her point of view, that is exactly what happened."

"God in Heaven above. So, the whole thing is known. And Sir Edward dead ... I am stunned. And yet we should have seen it coming. We all knew ..."

"Oh, the servants knew, too. That much is clear. They won't come right out and say it, but nobody at Red House Farm was surprised."

Nat brought his hand to his mouth. "John, we must protect Lyn. As much as I would like to see this festering wound exposed to the light of day, now that he is dead he can no longer do any harm. It is Lyn and the family's reputation that I must think of. Is there any way of covering this up?"

"It has already been done, Nat. Your father was floored and too overcome to act. I told him to stay at the hall and keep any scandal from Bess. I followed the messenger back to Red House Farm and said, (forgive me), that I was acting on Lyn's behalf. Alathea was still incoherent, but I assembled all the servants and read them the riot act. I told them that if they valued their futures they must memorize, and memorize quickly, the following tale: that Sir Edward Duke was visiting his daughter, as was his custom; that he spent the night in his own chambers, as usual; and that unfortunately he passed on in his sleep and was found dead by the girl who brought up his morning tea. A few gold coins greased my presentation. It wasn't long before we made the body seemly, placed it in the bed where it belonged, cleaned Alathea's room and otherwise set the stage for the coroner. I sent off a messenger for a physician and for Reverend Clement and was about to leave when I thought I should probably speak to Alathea. They had stripped her bed and made it up with fresh linen and when I found her she had gone back to bed and was nursing her new baby, the one which was born a few weeks ago. She was dressed in white, with a blue over-gown, and she looked like a Madonna with the Christ child. I found myself speechless. Finally I stammered out a few words. She merely looked at me oddly, thanked me for helping under the terrible circumstances of her father's sad death in his lonely bed, with Offley unfortunately away from home, and dismissed me like a servant. As I left I saw the older child, a little boy, lingering in the hallway. He was the image of Sir Edward Duke."

Nat leaned back, glad that the sun had crested Hazelwood's ridgepole. At least his body was warm, if not his soul.

"John, I am deeply in your debt. Not only your friendship, your support at Gray's Inn, but all of this ... Lyn ... the stain on her family ... Father and I could not have coped without you."

John's fresh face turned deep red. "Nat, I have done nothing. If I have helped in any way it is for the love I bear you ... all of you. I almost feel that your father is mine, that your family is mine. I will always be there for you."

Nat sat up, startled. Those words! Where had he heard them before? It was on the strand, in the golden path ... Lyn was walking into the water, disappearing from his life. He had cried out, in great need. And she? She too had said that she would always be there for him. Tears came to his eyes. He deserved neither her love, nor John's. Whatever the future held, he would conduct himself so as to be worthy of both of them.

Nat rose and pressed John to his breast. "Well, thank God you were there last night. Perhaps you should return to the Hall. I'll wake Lyn and break the news to her and we'll follow you within the hour. What a devil Sir Edward was to harm his daughter even in death. Well, he may have shortened our honeymoon, but he did not mar it. Good-bye, John. We'll see you shortly."

CHAPTER 6

APRIL-MAY 1674

The ice had melted from Hazelwood Mere everywhere but along the banks where it clung like a wreath of crystal. Lyn tossed a stone into the dark heart of the pool, heedless of the waterfowl which circled aimlessly, anxious to reach the reed beds and start nesting. Spring was late this year. Everything around her was dark and drear except where last week's snow lay, and even it was soiled at the edges and unsightly. Lyn slipped on a sheet of ice and came down hard on one knee, muddying her skirt. It was the final indignity. Furious, she seized a handful of pebbles and hurled them at the water. The birds rose in an anxious flurry and fled south towards the estuary. Angry with herself and the world, Lyn let the tears come and found some relief. She sighed and retraced her steps to Hazelwood.

She stepped through the front door to find nothing changed. The damp wood whose smoke had driven her from the kitchen still smoldered sullenly in the fireplace, roiling the thick air. The papers she had pulled from Nat's desk last night still covered the work table in disarray. If she went upstairs to the bedrooms she would find the linen which she had washed so carefully in anticipation of Nat's homecoming still hanging from the drying rods, still too damp to use. Well, it was her own fault. Her husband had asked her if Jemmy might accompany him to London and she had said "yes," so the fact that all of Hazelwood's cares lay at her feet was of her own making. Nat could not know that Rose's weekly visit would be cancelled due to the snow and that Lyn would be marooned in a sea of troubles. That was just the way it was and tears and tantrums would not help. Tears and tantrums would not dry the wood nor the linen nor, God knows, would they help her understand Nat's accounts and determine where all their money had gone. That must be her first concern. Nat and John would arrive tomorrow and she had only today to delve among his papers and fathom the mystery of their poverty.

Lyn flew at her tasks with a will and an hour later sat at the kitchen table in a clean house, with a bright fire blazing on the hearth, and with fires in all the bedrooms, economy be damned. All the beds would be made up fresh and snug by the time she sought her own couch tonight. John Grey would find nothing to criticize in her housekeeping. Turning to her task, she located a much-used piece of paper, reversed it, and found a clean corner to make her calculations. It had all been explained to her four years ago, just before the wedding. Could she have forgotten what they told her? First and foremost Nat had made over Hazelwood, the house and all sixty acres, to her, as her sole property. The Squire had not liked that one bit, but the farm was Nat's, from his mother, and he could do what he liked with it. Distracted, as always, by the fear of her father-in-law's disapproval, Lyn rose and went to the fireplace where she stirred the soup which bubbled gently on the hob. Hazelwood was her own: it was a constant balm to her cares. Why, one could live here comfortably with no income at all! They had a kitchen garden and an orchard ... sheep pens ... a cow in the barn. If things took a turn for the worse, her little farm was their refuge.

Now for their other assets. Squire Thomas, bless his heart, had not only settled five hundred pounds in cash upon them, but had given Nat Hinton Hall Farm, one of his finest holdings. Hinton Hall, she recalled, stood in Nat's name alone. She had no interest in it except for benefiting from the sixty pounds a year which it produced. Lyn toyed with the feather of her quill. She remembered how furious Nat had been when he learned that the gift of the farm was conditional. Squire Thomas had stipulated that Farley, the sitting tenant, be permitted to remain there until he died in recompense for his outstanding improvements to the land, wresting it from a gorse-filled wasteland and making it the model farm that it was today. Nat had planned to give Farley sixty days notice and then settle at Hinton Hall with his bride, but Squire Thomas disabused him of the notion. Farley was to stay; the spacious brick farmhouse might not be available to Nat and Lyn for years. There had been quite an argument. The Squire had used words which had remained with her: in a rare show of temper he had reminded his son that when one married in haste, one repented in leisure. Lyn sighed. Despite those words Squire Thomas had always been kind to her. If he regretted his son's marriage, one would not know it.

Lyn looked at her notes. Where was she? She owned Hazelwood, free and clear. Hinton Hall brought them sixty pounds a year and might be their future residence, but only when Farley died. Then there was the five hundred pounds the Squire had given them in cash. Yes, that was the Bacon side. It was a nice little fortune, and one which should have made them quite comfortable. Now for the Dukes. Her father, of course, had not only denied her a dowry but had denied her an inheritance. Lucky for him that he had redrawn his will so quickly after she fled Benhall Lodge, for he had died within the month. So, nothing from Sir Edward Duke. But her brother, bless his heart, had somehow managed to make them a wedding gift of eight hundred pounds, an impressive sum. He must have pressured Jane and Alathea into making a contribution, but she would never know, as she had not communicated with her family since the wedding. The breach was complete. True, John had made her sign a document which prevented her from ever contesting her father's will or making any claim on the Duke estate, but under the circumstances he had, she thought, been more than generous.

What did it all come to? Two farms totaling some three hundred acres; thirteen hundred pounds sterling; and sixty pounds a year flowing from Hinton Hall Farm. They were far more fortunate than most. Why, then, were they always strapped for cash? Nat had let her renovate Hazelwood as she liked, even agreeing that the Norman tower could be turned into living quarters for Jemmy, but the cost had been quite modest. Yet now that she wanted to do the last bit, repair the stable, he said they could not afford it. And there was no discussion of the matter ... it was just a fact. Indeed, it had been long since she had really had a discussion with Nat about anything. Even about her ... barrenness. This past January, on his birthday, when they had lain so long in bed watching the snow fall after ... after a full night of love play, when she told him her fears about not conceiving after four years of marriage, he had just laughed and told her that most girls would consider themselves lucky. Did he really not care? Or was he simply content to wait until they were more settled before having a family? Restless, Lyn rose again and poked idly at the soup. Why did she bother when she had no desire for dinner? She took the pot off the hob and placed it in the scullery. It would do for supper if she regained her appetite.

Pacing the kitchen, she let her thoughts wander to her marriage. There was no doubt that Nat was fading away from her, going down a different path. And she was not the only one from whom he was drifting. He spent so little time with his father now ... and rarely saw Bess, though Bury St. Edmund's was an easy day's ride and he got along well with his in-laws, the Hoveners. He was constantly in London but she was sure that John Grey did not take up all his time. How could he? Nat said he worked like a slave. Well, that was done. John had finished his studies at Gray's Inn and Nat was bringing him back to Suffolk for a whole week of relaxation and celebration. Then, it appeared, he was going to decide which London firm to join. He was in great demand. No, it was not John who filled Nat's London hours, it was Henry Bokenham. Nat did not guess it, but Lyn knew quite well about Merry Meg's. Lank Harry had taken great joy in confiding in her, though she had not asked for his confidence. Meg and her cards and her drink and her girls.... Lyn was no fool. She could tell when Nat had tried a new partner ... his caresses informed on him. As for their fortune, perhaps Meg had swallowed it up along with Nat's vow of fidelity. She would do her best to find out, but whatever she discovered would not change the fact that thirteen years ago she had sworn an oath which she would honor until the day she died.

Lyn crumpled her notes into a ball and tossed it into the fire. She gathered Nat's papers and replaced them in his writing desk, which he kept in the parlor. He was so careless with his papers that he would never notice that she had looked at them. As she tidied the downstairs rooms she chided herself for her dismal mood. The sun had come out and a triangle of bright blue sky peeped from behind the clouds. She would treat herself and Fancy to a ride, go early to bed and greet Nat and John and Jemmy with a smile when they arrived tomorrow.

The black and the bay had trodden many miles together and once again they paced happily, side by side, over the new snow as Nat and John rode from Hazelwood to Hinton Hall Farm. The atmosphere at Hazelwood had been somewhat subdued yesterday, but the beauty of the morning was infectious and the friends smiled at one another and urged their horses to a canter. The snow and mud was tiring and after ten minutes or so they stopped to rest.

"Do you always have snow in April here?" asked John. "I can't remember it in Ipswich."

"Nor can I recall such a late spring, but Father can. Last night was probably the last of it. Look – the sky is perfectly blue and cloudless and the sun feels almost hot."

"It is delicious. Thank you again for this week in the country."

"You know that you have a home both at Friston and at Hazelwood. Anytime ... anytime at all."

The bay tugged on John's reins as the animal sought some early grass under the drifts. Grey soothed him and glanced at his friend.

"Is anything amiss with Lyn? I thought her depressed ... distracted."

Nat doffed his hat and wiped his brow. "She is, with good reason. The truth of it is, John, that we are going to see Farley to convince him either to pay a higher rent or to vacate Hinton Hall Farm before his term is up. Unfortunately I don't have any legal legs to stand on because my father set the terms of his tenancy and I don't think I can change them. Under the contract he can stay until he dies and he must pay me only sixty pounds a year regardless of how much he makes. That's one reason I asked you to come with me ... to see if you can persuade him to accept some different terms."

"The contract is between your father and him. We would have to convince Farley and he would have to convince the Squire."

Nat frowned. "Well, that's not going to happen. Like Lyn, my father is not happy with me."

"What is the problem, Nat? We really haven't talked since Christmas and even then you seemed distraught, as though you were keeping something back from me."

78

"I was. It's time for the truth. Perhaps if you know everything you will help me with Farley. You know what assets and income I had when Lyn and I were married?"

"I should know, as I drew up the settlement. The two farms, the income from Hinton Hall and the good round sum of thirteen hundred pounds sterling. Not princely, but not bad for someone with your expectations. I trust you have not been invading your capital."

Nat spurred Prince and laughed bitterly. "No, I have not invaded it ... I have squandered it."

John was at a loss for words. He drove the bay forward and snatched Nat's rein, forcing his friend to look him squarely in the eye. "Is that a joke? Did you really mean what you said? Are the thirteen hundred pounds gone?"

"Gone, gone, gone. Nary a groat left. Some of it's in Meg's pockets, but most of it has vanished in Bokenham's maw."

John turned quite pale. "Bokenham? I didn't know you still saw him."

"Oh, I never stopped. He and I have visited every stew in London, but I lost most of my fortune right here in Suffolk, at *The Crown* in Southwold."

"Nat, you are serious."

"I am deadly serious. That's why Lyn has a long face. I told her yesterday. She confessed to having looked at my papers and said she could make neither heads nor tails of them. No wonder ... the gold is gone and I certainly didn't keep a record of my folly."

John released Prince's reins and wiped his face with his sleeve. "What a blow. What will you do? Some could live at Hazelwood on sixty pounds a year, but I doubt that you could."

"Well, Father will say I must. Besides, what options do I have? Only Hinton Hall. The farm is my golden goose. That's why you have to put the thumbscrews to Farley."

John pondered. "If I help you it will be on two conditions. The first is that you tell me everything about your finances so I know what I am dealing with. The second is that you have nothing more to do with Bokenham ... nothing at all."

"As for the first, I *have* told you everything."

"You have no outstanding debts?"

Nat flushed. "I have thrown my gold away but I have not borrowed. No, I owe nothing."

"And my second condition?"

"Why, it's a bit hurtful to be treated like a schoolboy, but I see your point. I agree. Harry Bokenham is a thing of the past. Of course, he is part of the family ... I don't suppose I must cut him if I see him on the street?"

"Don't quibble with me, Nat. You know what I am talking about. Think of Lyn! You owe it to her to sever your ties with that ... scoundrel."

Nat looked directly in John's eyes, those eyes which joy could turn sea-green but which now, in anger, were gun-metal gray. "I swear it. I'll have no truck with Bokenham from this day forward."

John leaned back in the saddle, satisfied. "Then I'll see what I can do with this fellow Farley. Come, the morning is passing. Let's ride."

When the friends reached Hinton Hall Farm the songbirds were twittering in the hedgerows and the snow was melting fast. The big brick house stood solidly on a gentle slope, all business. Saxmundham lay uphill to the left and to the right, visible in the pure air, was the sea, some five miles distant. Blue smoke rose from a forest of chimney pots and some busy soul was throwing open the first-floor casements to air the bedding. The farm spoke of industry and thrift, if not of grace.

As Nat and John crossed the muddy yard the front door opened and a freckled pointer leapt out, startling the horses. The dog was followed by a sturdy man with an antique musket in the crook of his arm. John's heart sank. Nat had always spoken of Farley as an oldster, practically in his dotage. It must have been wishful thinking, for the fellow standing before them was just past the prime of life and looked good for another twenty years.

"Mister Nat, sir! What a surprise. Good-day to you. And isn't it a beauty?"

Nat doffed his hat and jumped down from Prince. "Hello, Farley. Indeed, it looks as though spring has finally come. Are you shooting?"

"Why, the snow will keep me from tilling the fields until tomorrow, so I thought I would find a pheasant or two for the missus. You know how good the sport is, down Leiston-way."

Nat laughed. "I should know, for you're the one who showed me the birds' favorite haunts when I was a lad. But it's hardly the season."

Farley smiled. "Why who's to know, Mister Nat? Your father would not mind ... it's his land and you can be sure that I'll send some of the birds to Friston Hall for his supper table."

John had dismounted and was standing quietly by his horse. "It's not quite accurate to say that it's the Squire's land ... it's really Nat's, is it not?"

Farley scowled. "Oh, aye, I keep forgetting. But it's one and the same. It's Bacon land." A shadow crossed his face. "The Squire hasn't changed anything has he? I'm still to stay here and pay the rent to you, Mister Nat?"

Nat spoke quickly before John could say anything further. The attorney, he thought, had gotten things off on the wrong foot altogether. They needed to warm Farley up, not alarm him.

"No, no, nothing has changed. John's staying with us at Hazelwood and we wanted a ride and thought we would come your way. It must be almost a year since I paid you a visit."

"Aye, last October it were, I remember it well. Your lady wife brought us that basket of apples and those tarts. I can still taste them. Speaking of which, won't you step inside for a taste of cider? The birds will wait. They have nowhere else to go."

Two hours and several glasses of cider later John finished reviewing Farley's meticulous accounts and he stepped into the hall to summon his friend to the farmer's office.

"Well? Can we squeeze blood from this turnip?" Nat asked, mockery covering his embarrassment.

"To be blunt, no. The market has been soft and Farley has done nobly to provide you with the sixty pounds these past four years. He's stinted his own family and what is worse, stinted the farm itself. That's not good business. You make money by spending money, and he has cut back to the bone. You won't get more until trade improves."

"I knew you would say that. Well, so be it. For my part, I broached the idea of his leaving Hinton Hall and taking another farm, but it is not in the cards. He came here as a single man of twenty or so, and he's poured body and soul into the place ... married here, raised his family here ... it is home to him. He'll leave feet first, as they say. And Father will let him stay ... I daren't suggest otherwise. So, we've both failed. I doubt that Lyn and I will ever call this place home and as for the income, well, I got my sixty pounds ten days ago on Lady's Day and that's the end of it."

"I fear so, Nat. But Farley is a good man ... would you have it any other way?"

"No, but Lyn and I cannot live on sixty pounds. It is already spoken for, what with one thing and another. I'll have to find another way."

John rose and replaced Farley's account books. "Let's thank our host for his hospitality and ride to Saxmundham for dinner. Between us, perhaps we can think of somthing."

The Crown called itself Southwold's finest inn, but Nat found the atmosphere poisonous as he waited for Harry Bokenham in the empty tap-room. The windows had been closed tight all winter and the place was dense with smoke and the odors of close living. The innkeeper was upstairs, crippled with gout, and his wife, with an irrefutable excuse for abandoning her duties, remained glued to her husband's bedside where she wrapped the fug around her like an old blanket. *The Crown's* ancient timbers were steeped in the ale which had flowed from its taps for two hundred years and the building settled into indolence like a drunk resigned to his vice.

Nat sighed and jingled his few remaining coins as he waited for his cousin. As he paced aimlessly his foot slipped on a smear of cold mutton fat and he fell to his knees. How symbolic, he thought. *The Crown*, where he had wasted his fortune, had brought him low not only morally but now physically. Indeed, he had never felt lower in his life. He rose and wandered to the casement which gave onto a mean alley. The intermittent rain had started again and now it beat mercilessly against the glass, blown straight from the sea. He pressed his forehead on the icy green quarrels in an effort to cool a brow which burned with fever. He closed his eyes and willed his cousin to appear with Jason's three hundred pounds.

Three hundred pounds! He must have been mad! With Bokenham egging him on he had sold Hinton Hall Farm for half its value to Robert Jason, a feckless Hertfordshire heir with money to burn. Bokenham! His cousin had a talent for evil. No sooner had Jason appeared at *The Crown* ten days ago, fleeing the tedium of his aunt's seaside villa, when the sharper speared and gutted him like a fish. They had taken him to hunt Farley's lands the very next day and the day after that the only thing the vacuous youth could talk about was owning a Suffolk shooting box, preferably Hinton Hall Farm. Bokenham urged Nat to strike while the iron was hot and, eager to recoup some of his losses, strike he did. The day after the hunt Nat deeded him the property in exchange for a promissory note for three hundred pounds and shortly thereafter Bokenham escorted the youth to Hertfordshire to collect the purchase price. And now where was Harry? He should have arrived last night. Really, nothing prevented the wastrel from disappearing with the gold. Nothing, that is, but fear of the law and hope for even more lucre.

Nat paced the cold, fusty room. The fire spat sullenly and imploded, choking itself. He was chilled to the marrow yet burned with anxiety. How had he let the black dog back into his life ... a life which held Lyn and a warm home and a loving father and sister and a future as the squire of all the Bacon lands in and around Friston? The black dog, the shambling mongrel which had shadowed him from childhood, nipping at his heels with needle-sharp teeth, teaching him that he was unworthy of his ancestors and that, whatever path he chose, he would be sure to fail. The black dog which had made him extravagant at Cambridge, unmindful of John Ray's teaching, dismissive of what Gray's Inn had to offer and, most terrible, hurtful to Lyn and the Squire and Bess and John Grey, those who loved him best. Nat strode from the window and gripped the mantel where an ancient clock ticked the minutes away. What if Bokenham did not come?

The clock struck three quarters past eleven. Nat would wait until noon and then ... then. The pendulum swung and Nat gripped the mantel with both hands and stared at it, mesmerized. *Three hundred pounds, three hundred pounds, three hundred pounds* the clock repeated. The blue veins in Nat's temple seemed to pulse with the desperate, obsessive rhythm. *Three hundred pounds, three hundred pounds, three hundred pounds....*

The front door creaked and Bokenham strode in with the bitter wind.

Nat whirled. "Do you have it?"

Bokenham laughed and drew himself a mug of ale from the tap. He had disposed of the Hertfordshire fish and it would not hurt, he thought, to play with the Suffolk fish for a few minutes longer. Life was unfair. Bacon had everything and he, Harry Bokenham, had nothing. Let the squire's son taste a little anxiety. It would be good for his soul.

Nat raised the back of his hand to his mouth and brought it away stained with bright blood. He felt as though he would explode. *"Do you have it?"*

Bokenham took a long swallow. "Look to that pretty nose, Nat. There's blood coming from it. You must be ill."

"Harry, I beg of you in God's name …"

"Well, in that case …. Of course I have it. Here." The sharper pulled a fat purse from his bosom and tossed it in the air. "It's all in gold … such pretty coins."

Nat staggered to a bench and put his head in his hands, staunching his nostrils with his lace cuff. "Thank the Lord. Why do you torture me so? All three hundred pounds?"

"All three hundred pounds. It is nothing to Jason. I daresay you could have gotten more."

"Well, give them to me and let me leave. You'll not see me again. I am a reformed man."

"All very well, but there is the matter of my commission?"

"Your commission? We never agreed on a commission."

"How can you think that I would not ask for a small reward? I brought the fellow to you and arranged the whole thing. And then the trip to Hertfordshire through all that muck? Every hour in that fool Jason's company should be well recompensed, don't you think?"

"All right, Harry, all right. I'm at the end of my tether. What do you want? Will three pounds do? One percent?"

"So cold and businesslike, Nat? After all we have been through together? No, here's my proposition. I'm still dry and what's more, I'm famished. I'll rouse the innkeeper to make our dinner and give us a bottle or two of claret. After that we'll play until the clock strikes five. Whatever I've taken off of you by five o'clock is mine; if you prevail you keep the entire three hundred pounds and owe me nothing."

Nat was a better player than Bokenham and had beaten him far more often than he had lost. Few of the vanished thirteen hundred pounds had lined Harry's pockets. The wastrel made a living not so much by play as by providing marks to his more skillful, and even less scrupulous, friends. The odds were heavily in Nat's favor. He knew he would win. In a few more hours he would have his three hundred pounds and he would ride home to Hazelwood, leaving all this behind him. Time enough to explain the sale of Hinton Hall to his family … that was a matter for another day. Nat's nose stopped bleeding and he began to relax.

"Done."

"Good. Why don't you prepare the card room while I run upstairs and rouse the innkeeper."

Five hours later Nat dealt his last hand. He had lost consistently all afternoon and now he lost again. Bokenham thrust the last of the gold coins into the fat leather purse and pulled the strings tight as though he would choke it.

"It's the wheel of fate, my dear," the sharper said. "A pity, but you still have that pretty little farm and that pretty little wife. All you have to do is wait for your inheritance. Some people have all the luck!"

Bright blood burst from Nat's nostrils and mouth and the warm salty taste of his own essence was the last thing he remembered except for the feel of the strong cords of Bokenham's throat which slipped through his fingers as he fell into blackness.

They took Nat to Friston Hall because they did not want to distress his wife. The physician who regularly attended *The Crown's* customers was not sure the young man was going to live. He burned with fever and the blood kept coming. The medic rode all the way with him, in a cart. After all, Squire Thomas Bacon was a warm man and one could reasonably expect a large fee.

When Nat awoke he was in his old room, still crowded with boyhood treasures. The stuffed owl in the corner had not moved since he was fourteen and the big table under the east window was still stacked with books, higgledy-piggledy, although someone had cleared enough space to set a tray and a vase of roses. He looked up to see Bess' plain face, filled with kindness.

"Natty! You're awake. What a scare you gave us?"

"Why am I here, Bessy? I don't understand."

"Don't you remember anything?"

"Lyn ... where is Lyn? I ... I quarreled with her and insisted on going to Southwold when she didn't want me to. Southwold! *The Crown*! Oh, my God, Bess. Bokenham!"

"Nat, you are to be quiet. Absolutely quiet. Father brought in Doctor Graham and he said he would not answer for it if you became anxious."

"But Bess, do you know what happened?"

"I know it all, Nat. Bokenham fled to Brampton but Father followed him and got the entire story out of him. The whole thing about Hinton Hall Farm was a nonsense. The deed you gave Jason was invalid because it did not tell about Farley's life estate ... I think that is what they call it ... and, oh, all kinds of other legal things were wrong. So Father sent Jemmy to Hertfordshire to make sure the papers are torn up or burnt and then he'll give Mister Jason back the three hundred pounds, most of which Harry Bokenham still had. Hinton Hall is still yours and nobody need know what happened. We put out a story that you rode to Southwold for the exercise and became ill ... very simple and straightforward."

"And Lyn? Does she know?"

"Well of course, Natty. She came at once … it was the middle of the night. She's been sharing my room; in fact she's there right now."

"And she knows everything?"

"How could we not tell her?"

Nat turned fretfully and looked towards the window. "How long have I been lying here?"

"Two nights and a day. You slept the whole night they brought you and all the next day and night and now it is morning again. Doctor Graham gave you something … I don't know what it was."

"Bessy, how am I going to live this down? What will I say to Lyn and Father?"

"You don't have to say anything," said a quiet voice and Lyn entered the room. She glided to the bedside and smoothed Nat's forehead with a cool hand. "I think you had a sort of illness, Nat, over the past year or so, and now it gone. Let's look forward, not back."

The tears coursed down Nat's face and Bess crept from the room.

"Lyn, my love. It is true. I lost my path … I wandered from you, and from myself. It seems like a terrible dream. Will it be right now?"

"I'll always be with you, Nat. The golden road is still before us if you will walk it with me."

Squire Thomas looked from his library window at his May garden and smiled wearily. The daffodils danced bravely in the stiff breeze, but the tulips were suffering, their tender cups torn to ribbons by the wind. It had been a bitter spring. The deep purple blossom for which he had such great expectations had come to nothing. Well, that was no surprise. It was sinful to want a black flower. Elizabeth Brooke would never have approved of it, and God had proven her right.

Nat and John were tossing a ball back and forth on the lawn. They made a brave show, both of them so well-knit and comely, though so different in carriage and character. John was steady and Natty … Natty had almost broken his heart. To throw away his fortune and toss Hinton Hall Farm, the best of the Bacon holdings, after it! And all because he had not found a purpose in life. It was the final blow. Tomorrow he would tell them his plan. John had already agreed, thank God, and little Lyn would go along with it and Nat? Nat had no other choice.

Lyn! Lyn was at Hazelwood for the day, seeing to her farm, but she would be back tonight and tomorrow she would join his son and John Grey right here, in the library, and hear his proposal. He had to admit it, he had been wrong about the Duke girl. She was not the cause of Nat's unhappiness. No, if anything, she might be the solution. She had a will of iron under that soft demeanor and she would use it to protect Nat come what may. God bless the girl. Growing up in the Duke household, how had she turned out so well? It must be her poor mother's influence ... the child was the image of the second Lady Duke.

The best thing he had done was to ask John Grey to return from London. The young man was trying to get his career started ... hadn't been back in the capital more than a week following his country vacation when Natty ran amuck and then fell so ill. He had asked Grey to return and the fellow hadn't turned a hair. He no sooner got the message than he jumped on a hired horse and didn't stop until he got to Friston. It reminded the Squire of four years ago, when little Lyn had come to him with circles under her eyes and bruises on her shoulders. Really, it did not bear thinking about. Nat and Lyn. There was something about them ... they were as different from Bess and Henry Hovener as night and day. Well, if he could get them off to Virginia, perhaps he could have some peace.

The next day dawned bright and Squire Thomas spent the first hour after breakfast putting his library in order. He arranged three comfortable chairs on one side of his work table and on the table itself placed all of his cousin's letters to his right and the map of Virginia to his left. When everything was as he liked it he threw another armful of apple wood on the fire and rang for Preston.

"Are the young people about?" he queried.

"Yes sir, they are waiting in the morning room."

"Well, please have them come up and then send the girl with coffee for four."

Minutes later Nat and Lyn and John were seated in the Squire's comfortable, book-lined room which was brilliant with morning sun. After coffee, silence fell. The Squire cleared his throat and felt ridiculous. Although he must play the patriarch, the role had never been an easy one.

"I have some important things to say to the three of you, but first let me be clear that I want to look forward, not back. We all know about the events of last month. I see no reason to belabor them, though it is those events which inform this meeting." Nat looked relieved and Lyn stole a glance at him and took his hand. John kept his gaze on his lap, where his hands were quietly folded. "The fact of the matter is that unless you," (looking at Nat), "live in a very small way at Lyn's farm, you have no means of keeping your family. I doubt that you want to lead such a life, and I would not wish it on you. Bacons have always been among the first families here and my son will not be the first to lower that standard." Nat squirmed.

"Now then, what do you know about my cousin, Nathaniel Bacon?"

"He was born at Bury, to your uncle James Bacon, the rector of Burgate."

"The gentleman who died the summer after our marriage?" interposed Lyn.

Nat glanced at his wife and smiled. "Yes, that's the one. Let's see....
Nathaniel is just your age, Father. He was in France when I was born but he
was back in England when King Charles was slain. Although a Parliament
man, the King's death shook him, (how could it not?), and that, together
with the need to make his fortune, drove him to Virginia."

"Yes," said the Squire. "He sailed in fifty and has not been back since."

"What else do I know? He married in the colonies, married well I
believe."

"He wed a charming widow with a nice fortune, Elizabeth Kingsmill.
Unfortunately they are childless, but otherwise the marriage has been a
great success. They live at King's Creek, one of the finest plantations in the
colony."

"He's quite a boy for the books and he loves to write." Nat swept his
hand in the direction of the letters stacked at his father's right hand.

"He wrote regular bulletins to his father and since Uncle James' death
I have become his chief correspondent." The Squire patted the letters. "For
the past four years I have received quarterly reports, as it were, on the state
of Virginia ... they are all here, and they make very interesting reading. It's
a pity," (frowning at Nat), "that you never took the time to look at them."

Nat tossed his head and glanced at John, who kept his eyes down.
"Well, I daresay I should have, but it all seemed so far away, you know. A
trip of three or four months ... it might as well be China."

"Well, Nat, I recommend that you make up for lost time and pay close
attention to Nathaniel's description of Virginia, for you shall be sailing there
next month."

Nat leapt to his feet and Lyn put both hands to her mouth. "Sailing ...
next month?"

"That is what I said. I have booked you and Lyn passage on the *Adam
and Eve*, under Captain Gardiner's command. It sails from London early in
June."

Nat was, quite literally, speechless.

"I've already sent Nathaniel a long letter, asking him to make you welcome and help you get off to a good start. It went on a ship which is leaving any day now ... perhaps has already sailed ... so, with luck, he will be in
Jamestown to meet you and will take you under his wing. He stands very
high in the government ... is one of Governor Berkeley's right hand men.
You could not have a better friend. Count yourself lucky."

"Father, I am astounded, it is so sudden. Can we discuss this?"

Squire Thomas hardened his heart. "That is one thing we cannot do,
Natty. I have made up my mind. You have not shown me that you can govern yourself, so I will continue to undertake that obligation. You will go
with a tidy fortune of eighteen hundred pounds, some of it in cash and some
of it in notes. I will not even tell you the sacrifices that Bess and I have made

to collect that sum. Suffice it to say that both of us will be living meanly for some time to come. But listen to me, lad. This is your last chance. I can do no more for you. If your Virginia adventure is a failure, then you are on your own. You have an entrée to the colony and you have the means to be successful. Whether you have the discipline and the will remains to be seen."

Nat turned his back on the others and strode to the east window. Lyn knew that he was hiding tears of shame. After a minute or two he collected himself and faced his father. The sun poured in through the casement and illuminated his rich, dark curls and his golden eyes blazed. Lyn's heart beat fast.

"It is fair, Father. I can see that it is fair. I shall do what you say. I am in no position to persuade you that I will succeed, but I know that I will." Lyn rushed to Nat and enfolded him in her arms. He smiled down at her. "I am glad you bought a passage for my wife; it appears that she wishes to go with me."

The Squire sighed with relief. It had gone better than he expected. "You will go with my fondest love and all my hopes and dreams, Natty. But I have another gift for you ... perhaps the best one of all."

Nat looked quizzical. "Have you equipped us for our new country, sir?"

"No. Far better. I have persuaded John to take you and Lyn as his first clients and to go with you as your man of business, so that your fresh start will be a good one. With Nathaniel to sponsor you and John and Lyn at your side, you must succeed."

Now John Grey looked up proudly and smiled. Nat rushed to his side and clapped him on the shoulders, speechless. Lyn hung back, but sent John a look of happiness which nestled in his heart. He had three solid offers from London firms and he might be a fool to start his career by turning his back on England, but the Bacons were his family and he would do his best by them. He loved Squire Thomas like a father and Nat like a brother and as for Lyn ... it was better not to think too closely of Lyn.

"Why then," said the Squire, "I believe this calls for a toast. Natty, fetch the sherry and the glasses from the sideboard and let's drink to the Virginia adventure."

They gathered around the Squire's work table and toasted the future. John chatted with Squire Thomas as Nat leafed through Nathaniel Bacon's letters, but Lyn was drawn to the map which lay at the other end of the table. She smoothed the paper with tremulous hands and looked at the country which would be her next home. Why, it was a network of rivers. Once you passed two mighty capes there was nothing but water. And the names! They sounded like Indian drums! Potomac, Rappahannock, Chickahominy, Pamunkey, Piscataway. What strange peoples lived on the banks of those foreign waters? But there ... there was the York. It was comforting to know that King Charles' brother, the Lord High Admiral, had a presence in Virginia. And the large river which plunged west like an arrow … why it was called the James, another happy name. And to the south there was an Elizabeth River, which made her feel at home. And over there was the Blackwater …that sounded ominous. Lyn placed her hand on her breast and felt the rapid pulse of her heart. She thought of her first day with Nat, so long ago. She knew then that he would bring her adventures, and her premonition was true. They called it the "new world" and, for them, it would be so.

CHAPTER 7

AUGUST 1674

Lyn stood in the waist of the ship ignoring the seamen's curses as they swarmed up the shrouds to release a cloud of sail to catch the fickle summer winds. Captain Gardiner had made a calculated gamble to take the short route to Virginia and, until the past few days, it had paid off. To brave the Bay of Biscay, flirt with the coast of Portugal, kiss the Canaries, hug the earth's girdle until sighting the West Indies and then let the currents and winds of North America waft the ship up the coast of Spanish Florida to the great Bay of Chesapeake took three months or more. To dart from The Sleeve like an arrow, skim the Summer Isles, and pierce the Bay through the Virginia capes straight to the heart of the colony could cut the trip in half. Until the winds failed him two days ago the Captain's instincts had proven correct: they were about to set a record. The *Adam and Eve* had left Gravesend in the last week of June and it was now only the first week of August. The flotsam and jetsam which danced around the ship in the choppy cross currents, by his calculation, showed them to be only thirty miles or so from the Virginia coast. But yesterday and today they had been becalmed and the record was in jeopardy. However, in the last hour the warm westerlies had begun pushing against the vessel like a soft hand and hope had quickened in the Captain's breast. It would take the very devil of a ship's master to tack into the bay under these conditions but he *had* the very devil of a master in Throgmorton and he thought they could pull it off. Right now the ship was pitching like a mare with colic, but the wind had shifted a few degrees north and he intended to take every advantage of that fact. The master screamed, the canvas flashed and the helmsman adjusted the wheel and the *Adam and Eve* rose from the befuddled seas and surged forward, northwest. The sails flapped confusedly, but then billowed out in nice, tight arcs and the shrouds hummed for the first time in two days.

Captain Gardiner sighed with happiness and left the quarterdeck for his cabin. He would give Throgmorton a bonus: two hogsheads of Virginia sweet-scented; that ought to keep him happy, though doubtless the gift would be squandered on liquor and whores and by the time they got back to London his master would have naught to show for his efforts except boasting rights. As the Captain ducked below his eye caught a flash of blue and he noted that the girl was in her usual place in the ship's waist. He normally could not abide a woman on board – it drove the men wild. And this one was a beauty. But Squire Bacon had paid in gold for the three passengers from Suffolk and, to his surprise, they had turned out to bring more pleasure than pain. The girl had behaved like a perfect lady – she moved about as though she were enclosed in a glass bubble and even the most vicious sailors treated her with respect. The Squire's son was unpleasantly imperious but, to his chagrin, he had proved to be the worst sailor of the three and had spent most of the passage below. Grey was a mannerly fellow and a scholar to boot; it had been a pleasure to have him at table. The young attorney had acquired a whole fund of literature on Virginia and though most of it was trash – mere puffery – it was clear that he was studying the colony as he must have studied his law books. Captain Gardiner wished his passengers well in Virginia, though it was not a place that he would care to live. All in all, the voyage had been most successful. Another day should see them at Jamestown, snugged up at one of the capital's stout wharfs. He would offload the silks and satins and fine woolens and books and furniture he had brought from the mother country and take on his tobacco and be home well before Christmas. A man could not ask for more.

Lyn studiously avoided Captain Gardiner's gaze and the sailors' bustle. She had found that if she focused on the middle distance that everyone was the happier for it. The ship had started to move and the jarring and rocking of the past two days gave way to a pleasant, purposeful surge. They seemed to be going north rather than west, but doubtless the Captain knew exactly what he was doing. Although the wind was in her face it did not have the refreshing tang she was used to, but was strangely warm, like a tepid bath. The air felt fecund as though it bore growing things. The color of the wind was green. Was Virginia, then, a jungle? John had told her that the climate tended to hot, rather than to cold, and that the forests were vast. They said you could grow anything there. She shivered slightly. It would not be long before she would see, feel and smell plants and creatures unknown to England. The prospect was delicious, but daunting. Hazelwood swam into her mind, so orderly and precise. In her four years there she had learned every field, every copse, every stone of her farm. She wondered whether Jemmy was keeping up the gardens and exercising Lark. Fancy and Prince had found a home at Friston Hall, but fat little Lark was to stay at Hazelwood to do Jemmy's bidding. Lyn's throat tightened. Suffolk seemed far away. In truth, neither she nor Nat nor John knew when they would see it again.

One of the sailors cried out and Lyn turned to see the cause. There, on a ratline, huddled a small blue bird with a rust colored breast. It was a songbird – a landbird. They were close enough to Virginia for one of the creatures of the forest to have found its way here! Lyn smiled as the sailor – just a lad in his teens – brought her the treasure. She removed her cotton head scarf and wrapped the trembling thing in the fabric, feeling its throbbing heart. She felt a kinship with the bird which had lost its compass and had been thrown into an unknown universe. She would take the thing to Nat as a token that their journey was almost over.

Nat was curled in his bunk, facing inward, denying the world. He was furious that he had proven such a poor sailor. John had suffered as well, but, true to his cursedly steady nature, he rarely complained. And Lyn, little Lyn, turned out to have a stomach of iron. He knew he should not dwell on the matter. After all, having sea legs was a vagary of nature, not a test of will, but it galled him all the same. They had planned to use the voyage to study that heap of material that John had acquired, but he had been too ill. Well, he would have to rely on Colonel Nathaniel Bacon instead. He could not wait to step onto the solid earth. Nat heard Lyn's step and sat up, groaning.

"Look, Nat, a Virginia bird. It has flown here to welcome us. We're very close now ... the Captain says we'll be in Jamestown tomorrow."

"What in God's name are you going to do with a bird?"

"My, you are in a temper. I'll put it in one of Captain Gardiner's cages and release it when we reach land."

"Cages? What are you talking about?"

"There, in the corner. You've been so ill that you haven't noticed them. When he takes the long route he goes by the Canaries and brings some of the yellow birds back for his wife, so he keeps some cages at hand."

Nat had to smile. "Well alright, let me see the pretty thing. If we're that close to land I'll drag myself on deck. Only one more day? It's the best news I've heard since we left."

An hour later Nat and John stood on deck, one on each side of Lyn, and the three of them eagerly breathed in the mild air with its land odors. As Nat inhaled deeply, eyes shut, John nudged him, pointing west. A line of blue, the color of the Virgin's mantle, lay against the copper sky. The colors of the bluebird. Virginia.

Twenty-four hours later the sun was once again low in the west as the *Adam and Eve's* last hawser was wrapped tightly around the stout piles of Jamestown's wharf. The tide was ebbing and the muddy waters of the James ran sluggishly along the ship's sides bearing the detritus of their long journey through Virginia's vast, uncharted forests. The heat lay like an oppressive blanket over the ship, the river and the little town which lay sprawled on its low peninsula, inert. The breeze which had danced attendance on the ship all morning had surrendered to the humid air and neither leaf nor grass stirred in the quiet evening. Action seemed impossible. The colony's energy was sucked dry by mere survival. Jamestown lay, not in repose, but in defeat at the hands of high summer.

Lyn wished she had heeded Captain Gardiner's advice and put on her simplest, lightest linen frock rather than her best red kersey; she could feel the sweat dripping down her back and gathering unpleasantly under her arms. Suffolk could sometimes be a furnace, but never with this enervating mixture of heat and moisture. Perhaps after their record crossing they had run into a bit of bad luck, that was all – surely the weather would freshen soon, with the dawn. Once again Lyn stood between Nat and John. She glanced at her husband. His expression was stony. He spoke across her to Grey.

"Wake me from my dream, John. Is this a heathen town, or are we looking at Virginia's capital?"

John smiled forcedly. "You know as well as I that this is Jamestown. I told you it was small, no more than two or three hundred permanent residents. But take heart. There, to the left, don't you see a stout church tower? And that row of brick houses is not unseemly. I imagine the government buildings are on the higher land. Give the town a chance."

Nat removed his hat and wiped his dripping brow. "Damn my blood," he muttered. "Saxmundham, nay, Friston village is more comely. You can paint a cheery picture, but the facts give you the lie." Nat paused and straightened his shoulders. "Still, you said that the colony's real business is done on the great river estates, not here. Well, what's next? Gardiner said *The Unicorn* was the only place to stay. Let's find the inn before it is dark."

Lyn winced inwardly at Nat's flat tone. However, if he was disappointed at their first sight of Jamestown, it was with good reason. The little town on the mud flat looked like it had been flung there by a fractious child. The huts near the riverside were makeshift affairs of wattle and daub, apparently used for storage and commerce. To her right a broad street ran up a gentle declivity at right angles to the river and she saw, with hope, a handful of neat brick homes on its upper reaches, striving for dignity. To the left lay the church which John had mentioned, its stout brick tower rising bravely in the dusk, a beacon of civilization. Yet the twin St. Marys of Benhall and Friston were more graceful and welcoming than this prosaic, boxy structure. In the far distance she caught a glimpse of some brick row houses which looked promising, but they stood naked and glaring in a field of mud, with no sense of order or connectedness. To the far left lay a curious mound or dike – some sort of rampart, she supposed. Altogether the place had a raw, striving look as though it were fighting nature to stay alive. She hoped *The Unicorn* would be an improvement.

The three newcomers descended the gangplank and set foot on Virginia soil. They turned right and followed the rough lane which bordered the river. The street was dry and dusty until they reached a communal well where constant usage had created a quagmire. Long-legged swine with intelligent, questing faces lay in the cool earth, their quick breaths marked by the rapid rise and fall of their slim sides. Thin ragged children, sent for water, stared at the new arrivals with black, fathomless eyes. All living things seemed hostile and alert and Lyn's heart sank further. At the end of the lane the trio turned left and took the broad street where the better houses stood. They walked up a mild incline for perhaps a quarter of a mile to where the street was joined by an east-west avenue which looked like the principal thoroughfare. The welcome astringent scent of pitch rose from the deep green mass of a pine forest which lay beyond, to the north. To their right, beyond the brick houses, fields and gardens occupied the middle distance and a formless mass of trees marked the horizon which was blurred by falling night. The newcomers turned left and walked west, following the setting sun. Humble cottages of wattle and daub lay on both sides of the avenue. Most had stout brick chimneys at their gable ends, but some had nothing more than smoke holes. Most appeared to have only one or two rooms, with a sleeping loft above. The roofs were of thatch, although some were of rough tile and some even of handsome cedar shingles. Few of the cottagers had attempted a garden; what passed for yards were largely dust and weeds.

Lyn looked eagerly for signs of human life, but it was supper time and she saw no one except a handful of thin children wandering aimlessly, darting quick glances at the strangers. Not far from the church, on higher ground to the north-east, the travelers came to a neat brick building with a large, palisaded yard containing several dependencies. A thick, square-chiseled post stood before the front door with a wooden sign hanging motionless from the crosspiece. The sign bore no lettering but on each side, in mirror image, danced a white unicorn, its mane and tail formed like sea-wrack and a fabulous horn thrusting upward from each noble forehead.

The three travelers exchanged glances and, in unison, stepped onto the shallow wooden porch. A brass knocker, in the shape of a unicorn, was appended to the oak door and Nat seized it and knocked loudly. The door swung open under his hand and the trio entered a large common room bifurcated by trestle tables set end to end. On the far wall a huge fireplace gaped wide, its maw filled with black iron hooks and roasting jacks. The fire had been damped down until it barely glowed and the room felt blessedly cool. To the right of the fireplace stood a large hutch crowded with blue and white Delftware and pewter mugs. To the left a recess led to a back hall and a well-formed staircase which rose to the upper floor. The short ends of the rectangular hall were pierced with doorways. To the left the open door showed a large communal bedroom with simple wood-framed beds strung with rope, each holding a thin mattress and each covered with bedding in bright, fanciful designs. The door on the west end of the hall was closed.

There seemed to be no one about. Nat stepped forward onto the brick floor and his boots rang with authority. A figure suddenly appeared from the dormitory, her hands wrapped in her white apron.

"Mercy, you took me by surprise. We just emptied the house and we were not expecting anyone today. May I help you?"

Lyn eyed the woman as Nat spoke. She was tall, but graceless. Though long-legged, her bust was heavy and her torso thick. Her neck was ringed with fat and seemed unwashed, though Lyn mentally chastised herself for the unkind thought; perhaps it was the effect of the twilight. The woman's hair, which straggled from a white cap, was mouse colored and her eyes light and protruding. Her undistinguished features proclaimed her middle-aged; she was perhaps forty years of age. As Lyn took her silent inventory Nat explained their presence and asked whether they could have supper and a bed tonight and then bed and board for as many days as it took for Colonel Nathaniel Bacon to convey them to King's Creek.

At the mention of Colonel Bacon the woman's face lightened. She dropped a deep curtsey and moved forward into the common room. "Why you must be young Mister Bacon! I was told to expect you, but I thought you would be coming in September! They said you were arriving on the *Adam and Eve*; you are never going to tell me that Captain Gardiner has arrived, and we not know it?"

Nat explained their speedy passage and begged pardon for their unannounced arrival, asking whether they should seek lodgings elsewhere. Their hostess reassured them and bustled about, seating them on the fireside settles and pouring them tankards of wine and water.

"'Tis no trouble, no trouble at all. But let me introduce myself. I am Joanna Lawrence, mistress of *The Unicorn*. We were full last night with outgoing passengers, but they left at dawn this morning on the *Concord*. Perhaps you saw her as you sailed up the river? In any event, the inn has been empty since … it is completely at your disposal."

Nat acknowledged that the *Adam and Eve* had passed an outgoing ship that morning where the James debouched into the bay and Mistress Lawrence continued. "Now, I've just finished making up the beds and there are more than enough for you, Mister Bacon, and for your friend, in the common bedchamber. As for Mistress Bacon, we let the ladies have Clarissa's room, there, on the other side of the hall. Two ladies used the room last night and they said they slept like babies. I have changed the linen this very day, and it is as fresh as you could wish – it's almost as though I knew you were coming!"

Lyn could not warm to her hostess, whose enthusiasm was patently professional, but she composed her features and smiled her thanks. She wondered about Clarissa, who was so unceremoniously turned out of her room for "the ladies."

"My thanks, Mistress Lawrence, but I would not care to drive your Clarissa from her room. Perhaps we could share a bed, like last night's guests."

Joanna Lawrence's face burned and the rings around her neck moved like rolls of pastry crust. "I am afraid that would never do. Of course you don't know, but Clarissa is a blackamoor!"

Lyn was taken aback. She had never seen an African in her life, though her brother had shown her some etchings of African kings and had told her that Barbara Villiers, the King's mistress, kept a black boy like a pet. Given her hostess' reaction, she decided not to push the matter further, but she looked forward to seeing Clarissa. Did Virginia abound with Africans as well as savages? The coming days would be full of interest, indeed.

With his usual aplomb John relieved her of her embarrassment. "Thank you, Mistress Lawrence. Your arrangements will suit us well. Perhaps we could do something about our luggage and you could tell us when you serve supper?"

"Oh my, of course. We sup late in the summer, because of the heat, but it will be on the table soon. It will all be cold … I hope you don't mind. We've no salad, but plenty of fruit, and there's milk and cream in the ice house. If you need a hot dish I can make you some eggs, though you may prefer those for breakfast. Well, enough of that – I'll send a boy for your luggage and then I'll call Mister Lawrence. He's upstairs in his chambers, talking with a friend."

An hour later both Lyn's appetite and curiosity had been appeased. Despite her personal appearance, Joanna Lawrence kept a good house and the supper had been excellent. Of even more interest, they had been served by Clarissa, a tall, stately black woman who bore herself like a queen, but said not a word. Clarissa and the dishes had disappeared and now Nat and John were handling the slender clay pipes which Mistress Lawrence had provided for them, laughing as they determined how best to indulge in Virginia's famous crop. They were crushing the aromatic golden brown leaves in their fingers and preparing the pipes when they heard a new voice.

"It's my finest sweet-scented. May I join you?"

All three travelers started in surprise. The newcomer had approached as quietly as a cat; they had not heard a sound.

"Mister Lawrence?" asked Nat, rising.

"The same. Forgive me for not joining you at supper, but I was otherwise occupied. You must be Mister Bacon and this must be Mister Grey. And," turning towards Lyn, "this charming lady must be Mistress Bacon."

The bright brass Dutch chandelier shone down on the master of *The Unicorn*. Although he was not much above Nat's height, and under John's, Lawrence had great authority. He was clad in a suit of gray, offset by a fine white linen shirt, the neck and cuffs of which were edged with lace. His stockings were of silk, and his shoes of soft black leather. He wore no jewels but an intricate braided golden ring on his right hand. His figure was firm and symmetrical, giving the impression of great strength and agility, but it was his face that drew the eye. His hair had once been light, not much darker than John's honey brown, but now it was a badger gray, mixed iron and silver. He wore it chopped carelessly, chin length, and it hung disordered about his face. His upper lip and chin bore the same gray pelt, though unlike his hair, his moustache and goatee were finely trimmed. His eyes gleamed silver as he scrutinized his guests. He was altogether a gray man. His skin was pale for one who lived in a sunny clime – perhaps his duties kept him too much indoors. Beneath his fine, seeking eyes a straight nose ran to a thin-lipped mouth and firm chin and his cheeks were scored with vertical lines. Even in repose the man quivered with life, like a lynx about to spring. Although he had moved and spoken quietly, his presence filled the hall with tension. Lyn looked down, afraid, but Nat's face shone with interest.

"Yes, this is my wife," said Nat. "And our friend John Grey is an attorney who, together with my cousin, will help us get established here."

"I have heard all about you from Colonel Bacon, sir. But nobody looked for you sooner than September. Gardiner must have made a fine run."

John looked at the innkeeper with interest. "Six weeks. He claims it is a record."

"And it may well be. Gardiner has made the Virginia run many times, and the *Adam and Eve* is a sweet sailor. So you are an attorney. You will be most welcome in Virginia. 'Tis a fractious and litigious society."

Nat laughed, claiming Lawrence's attention. "'Tis a fractious and litigious world."

Lawrence smiled slightly. "As you say." He turned to Lyn and extended a hand. "And how did you find the journey? You seem somewhat fatigued. The climate can have that effect ... they call it 'seasoning.'"

Lyn took Lawrence's hand and quickly dropped it. The man's flesh burned as if with fever. Was he consuming himself and was his gray coloring that of ash? Would he disappear before their eyes like the dim fire across the room? What a strange conceit. She felt suddenly exhausted and longed for bed. Lyn turned to Nat.

"You must forgive me, dear, but I should like to retire. Perhaps someone could attend me and show me the ways of the house."

The three men were all solicitude. Nat escorted his wife to the little bedroom which they called "Clarissa's" and the innkeeper rang a bell. Within minutes the stately black woman appeared from the back of the inn and disappeared through the western door to assist the new guest. With the women gone, the three men seated themselves at the trestle table and relaxed, each taking up a pipe. After some minutes sweet blue smoke scented the great hall. Lawrence scrutinized his guests; they might have been stripped naked and flayed.

The innkeeper addressed Nat. "Are you as weary as your charming wife, or can I entice you to share a bottle of wine with me in my private chambers? I have been spending the evening with a friend who would be delighted to meet you. We are such an idle, gossip-mongering society here in Jamestown that as soon as Colonel Bacon told us that his young cousin from Suffolk was going to join us, we have been quite beside ourselves."

Nat and John glanced at one another. It was clear that Nat wanted to accept, and John to decline, Lawrence's invitation. John deferred to his friend. This was Nat's Virginia adventure; he must set the pace. Pipes in hand, the three men mounted the staircase. As they reached the first landing they heard a door slam below and they saw Joanna Lawrence appear from the dormitory. Her foreshortened face scowled up at them sourly, and she disappeared into the hall, frowning. Mistress Lawrence did not appear to favor private entertainment for the guests of *The Unicorn*.

When they reached the upper floor they followed Lawrence down a corridor which ran the length of the inn, forming the long leg of a T. At the end of the hall a door gave onto a large chamber which formed the short leg of the T. The innkeeper knocked quickly and swung the door open and ushered in his guests. Nat and John gasped audibly. Before them lay a large room which ran the width of the *The Unicorn's* west end. The room had no ceiling, but was open to the rafters, which gave it great height and airiness. A simple yet capacious bedstead lay to the left near a dormer window which gave onto the yard below and next to the bed stood a pine clothes cupboard. The floor was planked with the same wood and covered with bright rag rugs. Directly opposite the door was a brick fireplace, the hearth cold and empty on this August night. Next to the fireplace was a table crowded with decanters and bottles and carafes and before it lay the shining skin of a lynx. To the far right, under a second dormer window stood a huge table in a shelved alcove crowded with books. Four comfortable chairs covered in Turkey work surrounded the table and in its center was a tray littered with bottles of ink, sheaves of paper, quills and dottles of wax. Seated in one of the chairs was a tall man with silver hair.

John's interest was kindled. Perhaps Nat had been right ... the innkeeper was undoubtedly a man of parts. This was quintessentially a man's room, and an educated man at that. John wondered, idly, whether the innkeeper slept here alone, or whether he shared his wife's bed. His thoughts were interrupted by Lawrence.

"Gentlemen, permit me to name my particular friend, William Drummond. Will, this is Nathaniel Bacon from Suffolk and John Grey, a London attorney. Mister Bacon plans to settle here with his charming wife and Mister Grey will help them with their business."

The innkeeper's friend rose. He was taller than any of them, substantially above even John's six feet. Age had added weight to an already sturdy frame but the whole was not gross, but harmonious and fitting.

Drummond's original coloring must have been fair, but his hair now shone silver above a ruddy face and brilliant blue eyes. His features were regular and blunt, soldier-like, and his skin was roughened by the sun and wind. He kept his hair short, like Lawrence, but unlike Lawrence wore neither beard nor moustache. Nat supposed him to be in his fifties, about the Squire's age. Something about him suggested that he was a fighting man.

Drummond puffed on his pipe and smiled at Lawrence's guests. "It is a pleasure to meet you both. I live not far from the harbor and I saw the *Adam and Eve* come in this evening, but I had no idea that you gentlemen were on board. Although come to think of it, the last time I saw Colonel Bacon he did say you were taking passage with Captain Gardiner. I should have put two and two together, but Lawrence and I had other things on our mind. Welcome to Virginia. I don't know what your plans are, but if you will be in Jamestown for several days I do hope that you will visit us. I live at the east end of town – you may have passed my house on the way to *The Unicorn*. It's the only one with a green door."

John was taken with their new acquaintance. The man had a pleasant way about him – nothing thrusting or forward, unlike their host who reminded the attorney of nothing so much as one of those agile and restless sheep dogs he had seen in a trip to the Border Country. He was anxious to know more about both men.

Nat spoke. "So you know my cousin. Have you been long acquainted?"

Drummond puffed contentedly on his pipe and glanced at Lawrence, almost as though asking his advice. John found the interchange odd and sat up straighter in his chair, his attention caught.

The tall man turned to Nat and answered. "Oh my, yes. We are of an age and we came to the colony at about the same time. Colonel Bacon's plantation lies on the York and my lands are scattered, but over the years we have met many times. Of course he is a member of the Council of State and I have never had that honor. But yes, I would say that I know him quite well. A fine, principled gentleman. You couldn't be in better hands."

Something about Drummond's tone belied his words and John caught another glance between the older man and the innkeeper. There was an unspoken agenda here, and John intended to learn it. Drummond scraped his chair back and rose, ducking to avoid a rafter. As he placed his hands on the table to steady himself John saw that his right hand bore just such a gold braided ring as Lawrence wore.

"I have wasted too much of your time, Dicken," he said. "I must go. Sarah will not be best pleased that she has had to manage all four children this evening." The big man laughed. "I'll pay for it tomorrow." He addressed himself to Nat. "I was quite serious when I said that my wife and I would be most happy to see you before you part for King's Creek. Don't stand on ceremony; just drop by. I am in the trading way and I conduct business out of my home, so you are sure to find me. Dicken can tell you the way."

"I daresay we will be in Jamestown for a day or two. It will be a pleasure to pay you a visit," responded Nat.

"Very good, sir. I look forward to it. Nice to have met you, Mister Grey. Dicken, I'll see myself out and I will be in touch with you soon about that other matter." Throwing a slouch hat upon his head the big man left the room and closed the door behind him.

Silence fell in Lawrence's library. Each dormer showed a slice of deep blue sky and a sprinkling of stars. Suddenly dogs yelped in the distance; perhaps they marked the path of William Drummond as he made his way home. The clock on the wooden mantel chimed ten. Lawrence opened the casements and John heard the thrum of insects and the piping of frogs. The night hung about them like velvet. Within minutes small, hard-bodied creatures pierced the darkness and threw themselves at the candles, dying for the light.

Lawrence laughed and closed the casements. "The summer is hard here. They didn't plant Jamestown wisely, but it is what we have and we must do our best with it. Now for that bottle of wine"

Accepting a glass of claret, Nat spoke. "Forgive me for asking, but I sensed that Mister Drummond and my cousin are not, perhaps, on the best of terms."

Lawrence looked at his guests as if deciding how candid to be with and then appeared to have made up his mind. "You must form your own impressions of the colony, but perhaps I can give you some guidance. What I say will doubtless be balanced by the comments of others, so I will speak my mind. The fact is that Colonel Bacon stands very well with the Governor and that, in a nutshell, is everything in Virginia. Governor William Berkeley is an institution here. He reigned, if you will allow the term, during most of the forties; he continued as *primus inter pares* during the fifties although, of course, he lost his post while Cromwell was in power; and he was reinstated by the General Assembly as Governor in sixty and confirmed by the King in sixty-one and has dominated the colony ever since, for fourteen long years. Sir William Berkeley has put his stamp on Virginia as Governor and as First Citizen for thirty-five years, as long as I myself have been alive."

Nat arched his brows. Thirty-five years ... it was a long time. Whatever the old man was like, he had certainly impressed his cousin ... that much was clear from the Squire's letters. But how old was Berkeley? He must be sixty or seventy. Was his grip as firm now as it had once been? They would soon find out. At least he knew how old Lawrence was. Nat would have thought him older; it must be that incendiary process. Nat smiled and drank deep and noticed that Lawrence was watching him closely.

"Well, go on. I will give you Sir William's ascendancy, but how does that affect my cousin and your friend Drummond?"

"Oh, as for Colonel Bacon, I will say no more than that he stands staunchly by the Governor in all things. As for Will and me, the truth of the matter is that we have both felt the back of the Governor's hand, so we are no friends of Green Spring."

"Green Spring?"

"Oh, forgive me. 'Tis common parlance for the Governor's party. It is the name of his plantation – a pretty place, which lies not five miles from here."

"The Governor's *party*? That suggests that the colony is divided into factions. Can you explain further?"

Lawrence sighed and looked at his companions. He rose and strode the length of the room, glass in hand. When he reached the lynx skin rug he stood on it and rose slowly on his toes and then balanced on his heels as he pondered his answer. Finally, draining his goblet, he replied. "I may rue this night, but you seem honest and I would like to help you if I can. Will Drummond can share his story with you, or not, as he chooses, but you are welcome to mine. If my little history is of assistance to you, I will be content. All I ask is that you keep what I am about to tell you in confidence. Much of it is known, but things have come to such a pass that it were better that you not divulge this meeting."

Nat and John eagerly agreed. Lawrence was an unusual man and they yearned to know what had brought him to Virginia and how it was that he had earned the Royal Governor's ire.

The gray man commenced his tale. "I was born in forty in Woodstock under an ill star. Imagine coming into the world on the cusp of the Civil War in the heart of the King's country! My father, a small farmer, was a staunch Puritan and he paid for his beliefs with his life. He died on the battlefield in forty-two and I have no memory of him; nor of my mother, who died within weeks of my birth."

Nat's heart was touched: here was another whose advent had brought his mother's death. He would have to know Lawrence far better before he told him the fate of Elizabeth Brooke Bacon, yet he already felt a bond with the innkeeper. Lawrence continued.

"I was the last of five children. My older brother was my senior by sixteen years and between him and me came three sisters, all plain of face and empty of pocket. When father died my brother was eighteen, and a man. All our little property came to him and he was sworn to look after the rest of us and to stay well away from the conflict which killed my father. Poor James had no choice. He had to manage the farm and be a parent to the girls and to little Dicken, who had just learned to walk and talk. So he gave up his dream of studying at Oxford, which lay so temptingly close, (he had the makings of a scholar), and he did his duty by us and did it well. None of the girls married – they had neither looks nor fortune and their Puritan ways discouraged suitors. But bless them, they kept house for James and me and taught me my lessons and so I scrambled my way to a scholarship at the local grammar school. I did well at my studies – some said superlatively – and James planned to send me to Oxford to fulfill his own dream. However my ill star shone and robbed me of a university education as it had robbed my brother. The Protector had died and the Stuarts were back in power and, given my Puritan background, I was denied entrance to the university."

Lawrence's ill star, Nat thought. *He himself had been born under a lucky star, had been handed everything, yet what use had he made of his good fortune?* He closed his eyes and clenched his jaw. *Nothing – less than nothing. And now he had been given one last chance. He knew he would succeed here in Virginia ... he must. Perhaps the innkeeper could point him in the right direction.* When he opened his eyes he found Lawrence reading his soul. After a moment's silence the narrative continued.

"I was young and vigorous and, if I was denied an education, Oxfordshire was not going to keep me. James had married and after that our little farm was not big enough for the two of us, as the three girls were still at home. What were my choices? All I knew of a practical nature was farming, but I knew little enough of that as my family had filled my head with Latin and Greek and made me think myself above such lowly pursuits. I had been trained to no trade. The Church was closed to me both for lack of education and for lack of inclination. I had no sponsor for the army or the navy even if I had been inclined to a military career, which I was not. Trade bored me and in any event we had no connections among the merchant class. I was at loose ends, making myself and all around me miserable, when one of my former teachers came to supper one night and brought some promotional literature about Virginia. Perhaps you have read some yourself?"

John smiled wryly. *He* had read everything he could get his hands on, but Nat had found a way to avoid that task. Seasickness had been a convenient excuse, but a poor one.

"Well, no matter. Generally they contain more fiction than fact. But James and I knew no better and we were quite taken with the idea of a Virginia adventure. There was a common theme among the tracts which appealed to us, namely that the colony was the ideal place for 'a younger brother.' By that the authors meant that any impecunious scamp who could scrape together the cost of a passage could claim fifty acres of land under the headright system. The emigrant then had but to plant and seat his holding and pay the annual quitrents which, it was stated, were nominal. If there was not enough land at home, there certainly was enough here! How could a vigorous, enterprising man fail? Surely all the younger brothers of England would seize the opportunity – and all the older brothers be glad of it!"

Lawrence's tone was bitter and once again Nat thought of his own good fortune and how he had abused it.

"Well, James and I brooded about the possibility of my emigrating for some time and I was able to get my hands on some more information – particularly Hammond's description of the colony. To shorten my tale, we became convinced that I could do far worse than to try and make my fortune abroad. My sisters were against it, silly geese, but under James' command Marion and Susan sold their butter and cream and Margery sold her cloth as though the devil was behind them and before long I had my passage money in hand. I sailed from Liverpool in sixty-two and had a difficult passage of three months – twice what you and Captain Gardiner achieved! I arrived in October of sixty-two only to find that Governor William Berkeley was still in London pleading Virginia's case against the navigation laws.

"My ill star continued to shine. As Sir William's return was expected daily, the Council insisted that I wait for the Governor to obtain my land patent and would not act in his absence. My purse was slim and was reserved for the tools and clothing and seed and suchlike that I would need when I had my land. I had little or nothing to live on, winter was coming on, and I was not well, having had a nasty bout of the fever in the West Indies. I gave myself a week to decide what to do and because I felt so poorly I treated myself to a room here at *The Unicorn* in order to recover my health.

"Despite my illness I haunted the Statehouse during that week and talked to whomever I could, hoping to find a friend. I learned that an excellent property in Charles City County had escheated to the state, as the landowner had died without a will and without heirs. Now, as you will learn, Charles City County lies just upriver from Jamestown and is a choice location. It was one of the first areas cleared and cultivated and, being on the river and near the capital, land there is coveted. The escheated land was not on the river, but it was watered by creeks, had a small dwelling and had been largely cleared. Moreover, it was approximately fifty acres, the amount which I had the right to claim under my headrights. Some nearby acreage was still available and if I was successful with the fifty acres I might soon add to my holdings. It seemed ideal and in my fantasies I was soon one of the biggest planters in Virginia, with a fine brick house and a wife and family.

"But my week *had* run and there was still no sign of the Governor and I could not convince the Council to act. I opportuned the Secretary of State, Thomas Ludwell, but he smoothed my anxieties over and assured me that all would be well as soon as Sir William arrived and that I would just have to be patient. In the meantime he probed me about my background and I told him my whole story, thinking that it would work in my favor. What a child I was!

"Now I was in dire straits as I had spent every penny save what I had set aside to purchase my equipment and I had sworn not to touch that hoard. With the cold weather approaching, even if the Governor arrived and I got my patent, I could not realistically improve my land until the spring. How was I to survive the winter? The innkeeper, Roger Trent, was an old gentleman in failing health. He took to his bed at just about the time I became a guest at *The Unicorn* and Mistress Joanna was left to run the inn by herself. As my week came to an end I approached him, with trepidation, and offered to trade my skill with letters and numbers for food and lodging, until my situation was resolved. The ailing man accepted my offer, with gratitude, and I was given the little room where your wife is now sleeping. It had been Mister Trent's office and counting room and Mistress Joanna fitted it up with a cot and a wardrobe so that within a day I had both a snuggery and a job. Poor Mister Trent never rose from his bed and passed on to a better world on the first day of December, 1662. Mistress Joanna, his sole heiress, asked me to stay on and added a small salary to my bed and board. I gladly accepted her offer but then felt badly as not a week had passed when Sir William Berkeley finally arrived and I feared that I would have to desert my landlady sooner than either one of us had expected. Kindly, Mistress Joanna assured me that if for some reason my plans did not work out, she would always have a place for me at *The Unicorn*. How much better she knew Virginia than I!"

Here Lawrence stopped and paced the room once more. His face looked haggard as he continued his story.

"Well, then I began my siege of Governor Berkeley. He had been away for almost two years and I knew that he would be sorely beset with business, so I did not grow discouraged even when, two weeks after his arrival, they told me that my petition for the Charles City County land had not been reviewed or acted on. It was my habit to sit in the hall of the Statehouse every morning, from ten to twelve. One morning, as Christmas approached, I had taken my usual post when Philip Ludwell, brother to the Secretary of State, happened by. He knew what my business was – I do believe it was known to the whole colony. He laughed at me and told me I was wasting my time as the Governor had decamped to Green Spring for the holidays and had not set a date certain for his return! I was furious. I decided to beard the lion in his den and force an answer. Not only did my own fate lie in the balance, but there was Mistress Joanna to think of as well. I begged a horse of her and rode to Green Spring on Christmas Eve. Never was a plan more ill-conceived.

"I arrived at the great house as the sun was setting. There had been snow and then a warming trend and the roads were beds of slush and mire. I arrived exhausted and begrimed and in a foul temper. I banged on the front door with my sword hilt and demanded admittance and the serving man turned me away as though I was a savage. I brushed past him into the entrance hall and demanded an audience with the Governor. The old man must have heard me because he came in from his office, a portrait in crimson and gold silk, a full wig of fine white hair rippling onto his shoulders. He looked at me as one would a cur and told me to get out or he would clap me in jail that instant. I know now what I did not know then: one of the outbuildings at Green Spring is indeed a jail and he would have acted on his word without a second thought. Speedy justice, you might call it. If you omit the fact finding and the impartial judge or jury you can get a quick result.

"Well, I knew my cause was lost already, but I pleaded it there in the hall, in desperation. Berkeley's voice was as cold as ice when he told me that he had read my request days ago and had turned it down as Colonel Hill had been granted the patent. Why? Because the escheated land lay near Hill's plantation and the disposition was thus 'convenient.' He told me that he supposed I had known – didn't word of these things always get bruited about? He then advised me that I should apply for land on the frontier, a more fitting place for a man of my quality. By which, of course, he meant *lack* of quality.

"I was in despair. I looked and felt like a fool and I had made an enemy of a man who held all the reins of power in his fine white hands. Sir William turned his back on me and I dragged myself back to Jamestown, lower in spirits than I have ever been.

"You doubtless have guessed the end of my story. I asked Mistress Joanna to take me in again and she agreed. We were betrothed in January of 1663 and wed that June and I have been master of *The Unicorn* ever since. You have seen how small Jamestown is just a village. I soon knew everyone and everyone knew me. *The Unicorn* had an excellent reputation under Trent and Joanna and I made it our business to keep it that way. All persons of quality stop with us when they came to the capital. In fact the inn has become quite a clearinghouse for information and gossip. It is not an unpleasant life, but it was not what I intended.

"No, my dreams died at the hands of Green Spring because I was Puritan, poor and proud. Colonel Hill comes from an old established Virginia family and he is a favorite of the Governor. Anybody could have told me that I had no chance of getting the land I wanted, but nobody did. Nobody wanted to cross Berkeley and the Ludwells. You will find that only a few families rule here in Virginia and it is not wise to earn their displeasure. Perhaps I will regret my candor, but I should not like you to make the mistakes that I made. That is hardly likely, given your background and your connection with the Bacons of King's Creek, but nonetheless I would advise you to watch your step here. One slip can be fatal."

Rising, Nat and John looked at one another thoughtfully. They thanked their host for his company and his advice and descended to the dormitory where Nat, at least, lay long awake listening to the hum of the insects and the occasional cry of a night bird. He thought of the old governor at Green

Spring and of his cousin at King's Creek and of the trackless forest to the west. Wild animals and heathens were not the only concerns in this strange land. He would have to walk more carefully than he had in the past. He was glad that Lyn and John would walk with him.

CHAPTER 8

AUGUST 1674

John buried his head in the feather pillow and, hardly conscious of what he was doing, brushed his right cheek repeatedly against the intruder. As he rose from sleep his senses tingled with new sensations. The room glowed with opalescent light; his bare arms and shoulders felt as though they were bathed in milk; the scent of growing things encompassed him like a cocoon. Memory seized him and he jerked upright. Virginia! They had arrived. It was their first morning in Jamestown. Still stupid with sleep, he turned to look about him. The dormitory was empty. No, not empty. There was Nat behind the screen, laughing at him. Why the laughter? Ah, that explained the touch on his cheek. Nat had a basin of water and was dashing his friend with droplets to rouse him from sleep. John stretched and smiled his slow, delicious smile. He thought of Richard Lawrence. Yesterday had been exhausting but informative. It was clear that he and Nat would have to study the human landscape carefully in order to make the right choices, the choices which would create the kind of life in Virginia that Lyn deserved.

John yawned until his jaws cracked, tossed the thin quilt to the foot of the bed and, in a flash, caught Nat by the shoulders as the smaller man approached him once more with the basin. Snatching the dish, the attorney poured its contents on his friend's head, flattening the glossy black curls and soaking the fine linen shirt. Nat gasped and then burst into laughter. John was finally awake.

"It serves you right," Grey said as he looked about for his shirt and breeches. It had been so warm last night that he had stripped to his small clothes. However the heat had not kept him from sleeping; he must have been dead to the world for eight solid hours.

"What o'clock is it? And have you seen Lyn?"

"It is eight on the button and Lyn has been up for two hours, as have I. She bathed in rain water, can you believe? She said she slept well and that the girl, Clarissa, was a gem. We've been waiting breakfast on you, can you hurry? There is a chamber pot in that cupboard and the necessary is out in back; not very pleasant in this heat, I promise you. I'll ring for more water so you can shave. When you're ready we'll be in the common room."

"Fair enough. I'll be with you in a trice."

"Good. When we have eaten I want to walk about and see if that fellow Drummond is home. And we need to be alert for word from King's Creek. There ought to be a message today, I should think."

Nat toweled his head dry, grabbed his coat and darted from the room, leaving John to wash and dress. A quarter of an hour later the three newcomers were seated over bacon and eggs and an aromatic pot of coffee. At this early hour appetites were still alive and the hot meal was welcome.

Lyn looked fresh in a simple cotton gown with her curls tied back and bound with ribbon. She smiled at John as the bacon and eggs and hot bread slid down his throat. Nat paced about, peering from the windows and muttering comments as he gulped his coffee. Yesterday's disappointment over Jamestown had vanished and the new day had brought new hope to the travelers.

"I told Mistress Lawrence that we intend to see Jamestown this morning and that we would likely be back at noon to see if your cousin has sent word," said Lyn. "Was that right?"

"Oh yes," Nat agreed. "That should work out. We'll walk while it's cool and then we'll hope for word from the Colonel."

"Where shall we go first?" asked John.

"I would like to visit the church," Lyn interjected, "and I suppose you two will want to see the government buildings. I know where they are – Clarissa told me. And that mound that we saw yesterday – that is the old fort. It goes back sixty or seventy years to when the first colonists arrived. Clarissa said there is not much to see now, but we can trace the fortifications." She turned to Nat who was still pacing the room. "Shall you call on anybody at the Statehouse?"

"No, I think not. Lawrence says the government is dormant in August. The Governor and the Councilors have scattered to their various plantations. The Burgesses meet annually and the next Assembly is not until September, so none of them will be about, unless on private business. Lawrence told me that often Thomas Ludwell, or his brother Philip, who is Deputy Secretary of State, can be found in case of need, but I think our first visit, (apart from King's Creek), must be to Governor Berkeley and his Lady and my cousin will arrange that. No, I believe we should wait on Mister Drummond. Lawrence assures me that he is a fount of information. Did you know that he was Governor of Albemarle County for three years? That's somewhere to the south, quite a wilderness. We should seize the opportunity to see him now, as he moves about among his various plantations. Come, let's go or we shall never complete our *programme*."

John noted Nat's constant reference to Richard Lawrence. His friend had clearly been impressed by the innkeeper ... perhaps too impressed. Time enough to make friends; one must make haste slowly.

The three friends decided to see first the church, then the old fort, and finally the Statehouse. If they did not idle such an itinerary would put them at the Drummond house by midmorning, a reasonable hour for a visit.

The modest brick church squatted comfortably on a gentle rise, southeast of the inn. It consisted of a nave, with neither transept, aisles nor side chapels, and an impressive west tower which reached three stories, topped by a belfry sporting a homely wooden cap. The three spent a few minutes in the cool interior with its simple altar and rustic wooden pews and then climbed the tower, hoping for a complete panorama of Jamestown. They were rewarded for their efforts. Although the dense summer foliage partially obscured their view, the capital lay largely exposed before them. As they looked east over the spine of the church they saw the bulk of the village, its eastern limit marked by Orchard Run, the broad street which they had climbed yesterday evening from the wharf. To the right Front Street ran along the river's edge and they had a crow's eye view of the *Adam and Eve*, resting comfortably, her sails furled and her decks a beehive of activity. To the left Back Street ran west from Orchard Run past a clutch of modest cottages, a row of glaring brick town houses, and *The Unicorn* with its neat yard and outbuildings, until it reached the ragged common which lay before the Statehouse. Not far from the junction of Orchard Run and Back Street stood an impressive, two story brick house with high Jacobean shoulders and casements with diamond-shaped quarrels which caught the sun like jewels. Nat exclaimed as he noted the glossy green door: it must be Drummond's. Garden plots and orchards stretched east behind the Drummond residence and beyond their neat geometry huddled a formless mass of vine-draped trees which, jungle-like, trailed down to the water's edge.

To the south lay the broad brown expanse of the sluggish James which coiled through the Virginia forests like a great serpent, careless of man's feeble efforts. To Lyn the river seemed, not hostile, but indifferent. She supposed that it had flowed from its source in the far western mountains long before any human foot had trod the forest floors and that it would continue to do so when man's presence was marked only by white bones. White bones such as those which lay below her, in the little graveyard to the south of the church. Virginia, it seemed, had already taken its toll on the thrusting English. But the river rolled on in silence. Lyn thought longingly of her beloved Alde which gurgled and chuckled under the high Suffolk sky as it obligingly escorted gentry and cottager alike to the broad pebbly strand and finally to the sea. The Alde was a kindly guide, open-handed and knowable. Here the scale was huge and the human touch insignificant. Would modest

Jamestown, spread below them, striving for authority, take root and flourish or would it slide back into the heartless river without a trace? Whatever God's plan was, she and Nat and John were part of it and only a higher power knew whether they would succeed or fail.

"Lyn, wake up, I've spoken to you three times!" cried Nat. "What lies north, beyond Back Street and the pine forest?"

She answered, guided by what Clarissa had told her last night as she was preparing for bed.

"There's a swamp and then the river. The James almost encircles the peninsula and they call that part of it the Back River. The town is connected to the mainland by a narrow neck – there, to the northwest. Clarissa thinks that in the past the neck has actually flooded and the capital has been wholly cut off, 'islanded' as it were. She says that everybody thinks they should move the town, for the situation is poor and unhealthy, but the will is not there. People have become attached to what they have and they don't want to change. Besides, the Governor and many of the great men live nearby and it is convenient for them to do business here."

Nat smiled, somewhat condescendingly. "It seems that Clarissa is a fount of knowledge."

Lyn answered sharply. "Indeed she is. She's very kind, very handy and very knowledgeable."

To her relief Nat did not take her up on the issue as he normally would have and the subject was dropped. Lyn turned east again and there, as if on cue, she saw a toy-like Clarissa cross *The Unicorn's* yard with a basket of laundry and begin to hang it on lengths of rope which stretched between two saplings. The stately black woman was soon joined by Mistress Lawrence who snatched the linen from her and sent her back into the inn with what appeared to be rough words. Clarissa had not dropped a hint to Lyn about her employers, but her expressive face with its liquid eyes had led Lyn to infer that her loyalties lay with the master of *The Unicorn* and not with the mistress. She intended to find out more about the African woman whose intelligence and demeanor contrasted so sharply with her position of servitude.

As they descended the tower Lyn indicated that she would like to visit the graveyard and read some of the memorials, but Nat was anxious to press on and John wanted to see what was left of the old fort so she deferred her plan and followed the men west to a flat, dusty area where bricks and lumber and other signs of abandoned construction lay about, higgledy-piggledy, in the strengthening sun.

"Surely these bricks are new," she said. "Was the old fort not built long ago, early in the century?"

John looked about him, perplexed, and then answered. "Oh, now I understand. Yes – you are right. The colonists built the first fort while James was king. It was a triangle, fashioned on the old plan, with batteries at each of the angles. There – that mound might possibly indicate one of the sides. But this lumber is recent. It must belong to the fort they began in seventy-two when the third Dutch war broke out. You know our tobacco fleet was burned in the second Dutch war, in the sixties? They did not want it to happen again, so they planned a new fort, but it was never built and the Dutch savaged Virginia again, just last year. What can the Governor have been thinking? The James is three miles wide at its mouth and a mile wide here and deep enough for a warship, yet the only defenses are the old fort at Point Comfort and they say that it is falling apart and its great guns are useless. Odd, the colony seems to be strangely vulnerable. Well, I daresay Colonel Bacon can tell us all about it."

Nat looked at his friend and laughed. "'*Our tobacco fleet?*' Have you already become a Virginian?"

John blushed easily and, (to Lyn's secret delight), he colored now as he answered. "I suppose you are right. I have read so much about the colony that I must have made it my own. Well, there is not much to see here. Let's visit the government buildings and then pay a call on Mister Drummond. The sun is beginning to take its toll."

A five minute walk north brought the trio to the Statehouse. The imposing brick building lay to the west of the village, not far from where the river curved north to form Sandy Bay. It ran on an east-west axis and consisted of five parts, each joined to the others by common walls. Four town houses lay to the west and to the east stretched the Statehouse itself, a handsome structure of two stories capped with a cunningly made shingle roof pierced with dormer windows. The rosy brick glowed in the August sun and the wooden tiles gleamed as if announcing that here was the true heart of Virginia. As the newcomers speculated about the functions of the various structures a thin man with wispy hair bound back in a ribbon and with badly protruding teeth emerged from the elegant double doors of the Statehouse. He darted down the steps as though in a hurry but then, catching sight of the trio, he pulled himself up short and made his way over to them.

Doffing his cap, the thin man smiled and spoke in a soft drawl. "Good morning, gentlemen and lady. Don't tell me: you came in the *Adam and Eve*. First time in the colony?"

Somewhat affronted, Nat replied "Why yes, we arrived last night. We're waiting for a conveyance to King's Creek and thought we would look at your little capital before we go."

The thin man fed Nat the deference which the name "King's Creek" was obviously expected to engender. "Oh, you're for Colonel Bacon's. Now that's one of the finest plantations on the Peninsula. And the Colonel is one of our finest gentlemen. Why I've carried messages there many a time and never left without a kind word, a bite to eat and some of Mistress Elizabeth's perry. She's as fine a lady as the Colonel is a gentleman. You're off to a good start, you are."

Annoyed by the man's familiarity, Nat was about to turn on his heel when John spoke up. "You seem to know your way around. Do you have something to do with the Statehouse? We are curious to know how it is laid out."

The thin man smiled toothily. "Oh, you might say I have something to do with the Statehouse. I am its caretaker! Have been these ten years, ever since it was built!" He stepped forward and seized John's hand. "The name is Pitts. The family's from Devon but I was born and raised in the colony – a native Virginian!"

Upon learning that the man might be of use Nat composed himself and rejoined John and Lyn. He jingled some coins in his pocket. "Why, what a stroke of luck! Do you have a minute to answer some questions?"

"Oh aye, sir, that I do. The government's all gone. Naught happens in August. Even Mister Thomas Ludwell has gone back to Rich Neck. Only Mister Philip is here in case of emergency, and he is about to leave for Green Spring. I'll be all by myself. I always use this time of year to wash the windows, polish the woodwork and clean the brass. That way the Christmas season does not take me by surprise. Now what was it that you wanted to know?"

Lyn smiled and won Pitts' heart. She asked him to describe the Statehouse and the attached buildings to the best of his ability.

"Well, Mistress, it's clear enough. You go through those great doors there and you are in an antechamber where all the petitioners wait – all those who seek redress or wish to file a paper or whatnot. It's open to all, even if Sir William do sometimes call them rabble. On each side of the antechamber are two offices for the clerks – one keeps the colony's books and one looks after the land records. Then if you continue straight on you step into what you might call the heart of the matter – the Council Chamber. 'Tis a great room, all paneled in walnut, with a fine table and enough chairs for the Council – twenty-four carved chairs, there are, though there be only eighteen on the Council now, as we speak. And Sir William sits up on a little throne like – raised up above the others, as is proper. 'Tis a splendid room and I would be honored to show it to you, but I am forbidden to let visitors in when the government is not in session."

Nat had become interested in Pitts' narrative and interjected a question. "Why, if you have looked after the Council room these ten years then you must know my cousin well."

"Beg pardon, sir. Your cousin?"

"Colonel Bacon."

Pitts stepped back and bowed. "You're *cousin* to Colonel Bacon? And I thought you were just visiting King's Creek. Why, I beg your pardon sir, I hope I have not been too forward."

Nat condescended. "Not at all, Pitts, not at all. Your description is most interesting. Please continue."

"Yes sir, of course, sir. Well, next to the Council Chamber is a smaller room for those who appear before the General Court. For of course you know, sir, that the Council acts as the General Court. Where there's been a murder or suchlike, (begging your pardon, Mistress), or where the planters are at each other's throats over tobacco, (that being our coin, as you know), well then Sir William and his Councilors must sit as a court and render justice."

John gazed at the handsome brick building and stroked his upper lip thoughtfully. The Governor of Virginia was powerful indeed. He executed the laws, (and probably wrote them, if all were known); he was Captain General of the armed forces; and he was Chief Justice. It would take a wise man to wear all those hats well. Apparently Sir William answered only to the King and to God. And perhaps not to them. John thought that Nat might be right about visiting Drummond. One simply could not acquire too much information about those in power. The community of gentlemen here was obviously circumscribed and it would be prudent to gather as many facts as possible before making any serious decisions. John turned his attention to Pitts once again. The man was clearly taken with Lyn, for he was directing his comments to her.

"Now, Mistress, should you return to the antechamber you would find a beautiful staircase which takes you up to the first floor. There you would find a monstrous chamber, as big as the Council Chamber, offices and waiting rooms below. 'Tis where the Burgesses meet."

"And what is a Burgess, Mister Pitts?"

"Oh never call me Mister, Mistress. I go by 'Pitts.'"

"Well then, Pitts, can you tell me what a Burgess is?"

"Oh yes, Mistress. There are two for each county, which we've got twenty counties, the colony has grown so fast. So that makes forty. Forty Burgesses. They elect them when the Governor sends out an election writ. All the freeholders can vote. 'Tis quite a privilege, according to Sir William. If you have enough property and pay your taxes and abide by the laws you can cast a vote, excepting of course the women and children and servants and slaves. Now I cannot describe an election for you, as there has not been one since about the year sixty, when Sir William took office again. I was just a careless lad then, and paid no attention to elections. The Governor thinks the people are very lucky to have their voice heard through the Burgesses. Which you would never know to hear the Burgesses talk. Always complaining, they are. Some of them come from quite far away – it might take a week to sail from Stafford or Westmoreland. They only meet once a year, if that, so you would think they would be glad to leave their farms and have a change here in Jamestown, but grumble, grumble is all I hear."

"And when they do come, what do they do?" asked Lyn, smiling, for she had still not gotten her answer.

"Oh, make the laws, you know. They say the laws have to start with the Burgesses. Of course the Governor and Council can tip them over, arsy-versy, (begging your pardon, Mistress), but the Burgesses do write them. And what a lot of gabble-gabble it takes for them to agree to anything: children could do better."

"My goodness, they must be very important. I shall look forward to meeting a Burgess."

"Why, so you shall, Mistress, for Colonel Bacon was once a Burgess before he was appointed to the Council of State. A very gallant gentleman. He can tell you anything you might want to know."

Time was passing and Nat was anxious to reach Drummond's. He slipped a coin from his pocket, (an action which did not escape Pitts' quick eyes), and asked the caretaker to briefly discuss the four structures to the left of the Statehouse.

"Why the far house, with the river view, that is Sir William's town house, for his use when he is too weary to travel to Green Spring. His office is on the ground floor, and he has a fine set of apartments above. He does not stay there often, as Lady Frances does not care for Jamestown and wherever Lady Frances is, that is where Sir William wishes to be. And the next one, that is Mister Thomas Ludwell's, our Secretary of State. And right next to his is Mister Philip Ludwell's, our Deputy Secretary. Mister Thomas is a Councilor and Mister Philip is likely to be one, they say. They're like sons to Sir William, who has none of his own. Speaking of which, poor Mister Philip just lost his wife to the fever. He took it like a man, though. I'm sure you'd never know he was grieving just to watch him. He does have the little boy and the little girl to look after; perhaps they solace him. Now, where was I? Oh, to be sure. Well the Ludwells use their houses for their dwellings and their offices when they are not at Rich Neck or elsewhere and often rent them out to other fine gentlemen, too. Now the next one, the one next to the Statehouse, is more of an office, you would say. It is stuffed with records, land patents and wills and so forth. You'd be surprised what an amount of paper there is. 'Tis not my place to say so, but some might think that they could be more orderly than they are. And, if I may put myself forward, 'tis my good fortune to have a room there, at the top. And the basement? Why that is my responsibility as well, for I am the colony's jailer, too."

"The jail!" cried John. "The jail is right there, beneath the house?"

"Why, yes sir. And handy it is too. If you should not be fortunate before the General Court you have only a short walk to your bedchamber!"

"And what does Sir William think, having the jailbirds so close?"

"I confess he is not happy. Calls them rogues and thieves, but says they are not much worse than half the population which is *not* behind bars, so what's the difference? Says he. Oh, you don't want to get him started on the people they send over from England, I don't advise it. Have you met the Governor, sir?"

Nat interrupted curtly. "No, as I said, we've just arrived. And we're not likely to meet him unless we move on and see whether my cousin has arranged for us to get to King's Creek."

He tossed Pitts a coin and the three friends turned east towards *The Unicorn* and Drummond's. Lyn looked back and waved at the little caretaker as he continued to bob and bow, all the time rubbing Nat's silver on his sleeve.

The white unicorn danced, unperturbed by the gathering heat, but Nat, Lyn and John decided to step inside the inn for five minutes to seek respite from the sun and to see whether there was any word from the Colonel. They had not seen Richard Lawrence all morning and Mistress Joanna was absent as well, but they found Clarissa in the common room wiping down the trestle tables. She smiled at the newcomers and told them that no message had arrived for them. They refused her offer of refreshment but Lyn did accept the loan of a sun umbrella and, thanking the lithe African, they returned to the dusty street and made their way east.

William Drummond's house was as impressive upon close inspection as it had been from the church tower. It rose two stories, in the shape of a truncated Greek cross and every brick and casement shone, as did the famous green door. Alone of the houses flanking Orchard Run, Drummond's had a front garden with a neat wooden fence, an aromatic boxwood hedge, and a pair of urns flanking the door from which honeysuckle spilled in falls of cream and gold. It appeared that Mistress Drummond had brought housewifery in Jamestown to a new level.

Just as Nat reached for the brass horsehead knocker the door opened and he saw his acquaintance of the night before. William Drummond smiled and, bowing slightly, ushered the three first into the cool hall and then into his sitting room from the casements of which they could see the busy wharfside and the rhythmic flow of the James.

"Before anything, let me apologize for the absence of my wife, Sarah, and the children. I got quite a lecture this morning when I told her that Colonel Bacon's kin had arrived and that they might be paying a visit today. 'How could I have forgotten,' said she, 'that we were sailing to Swann's Point right after breakfast to visit Sarah?' My oldest, you see, named after her mother, is married to Sam Swann, Colonel Tom's boy. They live just over the river. See there, where the trees are the highest? That's the Swann plantation. Well, what could I say? Of course I had known about the visit for at least a week, but I wholly forgot. I find that it happens more and more as I get older. That's something that none of you would understand!"

Lyn was quite taken with the large man who spoke so gently and who obviously took pleasure in pointing out his own shortcomings and turning them into a joke.

"Oh dear me, I am so sorry that we have caused you to miss a family gathering. Perhaps if we leave you might still have time to cross the river and join them?"

Drummond laughed heartily. "Bless you, my dear. To tell you the truth the house has been so quiet this morning that I thought that I had died and gone to Heaven. No, I see the Swanns all the time. We're back and forth across the river weekly. What I do look forward to is word of England and learning more about your plans for Virginia. I fear that we are dreadfully parochial and the arrival of a ship is a great event, especially if it brings somebody of quality who plans to stay in the colony. No, we should seize this opportunity to have a good talk. With luck you will have many opportunities to meet Sarah and the brood."

With these words their host rang a handbell and, when a serving girl appeared, took his guests' orders for refreshment. The four of them settled on cider and soon the girl was back with a tray holding a great ceramic jug, four goblets and a plate of savories. Etiquette having been served, Drummond turned to Nat.

"So you are cousin to Colonel Bacon. Was it his siren song that brought you to Virginia?"

The three friends had long ago agreed on the answer to that question. After all, it surely would be posed again and again, in one form or another, and it was vital to their reputation to have a credible and consistent response. Nat's tale was that he was an inveterate traveler, (witness his three year tour of the continent, cut short only by illness), and that, having found Suffolk farming less than inspiring, he was going to indulge in a Virginia adventure. After all, if he found the colony not to his liking he had a handsome inheritance waiting for him in the mother country. The names Bokenham and Jason were expunged from his lexicon. The story was close enough to the truth that it was unlikely that he would be caught out unless word came to Virginia from their little corner of Suffolk and the chance of that happening was so remote as to be virtually impossible. As for Lyn, the stain on the Duke name was banished from the new world. For a woman, inventing a gentle fiction was easy. All she had to do was show the colony the dutiful face of a doting wife. She had married her neighbor, Nat Bacon, for love, (how romantic); he had become restless and was tempted to try his fortune in Virginia where he had kin, (how exciting); as a loving wife, it was her duty to follow her husband wherever he chose to go, (how seemly). As for her own family, regrettably both her parents were dead but she would, of course, correspond regularly with her brother, the new baronet, and her sisters – isn't that what all Virginians did? Nobody had to know that since

Sir Edward's death John and Jane had cut her off completely and that she herself would have died sooner than have any contact with Alathea. John's tale was the closest to the truth and thus the simplest of all. As an impecunious attorney beholden to the Bacon family he had crossed the ocean to help Nat and Lyn establish a plantation. If business opportunities presented themselves he would consider staying; if not, he would return to begin the grind of establishing a London practice. In shading the truth, would the three friends be doing any more than ninety percent of their compatriots? Surely not. And such was the tale which William Drummond heard.

If Drummond sensed that the newcomers' stories had been flavored for Virginia consumption, he gave no hint of it. He listened with interest, asked appropriate questions, and then offered to do anything he could to assist the emigrants. Nat seized the opening.

"You will forgive me, sir, if I touch on the personal. We sat long with Mister Lawrence last night and he suggested that you and the current government do not see eye to eye. Would you be willing to give us your view of Sir William's administration? If you have any concern that you are tipping the scales against Berkeley you cannot doubt that Colonel Bacon will right them. Our minds are open; we wish to hear everything which might bear on life here."

"Well, laddie, (pardon the word, but you are young enough to be my son), I would like to oblige you, but I hardly know you. Sir William and I have tilted over many issues over the years and recently we have had a complete falling out. The whole colony knows it. I'm sure your cousin can enlighten you – or the Governor himself."

John spoke up. "Oh, but sir, that is precisely the point. We don't want to hear only from the Green Spring faction. We want to learn everyone's point of view and then make up our own minds about our future. You *know* what they'll say at King's Creek. Can you not give us an antidote in advance? If it would make you more comfortable I am sure we would be happy to keep this conversation confidential." Nat and Lyn murmured their agreement.

The big Scot rose and stared out the casement at the wharf. Men were unloading the *Adam and Eve* and the riverside was crowded with merchants and sailors and idlers. The irregular glass caused their images to dance crazily in the morning sun. After a moment Drummond turned to his guests, a smile on his broad face.

"Well, Sarah has called me a fool many times and she may do so again, but I'll take a chance on you. If my story helps you in any way I shall have done my duty. I always had a soft spot for young ones, and I would hate for you to go wrong when you are about to start a new life. But I *will* ask you to keep what we say to yourselves, though, God knows, there is probably nothing in my life which has not been chewed over and digested from the Chowan to the Potomac." He chuckled ruefully. "You'll learn soon enough what a small world Virginia is."

Drummond reseated himself and without further ado began his narrative. "I am one of many – too many — younger sons from a large Inverness family. Though Presbyterians, we were staunch supporters of the Stuarts during the troubles. I saw action during the Civil Wars and just at the time that the tide began to turn against Charles I my own personal fortune ebbed as well. Though my father was a gentleman his lands were small and barren and his children were many and needy. By the year forty-seven I had naught to my name but my pride, a horse and some ancient arms which caused my friends, (and likely my enemies), to tremble with laughter rather than fear. When one of my mother's sisters offered to pay my passage to Virginia I leapt at the offer and never looked back."

"Did you say forty–seven? 'Tis the year of my birth!" burst out Nat spontaneously.

Drummond smiled. "Was it indeed, laddie? Well, it was a lucky year for both of us then, for until recently I have never regretted crossing the ocean. After all, I met my dear Sarah right here in Jamestown and all good things flowed from that happy moment. Sarah Prescott she was, and owned a cottage on this very spot. We tore it down in sixty-three and built this place, but I confess that I wish it still stood as a memorial to our marriage. I hope I do not shock you when I say that Miss Prescott was wooed and wed within three months of my setting foot on Virginia soil. It was not so rash as it sounds as I quickly had a patent for some fine land in Westmoreland County, way up on the Potomac. It was on the frontier then, and going begging, because few would live so far away. Sarah and I set out bravely and fortune was with us, for over the years our little farm grew into quite an impressive plantation. It is still our largest holding, though we are rarely there, preferring the comforts of our James River lands. We have this place and, at one time, we had the lease on quite a few acres of the Governor's Land up by Green Spring. Sarah prefers to stay here because she grew up in Jamestown and now we have the connection with Swann's Point as well, but we also have a plantation on the Southside, on the Blackwater. You couldn't find a prettier place and so peaceful the only thing you hear is the song of the birds."

"It sounds lovely," said Lyn softly.

"Why so it is, my dear. And if you like you are welcome to visit there any time you care to."

"What is 'Governor's Land'?" asked John.

"Why, Sir William has the right to lease some choice pieces which lie right next to Green Spring at quite a favorable rate. I got a foothold there in forty-eight and then leased a far larger parcel in the sixties, but it all came to naught."

"How is that?" persisted the attorney.

"Why 'tis one of the bones of contention between Sir William and me ... part of the reason that we don't speak today. Shall I tell you that story, or shall I let the whole tale unfold from the beginning?"

"As you like," offered John. "But perhaps if you started at the beginning we could understand it better."

"You have a tidy lawyer's mind. That's a good thing. Very well. Let me pour you all some more cider and then I'll go back to a time when I was younger, slimmer and ... what shall I say? ... more hopeful. Let's see.

"Well, when I arrived and married Sarah and we went to Westmoreland Sir William was in his first term as Governor – I believe he bought the position from Wyatt in forty-two or thereabouts. He was in his prime, some forty years of age, vigorous, and wholly in command. He was well enough liked, though many found him haughty and over-proud. In truth, he traded on the Berkeley name and on his knighthood and on the fact that he stood well with the King. The colony was much smaller then and he gave the people a lot of personal attention, riding to the frontiers, visiting on the Southside, staying at the various plantations. That kind of thing is worth its weight in gold, as doubtless you know. And of course he did nobly in putting down the Indian uprising in forty-four. You'll hear no criticism of that action, nor of the protective laws which were enacted shortly after, restricting the savages to certain lands and setting up a perimeter of frontier forts to guarantee our protection. Indeed, some would say that it was Berkeley's finest hour.

"Well, all that came to an end with the Protectorate. Cromwell sent his fleet over and Sir William had to kneel (literally) and kiss the Puritan's hand (figuratively). I think that broke something in the man; he's never been the same since. He'll have no truck with rebels – rules with an iron fist now, as though he still carries the wounds of the Civil Wars and the King's execution. In any event, in fifty-two he turned the reins of government over to the General Assembly and retired to Green Spring with his first wife. The first Lady Berkeley was a Ferrar, just a wisp of a thing, couldn't stand up to her husband at all. People felt sorry for her; in fact many don't even know he had a wife before Lady Frances. She brought him a handsome fortune, but no children, so that was a pity too. Which was hardly the case with Sarah and me. God bless your soul, little Sarah arrived in Westmoreland and then came little William and John and after them two more girls. But I am getting ahead of myself. The point is that in the fifties Sir William and his Lady were at Green Spring improving the original house and turning the gardens into a showcase, and Sarah and I were doing much the same in Westmoreland, though we added babies to the mix. I served as Justice of the Peace in the County Court and Sarah wanted me to run for Burgess, but the magistrate's job was all I could handle in addition to my plantation and my family. At that time all the Royalists kept their heads down and minded their own affairs. We almost never came to Jamestown and rarely saw Sir William. It was not until his second term, in the sixties, that the sparks started to fly.

"As soon as we learned that Charles Stuart was restored in sixty the General Assembly promptly elected Sir William Governor again. Some, at least, thought well of him. The King confirmed him in sixty-one and sent him a new set of instructions. His Majesty was eager for funds and he had a plan to wean Virginia from the tobacco teat, (begging your pardon, my dear), and compel diversification. And Sir William was not averse to the idea – quite the contrary. He had made Green Spring quite a showcase: had a whole orchard of mulberries and produced some decent silk; grew a little flax and a little hemp; even tried his hand at wine making ... you get the picture. Well, if the King thought Virginia was an Eden which was suddenly going to produce a bevy of cash crops, the Governor had a hobby-horse of his own to ride. The funds were not going to flow, said the Governor, unless Cromwell's Navigation Acts were changed and Virginia was allowed to trade in free markets. As it was, our staple, tobacco, could only go to English ports and only in English bottoms. We were denied the rich Dutch and Scandinavian markets as well as those of France and Spain and the Middle Sea. The New Englanders flouted the laws with impunity and were making money hand over fist, but the loyal Virginians were being strangled and only the London merchants profited from things as they were.

"Soon after he began his second term Sir William took his case to London in person. After all, he knew the King, though His Majesty would not likely remember him, having been just a child when Berkeley served in the court of the first Charles. But far more important, Sir William's younger brother John was one of Charles' inner circle and had been made a peer, Baron Stratton. Oh yes, Sir William had the perfect entrée to Whitehall and he seized the advantage, but it came to nothing. In the end both the King and the Governor tumbled from their hobby-horses, both losers. Virginia never diversified. Tobacco remains the cash crop here and, in my opinion, always will be. It is, literally, the coin of the realm: we trade in hogsheads of tobacco. As for the Navigation Acts, they were strengthened rather than repealed. Though many think it foolish, and argue convincingly that huge revenues are lost not only to the planters and merchants but to the Crown itself, London decided to keep its colonies on leading strings, and so it is. No, Sir William might as well have stayed in Virginia for all that he gained. And they say that he lost personal prestige in London – the King never warmed to him, found him tedious and self-righteous.

"Well, I am being tedious myself. The point is that after his fruitless sojourn in London Sir William returned, a hardened man. In my opinion, (though others will differ), he came back disillusioned and determined to use Virginia for his personal advantage in the way that he saw Charles Stuart using,(or abusing), his kingdom. Remember, the Governor was in his fifties, somewhat long in the tooth, and although some, (myself included), might have considered him well-off, his fortune was paltry when compared to those of Clarendon or Albemarle or even his brother. When he returned to Virginia late in sixty-two Sir William seized the reins of the colony and dug in his spurs and his battle cry was 'For Berkeley and Green Spring.'

"Now to return to my own story. In sixty-three Sarah and I decided to leave our Westmoreland plantation in the hands of an overseer and return to Jamestown and build handsomely on the site of her old cottage. We had many reasons to do so. Our plantation was thriving and was in such a condition that it almost ran itself; it did not need my constant personal attention. Additionally, over the years I had developed quite a nice practice as a merchant, buying and selling for others as well as for myself, and Jamestown, being the center of the colony, was the best place to develop my business. We had four children by then and little Sarah was already fifteen and would be looking for a husband. She and all the children would be advantaged by living in the capital rather than in our quiet backwater, and my wife would be returning to the home of her childhood which she still thought of fondly. We waited for spring and when the weather made sailing a joy rather than a peril the six of us piled into our sloop and made for Jamestown. We began construction of this house in April and, for our temporary quarters, took up residence at *The Unicorn* which Dicken Lawrence had just taken over. He gave us such a good offer that I think Joanna still holds it against us – I doubt they made a penny on us. But I was a winner in all respects. We got excellent bed and board for the six months that our house was abuilding and I met one who is as true a friend as I shall ever have in this world."

Nat and John glanced at one another. Clearly Lawrence's admiration for Drummond was returned in full measure.

"Well, we moved into this house by the time the cold weather came and it has been our main residence ever since, except for our years in Carolina, which I will tell you about, if you are not bored to death. I would have no complaints if, shortly after our move, I had not crossed swords with Green Spring."

"You seem to have gotten along well enough with the Governor at the beginning, though," commented Nat.

"Yes, because I had little or nothing to do with him until we moved to Jamestown and he returned from London, embittered. But even at the beginning there was some personal animosity. At our first meeting he made it clear that a penniless Scots Presbyterian was not much higher on his social scale than an indentured servant. However, I got my Westmoreland land without incident and a year later he let me lease twenty-five acres of Governor's Land. I would say that in the forties our relationship was ... what? ... neutral. In the fifties we didn't see one another more than half a dozen times. It all started in sixty-three. Berkeley is a great builder and he was most interested in what Sarah and I were doing with this house, particularly as one of the King's instructions was to establish handsome towns throughout Virginia, starting with the capital. If you think Jamestown is small now, you should have seen it a dozen years ago. The only building of interest was the church, which looked much as it does today. The Statehouse was in a different location, and was a hodge-podge brick thing of little merit. I believe everybody was glad when it burned down and they built the new one to the west of town. Well, in sixty-three Sir William used to drop by our house site regularly and one thing led to another. He ate many a dinner with us at *The Unicorn* and he got to know my family. Next thing you know Sarah and I were invited to Green Spring for a week. To tell you the truth, I was mightily impressed. His first wife had slipped away of the fever when he was in England and he was at loose ends so he had continued all the improvements he had begun when he was in private life. His greatest success came with silk and to this day you will see a fine mulberry orchard, though he has long since given up tending the worms. He had a vineyard which he still touts, though nobody I know thinks much of his wine. And back then, (and perhaps now – I don't know), he even had a glass house and grew lemons and oranges and was hoping for a pineapple. Oh, back in sixty-three he spun off ideas like sparks from a grindstone. Most of them seemed a little far-fetched, but I have to say that Green Spring is a credit to the man – it's as nice a seat as you will find in Virginia.

"And the Governor's hospitality did not stop there. After our visit to Green Spring we received invitations from all in his inner circle –the Pages, Tom Ballard, Sir Henry Chicheley, that hothead Beverley – you'll soon meet them all. And of course the Ludwells were always about – almost part of the family. They come from Bruton in Somerset, like Sir William, and the three of them cling together like burrs. And then there was Sam Stephens' wife, who was born Frances Culpeper. Sir William had asked Sam to open up Albemarle County and he was doing his duty down there in the swampland, trying to govern the ungovernable, and his wife was at loose ends at Balthorpe. She had a standing invitation to stay at Green Spring, but of course that would not have been right as the first Lady Berkeley had passed on, so Frances Stephens would use the Ludwell house in Jamestown when they were not in occupancy. Oh yes, she was an active member of the circle."

"I am confused. Wasn't the current Lady Berkeley born Frances Culpeper?" asked Lyn innocently.

There was a heavy silence. "Quite, my dear. It is the same lady. Sam Stephens died in March of seventy and by July of that year Frances Culpeper Stephens was the second Lady Berkeley. She has nine lives and always lands on her feet."

The implication was clear: at least in Drummond's mind Frances Culpeper Stephens and William Berkeley had had an understanding before Sam Stephens died in the swamps of Carolina. The Scot stirred in his chair and once again walked to the casements. He thrust one open and as quickly closed it.

"The heat shows that it is midday. Am I keeping you too long?"

The three guests spoke simultaneously but Nat's voice overrode the others'.

"No sir, we are fascinated, truly. We plan to return to the inn for dinner and to see if my cousin has sent word, but we are in no hurry. Mistress Joanna said the meal would be cold and that she could serve it anytime after twelve, so we are happy to hear you out."

Their host smiled his gentle smile and rejoined his guests. "Well, I suppose it is time to tell you about Carolina. I become agitated every time I think about it and Sarah would rather that I forget the whole thing, but she's not here and you might find the tale instructive. If the truth be told Sarah and I were of two minds about being taken up by Green Spring. Despite the dinners and the card games, the archery and the horse races, the sailing and the balls, somehow the Greens never let us forget that I was a Scot, a Presbyterian, and that I had come to the colony penniless; and that Sarah was the daughter of a humble Jamestown shopkeeper. We both had the feeling that when the gentry was tired of our novelty that we would be dropped mercilessly. Still, to be part of Green Spring, even on those terms, was an advantage not to be taken lightly. My business grew by leaps and bounds and the children were making contacts which would stand them in good stead in the future. After all, Tom Swann is Green. If we had not been part of the Governor's circle for a time I doubt that his son Sam would have developed the interest in my oldest girl which led to her marriage. Whatever our reservations, Sarah and I decided to let things unfold, taking the good with the bad, as one does in life.

"Well, not long after we had moved to Jamestown and while we were still all the fashion, if I may put it that way, King Charles made the great Carolina grant which doubtless you heard of back home. Even now I am staggered when I think of it. For their loyalty through the Civil Wars and through the King's painful years of exile eight favorites were given, as proprietors, all the land between Virginia's southern border and Florida's northern border, stretching from the Atlantic to the Pacific Oceans. Imagine having the power to carve up the world in such a way: it is almost beyond comprehension."

"I remember my brother talking about it, but I don't remember the men who were given the gift," admitted Lyn.

Drummond laughed. "Why that's easy. Sarah made up a memory device for our children and I shall tell it to you. Sarah called the eight Lords Proprietors the ABCs, as they were the mightiest in the land and all England seemed to depend on them as our tongue depends on the alphabet. There is one "A" — Albemarle, the great duke who restored Charles Stuart to the throne. There are five "Cs" — mighty Clarendon, crafty Ashley Cooper, Carteret, Colleton, and Craven. I have saved the two "Bs" for last, as they are our special concern. There are two of them – Lord John Berkeley, Baron Stratton, the King's favorite; and our very own Sir William. These eight men were given absolute dominion over a great slice of the new world. What they did with the gift was up to them, and Sarah and I became caught up in their coils."

"How is that, sir?" asked John.

"For several years before the King's gift men had been drifting down to Carolina which was, you understand, simply the far reaches of Virginia. It was a lawless land, peopled by those who had fled justice and seized land from the savages. You could carve out a little farm in the pine forest and live for a year without seeing another white man. The settlers took the law into their own hands. And Carolina was less hospitable than Virginia. The rivers changed their courses at will, the harbors shifted, the swamps stretched for miles, breeding fever, and the forest was boundless. Savages and wild beasts roamed as they might have in the first days after man's fall.

"Sir William had always been keen to develop the land even before he became a proprietor, just as he was keen on exploring the west. But in the early sixties governance of the wilderness was virtually impossible. There was not a harbor, not a road, not a house worth speaking of, not a plantation, not a church in all of Albemarle.County. Nevertheless, in sixty-two Berkeley sent Sam Stephens down to bring order to the settlement and to plant a seat of government. Many asked why Stephens was chosen – he was a mild gentleman who was better suited for growing tobacco at Balthrope than for dealing with renegades and savages. Nevertheless, off he went, leaving his wife behind to serve as hostess for the Greens. A year later he returned in poor health and with a report that Albemarle was likewise sickly. He had improved the settlement of Edenton on the river Chowan and had made it the seat of government, but apart from that little had been accomplished: by his report, Carolina remained wild and lawless.

"By the time Stephens returned Berkeley was not only Governor of Virginia, he had become a Lord Proprietor of Carolina and, to him, Albemarle County was more than simply Virginia's southern border – it was a land where he could rule like a king if he could get his arms around it. It goes without saying that his fellow proprietors, who all remained safely in England, gave him *carte blanche* to lay down the first lines of government: he was physically present and he had unparalleled experience in the ways of the new world. Who better to manage their affairs? As soon as he got Stephens' report he knew what he had to do: find a fighting man to serve as Albemarle County's first governor. He needed somebody with a military background, someone who had the common touch, and one who would cast a blind eye on religious dissent, for the King had stipulated that Carolina should be tolerant. He measured this cloth against me and, much to my astonishment, found that it fit. I had proven myself on the field; I had a reputation of being able to deal with men from all walks of life; and, as a Presbyterian, I would tolerate religious practices outside of the mother church. We were sitting in this very room when Sir William offered me the job. I do not speak with false modesty when I say that I was floored.

"I asked the Governor for a week to think it over and forthwith consulted with Sarah, the friend of my heart, and Dicken Lawrence, the friend of my conscience. I knew I was going to reject Sir William's offer and I only asked for the week to make the dose palatable. I was confident that Sarah and Dicken would second my decision, but once again I was floored. Both my counselors urged me to take the offer and make the best of it. This is how they argued: if I refused the Governor I would undoubtedly earn his lifelong enmity, for such was his character. If I accepted, even if things went awry, as long as I gave it a good effort I could expect his continued friendship and support. And, if I accepted and succeeded not only would I have Berkeley's support, I would stand well in the eyes of the men who effectively ruled England. Politics shouted down reason and when I returned my answer to Sir William it was 'yes.'"

Drummond turned to Lyn and smiled. "Now, lass, what would you have said if Mister Bacon had come to you with the same proposition?"

Lyn was taken back by the question, but she had a ready answer. "Truly, sir, if Nat wanted it, so would I. And if he left it to me, I think I would say ... let's try it. If we give it our best effort, nobody can complain even if we should fail. And if we should fail, we'll return to Virginia and live out our days."

"Bless you, lass!" cried Drummond. "Just what Sarah said. You women – you are rarely given enough credit for your brave hearts.

"Well, I was hoisted on my own petard, as they say. In October of sixty-four I found myself, my wife and four children, and four servants, together with a great passel of goods, on a neat little pinnace, (the *Sarah*), headed for Albemarle Sound. We had a pleasant voyage – you haven't lived if you have not smelled the great wafts of pine scent which roll off the land far out to sea. But the voyage was the best part of the whole adventure. Thereafter, things went downhill and I fear that my trusty counselors were proved wrong and I was proved right.

"We sailed up the Sound until we reached the Chowan and put down our roots at Edenton which was not much more than a makeshift village. God bless my soul, never was a place worse named. The wharf was sinking into the sand of the ever-shifting shores; the Governor's house was a log cabin which stank in summer and was icy cold in winter; and the whole family had to become field hands to wrest enough crops from our nearby plantation to prevent starvation. I thought I had left such a life long ago in Westmoreland County. Sarah, (who was expecting our fifth), and the children were heroic. They helped us keep body and soul together. And the boys still tell me that they enjoyed the adventure! Indeed, we were bound closer as a family, but my, it took its toll.

"Some of the settlers were glad enough to see the beginnings of law and order but it was, in truth, more of a fantasy than a reality. A few men would come in monthly with their fusils and practice arms under my instruction, but if the savages or renegades had risen up they could have slaughtered us with ease. In general the savages stayed in the west, but a number of the remoter farms still suffered thefts and murders and the fear was always with us. I held some court sessions and had some successes, but more failures. I was charged with seating the land, but applicants for land patents were slow to come since an enterprising man could avoid the government process by moving west and buying land from the savages rather than from the proprietors.

"However, in my second year business began to pick up and I became more hopeful. But the wheel of fortune never raises you up but she throws you down. Settlers were coming because I had relaxed two of the strictures on which the proprietors were adamant. First, I sometimes granted land on the promise that the land would be fully seated without insisting on an actual head count. We all knew that there was room for fraud there – a man might get acreage who never intended to provide the bodies which would clear it and improve it. I used my own judgment in assessing the applicants' character, but doubtless I made some grants which were technically impermissible. Still, in the greater scheme of things, Carolina would have benefited had I been left to my own devices. A second problem was the quitrents. The proprietors were avid for a profit and they set the quitrents far higher than those in Virginia, which I thought a foolish thing to do, given that land was generally much poorer. And the settlers had to pay in coin – no tobacco, no barter, no notes. The proprietors wanted cold, hard cash and they wanted a lot of it and they wanted it yesterday. Well, Carolina was never going to grow unless there could be some flexibility in the rules. I felt strongly about it and, after I was about two years into my term as Governor, I decided to argue my case to Sir William personally, for he had sent me an angry note about my lax practices. I sailed up to Jamestown and had my meeting and it was a disaster. Berkeley forbade me from deviating from my instructions. He, of course, lived in fear of antagonizing men such as Albemarle and Clarendon; he had no brief to exercise his discretion in Carolina and he was certainly not going to permit me to exercise mine. My arguments were fruitless and I returned to Edenton with orders to finish out my three-year term as directed and then to relinquish my post to 'a more worthy and faithful' man.

"Foolish me, no sooner had I arrived in Edenton when I poured out my troubles to Dicken in a scathing letter, abusing Berkeley for his shortsightedness and cowardice. (Dicken had been away when I was in Jamestown or I would have discussed the matter with him personally instead of committing myself in writing and thereby saved myself some grief.) A month later I received a command from Berkeley to relinquish my post forthwith *as he had evidence of my treachery.* I dragged the family back to Jamestown and asked for another audience with the Governor. We met in private and he waved my letter to Dicken in my face and called me a traitor. I asked him how he had gotten hold of my private correspondence and I thought that he would have a fit his face grew so red. He claimed that no governor appointed by him had a right to a *private* correspondence and that he was fully entitled to read anything I wrote. He thereupon dismissed me from my post and told me that Sam Stephens was already on his way to Edenton for the second time, as Albemarle's next governor. When I asked him pointedly whether Frances Stephens had accompanied her husband or was remaining in Virginia I believe that if he had been armed that he would have drawn his sword and spitted me on the spot.

"Well, I need to finish my tale and you need your dinners. Things have gone from bad to worse between Sir William and me ever since my return to Jamestown. He had the gall to send me a bill for the use of our home in Edenton, which I sent it back, unpaid, with an accounting scribbled in the margin detailing how much Virginia owed *me* for those disastrous years in Carolina. He groundlessly revoked my lease of three thousand rich acres of Governors' Land and gave the contract to Colonel Hill, who harvested and sold *my* fine tobacco crop and who still farms the land – some of the best in Virginia. What little business I had left after three years in Carolina fell off sharply as Green Spring took their accounts elsewhere. Our social circle contracted in sixty-eight as rapidly as it had expanded in sixty-three – but that's only to the good, as we now know who are true friends are. And finally, to add insult to injury, just last year I was forced to kneel before Governor and Council and own that I had failed in a contract to rebuild the old fort to protect Jamestown against the renewed Dutch threat. That's a tale in itself which I won't burden you with. Suffice it to say that I made the mistake of standing surety for Theophilus Howe who had the fort contract and when he failed to perform as required I stood in the dock next to him to answer for his failings.

"There you have it, my friends, or at least some of it. I could go on, as could Dicken Lawrence, but enough is enough. The fact is that even though I see Sir William often, living as close to the Statehouse as we do, the two of us have not exchanged a civil word for the past seven years. Virginia is his kingdom and Green Spring his Whitehall. He has a queen, (Lady Frances), who is treated better than Charles treats Catherine; and courtiers who lick his boots as readily as any in London. Your cousin will tell you a different story, and I hope you listen, for I freely admit my bias, but I advise you to tread carefully in your first months here as your standing with Sir William Berkeley and the Greens will determine your fortune."

Silence fell in Drummond's parlor and the three friends looked at one another with long faces. Richard Lawrence and William Drummond had given them much to ponder. In each heart rose the hope that Colonel Bacon would serve as a worthy guide through the shoals of Virginia politics. As one they turned towards *The Unicorn*, covetous of the expected summons from King's Creek. Whether for good or ill their Virginia adventure would truly begin at the plantation on the York.

CHAPTER 9

AUGUST 1674

Lyn pressed her cheek against Nat's shirt and took in the familiar smell of him. She tightened her grasp around his waist and felt the caress of his right hand on the loveknot of her locked fingers. It was good to be on horseback again, even if they were riding double and their mount was Richard Lawrence's old cart horse. Mistress Joanna could have loaned them her high bred mare but, for reasons of her own, she chose not to do so. It was typical of Nat to come up with this crazy scheme – it was the best part of him, a part which had been long dormant, at least as far as it related to her. Dusk settled its cloak around the riders and a nightjar called as Lyn's thoughts wandered back to the events of the afternoon.

They had returned from Drummond's to *The Unicorn* stunned alike by the oppressive heat and by what the big Scot had told them of Green Spring. No sooner had they sat down to a meal which none of them wanted, when a lad in a wagon had pulled up in front of the inn and whistled his way into the common room. Mistress Joanna knew him well – he was Timothy from King's Creek. The freckled boy doffed his cap, delivered an elegant letter to Nat, and joined the trio at table, uninvited. Lyn happily passed her plate to him and his youthful appetite made short work of her cold pork and greens. Nat ripped his cousin's missive open and read aloud. Colonel Bacon apologized profusely for failing to meet his kinsmen at Jamestown, but his lady was recovering from a fever and he himself was preparing for the harvest and dared not leave his plantation, even for a day He had sent Timothy who was sharper than his years might suggest. The lad had orders to collect from Captain Gardiner some merchandise which Mistress Bacon had ordered from London together with the newcomers' luggage. To spare his guests and his horses the heat of the afternoon he suggested that they spend one more night in Jamestown and press on to King's Creek in the cool of the morning. Timothy could doss in the wagon which would both save the cost of night's lodging and protect their chattels. The Colonel looked forward to seeing his guests by noon the next day and they must plan to stay as long as they liked – even months – as the search for a suitable plantation was not to be undertaken lightly. Both he and his wife were deeply stirred by the prospect of seeing their kin from Suffolk.

The three friends were encouraged by Colonel Bacon's generosity and the refined tone of his letter. It was what one would expect of a Bacon, but one did not know. They had seen and heard much in Jamestown and now they were anxious to sample plantation life. If they were to plant tobacco, it was a tobacco plantation which they must see, and King's Creek was universally proclaimed to be one of the finest. Things were coming together nicely. Lawrence and Drummond had painted one picture of the colony – now it was time to balance the scales and look at things from a different perspective. John, who seemed the least affected by the heat, offered to accompany Timothy on his errands and make sure that the rest of their luggage was retrieved from the ship and packed on the wagon in good order. Nat was once again claimed by Richard Lawrence and disappeared upstairs after assuring himself that Lyn had no objection. Lyn gladly sought the cool of Clarissa's room where she inspected and repacked the contents of her valise, including their gift to Mistress Bacon, a length of fine Flemish lace. When all was in order she lay down on Clarissa's cot to rest. She was reviewing the morning's events when, suddenly, she remembered the bluebird, the little messenger which had first brought them greetings from Virginia. Appalled, she sat up and began to lace her boots. The bird must still be in the ship's cabin, without food or water. She must hurry after John and release it. She was tidying her hair when the door opened and Clarissa stepped inside with jug of water and a pile of towels. Lyn explained her dilemma to the black woman who immediately offered to take care of the matter herself. She was well known to Captain Gardiner and most of his crew. She could board the *Adam and Eve* without any problem and release the little prisoner forthwith. Lyn, who was smitten with remorse for her carelessness, was almost speechless with relief. Dark eyes and violet eyes looked at each other with mutual respect and Lyn thought that a friendship had been born.

Lyn resumed her nap and later in the afternoon Nat tapped on her door with his surprise. He had had another long and interesting conversation with the innkeeper which he would share with her later, but more to the point Lawrence had drawn him a map of Jamestown and the surrounding area and had offered to lend him a horse if he cared to venture out in the cool of the evening. It was light until almost nine o'clock; if they left in the late afternoon they would still have hours to explore. Smiling, he tossed Lyn his oldest shirt and britches – she was going to ride double, as a boy, as she so often had in their first days at Hazelwood. With a slouch hat over her curls, nobody would notice such a daring breech of etiquette. Lyn's heart danced:

this was the Nat she adored, the one whom she thought she had lost. If Virginia returned her husband to her, she would risk any venture.

And so it was that the two of them were in this bosky dell, with the river to their left and the highroad on their right and the Virginia forest all about them. Pines scented the air and soft leaves touched her face like welcoming hands. Lyn sighed with happiness and pressed closer to Nat as the nightjar repeated its mournful cry.

"When we left the road did you take a trail, or are we finding our own way?" she asked.

"'Tis a trail, though clearly not much used." Nat answered. "I want to get to the water and I thought this path would take us there, but it seems to have disappeared. The trees are getting thicker and so is the undergrowth. Shall we turn back or dismount and see if we can find the river on foot?"

"Oh, I should love to see the river. Listen – I hear it. We cannot be far away. This horse is a bag of bones – let's leave him and stroll about. There is no danger, is there?"

"Oh no, Lawrence said we had nothing to fear this close to Jamestown. The beasts and savages have long since been driven away and we are not far from the main road. Come on, slide down and we'll let the hack rest. I feel muscles that I had forgotten I had."

Lyn slipped to the forest floor and felt a soft carpet beneath her feet. She leaned down to see what was cushioning her and picked up a dense swath of brilliant green moss. "Look Nat, how soft. We might be indoors, it is so fine underfoot," she murmured.

"It must be an old forest – look at the height of the trees. Here is one I don't know, already turning yellow. Look, the leaves shimmer in the breeze – they have a different shape with one, two, three, four points – and they feel as soft as fine cloth. Won't it be a pleasure to learn the names of all the new plants and creatures. How Ray would envy us. We might be in Eden!"

Lyn looked up and saw Nat's face alight with wonder. Tears trembled in her eyes and, tossing her hat aside, she hugged him close, her cheek tight against his breast where his heart beat fast. As she listened to his life's blood she silently prayed that this spark of enthusiasm would take hold and burst into a bright flame which would continue ever brighter.

Nat smiled down at Lyn, cupped her chin and kissed her brow. "Come, let's find the river. I should love to play the child for one evening and dabble my feet in the James. Tomorrow we'll put on the mask of duty, but tonight is ours."

Nat knotted the reins of their reluctant steed around a sapling and the two of them pushed through the undergrowth towards the rush of the river. Wild grape coiled about them with green clinging fingers and they tried the fruit, laughing as each made a sour face when they discovered that the dusky globes had not yet ripened. Their feet sank into pine mast and moss as they skirted forest giants which it would take three men to girdle. Interspersed among these ancients were smaller evergreens which, like faithful acolytes, attended their superiors, spreading spicy incense as if from censors. The nightjar called again and the violets and golds of late afternoon turned to purple and silver. Far above the moon's cutting edge sliced the velvet sky and released a flood of silver starlight which enveloped them.

Before long Nat and Lyn found the river bank. They pushed through the last of the underbrush, descended a gentle declivity, and found themselves on a pebbly shingle which disappeared into the great muscular coil of the James. The murky water was all but invisible save for where the ripples sparkled in the light of the moon and stars. Beneath their feet the pebbles danced like diamonds.

"Off with your slippers, Lyn. Let's feel the flood. The James is one of Virginia's great highways and we should learn it well."

"Is it safe, Nat? What if it should pull us in?"

"That does not sound like you, brave heart. Why so timid?"

"It is all so strange – so warm and ... I can almost hear things growing. And what lies to the west? Is this land knowable?"

"Do you already miss Suffolk?"

"Yes and no. Rather, no. But you must admit that it is a strange land. And the river is mightier than any I have seen except the Thames."

"Well, and look how man has tamed the Thames. If it lies docile at our bidding, why not the James?"

"Well, you are doubtless right. Come, let's see what the water feels like."

They walked gingerly over the pebbles and slid their slim white feet into the flood where it lapped upon the shore. The water was neither warm nor cold, but tepid like blood. They reached down and splashed their own faces and then one another. Lyn's foot slipped on a river-drenched rock and she reached for Nat's shoulder. He pulled her to his side and slipped his arm around her waist and held her fast. Wordlessly the pair moved back across the shingle to the shelter of the gentle bank which they climbed, heedless of their abandoned shoes and stockings. Still without a sound they fell upon the soft moss under the spreading arms of a tulip poplar. Golden leaves danced above them and an emerald carpet spread below them. Nat shucked Lyn of her boy's clothes like an ear of corn from its silken wrapper. Before he himself stripped he wooed her with his hands as he had done when they first lived at Hazelwood. Hunger rose in her and she eased him of his garments. They stood in the moonlight as God had made them and soon the two of them were one. Once more the nightjar called like the tolling of a bell and then, for one long moment, a perfect silence fell.

Nat whispered in Lyn's ear. "Remember our oath. I renew it now."

Lyn replied. "I shall always be here for you, Nat."

John's first view of King's Creek came as the wagon emerged from the dense forest and before him, in the glow of the late morning sun, lay fields of green and gold. Across the fields to the north the plantation house stood, outlined against the dark green of yet more forest. Dots of white, in all its hues from cream to snow, fluttered about like so many moths in the rich foliage: the shirts of the field hands who tended the ripening tobacco plants, stripping the unwanted leaves to bring on a perfect harvest. In the center of the tapestry stood a horse painted with great blotches of red and cream and on the horse sat a figure dressed all in white wearing a broad-brimmed straw hat like a golden crown.

"There's the Master!" cried Timothy, who switched the great haunches of the cart horses with vigor. The animals shuddered but kept to the same steady pace which had brought the conveyance from Jamestown.

John saw the rider in the fields doff his hat and wave it slowly back and forth in recognition of his guests' arrival. The attorney was seated next to Timothy on the driver's bench, Nat and Lyn having chosen to make a nest on the wagon bed among their luggage and the crates which were marked for King's Creek. It had not escaped John's notice that since the Bacons had returned from the mainland to the inn last night that a new sympathy seemed to lie between them. He turned to tell them that they were nearing their destination and found them in close conversation, oblivious of their surroundings. He reddened and faced forward again, silent, a pain in his heart. As different as they were, there was a deep bond between Nat and Lyn. They had drifted apart in Suffolk and now Virginia was bringing them together again. John might love them both, but he would never share that bond. The bright scene before him dimmed and he ran a hand over his face lest Timothy see his tears. He would help Nat and Lyn settle quickly and then, he thought, he would return to England as soon as his duty to Squire Thomas was done.

Lyn saw John's distress and guessed its cause. A woman knew when she had a worshipper and John had been hers since he had taken her hand in the dining room of Friston Hall more than four years ago. He was feeling excluded and she sought to engage him. "Why look, John – that must be Colonel Bacon waving to us."

John turned again, forcing a smile. "So Timothy says. We're almost there, and here comes the Colonel to meet us."

Nat had stood up in the wagon bed, clinging to a large crate to keep his balance. "Sure enough, 'tis my cousin. What a fine horse! I can't see him well enough to see if he looks like Father, but he has a good seat. And what glorious surroundings! I suppose that green stuff is tobacco."

John smiled in earnest. "Indeed, that 'green stuff' is why we came. You had better look at it long and hard, for it will be your bread and butter for years to come. Here's the Colonel."

Timothy brought the wagon to a halt where the drive from the plantation house met the main road. There, on the painted horse, sat the man in white. He was clean shaven and had cropped his grizzled hair to chin length, shorter than the fashion, but long enough for a Virginia summer. He had the look of Squire Bacon, but his regular features gave the impression of greater strength of character and less diffidence, and his eyes were a clear hazel, not blue. The Colonel swept off his straw hat, placed it on his breast and bowed deeply as a generous smile played on his intelligent face.

"You cannot imagine how delighted I am to see you," he exclaimed. "Forgive me for not dismounting, but I think it best if Timothy continues on to the house with you all and this mountain of luggage. I will follow right behind you and we can exchange proper greetings on the front porch. My wife is much recovered and doubtless will join us. You have made excellent time, Tim, now move along to the house."

As they drew up to the front porch Lyn noted with surprise that the Bacons' home was modest, both in size and in materials. Its weathered clapboard sides sprawled at random as though a child had formed it from toy bricks. The main wing bore a dormered second story above the ground floor, and the whole was charmingly bound together by a great porch. Clematis and honeysuckle clung to the porch columns and flower beds hugged the entire structure, crowded with lavender and verbena and wild rose and with shrubs which were new to Lyn. Behind the house, to the west, rose a large barn and a clutch of outbuildings like a hen and her chicks. To the south, between the house and the tobacco fields stretched a neat kitchen garden and a small orchard in which Lyn thought she could identify apple and pear trees.

Before she had time to notice more Colonel Bacon handed her down from the wagon and her hostess emerged from the front door. The senior Mistress Elizabeth Bacon was small and plump and had a head of beautiful white hair caught up under a dainty cap. Her golden brown eyes gleamed with excitement and her soft cheeks flushed. She was drying her hands on an apron which covered a gown of sprigged muslin. A single pink rose nestled in the lace at her bosom.

"Oh my, you're here at last! I'm so excited that I forgot to take off my apron. I make the pies myself – I don't trust the slaves with the crust. And right on time! There's a good hour before dinner and you shall have as long as you need to refresh yourselves. I've put you upstairs, I hope you don't mind. It is a little close in the summer, but if you open the windows at night it should be fresh enough, and there is so much more privacy. Otherwise you'll be tripping over the servants and slaves and that is such a nuisance. Come in, come in. Oh, my dear cousin, what a charming wife you have! No wonder she caught your fancy – no man could resist, I am sure. Now come in, come in and tell me all about Suffolk and the trip over. We know Captain Gardiner well and I am sure he took good care of you."

Nat and Lyn and John shared amused glances as their hostess babbled on like a shallow brook. They stepped inside the cool front hall just as the Colonel mounted the steps behind them, having offloaded their luggage and sent Timothy around to the back of the house with the crates of English merchandise. Well polished wood floors stretched about them covered with a miscellany of Turkey rugs worked in deep blues and reds. The furniture appeared to be a mixture of old Tudor pieces and lighter, modern items, the whole blending in a charming mélange. The scent of roses was everywhere and Lyn knew, already, that she would always associate the scent with her delightful hostess who must, herself, have been a rosebud as a young girl.

"Now, my dear," insisted the Colonel. "You don't have to prove what these poor young things have probably already heard in Jamestown – that you hold the Virginia record for volubility. I expect that they would like to find their rooms and have a little privacy." He turned to his guests. "I'll leave you in the capable hands of Sukey, our housekeeper. She will show you everything and then we shall meet in the parlor in ... shall we say thirty minutes? That will give us time for a cool drink before we sit down to dine. I hope you brought your appetites, for Betty's table is famous throughout the colony."

The chimes of a silver handbell brought a tall, stout black woman from the back of the house. She was immaculately clad in blue and white striped cotton and wore a white turban on her head. Although she smiled a welcome as she indicated that the guests should precede her upstairs, Lyn saw none of Clarissa's quick intelligence in her dark eyes. Rather, Sukey seemed to look through the new arrivals as though her deepest thoughts were on wholly other matters. Lyn shook herself at her fancy and rapidly mounted the stairs where two bedrooms awaited them, each redolent of beeswax and the ever present scent of roses.

The midday dinner proved the quality of Betty Bacon's housewifery. There were three kinds of meat, including a cunningly prepared chicken dish with a crust. There were six vegetables, from comfortable English peas and potatoes to golden Indian corn. There were hot breads made by their hostess' own hands. There were pitchers of icy milk and cold tea and the Bacons' famous perry, together with red wines and white, for the Colonel had a well-stocked cellar. After a brief pause Sukey and her helpers served a choice of apple pie or huckleberry pie with pitchers of cold, thick, sweet cream for those who still had the stomach. When the four Bacons and John had retired to the parlor, Mistress Elizabeth rushed from the room and returned shortly with trays of tea and coffee, compliments of Captain Gardiner. The guests groaned with pleasure and asked if they might fast the next day.

Colonel Bacon, whose appetite had not flagged throughout the meal, laughed. "This is only the beginning – the appetizer, as it were. We'll let you sleep it off and later in the day you can take some exercise to prepare you for tomorrow. Twenty-four hours from now I expect to be joined for an even more extravagant dinner by two of my neighbors, Tom Ballard and John Page. Each of them is an experienced planter and each has served the colony well in government and in the militia. They will be a resource to you, for I am sure that you are as full of questions about Virginia as you are of Betty's dinner." The Colonel turned to his cousin. "In addition, Nat, Tom Ballard owns some land which he is thinking of selling – it is on the James, quite a way up river. I suggest that you discuss it with him – it may be just the kind of thing you are looking for. Now I believe we would all profit by a short nap. When you hear the bell ring that will be a sign that I am ready to ride out in the fields again. If you two gentlemen would like to go with me I will have horses prepared for you and I can introduce you to the mistress who keeps the whole colony in thrall: *Nicotiana*."

Nat tossed restlessly in the heat and leafed idly through some of the booklets John had collected, but Lyn fell into a profound sleep and only roused when she heard Nat cursing as he pulled on his boots. She helped him dress for riding and gave him a kiss as he hurried downstairs, joined by John. She was glad for his eagerness and, once again, hoped that it would last. She felt more herself after she had poured a basin of water and washed her hands and face. After changing her frock and redoing her hair she went in search of Mistress Elizabeth who, doubtless, was waiting to show her the house.

Lyn had guessed right. The Colonel's lady was seated by the west window of the parlor to catch the afternoon light, a pair of spectacles balanced on the end of her nose, working on her embroidery. When Lyn appeared the older woman tossed her work into a basket and rose with a cry of joy.

"There you are, my dear, as dewy as a violet. That must be your flower, with your beautiful coloring."

"And yours is certainly the rose," smiled Lyn.

Mistress Elizabeth blushed. "Do you think so, my love? How kind. The Colonel has always said the same, and it is my favorite. I brought many with me from England and most of them do very well here, though August is not the best month to show them. Come, I'll give you a tour of the house and as much of the garden as you care to see. The heat is lifting and the evening should be quite pleasant. We often have thunder storms in the summer, but you can feel them coming on and I know that we shall not be plagued with one today. And now, my dear, how do you like to be called?"

"You know my name is Elizabeth, just like yours, but I have been called Lyn for as long as I can remember and, if you please, I should like to keep it so."

"Bless you, my case exactly. They called me Betty from the cradle and Betty I am to all of Virginia. I hope that you will follow suit."

"If I may, I should be honored."

"Well then, Lyn and Betty it will be. Now come see the room where I make my simples and syrups. You will have to become quite an apothecary, like me, for there are few doctors in the colony and those who call themselves so are not worth a groat. Home remedies are always best."

An hour later Lyn had seen jars and boxes of sassafras, jalap, ipecac and Peruvian bark; hyssop, lavender, comfrey and fennel; rattlesnake root and swamp root; the bark of the wild cherry and of the prickly ash, which were alleged to have the virtues of *Cortex Peruviana*; and the notorious Jamestown weed which was kept under lock and key, as a curiosity.

"Never touch the weed, my dear," warned Mistress Betty, "unless you are learned in herb lore. A concoction in the right proportions makes a wonderful cooler, but if taken wrongly you will have dreams inspired by the Devil and you may never come right again."

As the sun set the ladies toured the kitchens, the ice house, the well house, the smoke house and Sukey's cabin, which formed a cluster of buildings just west of the main house. Further west stood a large barn and the slave cabins; and beyond those again several tobacco barns the open sides of which let in drying breezes when the leaves were picked and hung for curing. Last Lyn and her hostess viewed the kitchen garden and the orchard, and the newcomer felt a wave of homesickness as the orderly rows of vegetables and herbs and the apple and pear trees reminded her of Hazelwood. They circled around to the front of the house and Betty pointed out the course of King's Creek, for which the plantation was named, and told Lyn that the house stood less than a mile from the York River where their warehouses and wharfs stood, ready for the give and take of Virginia commerce.

"And such a blessing it is, my dear, for we simply take the tobacco to the riverside by wagon, the coopers make up the hogsheads on the spot, the leaves are carefully placed in them, they are bound tight, and the tobacco fleet kindly calls and takes our crop. We are lucky to have river front property. Others have to roll the hogsheads – what a chore, and how it digs up the roads! – or make some other arrangement. The Colonel would not want me to interfere, but I suggest you tell your husband to look for a plantation with a good river frontage, such as Ballard's. Oh now, I've done what I said I would not. I told Natty that I would stay out of your business and leave it to the men. But I am sure you agree, my dear, that most men would be in a sorry pickle if they were not firmly guided by us women." Which sentiment Lyn did not dispute.

The two women returned to the house where Sukey had thrown all the windows open and where a pleasant breeze stirred. The faint scent of roses was everywhere. The dark woman served them with cold tea garnished with fresh mint and Lyn was grateful for the liquid, as the heat was still a novelty and she felt it draining her energy. Betty ordered the candles lighted and picked up her embroidery again while Lyn sat in restful silence. A small, cold evening meal would be served whenever the men returned from the fields: such was the tranquil rhythm of King's Creek.

Colonel Bacon proudly bestrode his painted gelding whose brilliant coat looked like snow on red Virginia clay. A young black boy held the reins of a dainty dappled gray mare and a leggy chestnut gelding and peeped shyly at Nat and John as the two descended the porch onto the gravel drive.

"Take your pick," called the Colonel as his steed tossed its head restlessly. "The mare belongs to Betty but she never rides now and I am thinking of getting rid of it, though it is high-bred and cost me a pretty penny. The gelding has just been broken and promises well. I may keep it to give my paint a rest from time to time, but I might sell it as well. It's one of John Page's colts and its blood lines are excellent."

John, who normally deferred to his friend in matters like this, moved toward the mare, leaving the larger, showier chestnut for Nat, but, to his pleasure, he was forestalled.

"No, John, you're taller and heavier and should try this beauty. The mare will suit me fine – look at those soft eyes. Lyn would love her."

The friends mounted and the three men road south through tobacco fields which stretched seemingly without limit.

"Are those men bringing in the crop?" asked Nat.

"Not yet, but we will harvest in a week or so. See how the leaves are starting to yellow – when they turn like that you have to watch them like a hawk. At the right moment we strip them and take them to the tobacco barns and string them up and let them cure for a few weeks before they are ready to be shipped. The leaves should be pure gold when they are placed in the hogsheads – I insist upon it. You will hear that King's Creek tobacco is among the best in the colony."

"And now – what are the men doing?"

"Oh, they're still pruning. From the time the plants are a foot high they must be pruned and stripped of their buttons and suckers or we would end with a bushy shrub of no quality whatever, its leaves quite depleted of flavor. We must prune right up to the time of harvest. Tobacco is very demanding, despite what you might hear to the contrary. To get a quality crop you want only eight or ten leaves when you harvest, and King's Creek prides itself on producing the best tobacco in the colony. " The Colonel pulled up his horse as it pecked and stumbled. "Many pernicious scoundrels throw in stalks and buttons and seeds and chaff and God knows what with the good leaves – 'tis a great crime and one which lowers us all. There should be a law against it, but the practice is spreading."

"Who are the offenders?" asked John.

"Why, I will not name them, for fear of being taken to court. You're an attorney, young Grey, you should know that I dare not speak ill of my neighbors. But generally they are the rabble, those recently arrived, with no breeding and no fortune. Or those who have scrambled their way up from servitude and scratched out a few meager acres where they grow trash. You'll find that there is a division in the colony, with planters like Sir William Berkeley and Ballard and Page and me on the one side and the rag-tag and bobtail on the other. One should not plant without the resources and skill to do it right." The Colonel turned to Nat, who was riding at his side. "That's why we are so extraordinarily glad to see you and your lady. It has been some time since anyone of quality has joined us. I look forward to introducing you to your peers."

Nat swiveled around and glanced at John. The attorney mouthed "Green Spring" and Nat smiled and nodded in agreement. Just then the Colonel let out a yell and charged at a black workman who had fallen to the ground and in doing so had crushed a dozen tobacco plants.

The planter leaped from his horse and approached the fallen man, whip in hand.

"Get up Eli, no more of your false fevers. You've just cost me a pretty penny – there's no saving those plants. There is another hour of sunlight and if you think you are going home early, you are sadly mistaken."

The black man groaned pitiably and John dismounted and walked to his side to see whether he could be of assistance.

"Get back, Grey," said the Colonel. "I know you mean well, but you are looking on the greatest malingerer that ever disgraced King's Creek. He's strong as an ox – he just wants to get to his liquor sooner than his mates. He's played this game many times before."

John reluctantly stepped back, though he did not remount his chestnut. The man looked ill and he felt compelled to speak. "With respect, sir, the fellow is an ugly color and the sweat seems to be pouring off him. You know better than I, but he does not look well."

The Colonel frowned and his lips thinned, but he approached the slave more closely and poked him with the butt end of his whip.

"Perhaps you are right. All these hands should be well seasoned, but sometimes they fall sick. If they slept at night instead of dancing jigs, and followed the generous diet we give them instead of swilling liquor, they would be the better for it. But they are poor heathens, and I suppose they cannot help themselves. God made them like children and we must treat them so."

The planter leaned down and examined Eli who lay, belly down, in the red soil, his sad face pressed into his hands. "Alright, my man. You have found an advocate and, against my better judgment, I'll listen to his plea. Get you home and send someone up to the house for some physic. Make sure Mistress Betty knows that I have given you sick leave. But tomorrow I expect to see you in the fields or know the reason why."

The Colonel remounted and signaled to an overseer who was given directions to see to the stricken slave. After the man had been helped to rise and make his weary way to his cabin, the three horsemen rode on, their initial gaiety dampened by the incident. After a few moments of silence Nat spoke.

"It appears that tobacco requires constant labor. When I find a plantation, how shall I best people it?"

The Colonel sighed. "Oh, my boy, you have put your finger on it. The weed *is* demanding, no question about it. We start the seedlings in the winter. Then the ground must be prepared, and well manured, for tobacco is a great glutton, gobbling the soil with abandon. You must carve new fields out of the forest every few years, or repair your old ones, so covetous it is of the earth's fat. Then once you have transplanted your seedlings there is no respite. They demand water, they must not be choked with weeds, and the pests must be kept away if possible. Children excel at these tasks, and it is good that the slaves are so prolific, for we have a goodly supply of little helpers. Then, as I have told you, when the plants are a foot high you must constantly strip them, leaving only the best leaves to take up and retain the flavor which makes Virginia tobacco famous throughout the civilized world. Labor, labor, labor. Your workers will be either servants or slaves. Some say the bound servants are best, as they know when they work off their indentures they will be free, so they have an incentive to please their masters and learn the trade. I have not found it so. I mean no offense to His Majesty, (God forbid), but lately England has been sending us human dregs: riffraff scraped from the streets and jail birds just out of their cages. The slaves may have less drive, but they are more docile. Betty and I prefer the Africans though, as you just saw, you have to treat them like children." The Colonel laughed bitterly. "'Tis just as well that we had no children of our own, for God has made us the unwitting parents of many."

Nat glanced at John's sober face. His friend's expression matched his own. Neither liked what he was hearing. Suffolk peasants had a hard life, but at least they could speak their minds to their masters, and frequently did. To be the lord of bound servants and slaves – human property – seemed an invitation to despotism. Richard Lawrence's and William Drummond's words floated through Nat's mind and he began to see how the lines of power lay in the colony. It appeared that the human animal in Virginia might be as different from those at home as the birds and beasts and fish and fowl and the verdure which shimmered around him as far as the eye could see.

The riders had reached the westernmost border of the King's Creek tobacco fields and they now turned their mounts with their backs to the sun. Long shadows fell across the Colonel's acres. In the distance the plantation house gleamed a pale gray. A bell sounded faintly and the white clad men made their way home like moths to a candle. The Colonel eased himself in the saddle and sighed again.

140

"It is not an easy life here, Nat. Authority takes its toll as surely as hard labor. Betty and I have nursed King's Creek from a starveling to what it is today: a model plantation. Merchants covet King's Creek tobacco and my word is as good as gold throughout the land, but my achievements are the result of a quarter of a century of unremitting labor. I cannot recall the last time I lay abed past sunrise. And I have tried to serve the greater good, rising from seats on the county court and the parish vestry to Burgess for York County and, most recently, as a member of the Council of State. There is no such thing as a day of rest. Sundays we go to church, of course, but the afternoon is not spent in leisure. When the great planters appear to play, they are actually hard at work. If it were not so, the colony would quickly come to grief. A good two thirds of the population is poor and ignorant and if they were not kept down they would be at our throats. And I am speaking not only of servants and slaves, but of freemen. You will, of course, take your rightful place among the elite, but even so you will have to look sharp to keep from stumbling.

"But, faugh, I sound like an old man. Our tables groan with food, our libraries boast the latest books, fine company abounds for those who seek it, and the Indian troubles are in the past. Virginia was a more perilous place by far when I first came: now it is like a paradise. You will do splendidly, with your charming little wife and your learned friend at your side. Come, let's return to supper. I want to tell you about Tom Ballard and his plantation at Curles Neck. I think it might be just the thing for you."

CHAPTER 10

AUGUST 1674

Sukey stood in the doorway and, by her expression alone, directed the serving girls as they removed the dessert course and set out the bottles of port and sherry and Madeira and arranged the dishes of fruit and nuts on the gleaming mahogany. Lyn and Betty had retired to the parlor to exchange confidences over their needlework. Colonel Bacon and Nat and John and Tom Ballard and John Page would join them later for tea, but the men would spend the next two hours at table, discussing the business which had brought them together. Sukey moved towards the door between the dining room and the parlor, took one last look to see that all was as it should be, and shooed the maids before her like so many geese. Tom Ballard eyed the smooth haunches of the youngest girl and winked at Nat.

"They run to fat, but get them young and there is nothing like it," Ballard said, loudly enough so that the women could hear. Sukey turned in the doorway and gently but firmly closed the door, her eyes focused on nothing at all and her mind seemingly a thousand miles away. John winced at Ballard's remark. The horse-faced man had been consistently coarse throughout the meal, and John was saddened that he, rather than the well-bred Page, might hold the key to Nat's future.

Taking a cue from Page and the Colonel, Nat pretended not to hear Ballard's remark, instead seizing a bottle of Madeira and making the rounds of the table, pouring each man a drink. *Well done, Nat*, thought John. *We don't want to make him an enemy, at least not now.* Before Ballard could say more Colonel Bacon raised his glass and proposed a toast to Nathaniel Bacon, Junior and his wife. The men murmured and touched glasses and the ugly moment was gone.

"Well then," said the Colonel, "we all know why we are here. Tom, I've given my cousin a preview of Curles Neck and he is interested in hearing more. I've asked John Page along to play Devil's advocate, for there is not a longer head in the colony than his."

Page smiled at his friend and acknowledged the complement. "I'm always at your service, Nathaniel." He turned to Nat and John. "The Colonel and I go way back. We arrived in the same year, took patents on neighboring land, and have gone through the same ups and downs over the decades. A man could not have a better neighbor. I'm flattered to think that my opinion might be worth listening to, but I can't imagine your needing more advice when you have a Bacon and a Ballard to consult with."

"Well, Tom's an interested party," insisted the Colonel, "so I brought you along to take the wind out of his sails if he starts puffing. After all, I've never been to Curles Neck, so if he tries to sell my cousin a pig in a poke I need somebody to speak the truth."

The three older men laughed, and discussions began in earnest.

"Well, my boy," brayed Tom Ballard, his meaty lips working over his slightly protruding teeth, "I've got just the place for you. Curles Neck is a beauty of a plantation, all cleared for tobacco and fitted out with house, barn, cattle and slaves, and with a fine James River frontage. You could move in tomorrow."

"Stop right there," interposed Page. "Let's discuss the location. It's on the James alright, but it is forty miles from Jamestown, right on the frontier."

"Nonsense," cried Ballard. "My little farm up by the falls is on the frontier, but not Curles Neck! Why it's closer to Jamestown than Varina ... just beyond Turkey Island. It's a day from the capital, whether you are riding or sailing."

"A long day ... a *very* long day. Come, Tom, admit that it is remote."

"Well, it's not Green Spring or Westover or Shirley, but Byrd and Goode live beyond it and they never complain of the distance."

"Byrd and Goode are not in government. They don't come to Jamestown once in a month. Byrd loves the wilderness – I sometimes think that he'd rather truck with the savages than with us."

"Oh come, gentlemen, stick to the point," urged Colonel Bacon. "Young Nat is not in government either, though we hope that he will be sooner rather than later. But seriously, Curles Neck is somewhat remote. It is a full day's travel from Jamestown, and that is something which must be taken into account. However, it has a superb river frontage, nobody could argue with that. Now, tell us the acreage and how fertile it is and what the house is like and so forth."

Ballard calmed down. "Well, Curles itself is a good twelve hundred acres and there are forty more in the little farm at the falls, which I might consider selling as well. Curles has been cleared for decades, so that work is done for you. It has lain fallow for some time but last year I grew a crop which was outstanding." He turned to the Colonel. "Remember, Natty, you said it was the best you'd ever seen, save your own."

"Of course I remember, Tom. That's why it came to mind when Squire Bacon wrote that his son was emigrating. What are the buildings like?"

"Well, to be honest, the house is only wood and it is not enforted, though I doubt the Indians pose a threat that far down river. There is a nice barn and the usual cabins for the men. I have forty men there now, half servants and half slaves. They are growing fat, for I did not plant this year, and all they have to do is look after the cattle and keep up the garden and orchards. If I don't sell the place soon I'll put them all on the market. To be honest, I am running the place at a loss now, and I am anxious to sell."

"Well, why did you buy it?" asked the Colonel brusquely.

"I over-extended myself, Natty, you know that. I had that wonderful overseer, the one who brought me my first crop, but after he died I have found nobody to take his place. I can't be running up there all the time – it's too far away."

John Page burst out laughing. "I thought it was 'just a few miles upriver'."

Ballard laughed as well. "Well, I admit it, Henrico is a stretch. But Nat and John Grey here are young and vigorous – what are forty miles to them?"

"Henrico?" asked John.

"Oh, 'tis the name of the county. Named long ago for the young prince who would have been king instead of the first Charles. Henrico County. That's where you'll be if you buy Curles Neck, and a fine, fat country it is, young and supple like yourselves."

Nat laughed. "Well, let's see. I've heard about twelve hundred acres of good soil and river frontage and a wooden house and forty workers. What about the cattle – will you sell them with the land?"

"For the most part. I have a nice herd of cattle; excellent swine which take care of themselves and only need a boy to prevent them from wandering too far; no sheep, I confess; and a fine black stallion which my wife won't let me ride. I keep it there to hold off temptation."

"A black? How old and of what parentage?" asked Nat eagerly.

"A pure black. You can see the dam if you like, but the sire died last year – my best stud, by far. He was famous in the colony – how he loved the ladies." Ballard's coarse laugh rang out again. Colonel Bacon and John Page took on the abstracted look which was their defense against their friend's crudity, but they agreed that the black stallion at Curles had excellent blood lines.

Ever since the horse was mentioned Nat's face had glowed with interest. John nudged him under the table, but it was too late. His friend had let his guard down and it might work to his disadvantage.

"You said something about another farm, at the falls," said John.

"Oh yes, I picked it up for a song, as part of the Curles purchase. It's a nice little property, overlooking the river, but it has not been developed yet. If the price for Curles Neck was right I would throw it into the pot as a favor to a friend."

"And had you thought of a price?" asked the attorney.

Ballard coughed and was silent.

144

"Well, spit it out, man," said the Colonel. "We've discussed it often enough – it's a fair price."

"For a friend, I would offer the whole for five hundred pounds."

Nat glanced at John and hoped that his face did not show his pleasure. It was much less than he expected. If he bought a working plantation for five hundred pounds that left him thirteen hundred pounds of capital to improve the place and weather the years before it became productive. He could hardly believe his luck. But did this mean that there was something wrong with Curles Neck? Surely his cousin would not let him make an unwise purchase. He turned to Ballard.

"The price is a bit high, but we have just begun to talk. I am interested enough to see the place. Is that possible?"

"Possible?" cried Ballard. "I've been waiting for you to ask. Tomorrow's Sunday, and my wife doesn't like me to travel, but we could start on the Monday. I have a sloop lying at Jamestown and, let's see, the tide should be right Monday afternoon. Yes, if we make an early start on Monday morning we'll be in Jamestown by midmorning, hoist our sails and reach Curles by the time it grows dark. If we should be delayed I know every planter on the river and we can be sure of a bed and supper. Who will come?"

"You know I can't leave my harvest," said the Colonel, "and Page is under the same constraint. Can you take the young gentlemen by yourself? If you cannot man a crew, I daresay I can lend you some of my hands for a few days, though I would be hard pressed to do so."

"Oh, the crew is no problem. I can pull three or four lads from the field – they'll be wild to go. If you trust me with your cousin it will be an honor to take him on his first sail up the James."

"Very well," said the Colonel, rising. "Nat and Grey will meet you Monday morning at the white oak which marks my southern border. God willing, we shall all emerge from this winners."

John sat his chestnut and played idly with the white oak leaves which danced before him, backlit by the morning sun. A pungent, verdant scent rose from the vegetation and he noted that each generous, hand-sized leaf was smooth on one side and velvet on the other. A few leaves were turning as the season advanced. The calm of late summer hung in the air. Nat was pacing the dirt road, switching at the undergrowth with his whip. He shielded his face against the sun and looked up at his friend.

"It feels right, don't you think? I believe Curles Neck was meant to be mine."

"It sounds promising, but even before we see the place I have one great reservation."

"Oh ye of little faith, what is that?"

"It's Ballard himself. The man is not only coarse but, I judge, untrustworthy."

"I don't disagree, but my cousin would never have put this opportunity in my way if he did not think it a good one. That's why Page was there. No, I think the scheme is sound at heart."

"You have been wooed by the black horse."

Nat laughed. "You think I'm a child. God knows I have given you enough reason to doubt my judgment, but you must trust me a little. Between us we cannot go wrong. Look, there's Ballard. We'll know within the next two days whether Curles Neck is a diamond or merely paste."

A thin, barefoot boy tossed Ballard the last line which bound the sloop to the wharf and the planter flipped him a coin in return. A crew of four lads trimmed the sails, cursing under their breath as they stumbled over Nat and John, and soon the vessel caught the favorable tide and moved upriver with the current. Ballard and his guests made themselves comfortable amidships and John watched first Drummond's house, and then the church tower, disappear below the horizon. It was nearly noon and all seven men had risen at dawn and were sharp set, so they did not stand on ceremony when Ballard began opening two great hampers and handing around cold chicken, soft wheaten rolls, meat and fruit pies, and fresh peaches for dessert. John drank cider with the crew, but Nat joined his host in finishing two bottles of sweet Rhenish.

The heat abated and the breeze freshened The sun shone through a thin cloud cover which dissipated as the afternoon wore on and soon a pure blue canopy arched overhead, anchored by brilliant green along the river's edge, with just a touch of yellow for contrast. Even the muddy James showed swirls of blue and green among the brown and gray. A perfect peace lay on the land and the only sounds were the slap of the water and the bellying of the sails as the sloop slid effortlessly westward.

Nat curled up like a cat and slept while John joined Ballard in the stern. The two sat in silence for some minutes and then John seized the opportunity to ask some more questions about Curles Neck. He glanced at Ballard's strong profile with its fleshy nose and lips and large ears. A choleric brute with a hair-trigger temper; he would not care to cross the man. He pondered how best to frame his questions.

"How long have you owned Curles Neck, Mister Ballard?" he queried.

Ballard started, as if drawn from profound thought. "Oh, going on five years. Between you and me I picked it up for a song from a widow who wanted to return to England. Longfields they called it. It was patented in thirty-eight, but it has lain fallow for years." The planter laughed cruelly. "The widow kept thinking she would find another man to run the place, but if you had seen her you would know why her dreams were dashed. A real scarecrow, she was – no flesh on her bones." Ballard faced John with a lively expression. "Now me, I like them round and juicy, like the Colonel's serving wench. What about you, Mister Grey?"

John blushed deeply and hoped that Ballard would attribute his color to the sun. Since he had met Lyn he had been all but celibate. He thought with distaste of his rare visits to Meg's. He was not ashamed of his appetites, for God had made men so. But lust had only marginally triumphed over revulsion the last time he had lost himself in the voluptuous, perfumed flesh of a purchased body. He needed a wife, but there was only one woman in the world whom he wished to marry and she was lost to him forever. He banished his thoughts.

"Oh, stout or slim, fair or dark, each has its advantages, don't you find?"

"Well said, lad. I was beginning to think you were a Puritan." The planter shoved his elbow into John's side. "I won't say it again, as I believe I offended your young friend, but there is nothing like dark meat. Do you take my meaning?"

As he made a perfunctory answer a wholly realized image planted itself in John's mind. He saw himself giving Ballard a huge shove off the stern of the sloop and watching the muddy water boil around the sinking face as the gross lips cried for succor and the fleshy arms thrashed about in the tide. This was not the way to find Nat's plantation – he must find another subject or join his friend amidships.

"Longfields, you said. And why Curles Neck?"

"Oh, the place lies where the river curls about most extravagantly. 'Tis strange – one can't find one's direction there by following the James for it runs thither and yon, to all points of the compass. 'Tis a beautiful spot, well watered, fertile, peaceful. You have Crewes on Turkey Island to the east and Varina beyond, (that's the county seat), but really it's quite a little kingdom, self-contained. No, as I was saying, the widow let it go for a song and I couldn't help myself, she sold so cheap, and threw in the little farm for nothing. But, as my wife keeps reminding me, I overextended myself and I will have to sell. That's how I can give your friend such a good price. Five hundred pounds is less than the place is worth, but I will still make a profit. There, I hope I have not damaged my cause by my honesty."

"Certainly not," John said truthfully. "I appreciate your openness. We are not overreaching, but we are new here, so we are somewhat at your mercy."

"Oh, never fear. I would never harm any kin of Colonel Bacon. Why, after the Governor I believe he is the best loved man in the colony. No, fair is fair. If you like the place, Mister Bacon shall have it."

"Tell me about the house and the outbuildings and the rest of it."

"Well, the house is quite old and it is just wood, so your friends will have to build, no doubt about it. But it will serve nicely for a year or so while they plan a nice brick seat. Allen has built beautifully on the Southside, in Surry County. You might want to talk to him about materials and a master builder and workmen and so forth."

"And the barns and cattle?"

"I should think the barns and outbuildings would do for quite some time, though they will have to be replaced eventually. As for the cattle, they are excellent stock. My overseer – the one who died – was one of the shrewdest farmers I ever met. 'Tis a pity the fever took him. Oh, don't worry – he died in Gloucester County while visiting kin. Curles is healthy enough – it stands on a bluff above the river and gets a nice breeze. There are some marshes, but they lie to the west and are nothing to worry about."

John glanced at Nat, still slumbering in the sun among the coils of rope. "And what about that black horse?"

"Ah, that should seal the matter if I read your friend rightly. 'Tis as fine a stallion as I have ever bred. The sire had some warhorse in him, and the dam is known for her speed. He's big and fast and will tolerate only the best of riders. Is Mister Bacon a horseman?"

"A consummate one. He left just such a horse behind in Suffolk. I am sure he would be interested in this one. Does it come with the plantation, or should we have to pay more for it?"

Ballard smoothed a hand over his fleshy lips and protruding teeth. "Why don't we see how far we get with our negotiations and then we'll decide about the horse?"

"Fair enough," said John, who stretched mightily and balanced himself as the sloop tacked. "I thank you for your candor. Now, I believe I'll join Nat for a catnap. Shall we reach Curles by sundown?"

"At this rate, certainly. You can get a glimpse of the place tonight before supper, then the slaves will give us a meal and find us some beds and tomorrow you can explore to your heart's content."

John moved amidships and settled down quietly next to Nat. Just as he pillowed his head on a coil of rope he saw his friend open both eyes wide and give him a broad wink. His whole conversation with Ballard had been overheard – they made a good team.

Curles Neck bluff rose, blunt-nosed, against the red orb of the setting sun. The breeze had died to nothing as the sloop bumped gently against the plantation's wharf. The James smoothed the shore like a sculptor's hand. Nat shivered as he stepped on the pebbly strand. It was just such a perfect evening as this that he and Lyn had come together again on the shore near Jamestown, joined as profoundly as they had been on the Suffolk shore so many years ago. And now this land might be Lyn's home, might be where he would find himself … might be where their children would run and laugh and play. He moved forward, John at his side. Behind them marched Ballard, followed by the crew. The seven men climbed the broad path which cut through the face of the bluff and brought them to the top.

As they reached their goal they turned as one and looked south. Below lay the serpent river, sparkling with the rubies cast by the sun's last rays.

Beyond lay forest which stretched endlessly to places only God knew. To the east the evening star rose over Jamestown. To the west the sun's chariot plunged below the horizon to bring day to new lands and night to Virginia. To the north lay Curles Neck plantation, verdant and welcoming in the soft dusk. Nat could make out a low wooden house not far from the edge of the bluff, and beyond it the peak of a barn. Candlelight sprang up in the slaves' cabins and voices pierced the gathering dark. As the men turned to walk towards the house the air was rent with the shrill cry of a stallion. Nat and John looked at one another and shared a smile. They felt as though they were coming home.

On the twenty-eighth of August, 1674, Nathaniel and Elizabeth Bacon, Senior joined Nathaniel and Elizabeth Bacon, Junior, Mister Thomas Ballard and Mister John Grey at *The Unicorn* for dinner. Over his wife's objection Richard Lawrence had reserved the entire common room for his guests. The occasion was the celebration of Nathaniel Bacon, Junior's purchase of the Curles Neck plantation, together with its buildings, cattle, slaves and servants.

Thrown in for good measure was the little farm at the falls of the James and the black stallion

Nobody, least of all Clarissa, was sorry when Mister Ballard left early in order to reach his plantation by nightfall. The four Bacons and John Grey were to spend the night at the inn as Richard Lawrence's guests. Early in the morning they would return to King's Creek from whence, on the first of September, they would proceed to Green Spring to pay their first visit to Virginia's Governor and his Lady. After having passed the night there they would ride to Curles Neck: they would ride home.

Lawrence watched the Bacon carriage disappear north, towards the isthmus. The Colonel's straw hat and his lady's white coif gleamed yellow and white, like a huge daisy, in the morning sun. Opposite the older couple the smiling visages of Nat and Lyn and John, who sat with their backs to the horses, formed a mosaic of buffs and blacks and browns highlighted with brilliant white and cherry red, until everything blurred and he could see nothing at all. A subtle smile crossed his own face and he turned to reenter *The Unicorn*. At this point young Bacon was content, having gotten Curles Neck and the outlying farm at the falls for such a pretty price. He had nothing on his mind but fitting out the plantation house for his cunning little wife and planting tobacco next spring. But time would take its toll – it always did in Virginia. Henrico County was a hotbed of unrest. For now, he and Drummond had planted the seeds of discontent with the young Squire and he felt confident that they would bear fruit. After all, Bacon and Grey had not yet met the Governor. After one interview with the peevish, brittle old knight the newcomers would remember their first conversations in Jamestown and would come begging for more information. Time enough then to introduce them to The Ring.

Lawrence closed the great oak door behind him and leaned upon it, deep in thought. The trestle table was still strewn with breakfast things and he moved forward to begin clearing them. Unlike Joanna, he had no false pride about housekeeping – all chores were the same to him as long as *The Unicorn's* reputation remained paramount. The inn was the very node of Virginia's news-web and he sat at its heart, spider like, among the silken threads of communication, and took it all in. One day soon it would be time to gather the threads together, read the pattern, and act.

Lawrence heard a door creak and he glanced to the right. Clarissa slipped from her bedroom, a pile of linen in her arms. Lawrence's smile deepened and he put down the tray of pewter cups. Business was so light at the end of August that he and Joanna had decided to close the inn after the Bacon party left and give themselves a three-day holiday until the first of September. The Assembly was going to meet later that month, then the tobacco fleet would be here, in full force, and the next thing you knew it would be Christmas. It had been a busy year, and it promised to continue so; they deserved a rest. Joanna had already left to visit a friend in Kecoughtan and he himself was going to sail upriver tomorrow, with Will Drummond, on special business. But today – today was his, to do with what he wished. Wordlessly the black woman came to him, proud as a ship, spilling white cloth like sea foam. She was as tall as he, and nobler by far. Their two mouths met in practiced union and she almost swallowed him whole. The great globes of her soft breasts met the hard cage of his ribs and he was on fire. Leaving the common room to take care of itself, the couple mounted the staircase, limbs entwined, Lawrence's hands sculpting Clarissa's body. They fled to the quiet of his chamber and banished all the world but that part which contained the two of them.

Drummond beat on the door again and again and, getting no response, opened it and stepped into *The Unicorn*. The common room was empty and there was no one about. He strode through the inn to the yard. He saw Clarissa pinning fresh-washed linen on the line and gave her a whistle. She smiled at the big Scot and pointed to the kitchen. Drummond found Lawrence with his shirt sleeves rolled high on muscular shoulders, his hands smoking with soapsuds.

"Whatever are you doing, Dicken? Where is Joanna?"

"What does it look like I'm doing?" snapped the innkeeper. "The breakfast things, self-evidently. The Bacons left this morning and with Joanna gone the chores have crept up on me. She left for Kecoughtan yesterday afternoon – didn't you know?"

"How should I know when I haven't seen you for several days? I thought we were going to dine together today and then leave for Bland's. Its past noon. Have you packed your valise?"

"All in good time. Let me finish the dishes and then Clarissa will find us something to eat. While she does so I'll pack. We'll be off within the hour. Are your boys ready with the sloop?"

"Of course. They can hardly wait. They have friends near Westover and are keen to visit them. Here, let me help you dry those things and then let's move along."

At dusk Drummond's sloop kissed the wharf at Westover and young William and John sprang onto the grassy bank with glee. They helped their father and the innkeeper over the side, fetched the luggage, and followed the older men up the path to the pleasant wooden plantation house which Councilor Theodorick Bland had built just before his untimely death three years ago, at the age of forty-two. Bland's widow had returned to England and his nephew Giles had come over to handle her affairs until the estate was settled. Shortly after his arrival the Governor had vested in Giles one of the honors his uncle had enjoyed: the position of Collector of Customs. The young man had seemed destined for success in the colony, but his fiery temperament had made him *persona non grata* with Green Spring and Sir William already regretted his generosity.

As Drummond beat on the door with Lawrence and the two boys behind him, the four heard the pounding of hooves and the scatter of gravel at one side of the house. A slim redhead with blazing blue eyes rounded the corner on a foaming mare and pulled up sharply. He flung himself from the saddle and threw his hands in the air.

"You won't believe it! He's done it again! Ludwell says he can't find all the documents he needs, and my aunt's affairs will have to be continued once again. And there's a rumor that he's going to England on the Arlington business, so how am I ever to settle my poor uncle's estate? I am beside myself."

Drummond seized the mare's reins and tried to calm the young man. "You've never come from Jamestown, Giles?"

"Where else? I rode there at dawn as I had word that Ludwell would be in town. He treated me like a dog, the son of a whore!"

"Why, my lad, I wish I had known! We've just arrived in my sloop – we could have brought you. I wish you had come by my house."

"Oh, it is all such a cuddy-cuddy, I wasn't thinking. Besides, I had the mare. Look at her, poor thing. I hope to God I have not ruined her. And I have done nothing to prepare for your visit! Have Byrd and Crewes arrived?"

"I haven't seen them. We just got here. Have you met my sons, William and John?"

The redhead glanced at the two boys. "Pleased to meet you, I'm sure. I say, would you do me a favor? Would you take Bella to the stables and see that the lad takes care of her? I will be wholly in your debt." He turned to Drummond and Lawrence. "What a way to greet my friends. Here, give me your bags. Let's go in and have something cool to drink. Byrd said he and Crewes would be here for supper and I haven't given the girls any orders yet."

Two hours later calm had settled over Westover. The Drummond boys had left to visit their friends; the Scot and the innkeeper had settled into a comfortable bedroom; and the two planters from Henrico County, William Byrd and James Crewes, had arrived and were unpacking their bags. The tantalizing odor of fricasseed chicken floated in the air and soon Giles Bland and his four guests were gathered in the dining room looking with interest at a sideboard spread with dishes, both warm and cold, and a formidable array of bottles. In the center of the great table was a huge watermelon carved in the shape of a boat and refilled with its own fruit, diced in neat squares, with the seeds removed. Around the boat other seasonal fruit had been placed in glorious profusion, and around the dessert medley silver candelabra blazed with myrtle candles. When all was ready Bland dismissed the servants and asked his guests to serve themselves. This was to be a business meeting, and idle ears were not wanted.

Thirty minutes later the five men pushed their chairs back from the table, sighing comfortably. Drummond pulled out his pipe and pouch and James Crewes followed suit. William Byrd rose and opened the casements which gave onto the lawn which stretched down to the river. Smiling, he said, "Your smoke will keep off the pests, so let's enjoy the evening air. I can't remember a finer day. 'Tis a pity to think what brings us together."

Giles Bland looked around his uncle's mahogany and determined that his guests' glasses were full. He raised his own goblet of golden sherry and proposed a toast. As he held his glass high the candlelight glinted from his right ring finger which was encircled with artfully braided gold. The metal flared in the light as the youth called out: "To the Ring!" Bland's four guests rose and drank deeply. The redhead spoke again. "Mister Drummond, will you take the chair, as usual?"

"Only if you call me Will, my lad."

"Very good, sir, but then what shall I call Mister Byrd?"

"Byrd," said the Henrico planter, tucking his honey curls behind his ears, his dark eyes gleaming with intelligence.

"Always a man of few words," laughed Lawrence. "Few words, but each of them worth its weight in gold."

"Why thank you, Dicken," said Byrd. "The Ring is a worthy cause and it deserves our best efforts." As he spoke he held his own right hand up to the light and dramatically twisted a gold circlet around his third finger.

Then James Crewes jumped to his feet and held his right hand high, his broad face flushed and his dark locks tumbled about in disorder. He pulled a twist of braided gold from his hand and held it close to a candle where it alternately flashed like fire and glowed like an ember. "Let's repeat the oath," he cried out, hoarsely.

Drummond sought to lower the temperature. He clapped his hand on Crewes' stout shoulder and eased the big man back into his seat. "We'll take the oath again when we leave, Jamie. Right now we have too much business to conduct. Dicken has drawn me up one of his famous lists and my life will not be worth living if I do not adhere to it."

"*Tout va*," muttered Crewes. "*Tout va.*"

Byrd frowned in annoyance. "Later, Jamie. The sooner we start, the sooner we'll finish. We have to leave by noon tomorrow. Go on, Will, call us to order."

The big Scot stood at the head of the table, drew Lawrence's list from his pocket and laid it in front of him. His voice was calm and clear. "This is the third meeting of the Upper James Chapter of the Ring, an association dedicated to the advancement of justice in the Virginia Colony. All members are present: Byrd for the falls of the river; Crewes for Turkey Island and its environs; and Bland for Charles City County. Do you gentlemen still have the confidence of your constituents?"

"We do," said Byrd, echoed by the two others. "We are empowered to act for our friends in Henrico and Charles City Counties, both on the north and the south banks."

"Very good. This meeting has been called to review and comment upon our proposed reform laws. It will be the third and, one hopes, the last reading. Earlier this year we met with the Northern Neck Chapter, the Middle Peninsula Chapter and the Lower James Chapter and the laws are final as to those bodies. Now is the time for you to approve or amend what has been written thus far. The three other chapters have given Dicken and me discretion to accept minor amendments without returning to them for further consultation. However, should you make major changes we will have to go through a fourth reading with the entire Ring. Please do not take that as a prohibition against substantive comments. Our laws have gestated for three years, and they may lie in the womb for a fourth before they see the light of day. If, however, you approve what has been written we shall be that much closer to our goal. I now call upon Richard Lawrence, our draftsman, to once again guide us through the laws."

Lawrence pushed his chair back and brought out a leather bound volume which he had been keeping beneath his chair. He placed it, unopened, before him. "These past three years have been busy, but productive. I am pleased with the result, but caution you that there is probably some language you will not like and some inclusions and omissions with which you will not agree. However, please bear in mind that I have been guided by two principles: first and foremost, the good of the colony, but second, and perhaps equally important, the reality of the political climate. As frustrating as it may be, our reforms must be incremental – we are not going to achieve everything we want at once."

The candlelight flashed on Bland's hair as the young man burst out. "I hope you have the one which makes the Secretary of State keep his house in order and fines the clerks if they can't get their business done? I've been trying to settle uncle's estate for more than three years! I never intended to stay here that long. I feel like I'm neither fish nor fowl, neither English nor Virginian. The situation is impossible!"

Drummond took control. If they let Bland rant they would never finish.

"Yes, Lawrence has written the law up nicely – he might be an attorney, he's so careful with words. But, begging your pardon, you mustn't interrupt or we shall never cover everything we need to discuss."

Bland gulped his sherry, but quieted down. Byrd's mellow voice was heard. "I wholly approve your approach, Will, but may I ask one question before we begin?"

"Of course."

"We've been working on this project, how long?"

"Why, three years, as you know."

"And each time we meet we discuss whether it is *these Burgesses* who are going to present the reform laws to the Grand Assembly."

"We have had that discussion more times than I can remember."

"Well, is it *this House* – the one that meets next month – that is going to propose our reforms to the Governor and Council? Or are we going to drag on for another year, and then another year, before we force Sir William and his coterie to acknowledge the miserable condition of the colony?"

"Hear, hear," shouted Bland.

Lawrence shoved the sherry decanter in his direction and spoke. "May I be heard?" He patted the leather volume. "As Will has explained, the gestation of our laws is almost complete and their birth is imminent. If you approve what lies in this book our first great task will be done. It will then be time to consider the transformation of the laws from idea to reality. Will and I have not been idle. We have employed, and are employing now, every means known to us to sound out the Burgesses and, yes, even some of the Councilors, about reform. It is premature to give you our report, but suffice it to say that it is clear to us that Berkeley's grasp is slipping from the reins of power. He has managed to avoid elections since he was reappointed Governor, but the Long Assembly of today is not the one he dominated in sixty-one. Many of the Burgesses may be the same, but they are not fools; their thinking has moved with the times. Moreover, there are many Councilors at whose opinions Sir William would be astonished. In my humble opinion should our laws be born this year they would enter the world untimely and would die a miserable death. But next year?...I will say no more, but I promise you that it will not be as long as you think."

Byrd stroked the soft golden hair on his upper lip. "Well, I'm disappointed, but how can I possibly argue with you? You and Will have been giants, heroes, in this enterprise. Surely you know best. It would be folly to come this far and then make a misstep. But I hope that we do not have to wait too long. Jamie and I have our fingers on the pulse of Henrico and, I tell you, it is a powder keg. Tobacco is so depressed that this latest proposed tax concerning the Arlington grant may be the final straw. I don't know how long the Upper James will wait for Green Spring to wake from its slumber."

"Aye, 'tis so," boomed James Crewes. He rose to his full six feet and lifted his glass, black hair streaming about his high-colored face. Black hair, black eyes, black mustachio and beard, black hair springing from the back of his hands. The man was a bear, a force of nature.

Drummond twisted his braided band and hurriedly picked up Lawrence's list. "Please gentlemen, to business. Dicken is going to read the laws one more time for your comments. Remember, if there are too many changes, we shall have to seek the approval of the other three chapters, and there will be more delay, something which you clearly wish to avoid. Dicken?"

Lawrence rose and opened the leather book. "Let's take the franchise first, as it is the keystone. Four years ago Berkeley stole the vote from all freemen and limited it to freeholders and housekeepers. It is intolerable that the people should not have a voice in their governance, as they did before. We now restore this fundamental right to all freemen. Are you in accord?"

Four voices cried "Yea!"

"Now for the sheriffs. We propose that they be limited to a one year term, as their abuses are notorious if left in office longer. As it stands now they are simply Berkeley's hounds, quartering the counties for levies, harassing the poor, threatening the needy. If they are ousted after one year the sunlight will be let in to one of Virginia's dark corners, to the advantage of all. Any comment?"

"Approved as written," the company cried out.

"Next we propose an end to the holding of multiple offices simultaneously. 'Tis another way the Governor has garnered support – he loads his favorites with honors and emoluments and thus binds them to him forever. Specifically, our law forbids one holding the office of sheriff, clerk of court, surveyor, or escheator from holding any additional such office concurrently. Any comments?"

The law was approved as written.

"Now Bland should like the next one. If you recall, we propose to assess fines against any government clerk or secretary who does not timely do his business, or who accepts extra fees for preferring the business of some over that of others. Here – look at my book for the exact language and for the amount of the fines. Do you like it?"

Bland laughed wildly. "Oh, 'tis fine. Had this law been in existence these past three years, I should be back in London now and my poor aunt would know whether she should buy silk or canvas for her drawers!"

Byrd spoke. "Have you included the requirement that the Secretary of State act more efficiently and not take illegal fees for issuing land patents?"

Lawrence looked over his shoulder and pointed in the book. "Yes, see there?"

"Ah – excellent. The Ludwell brothers have made a fortune from bribes and some men have been ruined, who have not been able to prove what land they owned. It is time to smoke the maggots out."

The hours passed. The hot food congealed and the cold food lay flaccid. The watermelon boat leaked a watery pink liquid onto the Bland mahogany. Candles guttered and the room became thick with blue tobacco smoke. White rings marred fine wood as bottles and decanters were emptied. As the hall clock tolled twelve, the five men closed Lawrence's book and sighed with relief. They had approved laws regulating the imposition of taxes by the county courts, which had no such authority; laws preventing sheriffs from abusing the colonists as they collected levies, a common practice; laws expediting probates and the issuance of letters of administration, so that the colonists would timely know the distribution of private wealth; and laws requiring the once-exempt Councilors to pay taxes, which seemed only just as those who sat on the Council of State had the greatest fortunes in Virginia. As issue after issue was taken up, discussed, and the proposed reform approved, the five men looked at one another, wondering how it was that their colony had fallen into such disarray and how it was that Sir William Berkeley had not been taken to task long ago.

At midnight Drummond gazed about him and laughed. "How we have fallen off! You four look as dissolute as a gang of highwaymen and I daresay I look like the ringleader. Well done, all, well done. The reform laws have now been approved by the entire Ring; it is cause for celebration. With this great task behind us Dicken and I will proceed to watch the September Assembly like hawks. It will be a rare Burgess who will not have dined at *The Unicorn* with us during the session. We will sing our siren song not only to our friends in the House but to some handpicked Councilors as well. After having taken the measure of this Assembly we shall follow up as we deem appropriate and consolidate our gains. Next spring, according to custom, we will bring our findings to the entire Ring, beginning with the Northern Neck Chapter and moving south, and learn your desires. By then we should have a good sense of who in the Assembly stands with us and who against us. If the climate is favorable and if it is the will of the Ring we shall play the midwife and attend the birth of our laws. Don't despair, my friends, the time for change is drawing nigh.

"In the meantime, you know how to reach Dicken and me whether we are at home or abroad. We are always glad to hear from you, but watch your step at all times. I hardly need to remind you that you remain under an oath of secrecy. Some might call our efforts treason and I, for one, should not like to meet my Maker before my time. Are there any questions? If not, I declare this meeting adjourned."

The five men rose and stretched. Drummond collected some bottles and placed them on the sideboard.

"How happy I am that we do not have to work tomorrow morning. Byrd, you and Jamie can catch the morning tide – you'll be home in no time. Dicken and I must wait for the ebb, so perhaps Giles can find something to amuse us until midday when my boys will have returned. Now, let us help our kind host clear his dining room and then find our beds."

"The oath!" cried Crewes. "Don't forget the oath."

The five men stopped what they were doing. Five hands, some slim, some broad; some soft, some calloused; some white, some weathered met across the table. Five gold rings glowed in the light of the last candles. Twenty-five grasping fingers intermingled like a coil of snakes. Five hands reached skyward.

"*Tout va*," growled Crewes. "*Tout va*," swore the Ring.

CHAPTER 11

SEPTEMBER 1674

Lady Frances Berkeley pushed her breakfast tray querulously to one side, slid from beneath the counterpane, threw on a wrapper and stepped into slippers of Spanish leather. The Governor had taken her by surprise last night: after supper he had asked her if he might share her bed, something which he had not done for several weeks. Unprepared, she had been unable to think of a convincing excuse to refuse him. The night had been a disaster for both of them. She had stayed up late, first working on her embroidery and then pleading that she needed to finish *The Practice of Piety*, which she had promised to return to Alice Page when they met in Jamestown for the September Assembly. But midnight came and Sir William was still awake, still waiting. They had gone upstairs together. How the servants had looked! She would have them flogged for their impudence. Servants should be no more responsive to their masters than chairs and tables – she would have to speak to her housekeeper about it. And after that? She could hardly bear to think about it. Without his wig, he looked a fool. And his breath was growing rank – there must be a bad tooth somewhere. Still, one could snuff the candles and let oneself respond to a practiced touch ... age did not matter so much in the dark. But in the past two years he seemed to have lost the finesse she had enjoyed for so long, ever since Sam had spent that dreary year in Carolina and she had been given the run of Green Spring. Yet she had been so needy that she had begun to respond! It had helped to think of Phil Ludwell ...once she did that she opened like a flower. And still the old fool had not been able to do a thing. After fumbling around he had muttered an apology and nodded off to sleep. He had not even had the courtesy to seek his own bed when it became clear that their love play was going nowhere. When he woke at dawn to use the chamber pot she had insisted that she be left alone, and he had shuffled off to his own suite, at the far eastern end of Green Spring house. She had managed to get back to sleep, but she woke in a bad humor and it did not help when the girl finally brought breakfast and her chocolate was tepid and her toast cold. As soon as she was dressed she would summon the housekeeper. A new and sterner regime was clearly needed.

Lady Frances sat at her dressing table and contemplated what she had to work with. Last year she had moved from Sir William's chambers and claimed this suite for her own. It lay at the western end of the house and it ran from front to back. Her sitting room faced south, so that she could keep an eye on the drive and see who was coming and going. Her dressing room formed a hyphen which connected the sitting room with the bedroom. And her refuge, her bedroom, lay in the northwest corner of the house. The northern exposure was somewhat gloomy in winter, but it was blessedly cool in summer. Moreover, as that corner of the house was carved from a high bank, her bedroom was really not on the second floor, but was almost at ground level. For that reason the builder had given the bedroom a little balcony and a neat staircase which descended to the grassy bank. Of all the rooms in the great house, only her bedroom had a private entrance. It was a feature she intended to take advantage of.

The glass gave back a reflection which caused the lines on Lady Frances' brow to deepen. She had celebrated her fortieth birthday this past spring, and she showed every year of it. She took an inventory, starting with her hair. It was mouse brown and straight, and had never been her best feature. Now there were clear strands of silver among the brown – it seemed unfair that she should be thus stricken, when Alice Page's black curls looked like they had on her wedding day and even the Ballard woman's light brown locks still gleamed with health. Well, she had an excellent lady's maid and a curling iron and coifs and caps could do wonders. What about her skin? This Virginia climate was killing. She had the sun to thank for those wrinkles which she could not smooth out and for that brownish color which looked so muddy in the wrong light. How wise she had been to cover the windows in pink silk and to repeat the motif in her candle sconces. If Phil ever set foot in her bedroom ... what was she thinking? Well, to be honest, she was thinking of Philip Ludwell lying in her bed, under her pink counterpane, with not a stitch on him. Philip, of the flowing chestnut hair, the sherry colored eyes, the legs turned as smooth as fine woodwork, the broad chest and the wicked laugh. She knew he wanted her. It had been months since his wife died, puny little thing. But he could not know how much she wanted him.

Lady Frances rose. My God, it had been a long time! She never thought that she and Billy would lose the trick of it. How ardent he had been, that summer of sixty-three when he had sent Sam to Carolina and she had played hostess for Green Spring. It had been hard to be discreet, and she supposed that some of their friends had guessed, but it was worth the risk. Oh, they had been a matched pair then. When Sam died in seventy and Billy had offered his hand she had not had to think twice. Virginia had buzzed when they married so soon, but it quickly wore off. And those first years were glorious. But time had taken its toll and now they had been brought to this pass. This thing with Phil... she would have to be very, very careful. After all, who knew better than Billy that she could put horns on a husband? But *she* was not seventy, she was in her prime, and she had no intention of giving up what she prized more than anything save wealth and rank.

Lady Frances returned to the mirror. She was not happy with her hair nor with her skin. What about her eyes? The lustrous brown orbs had been highly praised, but now they seemed to have sunk into their cavities and the skin around them looked dark. Well, a pencil could do wonders with eyes, what about her nose and lips? Ordinary, quite ordinary. But, again, a little paint would work its usual miracles. One had to admit the ravages of time and deal with them. In any event, her face had never been her fortune. It was time to reveal her true treasures.

Lady Frances slipped to the bedroom door and secured the lock and then moved into the sitting room and did the same. The curtains had not been opened and she left them so. Standing in front of the glass, she dropped her wrapper to the floor and slowly pulled her shift above her head, tossing it from her. She gazed in the glass, nude save for her slippers of red Spanish leather. There – those were her treasures, and they were still beautiful. Her perfect breasts sloped downward, dense with milky skin and blue veins, and then sprang up impudently, as if waiting to be grasped. She arched her back and watched the play of light on the splendid globes. She felt her nipples tighten and rise. Crossing her arms, she placed a hand on each proud projection. Her body stirred in response. Something like a blush crossed her face as she reached down between her legs and felt the heat. If only Phil Ludwell were here – but he was not, and Lady Frances chose not to wait for him.

The Governor paced the sitting room, gazing idly through the new casements which brightened the north-facing chamber and permitted a clear view of the terrace and the forest beyond. He noted that the tulip poplars were starting to turn and that even some of the oaks and maples had a bit of color to them. Well, no wonder, it was the first day of September. Indeed, he thought he had felt a touch of fall in the air when he had left his wife's bed early this morning. But then, perhaps it was just his imagination. It seemed that all of his senses were dulled now, on the cusp of his seventieth birthday, and he could not really rely on any of them. His memory was not what it used to be, either. The last three years in particular had taken their toll. His marriage to Fanny had given him a new lease on life, but that false spring had not lasted more than a year. Since then he had fallen off, there was no doubt about it, and the effort to deceive the world about his condition sometimes seemed more than he could bear. Thank God for Tom and

Phil Ludwell and old friends like Henry Chicheley and Nat Bacon. Without them he doubted that he could get through each day. And, above all, thank God for dear Fanny. It is true that she had been disappointed last night, but that was of no consequence. She was not a grasping, carnal woman like those harpies who surrounded the King. He and Fanny had had their moment in the sun in the sixties. Those had been heady days – perhaps his best. But now she herself was forty years of age and no longer needed a romp in the sheets to feel fulfilled. Being the second Lady Berkeley surely was sufficient for her; what else would any well-bred woman need? And how well she acquitted herself! Green Spring had never looked finer; his table was the best in the colony; and she kept herself (and him) looking their best.

Sir William strode to the looking glass and ran his hand over the deep red silk brocade of his matching coat and vest. The buttons were real gold, not cheap gilt things, and they glowed with the inner fire that only real metal had. He wore his finest wig as well – the one with the cascading white curls which seemed to give his face a little fullness and color and shave a few years off his three score and ten. The Governor turned from the glass and glanced at the fireplace which was centered on the north wall, graceful with scroll work of Purbeck marble. Above the mantel hung Lely's portrait, the one he had commissioned in sixty-one when he had spent that fruitless year in England. Lely had done him proud. His attitude was forceful and aristocratic, his left shoulder shrugged at the onlooker above the hilt of his ornamental sword and his right hand held his baton of office as the scene opened to the far distance, depicting an idealized Virginia. His face showed breeding in every aspect, from his broad forehead to the fine Berkeley nose to the firm lips. Yes, he had looked like that a dozen years ago and he did not look so different now.

The Governor straightened his shoulders and tucked in his stomach until the familiar pain in his abdomen returned and forced him to relax. A grim smile played over his pouched face and he seated himself wearily in one of Fanny's French chairs. They were so delicate that she did not care to have them used, but if you could not sit in a chair, what was the good of it? A clock struck ten. He hoped his wife would be down soon, as those relatives of Colonel Bacon were due at noon and he did not know what instructions had been given about dinner. What had Nat said about the young man? He was some kind of cousin, but Sir William could not recall the exact nature of the relationship. The youth was married – that much he remembered. And he was bringing a hanger-on, a poor relative or something of the kind. In any event, there were three of them and the Colonel had asked him to be particularly kind to them, as he hoped that they would stay and settle and swell the ranks of Green Spring. Well, that would be a wonder! Sir William could not recall an emigrant in the past ten years who came close to being a gentleman. They were all young and underbred and striving, like that puppy Giles Bland. Imagine, old Theodorick having a nephew like that! Well, it really was no surprise. The first King Charles had been a king indeed, gracious and impeccably mannered, poor martyr. But he had been brought down by the rabble like a noble hart seized by a pack of mongrels, and England had fallen off mightily since. The second King Charles surrounded himself with strivers and whores – who could expect gentlemen to grow up in such a depraved climate? Of course his brother John had done well enough. Fancy, Baron Stratton and now Lord Lieutenant of Ireland. But he was not one of the King's true intimates – there was some distance there. The Governor heard a light step on the staircase and Fanny appeared, like a vision, smiling. Clearly she had forgiven him last night.

Sir William rose and kissed his wife's hand. "My dear, you look splendid in that dull green – it seems shot with light. You are positively glowing."

Lady Frances stroked her husband's soft cheek. If this thing with Phil Ludwell was going to work, then she needed her husband to eat from her hand. He liked his women noble, well-bred and tigers in bed. If the tigers were no longer going to play a part in their menagerie, then she would have to work on her nobility and breeding. The breeding came with the Culpeper name. The nobility would come if he could ever get himself made a peer, like his brother. The tigers would wait for Phil.

"Billy, you are a picture. I had no idea you were going to wear the silk brocade – didn't you want to save it for the Grand Assembly?"

"Yes, but Nat Bacon has made a point of my helping his young cousin, and I thought it could do no harm to show him how the quality live here in Virginia."

"Why, you are kindness itself to do so much for the Bacons. I wonder if they would do as much for you? You look perturbed. If you are fretting about the menu, I settled it days ago. We'll dine early, at one o'clock, and that will give you all afternoon to talk to the young man. I'll entertain the wife; I do hope she is not a bore. The weather is fine and we can spend an hour or two in the garden, which will give us something to talk about even if she has an empty head. I am so glad they are returning to Jamestown this evening – we have had enough overnight guests this year." Lady Frances smiled her special smile. "Wouldn't it be nice to have a little time to ourselves for a change?"

The Governor kissed his wife's hand again. "Bless you for that thought, Fanny. I would love it. But don't you recall that Tom and Phil are coming for supper tonight? Regrettably Tom must return to Jamestown after our conference, but he said Phil could stay for a few days. I thought that you would like some company, someone to play cards with. Would you rather that he not stay?"

"Oh, I had forgotten about the Ludwells. No, no, don't change your plans. Phil is always able to entertain himself – they are like family. I suppose you want to give Tom his instructions about the King's grant to Arlington and my cousin Tom."

"Precisely. And I have a few words to say to Phil as well. I do appreciate your letting him stay; you have been an angel to him since his wife died. If Tom goes to London with Smith as I hope, I'll keep Phil so busy that he won't plague you, I promise."

Lady Frances played with her fan and pouted slightly. "Really Billy, it's alright. Whatever you want is fine with me. My, it is going to be a busy day – those Bacon people for dinner and the Ludwells for supper. I must see if everything is ready. When we've gotten rid of this crowd, perhaps we can have a bit of a rest before we go to Jamestown."

"I promise it, love," said Sir William Berkeley as he watched his wife sail from the room. She always did him credit. It was a good marriage; he felt sure that she would not regret it if their next years were more sedate than those which had preceded them.

On the last day of August Nat and Lyn and John said goodbye to Colonel Bacon and his wife and arrived at *The Unicorn* in time for supper. Although the Colonel had pressed them to accept the Governor's invitation to stay for several days at Green Spring they had heard enough about the old man to think it more prudent to limit their first contact to a few hours. Moreover, Nat and Lyn were wild to get to Curles Neck and claim it for their own. At this point Green Spring represented a necessary, but unwanted, diversion. Still, it was critical to make a good impression on Sir William and his lady and all three vowed to be on their best behavior when they dined with them the next day.

When they got to Jamestown they were somewhat surprised to find that Joanna Lawrence was away and that Dicken and Will Drummond had just returned from some kind of outing upriver. They were greeted with enthusiasm and given their old rooms, despite Lyn's plea that Clarissa not be turned out of her bedchamber. Lawrence assured her that the African had a comfortable corner upstairs, and Lyn had no recourse but to claim the little room again, which she did happily.

Will Drummond and his two boys joined Nat's party and the innkeeper for supper, and the seven of them made merry until late in the evening. No one said it, but all felt the more comfortable for Joanna's absence. The Drummond boys chattered on about the horses which Colonel Bacon had sold his cousin: Lyn was now the owner of the dappled mare and John of the chestnut. When they asked Nat why he was without a mount he told them about Ballard's black stallion at Curles and the boys grew so excited that before he knew it he had invited them to visit. Drummond smiled and tried to restrain his sons, but in fact their presence turned out to be a boon. It was arranged that on the day following the Green Spring dinner the boys would ride the gray and the chestnut to Curles, while Nat and Lyn and John sailed to their new home in Ballard's sloop. Ballard kept the boat permanently at Jamestown and he had pressed them for days to accept its use, together with that of his crew, who, according to him, were underbred and under worked dogs. Curles Neck was most comely when approached from the river and both Nat and John envisioned Lyn's face as she rounded the great loop in the James and first viewed the promontory which marked her new home. When the sailing party and the riding party converged at the plantation, Billy and John Drummond and Ballard's crew would spend the night at Curles and sail back to Jamestown together the next morning, leaving the Bacons and John Grey and their horses at the plantation.Nat and Lyn smiled happily as these plans unfolded, feeling that Lawrence and Drummond had already become old friends. As the evening came to an end the Scot simplified their lives even further. When he heard that they were planning to ride to Green Spring he laughed and claimed that they would be forever in Sir William's black book if they did so: to the Governor, a lady who rode in anything other than a carriage was no lady. It was not the way to introduce themselves to the colony's elite. Drummond insisted that Billy drive Lyn in his little gig; Nat and John could follow on the gray and the chestnut.

Lawrence looked oddly at his friend as the Scot smoothed the newcomers' way to Green Spring but he soon put his thoughts aside. Drummond was such a fair man that he probably wanted young Bacon to assess the Governor starting with a clean slate. It would do no harm. The innkeeper knew that the new owners of Curles Neck would come to the Ring in time; what thinking man could not?

And so it was that just before noon on a glorious first of September the Drummond gig rolled up the smooth gravel drive of Green Spring, with Lyn, in pale blue, seated in state behind Billy and with Nat and John, handsomely mounted in their best finery, riding attendance behind her. The little gig stopped with a flourish and Lyn gazed at the great house which she had heard so much about. She was disappointed. Green Spring had none of King Creek's homely charm nor was it neat as a pin, like Sarah Drummond's Jamestown home. The stolid building rose two stories, its cedar shingled roof pierced with multiple dormer windows. Its brickwork was somewhat clumsy and the courses looked as though they had been laid haphazardly at various times. The house was higher in the front than in the back, as its site was carved out of a gentle slope, and the bottommost tier was a galleried arcade, which gave the manse a marketplace look. Nonetheless, Green Spring was far and away the largest and most imposing building which she had seen in Virginia and she supposed it befitted the colony's first family. Before she had time for further scrutiny a large black man in brilliant green silk descended the staircase and handed her out of the gig. Two black boys appeared as from nowhere and took the horses, indicating to Billy that he should follow them. Nat and John joined Lyn on the steps and the three followed the butler up the steps and into Green Spring's hall.

The hall opened directly onto a large room in which Nat and Lyn and John saw two figures standing: a tall man in deep red with a fussy face almost lost in his pure white wig and a plain looking woman with a muddy complexion whose gown of sage green was cut low to reveal a formidable bosom. In pride of place above the mantel was hung a formulaic adulatory portrait. Nat had seen a dozen such in London: Lely cranked them out upon demand. The bodies all looked the same; he, or his students, simply changed the heads, called the thing a masterpiece, and raked in the guineas. In this case, however, the artist had caught the imperious look and the vanity of the sitter: the man in red and the man in the portrait were one and the same, and they both looked as though their opinions of their own worth were not subject to examination.

Appropriate greetings were exchanged as green-clad footmen appeared and handed sherry and savories around. After some vacuous conversation about their crossing, Virginia's summer climate and the state of health of Colonel Bacon and his wife, the party moved to the dining room, Nat going first with Lady Berkeley, followed by Lyn whose hand rested on Sir William's arm, with John bringing up the rear, trying to keep his countenance respectful. It did not take a genius to see that Green Spring pathetically mocked Charles' elegant court. In truth, despite the mansion's vaunted reputation, it was hopelessly provincial. John could not wait to reach the solitude of Curles Neck which promised a hard life, but an honest one. He moderated his thoughts. He was the one who had insisted on the importance of this audience; he must be a good scholar to his own teaching and walk carefully for the next few hours. Tomorrow they could put Green Spring behind them and sail west to create their own life.

Two hours later Lyn walked out with Lady Frances to view the gardens and, doubtless, to hear the Culpeper pedigree. The Governor escorted Nat and John upstairs to his private office, which formed the southern-most room of his eastern bedroom suite. It was a handsome chamber, done in tobacco brown and gold, and containing a surprisingly large library which John would have liked to peruse. The three men made themselves comfortable on a settee and matching chairs which were placed to permit a view to the south, or front of the house. Just before they seated themselves they saw Lyn's neat little figure next to Lady France's taller form, wandering through the simulacrum of a formal garden.

Sir William smiled and turned to Nat. "We are blessed in our wives, are we not?" he asked.

Nat was startled. His impression of Lady Frances was one of overweening vanity and excessive temper. Who could possibly be blessed in her? He answered without thinking. "Indeed sir, what would we do without the ladies?"

Clearly the Governor approved the stock answer. The old knight chuckled, seated himself and lit a pipe, offering the same to Nat and John, both of whom graciously refused. "So, my young friend, you have purchased Longfields – a wise choice. Tom Ballard never could pass up a bargain, but we all knew he was overreaching when he bought the place. It is far from Jamestown, but a handsome plantation. You will do well. Will Grey here be your overseer?"

Nat and John exchanged glances. Had the Governor not been paying attention through that tedious two hour dinner? Nat and Lyn's ancestry and John Grey's status had been chewed and mumbled like so many bones. Had Sir William already forgotten that John was an attorney? Did he think him a mere farmer? Still, they had vowed to tread carefully, so the answer must be politic.

"Why, no sir. John has kindly consented to help me establish myself here and then he will look about him to see whether he wishes to stay or return to England. Though we both come from Suffolk, neither one of us would claim much expertise in farming. Once we settle at Curles Neck I shall look to hire those who know how to grow and sell tobacco. As winter is not far off, we plan to spend these next months improving our dwelling and then, in the spring, we shall see if we can make our mark as planters. Doubtless we shall draw upon your rich experience, should you be willing to guide me, along with my cousin."

Nat had struck the right tone and the Governor was pleased. "I should be delighted to help, my boy. Any time, any time. Over the next weeks few weeks I will have my hands full with the Grand Assembly, but after that you are welcome to visit whenever you are in these parts. We have an hour or so now – do you have any questions which the Colonel has not answered?"

It was the signal Nat and John had been waiting for: now they could ask the Indian question. It had better come from Nat; John had effectively been dismissed from the Governor's universe.

"Why, if you please sir, my cousin said that I should ask you about the savages, as Curles Neck lies not far from the frontier."

Sir William smiled broadly. "You have nothing to worry about, my boy. The savages have long since been brought to heel. They have not plagued us since forty-four when old Opechancanough rose up again. I led the militia against him and quelled the riot and he died soon after, a complete failure. Since then the colony has raised forts to keep out those tribes which lie beyond the fall line, and has tamed those savages who live this side of it. Why, my darling Indians honor King Charles – they bring me twenty beaver skins each year to show their allegiance. We have been generous in giving them certain lands above the York and below the James and they live there happily, safer, no doubt, than when they did not have Christians to look after them."

Based on what he had read about Virginia's history, John thought the Governor's statement somewhat too good to be true and he ventured a question, hoping that he would not offend the old knight.

"You must forgive my ignorance, sir. Could you explain a little bit more about the fall line and the forts?"

Sir William looked at Nat rather than at John, but he answered the question. "I suppose you know our rivers? Look, 'tis simple. Put out your left hand." Nat and John did so. "Your thumbs stick up straight, do they not?" The friends agreed. "Well, call that the Potomac, the great river which forms our northern border. Now go to the next finger – what river is that?"

"Why, that should be the Rappahannock," said John.

"Very good, young man. And what is the next?"

"I see your scheme. Well, next is the York and then, of course, the James. But what do our little fingers represent?"

"That is the Appomatox – you'll know it well once you move to Longfields, for your plantation lies just beyond where it empties into the James from the southern reaches of the colony."

"'Tis a clever device," cried Nat. "Now I shall never forget my geography."

"I am glad you like it – I have used it many times to explain the colony to newcomers. Well, to return to the fall line. Put your hands out again." Nat and John complied. "There, where your knuckles are, half-way up your fingers – that is the fall line. That is where the rivers narrow and our ships can go no farther. 'Tis perilous to live beyond that line, and few do so. But this side of it – that is where the great plantations lie and the ships ply their trade. That is where civilization flourishes. That is where you are as safe as if you were home in Suffolk."

"Do the savages stay on the far side of the fall line?" asked Nat.

"Oh no, my boy. My darling Indians, such as the Pamunkeys, live this side of it. You must understand that they are our friends. They know and respect us and we know them and keep them on a short lead. Now, there are savages beyond the fall line, please do not misunderstand me. But they are of another kind altogether, speak a different tongue, and have different ways. They come and go in their skulking manner, but rarely do they venture near us. You will not be bothered by them at Curles Neck – only men like Wood and Byrd venture into their territory and they know what they are doing." The Governor turned to John. "Does that answer your question, Mister Grey?"

"Indeed, sir, it is a marvelous explication. And the forts? Do all the rivers have forts on their upper reaches?"

The Governor looked querulous. "Well, enough, young man. Well enough. The Assembly voted to set them up and I have not heard any complaints." He frowned and turned again to Nat. "Now then, do you have any further questions?"

It was clear that the subject of Indians – and Sir William with it – had been exhausted. The friends decided to lay the ground for their departure.

Nat spoke with honey in his voice. "With my cousin's help and your gracious hospitality I feel singularly well-informed. With your permission we shall take our leave and make our way back to Jamestown. We are going to sail to Curles Neck tomorrow. I am sure that when I next see you I shall draw upon your wisdom again."

Years of high breeding could not keep the signs of relief from Sir William's face. He extinguished his pipe, rose and escorted his guests downstairs to find that Lady Frances and Lyn had returned from their garden tour and were seated in the great parlor over cups of tea. Nat and John could see that Lyn was exhausted from her audience with Virginia's first lady. The nervous tension was almost palpable and five people sighed with relief when Billy appeared in the front drive with the gig, the gray mare and the chestnut tied behind. The pleasure of parting lent the words of farewell a certain authenticity and by five o'clock Green Spring lay in peace as Nat and Lyn and John disappeared into the green arch of the forest, on their way home.

Sir William massaged his stomach as the familiar dyspepsia rose up to plague him once again and Lady Frances dropped back into her chair, fanned herself and burst out laughing.

"Have you ever seen such a thing? What bumpkins. Who would believe that the girl's sister is married to a Wyatt? She is underbred and overly pert. And what a sense of fashion – she must have invented that frock, for it is in no mode known to me!"

The Governor was somewhat surprised at his wife's reaction. Grey was a nonentity, but young Bacon was attractive and sprightly. True, his family had followed the Puritan cause, but the youth looked the perfect cavalier and was a promising candidate for Green Spring. The Colonel had asked Sir William to look on the boy with favor and he intended to do so. As for the little wife, she was charming – dewy, fresh, and quite womanly. Should he defend her to Fanny? Sir William sighed. On another day he might have taken up Lyn's cause, but Tom and Phil Ludwell were due this evening and he simply did not have the energy. He turned to his wife, thanked her for the fine dinner, kissed her hand and retired to rest until the Secretary of State and his Deputy arrived. They would have to wrestle with the matter of the King's improvident grant to Arlington and to Fanny's cousin, Tom Culpeper, tonight, and he would need all his energy.

Lady Frances watched her husband retreat into the hall and heard his weary steps as he mounted the staircase. She herself would rest now as well. Phil Ludwell was going to spend the night at Green Spring and, if she had anything to say about it, he would not be staying in the blue room. She thought of her pink bedchamber: a most becoming color to one whose complexion was less than fresh and dewy. She smiled and went upstairs.

The Ludwells pushed back their chairs and stood as Sir William touched his lips with his linen napkin and signaled that supper was at an end. Lady Frances had already left to prepare the tea table and make sure that cards were available in the little parlor. The Governor always felt better with Tom Ludwell about – so reliable! – and Phil, the fiery cavalier, was quieting down too, as he approached his fortieth year. Both of the boys were like sons to him – like family. He felt much better than he had this afternoon when he had worked so hard to make a good impression on Bacon and his wife. Strange that he had done so, but then Colonel Bacon was a good friend and it had been his duty to help his kin. Why the Colonel had even indicated that if thing worked out he might make the young squire his heir! Odd that both he and Natty had each had two wives and yet neither one of them had children. It was one bond, among many, that bound Green Spring to King's Creek. Now Phil was going to entertain Fanny and he and Tom could decide what taxes to wrest from the Grand Assembly to pay for the necessary agents to plead Virginia's cause concerning the King's latest improvident land grant. Sir William pulled himself up short. He should not allow himself to think that way. Charles Stuart was his master and could order his dominion as he saw fit. That he saw Virginia as an unending source of revenue to placate his favorites was simply a fact of life. A Royal Governor should be prepared to take the bad with the good, or relinquish his office. And he had better not permit himself to think about *that* – the temptation to lay down his burden was growing on him daily, but if he ever mentioned the scheme to Fanny all hell would break loose. The Governor shook himself and he and Thomas Ludwell went upstairs to his private office.

"Tom, thank you for coming on such short notice. Do you insist on returning to Jamestown tonight?"

"I fear that I must, as my day starts at eight o'clock tomorrow morning. I brought two men with me and they will see me safely home, even in the dark. Now, shall we finish this business? It should not take us long. After all, if the people want to send agents to petition the King, they must pay for it."

"Well, of course, but the whole thing is galling, you must admit. I tell you, I fear to impose yet one more tax, given the current price of tobacco. I should not be surprised if it had not fallen below a penny a pound."

"I fear you are correct, but what can we do? The King has curtailed our markets and the people plant too much. The wise ones will stint for a season or two, but it is too much to ask of the small farmers. How else can Smith and I afford our passage to London and how else can the two of us and Francis Moryson afford to live there as gentlemen without a special tax? You know that we will work our finger to the bones for the colony."

"I *do* know that Tom, and so does every other Virginian. It has been a year now since the King granted Virginia to the two Lords Proprietors for thirty-one years and although neither has taken any action, who knows what they may choose to do in the future?"

"You know they only want the quitrents and the escheats – they will never dispossess us."

"You and I know that, but tell it to the men who have staked their all on Virginia land patents. I should guard my tongue, but this folly of the King's is beyond belief."

"Well, the three of us have a fair chance of straightening it out, but Smith and I must sail as soon as possible and we cannot sail if we do not have passage money. Moreover when we join Francis we must all live as gentlemen or we shall be shown the door at Whitehall. I have worked with the figures, as you requested, and here is what I propose: a further poll tax of fifty pounds of tobacco on all tithables, and a further tax on all lawsuits, depending on their gravity. The most weighty actions will be taxed seventy pounds of tobacco; the middle range fifty pounds; and the lesser causes thirty pounds."

"I like the plan. Perhaps we shall see this growing trend to litigate all arguments dampened if we make it more costly to go to court. What is the temper of the Burgesses who must, after, all propose the tax?"

"Well, of course I have talked to all who count themselves our friends and they think it will pass. The people really have no choice – they can either accept Lords Arlington and Culpeper as their Lords Proprietor or they can tax themselves and bring back the *status quo ante.*"

Sir William sighed. "'Tis a wicked world, Tom. Well, push it through. You and Smith must sail with the tobacco fleet. Will you stay with Francis?"

"If he has room for us. From what I have heard he has a handsome town house. We shall see when we get there. We must at least make a show of saving the people as much money as possible."

"Very good. The Assembly will meet on the twenty-first and Fanny and I will arrive the day before. I should like a respite from business until then; I count on you to act for me."

"You have my word on it. Phil and I will both be at Jamestown through the session and until I take ship."

"He's going to stay here for a few days, do you mind?"

"Not at all. He misses Lucy dreadfully and is poor company at Rich Neck. Please thank Lady Frances again for her kindness to him during this difficult time."

"I shall do so. I am sorry you must rush off. You are a good friend to me, Tom. You know that I depend on you."

A smile crossed the Secretary's worn face and he waved goodbye as he strode from the room, rushed downstairs and collected his hat and cloak and sword from the green-clad butler. He supposed Phil and Lady Frances were still playing cards. His brother was never happy unless there was a woman about, but as for him, it was business which kept him going. Even this sorry Arlington matter had a certain interest to it – he did not doubt that he and Moryson and Smith could bring it right. As he thundered down the drive followed by his two torch-bearing retainers, a pink curtain was drawn aside in Lady Frances' sitting room. The Governor's wife and Phil Ludwell peered out into the dark, then looked at one another and closed the curtain. There was not a star in the sky. It was going to be a long, dark night when one would want comfort in bed.

Chapter 12

September 1674 ~ January 1675

Salt water clashed with fresh as the flood tide met the rushing stream from the headwaters of the James and Lyn reached for the rail as the sloop danced on the wavelets like a high-bred horse. A brisk sea breeze dispatched the heat and the day quickened with a touch of fall. The four lithe black boys who made up the crew whistled at the wind and smiled broadly as the sails bellied taut and true and the little vessel surged forward. With the favorable wind and tide, the crew promised, they would reach Curles Neck well before dark. Among themselves the boys spoke with a soft, lilting tongue wholly foreign to Lyn. John told her that Ballard had bought the sloop's crew right off a Dutch slaver and that they were from a seagoing tribe somewhere on Africa's west coast. When the planter had learned that the young men were trained for the sea he had asked no further questions and snapped them up like so many fresh mackerel. John's face had showed his distress as he told Lyn what he knew of the black boys and she looked at the crew with compassion. If she felt apprehensive about settling at Curles Neck, what must they feel, snatched from their homes and bought and sold like chattel? John told her that Virginia law had permitted slavery for over a decade and that the issue had been a divisive one for the Assembly, but that lucre beat down conscience as it often did. She and Nat had never discussed the matter, but they had purchased two score slaves when they bought Curles Neck. Lyn glanced at the four slim backs, glossy as ebony. The boys were as beautifully made as chessmen. What must they be thinking? When she and Nat were settled they must decide how they would deal with the moral issue of owning human flesh. Like Circe, comely Virginia enticed strangers to her shores and then put them to strange tests. Lyn vowed to resist seduction: the dark goddess would not corrupt her; she would free herself from the taint of slave-owning at the earliest opportunity.

The black boys burst into song as the last clouds parted and the sun shone high and fine above the river. Dense verdure clothed the banks and slender willows kissed the water, their feet clad with silvery reeds. Behind the water-seeking trees clustered thirsty maples, already touched with scarlet and gold, and behind them stood row upon row of noble oaks and hickory and chestnut and the slim gray-clad tulip poplars which Nat loved for their grace. Far above an arrowhead of geese cleaved the sky, flying south: fall was upon them and winter would not be far behind. Lyn looked upriver and was suddenly pierced with a deep happiness which came from nowhere, like a dart from Eros. The day spread about her, an endless tapestry of green and gold and scarlet and silver. The world stood still and she was the center of the universe, all living things revolving around her, fueled by the beating of her heart. She was breathless, just as she had been on that far-off day in Suffolk when she and Nat had stood on a sea-path of liquid gold and vowed never to part. She turned and looked at her husband. He was standing by the mast gazing at her. Their glances arced across space and fused. They smiled. They were on their way home.

The magic faded but the day remained clothed in grace. The boys laughed and sang in their melodious tongue as they struggled to man the sloop with the young Squire standing always where he should not be. Lyn looked about for John and saw him at the stern, his back to them. His hands were clenched on the rail and he looked like he was in pain. Nat went to him, sliding precariously as the sloop tacked.

"Come John, let's eat. I have never seen a more splendid day and miraculously my appetite has not yet vanished as it usually does the moment I set foot on anything which floats. Clarissa put enough in those hampers to last us for a week. We'll dine and give the rest to the crew. I love them for their gaiety, poor fellows. Aren't those the boys that Ballard bought like cattle? Whatever their plight, they seem to be making the best of it. Lyn – come to the back here where we are not in the way. We're going to dine."

Nothing could diminish the beauty of the day. The sloop followed the sun and the river was molten gold. From time to time the verdant banks gave way to fields and farms and Nat and Lyn and John spied wharves both on the right and left banks, but they met no one. That day Virginia was theirs. Late in the afternoon they rounded a great bend in the river and the black boys broke out in laughter, pointing urgently to the left, or northern, bank. They had come to a low-lying area shrouded with reeds and rich with duck and teal. Beyond the marsh the land rose slightly and then seemed to dip again. Where the greensward rose highest Lyn saw a flock of great black birds, their feathers tinted with white and gray, their heads flashing with blue like Indian roanoke. Suddenly one of the great fowls spread its tail like a god's fan and bowed low to the lady it was courting. A cowl of red tumbled down its chest and blazed in the setting sun.

As the birds danced, the sloop passed by and Nat and Lyn and John stood breathless in the waist.

"'Tis a noble sight," cried John. "What birds are those?"

The black boys had heard the question. "Tur-kee, tur-kee," they cried, gesticulating and rubbing their stomachs.

"Why they are never turkeys?" said John. "Those great things? Is that what the Colonel served us for our last dinner? If I had known, I never would have touched my plate. They are too splendid to consume."

Nat laughed and Lyn had to join him. The attorney had dined well on their last night at King's Creek and now his face was a study. John joined the laughter and in the low comedy of the moment the three friends regained the normal equilibrium of their relationship. The crew made shooting motions, holding imaginary fusils to their shoulders and popping their mouths to mimic gunfire. Nat laughed again and explained that his weapons were stored below and that the turkeys would have to remain unmolested for the present, but he pulled out an apple tart and a jug of cider from Clarissa's hamper and the crew happily picnicked as the sloop tacked gently on the last leg of the journey.

Curles Neck bluff rose on the right as the sun slipped behind the western mountains. The river was as calm as glass, as if to ease the strangers' way home. The sky was a bowl of blue and mauve and violet set against a backdrop of bronze. As the sloop touched the wharf the only sounds in the whole world were the slap of the river against its prow and the call of a nightjar.

Lyn looked at Nat with pleasure. "'Tis the poorwill. Remember?"

"How could I forget?" asked her husband and reached for her hand.

"It is a mournful sound," said John, whose back was to his friends as he helped the crew slide the gangplank over the side. "I prefer the lark."

"Of course you do, John. You are a creature of the day, not the night," Lyn said, smiling.

John looked quizzically over his shoulder at the girl and held out his hand to help her disembark. Nat took her other hand and Lyn set foot on her own land, her husband on the left and her friend on the right.

Before her rose the dark face of Curles' Neck bluff, scarred with the great diagonal cut of the path which would take her to her new home. Nat urged her to go ahead, so that she would be the first to see the plantation house, while he and John walked behind her, side by side. The day was fading fast, but there was still enough light to see, and it was not long before the three stood on the top of the bluff. The house and outbuildings glowed with welcoming candlelight but before going indoors Lyn turned toward the river. The sloop bobbed like a toy, some fifty feet below them. The crew had finished unloading their goods and two of the boys had begun to climb the path to the house. Beyond them the James made its stately way to the sea, neither sullen nor fractious, but showing its gracious face. Beyond the river the south bank stretched dark and mysterious, disappearing into the shadows. The east lay shrouded in purple and only a touch of gold quickened the west. Curles Neck was silent, waiting to be possessed. As the three friends turned towards the house the air was rent by the shrill cry of a stallion. Lyn shivered involuntarily and Nat put his arm around her shoulders.

"'Tis only the black horse. I must find him a name."

Together the two men and the woman stepped through the door of their new home where a fire blazed and supper scented the air. Their journey had ended...and begun.

Lyn's *mind* could recall the assault of the heat and the damp on the August day they arrived at Jamestown, but her *body* could not. She huddled near the fire and wondered how it was that the winter wind could find her despite the rough plaster on the walls and the hangings she had placed everywhere. She shuffled her slippers in the aromatic reeds at her feet and piled the grasses higher so that her feet would not touch the floor, but her toes still cramped with cold. She pulled her shawl closer and smiled. It did not matter. Nothing mattered. This was Christmas morning and it was also the first day that she had not been able to fasten her skirt.

Today the baby had decided to show itself to the world, if only as a bump on her abdomen. She had known, of course, last October, but she had told only Nat until she was as sure as she could be that things were going well. In November they had informed John and he had smiled and said he knew. Nat laughed and called him a liar but Lyn believed him. She knew that John watched her every move; he could not help himself. And last month he had moved away, taking possession of the little farm at the falls which they called Bacon's Quarter. He said that he would only stay to supervise the building of the cabins and to clear the land for planting and that when Nat was suited with an overseer he would return to Curles, but Lyn wondered. Bacon's Quarter. It was beautifully situated, overlooking the falls. Nat and John had high hopes for the place, with its virgin soil and rich natural grass. They had already moved a small herd of cattle to the Quarter and both men had helped the hands put up the sturdy log cabin where John stayed. Lyn knew in her heart that he would be better there, by himself, than he would be at Curles Neck but she missed him sorely. The sad truth was that as Nat and Lyn flourished, John diminished; as they waxed, he waned. She wrung her chill hands. How unkind of fate to have spun the triangle which united them. Each loved the other two, but only Nat and she could perfect their love, so John stood the loser. Lyn wondered how long he would stay in Virginia; perhaps he was secretly thinking of returning home. But at least they had his promise to remain through the first spring to see the tobacco blossom and the baby arrive. Lyn shivered.

Like the other creatures of God, when the spring came she would be a mother. It was a great blessing.

She felt Nat's hand on her shoulder and she looked up and smiled. So far he had seemed content at Curles Neck. In truth he had been so busy, laying out Bacon's Quarter, supervising the germination of the tobacco seedlings, making drawings for the new house and taming that great black horse that he had not had time for boredom. Yet...she remembered Suffolk. All had been well until they had completed Hazelwood and life had become routine. Then he had started chafing at the bit and things had gone from bad to worse. Well, she had learned a lesson. She would have to help him keep occupied. Surely running a large plantation and fatherhood would fill his plate! If not, she would find things to wile away his hours. Their experience in Suffolk was not going to repeat itself.

"Have you had a ride, love?" Lyn asked.

"Yes, the brute is shaping nicely, but I still cannot find the right name for him. He's a devil, but there is an angel inside, I know."

"I insist on 'Folly' – that is what the beast is."

Nat laughed. "You may be right. I have begun to call him so, and the name may stick. The sun's out and the snow has almost melted. Come out to the barn later and take a look at him – I swear he is becoming docile."

"Well, you tamed Prince Rupert, so I don't doubt that you can master Folly."

"You are an angel to say so. Now, how is the young squire, or lady as the case may be?"

"Very well indeed, although my skirts no longer fit. I shall have to rummage through my trunks and find that kersey which Bess gave us to make winter clothes. I don't know what I'll do when it turns hot again. May I have Hannah to help me run up some frocks?"

"Of course. You know she is yours. When the new house is built I intend that she and Abraham do nothing but indoor work."

"And then we will revisit the issue of their freedom?"

"I have promised it. Don't look at me like that! They are the ones who wanted to wait a year before discussing it. There are two sides to the coin, after all. Free or bound, one has to eat and sleep. They are wise to take their time."

"Well, we have agreed to wait until the brick house is finished, but I will not let you forget it."

"You won't have to remind me. I take no pleasure in owning my fellow man, but we must have a plan which permits both us and them to survive."

"I know it, Nat," said Lyn softly. "I am talking to myself, not you."

"Now then, how is dinner coming?"

"Very well. I have built it around a saddle of beef which I shall cover in a crust. We have Mister Drummond's great sturgeon for a first course and both chicken and turkey for fowl. Hannah is making bread now and there is milk and butter and cream aplenty. The potatoes are tasty but I shall have to cream the carrots and turnips as they are past their prime. Hannah and I made the pies yesterday, and there are more than enough. Did you bring me the walnuts and hazelnuts as you promised?"

Nat slapped his thigh and looked truly contrite. "I confess I forgot. I'll ask Abraham if there are any in the storehouse. If not, I hope that we can do without."

"Well, what about the wine?"

"Lawrence sent us a dozen of Portuguese red and a dozen of white Bordeaux. More than enough."

"What am I forgetting?"

"It is only you and me and John and the Byrds and Mister Crewes – that's six, isn't it?"

"Well, there's the baby."

"Our baby?"

Lyn laughed. "Don't you remember that Mary Byrd asked if she could bring little William?"

"Why, how old is the child? Is he going to eat like a man?"

"Don't be a fool, Nat. He has not even reached his first year. Don't you remember him from church?"

"Oh, we saw him at Varina? Well, they all look the same to me."

"I hope you do not say that next spring."

"Ah...ours will be special."

"You had better say so."

"Now then, love, time marches on. Are you going to warm your feet all day? Come outside and get some fresh air."

"I shall come and see Folly and then change to my good clothes and lay the table. When do you expect John?"

"Byrd said that he would fetch him in his sloop, as they live just across the river from one another. Its ten o'clock now and they should be here by noon. Jamie Crewes is riding from Turkey Island. Let's step outdoors and then I will help you put the house to rights and we can have our Christmas."

The sun had set and Nat built up the fire until it roared. The branches crackled and spat and the spicy scent of cedar filled the room. Lyn lay back in her chair and stroked the rich beaver cloak which lay on her shoulders. She had never felt anything so dense and silky. She had been overwhelmed when Mary Byrd presented it to her, wrapped in paper which the young woman had decorated herself with clever drawings of Christmas holly. The gift was truly fit for a king, and she had been speechless until William Byrd smoothed the moment over and explained that he was deeply involved in the Indian trade and that these two pelts had been a gift to him from an Occaneechee werowance who owed him a favor. The others had exchanged mere tokens and Lyn still felt somewhat abashed at such luxury, but she coveted the warmth of the skins.

The dinner had gone splendidly. Each dish had been a success, and the profusion of food had been almost laughable. When the party pushed back from the table she sent the remnants with Abraham and Hannah for the servants and slaves to enjoy, and now she sat before the fire to sip Lawrence's wine and dip into the sack of nuts which John had providently brought from Bacon's Quarter. She was glad her guests had agreed to spend the night. Mister Crewes would doss down with John in the cabin the latter used when he was at Curles Neck, and the Byrds would share the loft with Nat and Lyn. It would do Nat good to spend time with a baby.

Earlier in the afternoon she had showed her guests their accommodations and had apologized for the little wooden house which was hardly big enough for two and which let in the draughts so dreadfully. She explained that right after Christmas the earthmaker and his men would arrive to dig their clay pit and begin the arduous task of making bricks and roof tiles. If all went well they should have a fine new house like Mister Allen's or Mister Page's by next Christmas and it would be situated right on the bluff to take advantage of the view. Mary Byrd had laughed and told her that she must visit their trading post one day, for it made the wooden house at Curles Neck look like a palace. Even the taciturn Mister Crewes had claimed that his own house at Turkey Island was nothing but a clapboard shack and that she would find nothing else "on the frontier." Lyn was comforted by her guests' lack of pretension and desire to make her feel at home. They seemed honest and forthright – there was none of the Green Spring gloss and glitter. She could not warm to James Crewes: such a man's man, a rough warrior. Doubtless he had a warm heart, but he did not have the means to show it. But she had been attracted to William and Mary Byrd ever since meeting them at church in Varina. Mary was a cheerful soul and had been a blessing ever since she learned that Lyn was pregnant. The Byrds, the Cockes, little Isham – they had opened their arms to the Bacons and made them feel at home. With a baby and a warm brick house and friends like these, Curles Neck would be home indeed. Lyn could not remember a finer Christmas, except perhaps the first one after her marriage. She thought of Friston Hall and Bury St. Edmunds and prayed that Squire Thomas and Bess were prospering. She would write them both a news bulletin when her guests had left and she had some time to herself.

Lyn woke from her doze to the sound of Byrd's mellow voice.

"So it is arranged that you will visit Bacon's Quarter in five days' time?"

"If Lyn can spare me and I can be home by the second of January. 'Tis my twenty-eighth birthday and my wife would take it amiss if I were not here, wouldn't you, love?"

"I beg everyone's pardon. I believe I fell asleep. You are going to John's in a few days?"

Nat laughed. "Everyone knows why you are tired, so don't apologize. Mister Byrd has a servant named Hartwell whose indenture is expiring. He is trustworthy and might be interested in the overseer's position at the Quarter. Mister Byrd has kindly offered to sail over from his trading post on the thirtieth and bring the man along for an interview. After that, if you permit it, I should like to stay on with John and get in some hunting. I could ride back on the morning of my birthday and still be in time for the feast I know you will insist on."

Lyn smiled her agreement. It would do John good to have some time alone with Nat and she would not mind a few days by herself to work on her wardrobe and write some long-delayed letters. She looked a question at John.

"I should like it of all things," he said. "I have hardly seen Nat since we finished the cabin in November. I think I've met Hartwell in Varina. If he is the fellow I am thinking of, then he will do very well."

Shortly after, the Christmas party broke up and sought their beds. She and Nat snuggled under the comforter and Lyn could not resist adding the beaver cloak to their bedclothes. She stroked the soft fur and rehearsed the day's events as she fell asleep. In Suffolk she knew every rill and every dale, but she also had experienced the pain of her mother's death, her sister's hatred, her father's perfidy and her husband's unhappiness. Virginia had not yet revealed its secrets to her but already she had made true friends. God willing the long journey across the ocean would bring them happiness.

Jacob Hartwell gripped Nat's hand and shook it hard. Five pounds a year and bed and board and clothing – it was not a fortune, but it was a good start. He would give the young Squire value for money. Martha and the boy would have to stay at Byrd's, but she had already agreed that it was best so. His wife had become indispensable to Mistress Byrd and the master had taken quite a shine to young Jake. They would do very well there, and he could see them every week, either here at Bacon's Quarter or at Varina or at Byrd's trading post. He would not be an overseer forever; one day he would have his own farm, as he had promised Martha. He raised his glass to Bacon and John Grey. He was glad the Squire was going back to Curles Neck and that he would be reporting to Grey. Young Bacon had a touch of arrogance and self-regard which did not sit well with Hartwell, whereas Grey seemed made for frontier life. And wasn't he an attorney? What was he doing in Indian country, clearing the land with his own hands? That would change when they finished the cabins and the ten slaves and servants Bacon promised had arrived from Curles Neck. Grey would have a few hours of leisure then. He, Jacob Hartwell, would make Bacon's Quarter a model farm. Only when he had done so would he and Martha and the boy seek their own fortune. They said that God helped those who helped themselves and the Lord would find a willing servant in him, he would stake his life on it. With a bow, he left Grey's cabin and sought his own. The winter sun was setting early, but he thought he could see for another hour and there was wood to cut and cattle to feed and supper to make for his new masters. One need never be idle in Virginia.

"That was satisfactory, John," said Nat.

"Most satisfactory. I have heard nothing but good of Hartwell. He worked off his indenture smartly and he already has plans for perfecting the Quarter. Byrd was most generous in letting him go, for I believe he could have kept him on easily. But perhaps he could not afford to pay him. Byrd is land rich, but perhaps he is cash poor. As for the Indian trading, it is all beyond me. He may be rolling in wealth or deep in debt – I wouldn't know."

"They say he is partners with the Governor," mused Nat. "If true, it seems an unlikely combination. Byrd does not strike me as Green, as Drummond would put it."

"Oh, you are right; he thinks and sounds just like Lawrence. But perhaps showing a tinge of green was the only way he could get a trading license. You know that the licenses lie in Sir William's gift, do you not?"

Nat's mouth turned down. "Yes, it's another way he keeps favorites. They say you can make a fortune with beaver. I should not be surprised if Byrd were a warmer man than he looks. He owns land on this side of the river, doesn't he?"

"Oh, a vast tract. I believe he will build here soon. But in the meantime he lives very simply at his trading post. It must be lonely for Mary."

"Yes, I should not care to be quite so remote. But he speaks the Indian tongues! He must feel comfortable with the savages. He's an interesting man, and I should like to know him better."

"Well, you'll have a chance to, if you like. When he dropped Hartwell off last night he gave us both an invitation to join him and a party of other planters at Goode's tomorrow at noon."

"Why, they'll just drink and carouse. I would rather hunt with you. If we gad about we shall not have much time together."

"I take that kindly Nat, but I sensed that there was a real purpose in Byrd's invitation. He speaks with his eyes. I know there is someone – or perhaps several men – whom he would like us to meet. I should like to go; we can hunt another day."

Nat looked surprised. Normally John was somewhat shy of company and loved nothing better than to spend a day with a good friend, a good gun and a good dog. Byrd's party must have real promise. They would go.

"Why so be it, if you like. We'll ride together and nobody, I trust, will be better mounted. Lyn has persuaded me to call the black Folly. Does your chestnut have a name?"

John surprised Nat again, by blushing. "You will laugh at me, but I call him Coke."

Nat did indeed burst into laughter as he splashed more sherry into their glasses and proposed a toast. "Coke and Folly — I say they go together."

John remonstrated and leaped to the defense of Sir Edward Coke, the distinguished jurist whom he revered. "I shall never get you to love the law, will I?" he said sadly.

"Never in the world," teased Nat. "I think I will grow tobacco and babies. It is not a bad life, is it?"

"No, it is not," answered John. He thought of Lyn and the child in her womb. Lucky Nat. Well, when his Virginia adventure was over he would find the law waiting for him, a stern mistress but one who was not likely to break his heart.

The black and the chestnut strode east toward the rising sun and breasted a hill below which lay Whitby, sparkling under a white mantle of new fallen snow. The world looked made again, so fresh and pure was the white blanket. To the left towered a stand of dark evergreens and to the right rolled the endless river which glinted and rippled in the winterscape. Blue smoke spiraled from the twin chimneys of Goode's manse, one at each gable end, as was the custom of the country.

Nat and John saw Byrd's sloop tied to the wharf and next to it a smaller, unknown craft. They saw no horses but their own; whoever the other guests were, they must have come by water. Folly and Coke proceeded down the hill, their hooves crunching through the icy crust of snow.

"We've met Goode at church, haven't we?" asked Nat.

"Yes, of course. He's a tall man, rising sixty. He wears his white hair like a Roundhead and has that scar on his left cheek – the one from the Indian wars."

"Of course. How careless of me to forget. I remember him as taciturn. He is a near neighbor of yours. Have you gotten to know him?"

"No more than you, at this point. He's not overly friendly – has never been to the Quarter. All I know about him is that he was one of the first to settle on the frontier and he has nothing good to say about the savages. Byrd says he has no love for Berkeley either. We'll know more soon."

Nat scrutinized his friend. There was something odd about this meeting, but they had reached the house and there was no time for more questions. As John said, they would know more soon.

A weathered, white haired man with a markedly scarred face stepped out on the covered porch and took the horses' reins as Bacon and Grey dismounted.

"Good morning, friends," he said. "Thank you for coming. I thought the snow might keep you indoors, but it was not much of a storm. My boy will put your horses in the barn – both of them are beauties."

Nat and John glanced at each other. For what it was worth they had made a good impression on their frontier neighbor. They walked into the large hall of an old log house and found it blessedly warm. Seated in front of a roaring fire were the familiar forms of William Byrd and James Crewes together with two young men who were strangers to them. One was of medium height, slim as a whippet, with fiery red hair and blazing blue eyes and the other was short and wiry with mouse-colored hair and eyes and undistinguished features. All four men rose just as Goode entered and made the introductions.

"I understand that Mister Byrd and Mister Crewes are well known to you, but permit me to make known Giles Bland of Westover and Henry Isham the Younger of Doggams. They have come up from Charles City County in Mister Bland's sloop expressly to meet you."

Byrd suavely intervened, speaking to Goode. "Now John, I must insist on one thing – that the word 'mister' not cross our lips. We of the Upper James are simple folk and we do not need to stand on ceremony. Let us use surnames only. There are so many Williams in the world that I refuse to answer to anything but 'Byrd.' What about the rest of you?"

"Call me Bland," laughed the redhead. "I have never liked 'Giles' in any event."

"And I can go by 'Isham,'" offered the small man. "My father has gone back to England on business and what he does not know won't hurt him."

"You all know me as Crewes," said the swarthy planter from Turkey Island, "but I answer to Jamie as well."

"Why then, we are Bacon and Grey," cried Nat heartily. "Let us not be formal."

"Excellent," said their host. "Now for the standing joke: I am 'Goode'."

The seven laughed and took their seats. A plain looking serving wench entered with a bowl of hot punch and the men chatted amiably among themselves for a few minutes, until Byrd rose and faced them, his back to the fireplace.

"Goode has obliged me by offering his home for this meeting as it lies somewhat in the middle of our several plantations, so that nobody's journey was too onerous." He paused and turned to Nat and John. "I have invited you to meet my friends at the suggestion of Will Drummond and Dicken Lawrence."

Open astonishment showed on Bacon's and Grey's faces.

"I know you think highly of them – you have both told me so many times. What I have not heard from either of you was an encomium of Sir William Berkeley."

Nat and John looked at each other and then looked around them. Understanding began to dawn on both their faces. John rose and walked to the fireplace and seized Byrd's right hand. The ring finger was encircled with braided gold. He turned to the others. Each held up his right hand; each was adorned with a twist of gold.

"What is this about?" he cried. "'Tis a Cabal!"

182

"The farthest thing from a Cabal, my friend," said Byrd quietly. "That pernicious word refers to those who fawn upon the King and are showered with favors in return. Our organization stands for the common man."

Nat was on his feet. "What is this?" he said urgently. "We came here in good faith, expecting to pass a few hours in conversation and play. Have we committed ourselves to some levelling plot?"

Byrd remained unperturbed. "Never in the world, my friend. Never in the world. We wish harm to no man, and good to all. Can you think that Drummond and Lawrence would involve you in something dangerous? We are simply a group of men whose ideas are not wholly congruent with those of Green Spring and who have formed a union, in the pure open light of day, to tell Green Spring so. We are neither plotters nor conspirators. There is nothing unlawful about our assembly. You are as safe as you would be at church. Our good friends in Jamestown took your measure and thought that you and we might have some common interests."

Nat glanced at John. As Byrd spoke they both relaxed somewhat, as if willing to hear more.

Goode rose. "We have alarmed you, haven't we, with our gold rings? 'Tis just a little symbol, a mark of identification. You will find men like us throughout the colony – many men. We have found it convenient to be able to identify one another wordlessly. The Governor has grown brittle and cannot stomach any opinion which does not stand foursquare with his. Those who wear the gold ring want to make some changes in Virginia, but we are not rebels, not Levellers. You have nothing to fear. See how we trust you? You are free to go. Within two days you could be at Green Spring or King's Creek reporting this meeting. As we are guiltless, we have no fear of disclosure. Come, have some more punch and learn something more about the Ring."

Both Nat and John took their seats, appeased for the moment.

John spoke. "Well, we are willing to hear you out. As you say, we are free to go and we are free to tell what is happening here. We heard enough in Jamestown to know that there is considerable unrest in the colony. If your group seeks lawful change, I for one see no harm in learning more, but what we do after today is wholly our decision." Nat nodded his agreement.

"Well then," urged Byrd in his mellow voice, "I shall tell you a little about ourselves and then we shall dine and in the afternoon we'll make ourselves available for questions. I assure you that we invited you to join us today for your benefit, not to bring you harm."

For the next hour Nat and John heard the history of the Ring: how Drummond and Lawrence had joined forces after the Scot's return from Albemarle, united in their hatred of the Governor; how they had subsequently found like-minded men by the hundreds as the colony reeled under natural disasters, foreign invasions and a plummeting tobacco market with little or no response from Sir William Berkeley; how over the past three or four years the disaffected small planters and yeomen had banded together and formed the organization which they called the Ring; how Lawrence began drafting laws reflecting the changes which the oppressed colonists craved; and how just this past fall the laws had been approved by the Ring's four chapters and now awaited introduction in the Assembly.

When they regrouped after dinner Goode spoke. "You six are all young, in your late twenties or early thirties if my guess is right, and some of you have not been in Virginia long," (nodding to Bland and Bacon and Grey). "But I am old enough to be your father – perhaps your grandfather — and I know by personal experience how the colony has fallen off since the forties. Why, Virginia did better under the Protectorate than it is doing now! Byrd has heard this speech, but let me give it to the rest of you. It explains why I, who have always supported our government, have become restive enough to join the Ring. As Byrd knows, I tell my story under four heads: Taxes; Terror; Troubles and Tyranny."

Nat and John exchanged smiles. Lawrence and Drummond had prepared them for this. They listened with interest.

"Like the camel of fable which soldiered on under its increasing burden, the colony has dutifully paid its taxes without complaint, until now. However the new tax imposed to send our agents to London to wrest back our land from Lords Arlington and Culpeper might well be the proverbial last straw – the one which brought the poor beast to its knees."

"Do camels have knees?" snorted Giles Bland. He was met with stony silence and quickly poured himself another glass of punch.

Goode looked directly at Nat as he proceeded. "As a substantial landowner you doubtless have learned the various taxes you will owe: a poll tax on all your tithables; two shillings a hogshead export duty on your tobacco; quitrents to the King at the rate of two shillings for every hundred acres of land; the county levies which fund the county court and county officers; the parish levies which fund the church; and various fees for registering deeds and proving wills and so forth."

Nat, who did not blush easily, blushed now. He had no idea what taxes he owed or would owe in the future. He had never given it a thought. "I leave that all to my attorney," he laughed. John smiled and said nothing.

"Each tax in and of itself is understandable, and doubtless necessary, but over time they have come to form a crushing burden. The Navigation Acts have essentially destroyed our tobacco markets: we are enslaved to our mother country and cannot take advantage of those, like the Dutch, who would willingly pay a premium price for our sweet-scented. With tobacco prices so low, many, (myself included), simply cannot afford to pay the levies. Here, look at these figures. I was playing with them this morning at the breakfast table and, let me tell you, they took away my appetite. It is not far off the mark to say that the average farmer cannot produce more than twelve hundred pounds of tobacco every year. Today you would be lucky to get a penny a pound for the crop. The numbers are simple: twelve hundred pounds of tobacco bring twelve hundred pennies; twelve hundred pennies make one hundred shillings; one hundred shillings make five pounds; reduce the five pounds by one-third for taxes and there is your profit: three pounds or so. Do you think that a man can support a wife and children on three pounds a year? Can you?"

Nat's mind was racing. Just yesterday he and John had felt badly about offering Hartwell only five pounds a year to manage Bacon's Quarter, but that was in addition to bed, board and clothing and the sum was tax-free, for Nat would be paying the taxes, not his new overseer. Moreover, Hartwell's wife and child would be provided for at Byrd's; the five pounds was for Hartwell's keep alone. The young Squire swallowed hard and envisioned the expansive fields at Curles Neck. In the spring they would be green with tobacco, promising wealth as the plants rippled in the wind. Was it a false promise? Would he and Lyn find themselves as poor after they sold a crop as before they had planted one? He frowned and looked at John, who sat placidly smoking one of Goode's pipes, his face impassive. Nat turned to Goode and urged him to proceed.

"I'll be honest with you, Bacon. I have paid my quitrents and my tobacco duties, but I have not paid my poll tax these three years. As for the county and parish levies, 'tis a joke; I simply ignore them. The sheriff could be at my door any day and what could I say to defend myself? My family has farmed Whitby since the thirties, but if things go on as they are I may lose this land that I love."

The seven men glanced at one another, silent. Goode's story was a familiar one. That was why they were here. Their host continued.

"But to go back to the new tax: I truly think that it will break many of our fellow colonists. Fifty pounds of tobacco per tithable does not sound like a great deal, but together with our other burdens it might as well be five hundred pounds. In addition, they increased the cost of going to law, so many a man who might have sought help from the courts will now find that door shut in his face. No, I am convinced that things have come to a crisis. Changes must be made."

"Hear, hear," cried Crewes, slapping his hand on his stout thigh. "I am in much the same straits, Goode. 'Tis a sorry plight. I have decided to pay nothing and see what happens next. Devil take the sheriff who seeks me out."

"Father is talking of staying in England and selling Doggams," contributed Henry Isham. "When he hears about the new tax I daresay that's exactly what he will do."

"I wonder if my aunt's estate will be worth anything, if I manage to get it probated?" queried Giles Bland. "Perhaps she should think of staying in England like your father."

"Well," said John. "You have told us about Taxes. What about Terror?"

"Ah," answered Goode. "We need to hear from Byrd on that."

The Indian trader shook his amber locks and smiled at the group. "When Goode says Terror he means savages. The afternoon is growing late and there is not time to tell you all that I have learned about the heathen above the falls and, for that matter, the heathen below the falls, whom Sir William calls his darling Indians. Suffice it to say that the Governor thinks that all is as it was when he defeated Opechancanough and the savages were brought to heel. It is not. Sir William has been buying beaver for firearms for twenty-five years and there are many bands which are as well-armed as the English. Should someone put a torch to that fire it would be many days before the flames died down."

"I should like to know more about the savages," said Nat. "Could you and your wife find the time to come to Curles Neck before the spring plant-ing and stay a few days, and help educate me? I am sure John would be glad to join us."

"I should like it of all things," agreed Grey. He turned to Goode. "Well, the Indians will wait. What falls under Troubles?"

"Oh, that's a catch-all category. There's the low price of tobacco, for one. Did you know that in Rolfe's day, the weed sold for three shillings a pound? The decline to a penny a pound is astonishing. And then you've doubtless heard about the Dutch raids which showed to the world that Virginia lies defenseless to any who care to ravish her. To the east our rivers and ports are exposed; to the west the savages have us at their mercy. Truly, we lie between Scylla and Charybdis. Sir William's stance on defense is a mystery. He is as vulnerable as any, living so close to Jamestown, but he turns a blind eye and a deaf ear to the whole thing."

"Oh, many say that he is beyond caring and that he and Lady Frances are about to return to England," contributed Giles Bland.

"Hmm," pondered Goode. "That's interesting. It may well be true. The Governor has aged greatly in the past few years." The white haired man turned back to John. "Let's see – what other troubles are on my list? Well, speaking of defense, many would argue that we have as much to fear from our own slaves and servants as we have from savages and foreign ships, their numbers have grown so great and their lot is so sorry. But the afternoon wears on and my litany grows tedious. You are probably thinking of your journey home and your supper."

"By no means," cried Nat, who had grown increasingly interested in the discussion. "I should like to hear about Tyranny."

"Why I have nothing to add on that subject that you have not heard already from Lawrence and Drummond. It is beyond dispute that Sir William runs the government by handing out favors to a select few who are then so indebted to him that they cannot say him nay. He has eyes and ears in every corner of Virginia – well paid eyes and ears." Goode laughed bitterly. "Why, gentlemen, for all I know you may be among them?"

Nat leaped to his feet, his face a deep red. "Never in the world, sir! I resent the imputation!"

"Now, now" soothed Byrd, rising as well. "You have taken Goode's statement wrong. All he meant was that Berkeley's hounds are everywhere and that although we know some of them, we by no means know all of them. You must agree that we have placed considerable trust in you. Although we meet lawfully, should you choose to report this meeting to Green Spring we would be the worse for it."

John spoke. "We will not breach your trust. I for one feel honored that you have included me in your very interesting discussions and I daresay Nat feels the same."

"Of course I do," said the young Squire. "When is your next meeting, and when do we receive our gold rings?"

At that the entire group laughed and the tension lessened. Byrd explained once again that the key reforms which the Ring supported had been wrought into proposed laws by Richard Lawrence and that the group's main function now was to breathe life into some, if not all, of them. He said that if Nat and John were interested in that process, that they would be welcome to attend the meetings of the Upper James Chapter and that he would take it upon himself to keep them informed of those meetings. As for the gold ring ... well, that was a little more serious. One had to take a certain oath and bind oneself to the group in certain ways. Bacon and Grey would doubtless want to think carefully about taking such a step, especially given their ties to King's Creek. Sir William's sword might be capricious, but it was powerful.

Nat and John left Goode's log house, deep in thought, as the sun dropped behind the western mountains. The others remained: clearly they were going to have continued, private discussions. Folly and Coke were brought around by a stable lad and the friends rode west, up the hill, to Bacon's Quarter. Hartwell had prepared a venison stew and corn bread which they fell upon heartily, asking the overseer to join them. As he washed the dishes and excused himself for the night Nat and John agreed that he had already made his mark. John's life at the Quarter was going to take a turn for the better.

"Perhaps I can entice you back to Curles now," said Nat lazily, as the two sat before the fire. "Lyn would like it, I know."

John was silent for a moment. "I think I shall stay here until the baby comes, Nat. You and she should have your privacy. I'll come as often as you need to help with your first planting – 'tis only twenty miles or so."

"And when the baby comes, what then?"

"Well, then I shall have to see how things are going. If all is well I might return to London. This has been a marvelous experience, but if I am gone too long my career will perish before it is born."

Nat struck his forehead with his palm. "I am a selfish beast, John. When I think of the future it always has you in it. I thought you would stay with us for some years."

John's heart smote him. He patted his friend's shoulder. "And I might, Nat, I might. Let's take it one month at a time and see what fortune brings our way. This business at Goode's – that should give us some food for thought."

"It should indeed. Curious how I feel at home with ... I guess I should call them the Ring. At Green Spring, and even at King's Creek, I feel as though I am in a masque, acting a part. These men are like Lawrence and Drummond – men of sense, men you can trust. Bland is a bit of a fool, and I don't have Isham's measure, but the others are impressive. Byrd is wise beyond his years and I should like to have Crewes at my shoulder in any fracas. And Goode has been here so long that he is a treasure of information. Well, perhaps we shall wear the gold ring one day."

"Perhaps we shall," said John. The two friends sat comfortably before the fire until it was time for bed. They would hunt the next day and put everything else out of their minds. Then Nat would ride home to Curles to celebrate his twenty-eighth birthday. It was a good friendship, thought John. It had been sorely tested and had survived. Still, he was not sure that he could continue his role as family counselor for much longer. Each time he saw Lyn it was like a physical blow. And Nat did not see it, he was sure. He turned in his narrow cot and saw that his friend had already fallen asleep. Wearily, he snuffed the candle and pulled the bedclothes around him. Lyn had stitched the counterpane by hand and he never slept without it.

CHAPTER 13

MARCH 1675

Nat sat Folly and watched the blackbirds. They were the exact shade of his great horse, just such a deep black with a glossy shine. Except for their red epaulets, their courting clothes: in that they bested the stallion. The males threw themselves into the spring sunshine like tumblers and flashed their wings. It was a brave show and it quickened his heart. Curles Neck was coming to life in the March sun. John said they could plant their tobacco soon, but not quite yet. They could still get frost.

Nat shifted in the saddle and thought back on the meeting at Goode's last December. It had been a watershed. Since then he and John had met frequently with William Byrd and the other frontier planters and they had received an intensive education in the benefits and burdens of life on a Virginia tobacco plantation. Now they had a much better grasp of what might lie ahead for Curles Neck and Bacon's Quarter. The picture was not rosy, but he did not regret his somewhat hasty purchase from Tom Ballard. He knew he would prosper. Look at Berkeley and his cousin and Bray and Page and Sir Henry Chicheley... the list could go indefinitely. All these men lived well, so why not he? True, they lived on credit and on their honor as gentlemen, but they flourished nonetheless. He still had a thousand pounds in reserve; he was doubtless wealthier than most of the great men. So he would plant, and time would tell whether it was worth the risk.

Of course the new house would put a dent in that thousand pounds might even cut the amount in half by the time all was said and done. But he had promised it to Lyn and he would never go back on that promise. Nat glanced to his left where the land sloped down to the marsh. They had dug the clay pit during the winter and now they were preparing to temper the soil. The earthmaker told him he would have bricks enough for the new house by summer. He had hired Allen's builder and the man had promised to start construction as soon as the bricks were ready. If they got underway in June he and Lyn would be in by Christmas, as they had planned. The house was going to be in the form of a truncated cross, somewhat like Allen's and Page's, but not an exact copy; he wanted to do something original. Lyn said the plan reminded her of Friston Hall and it was true – Curles Neck mansion would have overtones of his boyhood home, but it would be his own. His father, bless him, was sending the marble for the fireplaces and the glass for the casements and those items should arrive in September; the timing was perfect. The old Squire had insisted on making a gift of the marble and glass, he was so pleased at the good reports he had received. Nat smiled. It was not the least of his joys that his father was happy.

Folly tossed his head and Nat looked up from his reverie and surveyed his fields. The distant woods were shrouded in pale green mist: the first promise of spring. His thoughts went back to Byrd and Crewes and Goode. These were the men that he respected ... identified with. They were honest, forthright, hardy and fearless. Next to them the old Governor and his sour wife seemed antiquated and wooden, relics of a past age. Even his cousin was stuck in the past ... belonged more to the age of the first Charles Stuart than the second. Nat smiled again and turned Folly towards home. He was now one of the planters of the Upper James and he intended to be first among them.

As the young Squire urged the great horse south towards the river he saw two riders approaching him: John on his leggy chestnut and Lyn on her little mare. He frowned. He thought John was planting at Bacon's Quarter and as for Lyn, they had agreed that she was too far along to ride. The baby was due in two months, perhaps less. Something must be amiss. He spurred Folly and galloped forward.

"Don't scold her, Nat," pleaded John, bringing Coke to a halt. "She is as safe as houses. Mignon is like a goat – she cannot take a misstep."

"I'm glad to see you, John, but Lyn really should not be riding. Whatever possessed you, love?"

"I had to get out in the fine weather, Nat. I feel like a grumpy bear coming out of its cave. Nothing could keep me inside. You know that riding Mignon is as safe as walking."

"Well, I suppose you are right, but take a care. What brings you, John? You were here only last week."

John laughed, dismounted, and helped Lyn from her horse. "That's a fine welcome. I came to beg another hand from you as one of our boys was bitten by a snake; he's fine, but will be in bed for a week. But just as I arrived at the house I saw a messenger in the Governor's colors puffing up the path from the wharf. I took the message from him and sent him inside to refresh himself and told Lyn. She had just saddled Mignon so we decided to ride down together and bring you the letter. It is from Green Spring – look at the seal."

190

Nat slid from Folly and took the missive. The three of them looked curiously at the thick parchment and heavy red wax seal. What could Sir William want? They had only seen him that one time, last fall. They had talked about visiting him again, but none of them wanted to and, with the winter weather, Lyn's pregnancy, and the burdens of Curles Neck and Bacon's Quarter, they never seemed to find the time.

Nat broke the seal and opened the letter. He gasped with astonishment. "This is no letter. It is an order appointing me to the Council of State! What can the Governor be thinking? I've not been here a year nor have I served in the House of Burgesses nor held any office? Could this possibly be a mistake?"

"How could it be a mistake? It's your cousin's doing," Lyn quickly surmised. "I feel sure of it. The Colonel wants to advance you as fast as possible. I really believe he intends to make you his heir. Oh Natty, is this a good thing?"

John was a good whistler and now he whistled long and shrilly. "What a coup, Nat! Councilor Bacon! The *second* Councilor Bacon! I'm sure Lyn is right – you have your cousin to thank for this."

Nat was seldom at a loss for words, but he was now. "But I don't want this – it is absurd. I've barely gotten my feet wet here and besides ... the Ring."

"Whatever do you mean?" asked Lyn.

Nat and John glanced at each other. Their meetings with the planters of the Upper James over the past two months had not concerned farming alone. They had been initiated into the deepest secrets of the Ring. Drummond and Lawrence had sailed up in February and they had renewed their friendship with the Jamestown twain and perused the text of Lawrence's reform laws. They knew which Burgesses and which Councilors were sympathetic to their cause and which were owned by Green Spring. At the last meeting – just a week ago – they had taken an oath of loyalty to the Ring and at the next meeting they were to receive the bands of gold which marked their allegiance. But Lyn knew nothing of this. The reform laws were to be introduced at the next Assembly and then things would take a dangerous turn. Nat and John had agreed that Lyn was to get through her pregnancy safely and then look to the child. With all the changes in her life she did not need the anxiety of knowing that her two protectors might be on the edge of political suicide.

Nat turned to his wife. "Nothing, love. It is just a figure of speech." He glanced at John whose face was alight with interest at this new development. "Come, let's return to the house. I want to talk to the Governor's messenger and see what light he can shed on the matter. Let's persuade him to stay to supper and he can return to Jamestown tomorrow with my answer."

Three hours later Sir William's man had been cross-examined to a fare-thee-well and had been turned over to Abraham who was charged to feed him and find him a cot for the night. Lyn had retired to bed and the little wooden house belonged to Nat and John who stretched their legs before the welcome fire, rum toddies close at hand. The friends brooded like conspirators.

"Well, it's no mistake," murmured Nat. "Sir William signed the commission this morning and sent his man off to catch the tide. He must bring my answer tomorrow – March the fourth – and if I accept I am directed to be in Jamestown on the sixth to take the oath and commence my duties. What a strange turn of events. Of course it is my cousin's doing, but why did he not let me know?"

"Perhaps he sent you a message which miscarried. But far more likely he assumed that you expected this ... and how should you not, connected with King's Creek as you are and fit in every way for the position?"

Nat looked at John, startled. "What do you mean, fit for the position? No Councilor has been appointed, to my knowledge, who has not earned his way by years of service in the county offices and in the House of Burgesses. 'Tis the highest position one can hold here, short of the Governorship itself."

"But how many Bacons have arrived on these shores recently, young, educated, wealthy, well-connected ...? You understate your gifts. And if your cousin means to adopt you, as it were, then surely that was all Sir William needed to hear for you to win his favor. It must be apparent, even to him, that he needs new blood on the Council. I daresay he has assessed you as one who will appeal to the younger generation yet who will stand firm against atheistical and levelling tendencies. In his eyes you are doubtless a youthful incarnation of your cousin."

Nat looked thunderstruck. John was right. What a supreme irony. Just as Nat was finding his true friends among the Ring the Governor, cushioned by the cotton wool of his old coterie, had assessed him as Green Spring material and believed that he would be an ally, not an enemy. The old man's spies must be less astute than the Ring feared.

John leaned forward eagerly and grasped Nat's knee. "Of course you must accept. This is a golden opportunity. I see the hand of God ... or fate. The timing is uncanny. As a Councilor you will be in a position to cultivate the soil for the reform laws. You'll get to know each of your fellow members personally and be able to feel them out in a way which the Ring never could. And you'll have the Burgesses at your beck and call. There is something large at work here. This was meant to be."

Nat shook his head. "I'm no politician, John. I don't have a silver tongue – who should know that better than you? I call a spade a spade and the devil take the hindermost."

"Well, you will have to learn. You can't lose this opportunity, Nat. This is not just about you, but about all the rest of us – Lawrence, Drummond, Byrd, Bland, Isham, Goode, Crewes ... young Hartwell. Besides, you cannot refuse. One simply does not refuse an appointment to the Council of State. The Ring can guide you ... you can do it. Think. This is your chance to look beyond your own needs and serve the greater good."

Nat's golden eyes looked long into John's silver ones. The attorney was right. God or fate had offered him the chance to forget himself in the service of others. Was it not what he had always craved? "If I do it will you stay to manage Curles Neck and the Quarter and be here for Lyn when I am absent?"

John's heart turned over. Why had he not seen this? Well, if Nat could make the sacrifice so could he. Irony upon irony. As the wheel of fate pulled his friend up he tumbled down, like Milton's angel.

"Of course I will, Nat."

The friends clasped hands and drank deep. The fire had turned from copper to ash before they sought their beds.

The wind whistled through the cracks around the casements of Richard Lawrence's snuggery and guttered the candles on the work table, plunging the room into darkness.

"Damn my blood, "swore the innkeeper. "Keep your seats. You shall have light in a moment."

The gray man walked to the fire and plunged a stick of fatwood into its depths. His torch burst into flames and he returned to the table where he lit the candles, shielding them from the spring gusts with his body. He handed a limp white cloth to Drummond.

"Will – take this old shirt and stuff it into the cracks. The wind is howling. The last few days have been a false spring and winter is upon us again."

"It will pass over," soothed the Scot. "It clears the pests away and freshens everything. Give me a spring breeze every time over summer's heat."

Lawrence laughed. "The Devil take me, I believe you could find a silver lining in the thunderheads of the Last Judgment. I look forward to seeing the day and the event which you cannot redeem."

Drummond lost his smile. "Don't even say it, Dicken," he muttered.

Nat looked at his two friends. The room was alive with tension. It was the fifth of March. He had risen at dawn and made the long ride to Jamestown, Abraham at his side for company and protection. Now it was late and he craved his bed but before he could sleep he must milk these two for every last drop of wisdom. Tomorrow he would be sworn in to the Council of State and he needed a roadmap to guide him on his journey – he, the covert representative of the Ring.

Drummond spoke. "Well, you'll take the oath of allegiance and supremacy and then you'll just sit there, looking competent and respectful. They won't expect anything of you this first session. In fact they would be most annoyed if you made yourself heard. In these circumstances, silence is golden. If I were you I would simply keep an eye on your cousin and follow his lead. That way, you cannot go wrong."

"But do you know what issues they will be discussing? And will they sit as the General Court?"

Lawrence intervened. "I don't believe they're going to convene the Court – at least not to my knowledge. If they do then you had better keep your mouth shut, begging your pardon, for unless Grey has taught you well about the law since last fall you won't know how to conduct yourself."

"Indeed, that is my fear. Well, if the Court is not sitting I suppose I can simply take the oath and make myself civil to the others and thus survive. Now, please tell me who might be inclined to our cause and who will never be, so that I do not foil our plan before it has a chance to unfold."

"Oh I think you know well enough how they fall out," said Lawrence. "But let's go over it again if it makes you feel better. There are three groups: the committed Greens, who number ten or more, and constitute a slim majority; two friends who support the Ring and are almost deep enough in our affairs to wear the gold band; and seven or eight independents who will blow with the wind."

"Speaking of which," said Drummond rising and fumbling in his vest pocket. "Hansford gave me these last week in advance of our next meeting at Whitby. But you have anticipated us, so I shall give you your prize now, and Grey's as well." The Scot pulled two braided circlets of gold from his pocket and held them up to the candle where they shone like fire.

Nat reached for the rings and cradled them in his hand. He slipped one onto his right ring finger and admired the effect. It was like taking his marriage vows. He was committed. He slid the fiery metal from his hand and carefully placed his ring and John's in his pouch.

"I think I had better not wear it tomorrow," he laughed.

Drummond and Lawrence laughed with him and the innkeeper proceeded to advise Nat about their friends and foes on the Council of State.

"In addition to Sir William himself the die-hard Greens are the two Ludwells, Page, Bray, Bridger, Sir Henry Chicheley, Spencer and Cole. Of course I must add your cousin to that list."

"What do you mean, 'the two Ludwells'?" The Secretary sailed for England last fall and his brother is not a Councilor."

"Well, my friend, you are in for a little surprise. Philip Ludwell is going to be sworn in tomorrow, with you. Sir William thinks he is strengthening his faction by two, but we know that it is only by one."

"You astonish me," said Nat. "Philip. Hmm. What sort of man is he?"

"Why a selfish, grasping rogue who is not to be trusted farther than you can throw him!" cried Drummond.

Nat looked more surprised. He knew the Scot disliked Thomas but apparently his feelings for Philip were even stronger. "What do you have against him, other than his support of the Governor?"

"It seems that the rumors have not reached you in Henrico. It is beyond doubt that Philip Ludwell and Lady Frances have put horns on the Governor's head."

Nat burst into laughter but quickly controlled himself when he saw Drummond's face. Infidelity was not a joking matter to the Scot. Nat spoke soberly.

"Well, I am sorry for it. No man should have to suffer that indignity. Is it known throughout the colony?"

Lawrence answered. "I doubt it. We have better sources than most. But you are dropping with fatigue. Let me finish my assessment of the Council and then you should seek your bed. It goes without saying that you must tread carefully with the Greens. Now for our friends. There are only two whom you may absolutely trust: John Pate and Tom Swann. All the rest, Place and Warner and Jennings and the others, we may be able to seduce, but for now I would leave them alone. For this session, you cannot do better than to be silent and respectful."

"And so say I," agreed Drummond rising from his chair. "It's been a long day for you, Nat, and tomorrow may be a longer one. Bless you my boy. Good luck, and leave those gold bands in your pocket. I know that you are of two minds about this endeavor. Every member of the Ring appreciates what you are doing for us." With those words the Scot left Nat and the innkeeper alone.

Lawrence clapped the young Squire on the shoulders. "I knew you would bring us luck the first moment I saw you. This is a *golden* opportunity, if you take my meaning. If we play our cards well you may help us achieve more sooner than any of us could have hoped. And there is a bonus for you. I daresay you have not even thought of it. As a Councilor, you pay no taxes! When you digest that piece of good fortune, will you still act for us?"

Nat gasped. It was perfectly true. One of the many burdens the people bore was watching the rich grow richer through tax avoidance. Only the great men – those least in need of tax relief – sat on the Council of State and for the privilege of oppressing the colony they were relieved of any tax burden. The Ring had drafted a law expressly to correct this inequity, but Nat had not given it a thought; nor, oddly, had John. Both had been so taken with the opportunity Nat now had to open the Council to the winds of change that they had missed the irony of the situation.

Nat yawned hugely and simultaneously tried for sarcasm. "Well Dicken, now that I have been raised to glory I suppose that I must forget my friends."

Lawrence smiled warmly. "I know that you will not. Now, we have given you Clarissa's room so that you may have some privacy and get a good night's sleep. Take this candle and you should find everything ready below."

Nat took the light and made his way downstairs. Closing the door on the common room and pulling the curtains, he placed the candlestick on the dresser and pulled the two rings from his pouch. Each glowed with inner fire. Smiling, he tucked them away, blew out the candle and gratefully crawled into bed.

From henceforth I shall bear faith and true allegiance
to the King's highness, his heirs and lawful successors;
and to my power shall assist and defend all jurisdictions,
privileges, preeminences and authorities granted or belonging
to the King's highness, his heirs and successors
or united and annexed to the Imperial Crown of the Realm;
so help me God; and by the contents of this Book.

The solemn words reverberated in the Council chamber. Nat slowly drew his hand from the huge Bible and looked around him. Immediately to his right Philip Ludwell was accepting a goblet of sack from the hands of the Governor himself. The Deputy Secretary's face shone with pride as he quaffed the drink in one gulp and whipped a dainty piece of white lawn from his sleeve and patted his ripe, red lips over which the silky gold of his mustachio played. Beyond Ludwell Nat saw his cousin's comely face and thought of his father. The Colonel tipped his head as if directing the young Squire. Nat started and realized that Sir William was offering him a goblet as well. He put on his best courtier's face, bowed low, and accepted the glass. The Governor clapped his hands and a thin toothy man rushed forward from the shadows to bear a tray of gold-filled goblets about the room so that each Councilor could toast the new members.

Nat smiled as he recognized Pitts, the caretaker who had shown them the Statehouse on their first day in Jamestown. Only six months had elapsed since that day and here he was, a member of the Council of State, entitled to enter this gracious walnut-clad room whenever he chose. It seemed miraculous. And yet, he was here on false pretenses. His conscience smote him; he felt badly for his cousin, but what could a man do? He must follow his heart. Here *was* Colonel Bacon, smiling broadly and bringing his neighbors John Page and Thomas Ballard over to offer their congratulations. Page: Lawrence had said he was a true Green. But Ballard was classed as an independent and that was a surprise. Apparently the horse-faced planter had some levelling tendencies. One would never have guessed it from his conduct.

The Council fluttered and stirred. Lady Frances Berkeley walked regally through the fine walnut doorway from the antechamber. All the gentlemen rose and bowed deeply. Nat peeped at the Governor's wife through the screen of his eyelashes and restrained a smile. The woman must be a fool – she walked as though she were Queen Catherine, as though her very presence should ignite worship and longing in every heart. Lyn was so far her superior, in body and soul, that it was not even a contest. Little Lyn, honest and true as a die. Lady Frances was all artifice. Nat stifled a laugh as he wondered what lay beneath the golden silk brocade and the gauzy tissue which softened her aging neck and shoulders. Well, Philip Ludwell might know. He glanced at his fellow honoree as the Governor's wife moved among the Councilors, offering her hand to some and soft greetings to others. Lady Frances approached Ludwell and held out her right hand. The chestnut-haired man bowed extravagantly, his sherry-colored eyes aflame. The full red lips sought the delicate hand and lingered long – too long. As quick as a striking snake Ludwell's tongue darted from the cave of his mouth and caressed the proffered flesh. Lady Frances closed her eyes and smiled.

All heads turned as the Governor spoke. "We shall repair to *The Unicorn* for luncheon and then we shall commence business at two o'clock sharp. Unfortunately Lady Berkeley must return to Green Spring and I have asked Philip Ludwell to attend her. He has agreed to miss this, his first Council meeting, and I take it kindly that he should do so. I do not know what I, or the colony, would do without the Ludwell brothers."

The assembly broke up and Nat shook his head as he watched the Deputy Secretary of State escort the Governor's wife to her caleche and seat himself next to her. Drummond's gossip was obviously true. The couple had not even been subtle about it. Taking his cousin's arm, Nat left the Council chamber, glancing at Sir William Berkeley with some pity. The whole thing was sad. The Governor might be a tyrant, but he was human.

The Governor called the Council to order and glanced at the list of topics which lay to his right. Most of the Councilors were present, but some of those who lived farthest away had not yet arrived or had perhaps declined to come altogether. He felt a certain unease; he was not sure how firm his grip was on this body which he used to own, wholly. Still, sixteen was a good number. They ought to be able to get their business done promptly and get back to planting. Sir William looked down the table and grimaced. He used to know the heart of every Councilor but now...now as many as half the group were enigmas to him. What did he know of Swann and Place and men like Ballard who was chattering away to young Bacon, careless of the call to order? He hoped he had been right to oblige the Colonel by appointing his young cousin to such an honor so quickly, but his friend had assured him that Bacon would be an active and useful member of Green Spring, and he had taken him at his word. As for Phil, he should have been on the Council long ago, but there had been some grumbling over how close he was to the Ludwell boys and he had thought it more prudent to wait. How obliging of Phil to see Fanny home; it was quite a sacrifice to make and he would see the lad recompensed. Thinking of the Ludwells recalled the Governor to his duty. He banged his gavel in order to silence Ballard and some of the other underbred members. How the world had fallen off since the death of the first Charles. He could not like the second one as well. Still, a King was a King, ordained by God and he would serve His Majesty well, to his dying day.

The Governor coughed. "I have a number of items I would like you to consider and then we will open the meeting for questions and for any business which may have fallen by the wayside. First, I have a bulletin from Tom Ludwell which is most encouraging. He and Smith and Moryson have found some friends in London who are not unsympathetic to the coil the King has created by the recent proprietary grant. Though I say it who should not, Lords Arlington and Culpeper are not universally beloved. Neither has any interest in setting foot in Virginia. It may be that their interests can be purchased for a reasonable sum."

"Another tax?" groaned James Bray.

Sir William sniffed. "That's as it may be. Tom will keep me apprized and I shall pass the information on to you. He has only been gone half a year – I am most heartened by his early success."

The Governor pushed his wig back on his forehead and shuffled his papers. "Next, you will be pleased to know that Howe is going to remove that lumber from the site of the abortive fort. Perhaps I was out of line, but I told him the Court would forgive the rest of his fine if he cleaned the place up. The site is a good one – I hope to entice someone to build there." Sir William looked around the room for candidates, but saw only blank and impassive faces.

"Must the Court take action on that?" asked Jennings, one of the newer Councilors.

Sir William frowned. "I suppose so, if you insist on the letter of the law, but it has been a common practice to handle things a little more informally, at least during my tenure as Governor. Do you insist that we convene as the General Court and bring Howe before us?"

Jennings blushed deeply. "Oh no, Your Honor. Forgive me for speaking out of turn. I am still learning."

"Well, well that's alright. Phil Ludwell knows his way around, but young Bacon there can profit from these discussions, so don't apologize. Shall I take it that you approve my action with respect to Howe?"

There was a chorus of "ayes" and the Governor smiled.

"Of course relieving Howe of his fine is, in fact, relieving Drummond," insinuated Page.

"I know it and I regret it. But that is between the two of them. It seemed worthwhile to have the site cleaned up. But I appreciate your point, John, and I thank you for the comment."

Colonel Bacon spoke next. "Do you have any thoughts about a future fort at Jamestown, or is it a dead letter?"

"I see no need now that England and Holland are at peace again. We have no active enemies – we shall have to rely on our good ships to keep us safe." It was clear that Sir William considered the topic closed.

"Now, Sir Henry, did you have something to say about the savages?"

Sir Henry Chicheley rose and bowed to his fellow Councilors. "Thank you, Your Honor. I have nothing specific to report but the planters in Stafford County have indicated considerable unrest in their area amongst the Doegs. It seems that the northern Indians – the Susquahannocks – are pushing down along the Potomac on the Maryland side and are fomenting trouble."

"Well, that is for Governor Calvert to deal with. Is there some action you wish us to take?"

The old knight stroked his beard and pondered. Ballard snorted. Chicheley drove him wild with his cautious approach to everything. God in Heaven, it took the old man ten minutes to wish you "Good Morning."

"Noooo, I think not at this time. But it is something to keep an eye on. The Susquahannocks are of another race than our tributary Indians; they are said to be tall, stout and fearless...quite formidable. It would be a problem if they push their way into Virginia."

"Well, let's not borrow trouble. If there is one thing I am satisfied with it is the current state of Indian affairs. The Powhatans, Pamunkeys, Mattaponis, Chickahominies, all within the fall line are our true friends and allies. If these Susquahannocks cause trouble we can count on the Virginia Indians to come to our aid. But thank you, Sir Henry. I rely on you to watch the situation and report to me at any time. Now then, what other business is there?"

John Page indicated that he would like the floor and when the Governor ceded it to him he rose to his full six feet and spoke in his characteristic raspy tenor. Page was thin as a whip and beautifully clothed in black broadcloth and an expanse of Flemish lace. Gold rings glittered on both attenuated hands. "My news is somewhat like Henry's – nothing specific, just a rumor. It has been long since I left Middle Plantation but last Christmas I went up to Westmoreland to spend the holidays with my daughter, as some of you know. Alice and I stayed on longer than we anticipated as the girl is breeding and was not feeling well and she wanted her mother with her. Time hung on my hands and I made a point of visiting as many of the northern planters as I could. I spent time with Mason and Washington and Allerton and Fitzhugh and even had dinner with little Tom Mathew at Cherry Point. Like Henry, I heard a good deal about the Susquahannock problem but of far more moment than that, none of them could keep off the subject of the general unrest among the lower classes. Fitzhugh went so far as to swear that the small planters and servants and even the slaves were being organized some how. No one could give me specifics, but Alice and I returned feeling most uneasy. I wonder if we cannot direct the sheriffs to investigate and prepare a report for us?"

The Council sat in silence. Page's news was serious and alarming. The Leveller cause had been crushed in England; had it found its way across the ocean?

Colonel Bacon spoke again. "Why must unrest among the lower class-es be organized? With the price of tobacco as it is, they have enough cause for unhappiness without our suspecting a Masaniello in their midst. Who among us would like to eke out a living on fifty or a hundred acres under current conditions?"

The Councilors murmured and talked among themselves. Sir William banged his gavel again. "You are too soft-hearted, Nat. Any man who can-not make ends meet in Virginia is a fool or a rogue. The colony is a paradise compared to what is was when you and I came over. No, I lay this to Cromwell and his ilk. It's Pandora's box. Once those levelling ideas were released to the world there was no getting rid of them. I shall tell the sher-iffs to keep me informed, directly, and if I hear anything interesting I shall let the rest of you know at once. God save me, I had hoped to spend my last years in peace, but if action is necessary then it shall be taken."

Unexpectedly Sir William leaned over the great table and skewered Nat with his icy gray eyes. "You, young fellow. You have an outlying plantation. Have you heard any grumblings and rumblings from the rabble?"

Nat was wholly taken aback but he found himself strangely composed and lied readily, without batting an eye. "Why no, sir. I get about a good deal in Henrico and Charles City County and I can't say that I have noticed anything untoward. Everybody complains about the price of tobacco and about taxes, but that is hardly news. Perhaps whatever is going on is con-fined to the north."

Sir William sat back, satisfied. Colonel Bacon had been right. Young Bacon would be a welcome addition to the Council; he would do just fine. He addressed himself to Page. "There you are, John. You have always been an alarmist; perhaps that is how you keep that enviable figure. I would swear the James River is free of taint. But still, I'll put the word out to the sheriffs and give you a report the next time we convene. Is there anything else? Hearing nothing further, I declare this meeting adjourned."

The Councilors rose and stretched and talked among themselves. Nat left the Statehouse with Colonel Bacon and the two of them walked to *The Unicorn*. The older man had planned to spend the night in Jamestown but now that the Council had adjourned so early he decided to ride back to King's Creek that very afternoon. He found his body servant in Lawrence's stable and within ten minutes he was on the road, extending a fond farewell to his cousin and urging him to visit as soon as the baby arrived. Nat watched the Colonel disappear down Back Road and then returned to the stable where Lawrence was grooming Folly.

"You don't have to do that, Dicken," cried Nat. "That's what Abraham is for."

Lawrence laughed. "Don't tell Joanna, but Abraham is in the kitchen drinking cider with Clarissa. You know that I love a good horse, and Folly is a fine one. Look at those shoulders and haunches. But what do you need with a battle horse?"

"Why I don't need one, of course, but he is pure black and he struck my fancy because I left a black in Suffolk which I loved like a maiden. Besides, Ballard gave me a good price for him, because he couldn't tame him. It took me all winter to bring him around, but now he is gentle as a lamb, though you would never think so to look at him."

Lawrence glanced around. The stableyard lay quiet as a tomb in the thin late afternoon sun. "How did it go?" he asked quietly.

Nat moved closer to his friend and stroked Folly's glossy shoulder. "For my part, fine. In fact I believe that Sir William thinks I am as Green as grass. But what a heartless bunch they are, Dicken, my cousin excepted. He spoke up for the 'rabble,' as they call the small farmers and tradesmen, but the rest of them care nothing for the plight of the little men. Do you know John Page?"

Lawrence snorted. "Of course I do. As selfish and malicious a whoreson as ever walked under the sun. Why do you ask about him, in particular?"

"Well, he has been in Stafford and Westmoreland recently and the great planters there told him that the rabble was being organized by some unknown force and that they feared an uprising. He knew nothing specific, but the Council was concerned enough to ask the Governor to direct the sheriffs to sniff out what they can and report their findings."

Lawrence put down the curry comb and wiped his forehead with his sleeve. "So that's the way the wind is blowing. Well, it does not surprise me. Our northern chapter is the least discreet of the four. Will is planning to sail up there soon on the pretext of visiting his plantation and I will make sure he talks to Brent and spreads the word for the Ring to lie low. Still, it must all come out one of these days. Perhaps it is time to abandon caution and let nature take its course."

"But then your laws will have no chance whatever?"

"We have chosen the path of law, Nat, but at some point the people are going to weary of our slow, incremental progress – if you can call it progress – and choose a more dangerous road. And who am I to say that they may not be right?"

Nat frowned and leaned down and scooped up a handful of gravel which he idly tossed, pebble by pebble, as the innkeeper ran a comb through Folly's mane. He had missed the horrors of England's Civil Wars and his loving father had protected him well from unrest during the Protectorate. Would fate even the score here in Virginia? He thought of Lyn and sighed. She had been victimized enough by the family wars waged by Sir Edward Duke. She deserved to live in peace and raise her children free from discord. If he believed in God he would pray that reform come to the colony in an orderly fashion. In fact, whatever Supreme Being turned the world on its axis and toyed with the lives of men, he would offer up just such a prayer. A plea for peace was never amiss. Nat silently sent his thoughts skyward and then turned back to Lawrence. He wanted to give him a full report.

"For what it is worth, I do not think the Governor owns the Council. It is pretty much as you have described it. Perhaps half are Sir William's men, but the rest think for themselves – or don't think at all."

"Well, I'm pleased that you confirm my observations. What else did you learn?"

"Oh. There is some problem with Indians in Maryland. Some northern tribe is moving south and causing trouble. I don't know if that is important or not."

"They must have heard about the Susquahannocks. They are reputed to be fierce warriors. It is neither here nor there as far as the Ring is concerned, but if the savages decide to move into Virginia then it is one more burden for the people to bear, and it may be one burden too many. Was any action taken?"

"No. Sir Henry Chicheley is to continue gathering information and report to the Governor. Sir William said that of all the issues which plague the colony the Indians are his least concern."

"Well, I am not sure that I agree, but time will tell. You see how valuable your presence on the Council has been already? We know to warn our friends in the north to be more discreet and we know to keep an eye on the savages and we know that Sir William's hand is perhaps not quite as steady on the tiller as he thinks. I would say that is a good day's work. There, isn't the horse beautiful? I'm going to have a bath before supper. Would you like one too?"

Nat felt suddenly fatigued and he followed Lawrence into the inn, grateful for the prospect of a good wash, a change of clothes, a good supper and an early night. He would leave for Curles Neck at first light and he wanted to stop at Bland's and Isham's and Crewes' on the way. He would tell his friends all the news and he would wear his gold ring.

CHAPTER 14

MAY - JULY 1675

The young tobacco plants rippled like wind-blown water. Nat turned to John. "Isn't it a grand sight?"

"If they don't succumb to the fly," the attorney grunted.

Nat was seized with annoyance. "Can't you enjoy the moment? You're always looking ahead and, for you, there's always a gray cloud on the horizon. Perhaps your name has rubbed off on your disposition."

John refused to take the bait. Lyn's condition had made Nat edgy: the baby was due at any moment. "I expect you are right. But I'm the one who has worked hand in glove with the men this past winter and spring and, believe me, if you think I have a gloomy cast of mind, you should talk to them. You would think that bringing in a successful crop is as miraculous as Our Lord's creating wine from water."

Nat regretted his temper, but he did not apologize. Recently his friend had turned more and more into himself and seemed always to wear a somber cast. Something was amiss, but he could not for the life of him tell what it was. Things were going very well at Curles Neck and at the Quarter. The weather had cooperated; the men seemed content; the tobacco seedlings were thriving; even as they spoke the builder was carving the foundation for the new house; the bricks were almost cured and they would begin construction by the end of May. Perhaps it was due to the beautiful spring, but even the people of Henrico and Charles City Counties seemed more sprightly and hopeful. John must miss his books and the mental challenges of the law which he loved so much; he was not going to be a farmer forever. Nat shrugged mentally and physically. Most likely his friend needed a woman. They had not discussed the matter; he assumed that the wives of the servants and slaves might accommodate single men. If John was lacking in that department, he had only himself to thank. He changed the subject.

"Did I tell you that I bought Ballard's sloop?"

John looked up in surprise. Nat was spending money right and left. He bit his tongue. Now was not the time to talk of economy; Lyn needed the new house and Curles Neck certainly required a sloop, but it would have been more prudent to wait for the harvest of their first crop. He strove to sound positive.

"It's a charming craft. Does the crew come with it?"

"Yes, they do. The whole package cost only sixty pounds – I think it a very good price."

"Why, that's not bad. Ballard loved the thing – why did he sell?"

"I suspect he is very hard up."

"I daresay you are right. When do you take possession?"

"The boys are going to sail up soon – they could arrive any day. It will make my trips to Jamestown so much easier. Forty miles in one day takes too much out of a horse and rider."

John smiled. "Land, cattle, horse, ship, house and baby. It will be a banner year."

A movement caught Nat's eye. He turned towards the old wooden house and saw Hannah waving a white rag from the back stoop.

"John! I wonder if the baby has come!"

The two men mounted speedily and galloped across the fields. This was the moment which each, in his way, had been waiting for.

That evening Lyn sat before the fire which had been damped down low because of the blessed warmth of the day. All the doors and shutters were open and a river breeze freshened the house. In her arms lay a tiny person who wholly owned her heart as no other ever had.

John had done his homage to little Mary and had already left for Bacon's Quarter. Hannah and Abraham had retired to their cabin. Now she shared the moment only with Nat, as was fitting. Her husband left his seat and came to her and reached down to touch a hand which was no bigger than a flower. The baby blinked and smacked her lips and squirmed.

Lyn smiled like the Madonna. "She's hungry again. What an appetite!"

"Mary," murmured Nat. "I have always loved the name. Bless you for thinking of my aunt, whom I cherished, as she was the nearest thing I had to a mother." He laughed. "And how would we have dealt with another Elizabeth?"

"I hope you don't mind, Nat, but I chose the name for Mary Byrd as well as for your aunt."

"Mind? I think the world of Mary Byrd. She saw you through the whole ordeal. I am just sorry she missed the great moment."

"I asked John to let the Byrds know and to tell them to come anytime, without notice. I feel remarkably well – Hannah said the birth was as easy as any she has attended. I would not call it an ordeal. It was as if ... I can hardly find the words. As if Mary were a precious gift which Virginia has given us in welcome."

"What a fine thought, love. Only this morning John said this was a banner year for us, and right he was. Now if we have a good harvest and move into the new house before the cold weather, life will be complete."

Nat watched the baby suckle and leaned down to kiss Lyn's brow. He would write his father tomorrow. How pleased and happy the old man would be.

Thomas Mathew pushed his chair back from the tea table and sighed contentedly. The miller at Cherry Point had finally gotten the knack of grinding wheat flour fine enough for pastry and the last churn of butter was the best he had ever produced – his herdsman must have managed to keep the cows out of the wild onion. Dorothy had made scones and he had drowned them in butter and elderberry jam. It was heaven. His wife's voice pierced his happiness.

"Mister Mathew, *please* do not scrape your chair on the wood floors. They may only be heart pine, but it took months to finish them properly and now there will doubtless be a gouge where you have been sitting."

The planter sighed again. Back to reality. How to deflect his wife's irritation?

"Dodie, have the trees come back after that plague of flies?"

"Of course not – the creatures crawled out of the ground and devoured all the tender green just when the leaves were forming. How would the trees have come back?"

"Well, the forest looks healthy enough. I can't see any damage."

"Then you haven't looked. All the maples along the river are like skeletons. 'Tis most unsightly. I wish we were back in Warwick."

"Ah Dodie, please. Northumberland County is not the end of the world. Warwick is overpopulated and overplanted. How can you compare the two?"

"Well, did we have comets in Warwick? And was the sky ever black with pigeons, so multitudinous that they broke the greatest tree limbs that ever were? And then the flies ... Your name might be Job, for all that has happened this year already. What will be next?"

Mathew mused. It *was* odd. The spring had brought just such portents as his wife had named and it was only July. But Dorothy was so prone to melancholy. If he did not bring her out of it she would retire to bed for the rest of the day and he would have no one to talk to.

"Well, at least we salted away enough pigeons to last us all winter. Come, tell me you are not unhappy at Cherry Point. Should you like to move to our place in Stafford?"

"Oh, Mister Mathew, you are cruel. Live at the end of the world, surrounded by rough men and savages? I hope you are in jest."

"Oh, Dodie, of course I am. But only think of your advantages. Not many have a house like ours, overlooking the Potomac where it is most picturesque. Our orchard has finally matured and our wheat and tobacco promise well if only we get more rain. What is there for you in Warwick now that your mother has passed on? You were the one who wanted to sell the old place since it made you grieve to stay there."

Dorothy Mathew moved her embroidery needle in and out of her work. Thomas was right. She *had* wanted to leave her childhood home when it was no longer animated by her mother's vigorous spirit. And Northumberland *was* indeed civilized compared to Stafford. In fact, she had very little to complain about. After all, when Captain Grantham tied up at their wharf again he would bring the mahogany dining table and the matching chairs – a whole dozen of them. Everybody said Cherry Point was charming – and it was. If only she had not lost the baby last winter ... and then those strange events in the spring. She shuddered as she thought of the buzzing of the flies that had seared her nerves for days until, miraculously, they were gone. She got a hold of herself and counted her blessings.

"Come, Mister Mathew, have some more tea. Then will you walk me down to the river? I think some exercise would do me good."

Mathew smiled. "No more tea, but I'll gladly walk with you. And when we return you must put up my things, for I am riding to Stafford tomorrow for a whole week. Are you sure you will be alright with Betsy Moore for company?"

"Of course. She'll be here by supper time. We do *her* a favor to invite her, as she has not had a soul to talk to since Henry died. I shall darn your old stockings – I don't want you wearing the good ones in the wilderness."

"Whatever you like, my dear. Take my arm and let us get some fresh air."

Mathew stood in the doorway of his Stafford plantation house and gazed at the dependencies. There was the smoke house, there the well house, there the kitchen. The place was laid out well enough, but it was all terribly primitive. He smoothed his hand over the log walls of the main house: the bark was still hanging down like the pelt of a rough dog. And Pierce had not even had the time to fill the interstices with clay. The place was comfortable enough on a sunny July day like this, but come winter it would uninhabitable. Still, the man worked like a fiend – Mathew could not bring himself to utter a word of criticism. He had a gem in the rough, for the fellow had been plucked from an English prison and was covering up his unsavory past with unremitting labor. Mathew had him for five more years when the indenture would expire. By that time the place would look better and doubtless would be profitable. Once Pierce finished clearing the fields the tobacco would flourish here, he could tell, the soil was so fat.

He wondered about Mistress Pierce. She had no wedding band and he supposed that her union with the overseer had not been blessed by God. He and the Pierce family were going to church together tomorrow – perhaps he could make a discreet inquiry. If Dorothy found out that the couple was living in sin she would keep after him until he got rid of Pierce, and he would not let that happen. How was it that the Lord let women like Mistress Pierce breed like rabbits, but had thus far denied Dodie a child who lived more than a few weeks? It was not right. The woman had two urchins clinging to her skirts and another, most obviously, on the way. Still, she seemed to care for them well enough, and Pierce said she acted like a mother to the swineherd's boy, Robbie Hen, so she must have a soul, though one would not guess it to look at her.

Mathew heard the jingle of harness and looked up to see Pierce seated on a rough wagon pulled by two equally rough looking horses. The overseer jumped down and doffed his cap.

"Are you ready to look at the swine, sir? It's a good mile, so I brought the wagon. But if you would rather ride your mare...?"

"No, Pierce, thank you. She needs a rest, so let's take the wagon. Didn't your wife want to send some things to Hen?"

"Oh yes, sir. He would not survive without Rachel sending him bread and fruit and vegetables and table beer and keeping Robbie in decent clothes. It's our bargain – he cares for the best herd in the county and we help him with the rest."

At these words Mistress Pierce appeared, laden with packages, a towheaded little boy and a smaller girl clinging to her skirts. Her great belly lifted her skirt and apron in front and exposed thick legs clad in dirty socks and shoved into rough pattens. Mathew thought of Dorothy's silk stockings and dainty little slippers and shuddered. Each to his own. He helped the woman load the various sacks and bundles and a small keg of beer and complimented her on her generosity. He was surprised to see her blush deeply and he thought better of her. Poor thing – perhaps nobody had ever spoken highly of her before. Pierce doubtless simply used her for ... well, for the purpose for which God had fashioned women. Mathew wiped the picture from his mind and climbed into the wagon.

Pierce clucked and whistled at the shaggy horses as the rough conveyance jolted along a well-worn dirt path which ran north through dense forest, perhaps half a mile from the Potomac.

"Why do you not use the river road? It must be smoother," Mathew asked the overseer.

"Oh yes, sir, it is, sir. But this way cuts off a good piece – 'tis like the side of a triangle, if you take my meaning. This is your own road, on your own land, sir. Besides, the gentry grow angry when they see farm wagons on the public road. I've been called many a harsh name when I've took the liberty."

"Well, I can't say that I like that. I pay taxes here. We shall take the river road tomorrow, when we go to church. We shall have to take the wagon, will we not, with your wife and children and all?"

"Yes, sir. I was planning to take the wagon and pick up Hen and his boy on the way, which is our custom. You could ride with us or take the mare, as you choose, sir."

"Excellent. You are as entitled as any to use the road, and I want to make that clear to whoever might think otherwise. My! Look at the forest. Those poplars are as large as any I've seen, and there are some handsome oaks as well. There is fine wood enough to improve the plantation – it is only a matter of time. Perhaps I can send you some men from Cherry Point to give you a hand with the house while you finish clearing. I should like to plant next spring. We'll talk about it tomorrow. Ah, that must be Hen's."

"Yes, sir. 'Tis only one room, but it suits him well enough. And he's a good father to the boy. Takes him to church regular and is trying to get him some learning, for Hen himself don't read nor write."

The swineherd's small cabin stood in a natural glade near a stream which had cut deep into the rich soil as it made its way to the Potomac. Age had weathered its log walls to a pale gray shot with silver and rough shingles of the same hue formed the roof. Mathew saw neither well nor necessary house – he supposed that Hen and his son took water directly from the stream and answered the calls of nature in the deep forest. Human life here was not that far removed from that of the swine of which Hen was the master.

"What happened to the mother?" asked Mathew as the wagon jolted to a halt.

"Died when Robbie was born, I've been told."

"And the child is how old?"

"Some eight years. Why, there he is now. Rob, my lad, come and meet your master."

A slim brown boy with dark liquid eyes and brown hair lightened by the summer sun approached the wagon, eager to see what was in the bundles, but apprehensive of the well-clad stranger.

"Hello, my lad, I'm Thomas Mathew. You're likely looking. Where is your father?"

The child glanced shyly at the planter and sketched a bow. "In the forest with the herd, sir, but he knows you are coming and will be here soon."

Robbie Hen took the horses' reins and Mathew and Pierce climbed down and began unloading the wagon. As Mathew wrestled the keg of beer to the cabin's stone stoop a footstep caught his ear and around the corner of the cabin strode a larger version of Robbie Hen. The swineherd stood straight and proud and looked directly into Mathew's eyes as the introductions were made: he was respectful, but his own man.

"I'm glad to meet you, sir. Mister Pierce has said such good things about you. Perhaps you would like to see the swine?"

Mathew glanced at Pierce. "Why, I should like it of all things. Pierce tells me that you keep them in an enclosure, unlike most, who let them run wild."

"Oh yes, sir. I take them out in the forest every day, but at night I put them in their pen. Of course they could get out if they really had a mind to it, but generally they are tired when I bring them home, and they are happy enough to lie in the cool earth. I've made them some houses and they do seem to like their yard. But sir ... did Mister Pierce tell you about last week?"

Mathew glanced at his overseer again. "What do you mean?"

Pierce looked somewhat embarrassed. "I was waiting until you could hear it from Hen, sir. Perhaps I should have said something sooner."

Mathew frowned. "Whatever are you talking about?"

Hen spoke up. "Just a week ago – I know, because it was the day before church, just like today – two Doegs crept up on the herd just as I was collecting them to return home. They seized one of your best sows and the devils had not gone two hundred yards when they slit her throat and began to carve her up to carry her off across the river to their camp. Daisy gave a great cry as she died and I came rushing to her. I carry no firearm, only a knife and a tomahawk, but I was caught up with a sort of madness and I threw myself on the savages, armed though they were. They were so taken aback by my fury that I was able to give one a wicked knife wound in the shoulder and throw my hatchet at the other before they had their wits about them. They could have slit my throat as easy as Daisy's, but instead they fled to the river and jumped in their canoe. I followed them and saw them paddling as though the devil was at their heels. I feared more trouble, but all has been quiet since then. I told Mister Pierce when he fetched us for church on Sunday and he took Daisy's parts back with him to cure. Poor thing will make good eating, but she was one of my favorites and I beg your pardon for the loss."

"Why, my man, what else could you have done? You got rid of the savages and saved the meat – I can hardly complain." Mathew reached into his pocket. "Not many carry good English coin on them, but it would be my pleasure to give you this shilling and your son this penny. You have served me well."

Pierce coughed. He had clearly been afraid to disclose the Doeg incident to his master and now he was relieved that the story had been told, and so well received. Mathew told the overseer to finish unloading the wagon and he and Hen and the boy strode into the woods to visit the swine. An hour later he returned, well satisfied. Pierce seemed to be doing a commendable job of carving the plantation out of the forest and Hen was a real asset. He might even think of bringing him down to Cherry Point – the man was capable of doing far more than tending swine in the fastnesses of

Virginia's forests. He would turn it over in his mind tonight and perhaps he would broach the matter to Hen tomorrow. All in all he was well served in Stafford. It was most satisfactory.

On Sunday morning they took the river road, Pierce and his brood in the squat wagon and Thomas Mathew on his mare. The day was fair: the oaks and hickories and poplars towered above them and the slim maples and willows graced the river bank like so many handmaidens attending the broad, stately Potomac. A flash of red pierced the dense green as a cardinal fled to protect its young from the intruders. Moments later Mathew thrilled to the sound of an impudent mockingbird. Dodie thought them pests, as they woke her too early, but he loved them for their smart appearance and bold song. He had taught one to mimic his whistle and he and the bird would tease each other every morning at the breakfast table until Dodie put her fingers in her ears and made them stop.

Pierce glanced back and pointed left where a dim track branched off from the river road into the depths of the forest. It must be the other way to Hen's. Mathew nodded and urged his little mare alongside the wagon.

"Shall we be in time for church?" he asked.

"Oh yes, sir. We always allow more than enough time. And Hen is never late. You'll see – they'll both be sitting on the porch, each clean as a whistle, for they bathe on Saturday night. We like to be early, for Sunday is almost the only time we see our neighbors. Rachel has put up a good lunch, so if you like we can join the others by the riverside after the service and I can introduce you to some folks. However, if Colonel Mason and Captain Brent are there, you'll likely be invited to join the gentry. Don't let us hold you back. We'll eat with our friends and then return, but you must stay as long as you like. Colonel Mason knows about Hen and the Doegs – we told him last Sunday. He would be the one to ask about the savages here in Stafford, but if you'll pardon my putting myself forward, I would watch what you say to Captain Brent for his uncle, the first Giles, married a Doeg Empress and his cousin, the second Giles, is half savage."

"You don't say!"

"Yes, sir, I tell you no lie. The Brents are proud of their heathen connection."

"Well, well. I shall watch my tongue. Look – there is the cabin, but I don't see Hen."

"Why, that's a first. Perhaps he and the boy are inside making themselves finer than usual in your honor."

Pierce put two fingers to his lips and produced a whistle shrill enough to wake the dead. Two warblers, startled by the noise, flitted into the forest but otherwise the glade lay motionless, in deep silence. Slanting sunbeams pierced the green canopy and dappled the bronze carpet of last year's leaves. Nothing moved.

Pierce handed the reins to his wife and swung down from the wagon, glancing at Mathew. "I daresay the pigs acted up and Hen took the boy up to the pens to see what was amiss. Please God it's not those savages again."

A chill seized Mathew's chest. "Why, he said he had had no further trouble ... still....." The planter dismounted and tied the mare to the back of the wagon. "You go up to the pens and I'll look in the cabin."

Pierce frowned and nodded his acquiescence and strode to the right of the cabin to follow the stream up to where the swine were kept. Rachel Pierce gathered her two children to her and sat stolidly, waiting for whatever fate had in store. Mathew swallowed and crossed the well-worn little dirt yard to the cabin. As he approached the stone steps he noted that the door was open and that somebody had left a bundle on the threshold. Had Hen rushed off to guard the swine, dropping his clothing in his haste? He mounted the steps and froze. There before him, half in and half out of the humble dwelling, lay the swineherd in his Sunday best, his hat tumbled to one side. His sun-streaked hair, so like Robbie's, lay lank and motionless on the dusty planks of the porch. Mathew stooped to see the man's face and cried out in horror. The entire right side of Hen's visage was crushed and was a mass of crimson blood and white bone. The eye was nowhere to be seen. In the shadow of the fallen man's shoulder lay a tomahawk, brilliant with red feathers and red blood. A bluebottle circled the swineherd's head and settled on his face. Robert Hen would serve Thomas Mathew no longer.

The planter's head whirled and his stomach heaved. He turned and signaled Rachel Pierce. She needed to see no more than his white face and awkward stance: hurling strict orders to her children to move not an inch, she threw herself from the wagon and thrust her ponderous form across the yard. Just as she reached the stone steps and saw what lay across the threshold a great yell came from upstream. Mathew and Rachel looked at one another, riveted, and then the planter gestured to the woman to attend to the dead man and rushed up the path towards the swineyard. It crossed his mind that Pierce might have been attacked by savages, but he thought no further and ran on. The overseer was armed with a sharp knife, but his own pistols were still in his saddlebags. Well, it was in God's hands. Relief swept over him as he saw Pierce's stout form standing near the stream, waving his arms. Mathew reached him, breathless. Before them lay the lithe bronze body of an Indian bowman, Hen's knife in his side, buried up to the hilt, right beneath his heart. The warrior lay on his back, his painted face to the sky. His dark eyes were still open, though sightless. The right side of his head was shaven so as not to impede his shooting arm and the rest of his midnight hair was braided, long and thick, entwined with shells and feathers. His handsome torso was bare and his manhood was covered with a doeskin

211

breechclout. His legs were strong and straight and his feet bare, but they would never again tread the forest floor, either in peace or in war.

Pierce breathed heavily as though he had run for miles. "That's Hen, for you. A knife to the heart! I only hope there were not more of them. Fetch your pistols – we must go to the swineyard. He may yet be in trouble, and there is the boy to worry about." Pierce had lost the gloss of servitude: he spoke to Mathew as though he were an equal. The planter noticed nothing.

"There is no need of my pistols," he said sadly.

"What do you mean?"

"Hen lies dead in his cabin, struck down by a tomahawk. I suppose this one here is the murderer." Thoughts jangled in his head. "But you are right – where is the boy? My God, perhaps there are others. Let's go back and arm ourselves and decide what to do next. I left your wife with ... the body."

The color left Pierce's face. "Hen is dead? God in Heaven above. We must find the boy."

Without further discussion the planter and the overseer followed the stream back to the cabin. As they rounded the corner they saw the wagon just as they had left it, the shaggy ponies hanging their heads low in the gathering heat and the two Pierce children huddled in the wagon bed among the food hampers. But there was one change. Rachel Pierce had taken her place again on the driver's bench and she was not alone. Pressed against her sturdy bosom was Robbie Hen, shivering convulsively as though his whole nervous system had been disordered by a bolt of lightning. As it had, thought Mathew ... as indeed it had. The boy had worshiped his father. And more: could the boy have been a witness to the murder?

Pierce and Mathew walked to the wagon and stared up at Rachel's impassive face. Robbie Hen was white, the life drained out of him. Mistress Pierce held him close and stroked his back, over and over, as one would gentle a colt. A soft heart beat beneath that crude exterior, thought Mathew. The woman was coarse and well nigh inarticulate, but when it came to children her instincts were sound. He would not forget it. Pierce had seen life behind bars and his wife probably much worse, but here, faced with the cruelty of the wilderness they had come into their own. In truth, would he and Dodie have acted as well? Almost certainly not. The planter refocused his thoughts. Perversely, all were looking to him for guidance; he, who was least able to deal with these horrible circumstances. He untied the mare and strove to look masterful.

"The first thing is the child. You all go on to church with Robbie and tell the people what has happened. If Colonel Mason is there, make sure he knows everything. Then send some people back to help me. I'll stay here with ... with Robbie's father. My pistols are primed and I have plenty of shot – I always ride prepared. If, God forbid, the savages are still skulking about, I daresay I can deal with them. But please hurry, not the least because ... we should take care of Mister Hen as soon as possible. Off you go then! Make haste and see to the boy."

Pierce clambered into the wagon, seized the reins, and began turning the horses. Mathew was proud of himself. Nobody had to know how reluctant he was to stay in this quiet glade alone with Hen. Dodie would be proud. The child ... how Dodie would feel for the child. He glanced at Rachel Pierce, who, no longer obsequious, beckoned him over. Turning her head from Robbie, she spoke softly.

"If you please, sir, I found the boy under the bed. He saw the whole thing and hid there, sure that he would die like his father. There was only one warrior – the one Rob Hen killed. He is a Doeg, no question about it – one of the two that killed the hog. Robbie has seen the fellow many times ... knows him well. Don't fear for the lad, sir. I'll take him home. He belongs to us now."

Rachel Pierce's eyes glistened with tears and so did the planter's as he watched the wagon recede, the white faces of the two Pierce children like bright dots as they stared back at him, their faces frozen.

Mathew tied the mare to a sapling and started to walk towards the cabin. No; it was too much. He pulled his pistols from their holders and leaned against the rough bark of a huge poplar. Quiet settled on the glade. The planter sighed and slid to the ground, his back still to the tree, the pistols in his lap. A brilliant blue sky was just visible through the canopy and a soft breeze moved the leaves. Virginia. Beautiful, but cruel. The colony tested people and it was not always the wellborn who survived and prospered. The warblers returned and busied themselves about their nest. In the distance the mockingbird jeered.

CHAPTER 15

SEPTEMBER – DECEMBER 1675

Ballard looked around the Council chamber and groaned inwardly. At the foot of the table, figuratively below the salt as befitted a newcomer sat young Bacon with his dark curls and handsome, arrogant face. Those eyes were remarkable – like a hawk's. The Squire's little wife – what was her pet name? Lyn? – would be mesmerized by that predator look. Would just freeze like a rabbit. Freeze and make herself available – freely available – to the hawk. Turn over and show a soft, curved belly ... a belly that called for stroking ... whereas his own wife.... Enough of that. But Bacon's wife was delicious, no question about it. Somewhat delicate for his own tastes, but a nice little piece. The Squire had a child now, did he not? And probably another one on the way. Those slim, ardent youths just could not get enough ... well, neither could he.

At the other end of the great table, just to the Governor's right, sat Sir Henry Chicheley. Ballard groaned again and this time a sound escaped him, for John Page looked his way with an expression somewhere between a frown and a sneer. Page thought he walked on water, damn him. Bacon and Page. A pox on both of them. Young Bacon had his upper plantation, his cattle, his servants, his slaves, his great black horse, his very sloop and now the upstart sat at the Council table. Page's plantation looked as though every leaf and lawn and tree had been burnished and polished. The man's tobacco was second to none, expect perhaps Colonel Bacon's, and he never let you forget it. But old Nat was a comfortable soul ... not judgmental like Page. If one's debts had grown a bit out of hand Nat would give you some advice, but he didn't have that prating Puritan way of talking that John Page did.

Ballard leaned back and sighed. It felt like the Council chamber had absorbed all of the summer's heat and relinquished none of it. He rose and threw open the casements and felt the September air stir. Thank God – a touch of fall. Berkeley expected them to listen to Henry Chicheley – *Sir* Henry Chicheley, (couldn't forget that the pompous ass was a knight), report on the savages. They probably would be here all afternoon and even then they might not finish. He wondered if Lawrence had a spare bed at *The Unicorn*. He personally could not tolerate the Whiggish fellow but he did keep a good house. Ballard started. The Governor was addressing him.

"Tom, have you finished airing yourself? We are ready to begin. If the subject of an impending Indian war bores you, perhaps you would rather be excused."

Ballard bit his tongue. The old fool could still sting like a scorpion. He really must get a hold of himself – they were all staring at him. It was just that his debts had become crushing and last week Ann had denied him her bed. Well, probably half the men in the room were in the same position. He must put on a good face and let the farce play itself out.

"I beg your pardon, Your Honor. The heat distracted me. Now I am myself."

"Very good," replied the Governor. "I have called this special meeting so that you may be informed of recent events in Maryland which may impact the colony. Sir Henry has been good enough to give me a full report and he will now do the same for you. I would ask you to give him your complete attention."

Sir Henry Chicheley rose and straightened the notes in front of him. A neat silver beard outlined his short-jawed face and a trim moustachio sat on his upper lip. He was altogether compact and orderly, the perfect soldier. He was not, however, a natural speaker and he frowned as he marshaled his thoughts. He must tell this sorry tale as impartially as possible – it would be for the rest of the Council to settle on the facts like vultures and pick them apart with their bloody beaks. He had never been able to fathom why one had to overlay facts with great swathes of emotion, but most men were made so; it was just the way things were.

"Let me begin with the death of Robert Hen. You all know – or I suppose you know – that last July a swineherd in Stafford was murdered by the Doeg Indians."

"Perfidious heathen," muttered Cole.

Oak met oak as Sir William's gavel crashed onto the council table. "I will tolerate no interruptions. Go on, Sir Henry."

The knight glanced at his notes again. "Colonel Mason and Captain Brent took immediate action. Shortly after the crime was committed they sailed over to Maryland to search out the perpetrators." Chicheley looked around the table. "Brent knew his way about – there is a family connection with those particular savages. He went one way and Mason the other. Brent found the murderer's band and exacted immediate revenge. He slew the *werowance* in recompense for Hen and stole the chief's son in recompense for what Hen's child had to suffer."

Colonel Bacon raised a hand and was recognized by the Governor. "Was the Hen boy molested?"

"No," answered Chicheley, "but he saw his father die by an Indian hatchet and they say he has never been the same since."

The Colonel sighed and studied his hands. Nat cast a sympathetic look at his cousin and thought of Mary. What a hideous thing to happen to a child – surely the terrible vision of his father's death would be with him for the rest of his life.

Spencer spoke. "Did they kill just the one savage?"

"Oh, no. Brent slew ten at least and seized the child for a hostage."

Despite the Governor's admonition the entire Council muttered its approval.

"Ten Indians for one English?" cried Page. "It should have been one hundred."

"Here, here," called out the Council.

Nat found himself in agreement with the majority. Robert Hen had been cruelly slain, without provocation, and his son had been mentally scarred. It was appropriate to wipe out the whole Doeg band – any savages who survived would think twice about attacking the English in the future. It would be interesting to see what the Governor had to say about all of this. After all, he was a veteran of the last Indian war, a conflict which most of the Council was too young to have experienced.

"There is more," continued Sir Henry Chicheley. "Colonel Mason had split off from Captain Brent, following a trail to a second Indian camp. He too was successful. He found the savages at home and opened fire as soon as they showed themselves. Fourteen died before the firing stopped. As his men were reloading a *werowance* stepped from the bushes and Mason recognized him – recognized him as a Susquehannock."

"Not a Doeg?" asked Colonel Bacon sharply.

"Therein lies the problem," answered Chicheley. "Mason had stumbled on a Susquehannock camp and, as you know, last spring the Susquehannocks made their peace with Governor Calvert and were named English allies."

The Councilors looked at one another askance. The Susquehannock unrest had just been put down; now it might flare up again.

"It's all the same," cried Ballard. "They are all one and the same. If the northern Indians did not commit this crime, then surely they are guilty of others. Two dozen Indians dead for Robert Hen and the chief's son captured? It is a fair trade."

"Let Sir Henry finish," urged the Governor. "The tale gets more complicated."

"Well, Mason was aghast at his error. Between ourselves, it was purely a mistake – he thought he was attacking Doegs. But it would have been fatal to admit as much – if you give the savages an inch they will take a mile. He put out the story that Hen's death could have been attributed to any of the Maryland Indians and the settlers agreed with him. Unfortunately the

Susquehannocks did not see things quite the same way. Like wasps whose nest has been pierced by a sharp stick, they rose up and stung some Marylanders, marauding and pillaging. I cannot tell you in all honesty whether they slew any English, but it is likely.

"In August Sir William and Governor Calvert agreed to send a joint force to put the Susquehannocks down before the thing got wholly out of hand. Late that month or early this month Colonel John Washington and Major Isaac Allerton and Colonel George Mason on behalf of Virginia and Major Thomas Truman on behalf of Maryland found the Susquehannocks at Piscataway Creek and pinned them down in that old English fort – you know the one."

"I've been there!" cried Spencer. "Why, our friends should have been able to crush the savages like vermin, enforted there."

Sir Henry paused and looked at Sir William Berkeley, who frowned. Chicheley continued. "Well, it did not play out that way."

"You will never tell us that we were defeated?" asked Tom Swann who had hitherto been silent.

"I'm an old soldier," said Chicheley quietly, "and I make it a practice never to fight other men's battles after the fact, so I will not pretend to tell you exactly what happened. At some point, however, the savages sent out five *werowances* to treat for peace and things got out of hand."

"Explain what you mean, "commanded the Governor. "They need to know what happened."

Sir Henry cleared his throat. "We think it was Truman, the Marylander, but whether he or another, the peace talks were of no avail and ... the five *werowances* were slain. The English simply knocked them on their heads and that was the end of it."

"There was a truce and we killed the savages' spokesmen?" exclaimed Colonel Bacon.

"It appears so. Governor Calvert blames Truman; the man is going to stand trial."

"Well, there are probably things we don't know," urged Spencer. "Perhaps the savages were going to strike first. Good riddance to bad rubbish, I say. Was that the end of the matter? What happened to the rest of the band?"

"Well, the siege continued for some time and then, regrettably, the remaining savages – several dozen I believe — slipped through our lines and gained their freedom."

"What?" cried Ballard. "We did not crush the rest of them after the chiefs were slain?"

"It appears not," said the Governor dryly. "Governor Calvert and I have corresponded at length. Neither one of us is happy."

"Well, all's well that ends well, I suppose," offered Page. "Mason and Brent killed twenty or so; and Washington and Allerton killed five more, at least. That ought to keep the savages quiet."

"That's just the point, John," said Berkeley. "The savages are *not* quiet. The Susquehannocks have taken the warpath. They have fled Maryland, crossed the Potomac above the falls, and are making their way down the fall line, killing and torturing as they go. I called this meeting because last week I received a report of the death of an entire family in Rappahannock County. What Maryland sowed Virginia is about to reap."

The Councilors looked aghast. The Governor had just announced the beginning of the third Indian war.

"It is our duty to decide what to do next."

The Council broke for dinner and Nat and Colonel Bacon walked slowly to *The Unicorn*, deep in conversation.

"I cannot get the thought of the Hen boy out of my head," said Nat. "I picture Mary. Children are so tender – they should not have to see such things. I shall have to tell Lyn about this...she will take it badly." The young Squire paused. "Do you think the situation is as grave as the Governor does?"

"Oh yes, my boy. Sir William has worked miracles with the tribes within the fall line. They are quite docile and swear allegiance to King Charles. But these Susquehannocks – they are a different matter. We have no treaties with them – know very little about them. Mason's error was most unfortunate and then it was compounded by that fool Truman. No, I expect that things will get worse before they get better."

"Will Sir William call up the militia and organize a force to seek the savages out? Will we build forts? What do you think will happen?"

"Oh, it is too early to tell. But, generally speaking, he is all for peace. He may start negotiations, if that is possible. If I had to guess, I would say that he will send Sir Henry with a force to locate their emperor and see if he can come to some accommodation with them."

Nat stood stock still. "Accommodation? They have slain a frontier family – why it might have been mine? Are these the circumstances under which we should treat with the heathen? It would be a coward's way out."

Colonel Bacon clucked his tongue at his cousin as they entered the cool, dim common room of *The Unicorn*. "We don't have enough facts yet, my boy, but one thing I do know. Keep those thoughts to yourself or you will incur the Governor's wrath. I have seen him angry and I do not wish it on you. Now, let's get something to eat. Tell me about Lyn and Mary. I cannot persuade Betty to visit you; she is so set in her ways, so you shall have to come to us."

Colonel Bacon's speculation proved correct. After three hours of discussion the Council approved the Governor's plan to send Sir Henry Chicheley and some hand-picked men to the Rappahannock plantation where the family had been massacred in order to "investigate" the circumstances and report back with a recommendation for further action. In the meantime the Councilors were asked to order a muster of the militias in their respective counties and see that they were ready to march, if called upon. John Pate's request that the actions of Mason and Washington and Allerton be investigated was denied out of hand – not even put to a vote. Sir William Berkeley was not going to borrow trouble. His last words were for each Councilor to look to his own affairs. In his opinion, those who chose to live on the frontier knew that they were taking some risks – nothing ventured, nothing gained. Nat left the meeting seething with rage. What about the Hen boy? What about the slain family? What about outliers like Byrd and himself? Were their lives less valuable than those whose lands were cradled by the Bay? In the face of the Governor's obduracy no one, least of all he, had asked those questions. But if the savages attacked again, his voice would be heard, whether his cousin liked it or not.

He stood on the Statehouse steps and watched Sir William walk to his townhouse, one hand on Philip Ludwell's shoulder. He spat with contempt and turned the other way. He would share his thoughts with Dicken Lawrence and tomorrow he would sail back to Curles Neck. The Ring was meeting next week at Whitby – he would seek their counsel.

Lyn held Mary up to watch the workmen's last wagon disappear east. She raised the baby's hand and made it wave "good-bye." The last brick had been laid, the wood floors gleamed, Squire Thomas' beautiful glass shone in the casements and the Purbeck marble mantle graced the parlor. It was an elegant little house, and all her own. The slaves would move the furniture from the old wooden house this afternoon and tonight she and Nat would lie in their new bedchamber, under the soft blue counterpane which complemented the blue and white striped curtains. The furniture was humble, but she had no complaints. All in all, it was perfect.

She held the child to her and kissed the fragrant head with its dark curls. She turned Mary around and looked into her eyes. Yes – they were going to be like Nat's. The girl was her father's daughter: he doted on her.

Lyn started back to the wooden house to give Abraham and Hannah directions about the furniture. Nat had promised to talk about the slaves when the new house was finished, and finished it was. She would let him enjoy it for a few days, but that discussion was not going to wait long. Their harvest had been a good one and should fetch a decent price. Nat couldn't have spent the balance of the little fortune they brought from England. Surely they could find the wherewithal to free the slaves and pay them a decent wage so that they would stay on as hired help. All of them would, she was sure. The Bacons were good masters – it was just that she did not want to own any human being, under any circumstances.

Lyn reached the wooden house and smiled. It looked so frail and tipsy, how could they have lived here for a year? More than a year really, for it was November now and they had sailed to Curles a year ago, September. Well, it had served its purpose and now it was John's. He was spending more and more time at Curles since Nat seemed always to be away, either in Jamestown or upriver with the Byrds or that fellow Goode. She did not know quite why Nat needed to attend all those meetings, but John approved and doubtless it would all become clear at some point. They both wore twists of gold on their right hands and said it was the mark of some society of friends. How like men – they always had to organize themselves in strange groups and decorate themselves with medals and ribbons and other symbols, ranking themselves one against the other. She supposed women did similarly foolish things, but at the moment she could not call any to mind.

Dear John. She would make the old house so comfortable that he would not want to leave it. She could read his heart and knew that he suffered but he had seemed somewhat easier this fall. It had been months since he had talked about returning to England – perhaps he had decided to stay. If so, he must marry. Lyn laid Mary in her cradle and snuggled a wool shawl around her, for the wind had just started up again and it carried a hint of winter. She felt a twinge in her own breast as she thought of John with another woman. Who could possibly be good enough for him? Nobody that she knew. In truth, John was hers. Lyn blushed. It was a wicked thought. She had enough – more than enough. Next Sunday she would pay a little more attention to the sermon and regulate her thoughts.

Hannah entered with the curtains they were going to hang for John and she asked the black woman to watch the baby for a few minutes. She felt fluttered and wanted a little time to herself. What had made her think of John as hers? She wanted to possess no one. She and Nat were equals, living out the pact they had made as children. Mary was a gift who was in her care until the child became a woman, but whom she did not possess, except in the most primitive sense of the word. But John ... Lyn recognized that she wanted his continued fealty. Her soul was scandalous. She should want John to have what she and Nat had, but she did not. If he found another woman it would wound her deeply.

Lyn put her hands to her cheeks and felt them burning. She strode to the bluff and looked across the river. The forest was ablaze with yellow and gold and scarlet. There – that was a black gum. She had never seen such noble reds and oranges – the tree might be on fire. This new land was beautiful and yet it was so strange. Perhaps if she could look at her heart it would appear the same, burning with desire. She wished Nat were home; she suddenly wanted him desperately. Lyn straightened her shoulders and looked at the river. He had taken the sloop – perhaps she would see him coming around the bend, white sails gleaming. A movement caught her eye. There was a craft on the water, but it was not a sloop. It was an Indian dugout with...one, two, three, four oarsmen. Lyn watched them steady the craft as the current caught it and idly wondered who they were and where they were going. The wind blew off the river and whipped her skirts about. She ordered her clothes and turned towards the houses, old and new. If she kept herself busy this afternoon she would not have to think too deeply.

Nat wrapped Folly's reins around the familiar porch rail at Whitby and looked around to see who else had arrived. Byrd's sloop was tied neatly to the wharf and on the other side was Giles Bland's. Bland had promised to bring Drummond and Lawrence from Jamestown and to pick up Isham and Crewes if they had decided not to ride. There were no other horses, so the Charles City County contingent must have come with Bland by water. Nat loosened Folly's girth and waved to the slave boy who approached to take the black charger to the barn. All the boys loved Folly: he was a great rock of a horse. As he mounted Goode's dilapidated porch Nat heard hoofbeats behind him. He turned and smiled broadly. There was John, coming from Bacon's Quarter. He had not seen his friend since the housewarming in November although the attorney had promised to move to Curles Neck soon after Christmas, leaving Hartwell to oversee the Quarter. Hartwell — that was one of the best things he had done. The man was pure gold. The Quarter prospered and John had been relieved of half of his duties there, if not more. He must thank Byrd again for the referral.

John jumped from Coke and tossed the reins to the waiting slave boy. His grin was as broad as Nat's and the two friends embraced and entered Whitby house together. He and Hartwell were trying to get all the cabins finished before the snow and it had been a month since he had seen Nat and Lyn. The Bacons had taken possession of the brick house and he had moved into the old place on the same day, and they had shared a celebratory dinner. Dear Lyn: the wooden house was as cunning as a child's toy, with its old pine furniture and hand stitched blankets and curtains and rag rugs. Against his better judgment he had promised to move to Curles permanently when the Quarter was finished and that day was fast approaching. He hoped he had made the right decision; how could he have done anything else when he saw the pleading look on Lyn's face?

Bacon and Grey entered the familiar great room of Whitby and saw the Upper James contingent of the Ring settled comfortably before the fire, flagons of rum in hand. Both Drummond and Lawrence had come, so the group was larger than usual. A gold ring sparkled on each right hand. Warm greetings were exchanged and then Byrd took the chair.

"All present and accounted for. Good. I suggest that we discuss the Indian problem first, as we have done all fall, and then move on to other business. But first, Giles Bland has asked for a special hearing."

Nat knew that Byrd thought little of Bland, who, with his flaming hair, was a hothead both literally and figuratively. He noted the dry tone of Byrd's last sentence and winked at John who smiled and winked back. For their part, Bacon and Grey found Bland refreshing in his complete candor, but he was wearing if you spent much time with him. John likened him to a hummingbird which flitted from flower to flower with a vast expenditure of energy for so little accomplished.

Byrd continued. "Giles? What is the news from Westover?"

Bland drained his toddy and leaped to his feet. "Our friends from Jamestown already know this, but the rest of you may not. I have lost my livelihood. The old man has removed me as Commissioner of Customs!"

Little Isham cried out and black Jamie Crewes frowned. Nat had heard the rumor, and had told John and Byrd, but he did not know any details. Bland looked at him.

"I wish you had been there when the General Court met in November – you could have pleaded my cause."

Somewhat taken aback, Nat apologized for anything that he had done or failed to do which had caused Bland harm. He explained that in November he had been wholly taken up with shipping his tobacco and finishing his new house and that he had yet to sit on the General Court, the ways of which were still a mystery to him.

"Moreover, Giles," he asserted, "the Council pays little attention to me, I am so new to it and to Virginia. So far I have hardly said a thing, on any subject. My cousin strongly suggests that I wait for a year before opening my mouth, otherwise I will be considered rude and pushing, not at all the thing. The watchword of the Council of State is: 'make haste slowly'."

Bland flushed. "You can laugh, with your new house and your new babe and everything going so well for you. I don't know what I am going to live on. And father will be furious when he finds out that I have blotted my copybook."

Nat frowned. "Why, I'm sorry that you take it that way, Giles. I did not mean to jest. I am sorry that you have lost your position. What is the story?"

"'Tis more of Berkeley's tyranny. You know what happened a year ago with that whoreson, Ludwell. It all started then."

"We had just arrived, so I don't know the facts, just gossip and hearsay. But I do know that you challenged the Secretary to a duel and that he failed to appear and the next day was off to London. Is that what lies between you and Berkeley – the quarrel with Ludwell?"

"Oh, it started before that, from the first day we met. He has never thought well of me ... calls me an upstart because my father is a merchant. At our first interview he said I was pert and thrusting, all because I was anxious to settle my aunt's estate which still, four years later, languishes unresolved. But the duel with Tom Ludwell didn't help."

"Do you mind telling us what happened?" asked John. It was obvious that Bland wanted to unburden himself and if he did not do so he would be useless the rest of the day.

"It was in the fall of seventy-four, just after you arrived. I was in Jamestown on my aunt's business and Ludwell was throwing one obstruction after another in my way. I snapped and called him a whoreson and a puppy. He threw one of his gloves at me and I took it as a challenge, though I later learned that he did not intend it that way. I was in a rage. I told him to meet me at dawn at the glasshouse and bring his pistols. That night I begged a bed from Lawrence – remember, Dicken? – and at first light I crossed to the mainland and waited for my adversary. I waited in vain. He never came. Everybody knows that he ran to Berkeley who put him on a sloop for Kecoughtan where he caught ship for England. I cooled my heels for two full hours and then went back to *The Unicorn* in a rage, not knowing what to do." At this point Bland laughed at himself. "Dicken gave me some good advice along with some paper and a hammer and nails. I wrote out a note to the effect that Ludwell was the son of a whore, a mechanic fellow, a puppy and a coward and I nailed the paper and the glove to the Statehouse door in the broad light of day. They wanted to charge me with libel and lock me up, but Dicken says that if you speak the truth, you can't be guilty. How did you put it, Lawrence?"

"Truth is the perfect defense to libel," laughed the innkeeper. "Giles was as pure as the driven snow – who could doubt that Ludwell was in fact a puppy and a coward, running away as he did, with his tail between his legs. The part about his parentage may not be true, but indeed, who knows about that either?"

The men burst into laughter. It was a good story. Unlike his brother, Thomas Ludwell had no personal courage, and the whole colony knew it. It was not the first time he had hidden behind the Governor's coattails and it might not be the last. Although if the Ring had its way, it would be the last.

"But surely Berkeley did not wait a year to take his revenge," commented Crewes. "Why did the General Court throw you out of office just last month?"

"Oh, they say it's more libel, but I had the same defense. The truth! The fact is, I was riding home to Westover with some friends and Edward Hill overtook us and, unluckily for me, heard me use some rather harsh words about the Governor."

"Come, come Giles. What did you say?" grinned Crewes.

"That he was too old and feeble to keep his wife happy and that he wore horns and was happy to do so, as it relieved him of a duty he no longer wanted."

"Phew. Strong. Very strong."

"But true."

"Nevertheless, they found you guilty and stripped you of your office," said Byrd seriously.

"In that court? Of course. I didn't stand a chance. And they were not going to let me show that what I said was true, I assure you! Although they all knew it – all of them, to a man." Bland glanced at Nat. "Only Colonel Bacon and Tom Swann and John Pate argued that the process had not been fair, not quite by the book, but they weren't going to press the issue. I've never seen Berkeley so furious – I thought he would fall down in a fit. And now, of course, they are going to come after me for my unpaid taxes, I don't doubt it. The joke is that they will never be able to figure out what I owe because it is they themselves who have made my aunt's affairs so cuddy-cuddy that no one will ever unravel them. I would laugh if I were not weeping."

"Indeed, it is a sad story," commented John. "'Tis no way to run a government, by the whim of an old man. All the more reason for us to press forward with our reforms."

"Would that we could," said their host. "But I fear that this Indian business is going to put a spoke in our wheels. Listen to Byrd."

Before Byrd began Goode clapped his hands and the girl brought more rum together with a pitcher of hot water, a bowl of sugar and a plate of butter. Those who wished fashioned toddies and placed them on the hearth to warm. Crewes and Goode took their rum straight.

"You know I have connections with savages up and down the trading path, from the Occaneechee islands in the south to Monacan country in the west and all the way to the land of the Iroquois in the north. Moreover, within the fall line, among the tributary Indians, my communications are inferior to none, though I do say it myself."

"Best Indian trader in the colony," muttered Crewes beneath his breath.

"I am therefore happily situated – although the word 'happy' jars when I think of where my remarks are tending – to hear news which few others have access to. I will keep this short. My sources tell me that since the unfortunate incident at Piscataway Creek that some fifteen English have been slaughtered by the Susquehannocks, and that untold property damage has been done. All along the frontier people are leaving their plantations and grouping together for protection. Many have lost their harvests, their cattle and their very homes. They live in fear; you can see it on their faces. Those who least can afford it have suffered the most – it is unjust.

"I have quizzed anyone with any scrap of information and, to my knowledge, so far the depredations can be attributed to the Susquehannocks, who have sworn to murder ten English for each of their five slain chiefs. But I fear that the revenge of these northerners is just the beginning. If the Susquehannocks are successful the tributary Indians could flare up as well, like dry wood struck by lightning. Abraham Wood of Fort Henry on the Appomatox, who knows more about savages than I have forgotten, tells me that the bands are making alliances against us that they never would have countenanced a year ago, as the Susquehannocks have proved us vulnerable.

"For what it is worth, it is my considered opinion that if we do not strike soon and strike hard, that we will reap the whirlwind. The message needs to get to Jamestown, now."

A profound silence filled Goode's cabin. It was heavy news. The colony had enjoyed relative peace since the death of Opechancanough. Must Virginia now add a third Indian war to the calamities which plagued it? Nat thought of what the Governor had said at the Council meeting in September: those were his very words: a third Indian war. But what was he doing about it? Nothing ... nothing at all. Had his courage failed him, or did he have some clever plan that he was keeping to himself until the time was ripe to show it to the world?

Nat was about to share his thoughts with the company when John spoke. "You have suggested that another Indian war would impede the efforts of the Ring, deflect our reforms. I don't see it that way. It appears to me that Berkeley is as remiss in failing to protect the colony from this gathering threat as he is in failing to make taxation equitable, failing to improve our markets, failing to open the government to the people and failing to provide for the needy, hungry and impoverished. Isn't it all one and the same thing? Changes must be made."

"Hear, hear," cried Isham and Bland together.

"Ah, John," said Nat. "It's why I love you. You cut to the heart of the matter. Of course you are right. The Indian threat is not a reason to *support* the Governor – it is a reason to get rid of him."

"Well, I don't know that we are talking about 'getting rid of' Sir William," cautioned Goode. "That is not within our power, but within the King's. We are creatures of the dust; we dare not look so high."

"Well, well perhaps I misspoke, but you know what I mean. We want to change the government, root and branch, and it is not too far off the mark to say that Sir William *is* the government."

"Go easy, Bacon," insisted Goode. "It is one thing to coax the Burgesses to propose some reforms; it is quite another thing to talk about changing governments. I suggest that you moderate your language – it smacks of treason." Goode lowered his voice. "Men have been hanged for less."

"Hanged and then left with enough life in them to see their own bowels twisted from them, and then pulled apart, their poor limbs scattered to the four corners of the earth. 'Tis the price of treason. I too suggest you moderate your language, Nat," said John quietly.

Bacon fell silent. Was the business of the Ring so risky? Proposing reforms was not a crime ... but if Goode and John thought him foolish then he would watch his tongue.

"It is a lesson to all of us," said Byrd. "Giles has already suffered for saying what all know to be true. I urge the rest of you to be careful, or we will endure the same fate and our work will come to naught."

The visitors from Jamestown had been largely silent. When they met with the various chapters of the Ring they came as guests and made it a habit to sit back and let the members have their say, without interruption; then they would offer a few words. Richard Lawrence finally rose.

"Grey has hit the target. The Governor's failure to deal with the Indian terror is just one more mark against him, among many. But Goode and Byrd speak wisely. Like the Council, we must make haste slowly. We cannot change the government overnight. We have laid down a plan to woo certain of the Burgesses and certain of the Councilors and we must stick with it, or we will imperil ourselves and accomplish nothing."

"But what about the savages?" cried Isham. "If the government does not protect us, who will?"

Lawrence looked at the group, their faces drawn with anxiety. He sighed. This land was so fair, why was life so hard? "Of course the Indian matter cannot wait. I suppose that it is possible that even as we speak Berkeley is setting some plan afoot. How difficult is it, after all, to muster the militia? But I would not count on it. Nat thinks he showed his colors in the fall when he sent Chicheley out to 'investigate' the first Susquehannock reprisals and nothing came of it. No, he must be pushed into action."

The innkeeper looked at Bacon and smiled. He did not have to say a word. Nat rose to his feet. "I'll do it, of course. As the only Councilor among you, it is my duty. Despite my cousin's admonition, now is the time to make my voice heard. I'll write something up – what shall I do, John?"

"We can write a petition – a petition on behalf of the entire frontier. 'Tis a simple matter."

"Yes, yes," called the men, stirring with hope.

"That's the thing, a petition. John and I will write a petition, telling everything we have heard about the savages. Byrd, you will have to help us." The trader nodded quietly. "We'll make it respectful and all that, but we will have to show that time is of the essence – isn't that how you say it, John?"

"Yes. Time is of the essence."

"I'll take it to Jamestown myself. If we get it right, he'll have to call a Council meeting and there are enough wise heads on the Council to insist on an Indian policy. Really, I don't see how we can fail. We will just be speaking the truth."

Crewes and Bland and Isham cried out with enthusiasm, but Drummond and Lawrence and Byrd and Goode shared skeptical glances. Drummond spoke for the first time that afternoon.

"It is a good plan, laddie, and I think you should try it. But in my estimation you risk failure and more – you risk Sir William's enmity. He put you on the Council and he can throw you off it as well, if you offend him. Still, I don't see any other way. We cannot sit and wait for the tomahawk to strike – it is intolerable, unmanly. If you are willing to take the risk, God bless you."

"And so say we!" cried the rest as the assembly broke up.

As they walked to the barn John clapped Nat on the shoulder and said, "Well done."

Nat's heart warmed to John's praise. The friends rarely spoke their feelings and he was moved that John expressed himself now.

"I cannot join you at the Quarter. I told Lyn I would be back tonight and, in truth, my heart longs for my wife and daughter. Can you come with me now?"

John thought of all that awaited him at his little farm and sighed. Nothing, however, was more important than stirring the government into action. What if something happened to Lyn and Mary? He shuddered.

"Of course I can. Goode will send word to Hartwell that I shall be away for a few days. We can write this petition in no time. You can be on your way to Jamestown early tomorrow."

"Will you stay until I return ... and watch out for Lyn?"

"You don't even need to ask."

The two friends mounted and the black and the chestnut, the one dark as coal and the other bright as copper, moved east into the shadow of dusk.

CHAPTER 16

JANUARY 1676

John watched Byrd mount the path to the Quarter. There had been quite a storm yesterday and the landscape glistened white. A soft sound caught his ear as a cedar bough released its burden of snow. The sun was brilliant and the crystalline powder was beginning to melt. The attorney glanced up. It was noon, or close to it: Byrd and Mistress Hartwell and young Jake would be just in time for dinner. Jacob Hartwell had risen at dawn to prepare the venison stew and bake the cornbread and simmer the dried fruit in maple syrup for dessert. They had no sugar, but the overseer said his boy loved sweets and he must prepare something special for him. John turned to go inside his cabin where the party was going to dine.

"They're here, Jacob. I guess the river didn't freeze."

Hartwell smiled broadly. "Bless you, sir. I am so pleased. I have not seen the missus since Christmas, as you know. I hope we have enough food. The boy eats like a wolf."

"He has the look of you. A likely lad. What do you intend him for?"

"Oh, he'll have to help us farm when we have our own place. But Mistress Byrd has taught him his letters and his numbers, so his future will be brighter than mine."

"Well, you'll have to ride to Curles with me soon to talk to the Squire about staying on here for a while. Now is not the time to go out on your own, with the Susquehannocks on the prowl."

"Indeed, sir, you are right. I'll see what Martha has to say about my staying. You and Mister Bacon could not be better masters. It is just that ..."

"I know, Jacob. Who could know better than I? You want to be your own man. Well, we both will get there, I daresay, but it might take a while. Here they are."

Byrd stomped onto the porch, ridding his doeskin boots of snow, and turned to help Martha Hartwell. Young Jake bounded up the steps and rushed into the cabin, doffing his fur cap to John.

"There you are, father." The boy hugged Hartwell close and the man's eyes glistened with tears.

"Hello, my boy. Where are your manners? Did you greet Mister Grey?"

"Beg your pardon, sir. Good morning. Thank you for having us."

John smiled and welcomed Byrd and Mistress Hartwell into his snug cabin. After exchanging greetings the company sat down to eat and for a good half hour the only sounds were the movement of jaws, sighs of content, and an occasional request to pass the bread or fruit. As they sat back, replete, John rose and replenished the fire and cleared the table, urging Hartwell to sit and talk with his family. As he mixed hot water and ash in the wash tub and plunged the wooden dishes in it, Byrd joined him. The Indian trader rolled up his sleeves to help John and spoke under his breath.

"I had evil news yesterday from one of my trappers. There was another massacre in Rapppahannock County – much worse than the first two. Some thirty or forty English were slain and the rest have fled inland. I have not told anyone yet. As you know, I sent Mary and the baby to Jamestown right after Christmas, lest anything happen to them. And I did not want to worry Martha and Jake, spoil this meeting. But I must tell them now, don't you think?"

John stood silently, his arms smoking with suds, his jaws grinding. When was this going to stop? No sooner did they have a brief respite than the savages struck again. It was almost a month ago that Nat had ridden to Jamestown to plead the cause of the frontier and he had come back utterly discouraged. The Governor had gone so far as to suggest that he was embroidering the facts, fantasizing. Berkeley had refused to call a Council meeting and had sent Nat home with the vague promise that he would talk to Chicheley and see whether the militia should be mustered. Of course nothing had happened. John doubted that Berkeley and Sir Henry had even spoken. The great planters were swathed in the comfort of their bayside plantations, cocooned in ignorance. My God, what was it going to take to rouse them from their poppy-fed slumber?

The toll on the frontier settlers was visible. Every Sunday he looked around him and saw fewer people, and those who were present looking gaunter, their faces gouged with anxiety and sleeplessness. He himself slept with his snaphance when he slept at all. And those fools in Stafford who had so mishandled the murder of Hen and then committed folly after folly at Piscataway Creek – they had never been called to answer for their errors. And now this news. Thirty-six slaughtered! Had the Susquehannocks met their quota? He had lost count. He turned to Byrd.

"Of course you have to tell them. Is there any chance that the savages are moving this way?"

Byrd picked up a towel and dried a bowl. "Don't share this with everyone, or there will be a panic. All my sources tell me that the Susquehannocks are following the fall line south. If that is so they will strike in New Kent next and then ..."

"Then they will be here. Of course we have to tell the Hartwells. And I must ride to Curles tomorrow. Did you say I was the first to know?"

"Yes. But I'll stop at Whitby and at Varina on my way home this afternoon and tell Goode and whomever I can find at the courthouse and the church. Yet I fear the reaction – there is going to be a panic."

"Well, you can't keep it to yourself. People have to know. Once I tell Nat he will doubtless go to Jamestown and see Crewes and Isham and Bland on the way. We'll sound the alarm. You are not responsible for how people react. Ramsey will have to call out the Henrico militia."

John had inadvertently raised his voice and Hartwell heard the word "militia."

"Are they mustering again, so soon?" he asked as he rose from the table.

Byrd glanced at John and then turned to face the family who were still seated companionably at the table. "No. But they will. I have something to tell you."

And he related the story of the Sittenborne Massacre. How all the plantations within ten miles of the falls of the Rappahannock were attacked; how some thirty-six settlers were slain; how scalps were taken, both of women and men; how bodies were mutilated; how the brains of small children were dashed out against stones; how seventy-one plantations were reduced to eleven; how the survivors left cattle and crops and fled inland, towards Jamestown, begging for help, their lives destroyed.

The Hartwell family sat, stricken. Finally Martha spoke. "When did this happen? Have they sent troops?"

"Approximately a week ago," answered Byrd. "My informant didn't know what action Berkeley took, but I have not heard of any counter-offensive."

John looked compassionately at the pale woman. "I'll ride to Curles tomorrow and Councilor Bacon will take charge. The Governor will summon the Council, if he has not already ... perhaps even order the whole Assembly to meet early. Why, there may be troops in the field as we speak."

The snow still sparkled in the bright winter sun, but the afternoon had lost its joy. Byrd was anxious to move on to Whitby and Varina and Martha Hartwell and her son reluctantly prepared to leave with him. Hartwell wanted them to stay at Bacon's Quarter, but he acknowledged that they would be as safe at the trading post as anywhere. Byrd was a friend of the savages and his home lay secluded in the forest; it was not a likely target, especially since he kept few cattle and grew few crops. The Quarter would be more tempting to the Susquehannocks, with its neat cabins, its cleared fields and its fat herds. Martha took her husband by the front of his leather shirt and pulled him close.

"Don't do anything foolish, Jake. We don't need a hero in the family."

"Of course not, Martie. But I must do my duty. Now you and Little Jake run along. Mister Grey and I have a lot to talk about. I'll find my way over the river to Mister Byrd's as soon as this has died down. I'll be there as soon as I can, but Mister Grey is going to Curles tomorrow, so I must stay here at least until he comes back. Jake – look to your mother. You're a man now, and you must act like one."

The boy straightened and nodded, but his face was solemn. Thirty-six English slaughtered, and some of them children. Life was harsh. He was glad he had his father's snaphance and knew how to use it.

John rang a handbell and a slave came running. "Help Mister Byrd saddle some horses. He finds that he and Mistress Hartwell and young Jake are going to have to ride this afternoon, unexpectedly. You go along too, so you can bring the mounts back once our guests have finished their business and you have seen them safely into their boat. Mister Hartwell and I are going to take Coke and the roan and ride to the far fields. You need to know that there has been some Indian trouble to the north. Everybody must be extra alert. Don't stand staring like that! Hop to it!"

John felt badly that he had snapped at the slave, but tension was gnawing at him, freezing his neck and shoulders. The cattle were in the far pasture and the hogs were running free. He and Jacob would have to reconnoiter and swing the men into action. Perhaps he should think of bringing all the animals to Curles. It would be a busy afternoon.

John glanced at Hartwell who sat the roan well. He called the animal Blue and, indeed, it was just the color of the snow where the shade of the pines fell on it, a kind of silvery azure. The two men pulled up. The swine had left their ordure smoking on the cold ground – they must be just ahead. Within minutes they heard the grunts of the beasts and soon came upon them, rooting in the pine mast. Small intelligent eyes looked at them askance, questioning. John pulled some ears of corn from his saddle bag and rubbed them together, making a familiar rasping sound. The nearest hog grunted and pricked up its huge, leaf-like ears. It soon rushed towards him, its neat feet puncturing the snow. Before long the entire herd was gathered around the chestnut, tempted by the promise of corn.

"I've got their attention, Jake. They'll follow me back now. Are you sure you want to ride on alone to see the cattle?"

"Of course. It's only mid-afternoon – we have two hours of daylight. The savages strike at dawn or dusk, never in the full light of day. I have my knife and Mister Bacon's second set of pistols. I'll be fine."

"Well, you count them and try and herd them together and wait. I'll house the swine and bring as many men back with me as I can find horses for. There should be enough of us. Once we get them back to the pens we'll have a job feeding them, but one thing at a time. I don't want to take a chance on losing any stock, we've brought them such a long way. Mister Bacon is most pleased ... says we have better herds than those at Curles."

Jacob Hartwell smiled. It was true. He had sworn to make Bacon's Quarter a model farm and he had done so. Mister Grey had helped, but.... He watched the swine follow John, jaunty haunches gleaming and curly tails dancing. He had to laugh. If Mister Grey could see himself, he would laugh too.

Blue pushed through the snow which was melting fast. His hoofs made sucking sounds in the mud and his silver coat was soon spattered. Hartwell wiped some mud from his face and drew off his cap. It was almost hot, out here in the open. In this weather the cattle had likely trampled the snow and found the grass underneath; they would be fine. Still, they needed to be brought home. Grey was right – it would be difficult to feed them if they were penned up for the rest of the winter. Good thing they had brought in all that grass last summer. It sat in aromatic rolls in the barn loft. It would keep the herd going for some time. The overseer glanced ahead. He had reached another, denser stand of pines. As soon as he entered the cool tunnel the temperature dropped considerably. He shivered. It was quiet among the evergreens. Blue's steps were muffled by the thick pine straw. No birds twittered here; no stream ran; no humble grass or flower graced the dank forest floor. The overseer was relieved to reach the end of the tree tunnel and see the far pasture spread before him. The black cattle were like silhouettes against the snow; they seemed to be huddled along the farthest fence, which was odd.

Blue picked his way across the open space and then followed the fence line, towards the cattle. Hartwell squinted into the westering sun. His eyes were not what they had once been and he could not quite make out the actions of the herd, but most of the animals seemed to be pressed together in a corner, and some of them seemed to be lying down. Cattle did not care to lie in the snow ... could they have eaten something and become ill? No, this grass was healthy – that was why they had built the pen here. Hartwell felt his gut clench. Something was wrong with the animals. He kneed Blue into a canter and within minutes he had reached the herd.

Broad faces stared at him, eyes huge and muzzles smoking in the cold. He slid from the roan and dropped its reins. The horse was so well trained that it did not need to be tied; it would stand there until doomsday. Hartwell followed the fence to where the cattle seemed to be lying in the snow. His throat closed. Now he knew what had happened. Several of the great beasts lay on their sides, stabbing the sky with their skeletal geometry. And the scene was no longer black on white: the snow beneath them was stained crimson, great swathes of blood sweeping the field like fallen banners. Hartwell sobbed. Of all the creatures at Bacon's Quarter, he loved these black beasts the best and now six or more of them lay dead, their pink tongues lolling from lifeless mouths.

The overseer scrambled over the split rails and knelt before the nearest sacrifice. He stroked the stiff hairs on its face, tracing the whorls. The long eyelashes were still, the dark eyes unseeing. He knew this animal well: it had been born last spring and was perfectly formed. He followed the pool of blood to its headwater: the beast's throat had been slit. Hartwell stood wearily and made his way among the other fallen cattle, the live ones huddled just beyond, keeping together for comfort. Everywhere the story was the same: each throat gaped, showing the soft pipes where life's breath had moved until the final stroke came. It was savages. He had seen such things before. They could be among a herd without warning and they would slash, just so, whether with stone or metal. Most likely metal. The foolish English: in their lust for pelts they had armed the Indians to the teeth and now they must reap the bitter harvest.

Hartwell started. Blue's bridle jingled in the still air and the horse was tossing its head ... was turning ... was leaping away across the snow in great bounds. Blue would never do such a thing unless.... The overseer's heart sank and he knew his fate long before his flesh felt it. There, from the pine woods, crept six braves, skin-clad, painted, fur cloaks tossed on the white ground as the came. They bounded forward like hounds, making almost no sound. Hartwell's pistols were in Blue's saddlebags; he had only the knife at his belt. As he pulled it from its sheath he realized how fruitless the gesture was. The first arrow pierced his right arm and the knife fell to the ground. The second struck him in the abdomen and he knelt in agony. They were upon him. One stood behind him and grasped him by the hair and drew his head back. Jacob Hartwell thought of Martha and his boy as the knife crossed his throat. His blood spurted to join that of his black beasts and soon his wasted body lay among them. The savages nodded silently at one another and stooped over the slain man. Minutes later they left as quietly as they had come, plucking their furs from the snow and disappearing into the evergreens. The white bone of Hartwell's skull glistened under the afternoon sun like snow.

Folly ate up the miles between Curles Neck and Jamestown, moving his great limbs at the slow canter which he could maintain seemingly forever. Nat felt a slight nausea as he rocked in the saddle and the skeletal trees whipped by him on either side of the river road. The forest lay as desolate as an old courtesan stripped of her padded silks and patches and pots of rouge, every secret exposed. Somewhere behind him Abraham rode with Jamie Crewes. Crewes had exploded when he heard the news; Nat had never seen such a towering rage. The Turkey Island planter refused to listen to reason and insisted on accompanying Bacon to Jamestown and bearding the government in its den. It was exactly what Nat did not need: this was his mission. He had swallowed his bread and cheese and poured down his tote of

rum and was off again before Crewes could coax his horse from the pad-
dock. As he left, Nat had caught Abraham's eye and the black man understood that he was to stay with the angry planter and try and keep him from
making a fool of himself. Given Crewes' reaction Nat decided to ride
straight through to the capital, skipping Doggams and Westover. The word
would spread like wildfire even if he was not the talebearer.

There – there was the glade where he and Lyn had renewed their love;
soon he would pass the glass factory and be on the isthmus; within a quarter of an hour he would be face to face with Sir William Berkeley and he
would have the Governor's promise to call up the Grand Assembly or he
would perish in the attempt.

Nat beat on Pitts' door in a rage. He had just been told that Berkeley
was at Green Spring and had left no one in his stead. Even that cockerel
Philip Ludwell was away, either at Rich Neck or at the Governor's seat. He
had pried the information out of Berkeley's servant like the meat out of a
clam; the ill bred dog had actually slammed the door in his face. Pitts' door
opened and the thin man's face showed his surprise.

"Why Councilor Bacon, sir! Fancy seeing you here. Nobody is in town
– nary a Councilor nor a Burgess. Sir William and Mister Ludwell left for
Green Spring several days ago. I don't expect Sir William back for weeks, but
Mister Ludwell will be with us soon to hold down the Governor's place. Can
I help you with anything?"

"Yes, Pitts, you can. Your eyes and ears are sharp. Has Jamestown received
word of the most recent Indian massacres ... the one in Rappahannock
County and the one at Bacon's Quarter?"

Pitts covered his mouth and paled. "No sir. We have heard nothing. I
am sure I would know. It has been that quiet here that I know everything
that is going on." The thin man paused. "*Was* there a massacre?"

Nat sighed wearily. "Yes. Two of them. Two score English were slaughtered in Sittenborne Parish by the Susquehannocks some ten days ago.
Then, no troops having been sent against them, they moved south and
struck my own plantation. Yesterday my overseer was slaughtered. The frontier cowers in fear. We are living on our nerves. I must get word to the
Governor. Are you sure that he is at Green Spring?"

The caretaker paused, carefully marshaling his words. "The gentry spent
their Christmas moving from plantation to plantation, enjoying the season.
Then Sir William was here for just a few days and when he left there was talk
of more festivities, even a wolf hunt that Mister Philip wanted to organize.
I cannot promise that he is at home, but it is likely. If he is not at Green
Spring you will find him at Rich Neck or at Mister Bray's or Mister Page's
or at your cousin's. It's late. Won't you pass the night at *The Unicorn* and
look for the Governor tomorrow, when you and the horse are fresh?"

"Thank you for the thought, Pitts, but I cannot. The Indians have declared war. The news can't wait; the Governor must act *now*. Dicken Lawrence will give me some supper and see to my horse and then I'll be off again. I expect my body servant, Abraham, and Mister Crewes soon. If you see them tell them that I am chasing down the Governor. Tell Abraham to wait for me at *The Unicorn*. Crewes will do what he likes, as usual. God be with you, Pitts. Good bye."

Every casement in Green Spring's impressive facade blazed with light as Nat emerged from the forest. Dark had fallen long ago but between the candlelit windows and the torches which lined the drive he would have no problem finding his way to the mansion's front door. Folly's great feet crushed the last crystals of ice which lay in the carriageway and Nat pulled the charger to a halt. The horse's mighty head dropped, his sides heaved and the steam came off him like smoke. Nat himself slumped in weariness for a full minute and then slid from the saddle. From the house came the chords of an ill-played minuet. The Governor had found a fiddler or two and the gentry were at play. Nat grimaced. The music was apt. Had not Nero fiddled while Rome burned?

Bacon mounted the steps of Green Spring and pounded on the door without response. The fiddlers had burst into a country dance – the servants likely could not hear his knock, probably were all in the great hall, enjoying the festivities. Nat opened the door and stepped into the elegant hall. He remembered his first and only visit here with Lyn and John and scowled. Entering Green Spring was like entering the past. The old man was stuck in the era of the first Charles Stuart like a fly in amber. His heart dropped. Would he receive a hearing? Or ... could it be that the Greens were so removed from reality that they would brush him off? The possibility had not even entered his mind until now.

Nat strode into the great salon and looked fiercely around him. He had thrown on the first set of clothes that came to hand this morning and fifty miles of winter road had not improved his appearance. Somewhere along the way he had lost his hat and his curls were dank and tangled. Mud dropped from his cloak and he was aware that his jackboots were marring Lady Frances' polished floor. The merry sound of the fiddles ceased and the dancers came to a halt. Forty flushed faces turned his way and forty pairs of eyes looked at him, aghast. Resplendent in silver and gold, Lady Frances Berkeley dropped Philip Ludwell's hand and swam toward him, her lips pursed in a thin, grim line in her peevish face. Her formidable bosom heaved and she tossed her head, setting a confection of ornamental gold butterflies dancing among her high-piled locks.

"Can it be Mister Bacon? Why, I hardly recognized you! Billy didn't tell me that he had sent you an invitation."

The crowd tittered and Alice Page held a hand over her mouth to keep herself from laughing outright.

"Your cousin isn't here, you know. His wife has a cold which has gone to her chest and he couldn't come. Was there something else?"

The mistress of Green Spring signaled a footman and a tall man in green with a sneer on his face gave Nat the slightest of bows and relieved him of his cloak and sword belt. Next Lady Berkeley had a wooden chair brought, lest Nat sully her upholstery, and there, before the forty dancers, he sat and pulled off his boots at her direction. He was given a pair of the Governor's house slippers and then asked to step into the smoking room. As the door closed Nat heard the music strike up again and a fountain of laughter rose and fell like water. He threw himself into the nearest chair and, elbows on knees, buried his face in his hands.

Five minutes later a servant entered with a tray of spirits and showed Nat where the pipes and tobacco were – he was to take his pick. He ignored the offer of tobacco, but recklessly splashed rum in a tankard and took a deep draught. As the liquid fire coursed down his gullet he heard the door open and turned his head. Sir William, in a flowing white wig and a brilliant crimson and gold costume, entered, a scowl on his face. Behind him glowed Philip Ludwell, his eyes pools of gold and his chestnut hair blazing with inner fire. Nat unconsciously twisted the gold band on his right hand and wearily stood.

"Sit down, Councilor Bacon, sit down," said the Governor coldly. "I must confess that I am amazed to see you … and to see you in such a state. Your appearance could hardly have been less fortunate, coming as it did at the very height of Lady Frances' ball. Would you care to explain yourself?"

A part of Nat wanted to dash his tankard of liquor in that proud, remote face and rush from the room, rush back to Curles, to Lyn and Mary and John and Byrd and Hartwell. No, not to Hartwell. Never to Hartwell. The searing image entered his mind once again: John, huddled on Coke and leading Blue, and on the roan the strangest burden Nat had ever seen. A long, stiff burden. A burden that sat ill on a horse which rolled its eyes and sweated in panic. A burden that was the body of Jacob Hartwell, his life ripped untimely from him and his scalp … his scalp at some savage's belt. Lyn had fainted, for the first time in her life. And when she recovered the first thought of the three was how to keep Martha and the boy away from the overseer's bloody, mutilated corpse. Nat shook himself and drank deeply.

"I beg your pardon, Your Honor. I have slept little and ridden much. I am truly not myself. You must forgive me if I have interrupted your ball, but I bring tidings that cannot wait."

The old man stiffened and seated himself by the fire. Philip Ludwell stood beside him, one hand on the back of the soft leather chair, his eyes glowing.

"Sir William *must* forgive you? Your tidings *cannot* wait? You forget yourself, Bacon."

Nat bristled. Bland had called Tom Ludwell an insolent puppy; the same applied to the younger brother. Here he was, standing by the Governor, and at the same time keeping Lady Frances' bed warm ... the whole thing stank. Nat stiffened and brought himself under control. He could not allow himself to show temper. He was fighting for a cause that went far beyond himself. He was here to plead for the frontier and plead he would.

"And I beg *your* pardon, Mister Ludwell, if I have offended. But you must know that within the past two weeks the Susquehannocks have slaughtered two score innocents in and around the falls of the Rappahannock and just yesterday they struck my outlying plantation and killed my overseer." Nat choked and hot tears came to his eyes. "Killed him and scalped him. They might have been slaughtering a hog."

Berkeley looked taken aback. He sucked in his cheeks and blew them out again. Ludwell put a hand on the Governor's shoulder.

"Why, 'tis the same story you brought me at Christmas! You and that petition! And nothing came of it ... nothing at all. Why is it that only you bring me these stories? You will make me sorry that I did Natty Bacon a favor and put you on the Council."

Nat could not believe his ears. Although his petition had been essentially ignored the old man had said that he would have Sir Henry Chicheley look into it. Had nothing been done?

"Thank you for reminding me of the petition, Your Honor. It gives me an opportunity to ask you what Sir Henry discovered."

"Discovered? Discovered? Why nothing at all. It is some bugaboo you have. You need to get out and about more, spend more time in Jamestown. You have missed several Council meetings and several court sessions. Do I take it that you are not interested in serving on the Council of State?"

Damn the old man's soul to hell. He was turning it all against Nat, misunderstanding everything. Bacon ground his teeth.

"May I ask what exactly Sir Henry did when we brought you news of the Susquehannocks' reprisals?"

Berkeley rose, his eyes darting fire. "No you may not. You may not ask! What insolence. Do you suggest that I lie?"

It was, of course, exactly what Nat was suggesting. No inquiry had been made in December. Doubtless the Governor and Chicheley had tossed the offensive petition on the fire and had a good laugh. Well, perhaps thirty-six dead in Rappahannock County and seventy-four plantations reduced to eleven and the death of Jacob Hartwell would catch their attention.

"I think you have misunderstood me, sir. I hope that my next words will be very clear. Thirty-six of your people have just been slaughtered at the falls of the Rappahannock and the whole frontier is fleeing inland, begging for your protection. Yesterday my overseer was barbarously slain at the falls of the James. We know the Susquehannocks are the murderers. They are moving down the fall line, killing as they go, in reprisal for what happened in Maryland."

Sir William's face burned as red as his coat. He stood up, spittle gathering at the corner of his mouth.

"You know! You know! You know nothing! I have lived here for thirty-five years and governed for twenty-five. I fought the second Indian war and prevailed! I brought Opechancanough to his knees! I tamed the savages who now owe fealty to His Majesty the King. Who are you to tell me that the Susquehannocks threaten my borders? Get out of my house!"

Nat turned alternately red and white. He burned as though with fever. This was beyond belief. Virginia's western border was being systematically shredded and the very ground dyed with the colonists' blood and the Governor would not believe that it was true.

Philip Ludwell, an unlikely mediator, stepped into the breach. "Come Will, I'd like to hear about Bacon's overseer. If the man was killed, it would be upsetting to anyone. Our friend here seems a little ... how shall I put it? ... overwrought, but let's hear him out."

The Governor sat down and dabbed his lips with a lace handkerchief. "Very well, Phil, if you like. But I don't want to hear about Rappahannock County. Do you think that I would not have learned if the settlers were fleeing? 'Tis absurd." He glared at Bacon. "You – tell us about your servant."

Coldly, without emotion, a stunned Nat Bacon related the story of Jacob Hartwell. He could see that neither the Governor nor Ludwell gave it any credence. Berkeley asked him why he was so sure the murderers were the Susquehannocks and Nat told him everything he had learned from Byrd and the Ring, to no avail. Ludwell laughed it off.

"You admit that no one saw Hartwell die and the savages left no traces, even taking the arrows with them. How can you possibly say that the Susquehannocks have reached the James? It was likely some skulking Appomatox or Pamunkey who was looking for dinner and tripped over your man. It is a pity, but hardly conclusive that the colony is under siege."

Nat's head swam. He was never going to convince these men. Berkeley wanted to get back to his guests and Ludwell doubtless wanted to get back to Frances Berkeley. He made one more effort.

"And the slain cattle?"

"Oh, some band was looking for meat and was interrupted. It should be a lesson to your man Grey never to go about unattended when you live on the frontier." Ludwell smiled and reached for a pipe which he carefully filled and lighted. He blew smoke rings as Berkeley sat, frozen, and Nat sat, stunned.

The door creaked and a head alive with golden butterflies swaying on jeweled wire peered around the corner.

"Billy, shall you be long? Those who are not staying the night are leaving already."

Berkeley sat up with a start. "Forgive me, my dear. I am with you. Young Bacon here has had an unfortunate incident out near Curles – one of his men was killed when he found a band of savages butchering some cattle. It has shaken him badly and he is full of nightmares." The Governor stared at Nat. "But he is just on his way back to Jamestown. Phil and I have reassured him that the colony is safe. A good night's sleep will do wonders for him."

Lady Frances smiled graciously. "Then let me take your arm, dear. We must see our guests off." She looked past her husband to Philip Ludwell. "I daresay Phil can do the honors for Mister Bacon. Aren't we lucky that he is going to spend a few days with us?"

"We are indeed, sweeting. Here, take my arm. I'm glad the ball is over; I'm growing quite weary."

Ludwell watched the door close behind the Berkeleys and turned to Nat.

"I think you have your cue. You have been losing sleep over the death of your servant. I am sure that when you are more composed that things will look brighter." The Secretary puffed at his pipe and watched Nat rise and pull himself together. "However, *this time* I will make sure that Sir Henry takes horse and looks into whatever has been happening in Rappahannock County. If I were you I would attend the next Council meeting and mend a few fences. Sir William's opinion can make or break a man here. I daresay you know that already."

Nat declined to answer. The insolent footman in green brought him his cloak, (unbrushed), and his boots, (still filthy), and tossed his sword belt and weapon on the floor. He jammed his cold feet in his boots, belted himself, and strode through the front hall, ignoring the chattering crowd. Flinging his cloak about him, he mounted Folly and began the weary trip back to Jamestown. The January moon was a mere sliver and clouds obscured the stars. The road stretched out before Nat, cold, dark and lonely.

CHAPTER 17

MARCH ~ APRIL 1676

Lyn tapped on the door of the old wooden house and it creaked open under her touch. A chill March breeze caused it to slam against the wall like a gunshot. John leaped to his feet, surprise written on his face.

Oh, you *are* here," said Lyn. "I see you so rarely. I thought you would be in the fields. Here – I brought you some preserved peaches to tide you over until we have fresh fruit."

"Bless you, I could use them, I am that weary of corn and beans. I *should* be in the fields, but Nat asked me to hold back on planting until he returns from Jamestown."

"Hold back! He did not tell me that. Is he worried about the drought?"

"That among other things. I hope 'drought' is too strong a word – is it a drought if you have had two dry months?"

"Why, I don't know, I'm sure, but we've had no water since January's snow. The earth is drying up – you can see the wind blowing the soil away. That cannot be a good sign. What else is Nat worried about? It's the savages, isn't it?"

John took the peaches and put them carefully on a shelf and settled Lyn in the most comfortable chair by the fire. "Of course. If this Assembly does not fashion an effective Indian policy we will not plant this year. It is too risky; we are too close to the frontier. Think of Hartwell … In fact, if things do not go well in Jamestown I think Nat wants to send you and Mary to King's Creek. We are going to palisade Curles. It will be no place for you and the child."

Lyn rose, her face flushed. "Never! I will never leave Curles."

John frowned. "Lyn, remember how Hartwell looked? I cannot erase it from my mind. I dream about it constantly … the blood on the snow and the white bone gleaming through the torn flesh … it was horrible."

Lyn spoke softly. "You cannot forgive yourself for his death, can you?"

"No. I should never have left him alone. I knew the Susquehannocks were on the warpath. Bacon's Quarter was an obvious target. I shall never forgive myself."

Lyn put her hand on John's forearm and was surprised and chagrined when he pulled away. "I can't convince you, can I? Jacob Hartwell's fate was in his own hands and God's. You did nothing wrong, nothing at all. You saved all Nat's cattle and brought them safely here together with the slaves and servants! Well, what's the use? We've gone over it again and again and you are determined to blame yourself. Oh, John ...."

"What is it, Lyn?"

"Nothing. So Nat thinks I should hide in York County with his cousin, does he? If I could bear to leave Mary I would send *her* to King's Creek, but how could I spend even one day apart from her? No, I will never leave Nat and you here by yourselves. We will have to take our chances together, even Mary. Do I sound harsh and unmotherly?"

John avoided the question. "Mary Byrd and little William have gone to friends in Surry."

"I am not Mary Byrd. She hates the frontier. She would return to England if she had a choice in the matter."

"You are a brave soul, Lyn. Nat told me you would put up a fight. Well, perhaps it won't come to that. Let's see what the Assembly does. The Council meets today does it not? And the House of Burgesses tomorrow?"

"I believe so. John, you know they will do nothing. How can we trust the government when Berkeley sent Sir Henry Chicheley out in February with that force and then disbanded it before it had even left the tidewater, without explanation? The Susquehannocks have a free hand and William Byrd thinks that there are other bands in league with them as well."

John paced in front of the fire and mused. "It is strange. Nobody can explain Berkeley's paralysis. Some call him a coward, but that is not the answer. I think he has been through so much that now, in his old age, he simply cannot bear the thought of another Indian war. Out of sight, out of mind. Certainly if he had not been so greedy for beaver the savages would not be nearly so well armed. Perhaps he is trying to ignore the wages of avarice."

"Do the Susquehannocks have firearms?"

"The ones that attacked us used bows and hatchets, but everybody knows the savages are well-armed with matchlocks and pistols. Virginia has been selling arms to its foes for years and now the colony is reaping the consequences."

"Well, if the Governor will not do his duty, dare we hope that the Council and the House will? After all, the threat is to the whole colony, not just the frontier."

"Oh, they don't see it that way, Lyn. You haven't heard them talk. Most of the Councilors and many of the Burgesses live well within the fall line and they really don't take this seriously yet. Besides, whatever you may think of him, Sir William still holds the government in thrall. They will be guided by him. I would not be optimistic about this Assembly's doing much more than making some fine speeches and perhaps agreeing to man the forts."

"The forts! You yourself told me that most of them have fallen down and that even if they had not they are useless as Indians do not fight like English and no fort can keep them from attacking us whenever they like!"

"And I spoke truly. Forts are useless against savages. They must be hunted down like wolves."

"John! What a thing to say!"

"But it is true Lyn. The English may have started this conflagration, but it is futile to assess blame. The fact is that the colony is in flames. Our task is to do everything possible to protect the lives and fortunes of those we hold dear."

Lyn pulled her shawl around her and slowly rose. "I am sure you are right. Well, Nat will be back in less than a week and then we shall decide what to do next. If he orders me to King's Creek, so be it. But John ... take care of yourself. Don't be careless of your life because of Hartwell. We can't do without you."

John did his best to smile. "It is in God's hands, Lyn. I am not presumptuous enough to think that I could influence His plan. May I join you for supper? I have not seen Mary for many days and I miss her. We'll keep each other company tonight and when Nat returns we will know better what to do."

Nat looked around Lawrence's familiar chamber. A brisk fire blazed on the hearth and nearby on a small table stood a tray of bottles and decanters together with a bowl of sugar and a plate of sliced lemons. Trust Dicken to have fine cane sugar and fruit from the West Indies! With his connections he always managed to acquire the best of everything. Nat wearily mixed himself a toddy and tossed it down as though it were spring water. Hoping that he was not abusing his friend's hospitality, he dropped onto the pine bed and within minutes he was sound asleep.

Lawrence shook Bacon's shoulder repeatedly. "Wake up, Nat! Will is here and we want to know what happened."

Nat rose from the depths of slumber and pulled himself to a sitting position. Lawrence held out a basin of hot water and a cloth and he thankfully bathed his face, rubbing the sleep away.

"I beg your pardon. It was more exhausting biting my tongue in the House today than it was fruitlessly arguing in the Council yesterday. I have never been wearier. Hello Will, it's been a long time." Nat looked at his friends. "What can I tell you? I'm sure you know everything."

"We have good sources, but we are human," laughed Lawrence.

"Not you, Dicken. You're not human."

The innkeeper grimaced. "Come, let's sit at the table. I have a platter of cold meat and bread. I've told Joanna not to disturb us and the inn is so full with Burgesses that she will be busy far into the night, so we are guaranteed our privacy. Now, help yourself to food and drink and give us an eyewitness account of the incompetence of our government."

"Well, the Council meeting went as expected. Nobody said a word about Berkeley's sending Chicheley out last month and then pulling him back. Nobody, that is, except me. I hadn't gotten a complete sentence out of my mouth when Sir William exploded and called me out of order. He said if I uttered another word that he would have me ejected. Ever since last winter I had done nothing but bring tales of woe, exaggerate, slander him ... it went on and on. You should have seen my cousin! He was ready to sink under the table. But Swann spoke up on my behalf. He wisely suggested that we not dwell on the past and that we move on to a comprehensive plan for dealing with the Indian threat as it now existed. Clever Tom: implicit in his suavity was the fact that there was, indeed, a serious problem.

"Berkeley took Swann's hook and I sat mute for the rest of the session, much to my cousin's relief. I won't bore you with who said what. The good news is that a distinct majority, including some died-in-the-wool Greens, recognized that we are truly in the middle of an Indian war the only question being how to deal with it. The wiser heads wanted to field a roving army of horse and foot which could travel light and follow the savages wherever they went. Of course I supported that contingent, though I could only show my support by raising my arm from time to time to signal 'yea.' Unfortunately a larger group wanted to fight the last war and establish forts on the rivers, each manned by both horse and foot. They claimed that if the soldiers ranged out from each fort that the forces would meet one another from time to time and would create a perimeter that the savages could not pierce. That is nonsense, as you know. Even assuming that the men could find one another in the wilderness, most of the frontier would still be exposed. Any savage with half a brain could slip through as easily as kiss my hand.

"In any event, the fort people won the day. Berkeley had created a fort system in the forties; why not do it again in the seventies? It goes without saying that the Governor was pleased. After that decision was made they started to name names and the ridiculous degenerated into the absurd. In essence, they are going to pull the troops from the older counties, (good luck!), and Berkeley will put his friends in charge of this little army. It is going to be a band of brothers. Shades of Charles the First!"

"What sort of names, laddie?" asked Drummond.

"Well, Knight is to have the Potomac; Claiborne the Mattaponi; Lyddall the Pamunky; Ramsey the James; Jones the Appomattox; Potter the Blackwater; and Wiggins the Nansemond. They are all Green, as you know.

More of the old guard – my cousin included – are responsible for pressing men and horses. And another handful of favorites were given commissions to deal with the friendly Indians, employing some as scouts, others to take hostages and so forth.

"The names Bacon Junior, Drummond, Lawrence, Hansford, Swann, Pate, Bland, Isham, Crewes, Byrd, Goode and Grey were not heard. Although he did not want an army at all, once one was forced on him Berkeley made it his."

The three men sat in silence, Drummond and Lawrence digesting what Nat had told them.

"It is ill conceived," said the innkeeper at last. "If they are serious about the forts, it will mean a new tax which simply cannot be borne. They'll have to pay for powder and shot and food ... it is going to be expensive. And you are right about the nature of Indian warfare. The distances between the proposed forts are huge. It is of no avail to set a mousetrap if the mice can slip around it. The whole thing is a mistake. Hardly a surprise, I suppose."

"Some of the men you mentioned will acquit themselves well," offered Drummond, "but I agree with you and Dicken. The plan itself is a bad one. Well, did the House endorse it?"

"Yes. I sat through most of the session today. They issued an unequivocal declaration of war – I suppose that is a good thing. Then they adopted the fort system pretty much as I have outlined it, but with more detail. The amounts of weapons and food are specified; transportation is described. But the more detailed the thing got the more of a fantasy I thought it. The laws seem to have little to do with what Byrd and I have experienced these past few months."

"You still grieve your overseer, don't you, laddie," said Drummond kindly.

"Yes, but it is not just me. Think of Hen's little boy and those poor folks in Rappahannock who lost everything. The survivors are never going to forget the horrors which they have seen. The government just does not seem to understand ... and I cannot fathom its ignorance."

"I believe it is a sort of wishful thinking," muttered Drummond. "The laws sound so grand that those who write them think that the words are the thing itself. If we had more real soldiers in the Assembly perhaps we would have had a happier result, but that is not the case."

"Well, they did at least forbid the sale of arms to the savages – they made it a capital offense. But, like the rest of it, that is mere rhetoric. The horses had long fled before the stable doors were closed."

Lawrence mixed one last round of drinks as the candles burned low.

"How do you think this will affect the Ring?" he asked.

"Oh, I fear that our reforms are going to go begging. Nobody talks about anything but the savages."

"Yes, you are right," replied Lawrence. "Once again, we shall have to be patient. And you? What will you do now, Nat?"

"Oh, go back to Curles and begin palisading. John Grey will stand by me whatever happens, but I may send Lyn and the baby inland. I will not plant this spring. Crewes and Goode are growing nothing but foodstuff and the rest are following suit. The times are sad. Last year was such a good one for us, and now this. 'Tis Dame Fortune's way, I suppose."

"Well, I've kept Clarissa's room for you, though Joanna is livid about it. She tells me she could rent it for gold. Is Folly here?"

"No, I sailed. Could you see your way to letting my crew sleep in your barn?"

"It goes without saying. Whatever I have is yours."

"You are a good friend, Dicken, and you too, Will. Despite these reverses I always feel better for seeing you."

"And we you, Nat," said the Scot and the innkeeper together.

"You've done what you can, laddie," added Drummond. "Put everything out of your mind and sleep the sleep of the just. Things may look brighter tomorrow. Good luck to you, and keep us informed of how things go in Henrico."

Sadly and silently Drummond left *The Unicorn*, Nat sought his solitary bed below and Lawrence turned down the counterpane of the pine bed. He would sleep in his own chamber; he was in no mood to face Joanna. Clarissa came and went like the night wind. If he was lucky she would find her way to him tonight.

The April sun pierced the blue and white curtains and streamed across Nat's face. He opened his eyes and then closed them again with relief. He was in his own bed, with Lyn beside him, and he could rest in comfort as long as he liked. Byrd was going to sail down later in the day and they were going to Doggams for supper, but until then he had no pressing business. He and John had decided not to plant and for the past month time had hung on his hands. In truth, with John here, he could be wholly idle if he chose. Under the attorney's supervision the servants and slaves grew more than enough to feed Curles Neck and he had never seen the herds sleeker or fatter.

The protective fort system devised by the Council and affirmed by the House had, so far, been just as ineffective as he had anticipated. Colonel Ramsey had come by once to ask questions about the Henrico plantations, but nothing had come of it. If James River was to have a fort, Nat knew nothing of it. And still reports came in of Indian murder, rapine and pillaging. The Susquehannocks had not moved south and the frontier lay at their mercy. Nat pictured the palisade which was creeping east across his land from where the western marsh met the river. He himself doubted that it would deter an enterprising savage, but it made the men happier and, more important, it calmed Lyn's fears for the baby.

Nat stretched and watched the dust motes play in the sunlight and listened to Lyn's quiet breathing. Blue highlights shone in his wife's hair and her shoulder was as white as milk. She had just weaned Mary and her figure was as perfect as when they had wed. He felt stirred. He stroked her cheek and watched the dark lashes flutter. Her brow was as finely cut as marble. Lyn sat up and smiled.

"Awake so early?" she asked.

"'Tis not early. Look at the sun. It must be getting on for eight o'clock."

"That late? I should rise and see about breakfast. Mary has not made a sound – that's why we slept in."

"I heard her earlier. I think Hannah has dressed her and taken her to the kitchen. Don't get up ... Hannah will manage breakfast without you."

Nat reached for Lyn and pulled her close. With Mary almost a year old and less demanding, his wife had started to relinquish some of the baby's care to others. Since his return from Jamestown, despite the turmoil around them, they had enjoyed a second honeymoon. Was this the calm before the storm? Nat put the thought away from him and held Lyn close. They came together gladly and saluted the soft April morning with the rites of love.

Nat watched John help Mary walk – the child was forward and could almost stand by herself. To Lyn, the little girl was the picture of her father but Bacon did not see it. He thought she was simply herself, and he was enchanted by her. He was surprised by John's devotion: who would have thought that the thoughtful attorney who kept his emotions so firmly in check would have such a soft heart? The child tumbled down and began to cry and John picked her up and held her far above his head until the wails turned into shrieks of laughter. Lyn stepped down from the porch and joined the party on the bluff.

"Whatever are you doing? I leave Mary with you two for five minutes and already there is a fracas. It is clear that men are good for little or nothing."

Nat joined John's laughter as Lyn caught up her daughter and held her tight.

"Now, love, where is it that you want your summer house?"

"There, to the left, in that hollow where it will be out of the wind. The view of the river is superb. But I don't think we should be planning a summer house, Nat. Not until the house is palisaded."

"You're right, Lyn," interjected John, "but I could level the ground and we could put an old wooden table and a couple of benches there until we build something grander. It is a pity not to develop the river view. There is none finer in Henrico."

"That's a good thought," agreed Nat. "Let's do something simple and improve on it later if things look brighter. It will be a nice place for the child to play now that the weather is warm. As usual, John has found the solution."

"Oh, 'as usual,' is it?" groaned John. "Perhaps after perfecting Curles I can perfect the colony."

"And I'm sure you would do a better job of it than this government!" cried Lyn. "If I could vote you would be a Burgess tomorrow!"

"If you knew what you were saying you would not wish it on me," answered John. The day was sparkling and he turned towards the river which pulled like a magnet. "Look, there's Byrd, before his time. And he's brought Jake Hartwell." The attorney looked solemn. "He's come to see his father's grave … what shall I say to him?"

"John!" cried Lyn. "You must leave that behind you. You are the only soul in Virginia who faults yourself for what happened that day."

"Lyn is right," said Nat. "The boy will understand. Why, Byrd lost two traders last month, not a mile from home, and nobody blames him for sending men out to bargain with the savages. Your conscience is too tender."

"Well, I must try and put it behind me, then." John glanced at Nat. "Thank you again for letting the boy have Blue. His father loved the horse and he will cherish it as well."

"And Martha is still content that we buried Mister Hartwell here?" asked Lyn.

"Yes. With the Indian situation there was no other choice."

"Will she stay at the trading post?"

"No, Byrd is sending her to Surry to help Mary."

"Then he'll be alone but for Jake. Should we ask him to stay here?"

"No, he'll never leave his little empire. He does not know the meaning of the word 'fear'. Besides he is talking with Ramsey about placing the fort on his land. It just might happen."

Byrd's sloop had docked and the party on the bluff watched as he and Jake Hartwell puffed up the path. The crew remained below; they would take their master and the boy and Bacon on to Turkey Island within the hour to pick up Jamie Crewes, and then sail to Doggams where Isham was hosting the Ring for supper.

Nat leaped onto the wharf at Doggams, glad that the trip was over. A brisk wind had come up and the journey had been choppy and rough; as usual, his stomach had showed its displeasure. He held out his hand to steady Byrd, but black Jamie Crewes and young Jake Hartwell managed for themselves, springing from gunwale to wharf as neatly as deer. Nat glanced at Jake's right hand where a gold ring shone in the late afternoon sun. The boy had craved action after his father's death and Byrd had rightly focused the young man's wrath not on John, and not even on the Susquehannocks, but on the government which had failed at its most fundamental task: defense. The boy was an avid disciple. Sharp as a whip, he already knew the lessons of the Ring better than hot Giles Bland, who was obsessed with his own cause, or inconstant Henry Isham who one day wanted to slay Indians and the next could not wait to take ship for England.

The master of Doggams stepped out of the gloaming and greeted his guests. "Did you have a good trip? With this wind, you should have made record time."

"We had a spanking trip, all but Bacon," boomed Crewes. Nat's tender stomach was well known to the Ring and the men laughed at his expense.

"Well then, there will be more Gouda for the rest of us," crowed Isham. "My stores came in yesterday – I can give you white bread and Dutch cheese and Rhenish and a host of other delicacies. The *Richard and Elizabeth* is in port; it could not have been better timed."

An hour later the friends had dispatched as fine a supper as any could remember and had moved outside with their pipes. Jake smoked with them, and they teased him mercilessly about his taking advantage of his mother's absence. The wind had died down and the evening was fine. Isham had some torches lit and they sat under a great oak which stood on a natural lawn which ran down to the river.

"What news from home, Henry?" asked Byrd, always courteous.

"'Tis strange that you should ask. The *Richard and Elizabeth* brought me a letter from Father. He wants me to sell this place and take the next ship home."

"Never in the world!" cried Crewes. "You will not leave us now, Henry!"

"I have little choice, Jamie. Father owns Doggams; I am just his caretaker. He has heard about the savages and he is worried. Besides, he has come into some property and ... to be honest, we are going to be very well off. But for the Ring I would not shed a tear upon leaving."

The men murmured and chewed over Isham's news at some length. Nat thought of Squire Thomas and his heart skipped a beat. What if his father called him home? Would he go so blithely? He knew he would not. Without quite realizing it, he had found his way here in Virginia and his fate was bound to Curles Neck. He felt that he had an important role to play. What role was still shrouded in the future, but one thing was clear: this was his home. Nat was strangely moved and he rose to compose himself. He extinguished his pipe and leaned upon the huge oak, its rough bark as comfortable as a homespun shirt. In the near distance the river talked to him. No, he would not go back to Friston Hall. This was where he belonged.

The wind had scoured the sky clean and the stars seemed strangely close. The moon was just past full and it looked benign and wise as it hung in the firmament like the eye of God. What was that across the river? He knew all the James plantations now, and no house lay directly across from Doggams, only fields. Yet that was surely a torch or a fire ... and there was another one ... and another....

"Henry! What is happening on the other bank? Is there some festivity? Surely it is not the militia? Come and look."

"Why, that is odd. I have no idea. It is a large gathering of some kind. Look at the lights flicker – they must be torches. It has the look of an army, does it not? Farlow was by the other day, asking questions about our county – do you suppose he has something to do with this?"

"Farlow?" asked Byrd sharply. "He's one of us, but from the Middle Peninsula Chapter. Quite a scholar and quite a soldier, too. What lies over there that might bring Farlow our way?"

"Nothing that I know of, nothing but fields. It's just Jordans' Point. Beggar's Bush is at some distance."

"Beggar's Bush?" laughed Jake. "What is that?"

"Curious name, is it not? The first Jordan named his house so, years ago, when he planted Jordan's Journey."

"The moon is full and it is almost as bright as day. Could we not cross the river and see what is happening?" asked the youth.

Byrd glanced at Nat. They both burned with curiosity. Why not adventure to the south shore and see what Farlow was up to? Crewes was wrestling with the tap on a keg of rum and he finally forced it open. The spirits splashed onto the grass and Isham cried out.

"Jamie, what are you doing? 'Tis my precious Jamaica rum!"

Crewes closed the spigot, but not before he had half filled his tankard. He drank deep, the liquor coursing down his heavy beard. "Ah, I have never tasted finer. Bacon, Byrd and you, child, come and help yourselves."

A giddy spirit claimed the men and they filled their glasses and drank deep. The night seemed made for madness. Prudent Byrd licked a finger and raised it in the air.

"The night is warm and the wind is fair. Who will sail across with me and see what devils Charles City County has raised tonight?"

Crewes hefted the keg of rum onto his shoulder. "I will, but only if this buxom beauty goes with us!"

"I'm with you," cried Nat. He and Virginia had exchanged vows this very night – it was time to consummate the marriage.

Jake Hartwell raced screaming to the wharf, his arms windmilling in ecstasy. "Me first, me first!" he called as he threw himself into the sloop.

Half an hour later Byrd had negotiated the rough waters where the Appomattox met the James and had found a small cove where he could snug the sloop right up against the shore. Jake leaped over the side and staggered up the muddy slope brushing willows and sedge aside. He turned and summoned the others and within minutes Bacon and Byrd and Crewes stood at his side, the latter bearing the keg of rum on his mighty shoulder. The four men penetrated a screen of brush and saplings and soon found themselves standing on the edge of tilled fields, though there was no crop that they could discern. Dry corn stalks rustled under their feet: last fall's growth which had not yet been plowed under.

"Look," breathed Jake. "It's a great meeting. The lights we saw were torches, but they've made a bonfire as well."

"There must be over fifty men," murmured Byrd. "How could we not have known of this?"

Nat gripped his shoulder. "Tell me about Farlow. Is this his doing?"

"He's from Dorset and his family was Puritan, though he was too young to have fought for Cromwell. He's a good ten years older than we are. He's adept at the mathematics and well respected in Gloucester County for his judgment, but being a small planter has never held any office of note. He's at the forefront of the Middle Plantation Chapter."

"Sounds like Dicken Lawrence."

"Aye, they know and respect one another. Perhaps this is Dicken's doing."

"Come on," blurted Crewes. "What are we waiting for?"

Byrd hissed at the big planter. "We're waiting for Jake to scout and make sure that these are not the Governor's men."

Jake took his cue and slipped into the shadows. A quarter of an hour later he returned with the assurance that he recognized at least half the crowd and they were all Charles City County men dedicated to, if not all members of, the Ring. There was someone in charge, who was lecturing the meeting near the bonfire, but he could not say it was Farlow, as he did not know the man.

Bacon and Byrd sighed with relief. What fools they would have been to step into a coven of Greens. With Jake leading the way and Jamie Crewes behind them with his precious rum, they strode forward towards the fire. The crowd was silhouetted against the flames like sooty demons in one of hell's pits. As they reached the outermost circle they saw that a handcart had been dragged in front of the bonfire and the crowd had gathered around it in a ring. Balanced on the cart, steadying himself with one hand and gesticulating with another, stood a man in nutbrown homespun. His head was bare and his brown hair hung about his ears while a neatly trimmed beard of similar hue marked a strong, square jaw. The crowd was mesmerized by what he was saying.

"'Tis George Farlow," hissed Byrd. "Shh. Listen."

"...wholly failed to defend us. Is it not the first duty of a Prince?"

"Aye, aye," roared the crowd.

"Moreover, he refuses to permit those who have stepped forward to defend us to have any say, whatever. Sir William cannot have it both ways.

Either *he* must lead an army against the savages or permit those who are able and willing to do so."

"Councilor Bacon's petition went for naught and then the Governor pulled back the army he sent out under Chicheley," called out a familiar voice.

Nat and Byrd exchanged glances. It was Richard Lawrence. That explained Farlow's presence: the innkeeper had recruited him to speak to those who lived south of the James. The only question was, why?

Nat thrust his way through the crowd, Byrd at his side and Crewes towering behind him. As they reached the front row Farlow had resumed his speech.

"And so we are met here tonight, once again, to petition Sir William Berkeley to lead forth an army against the Indians. We all know the fort system will not work. It has been a month since the Assembly, and has anyone seen a fort, anywhere?"

"No, no," roared the crowd. "We need an army. We must have an army."

"Well then, if you are so resolved," continued Farlow, "come forward and put your name or your mark on this paper and Mister Lawrence and I will fasten it to the petition I have just read you and deliver it to the Governor tomorrow."

Farlow reached down over the back of the cart and Nat saw an arm stretch up with a great sheet of paper. It must be Lawrence. He stepped out into the center of the circle, Byrd and Crewes at his heels. Farlow turned in surprise and the innkeeper stepped around the end of the cart, surprise and then delight registering on his stern countenance.

"Nat Bacon! William Byrd! Jamie Crewes! It could not have happened better."

Nat gripped Lawrence's hand. "Whatever are you doing, Dicken? And why were we not invited to the party?"

"This concerns the Southside, Nat. George Farlow has become my at-large lieutenant and he's coursing the colony for recruits for a citizen army. Surry and Charles City County have risen to the call. You folks in Henrico were next on my list, I assure you. How did you find us?"

"Why, we were supping at Doggams and the whole countryside seemed ablaze," Nat hissed. "I take it this is not a secret meeting!"

"Does it look that way? I want the government to see and hear. How else are we going to get their attention?"

"And you think that sending another petition will do the trick?"

"No. It is just a ruse. We are seeking a leader to force the Governor's hand. We need some one to fight the savages while Green Spring stays home wrapped in lamb's wool. That is the only way the frontier will be protected this side of Doomsday. The General Assembly's plan has already become bogged down with issues of rank and precedence and lack of funds ... just what we expected."

"Hmm," mused Nat. "'Tis simple and clever. But you will never force Berkeley's hand."

"You may be right, but what else can we do?"

A roar burst forth from the crowd and both Nat and Lawrence jumped. Jamie Crewes had handed up the keg of rum to George Farlow and the brown man was acting as tapster to anyone who was lucky enough to have a cup or mug. The entire crowd surged forward, many offering their hats as vessels, and spirits and voices rose as the liquor flowed. Nat spotted Byrd in the distance, talking to some friends, and he was glad to see that he had Jake under his wing. Bacon turned back to Lawrence who was stroking his upper lip as he always did when he was deep in thought.

"Do you have a cup, Dicken? It's good rum; I can swear to it."

Lawrence smiled, but his mind was a thousand miles away. "No Nat. I would have you swear a different kind of oath."

"Whatever do you mean? Do you want me to sign your petition? I will, though it is futile."

"Oh, no. No – something a little more interesting than that. I think fate has brought you here tonight. This was never in my plans, but now it lies before me, like a beautiful chess-board. Why did I not see it before?"

"You talk in riddles. What do you mean?"

"How would you like to be nominated as ... what shall we call you ... General Bacon, by consent of the people?"

"*General Bacon?* It is absurd, Dicken. I've never fought anything except in the hunting field."

"But you know history, including the history of warfare; you know weapons; you know the savages; you know the frontier; your own plantation has been attacked; you, a Councilor, have urged the government to act, though fruitlessly; and ... above all ... you are what the people need."

Nat flushed. "What are you saying? You want someone to lead a volunteer army ... yes, I see it. With the Governor's blessing ... but if necessary, without it. Someone of rank; someone who is committed to the people ... I think I know what you are saying ...."

"You will do it! I hear it in your voice!"

"Yes, he will do it," said Byrd quietly. The trader had slipped up behind Nat and listened to the last part of the conversation. "He will do it because he is just the man to do it and he will have the support of every planter, large and small, in Henrico County and beyond. I like your plan, Lawrence. The time is ripe and the moment for action has come. Let's not wait any longer. Let's do it now."

Nat stood stunned as Lawrence caught Farlow's attention and Byrd moved through the crowd, bringing it to order. Earlier at Doggams ... when he had felt that sense of destiny ... was this what fate had in mind? It *did* make sense. The pattern was so strong and so perfect.... *General Bacon by consent of the people.* Yes. He would be that man. And he would lead an army against the savages and there would be no more Hens, no more Sittenbornes, no more Hartwells. His thoughts spun as the crowd quieted around him. Soon the only sounds were the spitting of the pine logs in the great fire and the call of a nightjar. Another omen: his bird. The poorwill approved his fate. He strode to the cart and mounted it as Farlow jumped down. Turning, he saw the men spread below, all eyes riveted upon him. He would speak to them. He began quietly, so they had to strain to listen.

"People of Virginia! I stand before you as your servant."

"No, our leader!" It was Jamie Crewes.

Nat ignored him. "Your humble servant. From the day that I set foot on your shores you have made me welcome. You have opened your homes to me ... and your hearts to me. I have no special gifts ...." (The crowd murmured its disagreement.) "I am a simple man." (The words 'Councilor' and 'Esquire' floated upwards.) "I want only to live in peace with my wife and child and cultivate the art of friendship." ("We too, we too.") "But the times are sad." (The crowd moaned.) "One greater than we has decided to test us." ("Savages ... heathens.") "And somehow you and I have come together at this moment." ("It was meant to be.") "Some among you have suggested that I, of all people, might somehow meet your needs as ... a leader." ("As a general. General Bacon.") "If it is really so ... if you trust me, despite my failings, how can I deny you my sword?" ("A Bacon. A Bacon.") "I stand ready to serve you in any way that I can. Now permit me to step down and wait your pleasure."

The crowd roared as the fire flamed high and George Farlow scrambled up upon the cart.

"Do I hear you say that you want Councilor Bacon as your general?"

"Yes, yes!" The tide of voices crashed over Nat like the Suffolk surf.

"Do any say 'nay'?"

The silence was absolute.

"Then gather round me and sign your name or your mark, not to a useless petition, but to a charm which shall wind up this plan and put it in motion. I shall guide your hands so that the names coil like a serpent and no man can be discerned to be either first or last, alpha or omega. Indeed, General Bacon will be our alpha and our omega."

Nat leaped from the cart into Crewes' arms and was whirled to the ground, a flagon of rum thrust into his hand. Byrd slid to his side and shook his hand heartily, Jake's eager face behind him. He felt Lawrence's iron grip above his elbow and the innkeeper steered him to one side.

"God keep you, Nat. This is your day. Enjoy it. But tomorrow come to me at Byrd's and the plot will reveal itself."

From there the night descended into madness.

CHAPTER 18

MAY 1676

Pagan that she was, Lyn loved May Day above all other holidays, but she was not going to celebrate this one. She had never been angrier with Nat, not even in Suffolk when the black dog of depression had worried at his heels and had driven him to the gaming table and the bottle. She watched Folly's gleaming haunches disappear down the drive. The set of her husband's back was inexorable. He was going to take an army south to crush the Susquehannocks and no one, not Lyn, not John, not Sir William Berkeley himself was going to stop him. And he had a disciple. At his side rode Jake on Blue. The boy worshiped the ground Nat walked on, thought him the apotheosis of chivalry. Young Jake Hartwell would probably end like his father, at the wrong end of an Indian hatchet, thought Lyn as she walked back to the house, her throat tight and her eyes blurred with tears. John stood on the porch, his forehead creased with sympathy.

"Well, he's gone," the mistress of Curles Neck said bitterly.

"Nothing will stop him, Lyn. And perhaps he is right. This is something he needs to do. Only he knows why he has taken up the people's banner, but it is the path he has chosen and he must follow it wherever it goes."

"Oh, it's clear enough, John. He has always felt guilty that life was so easy for him – you know that better than anyone. Now he is going to right the scales. I only hope that the price he pays is not his life. It is not fair to me and Mary. We could have withstood this Indian war. Curles is safely palisaded and we are not directly on the frontier. If the Susquehannocks have truly fled south to the Roanoke River as Nat says, what do we have to fear? Unless the Powhatans rise up the worst is almost certainly over. The whole thing is ridiculous ... and futile. The accolades of that crowd went to Nat's head. I trusted William Byrd. I am bitterly disappointed that he let this happen, nay, was instrumental in its happening."

"Well, Nat is in good hands. George Farlow will teach him how to lead an army; Jamie Crewes will keep him safe; and Jake will guide him through the forest without harm. Remember, the boy has taken the trading path to Occaneechee Island half a dozen times with his father, and he is wise in woodcraft. Besides, they're going first to Fort Henry to see Abraham Wood and, according to Byrd, no one knows more about the savages than Wood. Perhaps he will convince them to go no farther and we'll see Nat back here the day after next."

"Byrd," spat Lyn. "I never thought I would be angry with him, but he is part of the problem, lending Nat the trading post as his headquarters, helping marshal this army of ragamuffins, giving him the boy to guide them .... Mary would never have let him get involved in this folly, but she's fifty miles away. Men are such fools."

Despite her best efforts Lyn burst into tears and she and John went into the house where Grey rang for tea. Hannah brought the tea tray and, sensing that Lyn wanted to talk with Grey privately, took Mary outside to play on the bluff where the summer house was to be. The slaves had built a cunning round table and matching benches from a huge fallen oak and placed them in the hollow above the river, where some redbuds grew, and the child had claimed the place as her own. Lyn composed herself and sipped her tea gratefully; she had had no appetite for breakfast.

After a few minutes John spoke. "I don't want to distress you further, but I wonder if Nat is not in more peril from the Governor than from the Susquehannocks."

Lyn looked startled. "What do you mean? They have certainly quarreled over the colony's Indian policy, but I daresay things will calm down when the savages have been dealt with."

John paused. Today was probably not the day to utter the word "treason," but Lyn was entitled to know everything that concerned her husband. It had to be said.

"You know that when Nat returned from Jordan's Point in charge of this volunteer army that I urged him to seek a commission from the Governor who is, after all, Virginia's Captain General."

"Yes, of course. He said that he didn't have the time to play games with the old man; he would lose his best opportunity to strike the Indians; and in any event it would be futile because the Governor was too pigheaded to commission him."

"Well, not having a commission could be a real problem. Arguably Berkeley and Berkeley alone can legally wage warfare in Virginia. Under general principles of law, and specifically under the statutes which the Assembly passed in March, he and he alone is in charge of this Indian war. No volunteers need apply."

"Why, that's nonsense. What has Berkeley done for us? Nothing. Do you mean to tell me that we must sit here like sheep while the foxes ravage us and that we cannot protect ourselves? I don't understand that, at all. Surely everybody has a right to defend himself."

"Well, Lyn, you'd make a good advocate. The law does permit self-defense; it has to, doesn't it? It's just common sense. But this is a little different. When Nat was chosen 'General Bacon' and when he and his friends assembled their little army at Byrd's, they were not under direct attack, not in danger of their lives and limbs. Despite the fact that savages might have been lurking, waiting to strike again, one could argue that any action against them would not be self-defense. Nat and his friends are operating wholly separate and apart from the militia; they are waging a private war, if you will. I am afraid that Sir William would have a strong argument that Nat's actions are illegal and possibly treasonous."

Lyn paled. "Treasonous, John? How can that be?"

"Treason is more than rising up against the king, Lyn. It was defined long ago as comprising an act, or even a thought, of deposing the monarch; waging war against the monarch; or aiding the monarch's enemies."

"But Nat has done none of those things."

"Let me finish. Since that famous statute was written the doctrine of constructive, rather than actual treason, has developed. In our lifetimes mere public riots, such as gathering to pull down brothels, have been held to be treasonous as they encompass raising forces against the sovereign, rather than permitting the sovereign to regulate his own realm."

"Gathering to pull down brothels! That would be a good thing. I don't see the connection."

"Well, you are not the first to think that 'constructive treason' opens the door to abuses. But our common law is organic; the parent at all times lives in the child. The fact is that within the last twenty years some forms of public unrest have been adjudged treasonous ... unrest not unlike the gathering at Jordan's Point. Do you see my concern? Berkeley is the King's representative here, his vice-regent. An action against him is an action against the King. Given recent precedent a clever advocate could easily tar Nat with the brush of treason."

"But John, treason is a capital offense."

"My point exactly."

"My God! So if Nat slays the savages and saves the frontier ... the Governor might bring him to trial for treason?"

"I fear it is so."

Lyn walked to the casement and pressed her forehead against the glass. If she did not lose her husband to enemies beyond the fall line, she might lose him to those within. When would she be able to care for her family in peace?

Mary plopped down on the soft earth and began to sob. The little girl was learning to walk and she had pulled herself up to a standing position by clinging to one of the benches and had then set off on the precarious journey which had ended in ignominy. The mother seized the child under her arms and held her up high, making kissing noises to distract her. Soon Mary's tears changed to laughter and she reached for her mother's curls and chortled as she seized the blue ribbons which Lyn had braided in her hair that morning. It was the third of May, Mary's first birthday, and she and John were going to celebrate the event with a cold luncheon on the bluff, the place the baby loved best. John was in the fields; he would arrive shortly.

Lyn heard hoofbeats. She could not see the horseman as the redbuds screened her view of the drive, but she supposed it was John. She sat up straighter. The hoofbeats had turned to thunder. There was more than one rider coming her way ... far more than one ... it was a whole troop. Holding the child close to her breast she clambered up to the drive and peered through the foliage, the soft roseate blossoms brushing her cheek. A cloud of dust rose high in the air as a small army pounded down the road, directly at her. Her heart stopped. Could it possibly be Nat? But why would he bring his troops? The horse cloths of the vanguard were brilliant green and above them streamed an emerald banner. She knew that the Governor had adopted the color in honor of his seat at Green Spring, but surely Sir William would not visit Curles with an army? Another rider caught her eye. There, to the left, streaking across the fields was John, stretched low on Coke's neck as the chestnut raced flat out for the bluff, directly towards her.

John reached Lyn at the same time as the leader of the troop. The green-clad rider signaled his followers to halt and sidled forward on a white horse which tossed its head and rolled its pale eyes as it champed its bit and flung froth from its pink muzzle. John slid from Coke and put his arm around Lyn's shoulder as Mary screwed up her face to cry.

"By God," he muttered under his breath. "'Tis the Governor himself."

Lyn felt as though a jolt of electricity had passed through her. "The Governor?" she cried out.

"The same, madam," intoned Sir William Berkeley as his pale horse danced.

"Why, who are all these men?"

"You had better ask your husband, 'General Bacon'," answered Berkeley, his mouth turned down like a fish.

Lyn immediately bristled and John tightened his grip. "My husband! My husband is away. He has nothing to do with armies. I don't know what you mean."

"Has nothing to do with armies, madam? That is not what they tell me."

Lyn caught her breath. So that was it. Exactly as John had said. The Governor was incensed that Nat had raised a force to fight the Indians. He must have brought this green-clad troop to put down Nat's volunteers. Had the word "treason" entered the old man's mind?

"I am afraid I do not take your meaning, sir. But forgive me. Won't you dismount and come into the house? Perhaps we can come to an understanding over some refreshment."

John squeezed Lyn's shoulders. Bless her stout heart. She was still furious with Nat but she would defend him to the death.

Sir William Berkeley smiled grimly. "Now is not the time for hospitality, madam. I have come to hang your husband."

Lyn cried out and Mary burst into tears. John turned them both about and sent them down the path to the hollow in the bluff. He faced the Governor. "I have no idea what you are talking about. Mister Bacon has business south of the river. He left several days ago without saying exactly when he would return."

Spittle formed on the Governor's lips, as it did on his steed's. He raised his whip and approached John as if to cut him down. "You dog! I've seen you before ... you're Bacon's friend. Why, you must be the one that left his overseer to die! That makes you a coward. A dog and a coward. Well, tell your master when you see him that he is a rebel and a traitor and that he will pay the price for thwarting me. What is your name?"

"My name is no business of yours. Get your men off our land. This is private property."

The whip came down, but John easily jumped out of its path. Seizing Coke's reins he lashed them against the neck of the dancing white horse, causing it to rear. Berkeley almost fell from the saddle; he saved himself by gripping the pommel, though he lost his reins. A rider with rich chestnut hair and sherry-colored eyes urged his mount forward from the vanguard and quickly brought the white horse under control. The Governor and the flame-colored man rode back to their troop. A signal was given and the horsemen turned their steeds and proceeded down the drive, green pennant flying. John stood in the drive breathing hard until the last man disappeared into the forest and the dust cloud settled. The noon sun shone, a lark called and the James River sparkled below the bluff. John walked slowly down the path where Lyn stood trembling, Mary pressed close to her heart. He took the little girl from her and smiled.

"Come, Lyn," he said. "It's time for luncheon. Aren't we going to celebrate Mary's birthday?"

Nat had never seen such a thick canopy. Surely this southern forest held every shade of verdure which God had ever made. The sun must be directly overhead, but you could not tell it for the trees. Underfoot lay an ancient carpet of leaves, the product of centuries. The silence was absolute but for the occasional call of a bird or the rustle of a squirrel and, of course, for the soft tread of the hundred men who marched along the trading path, two by two, like Noah's creatures. He felt young and foolish and full of wonder. They were only three days' march from the James, but it might have been three hundred days, the forest seemed so remote and the affairs of men so insignificant. Still, it was his business to find the merchant Indians, the Occaneechees, and see what they knew of the Susquehannocks. His countrymen had made him General Bacon and General Bacon he would be.

After lunch Farlow and Crewes had moved to the van and he and Jake had dropped to the rear. He watched his men snake through the forest, awed by what they saw. He had questioned Jake's wisdom in following the Indian trading path, but the boy had convinced him that they were as safe there as anywhere, for the heathen could find them whether they were on a known track or in the wilderness. Nat shivered. It was an unpleasant thought. At any moment an arrow could slice through the green air and bring one of them down. A few men had old body armor and most of them wore leather, but they were rapidly shedding what clothing they had as the day grew hot and humid and he did not doubt that some would die if the savages struck. And of course the same went for him. True, he and Farlow and Crewes and Jake were mounted, but that made no difference. Horse or foot, a well-placed arrow would do its ugly business.

Folly snorted as Blue emerged from the forest like a ghost. Jake had stripped off his shirt but had paid the price: his slim torso was riddled with insect bites. He had found a creek and gathered some mud and was slathering it on his brown skin as he guided the roan with his knees. Nat smiled. Jake Hartwell was a centaur, part man, part horse. And he knew these woods like the back of his hand. Nat felt a twinge of envy and quickly quelled it. He was old enough to be Jake's father – was it seemly to feel jealousy towards the boy?

He broke the silence. "What do you think of what Wood told us?"

Jake laughed. "Oh, that old man. He thinks he knows more than anybody about the savages and the southern forests. 'Tis true that he has roamed about and that he can speak more Indian tongues than anyone else I know, but father was his equal."

Nat frowned. "I am sure he was, Jake. How many times have you been to Occaneechee Island?"

"Why, half a dozen times. Rossechy is a great king – father thought highly of him. But you have to watch him; he's a clever devil and will take advantage of you if he can."

"That's what Wood said. Said he and Berkeley had been in league for years, the Governor lusting for beaver and Rossechy lusting for firearms and powder."

"Oh, everybody knows that. You see, Rossechy manages to be friends with everybody, if he can make a profit by it. Mister Byrd says he is the shrewdest merchant in Virginia. He has been trading furs for English goods for a long time. But he trades with the other savages, too."

"Do the Occaneechees pay fealty to King Charles?"

"Oh, no. They are not related to the Powhatans, speak a wholly different language. But they are not related to the Monacans either, and certainly not to the Susquehannocks. I suppose they came from the south. Their great advantage is that they camp on the three islands where the Roanoke River crosses the trading path and so they are in the center of everything. All come to them, and that is how they grow rich."

"How many islands are there?"

"Three. First Totero, then Occaneechee and then Sapponi. The river runs swift between them. Occaneechee is the largest."

"Strange names."

"Father said they are separate bands of the same tribe, so each claims his own island. They are friends and speak the same language, but some of their customs are different. The greatest of them are the Occaneechees and the greatest of the Occaneechees is Rossechy. Why, he's as famous here as King Charles is in England."

"And when shall we see him?"

"Three more days; we have come half way."

Nat and Jake rode on in companionable silence for some time. At mid-afternoon Farlow called a halt and he and Crewes rode back to join Bacon and the boy while the men threw themselves on the ground to rest or wandered about looking for water. The four horsemen dismounted and loosened the girths of their weary mounts. Jake found a convenient fallen tree and they pulled out their pipes and smoked, the woods stretching around them without end.

After a few minutes Jamie Crewes spoke. "Did you believe that fellow Wood about these trading Indians?"

"What do you mean?" asked Nat.

"That you can trust them? I don't like the sound of it. They've been friends of the Governor for years."

"I think he meant that the Occaneechees are friends to all, but when push comes to shove they think only of themselves. As far as I can learn they trade with the Governor not for love of him, but because he can give them powder and shot and firearms. Wood said they would turn on him tomorrow if it was to their advantage."

"And we are supposed to trust such people?"

"Not trust. Do business with them."

"What business?"

"Well, they are more likely to know the whereabouts of the Susquehannocks than anyone else. They say that Rossechy knows everything that goes on in southern Virginia and beyond, wherever this forest goes. He sits on his island like a great spider and gathers information."

"Then why cannot the Susquehannocks use them against us?"

"Because they hate the Susquehannocks."

"How do we know that?"

"Not only from Wood. All of Byrd's men told us that as well. The southerners hate and fear the northern savages. Do you doubt that?"

"Not the way you put it. But you said this Rossechy would sell himself to the highest bidder."

"Well, who can buy him better? The Susquehannocks, who are on the run and who have nothing but the clothes on their backs, or we who have four pack horses laden with cloth, glassware, blue beads, copper wire and, above all, iron tools and knives."

"So you mean to buy him."

"Well, I suppose so."

"But what if the Governor has bought him first?"

"The Governor? What do you mean?"

Farlow emptied his pipe, knocking it against the log and carefully disposing of the ash so that it would leave no trace. "Why are you being so cryptic, Jamie? Come out with it." Farlow turned to Nat. "Jamie is worried about that Irishman that Wood told us about."

"Ahhh," breathed Nat as he rose and stretched and extinguished his pipe as well. "That is what this is all about. The fox-faced fellow who left Fort Henry just as we arrived. Did any of you get a glimpse of him?"

"I did," said Jake proudly. "I know the man. I've seen him twice at Occaneechee Island. He takes messages back and forth between Sir William and Rossechy. Father said he is fluent in the common Indian tongue and many other languages as well. He's spent a lot of time with the savages and is very clever."

"What's his name?"

"I don't know. Everybody calls him the Irishman, 'tis so unusual to have one of his kind here."

"It *is* unusual. What else do you know about him."

"Well, father said the Governor owns him, body and soul. I don't know what that means, but I think he did something bad in Ireland and Sir William holds it over him"

"Aye," growled Jamie Crewes as he cleaned out his pipe with a twig and put it back in his pouch. "I've heard something of the fellow. They say he was transported and owes his freedom here to the Governor. I've never seen the man, but he is known to run Sir William's errands with the savages. I must have missed something at Fort Henry. Did you say that he left as we arrived?"

"That's what Wood said, and I guess Jake saw him as well."

"Yes, sir. I saw him with my own eyes. He slipped out just as we rode in. I didn't make anything of it, as he runs back and forth between Jamestown and the Roanoke as you do between Curles and Bacon's Quarter, but now that you mention it, it almost looked as though he left *because* we had arrived."

"Humph," muttered Nat as the four men walked back to their horses and remounted. "Let's keep an eye out for him. His errand to Rossechy may be innocent, but what if he was sent ahead to do us some harm? I don't believe in coincidences. George, Jamie – describe this fellow to the men and tell them to watch out for him and let me know anything you learn."

Nat's two lieutenants agreed and rode forward, stirring up the somnolent soldiers and passing the word through their ranks. Jake grinned at Nat and flew up on Blue like a bird. They would march for two more hours before they made camp.

Three days later, early on a splendid May afternoon, Bacon's army arrived on the banks of the Roanoke River a mile or so upstream from the Indian islands. The largely deciduous forest was in full leaf and the trees murmured whenever a breeze came off the river. Slender pines were intermingled among the hardwoods, reaching high for sun and air, and their spicy scent enlivened the afternoon. The Roanoke rushed deep and true between steep banks, its bright water clear unlike that of the muddy James.

Nat signaled Farlow and Crewes to join him and Jake, and the four of them rode to the very brink of the steep bank which plunged down to the rushing flood below. Nat gazed right towards the river's distant source and left towards Rossechy's island kingdom. It was a land of stunning beauty; a man could be happy here.

"Well, it's time to execute our plan. Jake and I will proceed with ten men and two of the pack horses. If all goes well the Occaneechee guard who watches this shore will greet us and secure us an invitation to see the King. If we are successful we'll tell the guard about you and the rest of our force and Jake will come back to fetch you. With luck we'll sleep tonight on Occaneechee Island as the guests of Rossechy."

"And if the Irishman has set a trap?" asked Farlow.

"We are in Jake's hands. He is the one with the key to their tongue. It is for him to test the guard and see if he senses that something is not right. At some point we have to take a risk. Suppose the Irishman has reached the King – what can he have promised that would put us in peril?"

"Unlimited firearms. Remember, Rossechy knows Berkeley well, but he does not know you. They speak as king to king. Where do you think his allegiance will lie?"

"You forget that for the past two months selling firearms to the savages has been a capital offense. Even the Governor would not play with that fire."

"Ah, but Rossechy knows nothing of our laws. And think of this: what if the Irishman told him that trading firearms had been banned, but that laws can change and who better to change them than Sir William Berkeley?"

"It is a stretch. The old man is a fool, but not such a fool as to commit a hanging offense in a country where every savage is now deemed an enemy. No, I think we have as much leverage as the Governor. Everyone says that Rossechy looks out for his own people first. It is entirely to his advantage to help us seek out the Susquehannocks and earn the rich goods we have brought. Besides, look at our force. Jake says there are never more than five score savages on Occaneechee Island and that includes the women and the children. Even if he thought he could buy the Governor's favor by harming us, is it likely that they would attack our army?"

Farlow looked sceptical, but Crewes snorted. "Nat is right, George. At some point you have to act. We didn't come all this way to be cowed by an Irishman. Jamestown is more than a hundred miles away. Let's get on with it. If this Rossechy acts up, he'll regret it or my name is not James Crewes. Come, the afternoon wears on. Let Nat and Jake go or we will be spending another night in the forest."

And so it was that despite Farlow's concerns Nat and Jake rode east along the river, each leading a pack horse, and behind them marched ten stout men dressed in fringed leather and carrying flintlocks on their shoulders and powder and shot at their belts.

Nat leaned back against the pile of furs, sated. A short woman whose forearms sparkled with copper bangles handed him a pipe and retreated to a dark corner of the hut. Bacon supposed she was Rossechy's main wife; only a very rich woman could wear so much copper. He glanced at his right hand and twisted his own gold ring. Rossechy followed the movement and smiled. The Occaneechee King spoke in the common tongue, using Jake as a translator.

"You prize gold as we do copper," he said, his bronzed face impassive but for a slight smile on his thin lips.

Nat looked at his host. Unlike the statuesque northern Indians, the Occaneechee King was only of middling stature and build, but there was something lively about his face which indicated a quick intelligence. His black hair was pulled back and bound in complicated plaits; a few strands of silver showing his advancing years. His muscular torso was bare and smooth, and around his neck he wore countless strings of *roanoke* and copper and bone and feather, so that his entire chest shone like a cuirass.

"We prize both. Copper is a worthy metal and I have brought much with me. It would give me great pleasure to show you the contents of my packs tomorrow. We have more than copper."

Rossechy's dark eyes gleamed. "You have firearms?"

Nat took his time and puffed on his pipe. Unlike the Virginia sweet-scented, the Indian tobacco was coarse and rank and he was hard-pressed not to cough, but appearances were critical and he mastered his breathing.

"I regret that I do not, although one never knows what can be arranged. As I explained this afternoon, the English are at war with the Susquehannocks and in an excess of caution our wise men made laws forbidding us from trading firearms with any Indians until the war is over."

Nat glanced at Jake to see if he had managed to convey some of the subtleties of his words. The boy looked at ease and Rossechy's face seemed to indicate an understanding of what had transpired.

"I have heard of this war," the King acknowledged.

Nat's ears pricked up. Had the news been carried by savages or by the Irishman? He would try and find out. "Then you have heard of the unfortunate prohibition on trading weapons?"

The King shifted his position and used his pipe, as Nat had, to delay an answer. "I have heard something like that, but it was not clear to me until now."

Nat was not going to learn whether the Irishman had reached the King's ear; at least not through this conversation. "Would it please you to know what is in our packs, or shall we wait for tomorrow?"

"It would do no harm to learn what you brought."

"Four whole packs, filled with red cloth, glass," (making hand gestures indicating bowls and pitchers and drinking vessels), "many blue beads, so like *roanoke* that few could tell the difference, much copper, and many iron tools, hoes and saws and hatchets among them."

Rossechy looked impressed. "It is much. Your King has never cheated me; I am sure the goods are the finest. What would you expect in return? Furs?" stroking the pile of beaver, otter, deer and lynx against which he leaned. "Or some service?"

"You have already done us a great service by feeding my men, who had exhausted all their food; by permitting us to camp among the great trees in the very center of your island; and by sheltering our beasts on your northern bank, with your own braves to guard them. But, yes, there is another service I would beg of you. After what we have already said, I think you know what it is. Nothing can be hidden from a king."

Rossechy bridled. Perhaps, thought Nat, he was not as subtle as Jake said.

"You want my help in finding the Susquehannocks."

Nat bowed his head as though mightily impressed. "Not only in finding them, Your Majesty. I should like to make an alliance with you to track them down and slay them."

For many minutes Rossechy smoked and pondered, his gaze unfocused as though his thoughts were a thousand miles away. Suddenly he stood and withdrew to the corner of the hut where his nephew and two councilors sat huddled in silence. The four braves spoke quietly together at some length and then the King returned to his place by the fire. He stared at Nat.

"Tomorrow at dawn we shall take our canoes to your camp on the north shore. If we like the contents of your packs we, and we alone, will dispose of the Susquehannocks. I know well where they dwell. There is a small camp not five miles upriver and a larger one five miles beyond that. They have killed our game, sullied our water and frightened my trading partners away. They are no friends of ours. We shall round them up like so many deer and lay their scalps at your feet."

Nat was startled by the munificence of Rossechy's offer and he had to compose himself before answering. Was there a trick here? If so, he could not find it. It made all the sense in the world. The Occaneechees could slip through the forest like the wind and be on the Susquehannocks like a hurricane, while his own troops would unquestionably signal their presence far in advance and frighten the foe into the forest, never to be found again. Look what had happened at Piscataway Creek: once the *werowances* had been treacherously surprised and slain, the rest of the tribe had escaped almost unscathed, even though the English had them cornered in the old fort. Yes, if Rossechy was willing to take the northerners on, why not accept the offer? Nat would give a great deal to see the scalps of those who had taken Hartwell's. He glanced at Jake and then replied.

"I am deeply honored by your offer. It is far more than I could have hoped. You have shown yourself a true friend to the English and you have my word that you will be repaid for your generosity. Although I am not directly authorized to speak for our Governor, you can be sure that he will join me in rewarding you appropriately should this venture succeed. I hope I do not offend you, but may I offer my hand on it?"

Rossechy was well used to English hand-shakes and he accepted Nat's grip and crushed it with his own. The two men smiled across the fire, each quite sure that he had the benefit of the bargain.

Occaneechee Island was larger than Jamestown peninsula, and at its heart a grove of great trees stood. Nat's troop – all but the ten men who guarded the horses on the north bank – had been permitted to camp there and now, as the sun set, they began making their camp fires, laughing and teasing the Indian women who brought them corn and beans and squash and venison. Many of the girls had not been averse to testing the prowess of the English in the arts of love on the preceding night, and the men were in a good humor.

Nat sat on a fallen log at the edge of the grove and smoked his own pipe, stuffed with the finest sweet-scented, relieved that he did not have to pretend to enjoy the Indian weed. Before him stretched a clearing dotted with garden plots and bordered by wild vetch. The prospect was pleasing – he might have been home in Suffolk, watching the cottagers finish their chores before heading home for supper. He heard a footstep and turned to see Jake striding from their camp site. The boy perched on the log next to Nat and drew out his own pipe. Bacon smiled. The lad knew far more than he about this wild land, but he looked up to "General Bacon" ... hung on his every word.

"They liked our goods, didn't they, sir?" Jake asked.

"Oh yes, I think they were more impressed than they expected to be. We have Mister Byrd to thank for choosing the things they covet. It didn't take long, did it? No sooner had they inspected the packs than they marched off into the forest. With luck the Susquehannocks will fall to their arrows and hatchets this very day."

"And to their matchlocks."

"Well, quite a few of them had firearms, but I wouldn't vouch for their quality. They don't know how to care for them properly. That's why Rossechy is so avid for more."

"The men weren't too happy to learn that the Occaneechees were going to do their job for them."

"No, but they quickly saw the sense of it. There is no way in the world that we could have crept up on the enemy – it is just not in our blood. Do you think I could have persuaded the men to shed their boots and stockings and tiptoe through the forest?"

Jake laughed. "Never. No, they would do well if we were attacked, but you can't learn to wage war like a savage in one day." The boy's face became somber. "I hope that father's murderer ... you know."

Nat patted Jake's hand. "I know, "he said softly, and looked for a new subject. "Did you make a tour of the island as you said you would this morning?"

The boy brightened. "Oh, yes sir!'Tis a beautiful place, so peaceful, except for the rushing water which is ... well, somehow it is peaceful as well. I think the Occaneechees could stay here all year, though I believe they winter somewhere else, where it is warmer. The Toteros and Sapponis have not yet come. It seems they camp here during the summer and fall and move elsewhere in the winter and spring."

"Is there more than the one camp, the one on the western end where we dined with Rossechy?"

"Yes. That is the main one, by far. There is no lodge so grand as his, and half the savages or more live there. But there is another camp at the far eastern end of the island, and a third one on the southern shore, perhaps half way in between."

"How many savages are there?"

"I suppose about the same as us – perhaps one hundred, but half are women and children."

"Did you talk with any of them?"

"The eastern camp was friendly and gave me lunch – such tender fish! – but the people on the southern shore seemed sulky and would not come out of their huts. I cannot say why. Perhaps I offended them somehow, but if so I don't know what I did wrong."

"Probably nothing. People are the same everywhere, even savages. Perhaps you interrupted their afternoon naps."

"I don't doubt. Look, sir! There, beyond that patch of corn! It is the King and his nephew! Do you suppose ...?"

Nat and Jake rose and soon they were joined by the English who trickled down to the clearing from the forest, Crewes and Farlow among them. Rossechy's long shadow preceded him as he walked in glory, the aureole of the western sun behind him.

"I bring you good news," said the King solemnly.

His nephew, One Ear, so named because he had lost his right ear to an enemy hatchet, stood beside him and smiled a vulpine smile. Nat was reminded of the Irishman: One Ear had the same foxy look.

"So soon, Your Majesty? I am anxious to hear."

One Ear held out a hand from which depended a long braid of silk grass. Entwined in the fibers were a dozen or more scalps, each black as a crow, and each bordered with the same pennant of flesh-colored stuff. Nat shuddered. It was what he had wanted, but it was still a gruesome sight. He did not reach out for the trophy.

"You have had a great triumph. I am impressed and grateful."

Rossechy signaled One Ear to retreat. Perhaps he could read the squeamish English faces for he looked at once quizzical and amused.

"We did well. My nephew took the smaller band and left no one alive. The Spirit permitted me to find the larger group; there is no one left who will tell their tale. There are now no Susquehannocks south of your James River. We brought twelve scalps back – the finest – the other twenty were not worth saving."

"More than thirty of the enemy! You and your men are mighty warriors. May we feast together tonight and hear your story? Tomorrow all that is in our packs shall be yours. This is a great day and the English are in your debt."

A look of feigned sadness crossed Rossechy's face. Nat was reminded of a mummer he had seen at Cambridge – what a strange connection!

"It grieves me to refuse. Permit me to explain. We have our own way of celebrating a victory, and although the English are our good friends, they have never been permitted to see this ceremony. We shall eat and sing and dance long into the night. Perhaps tomorrow, after the gift-giving, we can join you for a meal and celebrate in your manner."

Nat was greatly relieved and he hoped he did not show it. The last thing he wanted was to be caught up in some savage rite where the ghastly details of each enemy death was retold and embellished.

"My King, of course we understand. Every nation has its own customs. Enjoy your feast and tomorrow, at your convenience, we will distribute our paltry gifts and do our best to feed you well, though it is your own bounty on which you will be dining. I think I can promise that greater and more fitting gifts will be provided at a later date. You have my word on it."

General Bacon and King Rossechy bowed to one another and the Occaneechee turned and made his way west to his village where even now the fires were burning and the drums were beating. The soldiers drifted back to their campfires, some grumbling that they had been denied a battle, but most overjoyed that the Susquehannocks had been put down with no English blood spilled. Nat's left arm was grasped above the elbow and he turned in annoyance to see Farlow's brown face. He smiled. George was always welcome.

"Never was a battle so easily won! Are you disappointed?" cried Nat.

"No. I believe the battle was fought, but it was not fought today."

"Whatever do you mean?"

"That string of scalps confirmed what I already knew. The Occaneechees did away with the Susquehannocks some days ago, on their own initiative. When you let them know that they could get the English to pay for their wars, they leaped at the opportunity. You have been gulled."

Nat seized Farlow by the shoulders and steered him to the fallen tree where Crewes was sitting. "Explain yourself."

"I had Pomfrey follow Rossechy and One Ear into the forest. He's my best scout, and even the Occaneechees never knew they were being tracked. No sooner had the tricksters walked a few miles than they found a nice glade with a running stream and spent the day eating jerked meat and dried corn and laughing with one another and telling tales. Late in the afternoon they returned as if from battle. They picked up the scalps from the King's hut where they had been for days and put on that little charade for your benefit. Tomorrow they will receive four packs of prime trading goods for nothing."

Nat's face was a study. He had never been so astonished and mortified. His first thought was to beard Rossechy in his den and bring him to task, but then he realized how foolish that would be. Finally he smiled, ruefully, and then burst out laughing.

"Well, as long as the Susquehannocks have been slain, how can we complain? Rossechy has lived up to his reputation. He is a master of guile. But are you sure they have killed the northerners?"

"Oh yes, the scalps were those of the Susquehannocks – you can tell from the way the hair is done and from the decoration. It is just that they are five or six days old. I would swear to it: I got a good look at them. Besides Pomfrey overheard them joking about their cleverness. He has enough of the language to understand; there is no question about it."

Nat sighed. "Well, I don't know how I am going to explain this at Jamestown. I wonder if we could bind the men to silence."

"I would think so – nobody wants to look like a fool."

Crewes grunted. "Maybe the savages have outsmarted themselves. We haven't given them their prizes yet – why should we do so now that we know the truth?"

Nat stroked his lip. True, he could march off tomorrow with his goods intact, but he did not relish the thought of Occaneechee arrows whistling through the dense woods as his troop marched north.

"No, Jamie, I think not. After all, we have the result we wanted – it just didn't happen quite the way we imagined. Come, let's have supper. Tomorrow we'll entertain King Rossechy and begin our journey home. Where's Jake?"

"He was on the heels of the King and One Ear like a dog after a bitch in heat."

Nat started. "That's a bad idea – Rossechy said this victory dance was private. He could take it very ill if he thought we were spying on him. George, stay here and keep an eye open for the boy. Jamie, follow me."

Bacon and black Crewes slipped through the dusk towards the Indian village. They had not gone far when they met Jake hurrying towards them, his face white in the fading light.

"Sir, sir! Oh, it's very bad!"

"What is it Jake? Shhh, come back with us to the camp. What has happened?"

"I wanted to see them kick up their heels, so I followed them back to the King's hut. You know it backs right up to the cliff above the river. Well, I slipped around behind the hut and hugged the face of the rock and found a place to peek through where there were no savages keeping guard. Not a foot away from me was the Irishman! They treated him like a long-lost brother, pressing him with food and drink and jabbering away so fast I could barely understand. But I *did* understand! He's been hidden away in the southern camp for four or five days – must have come directly after he saw us at Fort Henry and left by the back door. Well, he has convinced Rossechy that Berkeley is going to give him a cache of new firearms – flintlocks! – if he murders us!"

"Murders us!" cried Nat, in spite of himself.

George Farlow appeared out of the dark and once again Nat felt his arm in a soldier's grip. "Shhh! Jake – keep your voice down. I heard what you just said, but I don't want the men to hear it yet. Go on."

Nat and Crewes and Farlow stood on the edge of the campsite, the frightened boy in their midst.

"What more is there to tell? Mister Farlow was right: the Governor set a trap for us. Rossechy was primed to do us in as soon as we arrived. He was supposed to attack last night, but he got sidetracked when he saw that in addition to the Governor's guns he could winkle us out of our goods. The Irishman was furious at the delay, for he wanted the trap sprung last night, when we were tired, but then he saw the humor of it." Jake paused, the three men riveted upon him. "They just agreed to do it tonight."

"Damn my blood," said Nat under his breath. "The traitorous bastard."

"Well done, boy," breathed Farlow. "Without you we would have been slain in our beds."

"Let's turn the tables on *them* and attack, tonight," urged Crewes.

The four looked at one another. Of course – it was obvious. The men were well-rested and well-fed. A three-quarters moon would be rising soon, casting enough light for them to see. All the Occaneechees would be gathered in the western camp to celebrate the false victory. It could not have fallen out better if they had planned it. Someone would have to alert their horse-guards on the northern bank, but otherwise no preparation was needed but for the men to finish their suppers, douse their campfires, load their weapons and march upon the King.

"Jake, take one man to help you paddle, purloin a canoe and row to the north shore and tell the guards to be ready to leave at a moment's notice. When you get there, stay there. No – don't argue. I won't have you anywhere near this battle. I have your father's death on my conscience, and that is enough. We'll join you tonight or tomorrow, when it is all over. That is an order. George, Jamie get your troops together. We march in half an hour. Silence is essential. I will personally garrote any man who makes enough noise to warn the savages. We are going to fall upon them and exterminate them, men, women and children. Now, go!"

The moon rode the cloudless sky, indifferent to the affairs of men, shedding light upon saint and villain alike. Bacon's men were quickened by the Indians' treachery like powder by a slowmatch. Their leaders were hard-pressed to restrain them. Crewes' troop filed to the south of the village and Farlow's to the north, with Nat striding next to his lieutenant. The Indian palisade was in disrepair and they were going to pierce it near the cliffside where there were fewer guards and where the King's hut stood. If they were lucky they would seize Rossechy in his den and use him as an example to dishearten the rest. If, as was more likely, the savages were in the center of their compound, dancing and celebrating, they would pounce on them from the rear and rend them to pieces. The rules of warfare had been tossed away; any act which brought death to the savages was condoned.

Nat's heart beat fast. His fate had been sealed at Jordan's Point. This was his destiny. He and Farlow reached the northern palisade without incident, but the moment they stepped inside a skinny cur burst into a torrent of barking. Hoping that the raucous cries of the celebrants and the thrumming of the drums would overwhelm the dog's warning, Farlow drew a knife and threw it, true as a die, into the animal's throat. Nat saw the blood flow as the creature gasped its last and Farlow retrieved his weapon. The two men turned and signaled their troop to follow. Within seconds they reached the King's hut and Farlow peered inside. His face showed his disappointment: the hut was empty. As Nat raised his arm to signal his men forward a movement caught his eye and there, on the other side of the hut, stood Jamie Crewes, huge in the darkness.

The two forces silently acknowledged one another and turned east, where a bonfire burned bright and the howls of the Occaneechees rose to the heavens.

Now they discarded any pretense of surprise and strode forward, firearms primed, knives sharpened, hatchets ready. Bacon's army burst into the fire circle, bringing chaos with it. Nat's flintlock brought down a brave and before he could reload a savage was upon him. Like Crewes and Farlow, he bore a sword and now it was in his hand, driven by a wild fury he had never experienced before. The Indian was down, his left arm severed from his body and his life's blood flowing to ground. Like a snake in a death paroxysm the warrior struck at Nat with the hatchet in his right hand, but even as he wielded the blow it lost its force and Bacon avoided it easily, without thought.

To Nat's right Crewes was windmilling death, his sword in his right hand, his hatchet in his left. To the north Farlow had grouped two lines of gunmen, one standing and one kneeling, each with a matchlock or flintlock at his shoulder. Nat prayed that no English would walk into the line of fire and then, with the prayer still in his throat, turned to fend off another savage. This brave died with Nat's sword in his heart just as the muskets cried out in the night and the women started to wail.

Nat and Crewes fell back together against the wall of a hut and looked about them. The guns had wrought havoc: it seemed that fully half the village lay dead or dying at their feet. Farlow gave the order again and the night was pierced with fire. The squaws who had rushed to their fallen warriors tumbled in the dust, some into the flames themselves. The stench of burning flesh filled the air and children screamed. Crewes speared a small girl with his sword and Nat thought of Mary and looked away, into the face of the Irishman.

The fox face grinned as a dagger flashed but before the blade touched Nat's flesh the Irishman crumpled to the ground, spitted by George Farlow's blade. Farlow nodded at Nat and pulled him to his side.

"I still haven't seen the King. Let's go to the gate and see if he is trying to escape."

Breathless, Nat nodded and signaled to Crewes. The battle was well in hand, the English triumphant. The three leaders rushed east to the main gate of the village. There they found Rossechy and One Ear, side by side, but not in flight. Both were kneeling by a fallen woman, a woman whose arms were covered with copper bangles. Her chest was dense with blood and her eyes were sightless. The two warriors rose and faced the three English, weaponless. Crewes advanced on One Ear, mercilessly, and soon the King's nephew lay on the ground, a steel blade in his heart. Rossechy stood motionless. He

271

looked at, and through, Nat, as though he saw something which was not visible to the rest. Farlow sprang on him like a tiger and cut his jugular with a bright blade. The blood streamed down the King's muscular torso, turning his strings of shells and bone and feathers and copper bright crimson. As he died he did not take his eyes from Nat but his spirit was already far away.

The sun strove unsuccessfully to break through a milky sky. It was going to rain. *Thanks be to God,* thought Nat, as he watched the last of the Indian village go up in flames. It was Rossechy's funeral pyre, and that of his entire people. No one had survived. The battle had lasted little more than an hour. It had taken his army far longer to dispose of the dead. They had labored through the night and now, in the early morning, it was over. The coming rain would douse the fire and Rossechy's kingdom would vanish from the face of the earth.

Nat turned to Jake. Despite his General's order to stay on the north bank, the boy had returned to the island at dawn, assuring Bacon that the horse-guard was safe and well and that the beasts and all the trading goods were unharmed. The English had no casualties – just some minor scratches and a few burns. In one sense, it was a great victory. The original cause of the troubles, the Susquehannocks, slain, some thirty of them. And the treacherous Occaneechees paid back for their deceit. They had counted the dead: some fifty braves and an equal number of women and children. Bacon could return to Jamestown claiming to have dispatched four score savages – nobody was going to care what tribe they came from, as long as they were dead and the frontier could rest in peace. As for the Irishman, Nat had sworn his army to secrecy over the traitor's death and none of them had a reason to break that vow. What was it to them that one of the Governor's henchmen had met his end in the wilderness? It had not come about as he had planned it, but it had come about. Nat should have felt elated. Then why did he not? Now, for the first time, he understood what John had tried to convey to him about Hartwell. He could not clear his mind of Rossechy's face. The King was a master of deceit and had earmarked Nat for death, but nonetheless ... he had been a man. And now he was dust.

He tried to smile for Jake, but could not. "Come on, lad. We're the last. Let's find a canoe and cross the river. It's time to start home."

Chapter 19

May - June 1676

When Nat finally arrived at Byrd's the first person he saw was Martha Hartwell, waving her apron at him. Then Jake sprang off the porch and came running across the yard, yelling.

"You're famous, General. They're gathering at Varina to welcome you home."

Nat slid wearily from Folly and handed his reins to the boy. He had sent Jake and half a dozen swift messengers on before the rest of the army to bring the news. Obviously they had.

"It is good to see you safe, lad, and to see you with your mother. Is she back with Mister Byrd?"

"No, sir. She came with letters and a package from Mistress Byrd and she's going back to Surry tomorrow. But wasn't it lucky that she was here when I arrived?"

Martha Hartwell approached Nat and curtsied. "Welcome home, General Bacon. Thank you for taking care of my boy. He can't stop talking about your adventure."

Nat laughed. "I can't get used to 'General Bacon'. As for Jake, didn't you know that he's a hero? He got us safely there and after we had stumbled into Rossechy's trap he saved us by overhearing the plot."

Bacon glanced at Jake who was shaking his head. It was clear that Martha Hartwell had only heard the sanitized version of the story and it was better so. The canonical script which had been drilled into the soldiers was that after the Occaneechees had formed an alliance with the English and honored it by eliminating the Susquehannocks, their lust for firearms had caused them to turn on their partners. God was with the Virginians and Jake Hartwell had learned of the plot and saved the day. The story was close enough to the truth to stick. Not one word was to be uttered about Sir William Berkeley's unholy alliance with Rossechy nor about the Irishman. Nat was willing to let bygones be bygones. Doubtless the Governor rued the day he had sent the fox-faced fellow on such an evil errand. His teeth were drawn. Better to let things rest as they were.

Crewes and Farlow dismounted and joined Nat and the Hartwells and soon Bacon's army was dispersed among the scattered outbuildings of Byrd's trading post. The troop had arrived precisely as expected and that morning Byrd had begun preparations for a great outdoor feast. The carcasses of deer and swine were roasting over vast beds of coals and slaves were spreading the rough wooden tables with platters of fruit and vegetables, baskets of bread, and jugs of cider and perry. The day was still cool under the canopy of oaks and hickories and Nat felt suddenly overwhelmed with relief at having reached home safely. Nothing could be better than this save being at Curles Neck. Tomorrow he would press Lyn and Mary to his heart and, God willing, bide with them for a while. He was not naive enough to think that he could mend fences with the Governor. He would ask leave to withdraw from the Council of State and would return to farming.

George Farlow organized his Southsiders and Jamie Crewes his Henricans and soon the feast was in full swing. One of Byrd's blacks had a fiddle and as the men gathered to eat, several of them broke into a jig, the others stamping and clapping in time to the music. Nat had plunged his head in a bucket of rainwater – he had not bathed properly since a symbolic cleansing in the Roanoke River after the funeral pyre. He shook his head like a dog. He could not rid his mind of the images of the slain Occaneechees, particularly the little girl who had met her death on the point of Crewes' sword. He wondered if he would ever really make a "general." As he groped for the towel which Jake held out to him he heard a familiar voice.

"Hail, Caesar!" It was Dicken Lawrence.

Nat toweled his face and broke into a grin. The gray man looked grayer, the furrows in his cheeks deeper, and his eyes more intense.

"Dicken! Well, you created a general and an army. How do you like it?"

"I like it well, Nat. Welcome home. Did you know that the whole of Henrico County is going to greet you at Varina tomorrow and give you a triumph?"

"I don't want a triumph. There are only three people in Henrico County whom I really wish to see, and you know who they are."

"Lyn, John and your child, of course. I stopped at Curles yesterday on my way here and told them the good news which I had just learned from Goode who was kind enough to sail all the way to Jamestown to bring it to me. That is a triumph in itself. I can't remember the last time the old man left Whitby. I hope you are impressed; you have the whole colony in your pocket."

Nat smoothed his hair and handed the towel back to Jake. "Are they well at Curles? Will they be at Varina?"

"They *are* well and they will *not* be at Varina. They want to welcome you in private, not in public." Lawrence put his hand on Nat's shoulder.

"You should have seen Lyn's face when I told her you were safe and were returning in a blaze of glory. And you have a friend in Grey – he shed a tear. I believe they suffered more at home than you did in the wilderness."

Nat's heart pounded. Thank God for Lawrence's news. Now he could relax, get through today and deal with whatever the people at Varina had planned for him tomorrow and then finally get back to Curles.

Jake joined the festivities and Lawrence took Bacon to one side. "Speaking of the wilderness, young Hartwell and the other advance scouts seemed to be a little unclear, a little contradictory when they told us the story of your campaign. Do I gather that there is a tale behind the tale? Truth is such a complex thing."

Nat spoke quietly. "I have a story that is only for your ears and Byrd's. Where is he? We've taken over his home like a swarm of locusts and I have yet to see him."

"Oh, he's in the main house, waiting for you. A lot has happened in your absence. Come, let's tell the slaves to make up some platters of food for us and join Byrd. We're going to be talking all afternoon."

Nat loved Byrd's house. It was large and simple, fashioned from huge logs, some of them still wearing their bark. The ground floor consisted of two rooms, the living quarters and the trading post itself. The affairs of one merged seamlessly with the affairs of the other, so that on the private side one might find piles of furs and strings of shell money and bales of red cloth, while the commercial side contained comfortable chairs and a great stone hearth which begged the visitor to sit and stay awhile. The bedrooms were upstairs, in the attic, reached by a steep staircase which was almost a ladder. With Mary and little William in Surry, Byrd had taken to sleeping downstairs in his living quarters, and it was there that Nat and Lawrence found him, pulled up to his desk, scrutinizing a document.

"I've brought your goods back unharmed, William," laughed Nat.

Byrd leaped up, the feet of his chair shrieking on the pine planks.

"Bacon! God bless my soul, what a victory. I couldn't believe my eyes when Jake and the others appeared. And then for a terrible moment I wondered if they were the only ones who had survived! But I soon learned the story ... or at least *a* story."

Nat glanced at Lawrence and back at Byrd. "There are two tales to tell and you have only heard one. You and Dicken will soon know the truth, and then it is in your hands how much to share with the Ring. The long and the short of it is that Berkeley had set a trap to kill us all."

Even cynical Lawrence and shrewd Byrd gasped at that bald statement.

"Sit down, Nat. Oh, there's food, good. Let's eat and drink and hash this thing out. We have some surprises for you, but I want to hear your adventure first."

An hour later the story had been told and Lawrence and Byrd were still digesting the knowledge that the Governor's *amour propre* was so great that he would rather kill a hundred of his own subjects than appear to condone their extralegal actions.

"Well, that explains things," sighed Byrd as he quaffed his cider. "The Governor took some rather extraordinary steps on the tenth of May and it all fits together with his plot to put down your army."

Nat pricked up his ears. What was he going to hear now? Byrd pulled out the document he had been perusing earlier and handed it to Bacon.

"I'll let Dicken summarize this for you while you read it. It is quite remarkable."

"It *is* remarkable. And hope for our cause springs up in my heart. I, who thought that sap would never again run in my veins. What you have there is a proclamation which finally dissolves the Long Assembly after fifteen long years; which calls for new elections of Burgesses; and which invites, *invites*, the citizens to state their grievances to the new Assembly in so free a manner that if His Honor himself is perceived to be the chief grievance, that the whole government, Governor, Council and House will jointly plead with the King to relieve Sir William of his post. *And, and* ... the vote is open to all freemen."

Nat sat in stunned silence. New elections? An expanded franchise? A new House? The Governor pleading for his own removal? It was too good to be true. He read the paper again and again and finally spoke.

"This is all theater. Berkeley is beating his breast and trying to drum up sympathy. He doesn't believe for one minute that the colony will ask for his removal. This is a little masque, a whim, a jest."

"Ah," said Lawrence. "But he *did* dissolve the Assembly and there *will* be new elections. The old man is so out of touch with the people that he has put cold steel in their hands thinking it only a toy sword. *He* may think it theater, but *we* do not."

Nat brooded silently. "Don't you see," urged Byrd. "The trap he laid for you is part and parcel of the whole thing! His arrogance has no bounds. He truly believes that he is justified in crushing the people's army for its failure to receive his blessing and he truly believes that a new House of Burgesses will be at his beck and call as the old one was. The man lives in a fantasy. Let's take advantage of his dreams."

Nat glanced at the paper again. "Two Burgesses from each county – 'two of the most sage, best experienced and most understanding persons ...' – you are right, Byrd. This proclamation might just be Berkeley's political death warrant. When are these elections to be held?"

"Why," smiled Lawrence, "in fact ... tomorrow."

"Tomorrow!"

"That is why there will be such a crowd at Varina. To greet you and to vote. The timing is perfect. I could almost believe there is a God if I did not have so much evidence to the contrary."

Nat groped for his glass and found that Byrd had given him a noggin of rum. He drank deeply. "Who do you suppose will be elected from Henrico? Goode? Cocke? You, Byrd?"

"Why Nat," insinuated the innkeeper. "There are only two men I can think of who meet the description of 'sage, best experienced and most understanding:' the heroes of our recent Indian wars – you and Jamie Crewes."

"I?" shouted Nat, leaping up and spilling his rum. "Jamie and I? 'Tis a raw jest."

"'Tis no jest at all. I have never been more serious in my life. Jake brought the good news just days after the proclamation was announced. Every since then there has been only one theme in Henrico: Bacon and Crewes, Bacon and Crewes. I daresay if Farlow was from Henrico you'd have a little competition, but he'll have to make the running in York."

Nat burst out in helpless laughter and would not be quieted until Byrd poured more rum down his throat.

"I do not believe what I am hearing. And you, Dicken, I suppose you will throw your hat in the ring for James City."

"You can be sure of it. It is already done. I must sail tomorrow or I will miss the event. Don't you look forward to sitting in the House with me?"

This time Nat was speechless. He looked from Byrd to Lawrence and back again.

"You are serious. You think the old man has unwittingly unleashed forces which will strike him down like a hurricane. Damn my blood ... it is extraordinary." He caught himself. "But you are forgetting one thing. I'm still a Councilor – I can't run for Burgess."

Lawrence's gray eyes glinted. "I wouldn't worry about that. Berkeley published another proclamation on the same day as this one. He named you and Crewes rebels and threw you off the Council."

Nat looked taken aback and then smiled. "Threw me off the Council? It is a pity that he was there ahead of me, for I was about to resign from that august body." He paused. "Which reminds me of my cousin. He is going to take this all badly. Well, so be it. Life must go on. What does it mean that I am called a rebel?"

"Well, nobody knows, but it can't be a good thing."

"When I left without the commission John was afraid they would level a charge of treason against me – is that where this is going?"

Lawrence and Byrd looked somber. "It is possible, "said the former. "The Ring has always known that it is a risk. Berkeley can always level the charge against those who disobey him. Whether he can prove it is something else again."

Nat stroked his upper lip. "So I'm off the Council and have been named 'rebel' – what makes you think the Henricans will elect me to the House?"

Lawrence laughed in earnest now. "Of that there is no question. You have no idea ... you are the hero of the day, the savior of the frontier. They would elect you in spite of yourself, and Crewes along with you."

"What should I do next?"

Byrd spoke. "Today ... enjoy yourself. Tomorrow ...bid Farlow and his troops farewell – they are anxious to return to their homes. I'll ferry you and Jamie across the river in the afternoon to attend the elections. You won't get to bed early – I suggest you plan to spend the night at Bacon's Quarter. Things will have calmed down by the next day. When all of Henrico is abed with sore heads then you can finally make your way to Curles and receive the reward that is closest to your heart."

Lyn knew she would find Nat under the maple, looking at the river. They had found the promontory on one of their many rides and it was a favorite spot. It lay a mile east of the brick house at a point where Curles Neck bluff sloped down to the edge of the James. The shoreline was dense with willows and sedge and waterfowl and now, on the first day of June, the fox grape would be running riot over the underbrush and fallen trees and the green fabric of summer would be whole once again. Under a splendid maple there was a small clearing where the rock pierced the soil and lay exposed under the Virginia sun. Lyn and Nat had spend many hours there, musing and talking as they idly threw pebbles into the James or, on occasion, tossed a fishing line into the water to see what luck would bring their way. It was where Nat would go to think.

She kneed Mignon onto the trace which led to the promontory and pondered the events of the past two weeks. She had been wild with joy the day her husband returned to Curles, flushed with his reception at Varina and his election as one of Henrico County's Burgesses. That first day had been wonderful. Every man, woman and child at Curles had attended a victory feast to celebrate General Bacon's return and the singing and dancing had lasted far into the night when she and Nat tumbled into bed, avid for one another. Then came the gifts: the stunning lynx skin saddle cloths for her and John, which matched Nat's own. The shell necklaces and bracelets for Mary which had sent the child into raptures. The bolts of red cloth for Abraham and Hannah, enough to garb them for years to come, and a dozen of their fellow slaves as well. John's relief, too, had been palpable. He was pleased for his friend's success and, like her, supposed that with peace likely, Nat would now settle down and farm. The anxious months were behind her; now she could live in peace.

Lyn's dream started to fray when the strangers came. Individual families and, from time to time, whole groups of settlers would wander up her drive as though they owned the place, asking for General Bacon. Nat would appear smiling and, rather than exchanging a few words with the unwelcome guests and then sending them packing, would invite them to stay for a meal ... offer them a bed in the barn. John had to share the wooden house with rough vagabonds on more than a few occasions and Lyn knew he resented it. Twice she herself had been forced to open her guest chambers to ill-clad, down-at-the-heel women and their wan, contagion-carrying children. She had had a furious argument with Nat when Mary had come down with a fever after playing with one of the ragamuffins. Her husband had called her heartless and selfish and she had charged him with thinking more of strangers than his own family. Each still bore the hurt of those recriminations.

And it had not stopped. It was not just a matter of Henricans gawking at an Indian-slaying hero until the novelty wore off. Most of the settlers were from the north, from New Kent and Rappahannock. They came because they thought that General Bacon was going to solve all their problems: protect them, find them land, feed and house them, tell the fools in Jamestown how to run the government. It was a contagion as virulent as the fever which had struck little Mary. And Nat responded! He let them camp in his fields, eat his stores, draw water from his wells. He sent them off with letters to his friends, asking that the strangers be given aid, perhaps a few acres of land, a job, spare clothes for their backs. Charity was one thing, but this was insanity. Because Nat had chased the Susquehannocks out of Virginia, (and what a tale the true story was!), he was now charged with the welfare of every ne'er do-well who was too feckless to till his own acres and protect his own borders. Lyn seethed and Nat smiled. He had found his *metier*. The people had elected him their leader and their leader he would be.

Lyn pulled Mignon to a halt and slid from her back. Before she reached Nat she wanted to think everything out clearly. She had ridden off in a storm of rage and anxiety and now it was time to collect her thoughts. Neither one of them needed another shouting match.

She looped Mignon's reins around a dogwood and found a mossy seat under a large oak. A cardinal flashed red above her as she closed her eyes to think. Attacking Nat about the stream of strangers who were gobbling up Curles like a swarm of field mice was a dead end. He owned Curles and he would do with it what he wished. But this proclamation that Giles Bland had just brought ... that was another matter! Giles Bland – what a shallow cockerel. She could not for the life of her see why Nat gave him the time of day. And Crewes ... the man was a brute. Yet William Byrd, for whom she had the greatest respect, ran with the same crowd and shared much of their thinking. Even John maintained that this Ring was principled and well worth supporting. She would never understand politics. To her it was ... what was the expression? All noise and no wool. But what of Nat?

Her husband had ridden out early after yet another silent breakfast. Lyn had attended to her housekeeping and sent Mary off to the henyard with Hannah to look for eggs when she saw a rider pounding up the drive. She scowled, thinking that it was another beggar come to disturb the perfect summer morning when she spied Bland's inimitable red hair and, as much as she disliked the young planter, actually felt relieved that it was he and not a stranger. As she stepped out to meet him John joined her from the wooden house. The hotheaded youth was waving a sheet of paper about and could hardly articulate his message, and it was not until they had coaxed him into the brick house and given him refreshment that they understood why he had come.

Three days before, on the King's birthday, the 29th of May, Sir William Berkeley had issued another proclamation. It was largely a bold defense of his administration and a challenge to the people of Virginia to identify how, if at all, he had failed them. But there was more, and that more touched Curles Neck closely. The Governor began by scoffing at Nat's victory over the Indians, claiming that he himself had achieved far more. He next expounded the precise argument which John feared: he claimed that under the laws of all civilized nations if a subject waged war in defiance of the direct command of his prince, the act was treason, even if the war was waged against the prince's acknowledged foes. Sir William Berkeley and the Council of State then charged Nathaniel Bacon, Junior with treason and called upon all loyal citizens to bring him to heel. The proclamation was to be read publicly at every county courthouse throughout Virginia.

Bland had tumbled out the words, handed the proclamation to Lyn, gulped his ale, and fallen silent. Fool that he was, Lyn's heart softened towards the young man who had rushed to Nat's aid, ignoring his own comfort and safety. Leaving John to look after him, she ran from the room, proclamation in hand, calling for Abraham to saddle Mignon.

Lyn opened her eyes and looked around her at the peaceful sylvan scene. Another cardinal flitted across the glade – they must be nesting. Sir William Berkeley and Nathaniel Bacon were nothing to them. She opened her fist and smoothed the terrible paper. She *must* convince Nat to resign from the House of Burgesses and mend his fences with the Governor. The Indian troubles were behind them. Surely if he stayed quietly at Curles Neck this storm would pass over as well and she could have a husband again, and Mary a father. Even John must agree that things had gone too far. It was time to confront her husband.

When she came upon him he was lying prone, peering at the river, like an idle boy. But when he rose and sat, cross-legged, staring out over the James his face was not that of a boy. His profile was clawed with care and his mouth turned down. The black curls in which he had taken such secret pride were dull and matted. He pressed his face in his hands. Lyn's heart turned over.

"Oh, Nat."

He whipped around and paused, like a dog expecting the lash. "Lyn."

Lyn rushed forward and wrapped him in her arms. How selfish she had been – he was as troubled as she by the events of the last weeks, and she had denied him a hearing.

Nat's face smoothed out as if brushed by an artist's hand. "Why Lyn – do you not hate me?"

"Hate you, Nat? Have I ever hated you? My anger comes from love. This country is eating you alive."

"Ah, Lyn I am torn between my duty to my family and my duty to ... my people. I know you do not understand, but Drummond and Lawrence and the other members of the Ring, my soldiers, the poor souls who are pouring in from the frontier ... to me they are like family and I am driven to help them. You would have me stay home and tend my garden, but I cannot. Truly, I cannot. And if I choose the larger stage I will lose you and lose Mary, the delights of my heart. Even John thinks I am making a bad choice ... I can see it in his eyes, though he says nothing."

Lyn thrust the proclamation at Nat. "Perhaps this will help you choose wisely, Nat."

Bacon studied the document for a full ten minutes and turned his gaze once again to the wide river. "Well, so be it," he sighed. "The line has been drawn. To Berkeley, anyone rash enough to defy him is a traitor, and you and I know that cannot be. His time is past. The people have spoken and the people are right. It is my fate to help their cause."

Lyn sighed and the emotions which raged within her drained away, leaving her spent but at peace. It was over. Nat had made his mind up and he would not change it. She had only one choice now: to love and support her husband. She leaned over and kissed his brow and smoothed his curls. He stood wearily and clasped her to his breast. For a full minute they stood in silence, listening to the song of the river. Then they turned as one, found their horses and rode home.

John joined them for supper that night and such a peace reigned in the brick house at Curles Neck as had long been absent. Like Lyn, Grey accepted without cavil Nat's decision to proceed to Jamestown for the June Assembly as a Burgess for Henrico County despite the gauntlet the Governor had thrown down. A confrontation between Green Spring and the Ring had been long brewing; it was time to bring it to a head. If God had chosen Nat Bacon as the champion of the people, man could not stay His hand.

"Will you go with Crewes?" Grey asked.

"Yes. I'll take the sloop and twenty or so of our Indian fighters and ask Jamie to do the same. Two boats and forty men should give the capital something to think about. Perhaps we should tie up at Swann's Point first before setting foot in Jamestown."

"You need to talk to Drummond and Lawrence. Why not send Jake first, on horseback, to arrange a rendezvous with them at Swann's Point?"

"'Tis an excellent idea. The Assembly convenes on the fifth. If Jamie and I sail on the sixth we can meet Will and Dicken that night and learn the lay of the land. If all goes well we'll take up our new duties on the seventh; if things go badly we'll sail home to return another day."

"If rumor is correct the House will be three-quarters yours and only one-quarter Berkeley's. Even he would not arrest you without the Assembly behind him."

"Oh, John, I don't know. He is capable of anything."

Lyn shuddered. "And if you succeed in taking your seat? What next?"

"Why, we'll push through as much of the Ring's business as we can. But my chief object is to persuade the old man to give me a commission to fight the savages. Our recent visitors ... the ones who have caused you such grief ... all say that the tributary Indians have taken fire from the Susquehannocks' example and that the troubles have just begun. Under that threat, Berkeley will have to legitimize me."

Lyn looked from Nat to John. "Will you stay with me and Mary?" she asked softly.

"It goes without saying," said John quietly. "Whenever Nat is away I shall be here."

Nat smiled at his wife and friend. Suffolk seemed far away ... another universe. But the three of them were still together and that was a good thing.

The ketch darted out from the left bank of the James like a bird of prey. Nat checked his sloop like a blood horse and Jamie followed suit. Both vessels bumped softly against the river bank and were made fast to the trees which lined the water. The Drummond boys snugged up against Nat's sloop and clambered on board, assisted by many helping hands.

"Billy! John! I thought to see you at Swann's Point. Is ought amiss?"

"Yes, General, indeed, sir. Father is in such a lather. He said if we did not catch you he would skin us alive. Colonel Swann won't give you a berth at Swann's Point – won't have anything to do with you. Father cursed him out good, but to no avail."

"And then Sarah burst into tears and Sam took her part and the whole family was in an uproar! But the long and the short of it is that neither you nor father is welcome at Swann's Point."

"God damn my blood, Tom Swann? He was always a moderate, good to me, not a Governor's man."

"Oh and he's not Berkeley's man yet, says father. He just doesn't want to be caught in the middle."

"I see. So the Governor is out for my blood, is that the way of it?"

"Oh, yes sir. People talk of nothing else. You are supposed to be a rebel – they call it a civil war."

Nat was silent, deeply perturbed by what the Drummond boys said. Well, one thing was clear: he and Jamie were not going to be permitted to enter Jamestown and take their seats in the House without a struggle. He patted the messengers on their shoulders.

"You are brave boys. Thank you, from the bottom of my heart. And thank your father when you get back. Will you be safe, returning by yourselves at dusk?"

"Oh, yes sir. Don't worry about us. Not a day goes by that we are not out in the ketch, fishing. That will be our story and nobody will give us the lie."

"Off you go then. And Billy ... tell your father to come to *The Unicorn* in the dead of the night. With luck I'll be there with Lawrence."

Nat leaped onto the bank and almost found himself in the river; the sedge and undergrowth were so thick that they threw him back like a line of foot soldiers. He forced his way through the greenery until he reached Crewes' sloop.

"Jamie, come here. I have something important to tell you."

Crewes' bulk crashed through the vegetation and the two planters walked a few yards inland where the forest opened up into a series of glades. They stopped under a large oak. The sliver-like new moon shed no appreciable light and the night was pitch black. Nat told Crewes what he had just learned and the big man cursed and then stroked his beard thoughtfully.

"Well, perhaps we should camp here overnight and arrive in Jamestown tomorrow, at midday, and disembark as innocent as lambs. What could the old man do to us in the full light of day with the whole town gawping?"

"He could throw us in jail, without a doubt, and he would. Especially with our forty armed men. He would call it a civil war and ... he might be right."

Crewes laughed hoarsely. "We should just attack the Statehouse and string him up. I swear that we could do it ... we would take them completely by surprise."

"Don't even say it. Do you want to hang? The old fool is like the great toad of the fable who puffed himself up with hot air. If we play our hand right he will back down. We'll get our commission. But we need to find a way to get into town and into the House without inciting a riot. I need Lawrence's advice, and I need it now. I may try and slip into town tonight."

"Why not? Jamestown is a sieve – it's laughable. If the Powhatans had the courage to strike they could wipe out the whole government before anyone had time to say 'boo'."

"I'll do it. The night is black. I'll borrow a rough hat and coat from one of the men, hide my curls, rub a bit of dirt on my face ... whatever will disguise me, and creep into town in the small hours. The dogs will bark, but what of it? They always bark at something. The isthmus is palisaded – is there a guard?"

Even in the dark Nat could see Crewes' face shine with excitement. "There is supposed to be one, but he'll doubtless be asleep. If not, make your way along the Back River until the palisade ends and go through the pitch and tar swamp – nobody will be about on a night like this."

"It's worth the chance. I must talk to Lawrence and with luck Drummond will join us. It won't take more than an hour to pick their brains; I'll be back with you by dawn."

Crewes seized Nat's shoulders. "Natty, let me come with you! I've never had more fun than on Occaneechee Island. You're the boy for adventure!"

Nat caught some of Crewes' giddiness and laughed. "You must stay with the men, Jamie. They wouldn't know what to do without a leader. But listen, it's possible that I may fall into Berkeley's hands – it could happen. If you don't see me by dawn I want your promise ... no, listen! ... I need your promise that you will sail upriver with the next tide. He's not going to hang me from the nearest tree, not with the whole Assembly in town. If I am caught they'll toss me in jail and I want you and the others free to come to my rescue. Do you understand?"

Crewes glowed and expanded with excitement. "You have my word, General."

"General? We're both Burgesses!"

The two men laughed and Nat returned to his sloop where he traded clothes with one of the soldiers, thrust his hair up under a rough cloth cap, smeared some mud on his face and melted into the night.

Diamonds in velvet – it was trite, but true. If Nat could cut the cloth of the night sky, what a gown Lyn would have! But good that there was no moon; he needed the cover of darkness. He crouched low and sped along the isthmus until he was near enough to the palisade to make out the guard-house. He saw no light, but that could be deceiving. On a mild night like this a guard would have no need of a fire, but he might still be lurking in the shed or pacing about, fusil in hand. Nat crept closer. He heard nothing but a shrill chorus of frogs. When he was within thirty feet of the palisade he slid cautiously down the bank of the isthmus and inched along the muddy shore of the Back River. He heard a strange sound and froze. The frog song continued unbroken, and that was reassuring; if the creatures were unperturbed there could be nothing amiss. He heard the strange sound again and almost laughed. It was unmistakably a snore. Some poor fool was playing soldier and had been caught by fatigue. It was a good omen. Nat continued along the shore, coming close enough to the palisade to touch it. He guided himself with his fingers until the rough barrier ended in the thickets of the pitch and tar swamp. Nat felt invigorated by the spicy scent of the pines. Now he was all but safe. He would slip through the swamp, dash across Back Road and enter Lawrence's yard by the stable. With luck the back door would be unlocked – it usually was. Then his last obstacle would be creeping upstairs and past Joanna's bedroom. How ironic if Lawrence had chosen this night, of all nights, to sleep with his wife, but Nat doubted it. Lawrence's devotion to the Ring had driven a wedge between him and Joanna and the innkeeper told Bacon that they had not shared a bed for many months. And, of course, Joanna's loss had been Clarissa's gain. Now for the pine woods!

When Nat reached the stable door his progress was checked for the first time. The heavy slabs of oak were usually kept open, as horse thievery was not a crime that kept the people of Jamestown awake at night. Tonight however, for some reason, they were tightly closed and he could not budge them without causing an ungodly racket. The problem was not irremediable – he would have to find a way over the little palisade which bordered Lawrence's yard and that should be simple enough. Nat stepped back into the street to reconnoiter and just as he did so a night-watchman rounded the corner, lantern in hand. In a flash Nat was around the far corner of the barn and over the fence. He crouched in the darkness and cursed his luck. To be caught so near his goal – it would be cruel! He knelt for a good five minutes, willing himself to be absolutely silent, acutely aware of every breath he took and even of the crack of his trembling knees. The night was perfectly still. Not a dog barked; not an owl cried. He eased to his feet and followed the line of the barn and the fence until he reached the back of the inn itself. The black night was blacker yet under the eaves and he crept unnoticed to the back stoop and, breathless, gently pulled the door. It opened without a sound and Nat was in the cool hall which led to the common room.

He stood silently for a moment, letting his breathing return to normal. He thought it exceedingly odd that the watchman seemed to have vanished without a trace, but there was nothing he could do about that now. He walked quietly down the hall into the great room and heard coughs and snorts issuing from the dormitory. Of course – the large bed-chamber must be full, stuffed to the gills with Burgesses. Joanna would be making money hand over foot, some solace for a cold bed, he supposed. Using his sense of touch he made his way up the great staircase, blessing the builder for creating treads which would not creak under a far greater weight than his. There was no light in the hall above, no wall sconce, no flicker of flame from under a door; all was dark and silent. He walked carefully past the Lawrences' private quarters until he came to the door he knew so well. He lifted the catch and slid into the innkeeper's sanctuary like a ghost.

"Is that you, love?" whispered Dicken Lawrence.

"Have you changed your preference from maid to man, Dicken?" grinned Nat.

The innkeeper sat bolt upright and cursed. "Bacon – you fool. For the first time since I met you I am sorry to see you. Doubly sorry. You are *not* my love, (though I love you well); and you are in great peril. Why have you come?"

"That's a fine welcome from a fellow Burgess. May I sit down? I've come three miles and more tonight to visit you and all I get is the rough side of your tongue. Why have I come? Jamie Crewes and I need to know if we can land here tomorrow and claim our seats in the House without being clapped in irons."

Lawrence lighted one of his bedside candles and beckoned Nat to sit next to him on the pine bed so that they could talk softly.

"The short answer is 'no.' Berkeley is out for blood. In his book you and Jamie are rebels and traitors and he would like nothing more than to jail you tonight, try you tomorrow, and hang you the day after."

All traces of humor left Nat's face. "You are serious. That's what the Drummond boys told me earlier today. Thank God they caught us in time. We are tied up well above Sandy Point and we can turn tail if we must. Hmmm. Well, what do you think I should do?"

"Hie you back to Curles and start negotiating with the old man on paper. You'll bring him around – with this Assembly, you'll bring him around. But right now he is spitting fire like a dragon and if he saw you he would lose whatever composure he has retained. The people are for you Nat, never fear. The people are for you. And the Assembly is ready to declare war on the savages once again, scrap the idea of forts, and field a real army to deal with the menace. But you are not going to worm your way back into Berkeley's graces without some masterful diplomacy. Lord, I wish you had not come tonight. I have a fear on me!"

"Dicken! That is not like you. Perhaps Drummond will make you feel better. If he can get away he will join us here and we can devise a plan. Although, in truth, you have just given me one, and I don't see what else I can do but follow it."

"Yes, you only have one choice." Lawrence's face flamed with eagerness. "But Nat, there is good news! By far the majority of the Burgesses are either members of the Ring or sympathetic to it. We elected Tom Godwin as Speaker and he is wholly behind our reform laws. We have a real chance of success!"

"Why Dicken, that's wonderful. And the franchise? Will they keep it open to all freemen? You may yet be able to vote!"

"I am hopeful. And we have solid support for the rest. Oh, I never thought this day would come."

Nat smiled at his friend. He was pleased to see that there was another, more hopeful man behind the grim facade. "I am happy for you. I only wish that Jamie and I could be there to participate in the debate and to vote. I should return now and give Crewes the bad news. He will be furious – I hope he does not do something rash. We'll make Curles our headquarters and I will start suing the Governor for peace. It sticks in my craw, but what else can we do?"

Lawrence rose and adjusted his nightshirt. "Be careful – there are watchmen about and it would grieve me to see you fall victim to the Governor when we are so close to success. Oh, how careless of me. I forgot to tell you that your boy Jake arrived safely and is sound asleep in the barn. That's why I closed the doors so tight – were you able to open them or did you jump over the fence?"

Nat was about to recite his night's adventure when Lawrence held up a warning hand.

"Shh! Somebody is coming down the hall!"

Lawrence must have the ears of a fox for Nat could hear nothing. The latch lifted and Bacon instinctively made towards the window as if to escape, but stopped in mid-stride. It was William Drummond.

"Will! You came!"

"Aye laddie, and you must go! They are on your heels!"

"What? It is not possible. Nobody saw me – oh, the night watchman."

"They spotted Jake Hartwell the minute he came to town and they have been dogging his footsteps, hoping he would lead them to you. That's why the watchman was hanging about the barn door. He spotted you and sounded the alarm. Not ten minutes ago they were pounding on my door asking if you were there, for we are known friends and for some reason they thought you had gone to earth at my place. They searched the whole house. Sarah and the children are in a state, and so am I. Nat – go now! *The Unicorn* is the next place they will look! I'm surprised they did not start here!"

"Bless you both, I'm off."

Nat crept back the way he came like a cat, his heart in his throat. Berkeley's men could burst in at any second. When he slipped out the back door he breathed a little easier. He followed the fence to the far corner of the yard and hopped over it with the help of a rain barrel. Praying that he did not disturb a dog, he cut through some garden plots until he reached the reassuring bulk of the church. He leaned against one of the buttresses and breathed a little easier. His best bet was to go west, skirt the town entirely, circumvent the Statehouse and follow the James to the isthmus. With the night so dark he had a fair chance of dodging around the palisade and racing across the causeway to the protection of the forest. He stuffed his hair in his cap more securely, licked his lips and disappeared into the shadows.

An hour later a sweat-soaked Nat reached the bank where the sloops were tied. Jamie would have posted a guard and he hoped his mouth was not too dry to give the signal. He paused and swallowed, letting his heart slow, and then whistled the characteristic first three notes of the mockingbird. Within minutes a shape darker than the dark forest was at his side.

"Pomfrey! Thank God! It was a near thing. They almost nabbed me. We are going to have to return to Curles Neck. How is the tide running?"

"It has just turned in our favor. Give it another half an hour and the sloops should do very well."

"Half an hour? I hope we have that much time. Are the men asleep?"

"Colonel Crewes posted six of us as guards and the rest are asleep or resting. I believe Colonel Crewes has dropped off."

Despite his anxiety Nat smiled. Crewes was no more a colonel than he was a general, but ever since Occaneechee Island that is what the men called him. Of course he was asleep – Jamie Crewes could sleep under any circumstances.

"Lead me to him. I'm going to have to explain why we're turning tail. He won't like it."

Forty minutes later Bacon's army was awake and standing to attention on the bank where the sloops were tied. Dawn had broken and the east was touched with gold and rose, like a peach. The day promised to be lovely, and Nat devoutly hoped that the journey would be as well.

Their view of Jamestown was cut off by the bend of the river; with luck they would not be seen even when they reached the middle of the stream.

"All right, Jamie. Load your men and cast off. We'll be with you in five minutes."

Crewes did as he was told and Nat was pleased to see the sloop's sails belly with wind as the little vessel moved out into the stream. If things continued this way they would be safely at Curles by dusk. Pomfrey's voice startled him.

"General," the soldier hissed. "Look there, to the east. 'Tis a three-master."

Not only a three-master, but a very familiar one. Silhouetted majestically against the aureole of the rising sun, the *Adam and Eve* breasted the James on the flowing tide. Even as his heart sank, Nat noted the familiar figurehead, a golden-tressed Eve kissing the air with seductively pursed lips. *His* ship. The home where John had studied and Lyn had nursed him for six long weeks. *His* captain. Captain Gardiner must be on the quarter-deck, doing the Governor's bidding, hunting down the rebel foe. It was a supreme irony.

"They're aboard, sir. Please go aboard yourself and I'll follow and cast off."

Nat darted up the gangplank and raced back to the tiller as Pomfrey shoved the plank under the gunwale, tossed the sheet into the sloop and joined the four black boys who were desperately pushing the sloop away from the bank with cumbersome oars. Slowly, slowly the vessel moved from its muddy embrace until finally, with a sucking sound, it was free and spinning on the tide. The sails blossomed in unison and the sloop caught a favorable breeze and righted itself, now moving swiftly west with the flowing tide.

Crewes' vessel disappeared around a bend and Nat sighed with relief as his little ship danced in its wake. That was when the great guns boomed. Not ten yards from the prow the James exploded into frenzied motion, water flying everywhere and waves slapping at the sloop's sides. The vessel staggered and lost its weigh, sails flapping fecklessly. It was now broadside to the *Adam and Eve's* foredeck chasers, a sitting duck. Another ball ruffled the water, just to the right of the sloop. The guns fired again: a palpable hit. One ball sheered the mast and the other mortally wounded the sloop just below the waterline. The river grabbed its prize like a terrier with a rat and the vessel went down with all hands.

As he disappeared into the river Nat's thoughts were not for Lyn and Mary, rather he was absurdly grateful that he had shed his jackboots and wore only the Indian moccasins which had carried him soundlessly to Jamestown. He was not a strong swimmer, but he could keep afloat. He would make Berkeley work for his victory, he thought, as he struck out for shore. As he struggled in the ochre water he looked desperately for his crew: some of them, at least, had already reached the shore, the black boys among them. God be praised that they had been tested against the West African surf – this little contretemps would be nothing for them. With luck they would scamper through the forest and make it safely home along with his soldiers. Just as his strength was leaving him he reached the bank, but at a place where the earth formed a rampart and the vegetation was too dense to pierce. He would have to float downstream before he could scramble up on dry land. He pulled himself along hand over hand and then saw a shelf where half a dozen of his men had dragged themselves out of the river and were even now dashing into the trees. A wild cherry drooped over the water and he grasped for a low-lying limb. Once he had seized that branch he ought to be able to find a foothold and reach the passage where his soldiers had scampered to safety. He stretched high and ... felt his arm grabbed by rough hands. His other arm was seized and the back of his head careened into the looming side of a longboat. The world went dark and he knew no more.

"Mister Bacon, Mister Bacon. Can you hear me, sir?" asked Captain Gardiner.

Nat opened his eyes and his head swam. His skull felt like it was split in two. He reached to the back of his head and felt a great lump and then flinched as he touched it.

"You can thank those curls of yours for saving you from worse, sir. I must apologize. My men did not intend to bang you about like that, it was an accident."

Nat groaned. "And you did not intend to sink my sloop, Captain?"

Captain Gardiner actually blushed and looked contrite. "I have never had to fire on a passenger before, sir. And I hope I never have to again. But the Governor ordered it, and he is Captain General of the colony, so I could not say 'nay.'"

Nat struggled up and looked around him. It was a familiar sight. He was in the Captain's cabin, in the man's very bunk. He had eaten many a meal at that table, and drunk many a dram from those decanters, and looked many a time at those charts. Ah, Dame Fortune. She had her ways.

"How did you find me out? I thought we were well hidden in that cove."

"So you were sir, but some fishermen were out early and they brought word that two sinister sloops were harbored in a place where ships rarely go. As you were known to have been in Jamestown during the night it did not take long to put two and two together. I was anchored in Sandy Bay and they roused me out just as dawn was breaking and told me to bring you down, you and all who sailed with you."

Nat groaned. Had he lost any of his men? He did not know who could swim and who could not. The sloop had sunk near the shore and he himself had seen at least ten escape, but that left ten more. Captain Gardiner seemed to read his mind.

"We've had you washed and tidied up. You're in one of my nightshirts, who would have imagined it? Doctor says you must stay there for the rest of the day – head wounds can turn nasty. If you are well enough tomorrow I am afraid that I must present you to Sir William and your fate will be in his hands. For now let me send your man Pomfrey in with a basin of gruel. He'll tell you about your friends."

Nat lay back, exhausted. Gardiner was a good man. Anyone would have done as he had under the circumstances. Pomfrey entered with a steaming bowl which he set on the table to cool. He knew what was foremost in General Bacon's mind.

"Just you rest there, sir, and never fret. As best I can figure none of our men drowned. I saw your crew of four and ten of my men make shore and disappear in the forest. That leaves ten to account for. I'm one of them, so that leaves nine. As we speak the nine are sitting in the hold, clapped in irons. They're not happy, but they're not dead. A miracle it was, that all survived, with the sloop cut up the way it was."

"Pomfrey, you could not have brought me better medicine than that news. Let's try the gruel. I should probably get used to it – it looks like the kind of thing they serve you in jail."

CHAPTER 20

JUNE 1676

Pitts leaned over the former Councilor and laid a hand on his brow to see if he had a fever. They said he had a great crack on his head and one never knew what would happen with those kinds of injuries. Still, the jail was cool and comfortable and Mister Bacon was protected from the hot June sun and the great black flies that plagued Jamestown in the summer.

Nat stirred and muttered and opened his eyes. "Pitts!" Bacon laughed weakly. "You once invited me to share your hospitality. See – I have taken you up on your invitation."

Pitts covered his mouth in the characteristic gesture which shielded his bad teeth. "Oh, sir, how can you jest? I never meant to be your host in such circumstances as these! Did you have an easy night?"

Nat sat up on the straw and looked around the dank cell. "Well enough. I guess Sir William did not think I was sufficiently secure on the *Adam and Eve*. Despite your kindness I would have preferred to stay there. I hardly remember being brought here last night, my head aches so, but I think it is better this morning. Is there any chance of my having a wash and a shave and perhaps a bite of breakfast?"

"Oh sir, I will try my best." The thin man blushed. "That there great bucket is for the necessities of nature. I wish it was behind a screen, but they would not give me the money for it. That there small bucket is for washing. I asked them for a china basin but they said 'no' to that, too. There is no hot water, but I will bring you some from my own kitchen, which is just upstairs. As for breakfast, you shall share my own, which I am about to go prepare it. How does hot bread and a rasher sound?"

"It sounds like heaven, but if you added hot coffee I would know I was in paradise."

Before Pitts could respond Nat heard a familiar voice.

"You can share a pot of coffee with me at *The Unicorn*, Nat," said Colonel Bacon quietly. "I've convinced Billy to let you out on your parole.

291

Come, Lawrence is waiting for you. He showed me his upstairs snuggery and he can hardly wait to see you down some bacon and eggs at his table and then tuck between his sweet smelling sheets. You'd think you were his long lost brother, he carries on so."

"Cousin! I'm always happy to see you, but perhaps never more so than now. I know I'm going to get a lecture. Can it wait until Lawrence has worked his magic?"

"Yes, of course. Come on, then. Here, Pitts, this is for you. Thank you for your kind attentions to Mister Bacon. I hope we do not trouble you again."

Two hours later Nat *was* stretched out on the pine bed between Clarissa's lavender-scented sheets. He had had a huge breakfast and a hot bath and he began to think that he would live to fight another day. Lawrence was downstairs, minding *The Unicorn*, and Colonel Bacon sat at the work table quietly reading a volume of sermons which had been gathering dust on the innkeeper's bookshelves. Nat looked at his cousin's profile and thought of his father. They were much alike, gentlemen both, but always swimming with the stream, never against it. Streams ... he silently cursed as he remembered how close he had been to evading Berkeley's grasp. What was going to happen now? Colonel Bacon glanced at him.

"Awake? Good. We need to talk." The planter walked to the bedside and pulled up a wooden chair. "Nat, I confess that I am greatly disappointed in you. You and your little Linnet were off to such a good start – a fine plantation, that new house I've heard so much about, your little girl ... But now you are letting it slip away. Tom lived through the Civil Wars – I would have thought he had taught you to keep your head low in a storm."

"He did, sir. All he wanted was for me to stay in Suffolk and grow wheat and tend sheep and ride to the hounds and provide him with a quiverful of grandchildren. None of this is his doing."

"Well, what is it then? Are you a storm crow?"

"I suppose I am, sir. It is my nature. I was never happier than when I was roaming about the Continent with Ray ... something new around every bend. Lyn, of course, brought me my greatest happiness, but even then I grew weary of the sameness. I should be ashamed to say it, but it is my restless nature which brought us to Virginia. She, like father, would have been happy enough to stay at Hazelwood and, in the fullness of time, at Friston Hall. But I need ... I don't know, constant motion. But I did not go to the Roanoke River seeking novelty, sir. Surely you know that the Susquehannocks held us under a reign of terror. Every day we lived in fear – it was not to be endured. You know my outlying plantation was attacked and I lost a good man and some cattle. Like father you survived the Civil Wars – surely you know what I mean."

"Ah, Nat, I don't criticize your intentions, just your actions. You could and should have worked with the Governor, not against him. And after I got you a seat on the Council! You were perfectly positioned to guide him. All he wanted was for you to respect his knowledge of the savages, give him some credit for having survived the wars of the forties and kept the peace for decades thereafter. But you and those ruffians started making demands, telling him how to do business ... I know he has grown prickly with age, but you could have won him over."

"Oh cousin, I beg to differ! He all but took the Susquehannocks' side in the Piscataway Creek disaster; he looked the other way when Hen was murdered; all last winter he ignored the devastation of the frontier; he as much as called me a liar when I asked him to avenge Hartwell's death; he pooh-poohed the Sittenborne massacre; and then he called an Assembly which marched to his drum and docilely adopted his useless fort policy. Why cousin, even then the people of Charles City County and Henrico begged him for permission to go against the savages before taking matters in their own hands! He cursed us and refused! What more could we have done? Would you like to see Lyn and Mary lying in their own blood, like Hen and Hartwell! No, I regret nothing."

Colonel Bacon shook his head and sighed. The young were so impetuous, and his cousin more so than most. "Well, you have brought yourself to a pretty pass. I have never seen Billy so angry. He feels that his whole career is being attacked. He has asked me to dine with him today and I shall do my best to bring him around. God knows, with the savages still restless on our borders, the colony does not need a divided government. But if I convince him to forgive your transgressions, you must meet him half way – perhaps more than half way. Promise me that if Billy withdraws the charge of 'rebel' that you will submit to his authority and make every effort to live in peace."

Nat turned his head and glanced through the back dormer. The sky was a pure blue and the limbs of the yellow poplar in *The Unicorn's* yard tossed in the wind. It must be a beautiful day. He wished he was riding through his fields, Lyn on one side and John on the other, the wind blowing in his face. Could he agree to Colonel Bacon's terms? The Governor was in error and the people knew it. He, Nathaniel Bacon, Junior, had the people behind him, without question. The colony needed a new regime. Still ... Berkeley would not go quietly. He need only plead for help from the King and Virginia's government would be in turmoil for years, at a time when, as his cousin had just said, it needed to be united. He looked at the sad face which was scrutinizing his own and thought of his father again. Something about the brow and the way their eyes were set ... Bacon blood.

"Do you know that just after I left for the south he came to Curles with an armed force and terrified my wife and daughter? Is this the man I am to kneel before and offer my fealty?"

The blue veins in the Colonel's temple pulsed. "I know, Nat, I know. I have spoken to him about it. Between you and me he rues that action, but you will never get him to say so." Bacon rose and paced about the room. "Damn, damn, damn. The two of you are so imperious! Nat, listen to me. Billy's teeth are drawn. Several days ago, before you came to Jamestown, he sent Lady Frances off to London with a letter to the King asking to be relieved of his position. He is even willing to return to England after all these years, if his wife agrees. Baron Stratton has a fine place at Twickenham – it would be a splendid place to retire. He's in the process of writing his will. He's an old man, boy ... be charitable."

"Oh cousin, that's just the point. He's an old man and incompetent to rule Virginia. But he's still Governor and can still do enormous harm! I doubt his sincerity – why didn't he sail with his wife and hand in his resignation when he got to Whitehall?"

"Don't be a fool! You are showing your ignorance! A Royal Governor cannot leave his post without the King's permission," the older man snapped. "I see that it is hopeless. You are like two dogs straining at their chains, mouths gaping, tongues lolling, froth dripping from your bared fangs! There is no reasoning with either of you! I'll cancel my dinner and return to King's Creek. The devil take both of you."

Nat had never seen his cousin lose his temper except that one time at King's Creek when he thought his slave was malingering, and he never wanted to see it happen again.

"Cousin, cousin, calm yourself. Surely I have a right to advocate my cause! I insist that I have the right of it, but I am agreeable to making peace. Tell me what to do."

Colonel Bacon smiled and took his seat again. He patted Nat's hand. "That's my boy. I know it is hard to swallow. To be truthful, if I were a judge I might rule in your favor. But sugar cured more than vinegar ever did ... let's see if we can't mend some fences. Virginia will be the better for it."

Nat nodded. "It is that which has decided me. If the Governor will work with this Assembly and be persuaded to a more effective Indian policy we will all be the better for it. Guide me."

"Well, I'll lay the groundwork this afternoon. You don't need to know the details – I'll convince Billy that your motives were good even if some of your actions were ... impetuous. I'll try and get an audience for you tomorrow – will you be well enough?"

"Oh yes, I could get up now. My head still aches, but it is much better. I'll see the old man tomorrow, if he is willing. What then?"

"Well, I suggest that you own yourself at fault and ask for his forgiveness. Can you do that?"

Nat grimaced. "With difficulty. What words do you suggest?"

Colonel Bacon mused. "Mister Lawrence is the man for words, isn't he? I'm glad he's in the House – he is fit for far more than keeping an ordinary. I know you and he are close. Do you think he would help you draft some kind of statement – something that you could live with, but which would placate Billy?"

Nat smiled. "I think you've found the key. With you to work on the Governor and Dicken to work on me, we ought to able to build a solid bridge. Lawrence has a house full of Burgesses, but I know he will help me. Would you be kind enough to speak to him as you leave?"

Colonel Bacon rose. "Of course, my boy. I'm so glad you see things my way. Not every difference of opinion needs to result in conflict. Follow my lead in this and later ... well, you know that Elizabeth and I are childless."

Nat felt his eyes tear. What a gentleman his cousin was! He gripped the Colonel's hand in appreciation. "Send me word when I should appear before His Honor – I'll make you proud."

The Governor's chair was at the head of the Council table on the raised dais which symbolized his supremacy. Ten stout oak chairs with Turkey work cushions stood on each side of the great table, awaiting the Councilors. The June sun shone brilliantly through the casements, flooding the handsome room with light. In the far left hand corner as one faced the Governor's seat was the entrance to his private office. The door creaked open and the Governor's clerk crept into the chamber obsequiously, bearing an armful of silk which glowed blue and crimson and gold. Sir William and the Council were due at any moment and the clerk was late in hanging the banner bearing the Stuart arms on the iron hooks behind the Governor's chair. If all was not ready he would hear about it for days. He laid the pile of silk on the dais and dashed back to the office for a stool. Mounted on the stool, he hurriedly fitted the rings which were sewn along the top hem of the banner onto the hooks and let the brilliantly hued cloth unroll. Please God, he thought, let there be no rips or tears or moth holes. He replaced the stool in the office and returned to the banner to straighten it and smooth it out. He had forgotten how glorious the cloth was. It almost brought the King into the Council chamber with it ... certainly conveyed the essence of his majesty. There, gold on crimson, were the proud lions *passant* of England and their kin, the fierce lion *rampant* of Scotland. Against deep blue the elegiac harp of Ireland spoke and the elegant lilies of France declaimed both grace and power. What it was to be a king! Forgetting his haste, he traced the motto with his forefinger: *Honi Soit Qui Mal Y Pense*. He had never understood that part – something about evil, though. He knew enough French to know that. And then the other part – that one he understood: *Dieu et Mon Droit*. God and My Right. The clerk shivered. Indeed! It almost made the

King equal to the Deity. He was glad he did not serve in the Royal Court; being the Governor's clerk was bad enough.

The clerk jumped as the double doors of the anteroom were thrown open and Councilor Philip Ludwell marched in, a vision in green and gold. Thank God the room was ready. Ludwell's tongue was almost as rough as Sir William's and the Deputy Secretary was, if anything, more impatient than the Governor. Ludwell glanced around.

"Where are the decanters and goblets? It is going to be a long, thirsty morning."

"Why, that's Pitts' job, sir. I am not responsible for refreshments."

"Well find Pitts then, you fool. Isn't that the way of it – something as simple as setting up a room and you spend all your time fighting over who is responsible for what, instead of getting the job done." Ludwell clapped. "Go, now! The Governor is on his way."

Half a dozen Councilors walked into the chamber, laughing among themselves and the clerk dashed out, cap in hand. How mortifying to be given a woman's task. He had been hired for his fine hand and his ability to keep records, not to be a barmaid. He scuttled to Pitts' lodging and banged on the door. As he waited he saw Sir William Berkeley strolling up from his town house with Councilor Bacon, (the real one, not the young one they had thrown in jail). Five or six other members crossed the yard; soon they would be assembled. Pitts opened the door and the clerk stepped inside with relief. He was out of it as soon as he delivered his message. He was anxious to return to his papers which were far more accommodating than the gentry who ruled Virginia.

Sir William and Colonel Bacon waited for the other Councilors to enter the Statehouse and then walked in together, arm in arm. Their appearance, so amiable and so peaceful, was a calculated demonstration of what was to come. The real business had been handled yesterday. Colonel Bacon had obtained the Governor's word that he would pardon Nathaniel Bacon, Junior if the master of Curles Neck owned his faults and showed sufficient contrition. The Governor wanted young Bacon's submission in writing, which seemed reasonable, and if he approved the document he offered, to the Colonel's astonishment, to restore Nat to his seat on the Council.

"I can keep a better eye on him that way," Berkeley had said with a smile which caused chills to run down Colonel Bacon's spine. Of course it was true: his young cousin was far more of a threat to Green Spring as a Burgess than as a Councilor. He would have to accept the offer and when he did so the rabble would fall away from him, thinking that he had shifted his allegiance from the people back to the ruling class.

Colonel Bacon had conveyed the offer to Nat who balked at first, but then, at Lawrence's urging, had accepted it. Lawrence and Nat had spent the afternoon drafting a flowery submission in language calculated to appeal to one who had served in the court of Charles the First. Nat quarreled over much of the verbiage but Lawrence became quite short with him and told him that he should promise the Governor everything but life itself – once he was cleared of criminal charges and reinstated on the Council he would be excellently placed to help the Ring which now dominated the House of Burgesses. Nat remembered his promise to Colonel Bacon and his allegiance to the Ring, swallowed his pride and followed Lawrence's lead. Country must come before self – he had sworn it.

Late in the evening Colonel Bacon brought Sir William a final draft of the submission and the Governor chuckled with pleasure. He had brought the young rebel to his knees – nay, more. The upstart was prone on the ground with the Governor's foot on his neck. The master of Curles Neck had owned his faults, pleaded for forgiveness, promised continued allegiance and pledged his estate for a year as a bond for his good behavior. Nothing was wanting. After approving the submission Sir William sent for Speaker Godwin and alerted him to what was transpiring. Godwin, who had the authority to speak for the House of Burgesses, was properly deferential and did not interpose a single objection. He praised the Governor's wisdom and indicated how pleased the House would be at the peaceful resolution of "these recent unfortunate events." Berkeley was pleasantly surprised; Godwin had certainly not been his choice for Speaker, but the man had actually behaved himself ... seemed to know his place. Colonel Bacon sighed. It had been a long day, but a fruitful one. Tomorrow, on the ninth of June, the principal actors would play their parts for all the world to see. He trusted both of them, at least in this. By noon tomorrow Nat would be a free man. What he did then was his own concern.

Sir William wore judicial black with a cascade of lace tumbling down his chest. John Page looked like his double, but all the others were brightly clad, no one more so than Philip Ludwell whose brilliant green suit proclaimed his allegiance to the Governor's faction. Colonel Bacon's deep blue became him as did Thomas Swann's tobacco brown with gold trim. Ballard wore a red that set one's teeth on edge – it was more orange than rose in tone and the horse-faced planter looked as though he were wrapped in a sunset.

The Governor brought the meeting to order with a crash of his gavel and Pitts threw open the double doors into the antechamber. In walked Nat Bacon in silver gray, with fine cambric at his throat and wrists, silk stockings of the purest white, and highly polished black shoes with silver buckles. His black curls glistened with health and his hawk eyes scanned the room. He did not look like a penitent. He looked as though he owned the Council chamber.

Colonel Bacon glanced at the Governor and then at his cousin and sighed inwardly. All these two had to do was play a part – were they going to bring it off, or was all his work going to be for naught? Nat bowed profoundly to Sir William and then again to the rest of the Council. Colonel Bacon expelled his breath. The boy was going to mind his manners – it was going to be alright. It was fortunate that the Hartwell lad had brought Nat's good clothes – he looked splendid, every inch a Bacon. Now, if he would just lower those eyes.

A false smile played on Sir William Berkeley's face; his eyes were as colorless and cold as ice. He gestured to the Council, who took their seats, but, like Nat, he remained standing. His light voice floated through the morning air, mellifluous but with an undertone of command.

"If there be joy among the angels over one repentant sinner, there is joy now, for we have a penitent sinner before us. Greetings, Mister Bacon."

Nat moved three steps forward, bowed again, and knelt on one knee. He pulled a roll of paper from his breast. "I am profoundly grateful, Your Honor, for the privilege of appearing before you and my former colleagues. I *have* sinned and I recognize it and deeply regret it. My folly did not spring from evil thoughts, but it was folly nonetheless. When the Governor speaks all the King's subjects must listen."

Sir William indicated that Nat should rise. "Phil ... Mister Ludwell ... do me the courtesy of bringing me that paper in Mister Bacon's hand."

Ludwell, who sat at the foot of the table as became a junior Councilor, crossed to Nat as the latter rose to his feet. His sherry-colored eyes glowed as he took Bacon's submission, carefully avoiding touching his flesh. As he turned to walk towards the Governor he subtly brushed the penitent's shoulder, causing him to stagger slightly. Nat composed himself and cast his eyes on the floor, but the hands which gripped each other behind his back were clenched so tightly that he bruised his own flesh.

Sir William took the paper from Ludwell and spoke to him *sotto voce*. The Deputy Secretary nodded and returned to Nat, indicating that he should take a seat at the foot of the table, opposite the Governor. Nat clenched his jaw and followed Ludwell. He took his seat, eyes cast down. Ludwell sat to his right and Jennings to his left. The room was wholly silent, all eyes on the former Councilor except those of the Governor who seated himself and read the submission. He nodded as he read and twice looked up and sent his chilly gaze Bacon's way. When he had finished reading he stood, handed the document to his right where Colonel Bacon sat, and raised his voice.

"A very proper statement. I am satisfied. You own the error of your ways in the nicest language. I am sure that henceforth we will live in amity. God forgive you, I forgive you."

The entire Council murmured its approbation. They knew generally what young Bacon's submission said, but they wanted to read it for themselves. The paper passed from one Councilor to the next, each taking his time as he perused it, each glancing at Bacon from time to time until he was finished. Ludwell had risen and must have summoned Pitts, for the thin man entered and began handing around silver goblets of Madeira.

The Governor took his seat again and drank deeply. He said a few words to Colonel Bacon and then raised his goblet, intoning once again "God forgive you, I forgive you."

The Councilors raised their cups to Sir William, a few of them toasting Nat as well. The submission made its way around the table and back to the Governor, who took it and placed it carefully in front of him. At his signal the Council fell quiet.

"The House has been considering our Indian policy among other things. The full Assembly will meet tomorrow to consider the Burgesses' proposals. There is much talk of discarding the fort system authorized by the prior Assembly and raising an army which will rove at will to put down any savages foolish enough to reject the hand of friendship. If such an army is raised I want to make it perfectly clear that *any* Virginian with the requisite skills will be welcome to join its ranks. Mister Bacon, you and your followers are free to join such a force – I shall be pleased to commission any of you who meet the qualifications. Let's let bygones be bygones. You are freely pardoned, young sir. And, lest there be any question, my pardon extends to those men who, however rashly, accompanied you to Jamestown. The slate should be wiped clean, do you not think so?"

"Here, here," roared the Council. This was munificent indeed. The Governor was rising to the occasion. The savages would not divide and conquer.

Nat rose and lifted his cup to Sir William Berkeley. "Never were fairer words spoken, Your Honor. Here is to a government united against the savage foe. Long may it prosper."

The Governor stood and raised his cup in turn. "God forgive you, I forgive you. Know that it is my intention that should you conduct yourself civilly until the next Quarter Court you may resume your seat at the Council table. One Bacon has devoted himself to the service of Virginia these many years ... why not two?"

The Council muttered, astonished at the Governor's benevolence; Colonel Bacon smiled in relief; and Berkeley and Nat smiled in perfidy. They were natural enemies and nothing that had happened today was going to change that. Nat knew that he had been restored to the Council to keep him on a short leash, little did the Governor know what he intended to do when he got there. Divide and conquer ... precisely! It would be his watchword. More toasts were proposed and as the noon sun beamed on Jamestown the Council of State adjourned for dinner and its prodigal son returned to *The Unicorn* to consult with his true ally, Richard Lawrence.

Saturday saw Lawrence and Nat rise with the sun, the former to attend the House and the latter to ride out with Jake Hartwell to exercise the horses and relieve some of the tension of the past few days. Lawrence had obligingly placed a cot for Nat in his snuggery. Being effectively joined at the hip with the leader of the Ring, Bacon would hear the latest news as soon as it happened.

Folly and Blue crossed the isthmus and turned east on this, another glorious June day. Their riders urged them to a gallop for the first mile, and then pulled them back to a walk, necks dripping and haunches steaming. The road was not far from the river and as the horsemen splashed across a creek two great herons rose from the sedge and soared south, across the river.

Nat smiled with pleasure. "What splendid creatures. I suppose they are nesting. This is like old times, isn't it?"

Jake grinned. "Oh, yes sir. You have no idea how worried we were. Mister Lawrence says you never know what the Governor is going to do."

"Well that's true enough, but that's all behind us now. By tomorrow I should have my commission and then we'll be off to Curles Neck and raise Bacon's army again, only this time it will be legal."

"What of Mistress Bacon? Should you like me to go on ahead and tell her that you are safe? If she got the news that you were seized and jailed she must be worrying herself to death."

"What a kind thought, Jake. But Lawrence thinks the Governor will sign the commissions tomorrow, after church, so why don't you wait. We can leave Sunday afternoon or, if there is some delay, on Monday. Then I can tell her the whole story myself."

"What shall you do about the sloop?"

"Hmmm. I don't know. I should like to get its cost back. I'll ask Lawrence what he thinks tonight. Right now there are more important concerns than that. I'd like to assure myself that all my men escaped injury, but that will have to wait until we're at Curles. Come, shall we gallop a bit more and then return to Jamestown?"

Lawrence was late returning to the inn Saturday night and when he did appear he looked drawn and haggard. Giving Joanna a perfunctory greeting, he ordered supper to be brought to his chambers and he and Nat closeted themselves in the snuggery. No sooner had they quaffed their first cup of ale when the latch clicked and Drummond appeared.

"I got your message, Dicken. Ah – bread and cheese. That's fine with me, now is not the time to fuss about food. Thanks, I'll have a cup. Here's to you both – Burgess Lawrence and Councilor Bacon (again)."

"Sit down, Will," urged Lawrence. "There's a lot of news. The Indian bill passed. We're to have an army of one thousand men, seven-eighths foot and one-eighth cavalry."

"Well done," said Drummond. "Who is to lead it?"

There was a dramatic pause. "Nathaniel Bacon, Junior, Esquire is to be General and Commander in Chief of the entire force!"

Nat gasped and Drummond pounded his fist on the table. "Well done, Dicken. How did you fellows pull that off?"

Before Lawrence could answer Nat interrupted. "Tell it to me again ... the bill actually names me as general?"

"Names you to head the government force, and then states that you are free to call upon volunteers and if your volunteers are sufficient you may do without the regular army!"

The enormity of what the innkeeper said brought silence to the room. Finally Nat spoke again.

"I hardly believe it. How did it come about? Is this your doing?"

Lawrence answered with what seemed at first like a *non sequitur*. "When did you and Jake return?"

"At noon or thereabouts. Around dinner time."

"As you rode back did you notice anyone or anything in the woods?"

"Not particularly."

"Well, had you ridden north a mile or so you would have found a huge camp – some five hundred settlers. They've swept in from the frontier to make sure their voice is heard by the Assembly. They're your men, Nat. Their cry is 'Bacon, Bacon.' They won't go until they know that you are going to lead the Indian fighters with Berkeley's commission in hand."

Nat looked at his friends, astonishment on his face. "It must be because of Occaneechee Island. It's ... it's a miracle. But Dicken, how did the Governor take this? It could set him off again, being told what to do by 'the rabble.'"

"You've taken the words out of my mouth. When Berkeley heard the form of the bill he frowned like Jove and looked about for his thunderbolts. Fortunately he could not find them. If he had the power he would clap the whole House in jail as surely as he did you. Even the Council felt his wrath, particularly your cousin. It will be some days before the name 'Bacon' will be palatable to our Governor."

"Well then, what's going to happen? Is it all a nonsense?"

"By no means! You have the support of most of the citizens, most of the Assembly, and a good part of the Council! The Governor's hands are tied. Whether he likes it or not, he will give you a commission ... likely as soon as tomorrow."

Drummond raised his cup to Nat. "Congratulations, General Bacon. I stand ready to serve you in any capacity that I am needed."

Nat looked almost frightened. Will Drummond, a proven soldier, looking to him for leadership? Five hundred men clamoring for him to lead them against the savages? The House of Burgesses crying for his aid? The Council now split, with some falling away from Green Spring? Dame Fortune was playing with him again.

"There is something wrong here. Berkeley set one trap for us on Occaneechee Island. This is another one, I feel it in my bones."

Lawrence and Drummond looked sober. "'Tis true, he would stop at nothing," agreed the innkeeper. "I have some thoughts about how to protect yourself, even with the commission in hand."

"And what are those thoughts?"

"Lady Frances has sailed for Whitehall, bringing a tale of rebellion. That being the case, in addition to the Indian act we should secure you an act of pardon and indemnity for your actions at the Roanoke River. That way London will know that your alleged transgressions are forgiven and forgotten, despite what they may hear from Berkeley's wife."

"Why not have the Governor pen a letter to the King himself, explaining that matters have been adjusted and that General Bacon is the authorized leader of our Indian forces, whatever rumors there might be to the contrary?"

"An excellent idea. Best to keep things simple."

Nat rose and paced the room. "So I'll be commissioned as general tomorrow or soon after, and then I'll have a blanket pardon for what happened in the spring, and it will all be explained to the King in simple terms?"

"Precisely. What do you think?"

"I like it well. I'm ... I don't know what to do next. One day in jail, the next day General and Commander in Chief of the Indian forces ... it is too much."

Drummond put his arm around Nat's shoulders. "Let's take it one day at a time. You'll attend church with us tomorrow. The Governor will be there and the two of you can shake hands and show the people that all is well. Then we'll have the commission ... that's the important thing. After that Lawrence and I can talk to the Burgesses and the Councilors, initiate some of these other matters. Why, laddie, by the middle of the week you and that great black horse will be riding out against the savages! Perhaps I'll go with you!"

Lawrence laughed. "You, Will? Sarah would never let you. I'd rather face the Indians than her wrath. Come, let's finish supper and I'll tell you what else is afoot. The climate is so fair that we have an excellent chance of getting all our reform laws passed ... I can hardly contain myself."

Sunday passed with the Governor and the budding general exchanging polite greetings in Jamestown church; no commission was forthcoming. Monday passed with the Governor's promise to sign the commission and his approval, in principal, of an act of pardon and oblivion protecting the Roanoke River Indian fighters from being charged with rebellion; no commission was forthcoming. Tuesday passed with word from Lawrence that in Sir William's opinion any commission he signed would be invalid as a product of duress and coercion; no commission was forthcoming. On Wednesday morning Nat could contain himself no longer and sought his cousin's counsel. Colonel Bacon had been staying in Thomas Ludwell's town house together with a number of other Councilors, and it was there that Nat strode as early as civility permitted.

No sooner had he banged on the door than he was looking at the austere face of John Page, immaculate in dark brown, his silver wig perfectly aligned although the day had just begun.

"Mister Bacon!" said Page. "What a surprise. I was just about to walk out in the cool of the morning. What can I do for you?"

Nat saw the contempt in the older man's face and had difficulty controlling his expression.

"Is my cousin here?" he asked, shortly.

"Colonel Bacon? Oh dear, no. No. He left yesterday for King's Creek. Didn't he tell you? A pity."

"Is his wife ill?"

"Why, not that I am aware of. He saw no need to stay, with the House in such turmoil and not much business getting done. I daresay he'll be back by the end of the week. May I help you in any other way?"

Page's expression indicated that, for him, helping Nat Bacon was probably as tasteful as weeding tobacco with his blacks. Nat ground his teeth. "Perhaps you know if the Governor is seeing visitors this early?"

"The Governor? Why, you are not keeping up with the news, are you? Sir William left yesterday as well. Those rabble in the woods finally decamped and he was able to make his way back to Green Spring without those villains annoying him."

"He left!" cried Nat, almost shouting. "What about my commission?"

"Your commission?" queried Page superciliously. "I know nothing of any commission. You will have to address yourself to the Governor. I'm afraid I don't know his schedule. You'll have to go to Green Spring."

Nat's temples throbbed. It was just as he expected. The old man was not going to bow down to the mob. The will of the majority would only make him more intractable. Controlling himself, he thanked Page and turned to go, but not before seeing the amusement on the planter's face. He would remember this exchange. If the day ever came that he and Page crossed paths again, he would remember this day.

By the time he reached *The Unicorn* his mind was made up. Neither Lawrence nor Drummond was available to advise him, the innkeeper being in the House and Drummond across the river at Swann's Point, but he felt no need of their counsel. Everything had become clear, as clear as the crystal waters of the Roanoke River. It was past time for words; it was time for action. The people had elected him general and general he was going to be. If Berkeley would not give him the authority which the law required, then he would take it by force. He ran upstairs, whistling for Jake as he went. Nat began throwing his things in a bag and when the boy appeared he told him to saddle Folly and Blue – they were going all the way to Curles Neck today.

He snapped his bag shut and looked around Lawrence's snuggery. When he saw it next he would no longer be an acolyte – he would be leading an army.

CHAPTER 21

JUNE 1676

Lyn had coaxed the wild honeysuckle to tumble down the bank above her still unfinished summer house and today it was in full flower, perfuming the mild summer air. Except on the stillest day a river breeze refreshed this refuge and today the gentle winds swirled around mother and child as they sat on their rustic bench, Mary's shells scattered on the table before them. An emerald hummingbird with a ruby throat darted among the gold and cream blossoms, dizzy with nectar. Mary screamed with delight and clapped her hands.

"Bird, bird," she cried.

Lyn held her close and kissed her cheek. "Yes, love, 'bird.' Good for you!"

The precocious child could already say ten words, and Nat had missed them all. Lyn heard the sound of horses and flinched as she thought of the day six weeks ago when the Governor had pounded up the avenue, threatening to hang Nat high, as a rebel. She hoped that he and Mister Crewes had been seated in the House of Burgesses and that both of them were keeping their heads down while the high winds of politics blew. Holding Mary close, she struggled up the path to the spot under the redbuds where she could see the drive without being seen. To her surprise the first thing she saw was Folly, with Nat astride, hatless, black curls whipping in the wind. Behind him streamed a small entourage – there was Jake, of course, on the roan; and the big fellow was Jamie Crewes; and that looked like Mister Byrd ... he must have crossed the river without stopping at Curles. Lyn lost count and stepped out onto the avenue, waving her garden hat.

Nat pulled Folly up in a cloud of dust, the other riders just behind him. He threw himself off the black horse and seized Lyn with a great laugh which made Mary burst into tears and begin shrieking. Lyn scolded Nat and was relieved to see Hannah descending from the porch of the brick house, come to rescue her charge from the brute men. With the child quieted in the black woman's arms, she turned to her husband and pulled his head down for a kiss.

"Back so soon, love? I *am* glad. Show your friends into the house while I fetch John. How many are there for luncheon – six besides myself?"

Three hours later Lyn sat in the parlor alone, a wiser and sadder woman. Nat, John, Crewes, Byrd and Jake had eaten and discoursed mightily. Silent among them was one she had heard much of but never met, John Goode of Whitby. Trembling, she heard the tale of the sloop's going down under the guns of the *Adam and Eve*; Nat's night in jail; Colonel Bacon's good offices; Nat's submission to the Governor and Council; his pardon and reinstatement; and then ... the duplicity of Sir William Berkeley who had fled to Green Spring leaving the clamoring crowd behind him and all his promises unfulfilled. That was bad enough. What was worse was that General Bacon was about to sally forth to raise an army and that all her luncheon guests, including John Grey, wholly supported him. To her, it was open rebellion which once again would put her husband's life in danger. To them, it was seizing their own destiny from a man for whom no Virginian could now have a shred of respect. The path was clear and it led to Jamestown.

The division of labor was also clear. Byrd and Goode would marshal their fellow Henricans, organizing a force which would report to General Bacon at the mouth of the Chickahominy on or about the twentieth of June. Goode was too old, and Byrd too pressed with his own cares, to accompany the force, but they would send them off well-armed, well-trained and well-instructed. Crewes was to ride north and find Farlow who was reputed to be in New Kent. The two Roanoke River veterans would pull men from New Kent and Rappahannock Counties and gather any others who sought to join Bacon's army, and they too would report to their General on the twentieth of June at the place where the Chickahominy met the James.

It went without saying that Jake would stay with Nat and continue acting as his body-servant. The relationship had been sealed at Occaneechee Island and only death would sever it. John had been persuaded to remain at Curles Neck to guard Lyn and Mary and to keep the plantation, now Nat's headquarters, running at a subsistence level. As usual, he said little and did not complain, but Lyn knew that the wish of his heart was to join Nat's army. Nat himself was going to cross the river to the Southside and ride east, stopping where he knew, from Lawrence and Drummond, that he would be welcome. He planned to ride as far as the Blackwater and among other things search out Thomas Hansford, whom Drummond spoke highly of. The man was reputed to be a fine horseman and Nat thought he might be interested in leading the cavalry.

And Lyn? Nat looked beyond her needs, seemed not to see them at all. He assumed, (and of course he was right), that she would support him, however tortuous his path. Nat was like one possessed: some spirit inhabited him and directed his every move. She had never known him so focused and self-confident and she sorrowed at the knowledge. She and Mary were much to Nat, but not everything. He was responding to a higher call and she had been left behind. She could join Mary Byrd in Surry or stay at Curles ... that was her choice. Of course she would stay. Curles Neck was her home and she intended to be there whenever Nat returned. Could anyone doubt it?

Nat lay supine under the tulip poplar and watched the soft green leaves turn in the wind. The chuckle of the Chickahominy was audible through the underbrush. In a nearby oak a gray squirrel ceased its chatter, reassured that the strange creature below was no threat. Nat brushed some midges from his face and turned over, his cheek pressed on a cushion of moss. The early afternoon was silent but for the call of the distant stream and the languid buzz of insects. He stretched hugely, luxuriating in this blessed pause, a hiatus between raising his army and tomorrow's planned action.

Things had gone far better than he hoped. He knew that Crewes and Farlow would acquit themselves well, but they had exceeded his expectations. Using the Occaneechee fighters as a core, they had quickly assembled a force of three hundred men from Henrico and Charles City Counties and as far north as New Kent and Rappahannock Counties. Crewes and Farlow were each put in charge of one hundred men, a mixture of veterans and new comers. He himself reserved the one hundred Roanoke River veterans for his own command. Nat smiled as he thought of the shouts of joy which rose from his Indian fighters when they learned that they would report to General Bacon himself. Pomfrey and Turney had drunk themselves under the table, and they were not alone. Somehow he had won their hearts; they would follow him anywhere.

Nat spied a hickory nut and pulled himself up to a seated position. He leaned against a tree trunk and idly tossed nuts into the undergrowth, smiling as the squirrel scolded him from above. What could he say about his recruits – they were wonderful ... beggared description. They gladly took responsibility for their own food and clothing and seemed unfazed by the gathering heat of summer and the thunderstorms which regularly rolled through the woodland, leaving the atmosphere moisture-laden. Most of the men were armed with serviceable matchlocks or flintlocks; those who had no firearms had knives and some even had swords. A handful of frontiersmen who held themselves apart from the others carried bows and arrows, their English skills honed with the prowess of the savages who were once their allies and now their foes. The Indians had turned English weapons against Virginia: now it was time to reverse the coin.

Yes, Crewes and Farlow had done well, but Nat too had unearthed some gold. In the past week he had visited more than a dozen Southside plantations and had received a warm welcome at each of them. At Drummond's Blackwater plantation he asked for, and was given, directions to Hansford's neighboring farm. When he reached the place, by a stroke of good fortune, the young planter was entertaining a visitor from Gloucester County, one Anthony Arnold. Arnold had grown up on the Blackwater and he and Hansford were boyhood friends. Like Hansford, Arnold was a charter member of the Ring and a sworn foe of Green Spring. The youngsters, one fair and one dark, drank up Nat's story of the Occaneechee campaign, each cursing loudly that he had not been part of the adventure. Both were eager to march on Jamestown and force a commission for General Bacon from Governor Berkeley's reluctant hand. Within an hour of meeting them, Nat had made them his lieutenants and given them assignments. Hansford was a noted horseman and he was charged with recruiting and leading one hundred horse. The blond planter crowed with joy and made plans to leave his farm that day 'to rouse up the boys' and meet Nat at the rendezvous on the Chickahominy not later than Thursday, the twenty-second of June. Swarthy Arnold was charged with returning to his home in Gloucester County and raising a force there and in neighboring Middlesex County. Jeering at his friend, he swore he would have a hundred foot soldiers on the banks of the Chickahominy before Hansford was there with his cavalry. Within another hour the new recruits had packed their saddle bags and were on the road, leaving a somewhat breathless Bacon to return to Drummond's where he spent the night before returning across the river to meet his army.

Five hundred men! Four hundred foot and one hundred horse. All called up within a week, and ready to march. Nat did not credit himself with the miracle – he and the rest of them were simply being swept along on a torrent, a torrent which was about to crash upon Jamestown peninsula and change it forever. Nat rose and stretched and glanced around. Tomorrow they would march – when, if ever again, would he enjoy the luxury of a quiet afternoon like this one? His camp was almost a mile away and he began the long walk back, sunk in thought.

"General Bacon, General Bacon!" the men cried as Nat appeared on the outskirts of the camp. Here, to the west, on the very banks of the Chickahominy, were the Henricans and the citizens of Charles City County, many of them part of his first army. They rushed forward to shake his hand, simply touch him as though he emanated some magic. He thought of the King's touch – how miserable beggars would seek the slightest brush of the royal hand, sure that it would cure their ills. He was ordinary, luckier than most in his birth, but just a simple man, and yet these soldiers saw something special in him. He would not disappoint them.

"Pomfrey – is it you? Do you have your red ribbons?"

"Oh yes, sir, Mister Byrd was as good as his word. But we had a terrible fight with them from Rappahannock as wanted the red – they had to settle for the orange."

Nat was concerned. "I hope you did not really fight? We must remain friends or we shall never prevail."

"Oh, not as to say 'fight,' sir. Argue-like. Mister Crewes and Mister Farlow got together and sorted it out. Your men are to have the red, which, between us, is the prettiest. Mister Crewes' and Mister Farlow's and Mister Arnold's men are to have the orange, which is a fine color ... they should be glad of it. And Mister Hansford's horse are to have the bright yellow, which makes them happy. They call it gold, so they feel superior."

"Why that seems fair enough. Let me see the ribbon. Oh, 'tis a fine color, a real crimson. And you shall wear the bands on your right arms, is that it?"

"Yes, sir. Seeing as how we don't have uniforms, it was the best we could do. Mister Byrd said it was all the colors of fire ... against the Governor's green, as it were. Said there was copper there, and gold, and all kinds of fine things. Had them dyed special, he did, being as how he could not be with us."

"We owe Mister Byrd a great deal. Remind me to send him thanks, will you? I'm going to be busy and I might forget."

Pomfrey swelled with pride. "Oh, yes sir! Yes, we're going to be busy, alright." The soldier burst into a raucous laugh shared by the group which had gathered around their General.

"Very good, men. Now, if you will excuse me, I want to find my captains. We will go over the plans one more time and make sure we leave nothing to chance. This evening, after supper, I will talk to you all so that you are clear about tomorrow. God bless you!"

At dawn they marched to Paspahegh Field, Hansford and the horse in the van, the foot soldiers in the rear. Nat rode next to Hansford, Folly looming above the rest of the horses like a dark shadow. On his right was Jake on Blue, his face shining as though it was his wedding day. Nat had never felt so stirred. The tramp of the horses and the jingle of their harnesses created a special music. It was a pity they did not have a war drum, but the men were so inspired that a drum seemed unnecessary.

They would reach the open space where the Jamestown isthmus met the mainland by mid-morning. Disaffected Jamestowners had assured Bacon's army that the Governor was in town together with the great majority of the Council and the entire House of Burgesses. Nat's march would not be in vain.

The morning mist cleared and the sun beat down upon as fine a summer day as any soldier there could remember. By ten o'clock the horsemen emerged from the forest road upon the green expanse of Paspahegh Field. As previously arranged, half of them encircled the great lawn to stand watch and half of them marched to the edge of the Back River with Hansford. These men were the lucky ones who would lead the army across the isthmus to Jamestown, march to the Statehouse itself and beard the Governor in his den.

Arnold's men assembled to the right and Farlow's men to the left. Jamie Crewes had drawn the lucky straw last night: his men, and General Bacon's, would seize the town; the others remaining on the mainland to stand guard. Nat's mouth was dry and his head spun from the heat. He could not believe this was happening, but there, all around him, were five hundred stout men, weapons gleaming, faces bright with anticipation, their right arms banded with the colors of fire. Bacon's army! It was true. And within the hour he and Berkeley would be face to face ... but under what circumstances? He moved Folly to the center of the field. The mainland force was properly assembled, ready for either an attack from the woods or a call for help from the peninsula. There was nothing to wait for. He rose in his stirrups and sig-naled with his right hand, his crimson ribbon fluttering as he waved.

Hansford fell in to Nat's left and Jake to his right, and they were off, fifty riders close behind them, surging forward in ten ranks of five. Nat turned and saw the red ribbons of his men and the orange of Crewes' as the foot soldiers marched in formation, eight abreast. Jamie followed in the rear, herding his soldiers like sheep. Nobody was going to straggle; nobody was going to cut and run. This was an army – Nat Bacon's army!

Nat knew he took a risk by leading his men: there could be sharpshoot-ers on the town side of the palisade, and somewhere Berkeley was reputed to have some canon, but he was confident that no one in Jamestown expect-ed the invasion. The townspeople who spied for them were wholly theirs and they said that the government was unwitting, caught up as it was in a mighty clash over legislation, the Governor and Council distracted by a spate of laws pressed upon them by the rabble. And if he fell at the head of his army? A vision of Lyn flashed through his mind. He would never say it to her, but in all candor ... what better death could one have?

The cavalry reached the palisade without incident and Nat held up his hand for a halt.

"What do you think, Tom? The gate is wide open. Should we march straight through, or send someone to reconnoiter?"

"The place looks wholly deserted, but I cannot take a chance with Your Honor. Let me send the first rank of horse through and see what happens."

"Very well. Proceed."

Hansford's cavalry was rough looking, and the steeds mismatched, but they were not lacking in bravery and vigor. Five horsemen grinned and pressed their mounts through the open gate at a canter, swords in hand. Nothing happened. The only sounds were those of the James and the Back

River lapping against the embankment and the horses snorting and stamping, their bridles jingling. Within minutes the five riders returned, disappointment on their faces.

"'Tis quiet as a tomb," said one. "There's not a person in sight all the way to where the road turns into the woods."

"Tom, do think it could be an ambush?"

"No, sir. Everything adds up to this being a complete surprise. I suggest that we march smartly forward and execute our plan: the foot to secure the town, the horse to advance to the Statehouse door, with you to follow with your twenty hand-picked fusileers."

"Let's do it." Nat raised his right hand and signaled 'forward' and Bacon's army marched into Jamestown.

They flowed through the capital like a freshet over limestone, coursing through the low ground of the streets and alleys, most of the men eventually finding themselves on Front Street, along the river. The town was completely surprised. The residents ducked their heads and stayed indoors, waiting for the political hurricane to blow over, but many of the transients cheered and eagerly questioned the ragtag soldiers about their quest for General Bacon's commission. There was no opposition, and some townspeople, like the Drummonds, opened their homes to the men and cheerfully served them food and drink. *The Unicorn* was overrun and Joanna Lawrence mercilessly stripped the hungry soldiers of whatever valuables they had in exchange for sustenance; nary a one was served for free and her face wore a permanent scowl. She thought of her husband in the Statehouse with the other Burgesses and her scowl deepened. If the inn was ever earmarked as a seat of rebellion her business would die, and if her business died her marriage would die with it.

Hansford sent half of his horse to patrol the town but the other half, the cream of his cavalry, followed him as he preceded General Bacon to the Statehouse green. The green was no more than an irregular piece of ground which lay between the government building and the river as it curved around the western end of the peninsula, but it was large enough for a parade ground and his troops made a brave appearance as they formed two lines behind him, facing the Statehouse. When his men were in position and he determined that there was no opposition, he raised his yellow-striped right arm and Nat kneed Folly forward from the clump of trees where he had been waiting, twenty hand-picked fusileers marching smartly behind him. Behind the gunmen rode Jake on Blue, his head in constant motion as he scanned the area for any sign of trouble.

Jamestown peninsula baked in the summer sun, silent but for the jingle of harness and the muffled tramp of General Bacon's fusileers. Nat moved Folly next to Hansford's bay and his fusileers formed a single line in front of the horsemen, guns primed and ready to fire. The Burgesses met on the second floor and Bacon's men soon saw the casements thrown open and worried faces peering down at them. The distance was not great and Nat recognized some of the legislators. He put his hand to his heart and bowed slightly as Folly shifted his great haunches and snorted. There! There to the far right ... it was Lawrence, the pink blob of his face split with a great white and cherry smile. Nat bowed to the right and then, not wishing to offend a group whom he believed to be largely his friends, bowed to the left. The silence was still profound, but a few of the Burgesses waved their white handkerchiefs bravely as if to encourage the invaders.

Nat glanced to the right where Jake was securing the road to town. He saw nothing alarming – not a soul was stirring. He looked quizzically at Hansford who nodded his head in silent agreement. Now was the time – General Bacon was going to dismount, walk through his line of fusileers, who would reform behind him, and proceed to the great double doors of the Statehouse and demand an audience with the Governor. Nat took one more quick look around him: all was quiet save for Lawrence's vigorously waving arm. He rose in his stirrups and began to slide his right leg over Folly's great, black back when he froze at the sound of a familiar voice.

"Mister Bacon!"

An elegant figure in emerald green whose chestnut hair flamed in the noon sun stepped from the shade of the Statehouse porch onto the steps and descended half way.

"Mister Ludwell."

Nat dismounted and strode forward, his fusileers parting like a stream around a rock, and reforming as he passed through their line. Ludwell still had the advantage of him; he stopped just in front of the soldiers, some thirty feet from the Deputy Secretary. The man in green opened his lips but Bacon spoke first.

"I really can't hear you from there. If you have a message for me, please approach and give it to me."

Ludwell paused, biting his lower lip. A full thirty seconds passed and then he descended and walked towards Nat. Bacon remained where he was, just in front of his fusileers, standing quietly. He glanced up without moving his head. The second-story casements were as stuffed with Burgesses as a Christmas goose with breadcrumbs and oysters.

Ludwell spoke, loudly enough for all to hear. "You have no business here, sir. You must demean yourself properly until the next Quarter Court before His Honor will even consider reappointing you to the Council. And what is this armed force? You are violating every law in the book, approaching the seat of government so violently."

Nat spoke as loudly as Ludwell. After all, this was theater, and they had a full house. "I am not come for a seat on the Council, I am come for my commission. The commission which the people of Virginia gave me, through their lawfully elected representatives. The commission which I should have had two weeks ago had Sir William Berkeley not fled to Green Spring to delay this moment. God damn my blood, I have come for my commission, and my commission I will have!"

The air was rent with cheers from Hansford's horse, from the fusileers, from Jake who paced the Statehouse green on his roan, and from the Burgesses above.

"The bill authorizing your commission is not yet law. The Governor is reflecting."

"Reflect me no reflections, Mister Ludwell. The people have elected me General Bacon. They have told the Governor their desires. *They* have commissioned me. Now I want that scrap of paper which will protect me from the charges of 'rebel' and 'traitor' which have already been thrown at me – charges which, doubtless, are winging their way to Whitehall even now. If you have nothing further to say then step aside, for I am going to see Berkeley and I am going to see him now."

The crowd fell silent and the June sun burned down. Nat saw beads of sweat on Ludwell's brow and hoped that his own remained cool. He took one step forward and his fusileers straightened and realigned their firearms, each flintlock slanting from left hip to right shoulder like rain in a high wind.

Ludwell swallowed. "I shall take your message to the Governor. Wait here."

Nat nodded silently and the green man turned in the dust, climbed the steps, and disappeared into the inky blackness of the Statehouse. From the corner of his eye Bacon saw Jake ride forward to catch his attention. The boy pumped his right arm in the air. It was slashed with crimson as bright as blood. Jamestown held its breath.

The double doors opened again. Would Ludwell bring a message of defiance? If so, Nat would give the signal, he and his foot soldiers would march into the Council chamber and Hansford would send Jake and half his horsemen into the town to summon the rest of the army, while the remaining riders stood guard, ready to fight where they were needed.

A figure stepped from shadow to sunlight: It was Sir William Berkeley himself. The Governor was once more dressed in sober black, lace at his neck and wrists, a full periwig of silver hair on his head. Oddly his hands were at his breast as though he were fussing with his clothes. Yes – it was true; the old man was unbuttoning his coat and his fine green silk vest. What was he doing? Was he ill? Was it something about his heart? Nat felt a twinge of concern and sympathy – was the old man about to drop dead before him? The Governor stood at the top of the steps, his eyes pouched, his cheeks pendulous, his thin lips turned down, fishlike. Suddenly, with a dramatic gesture, he dropped to one knee and tore open his vest and shirt and bared his breast. Nat watched in horror. The Governor's flesh was as white as lard and the hairs on his chest were silver.

"'Fore God, shoot me. 'Tis a fair mark. Shoot!"

Gasps came from the Burgesses above and the soldiers below, but Nat hardened his heart. This was theater, indeed; the Governor was inviting him to step into a melodrama. Hadn't they performed once before to much acclaim, the one pretending submission and the other graciously conferring pardon? They had won their audience over then, surely, though it had all gone up in smoke. And now Berkeley was playing the pitiful old man, the one who had given his life for Virginia. Nat would decline the invitation to join the farce. This was a day for reality, not dreams. He must pierce the thin tissue of illusion with cold steel and wake the spellbound audience.

Nat kept his voice level but it rang loud and clear in the still afternoon. "Rise up, Your Honor. We will not harm a hair of your head. We come for the commission and the commission we will have."

A collective breath was exhaled. No blood was going to be spilled unless, perchance, those fools in the Council chamber rushed out with their swords drawn in a frenzy of patriotism. Quiet reigned and Nat stood his ground. The longer he waited the more ludicrous the Governor looked. Already he was unsteady and he had to put a hand to the ground to keep his balance. Once he put his hand down the breast-baring gesture lost its dramatic effect and he seemed simply like an old man who was looking for something he had dropped, perhaps his spectacles. Nat waited for the tragic mask to slip further and then mounted the steps and approached Sir William. He held out both his arms and the old man grasped them and rose clumsily to his feet, avoiding Nat's eyes. Without words the two of them disappeared into the cool darkness of the Statehouse.

The fusileers grounded their guns, unsure what to do next. Fortunately Jamie Crewes rode up at that moment, dropped to the ground like a stone, and quizzed them. When he heard what had happened he burst into a great roar of laugher which was echoed from the windows above. More white handkerchiefs fluttered as the Burgesses relaxed, at least for the moment. Crewes and Hansford conferred and decided to marshal all the foot soldiers save Nat's fusileers in the area between the Statehouse and the town so that they could respond in either direction should trouble arise. The horsemen who were still guarding the town would remain there. The two captains called Jake over and he sped off with the orders, leaving a cloud of dust in his wake. The sun was fierce and Crewes and Hansford drew their men back a hundred feet into the shade of some trees. Ten minutes had elapsed with no sign of Nat; they must determine how things stood in the Council chamber. Using some subtlety for once, Crewes persuaded the blond planter to take some men and follow Nat; Hansford was a natural gentleman and would not add fuel to fire as Crewes might.

His cornsilk hair shining in the sun, Hansford approached the fusileers and counted off ten to follow him. The little group marched across the green, Burgesses still hanging from the casements, watching their every move. The great doors had been left open. The men thrust their way inside and saw the entire Council drawn up, each man beside his chair. The Governor had seated himself in his usual place, but his face no longer bore any trace of authority. He was as pale as a star and his features held no expression whatever. General Bacon was standing at his right, next to his cousin. Colonel Bacon's hands covered his face and his head was bowed. When Hansford assured himself that his general was unharmed and unthreatened, he halted the fusileers and they stood quietly, waiting. No one spoke until Sir William choked out some words, so low that it was difficult to catch his meaning.

"You shall have it tomorrow. Your commission and thirty more. Send Godwin to me and I shall instruct him to draft the bill of pardon and oblivion and deal with the matter of your sloop. The Council and I will write the letter to the King."

Nat bowed. "It is most satisfactory, Your Honor. Thank you. If the laws are signed and read on Sunday I shall march on Monday, you have my word on it."

Nat withdrew, walking backwards as one would exit the royal presence, watching the Governor's face as he went. Berkeley clutched at his stomach as though a dagger had been thrust into his vitals, as in a sense, it had. Colonel Bacon helped him from his chair and escorted him to his office. As the door closed on the old man Nat turned and saw Hansford. He clasped his captain's arms and the two left the Council chamber and entered the anteroom just as Richard Lawrence appeared at the bottom of the great staircase. The three members of the Ring looked at one another and smiled.

"We got it all, Dicken," said Nat quietly. "I'm to have the commission together with thirty more for soldiers of my choice. The House is to draw up a bill of pardon and one awarding me seventy pounds for my poor sloop. The Governor and Council will jointly send a letter to the King exonerating me from any taint of rebellion. My God, I can't believe it."

Lawrence was so moved he almost cried. "And the Council of State is going to approve all of our laws, every last one of them. It is a complete victory. I never thought I would see this day."

"Give Sir William some time to collect himself and then send Mister Godwin to him, will you? It is his request."

"Of course, Nat ... General Bacon." The innkeeper turned to mount the stairs to the House chamber and then paused. He rushed down again and clasped Nat in his arms. "You are a hero ... I'll never forget this day. Now ...

can I persuade you, at least, to stay in town, even if your army camps on the mainland?"

Nat looked at Hansford with confusion. The day had held too much; he was too spent to think or plan further.

The blond planter smiled, his blue eyes shining. "I'll take care of everything, General. We'll set up your headquarters at *The Unicorn*. You don't have to worry about a thing."

Nat's head spun. So this was what it was like to be a general! He watched Dicken Lawrence climb the great oak stairs and gave him one last wave and then walked out into the sunshine, Hansford at his side.

CHAPTER 22

JUNE - JULY 1676

She walks like a cat, thought Nat sleepily as he watched Clarissa place the breakfast tray on Lawrence's work table and open the simple cotton curtains which covered the casement overlooking Back Street. The majestic woman turned to leave and Nat shut his eyes and mocked sleep. If she knew he had been scrutinizing her she might mistake his intentions. Yet she *was* eye-catching and alluring in just that way ... the way that had Lawrence in thrall to her. But that was unfair to Dicken. Nat sensed that Lawrence had a strong emotional attachment to the African woman, as well as a physical one. The innkeeper was mismatched with Joanna in all respects, which was a tragedy as he owed her everything and obviously felt his betrayal of her keenly. Yet not keenly enough to stay away from Clarissa. Clarissa: the perfect mate for Richard Lawrence except for that one fatal impediment – the color of her skin. But Nat did not think that would stand in Dicken's way if he had not been tied to the mistress of *The Unicorn*. Clarissa was a free black and, as far as Nat knew, able to marry anyone she chose. Free to marry in a legal sense ... what Virginia would think of such a match was something else again. Yet Dicken, of all people, would tell public opinion to go to the devil if it stood in his way. No – it was his tie to Joanna which held him back. It was a great pity for all of them ... kept them locked in a bitter triangle.

Nat stretched and sat up as his thoughts wandered to Curles Neck. He had never told Lyn of Dicken's dilemma – it would have upset her so. Not that she would have censured Lawrence for his *affair de coeur* – she would have pitied all three of them for being denied their heart's choice. Although proper, Lyn was no prude. Sweet Lyn. Lucky him, that he was *her* heart's choice. John's face flashed before him briefly and he brushed it away like a moth. What had made him think of John? He leaped out of bed and poured a basin of water from the pitcher Clarissa had brought, while the steam still rose from it. A cold shave was no way to start the morning.

By noon on Saturday General Bacon's four captains — Crewes, Farlow, Hansford and Arnold — had climbed *The Unicorn's* stairs and Nat had a clear picture of how things stood with his army. Half the cavalry and all the foot save his own men occupied Paspahegh Field, securing the entrance to Jamestown peninsula. The rest of the horse and Nat's company patrolled Jamestown itself, the select squadron of fusileers stationed in and around the Statehouse lest a disaffected Burgess or an unhappy Councilor slip away and summon help. The men were ravenous and one of the squadrons had taken it upon itself to raid Green Spring for provisions, but Farlow had put out that fire with harsh words and the flat of his sword. If Bacon's army was not a model of propriety they would quickly lose the goodwill of the people. Each captain had designated a file to obtain food and the men were on strict orders to be civil and to walk away in peace if their requests were refused. Nat was not overly concerned about provisions. Jamestown could supply man and beast today and tomorrow and on Monday the entire force would be on its way to the frontier, marching through friendly territory where the colonists would doubtless flock to feed them. Other than the issues of supply, the captains had no concerns. Most of the citizens seemed to support Bacon – or at least that is what they said. Not a man, woman or child had raised a weapon in defense of the Governor. Still, they would remain alert for trouble; success would not be theirs until they were on the road west, commissions in hand.

The yoke of command still sat strangely on Nat's shoulders and when he had sent the last captain back to his post he stirred restlessly, wanted to leave Lawrence's attic which, once a refuge, was beginning to feel like a prison. Most of the inn's guests were Burgesses and they were all in session at the Statehouse, so when Nat slipped downstairs as the clock chimed twelve noon there was no one about but Joanna and Clarissa. Joanna told him that Lawrence was returning at one o'clock for dinner and had asked if Nat would join him for the meal which was to be served upstairs in his private quarters. Nat agreed readily and, thanking both women for their hospitality, left the inn by the back door to visit Folly and then to walk by the river for an hour or so.

Nat returned to the inn just after the appointed time and mounted the stairs with a good appetite. He had entered by the yard and on his way had ducked into the kitchen to thank Clarissa once again for all she had done for him. She smiled and told him that Jake and the Drummond boys had snared some wild ducks at Swann's Point and that if he hurried he might find that Lawrence and his guest had left him a few bones to mumble on. Lawrence and his guest? Who could that be? Nat tapped on the familiar door and entered, greeted by the sweet-tart scent of cherry sauce.

"There you are, General. Sit down, sit down. Clarissa has outdone herself."

"Hello Dicken. I missed you this morning – you rose with the dawn. Are you going to introduce me to your friend?"

"Certainly. General Nathaniel Bacon, Mister Thomas Mathew. Mister Mathew, General Bacon."

An undersized gentleman with a youthful face, an eager expression, and grizzled hair at odds with the rest of him stepped forward and seized Nat's hand and shook it vigorously.

"General, this is an honor ... an honor indeed."

"The pleasure is mine, Mister Mathew." Nat's face showed his dawning understanding. "Ah, Mister Mathew! You are Hen's master and it all started on your plantation!"

"I am afraid that is so. I saw the murdered man myself, the very morning he died. The boy has never been the same since. Robbie, you know. We brought him down to Cherry Point but he felt more at home with the Pierces, so we sent him back. Mistress Pierce says he still wakes in the night screaming, and it has been almost a year ..."

Nat sighed. He had thought of the boy often ... every time he thought of his own daughter. Perhaps some day Robbie could meet Jake ... Jake, whose father's death had seemed to fuel his life rather than quench it. Such a thing would affect people differently ... it was a matter of character.

"Well, welcome to Jamestown. What brings you here?"

Lawrence interposed. "First of all, Nat, wash your hands and join us or the duck will not be worth eating. Mister Mathew is a Burgess from Stafford County, did you not know? He and Colonel George Mason distinguish themselves in the House on behalf of the northern frontier."

Nat shook the water from his hands and took the towel that Lawrence offered him. "Colonel Mason? He led the Indian raid, did he not ... the one that set the spark to the powder train?"

"Indeed he did, sir, and acquitted himself nobly. They slander him who says that he knowingly killed the Susquehannocks. How could he have distinguished them from the Doegs? He has not been treated fairly and I hope that history will redress that error."

"Why, you speak strongly, Mister Mathew. You have a decided opinion on the subject."

"I do, sir. The men from Stafford are as fine a group as you will ever meet. Many a false rumor has flown about ... 'tis a pity."

The three men were silent for several minutes as they demolished the duck and a bottle of Rhenish. Lawrence excused himself and returned with more wine and a basket of nuts, while Clarissa slipped in behind him and quickly cleared the table, placing a bowl of strawberries and a pitcher of thick cream on the table before she left.

"This is a noble sight, Dicken," said Nat. "I hope you don't expect me to work this afternoon."

"Ah, but I do, General. Let's smoke a pipe and settle our stomachs and then we'll give you a report from the House."

Lawrence opened both casements and a soft breeze freshened the attic as Nat and his fellow Burgesses puffed in silence.

Nat turned to Mathew. "Is this your first foray into politics, Mister Mathew."

"If you care to, you may call me Thomas, General Bacon. Yes, sir, it is – my first and last."

"I'll be glad to call you Thomas, (I love the name well, as it is my father's), if you call me Nat. Now, why is your public career ending just as it begins?"

"I was not meant for such turmoil, sir. It has taken its toll already. I've lost flesh – look how my breeches gape at the waist. Dorothy said this would happen, and she was right."

"Bless my soul, Tom, have some more berries and cream! I know that soldiering can strip a man of flesh, but politics? Most men seem to grow stout with discourse. Except Dicken here ... he has some engine burning inside which keeps him slim."

"You may laugh, sir, but some pounds were shed yesterday when we saw you on that great black horse, with your fusileers lined up so proper. And that blond fellow behind you with the cavalry – looked like the angel of death."

Nat laughed. "Why, bless my soul, I had no idea we made such an impression. We were wondering if shot would start raining on us from above, I assure you. If I hadn't seen Dicken there, waving his handkerchief, we might have all retreated as soon as you showed yourselves!"

"Why, General, you have the House behind you, surely you know that. A handful of men were grumbling, but very few, and they soon stopped when they saw the rest of us cheering. No, you have nothing to fear but the Governor and I don't believe he could raise more than a few hundred souls if he tried. I could almost feel sorry for him, but then I think of Robbie Hen and the others who lost their families and my heart hardens."

The trio fell silent, remembering the terrible events of the past year. When they had finished their pipes they knocked the ash into the fireplace and Nat looked expectantly at Lawrence. The innkeeper never did anything by chance; there was a reason that he had invited Thomas Mathew for dinner.

"Let me tell you the situation in the Statehouse, General. Every reform bill has been approved and awaits the Governor's signature: the checks on the sheriffs, the reorganization of the Secretary's office, the reduction of government fees, the tax on the Councilors ... everything we've worked so hard for. And, above all, the franchise. Just think, when the next election writ is issued I will be able to vote, for the first time since I set foot in

Virginia. You cannot know how happy that makes me."

"I believe I can, Dicken. And it warms my heart as well. Too many Virginians have been silenced for want of owning sufficient property. Redress of that evil is long overdue. You and Will deserve a laurel crown, a medal ... something."

"Well, we're not going to celebrate until the laws are signed and read, I assure you. Berkeley is seething with rage as his hand slips from the reins of power. He is capable of anything. But that brings me to my next point. I've introduced you to Tom Mathew not only because I knew you would like one another, but because Tom writes a fine hand and is well known for it. The only task left, apart from tomorrow's signing and reading of the laws, is the signing of your commissions. I understand that you want thirty of them, besides your own."

"Yes, all my men are volunteers and I need to protect them from the taint of rebellion. Jamie ... Tom Hansford ... the Arnold boy ... George Farlow ... should the tide turn they could all be labeled traitor, just as I was, for want of that magic paper. We must have them."

"Well, of course. But Godwin confided that just this morning the old man was looking for a way out, like a rat in a corner. He claimed he could not possibly have the commissions ready ... you would have to wait ... it might be a week or more before it could be done ..."

Nat flushed. "That is intolerable. If necessary we'll occupy the Statehouse and I'll stand over him with a pistol until he writes and signs every one of them."

"Agreed. But there's an easier way. All the world knows that Berkeley has agreed to give you the commissions and has agreed on their language. He is now buying time by pleading his clerk's absence; why not provide him with a clerk and present him with thirty-one nicely drawn up documents ready for his signature? How can he then refuse to sign?"

Nat was torn between chagrin and laughter. The Governor was impossible ... if only Berkeley would take ship for England and leave Virginia to its own devices. Men like Drummond and Lawrence could govern it well ... but that was a fancy and he needed to address reality.

"An excellent idea, if Tom Mathew is agreeable. Are you, sir?"

"Oh yes, General. That's why I came ... I worked it all out with Mister Lawerence this morning. See that pouch? I've already written half the commissions, and it won't take me two hours to write the others. We can present ourselves to the Governor by four o'clock and, as Mister Lawerence says, what can he do then but sign?"

Governor Berkeley sat behind his desk in his private office behind the Council chamber and gazed, unseeing, out its single casement. His whole abdomen burned with fire. It happened whenever he was crossed, but never,

never had he suffered such an acute attack. If Fanny were here she would know what to do. Two silver tears crept down the old man's soft, pouchy cheeks as he thought of his wife. My God! If only he were home at Green Spring, with Fanny by his side, the rest of Virginia could go to perdition. The colony had all but cost him his life – perhaps it would kill him, he wouldn't be surprised, not given how he was feeling now.

Natty Bacon's cousin ... who would have ever thought? Poor Natty, he felt so badly about the whole thing that he had gone back to King's Creek, couldn't face Billy Berkeley under these circumstances. The Governor shifted in his chair, trying to relieve the pain in his belly. He missed Tom Ludwell almost as much as he did Fanny. Phil was fine, but he was a man of action while Tom was a thinker. He needed a thinker ... someone to help him get out of this coil the rabble had caught him in. At least he had managed to get rid of his clerk, sent him down to Kecoughtan on a trumped up errand. But that wouldn't stop them ... it would only buy a little time until they found someone else who could write the commissions. Then he would have to sign – he, the Royal Governor, would have to bow to the will of the Burgesses and the fools and knaves who had elected them. God in Heaven above, what had possessed him to call new elections? He had misread the country, there was no doubt about it. Misread Virginia just as Charles the First had misread the homeland. And look what had happened to the Blessed Martyr! He supposed there were some here who would like to see *his* head on the block, damn their souls. Well, there was fight in him yet. He might be forced to give Bacon his commission but that was not the end of the story.

The Governor heard a tapping at his door and he stood, grimacing with pain. There was a looking glass in the corner and he quickly dried his face and straightened his wig and rebuttoned his vest and coat. It would not do to let anybody know how distressed he was.

"Enter!"

The door opened just wide enough for Pitts to thrust his head in. Upon the Governor's nod he opened the door wide and entered the office.

"What is it, Pitts? Has that fellow Bacon come?"

"Yes sir, he is waiting in the antechamber with one of the Burgesses, but just before he came a messenger from New Kent arrived. Says he has something urgent for your ears only."

"Show in the messenger and tell Bacon to wait."

"Yes, sir."

Within minutes a square, brown man covered with dust entered the office, apologizing for his appearance. Berkeley recognized him – he was a lieutenant in the New Kent militia called Smith or Thompson or something ordinary like that.

"Ralph Rodgers, sir, sent by Colonel Claiborne."

Rodgers, that was it. "Come in Rodgers. What do you have to tell me?"

"Nothing good, sir, I fear. Colonel Claiborne would like you to know that yesterday at dawn the entire Liddell family was slain by savages ... all eight of them, tortured and slain."

The Governor groped for his chair and sat down. The pain in his gut was almost beyond bearing. "I am sorry to hear it, Rodgers. Where did this happen? And does Colonel Claiborne know who is responsible?"

"They had a small farm on the Pamunkey, Your Honor. There weren't no witnesses left, so to speak, but we in New Kent know that the Pamunkeys are to blame. Their braves have been seen in war gear and many of us have heard them howling at night as they prance around their fires and work themselves up for murder, if you know what I mean."

"Ah. But nobody actually saw the Pamunkeys attack the Liddell place?"

"No, sir, but that's neither here nor there. We know they did it."

The Pamunkey Queen was a staunch English ally and Berkeley doubted that her people had anything to do with the recent massacre, but he also knew that in the current climate he would never be able to persuade the colonists otherwise. Once this story got out the Pamunkeys' death warrant would be effectively signed. Berkeley sighed and looked at Rodgers.

"Thank you Rodgers. It is heavy news. Tell the man who let you in to give you some refreshment and a bed for the night and report back to Colonel Claiborne tomorrow. Tell him the matter has been noted and will be taken care of."

"Yes, sir. Thank you, sir."

Shortly after the New Kent messenger left the Governor followed him, crossed the Council chamber and entered the antechamber. Bacon and a Burgess whose name Berkeley could not recall – one of those new, Masaniello-like ones – sat cooling their heels. They rose and bowed as the Governor approached them. Bacon hardly bent his head at all, but the other Burgess at least had the breeding to make a proper obeisance. The game was up and the Governor knew it, so he would spike their guns ... pretend he was expecting them.

"Mister Bacon, have you brought me the commissions?"

There was a moment of astonished silence. "Yes, sir. Mister Mathew has them right here – one for me and thirty for those of my men whom I designate."

"Very well, give them to me. My clerk is away and I shall have to play my own secretary. Give me half an hour to sign them and then you'll be on your way. The laws will be signed and read tomorrow, after church. Will you be present?"

Nat struggled to regain his composure, such was his surprise at this easy victory. "Yes, sir. My men would not miss it for the world. And, with commissions in hand, we shall be off early on Monday to fight the savages."

"Very good. Wait there and I will return shortly."

The Governor took the pouch from Mathew and returned to his office. He could not bring himself to tell the young upstart about the Liddell massacre – the news would be out soon enough. Monday would see Bacon marching to New Kent. Perhaps he would not return.

Governor Berkeley stood on Green Spring's broad porch, surveying the drive and the ornamental garden and mulberry orchard beyond it. The heat was intense; he was glad he was wearing his lightest wig, but even so he was uncomfortable. Too bad he could not go about in his natural hair and a straw hat, like the slaves in the garden across the way, but it would not do. He was about to leave for Gloucester County with Phil Ludwell and Robert Beverley to raise a force of loyalists and he must look every inch the Captain General that he was. He adjusted his sword belt and once again drew the bright blade and made a few cuts in the morning air. It was a good thing he had turned out his kit yesterday: they had found moths in his stockings and rust on his sword. His valet had taken a beating for that carelessness, and was doubtless a better man for it.

Berkeley saw a cloud of dust rise up where the drive disappeared into the dark forest. Two riders raced up the road and pulled to a dramatic halt below him, at the foot of the great cascade of stairs. Phil Ludwell looked dashing in his usual green, on a chestnut mare that matched his hair. Beverley rode a sorrel – a good, stout soldier, nothing distinguished about his appearance, but a tiger when it came to a fight. Middlesex County was lucky to have him. The Governor waved, stepped indoors to order his horse, and descended the stairs to welcome the Colonel and the Major.

Within the hour the Governor and a small force of some thirty men were on the road to Gloucester County. The cards were finally starting to fall his way – report had it that the people of Gloucester were not happy about Bacon's recruitment tactics nor about the levies he exacted to pay for his Indian force. Berkeley smiled grimly. The upstart thought he could fight with volunteers, but within two weeks of his marching off against the Pamunkeys his men were grumbling and he was milking the colony for funds to pay them ... bribe them, would be a better term. Bacon was beginning to taste what it was to be a leader – it took a little more than a wish and a prayer. The Governor would not be surprised if his army fell away from him and the whole thing petered out within the month. However, at this point, in mid-July, the young man and a substantial force were still quartering the frontier, looking for savages. Who knew what the future held? Green Spring had decided that it needed to field its own army. Whether that army would march against Bacon or against the Indians, circumstances would dictate.

By noon the Governor's force had reached the York River not far from Queen's Creek. They took refuge from the sun in a grove of poplars and ate and drank well from the baskets carried by the four pack horses. Berkeley was pleased that his appetite had returned and that terrible burning inside had abated. It was either the exercise, (he should take more), or, more likely, the fact that he was about to bring Bacon to heel. The rebel had had his day in the sun; it was time to bring him down.

"Did you arrange for the ferry, Phil?"

"Yes, sir. See those boats over there, to the left? They should get us across easily enough. The day is fair and the water is still – I see no problem."

"And when shall we reach Tindall's Point?"

"Within an hour after landing – perhaps less."

"Do they expect us?"

"Well, the fort does, of course. And Colonel Atkins should have directed the sheriff to read your order on every plantation and farm, so we should have a good crowd."

"When are the citizens ordered to appear?"

"Ten o'clock tomorrow morning, at the fort."

"Will Colonel Atkins be there?"

"Oh, I should think so, sir. How could the head of the militia not be present for a muster?"

"Who is in charge of the fort?"

"Major Wiggins."

"Do you know him?"

"No sir. I have been working through Colonel Atkins."

"And what is he like?"

Ludwell paused. Atkins had been a reluctant ally, but Billy was enjoying himself and he did not want to dampen the old man's enthusiasm.

"Oh, well enough, I suppose. I hardly know him."

After luncheon the Green Spring force made its way to the ferry landing and by three o'clock all were safe on the north bank of the York River. York Fort at Tindall's Point was an easy ride away, and they set off in good spirits.

Colonel Atkins adjusted his sword belt and rubbed the back of his neck. His muscles were as tight as a drum and he felt a headache coming on. York Fort was nothing much to look at: a wooden palisade surrounding some ill-built cabins which barely kept the weather out. He had two great guns, little powder, and almost no shot. He could not remember the last time the guns had been fired; he was afraid to try them lest they explode. And now the Governor himself was arriving with an entourage. What did they expect to see, the Tower of London? If the King would not send weapons, how could Virginia defend itself? But one thing was sure ... he would take the blame. There was another problem ... how many of his militia would report for duty? When the word got out that Berkeley wanted a force to go against Bacon, the whole county was aghast. Wasn't General Bacon all that stood between them and a hideous death at the hands of the savages? Why would the Governor want to start some kind of civil war when the heathen were breathing down their necks? The whole thing was incomprehensible. His own three boys swore they would not report and though he yelled at them, they just laughed and disappeared into the woods. He supposed it was the same everywhere. So even if he got through this afternoon, managed to actually fire his canon, feed the Governor a decent meal and bed him down without the lice devouring him, tomorrow's muster could be a disaster. Now the headache had reached his temples ... it was going to be one of those bad ones.

"Colonel Atkins, sir."

"Yes, Wiggins."

"Oh, my sir, you look poorly. The Governor is on his way. Do you want me to fire the great guns?"

"Thank you, Wiggins, I'll see it through. Are they at the gate?"

"Yes, sir."

"Very well, let them in and whatever happens, happens."

Sir William tossed on the thin mattress that stank of sweat and God knows what else. A thunderstorm had passed through just at bedtime and the cabin's roof still dripped. There! A plash right on his head. He sat up and scratched his ankles. It must be lice ... something was eating him alive.

"Phil," he hissed.

"Yes, sir?"

"Are you awake?"

"I am and shall be all night, I am sure. I can't remember being so uncomfortable. We should have stayed at Warner Hall. It is my fault; I apologize. I had no idea the fort would be like this. What a joke! Why, the Dutch could sail right up the York with no one to stop them!"

"When do you expect the *Adam and Eve*?"

"Captain Gardiner is supposed to arrive tomorrow morning, at the same time as the muster, to make a show of force. I hope to God that he arrives on time."

"When he comes, we'll stay on board with him."

"That's a wonderful idea. I'll arrange it as soon as I see his sails."

"What do you think of Atkins and all of this?"

"A huge disappointment. The canons won't fire unless they are thoroughly overhauled and the palisade is a joke – wouldn't keep out a child."

"Atkins seemed lukewarm, at best, about raising a force."

"Well, we shall see tomorrow. Do you think you can sleep? I am going to try."

Governor Berkeley sat his white horse and tried to look as Lely would have painted him. The beast tossed its head and slobbered and Sir William checked it viciously. He was so tired that there was only a hair's breadth between him and mayhem. He had never seen Ludwell less than elegant, until this morning. The Secretary's hair was matted and one of his eyes was red, as though it were infected. Both men felt filthy and ill at ease. The fort's sanitary facilities were almost nonexistent and Major Wiggins' idea of breakfast had been reheated porridge. Neither coffee, tea, nor chocolate could have been purchased for gold – there was none to be had.

Still, the morning was fine and the three elegant masts of the *Adam and Eve* promised solace, outlined as they were against the morning sky at the nearby wharf. Berkeley could just see Captain Gardiner's dapper figure as he walked his quarterdeck. He would give them a good meal, a bath and an afternoon nap. After that, the world would look a little brighter.

Major Beverley rode up to the Governor and doffed his hat. The man looked bright and fit – perhaps the cabin where he and Atkins and Wiggins had slept had been free of lice.

"Well, Beverley, did you see anyone coming? It is well past ten o'clock."

"Yes, sir, there is a small troop just down the road, but ... well, I talked to them and they say that they are twenty in number and no more are coming."

Berkeley paled. "Gloucester will only muster twenty men?"

"That is what they say, sir. I am sure Colonel Atkins can tell you more."

The Governor turned in his saddle and stared at the fort. Atkins and Wiggins were riding out that very minute. He waved his arm and Atkins pressed his nag into a gallop and soon was beside the Captain General.

"How many men do you expect, Colonel?"

"Two hundred, easily."

"That is your full force?"

"Yes, sir."

"And if I told you that only twenty are coming ... what then?"

The blood drained from Atkins' face. How could he have a pounding headache when all his blood was curdled in his stomach? "It ... it is not possible, sir."

Just then those of the Gloucester militia who had chosen to oblige the Governor arrived, a ragtag force, some bearing firearms, but many with no weapons but knives. Colonel Atkins straightened his shoulders and looked stern.

"Men, you are late ... you have kept the Governor waiting. When will the others be here?"

A swarthy fellow with a pair of pistols in his saddle holsters spoke for the rest.

"We're all you've got, Colonel. The rest have gone with General Bacon or have taken off to parts unknown. We got the word long ago, but what you see before you is all you *will* see, should you wait here a week."

"Thank you. You men – go over there, in the shade. I'll be with you shortly." Atkins turned to the Governor. "What can I say, sir? That is the way it is. Ever since Gloucester heard that General Bacon was taking the field against the Pamunkeys, they were his. I can't force them to muster – only the law can do that. You are free to bring them up on charges, if you can find them. I'm sorry, sir. I did my best."

Governor Berkeley declined to reply to Atkins. He pushed the white horse out onto the green field where the muster was to have taken place. Beyond the field the *Adam and Eve* bobbed in the ebbing tide. He threw an arm into the air and within seconds Ludwell appeared on his right and Beverley on his left. He was so enraged that he could hardly speak.

"Major – seize the canon and get them on board the ship as quick as you can. Leave nothing in the fort – not powder, not shot, not food, not blankets ... strip it bare. Phil – choose five men and tell them to take our horses back to Green Spring – all our horses. Then tell Captain Gardiner that within the hour he's to carry us to the Eastern Shore."

Ludwell and Beverley exchanged startled glances, but said nothing. The Major hurried off and the Secretary urged his horse closer to Berkeley.

"Sir ... you look ill. Can I help you to the ship?"

The Governor's icy gray eyes glared at a world which no longer did his bidding and then turned up, blind. Sir William Berkeley slipped from his saddle, unconscious, into the arms of Philip Ludwell. The Secretary cradled the old man in much the same way that he had cradled his wife, and, for once, blushed to think of it.

Nat made the Liddell plantation his headquarters. In doing so, he reasoned, he would have a daily reminder of his mission, not let the July heat and the dissension in his army distract him from his purpose. Eight simple wooden crosses marked the family's graves: the Liddells were buried on the edge of one of their fields, where it met the woods. His men had enclosed the site with a split rail fence and he made it his business to tend it, personally. It had only been a month since the massacre and already the Virginia forest was reclaiming the farm and its fields. The loamy soil of the grave site was dense with brilliant green grass and grasping tendrils of fox grape and honeysuckle had already seized the wooden fence and begun their work of destruction. The fiery summer sun had finally disappeared in the west, leaving an afterglow softened by the dense green of the endless woods. Nat cleared a space around each cross and then stood and stretched his weary muscles and looked around him. Here in New Kent the forest went on forever, one tract of oak and hickory and poplar much like another. The landscape was not unlike the southern woodlands, but there Nat's army had followed the trading path and somehow the simple fact that man had traced a road from the James to the Roanoke gave a comforting structure to the wilderness. Here, in contrast, there was no pattern. One could not tell north from south nor east from west except by tracing the arc of the sun. The forest was as vast as the ocean. No wonder they had not found a single Indian in thirty long days of looking.

Nat retraced his steps to the Liddell cabin and climbed the rickety steps to the porch which creaked under even his slight weight. The place seemed made of matchsticks. Next year at this time the forest would have reclaimed it, unless another poor soul took up the battle against nature and tried to coax a crop of tobacco from these pitiful fields. Bacon entered the cabin and thrust his face in a basin of water, to no avail. The cool well water of the morning had grown tepid and stale and the basin was full of the bodies of dead insects.

George Farlow looked up from the table which, together with four stools and some benches, constituted the entire contents of the one-room dwelling. The sleeping loft, which Nat and his captains shared at night, contained a chest and some thin mattresses, some stuffed with feathers and some with corn cobs, but nothing more. The Liddells had not been murdered for their possessions, but for who they were – interlopers on Pamunkey land.

"Good evening, General. Do you feel better for your walk?" asked Farlow.

"I do, George, thank you. But I'll feel even better if Jamie and Tom and Tony keep their supper appointment and tell me that Brent has left with his band of ruffians."

Farlow rose and sloshed some rum in a thick glass, topping it with water. "Here, this will keep the juices flowing. The heat is extraordinary, is it not? We're not far from the river, but it doesn't cool you like the York or the James. No wonder the savages run about in their bare skins."

"Why haven't we found them, George? Not a Pamunkey, not a Chickahominy, not a Mattaponi – where can they have gone?"

"It's as I've said before, General. They are the masters of woodcraft ... they can move through the woods like smoke."

"But surely we should have found a firepit, a clearing, a garden ... But nothing, nothing at all. I was going to wait for the others, but I might as well tell you now that I have decided to let most of the men go. They are needed at home and their patience has worn thin. I can't keep them marching through these interminable forests in mid-summer when we have had no success."

"Well, sir, I could see it coming, but we must keep some force intact. Let's see what the others say. Tom will bring us news from the Southside and the lower James, Jamie from the upper James, and Tony from the York watershed. We'll know better what to do when we have their reports."

"Of course, that's the plan. Look! There's Jake! Now we'll have some news from Curles! And there, behind him, there's Jamie ... the others are coming. Ah, they must have met at the crossroads. Now we can finally plan!"

The six men hurried through a meager supper and settled on the front porch with the jug of rum as the last light faded in the west. The night was clear and star-studded above the Liddell fields, but otherwise the great trees cut off even the sky and Bacon and his captains were wrapped in darkness. Jake had brought long, comforting letters from Lyn and John which relieved Nat of some of his unease. Now it was time to hear from his captains.

"Tom, what news from the Southside?"

"To be honest, sir, almost none. They are just beginning to hear about the new laws, and while some are enthused, many think that the Governor should be left alone. They approve your leading an Indian force, but only with the Governor's blessing. We won't get much help from the Southsiders. 'Tis most disheartening. Still, I did drop by Swann's Point and Sam and Tom Swann say they are yours to command."

"Well, that's a change! We'll see what speaks louder: their words or their actions. Jamie, what's the word from Henrico?"

"Oh, as you'd expect Nat ... General. It's your home country and the people love you. Byrd and Goode keep them razor sharp. They'll join you whenever you whistle, never fear."

Nat sighed. *That* was good news ... if he ever lost the support of his neighbors, things would be in a bad way indeed.

"Now Tony, I apologize for leaving you to the last. What about the counties on the York? "

Arnold had been fidgeting all evening and it was clear that he had something urgent to say but, of all the captains, he was the one Bacon knew least, so he bided his time.

"I've important news, General. While we were Indian hunting the Governor, Mister Ludwell and Major Beverley went to Gloucester to raise troops against us! He planned to attack us from the rear and wipe us out! But Gloucester wouldn't muster ... they've declared for General Bacon. Crushed, the old man took to his heels and sailed to the Eastern Shore, leaving the Western Shore for Bacon's Army!"

Nat leaped to his feet. "Damn my blood, Berkeley fled? Why ... Virginia is ours! It is only my army which stands between the savages and the people. The coward! Who is a traitor now, to leave his sheep at the mercy of the wolves?"

"What shall we do next?" asked George Farlow.

"Well this puts a different complexion on things. Our course is clear – we must return to Jamestown and seize the reins of power."

"Hooray," cried Jake, and tossed his cap in the air.

"Don't be a fool, lad," cautioned Farlow. The old soldier turned to Nat. "General, with respect, you're talking about a civil war. No commission is going to save your neck if this venture goes wrong."

"It is not I who cast the die, George," crowed Nat. "Berkeley has abdicated his post. *His* is the hanging offense, if you like."

Fair Tom Hansford spoke. "Why not compromise? Why not march, say, to Middle Plantation and summon the great planters to a conference. General Bacon can put himself at their disposal. If Berkeley has truly left the field empty it should not be difficult to convince the gentry that Nat is the man of the hour and that he should lead the colony until we hear from England. That course does not smack of rebellion."

"Well said, Tom!" cried Farlow. "It is an excellent, politic plan."

"Indeed it is," Nat agreed. "What say you all? Shall we trade Indian fighting for diplomacy?"

"If General Bacon becomes Governor Bacon," boomed James Crewes. "What are we waiting for?"

CHAPTER 23

JULY - AUGUST 1676

The spearhead of horsemen pressed towards the Middle Plantation with General Bacon at its tip. He rode coatless, his fine linen shirt bright in the midday sun, crimson ribbons fluttering from his sleeves and from Folly's mane and tail. At his right was Tom Hansford, fair as Lucifer, and at his left loomed the Hephaistean bulk of Jamie Crewes. One hundred riders curvetted proudly behind the General and his two captains, yellow ribbons banding each right arm and dancing from bridles and saddles.

Behind the cavalry marched one hundred hand-picked infantry under the command of George Farlow who rode beside them, vigilant for any sign of sloth or insubordination. The foot not only wore orange bands on their upper right arms, but had fashioned cockades which graced their headgear, whether it be cap or hat. Next came Anthony Arnold's hundred, who proudly displayed orange ribbons at both wrist and buttonhole. Last, but far from least, marched General Bacon's special force of fusileers, twenty proud men clad in black breeches and white shirts like their leader, with broad bands of crimson encircling each muscular upper arm. In General Bacon's absence, they reported to Captain Crewes.

Dashing around Bacon's army like a hummingbird in Eden rode Jake Hartwell on his silver horse, ecstatic as his hero approached the Middle Plantation whence – who knew? – he might emerge as Virginia's leader.

A thunderstorm had cleared the air and the forest was a vibrant green, the dense leaves still glistening with rain. The army reached a crossroads where a right turn would take them to Jamestown peninsula which lay in reptilian slumber, a mile or so to the south. Nat called a halt and whistled for Jake. When he saw the boy he guided Folly to the right where the grass grew long and lush and signaled for Blue to follow, indicating to Crewes and Hansford that they should proceed without him.

"Are we going to Jamestown, General?" asked Jake eagerly.

"*You* are," smiled Nat. "I must press on. I want to reach Middle Plantation before dark and set up my headquarters before we sleep tonight. But there is heady business to conduct and I need to consult with my oldest friends, Mister Lawrence and Mister Drummond. I need you to find them both and urge them to attend me tomorrow, no later than noon. Lawrence is sure to be at *The Unicorn* and, with luck, Drummond will be home, though he might be in Westmoreland or at his Blackwater property. If so, I'll have to make do with Dicken alone."

"And where shall you be in Middle Plantation?"

"I don't know – in whichever is the best house. There are only a handful to choose from, so you ought to find us with ease. Don't fail me Jake, this is important. Here – let me scribble a note. Tomorrow is July the thirtieth, is it not? Tell them I must see them by midday ... it is vital. Choose a couple of Hansford's men as an escort – you shouldn't go alone. Now, good-bye. Stay at *The Unicorn* tonight and I'll see you tomorrow."

"I won't fail, sir. Good-bye."

Although Otho Thorpe's was the finest home in Middle Plantation, it could not hold a candle to Curles Neck, thought Nat as he paced the dining room where he had established his headquarters. He was in the older, wooden wing which was divided equally between parlor and dining room. A new brick ell projected in the back, making a squat "T," and providing bedrooms sufficient for him and his entire staff. Although Thorpe was in England on business, he had left his house servants behind, including a first rate cook, and they had all been drafted by Bacon's army before they knew what was happening. Nat and his captains had dined and slept better last night, and breakfasted better this morning, than they had for many a long day.

Now Nat awaited Drummond and Lawrence. He did not doubt that they would come if they were both in Jamestown. They had no business which could be more pressing than analyzing the implications of Governor Berkeley's rape of the fort at Tindall's Point and flight to the Eastern Shore. He himself was formulating a plan which included issuing a declaration, to be read in each county, charging the Governor with treason for having abandoned his post; and summoning, (perhaps "inviting" would be more politic), the first men in the colony to Middle Plantation to discuss – how should he phrase it? – the new leadership of Virginia. These were treacherous waters and he needed Drummond's sound good sense and Lawrence's clever mind to guide him through the shoals lest he perish on a hidden reef.

Nat had set the dinner hour at two o'clock; such a schedule permitted him and his staff to use the cool of the morning for business and to slumber during the sultry afternoon. All would then be refreshed to resume work in the evenings when, with luck, a breeze might lower the temperature and humidity and disperse the insects whose strange, primordial voices thrummed in a perpetual chorus as summer reached its zenith.

Nat peered out of the thick diamond panes of Thorpe's casements once again. There! Finally! One, two, three ... five horsemen were dismounting at the front door. He recognized Blue ... it had to be Jake and his guards and Drummond and Lawrence. Nat threw open the front door, ahead of the servant who had just stepped into the hall from the parlor.

"Will! Dicken! You came! Of course I knew you would. Come in out of this terrible heat – it is no day to be riding. Good boy, Jake. Look after the horses and see what they have for you in the kitchen, and then join us in the dining room. Hansford's men can find their way to camp – it is just down the road, but make sure they have something to eat and drink first. Come in, come in. You cannot know how glad I am to see you."

Unbidden, the servant brought a pitcher of fruit juice and a set of thick glass tumblers into the dining room. The juice even had a sliver of ice in it, for there was still a block in the ice house, although it would soon be gone. Drummond and Lawrence shed their dusty coats and ran their fingers under their shirt collars which clung to their necks, soaked with sweat.

"Are you planning the Devil's work for us, laddie?" asked Drummond. "Certainly it is as hot as Hades."

"When I tell you my thoughts you may decide that they are touched with brimstone," replied Nat. "We dine at two; will you take anything now to stave off the pangs? You must have left Jamestown early to be here so promptly."

"We wanted to leave yesterday, as soon as your boy delivered your message," laughed Lawrence. "He said he was under orders to spend the night in Jamestown, so that is what we did. But nothing could keep us back this morning – I think Will and I both rose in the dark, we are so eager to know what is afoot. I, for one, need nothing until dinner – do you, Will?"

"No, no. This juice is most refreshing – it will tide us over nicely. Come, Nat, we didn't ride all this way to discuss food. Give us your news."

"Well, I suppose you know about the Governor ..."

"We have reliable information that his pique at not being able to raise a force against you in Gloucester caused him to have a fit and then to lash out at York Fort, strip it bare. Why he sailed across the Bay, I have no idea, but he is at Arlington as sure as eggs is eggs," replied Drummond.

"Why then you know more than I! What is Arlington?"

"You don't know Arlington house? 'Tis a fine mansion in Accomac, overlooking the Bay. Custis owns it – he is wholly the Governor's."

"Custis? Strange name. I have never heard of him."

"He's a Hollander ... or at least his family is. They are among the greatest merchants and planters on the Eastern Shore."

"Why then, that explains it. Berkeley's going to gather a force there ... raise some kind of navy ... and sail back to hunt me down. The mystery is solved."

Drummond stroked his chin. "It is entirely possible. Accomac has, of course, not suffered a whit from this current Indian war, and they have always been staunchly behind Green Spring. Yes ... if he can find the ships he might well be planning just what you said."

"Why then it's clear as crystal, it will be a second civil war."

"Precisely," said Lawrence. "Berkeley is putting it out that you were never truly commissioned to go against the savages, that you forced his hand. Therefore you are still a traitor and a rebel and he is justified in exterminating you. Unfortunately, many will believe him. What do they know of commissions? If the Governor says you twisted his arm, who will doubt it?"

Nat paced the room as his friends made themselves comfortable at the dining table and drank deeply from the thick tumblers. "Then I must execute my plan ... it is the only way I can protect myself and my men."

"What plan is that, laddie?" asked Drummond.

"I need to write a declaration –or rather, Lawrence needs to write one for me – explaining the Governor's perfidy, how he has abandoned his sheep to the wolves. It needs to be sent out this very afternoon to all the counties on the Western Shore and declaimed at the court houses. I'll send my own men to read it; we can count on the support of some of the county sheriffs, but not all of them. It needs to be strong ... needs to counteract Berkeley's fable of coercion. And then we must summon the gentry here as soon as ever may be and convince them that by abandoning his people the Governor has, in effect, abdicated. Someone must lead Virginia ... the great men must help us find a way to fill his place."

Drummond and Lawrence looked at each other. It was a formidable task and if they undertook it they were on the road to treason. Only the King could remove a Royal Governor – to do otherwise was a usurpation of the royal prerogative. Still, under the circumstances, what choice did they have?

"In over shoes, in over boots," cried Drummond. "This has been building for many years. My heart tells me that this drama will not be over until your army and Berkeley's have met in battle. Only God knows how the story will play out ... I, for one, am willing to take my chances."

"And I," said Lawrence crisply. "Berkeley *did* abdicate. Virginia *has* no leader. Your plan is a sound one. Let's do it."

Nat smiled at his friends. Whatever the future held, these two would be with him until the end. He clapped his hands for the servant and ten minutes later a bowl of punch stood on Thorpe's dining table, thin slices of orange and lemon floating in the aromatic brew of juice and rum. The three toasted each other and their cause and then settled down to work.

Late that evening the candles still flared as Nat and his two counselors threw themselves back in their chairs, exhausted but content. Bacon batted idly at the moths which were inexorably drawn to the candle flames and then gave up the effort. If the frail things chose to kill themselves, it was their fate, and there was little that he could do about it.

"Well, that's a good day's work," he exclaimed.

"It is indeed, laddie. Lawrence's pen might be tipped with acid."

"Go over the points about Berkeley again, Dicken, will you? If this goes out under my name I had better understand it."

The innkeeper laughed. "Of course. One: Berkeley has not followed the royal instructions, has not built towns, has not diversified Virginia's economy, has ruthlessly raised and then viciously squandered taxes, often to the benefit of his favorites and to the detriment of the people."

"Here, here," said Drummond, pouring another cup of punch.

"Two: he has filled the courts with ignorant fools for the sole reason that he owns them and thus controls the course of justice. Three: for years he traded firearms for beaver, thereby arming the savages and usurping the King's monopoly in the fur trade."

"I like the way you put that ... it ought to catch the King's eye," murmured Nat.

"Four: Berkeley has wholly failed to protect Virginia against the savages, whether foreign invaders or former allies. Five, (here's where you come in, Nat): when the people raised their own army to protect themselves, Berkeley so hampered its efforts as to prevent it from being effective."

"How true that is," said Bacon.

"Six, seven, and eight: knowing the peril posed by the savages and knowing the will of the people, nonetheless the Governor has raised, and is raising, his own army to cut down the people's army, to the great detriment of all."

"Every word is true," said Drummond.

"Then I sum up by saying that for all these reasons Sir William Berkeley is guilty of traitorously injuring His Majesty's interest in Virginia."

"Excellent," said Nat. "Well done. And then we list his most pernicious counselors as fellow traitors. Are you quite sure that is a wise course?"

"All Green Spring is of the same stripe. I think it politic to cast blame widely ... it sounds less personal."

"Say again whom you have listed as his most pernicious aiders and abettors."

"Here – read it for yourself. Ludwell, Chicheley, Spencer, Bridger, Beverley ... the obvious ones. We end by calling for the arrest of all these men, starting with the Governor, within four days of the reading of the declaration, and request that the scoundrels be brought to Middle Plantation for further disposition."

"And you have stated that the arrest warrant issues under His Majesty's name, have you not? I feel strongly about that point. In bringing a rogue Governor to task, we are acting on behalf of the King."

Lawrence pointed to the declaration with the feather end of his quill. "There ... see? The people are charged with seizing the miscreants in the name of the King. It could not be plainer."

"It takes the sting from it, Dicken, don't you think? All my actions have been to further the King's interests here, not to oppose them. That must be very clear, lest His Majesty take offense at what we are doing."

"Your point is well taken, Nat. I have said it as clearly as I can. See here? You will sign as Nathaniel Bacon, General By Consent of the People. For that, my friend, is surely what you are."

Nat shivered despite the heat of the night. Once this declaration was read, there was no going back. But it was the right thing do; his heart told him so. He turned to Drummond.

"You said you have a man who writes a good hand?"

"Yes, I recognized Perkins among the foot soldiers when I rode up. He's a farmer now, but he was trained as a clerk. He's waiting in the parlor."

"Very good. We'll give him a pot of coffee to keep him awake and he shall make a copy for each county. I'll keep the original. I want it to go out as soon as he is finished, no matter what the hour." Nat clapped his hands and Jake entered from the hall where he had been dozing on a stool. He rubbed the sleep from his eyes and yawned hugely.

"Yes, sir?"

"Jake, wake Tom Hansford and tell him to report to me. He's to choose horsemen sufficient to ride to each county seat, no matter how distant. They must be ready in two hours' time. Each is to take a document which I shall hand him personally, and when they arrive they must read it themselves, or arrange to have it read, so that all the people know its contents. This is of the highest moment. Tell him to choose his best men."

"Yes, General. It shall be done exactly as you say." The boy dashed from the room.

Nat looked at his weary counselors and held his silver punch cup high, in a toast.

"Here's to the Ring ... and beyond."

Drummond and Lawrence rose and toasted General Bacon in return. "To the Ring ... and beyond."

Nat dreamed that Lyn lay in his arms; he thought he could feel her cool white arms around him and smell the scent of her – that mix of rose attar and new mown grass which was her essence. Then, strangely, John's face drifted into his mind's eye. Grey looked wise and sad and distant. He seemed almost to be weeping. Nat rose to consciousness, fighting the forbidding image. He found himself prone on his cot in Thorpe's best bedroom, a fall of netting all about him to keep off the insects. His head was cradled in his arms and the salty tang of his own sweat assailed his nostrils. Nat sat up and wiped his brow. His head was soaked; at times like this he was tempted to shave his black curls and adopt the fashionable peruke, but he knew that he would never do it. The Middle Plantation was stifling, buried as it was in the summer forest. He thought once again, as he had so often, how lucky he was to have a riverside home. He would never live far from the sound of water. Tatters of his dream stayed with him and his mind reached out for Lyn and John. He had just written them both – that must be why they seemed so close. But why was John so sad? Were things not well at Curles Neck? His messenger should return tomorrow and if there was bad news, he would learn it then. God forbid that it be so; he had worries enough to deal with here.

Nat rang the handbell and Jake, who shared the room next door with Hansford and Arnold, responded quickly. "What can I do for you, General?"

"What o'clock is it, Jake?"

"Close to four, sir."

"I hate this hour ... the whole world seems sunk in torpor. Do you think I could have a bath? The gentry will arrive between five and six and I must be at my sharpest."

"Of course, sir. There's still some rainwater from the last storm and it should be fresh enough. We'll bring you the hip bath right away; it will be almost as good as a dip in the James."

Nat smiled. Jake was a godsend. Despite his hard life and his father's tragic death, young Hartwell met the world with joy. It was his nature ... what a wonderful gift.

"Excellent. Are the great rooms prepared for our guests?"

"Oh, yes sir. We've arranged the parlor and dining room so that there are seats enough for thirty. It may be crowded, but it should do well enough. They are preparing the drinks now and they'll serve a cold supper at eight. I'll check again when I go for your bath."

"You're a good lad, Jake. I hope you'll join us tonight."

"I wouldn't miss it for the world, sir," cried the boy as he dashed out the door.

General Bacon was dressed in what had become his uniform: slim black breeches and a dazzling white shirt, generous in sleeve and collar. Normally he bound crimson ribbons on both arms, but tonight he wore his colors in the form of a broad sash which crossed from his left shoulder to his right hip. After his bath his hair had regained its sheen and his luxurious curls played on his shoulders as he circulated among the gentry, noting Ballard's horse face, Beale's subtle smile, Bray's enthusiasm, (once reserved for Governor Berkeley), and, most welcome, Colonel Swann's quiet, approving presence. Drummond had Swann by the elbow, and the Scot steered his son-in-law's father to an alcove, simultaneously indicating to Nat by a motion of his head that he should join them. The three men stood apart from the crowd where it was quiet enough to converse in normal tones.

"Will Drummond tells me that I am deeply in your debt, Colonel Swann," urged Nat.

"Indeed, General, I am in Will's debt. He is the one who helped me understand your cause. Once the light dawned, duty dictated that I recruit on your behalf and help you in any way possible. The Governor's abandonment of the colony is shocking. I should never have thought it possible of Berkeley. He has been a changed man these last two or three years ... I believe that he may be ill. In any event, new leadership is needed ... that much is evident."

"I am pleased that you see the issues so clearly; as others may not. I seek only to serve the King's interests. If a prince's servants fail to do his bidding, others must fill the gap."

"Well said, sir. As soon as Sam and I knew you were camped here we scoured the countryside, urging men of quality to come and meet you." The planter looked about him. "I see that we have been successful."

"Indeed sir, you have. I sent out my messengers only three days ago, and look what a response we have had! All the counties are represented, except for the far north and perhaps a few on your side of the river."

"Oh,' tis the devil's own work to stir the Southsiders. But most of the colony has delegates here, without question. What is your plan?"

"All will be revealed in a few minutes when I speak, but let me give you a preview. Are you familiar with my declaration, the one which was read in every county within the past few days?"

"Certainly, sir. Everyone of consequence in Surry heard it; there was quite a crowd, I assure you."

"I am glad to hear it. Well, I am going to follow the declaration with an equally strong statement which I call my manifesto. I shall read it tonight, for I want the gentry's reaction. The message will not surprise you. I remind the people once again that it is not we who are traitors, but Berkeley and his followers. I cannot say it too often, for so many are fearful of crossing a man who has lived here for thirty-five years, and ruled for twenty-five."

"I commend your prudence. You *cannot* state it too often. Many have told me that they agree with your positions but that they dare not act for fear of being labeled a Cromwell."

"I hope that I can convince them, for my thesis comes from the bottom of my heart."

"What else do you plan beside the manifesto, laddie?" prompted Drummond, who knew Nat's scheme perfectly well as he had helped devise it.

"If the manifesto is well received I shall send it out to be read throughout Virginia as I did the declaration." Nat paused and eyed Swann. "However this time I shall promulgate it accompanied by a letter signed by all the great men who support my cause. Such a letter ought to have a powerful effect. Do you think those gathered here tonight will sign such a letter?"

Swann looked unperturbed. "Whoever follows you should have the bowels to state it publicly. My signature is yours ... just show me where to write."

"It is noble of you, sir. I hope the others are of your thinking."

"And what of the election, Nat?" urged Drummond.

"Ah, yes. The third part of tonight's *programme* is to convince my guests to join me in instructing each county to send delegates to meet here, at Middle Plantation, on the fourth of September to hold new elections. We shall need the House solidly behind us to weather the many months it will take for London to send us a new Governor and for our new leader to select a Council of State. During that time the government will necessarily be in the hands of the Burgesses."

"A new Governor," breathed Swann. "And what do you propose to do with the old one?"

"Should he survive," said Nat, quietly but firmly, "I shall put him and his henchman on a ship for England to be tried for treason."

Swann paled. General Bacon's vision was large and it was frightening. It was also moving quickly from the abstract to the concrete. If Bacon really had the people behind him, (and only time would tell), then Virginia would soon be in the throes of a civil war and he, Colonel Thomas Swann of Swann's Point, hoped to God that he had chosen the right side. What did Will Drummond always say? In over shoes, in over boots.

"I am with you, General. Undoubtedly we must have new elections. What role shall you play in a new government?"

"I cannot know until the day comes, Colonel. Should Henrico want to elect me Burgess again, that is one possibility. Should the new Governor honor me by a position on the Council of State, of course I would consider that. Should the people wish me to remain their General, you can be sure that I would listen attentively to their desires. Man proposes, but God disposes. As for now, I can only let the plan unfold like a great Turkey carpet; how the pattern ends is in greater hands than mine."

The three men looked at one another solemnly, gripped by the feeling that the wheels and cogs of history were moving and that they were only a small part of an unknown and unknowable process. Their silence was interrupted by Jake's voice.

"General, sir ... they are waiting. They are anxious to hear what you have to say."

"Very well, Jake. I shall speak from the staircase, as we planned. Are you sure I can be heard from there?"

"Oh, yes sir, if they will stop talking. They gabble like turkeys." Jake caught Colonel Swann's look and blushed, but the planter only smiled.

Drummond seized the handbell that stood on the dining table and rang it loud and clear. Within a minute all voices had ceased and there was no sound but the creak of the floor boards which groaned under the combined weight of forty men. Nat glanced about him and felt a surge of energy. He strode to the staircase and mounted just high enough to see most of his audience. A large candelabrum stood next to him and the hall blazed with light. Lawrence slipped to the foot of the stairs and winked at him in passing. Drummond stood next to the candelabra and rang his bell again.

"Gentlemen, I give you General Bacon," the Scot called out in trumpet tones.

Nat waited briefly as a palpable tension rose, and then he began the most important speech of his life.

"If virtue be a sin, if piety be guilt, then all the principles of morality and goodness and justice are perverted, and we who gather here tonight may rightly be called rebels though our hearts be true to our prince ..."

Lawrence's prose rang in his brain like church bells and he felt elated, inspired, seized by a force wholly outside himself. Truly, he was no more than a tool, a vessel with no purpose but to swear these men to fealty and convince the people of Virginia that, if they seized this moment, they could shape their own future. It was his destiny.

"They're all gone, laddie, every last one of them," Drummond crooned as he poured Nat a tot of rum. "You were brilliant ... there's no word for it. I thought Dicken was the word-man, but you outshone him tonight."

"Why, they were Dicken's words," protested Nat, drinking deeply.

"That's as may be," crowed Lawrence, "but you breathed life in them. Why it was splendid ... you won them all over, to a man. They couldn't wait to sign the letter of support and the orders for new elections ... you had them in the palm of your hand."

"Do you think we shall really have elections, called thus improperly?"

"Who can say? There is nothing to lose by trying. We shall know in thirty days."

The friends relaxed in silence. It was early on the morning of the fourth of August; although Thorpe's parlor clock had struck three they could not bring themselves to go to bed, exhilarated as they were.

"Do you think they will all find lodgings?" yawned Nat.

"Ten or more live close enough to ride home; the rest will prevail on the householders to let them have a mattress or a pile of straw. I don't think they much care, they are so pleased that things are moving forward in this way. I must confess that I was surprised to see Tom Ballard and James Bray, but most of the others have long had a bone to pick with Berkeley and are pleased to finally show their colors."

"What do you think about this Captain Carver that Swann told us about?"

"I don't know the man," responded Lawrence. "Do you, Will?"

"Oh, yes, he's an old sea dog. Rough around the edges, but with a wealth of experience. He and Swann go way back, but I've only met him a couple of times. He has some deep grievance against Berkeley, so doubtless he would be pleased to serve you."

"But is he trustworthy?"

"I don't know, laddie. You'll have to talk to him. Swann can tell you anything you need to know. Why don't you come to Jamestown when you can get away from here and we'll sail across and pick Tom Swann's brain. What I *do* know is that you'll need a navy of some kind. Berkeley has the advantage there. He's got the *Adam and Eve* and, rumor has it, a second ship and a couple of sloops. Situated at Arlington as he is, he can command the capes and direct all the naval traffic his way, if he is clever. That's what you need to fear ... the old man's gathering a large enough navy to return to the Western Shore and give you a run for your money."

"I *do* fear it, Will. My army far outnumbers his, but we have only a handful of sloops to our name, and mine is not among them!"

"You still grieve your sloop, don't you," laughed Lawrence. "Well, someday perhaps Gardiner will disgorge that seventy pounds and you can build a new one."

"*You* can laugh, Dicken. You don't give a fig for sloops or ketches or three-masters, but I was fond of the thing and I could certainly use it now. We must get somebody over the water to spy on Berkeley. How else will we know what he is doing? They say the people of Accomac will stand by him and we won't get any help from turncoats."

Drummond rose, finally ready to seek his bed. He was gathering cups and glasses neatly and putting them on the sideboard, when he froze. Nat yawned again and looked at the Scot quizzically.

"Am I dreaming, or is that a knock at the door?" the big man asked.

"You're not dreaming!" cried Lawrence, who sprang up and slipped to the front door, opening it a crack to see who was there. A torch still flamed in its socket and illuminated the front steps brilliantly. There, a twin to the fiery flambeau, glowed Giles Bland's red head.

"Giles!" said Lawrence. "Whatever are you doing here, in the middle of the night? Come in, come in. God preserve us ... are you the bearer of bad tidings?"

"Hello, Dicken ... Drummond. At your service, General Bacon. Bad tidings? Not I! I've been in Jamestown for the past two days, well served by your charming wife, Dicken, I must say. And guess what? The *Rebecca*, Captain Larrimore, has just berthed. Your slave convinced me that you would want to know the news forthwith, although for the life of me I do not know why. She is a most insistent woman ... what's her name again?"

Lawrence looked daggers at Bland. "Her name is Clarissa. And she is not a slave. She is a free woman and serves me ... serves us ... out of loyalty."

"Well don't bite my head off. It's neither here nor there to me. Don't I get a few thanks for having ridden eight miles in the dark when I could have been snug in bed?"

"Of course you do, Giles," said Nat, taking over the conversation. "These are excellent tidings, and most opportune. We were just discussing shipping. Come in and sit down and have some rum. Can you stay awake a few hours longer? I have a proposition for you."

Late the next day, after a refreshing morning's sleep, Giles Bland mounted his horse to return to Jamestown, an elaborate set of instructions in his saddlebags. To Nat's knowledge the *Rebecca* was the only ship in Virginia waters not under the control of Governor Berkeley. Could he capture it, he would have the basis for a navy. And if he had a navy he could take the fight to Berkeley, beard the old man in his den, clap him in irons, and send him to London with his henchmen to stand trial for treason. Although it was a long shot, the opportunity was too good to pass up.

He and Lawrence and Drummond had quizzed Bland closely concerning Larrimore and his crew. Bland swore that the newcomers were wholly ignorant of how things stood in Virginia, had heard nothing of the Indian depredations nor of the brewing civil war. Pure chance had guided them through the capes unnoticed by Berkeley and they had not touched shore until they reached Jamestown. Once there, their only contacts had been with folk who were themselves ignorant of the winds of change or were devoted to Bacon's cause and revealed nothing, fearing that whatever they said might reach Berkeley's ears through the *Rebecca*. When Bland finished his report the General, the innkeeper and the Scot shared such a look as you might see on a lioness as a tender fawn wobbles from its protective thicket into the cruel light of day, almost begging to be taken.

Dawn saw Bacon's four captains seated at the dining table, still somewhat stunned with sleep, but their faces brightening with interest. One of them was about to be awarded a plum: an order to seize the *Rebecca*, her captain, and her crew. To whom should the prize go? Nat silently assessed his staff. Jamie Crewes would always be closest to him: they had been friends and neighbors since he and Lyn first moved to Curles Neck and those tender ties had been forged in iron during the Occaneechee campaign. He needed Jamie by his side ... always would. George Farlow was another Occaneechee veteran and the best soldier there, himself included. He could not do without Farlow's expertise and sense of duty. Hansford ... ah, how he loved the man. Tom's blond beauty and generous spirit endeared him to all. Nat was uncomfortably aware that, without thinking, he had made

Hansford a favorite and that Tony Arnold felt the slight. For the past week Tony had seemed restless, ill-at-ease. Although he was the friend of Hansford's heart, Nat thought it likely that he had always suffered in comparison to the young Apollo, always fallen a little short in looks, in intelligence, in skills. And yet Arnold was tough as nails and true as a die. Perhaps this was the time to let him shine. Yes, that was it. Anthony Arnold would be permitted to handpick a force from the whole of Bacon's army; he and his men would drift into Jamestown dressed as farmers, tradesmen and casual laborers; and when the moment was right Arnold would spring the trap and the *Rebecca* would be his. With the aid of Giles Bland and William Carver the ship would be transformed into a waterborne Trojan horse and soon it would speed across the Bay on its white wings to coax Berkeley from Arlington and bring him down.

Nat spoke. "Tony, I want you to meet Giles Bland, an old friend of mine from the upper James. You and he are going to work together on something of great moment. Listen carefully and I'll tell you what I have in mind..."

At dusk Bland reached the crossroad which would take him to Jamestown. Unconsciously he reached down and patted the saddlebag which held his instructions. He didn't need the thing in writing; that was for the benefit of Colonel Swann and Captain Carver. As for himself, the plan was burned into his brain. Nat Bacon — *General Bacon* – had entrusted him with a great enterprise ... perhaps too great. He was to get himself across the river tonight and hunt out Colonel Swann, wherever he might be. That done, he was to direct the Colonel to summon Captain William Carver to Swann's Point as soon as ever he could. God forbid that the old salt had disappeared into one of his haunts; they would soon know. Once Carver had been located he, Giles Bland, was to cross examine the man and assess his competence to sail the *Rebecca*. If Carver passed the test, Bland was to get word to General Bacon immediately and that arrogant, swarthy fellow – Tony Arnold – would slip into Jamestown with an armed force, whatever the hour of day or night. God willing, they would seize the *Rebecca* without incident and lock up captain and crew in the hold, keeping a handful of sailors on deck with pistols at their heads, the ones who best knew the ways of their ship. Once the prize was seized he and Carver would go on board, the old captain to sail the ship and he to orchestrate the capture of Governor Berkeley.

Bland's mouth grew dry and he swallowed hard. He, Giles Bland, was to be the Odysseus who would ride Bacon's Trojan horse to the Eastern Shore. It was all a bit overwhelming. Well, it was getting darker. Time to get on with it. He would leave his mount at Drummond's and Billy and Johnny would take him across to Swann's Point. The ball had started rolling now, and nothing was going to stop it. John Bland's son was going to be a hero.

CHAPTER 24

AUGUST - SEPTEMBER 1676

The sun's orb pulsed in the sky and Virginia burned. All living things hid under the forest's dense green canopy and waited for the universe to right itself. Nothing with sense would stir; it was time to rest. Nat paced Thorpe's dining room. He was starved for exercise, but he would wait for the cool of evening before mounting Folly and riding until his cares dropped from him. This business of being a general ... it was taxing beyond belief. The army looked to him for everything: how could they get fresh wheat bread, who would mend their stockings, what to do with the well which had given some of Farlow's men the bloody flux, how to cure the dainty mare which had gotten into the clover at Rich Neck and blown up like a balloon, poor thing. Crewes had finally shot her and the soldiers had dined on her flesh. Nat shuddered. If only he could focus on essentials; his captains should really take care of the rest. And generally they did. All in all, the men were splendid. But the questions came at him as fast and thick as the relentless rhythm of the cicadas which thrummed endlessly in the summer woods, and it was rare that he had a moment to himself.

What news there was, was good, but there was not enough of it. Arnold had done splendidly in taking the *Rebecca* last week. Nat himself had stood on Jamestown wharf and waved good-bye as Captain Carver sailed off in the pretty ship with Bland's red hair shining like a beacon from the quarterdeck. But that was five days ago and there had been no word since. Had Berkeley been enticed aboard on the pretext of talking peace and thrown in the hold to keep Captain Larrimore company? Or had the *Rebecca* herself fallen into a trap, putting Giles and Carver and Tony Arnold's men in jeopardy? He must wait and see.

His four captains, (for Arnold had placed his men under Bland and remained with the army at Middle Plantation), had seized all the surrounding plantations without incident, including the Ludwells' fine place at Rich Neck. Tom Ballard must be thanking his lucky stars that he had joined the rebels, for by doing so he had saved his farm. Hansford would have snapped it up like kiss-my-hand if the horse-faced planter had not come down on the right side of the quarrel. Nat smiled as he continued to pace. The best thing was that just this morning Jamie had returned from a five-day foray with the news that he had taken Green Spring. Apparently there had not been much of a struggle; the house servants could hardly wait to surrender and those who worked in the fields and gardens had taken to their heels with as much of their master's goods on their backs as they could carry. Jamie had urged him to make Green Spring his headquarters, as the symbolic significance of occupying the Governor's mansion would carry such a strong message, but Nat wanted to stay at Middle Plantation through the September elections. After that ... well, who knew what would happen? He might well take up residence in those bright rooms where Sir William and Lady Frances Berkeley had treated him like a dog.

Nat sighed and poured himself a glass of water to which he added a tot of rum. What he really wanted was to go to Curles. He had not been home for almost two months and he craved Lyn's caresses and John's strong hands on his shoulders. And his daughter! Little ones grew by leaps and bounds at her age; she had been walking when he last saw her and doubtless she would be running about now like a little lamb. Additionally, there was something about Lyn's last letter which nagged at him – a certain coldness, a lack of candor. It was probably nothing, but still.... And John was profoundly worried that the Indian war had taken another direction and become a rebellion. He didn't say much, for fear that other eyes than Nat's would scan his lines, but it was clear that he thought that Nat was flirting with disaster. He needed to put things right at Curles, but now was not a good time: he must wait here until he learned the fate of the *Rebecca*.

Nat heard a familiar footstep and Jake Hartwell appeared from the hallway. It was the first time Bacon had seen his body servant less than fresh; the boy looked haggard and spent. Nat chastised himself silently. Jake was just a lad – he should not be driven so hard.

"You're a sight for sore eyes! Pull up a chair and here, take my glass, I don't need this and you do."

"Oh, thank you General. This heat does take it out of you, no question."

"You've been with Arnold, haven't you? What's the news?"

Jake buried his face in the thick tumbler and drank deep before he answered. He smiled as he looked up. "Splendid news, General. Tony caught Sir Henry Chicheley and locked him up in Green Spring jail."

"You don't tell me! The old knight himself! Why, that's excellent. Poor old man, I could almost feel sorry for him. How was he so careless as to fall into Arnold's hands?"

"We think he was coming to Green Spring to fetch some of the Governor's things for him ... some errand of mercy. He won't say. But there he was, riding through the woods all by himself, as though he had never heard of General Bacon. He drew his sword and put up quite a fight, but there were about fifty of us, so it was just a matter of time before he grew weary and Tony – Captain Arnold – disarmed him and put him on parole not to flee and escorted him to Green Spring."

"And you put him in that little brick house that the Governor used for a jail?"

"Yes indeed, sir. Captain Arnold wants to know what to do with him."

"Why, we'll leave him there to learn what it feels like not to have a mansion at your disposal. Is Tony still at Green Spring?"

"Yes, sir. He said you told him to guard the place with a small force until further orders."

"Yes ... I sent him out this morning right after Jamie told me that Green Spring was ours, but I had no idea he would be so successful so soon. We'll let Sir Henry stew in jail for a while and then decide what to do with him. Do you know, Jake? It crosses my mind that if Bland's mission goes awry, with Sir Henry in our custody we'll have a bargaining chip to play in the hostage game. I am most pleased. Why don't you take the afternoon off and get some rest? I'm going to find Captain Crewes. I might visit Green Spring myself and arrange the fate of Sir Henry Chicheley."

Minutes later Nat found Jamie Crewes entertaining his men with the news of Chicheley's capture. Figuratively speaking, the old knight was tossed about roughly, and Nat was somewhat put out by the men's coarseness, but that was the nature of war. The General caught the Captain's attention and the two men strolled into the forest as the sun relaxed its grip on the colony and blazed west like a flaming chariot.

"All four of you have done splendidly, Jamie. I am so glad that a little glory is going Tony's way; he was suffering a bit, as I'm sure you noticed."

"Thin-skinned as a girl, he is. Brave withal, but sensitive as a maiden. People will love Tom Hansford, it's just the nature of things. He's a young god. But after the *Rebecca* and Sir Henry? Tony's full of himself now – you should see him."

"I plan to. I want to ride over this evening and make sure that things are as they should be at Green Spring. Will you come with me?"

"Aye, Tom and George can handle things here, if something comes up. We should be back by bedtime. I don't see the harm in it."

"Very good, let's start now. Cook can put up a cold supper for us and we'll eat on the way. That way we'll have a chance to discuss something which I've been brooding about. I've decided I can't wait for news of the *Rebecca* to recommence my Indian campaign. The scouts are fairly sure that the Pamunkeys have fled to their village at Dragon Swamp and I want to march against them as soon as we can put a force together. I want your advice on how many men to take, how many horse, how many foot and so forth. It is in my mind to marshal the troops tomorrow and start out at dawn on the following day. What do you think?"

"What do I think? I think you should have left a week ago! The best way to draw the people to you is to bring them some Indian scalps. You know I am yours, Nat. Just tell me what you want and it shall be done."

Nat clasped Crewes' huge hand and the two men returned to camp, shouting for their horses.

Queen Cockacoeske played idly with the deep fringe of her deerskin skirt as she sought Totopotomoi's spirit. If she put everything else out of her mind and concentrated hard enough, he would come to her. The moon had waxed and waned many times since her husband had laid down his life for the English at the place they called Bloody Run, and how had they recompensed her loss? By taking her lands and pushing her ever farther into the forest. By charging her to raise warriors to fight the tall, fierce Susquehannocks who had swooped down from the north and lit the powder train which was still burning out of control. By falsely accusing her of murdering the poor souls they called Liddell whose woodcraft was so deficient that they were starving to death right on the banks of the Pamunkey where the berries were lush and the corn grew without effort and the game teemed so that even a child could fill the pot. It is true that the sickly whites had been slain by her tribesmen, but not at her order ... never at her order. The massacre had been committed by a group of young men who had since been banished; she would have nothing to do with wanton slaughter. She had been ever true to the English and she would remain so, as it was Totopotomoi's dying wish. He said that such a power burned in the white men as no Pamunkey could ever quench; it was better to go with them than against them. Cockacoeske closed her eyes and leaned over the tiny, aromatic fire, drawing in its essence. Ahh ... finally she felt him, felt Totopotomoi reaching out for her. He looked sad and shook his head at her. It was all she needed to see. She would not dishonor her alliance with the English, whatever happened. Totopotomoi told her so. When she passed on and she and her husband walked the fields in the sky, hand in hand once more, she would be able to look him squarely in the eye and tell him that she had kept her word.

The Pamunkey Queen rose and placed her finest head band of black and white shells upon her brow. She looked about her hut with displeasure. Her people had not had time to build their summer camp properly; they had been rushed here, with the English nipping at their heels. The English ... always in a hurry ... wanting so much, so fast. The hut was ill-built; she would have it reconstructed soon. Still, it would have to do for today's council. The Queen crouched and pushed aside the deer skin which covered the door to the hut and stepped out into the sunshine. Her little nephew knelt by the door, ready to do her bidding. Cockacoeske smiled at Squirrel and spoke.

"Tell the elders I am ready for them. Tell them we have all day to talk, but I shall not change my mind. No weapon shall be raised against the English. Totopotomoi has spoken."

Folly shoved his huge muzzle into the Piankatank River and sucked up the moisture. Nat slipped from his back and made his way awkwardly across the river stones and muck, trying to find a clean pool where he could wash the sweat from his face and, perhaps, drink as well, unless the water was too foul. It was the ragtag end of August and the river was low. It probably was not a good idea to drink the water. He splashed his face and returned to Folly where he pulled a flask from his saddlebag and finished the last of his berry juice and rum. The liquid was warm and sticky and it clung to the bristles which darkened his upper lip and cheeks and chin. He had not shaved for several days, as the scouts had suggested that the army build no fires lest the savages see the smoke. Without hot water, how could one clean oneself properly? All the men were uncomfortable and disgruntled. If they did not find the savages soon, Nat knew there would be deserters. He had no power over them – they followed him of their own free will and they would leave him on the same basis. This was where leadership counted – he must bring them to battle soon.

Crewes crashed through the underbrush, grinning. "Good news, Nat. The scouts are back and they have found the Pamunkeys. They are at Dragon Swam, sure enough. It's just across the river, a miserable place full of thickets, brambles, scrub oak and chinkapins. It is one of their summer camps – the one they use when they are hiding from an enemy, for the vegetation makes a natural fort. You must come back to camp right away – they may have spies along the river who could see you."

Nat's depression fled. Thank God! These past ten days of beating about the trackless forest were at an end. He longed for action as much as his men. After considerable debate he and his staff had agreed that the most effective Indian force would be small, (less visible and more manageable), and mounted, (horses were an inestimable advantage over the savages, who feared and hated them). Accordingly he and Jamie Crewes had taken fifty of Hansford's best horsemen and left the others behind. Tony Arnold was still at Green Spring, a new man after capturing both the *Rebecca* and Sir Henry Chicheley; Farlow remained at Middle Plantation and spent his days drilling his men and scouring the countryside for food and supplies; and he had given Tom Hansford the responsibility of holding Jamestown, on the off-chance that Berkeley would abandon the Eastern Shore for his old capital. Time was of the essence. He must return to Middle Plantation soon for the elections and he could not return without an Indian victory. God was good ... it was all going to work out perfectly.

Nat seized his horse's reins and followed Crewes away from the river and into the forest. "How many Pamunkeys are there?"

"The Queen herself, ten or twelve elders, and perhaps thirty or forty others, both warriors and women. As it falls out, we are evenly matched in numbers, but our horses and light armor give us a huge advantage. It should be a slaughter."

"Can we surprise them?"

"Up to a point. The river is low and easy to ford. I suggest that we split the force, that I cross to the north with half the men and come down on them from that direction while you take the other half and attack from the south. It has been so dry that I do not think we'll have a problem with the swamp, but we should tell the men to be careful – they may have to leave their horses and cover the last yards on foot."

"Do the savages know we are here?"

"Not that the scouts could tell. The elders are all in conference with the Queen in the main hut, the warriors are lying about, and the women are cooking and doing other chores. They seem wholly unwitting."

"Then we must attack now!"

"*Tout va*, General! Let's brief the men and be off. Within half an hour the Pamunkeys will wish they had never been born."

Queen Cockacoeske closed her eyes and let her mind drift to Totopotomoi as the elders murmured among themselves, endlessly debating whether to try and form a confederacy to go against the English with other Powhatan bands which, more often than not, had been their former ene-mies; or whether to maintain their longstanding alliance with Governor Berkeley and tamely submit to whatever he imposed upon them. The coun-cil was evenly split. They would not finish today, or perhaps even tomorrow. But *her* mind was made up. Ultimately her people would have to stand by the English. It was written.

The Queen frowned, her meditations disturbed by unusual sounds. She heard the screams of women and a great yell as one of her warriors sound-ed a war whoop. As she rose to her feet the clarion cry of a war horse rent the air and before the council could collect themselves, thudding hoofs pressed them to the earth like sea waves and the thin withy frame of their hut was slashed by English steel, leaving them exposed to the brutal sum-mer sky. The Queen crouched by the pile of pelts which formed her sleep-ing bench and from the corner of her eye saw her brother-in-law fall beneath a horse, his skull crushed and his brains dashed upon the stones of the hearth. When she saw that the great beasts had passed her by she dashed to the next hut which miraculously still stood, unharmed. Squirrel cowered inside, shivering with fear.

"Come child, lead me to the woods. Could it be that I misread

Totopotomoi's mind? Quickly, quickly, before they come back. May Oke save us."

Nat sat Folly in the very center of the Pamunkey village, surrounded by devastation. All the huts but two were flattened, and under the withies and grasses bronze limbs still twitched and cries and groans could be heard. It had been a total success. He and Crewes had crushed the savages like corn between mill stones. In a clearing to the south, where the Indians had their garden, Crewes was dealing with the survivors, some fifteen warriors and women. They would be taken to Middle Plantation to be exhibited at the next Assembly, guarantors of General Bacon's success. As for his men, none had been killed and the injuries were minimal, many of them caused as the two English forces met one another like the two halves of a nutcracker.

He would like to take some plunder, if there was anything worth having in this miserable place. Perhaps he could find a few furs or some shells or beads which he could display as he returned, triumphant. The two standing huts might yield something interesting ... he would see. Nat dismounted and patted Folly's neck. It was all over so quickly that the animal had hardly broken a sweat. He approached the nearest hut and stopped suddenly, his hand on the hilt of his sword, as he heard grunting noises from within. Could it be a savage? Perhaps one in the throes of death? He approached the hut, stooped, and carefully drew aside the animal skin which covered the door. He almost laughed. There was nothing to fear. It was only the beast with two backs. One of his soldiers was displaying the pale twin globes of his buttocks for all the world to see, as he plunged his member into the smoky flesh of an Indian lass. Nat turned to withdraw and leave the man to his pleasure when he saw the soldier raise his right hand. Curious. Was the man in trouble? Perhaps the wench was fighting back. Nat saw the man's hand descend and then he heard something like a sigh. Everything must be in order; the situation was growing awkward and he turned to go. As Nat was leaving the soldier stood awkwardly, hobbled by his breeches which clung to his ankles. He fumbled with his clothes and when he was dressed he retrieved a knife from the ground, sheathed it, and turned to leave. His face dropped as he confronted his General.

"Beg pardon, sir, I didn't know you were here."

"It's nothing," said Nat. "I was looking for some treasures and ... look what I found!"

The man looked confused and perturbed. "I was only getting my own back, if you take my meaning, sir."

"It's alright. Better go join the others now. We'll be off home as soon as Captain Crewes arranges for the captives."

The man shuffled off, head down. Nat decided to see whether the woman had recovered. If she was of sufficient rank she would have to join the other captives, otherwise he would just let her go. He stepped into the hut and let his eyes adjust to the darkness. The woman's skins had been shoved above her waist, leaving her legs and sex exposed. Her flesh was dusky and the seductive triangle of hair was dark and thick. She lay curiously still … perhaps she was in shock. Nat leaned closer. The Indian seemed not to be breathing, for her breast did not rise by so much as a hair. Truly, she lay as still as death. Could it be? Nat caught his breath and leaned over the woman. Her head was at a curious angle and around her neck was a broad band of beads or dark shells … unless. Nat leaned closer still. There was a curious smell. The beads that made up her necklace were beads of blood. The soldier had used her and slain her, all within the space of a minute. Nat sighed and stood up, his head brushing the rounded top of the withy hut. He thought of Robbie Hen and Jake Hartwell and Lyn and Mary. He crouched and left the little dwelling, carefully pulled the deerskin over the door opening, and returned to Folly. Mounting, he rode south to the clearing where his army awaited him. He was General Bacon and they were waiting to be told what to do.

As they pushed their way through the forest the victors of Dragon Swamp looked more like the defeated. Their cornmeal, bacon and rum had long since been consumed and they were reduced to dining off squirrels and blackberries and sour fox grapes, a diet which, at any given time, sent half the men into the forest, busy with the calls of nature. The horsemen were held back by the slow pace of the captives, one of whom was assigned to each three riders. Bacon's army took out its bad humor ruthlessly on the Pamunkeys and Captain Crewes looked the other way at this behavior, as did the General, except when it came to the women. Bacon was clear that no woman would be molested; the image of the squaw with the bright necklace of blood was still with him.

Nat stared mindlessly at Folly's mane which draped to the right of his neck except near his head where a perverse tuft of hair insisted on falling to the left. The General thought of nothing. This endless journey must simply be endured until they reached the road which followed the left bank of the Chickahominy; then they would be within striking distance of Green Spring, Jamestown and Middle Plantation and he could plan his triumph as the protector of the people and determine how to manipulate the elections which, by his calculation, were only three days away.

Nat heard the jingle of a bridle and looked up to find Jamie Crewes at his side, grinning broadly as usual. "We're almost there, General. The river road is not half a mile ahead. Now it will be easy going. We can reach Green Spring, or even Jamestown, tonight."

Nat sighed in relief. "My God, I am glad to hear it! I've decided to rest at Green Spring where we can refresh ourselves before making a public appearance. We'll leave the savages there; they'll be safe enough in one of Berkeley's big barns until we decide their fate. Above all, Arnold should have news of the *Rebecca* and he will likely know how far advanced the elections at Middle Plantation are. How far do we have to go?"

"Oh, not five miles. We'll be there well before supper."

Not a mulberry tree was left in Sir William's orchard and Lady Frances' garden grew, not peonies, but canvas tents. The Governor's fences had been ripped down for firewood and his sheep and hogs slaughtered to feast Captain Arnold's men. Soldiers lounged on Green Spring's broad portico and the Berkeleys' delicate walnut chairs baked in the sun as Arnold and his staff sat at the top of the great staircase which rose from the drive to the front door, idling in the shade as they smoked the Governor's pipes and drank his cellar dry.

Suddenly Arnold leaped to his feet. "It's the General!" he cried. "Sound the parade!"

A youthful subaltern rushed into the house and emerged with a drum which he slung at his side by means of its broad green sash. Soon the sleepy afternoon was rent with a brisk rat-a-tat and men appeared from house, barn, lawn, garden and orchard, arranging their clothes and checking their weapons, as they formed their files in front of the mansion. General Bacon and Captain Crewes and fifteen miserable savages sandwiched between two troops of horse made their way up the gravel drive and halted to receive the smart salutes of Arnold's men and then spontaneous cheers as the Pamunkeys were discovered.

Captain Arnold descended the staircase, his heart thudding in his breast. This was the moment he had been dreading for a week.

"Welcome, General. It does my heart good to see you and ... what looks to be your whole force. Please come into the house. I'll order supper immediately."

"Thank you, Captain. We have been fortunate enough to return unscathed but for a few scratches and broken bones. With your permission Jamie – Captain Crewes – will look after our captives tonight. He'll lock them up in one of the barns and post the first guard, but then I'll ask you to guard them. Supper can wait. I should like to receive a report from you as soon as possible." Nat swung off his horse and handed the reins to one of Arnold's men. "Where is your office?"

"I use the Governor's room; it's just to the right after you enter the hall."

Nat thought back to the night of Lady Frances' ball. He had spent an unpleasant few hours in that room and he did not care to see it again. "Doesn't Sir William have a bedroom suite with a sitting room?"

"Oh, yes sir. It's up the stairs and all the way to the right ... forms the whole east wing. I've ... I'm afraid it's where I have been sleeping, but I'll have my things removed right away."

"There's no hurry, Captain Arnold. I'll meet you in the Governor's sitting room in fifteen minutes."

Nat ascended the staircase as Arnold dismissed his men and Jamie moved his cavalry and the Pamunkeys past the house and towards the outbuildings to find a suitable prison for the captives. *Speaking of prisons,* thought Nat, *was Chicheley still here?* He must ask. His heart beat fast. What was the news from the Eastern Shore? All else was insignificant.

Nat shed his coat and tossed it, and his sword, on the bench which stood at the foot of the Governor's bed. The bed was unmade, the sheets and counterpane tangled together as though wildcats had fought among them. Mud was tracked on the polished wood floors and on the Turkey carpet. Arnold's washbasin was still full of soapy water and black bristles coated the basin's sides, while the Captain's razors lay negligently on a walnut dresser, staining the dark glossy wood. Nat would have these things attended to in due course. He hoped that Arnold's mind was tidier than his bedroom and that the Captain would have some reliable intelligence. The Governor had placed a settee, some armchairs, and some low tables just under the south windows of his suite, and Nat sat here, idly leafing through a spill of documents which lay on one of the tables. Anthony Arnold might be a fighter, but he was no administrator.

A soft knock sounded at the door and a slave appeared with a tray of assorted liquors and crisp breads. Arnold appeared immediately behind him, seized the tray, told the boy to leave, and closed the door into the hall with his foot. He set the tray carefully before General Bacon, avoiding his gaze.

Nat pounced. "Well, Tony, the news must be bad. If it had been good you would have said something by now. What is the fate of the *Rebecca*?"

Arnold was relieved that his silence had betrayed him. "We've known for a week, sir. I would have sent a message but we did not know how to find you. Captain Carver sailed the ship to Arlington neatly enough. They anchored just off the Arlington plantation and Mister Bland opened negotiations with the Governor, the messengers rowing back and forth under a white flag, as it were. Within a couple of days they had arranged that Captain Carver, (whom the Governor knows well), would go ashore and dine with Sir William and try to win him over, convince him that his best course was to return quietly to England so that his case could be put in the hands of the King and the Privy Council. Carver was to harp on the size and strength of your army, how you held the entire Western Shore with the populace staunchly behind you, how the people accused the Governor of treason for abandoning them to the heathen ...generally make a strong case and frighten him into submission.

"Well, Carver went ashore with a good three quarters of your men, some one hundred and fifty or so. They camped outside Arlington while the good Captain and the Governor dined as planned, but instead of the Governor succumbing to Carver's blandishments and show of force, things went badly awry. Somehow Captain Larrimore got word to Sir William that Bland had only forty men on board and that the *Rebecca* could be taken easily if the Greens could reach the ship while Carver and his force were still tied up in negotiations. Colonel Philip Ludwell and a small force slipped out of a hidden creek in a longboat, or boats, and reached the *Rebecca* at midnight. When the boats reached the ship your men likely thought it was Carver returning from his feast, though that is speculation only. In any event, the Greens got on board, overwhelmed Bland and your men, freed Larrimore and his sailors from the hold, and took the *Rebecca* without spilling a drop of blood. Bland was clapped in irons ... is probably still in the *Rebecca's* hold where Larrimore had just been, such being the quirks of fate."

Nat had sat frozen and silent all through Arnold's tale. Finally he sighed hugely and spoke. "It is a disastrous result. No navy, no Carver, no Bland. There must have been a traitor among Carver's men ... how else could Larrimore have sent a message to the Governor?"

"It seems likely, sir," said Arnold meekly.

"But what has happened to Carver's force ... the men who went with him to Arlington?"

"Well, fortunately many of them escaped by going north and crossing over from Accomac to Gloucester. The Eastern Shore is wholly the Governor's, so their passages were made at the point of a gun or sword. It was they, of course, who brought us the news. We can't account for more than half of Carver's force, however, so we have to assume that the rest were taken prisoner or ..."

"Or what? Slaughtered?"

"Well, the men who made it back said that some of their mates were talking freely of changing sides, swearing allegiance to Berkeley."

Nat paled. Seventy or eighty of his soldiers thought so little of him and his cause that they broke their vows at the first sign of trouble? What did that say of the rest of his force, those on the Western Shore? Did this whole enterprise hang by a thread? Perhaps they needed to be sworn to a stronger oath.

"So Bland is in irons ... poor Giles, he's no stoic, he will take it very badly. Thank God we have Chicheley ... we do still have him, do we not?"

"Oh yes, sir. He's still in the little jail, but we let him out to exercise. He hasn't said a word ... quite a martyr, he is."

"Well, double his guard. Berkeley loves him dearly and I daresay will relinquish Bland to get him back. Where does this all leave us, Tony? How many ships do they have now?"

"Four, sir, and a great many sloops and small craft. And of course the *Rebecca* has sixteen guns ..."

"Then Berkeley is a formidable foe. If he plays his cards right ... I hardly like to think what he could do. Certainly take Jamestown, back."

The two men were silent, the drinks untouched. Arnold had not even sat down, but he did so now. Forgetting for a moment that Nat was his General, he reached out and touched his knee.

"There is something else, sir."

Nat groaned. "What?"

"It's Captain Carver ... they hanged him from one of Arlington's oaks the day after the feast. It seems he was a little overcome with wine and he fell asleep, only to wake up a prisoner. They didn't even shoot him like a soldier ... strung him up like a common criminal. They say that Berkeley served as witness, judge and jury and then watched the execution avidly."

Nat buried his face in his hands. He hardly knew William Carver, but had taken to the old man, who was full of tales of the sea. Now he dangled from an oak, the crows picking his bones. Had he even had a trial? If so, it must not have been much of one. But then Berkeley had belonged to the court of the first Charles Stuart; perhaps he had been taught the workings of the Star Chamber.

"I should like to be alone for a while, Tony. That is the Governor's dressing closet beyond the bedchamber, is it not? I'll bathe there – would you kindly send me up a hot bath? And find Jake and tell him to bring up my things. And do you suppose you could get me some fresh linen and have them put this room to rights? I'll be down to supper later and we'll discuss what to do next."

Nat supped with Arnold and Crewes in the Berkeleys' great dining hall, the three men huddled at one end of the massive mahogany table. They disdained the Governor's silver with its flamboyant design and pretentious coat of arms, and used the kitchen pewter instead. Nat ate nothing, but his Captains worked their way steadily through the sequence of dishes which the slaves handed Jake, who insisted on serving his General personally.

"I don't know whether I should go to Jamestown first, or Middle Plantation" mused Nat. "I must see how the preparations for the elections are going, but Berkeley could attack us at any moment ... I really must see Hansford first. That's it ... I'll see Tom tomorrow and then go on to Middle Plantation unless there is a pressing need to stay in the capital."

"Tom sends me a daily bulletin, sir. So far there is no word of Berkeley, and we have spies all along the coast, so we'll know when he sails."

"What can the old man be waiting for?"

"He must be gathering an army. He now has sufficient transports to bring a force of five or six hundred men."

"But what is taking so long? If he owns the Eastern Shore, they must be flocking to his colors."

"Well, the great men are his, but who knows about the common folk? If they leave their fields for a day it might spell ruin. Remember, the harvest is near."

Nat perked up. "You think his following is thin?"

"As it is here. The truth is, sir, that I believe that many Virginians ... how shall I put it? Blow with the wind. They are going to seek their own advantage ... measure things on a small scale, not as you and Berkeley see things. Just as some have fallen away from you, the Governor runs the same peril. I take it as a good sign that he did not act as soon as the *Rebecca* was once more his."

"I like your thinking, Tony. It sounds right. Well, I can be in Jamestown by midmorning. With luck, Tom will be able to paint a complete picture for me. Now, what have you heard from George?"

Arnold glanced at Crewes, but the big planter was working his way through a boiled fowl and was no help at all. "I hate to add to your gloom, General, but I trade messages with George every day, just as I do with Tom, and the word is that these elections are not going to happen. Whether the people are confused, or the Burgesses are frightened ... I don't know. Only a handful of delegates have shown up so far and they have all left, fearful of becoming caught in the crossfire of a civil war. You may have to send out another order or writ or whatever it is you do to have an election."

Nat stared in his wine cup and refilled it from a bottle of claret which Jake had just brought up from the Governor's cellar. "So there is a falling off there, too? Virginia is going to sit on the fence until they see which side to come down on, is that it? I own, it is most disappointing."

Arnold did not respond. He had brought his General nothing but bad tidings ... better leave him alone to digest the news. Crewes shoved his plate aside and wiped his face and hands extravagantly on one of Lady Frances' fine linen napkins.

"Men are men, wherever they may live, Nat. It'll look better in the morning. I'd put my money on Bacon's army any day. It will come right, you'll see."

"Ah, Jamie, what would I do without you? Your very presence chases the black dog away. You're right. Let's get a good night's sleep and see what Jamestown has to tell us tomorrow. Tony, thanks for everything. Have you found yourself a bedroom, now that I've dispossessed you?"

Laughter was finally heard at Green Spring on this day of gloom. "Oh yes, sir. Captain Crewes and I are going to share quarters. You'll find us in the west wing ... in Lady Frances' pink bedchamber!"

Jamie Crewes burst into a roar of laughter and the three men parted for the night.

Jamestown wore a peculiar aspect as General Bacon and Captain Crewes and twenty veterans of the Dragon Swamp trotted across the isthmus, the Back River at their left and the James at their right, primordial twins nibbling at the land bridge in a never ceasing effort to reduce the peninsula to a watery grave.

The palisade was derelict and untenanted and not a soul stirred as the little troop made its way towards the town, until they reached the pine forest. No sooner had they entered the dark aromatic grove when they heard the jingle of harness and the click of muskets and Captain Hansford's guard came at them from the right and the left, with menacing faces.

"It's the General!" called the leader of the guard as he quickly identified Nat and Jamie Crewes. "Welcome, sir! Captain Hansford will be overjoyed to see you."

"It's Digby, isn't it?" smiled Nat.

"Yes, sir," cried the man gladly, proud that General Bacon knew his name.

"Why did we not meet your men on the mainland or at the palisade? What if we had been Governor's men?"

Digby blushed. "You came on the very day that Captain Hansford called a muster. You'll find the whole force on the Statehouse green; he's reorganizing us to meet a naval attack. He posted us here, just in case ... and ... there you have it, you did catch us by surprise."

"Alright, Digby, fair enough. I'll soon find out what the Captain has in mind. But I suggest that you and your men position yourself at the palisade; everything is uncertain and we would look like sorry fools if Berkeley attacked us from the land rather than the river."

Two hours later Nat and Jamie Crewes were dining in the common room of *The Unicorn* which Hansford had made his headquarters. General Bacon sat at the head of the table with Dicken Lawrence and Captain Hansford to his right and William Drummond and Captain Crewes to his left. Clarissa plied the men with food and drink in the absence of Joanna Lawrence who had returned to her friends in Kecoughtan when Bacon's army had taken over her inn.

"So you hear that Berkeley has five ships and ten sloops? 'Tis more than Tony thought."

"Aye," admitted Hansford, who looked worn and discomfited. "If he raises the men he can ship five or six hundred, easily. That's why I decided to reduce the force here and place more men along the river to give us plenty of notice."

"Where do you think he will land?"

"That's the Devil of it ... we don't know. If we knew he was sailing for Jamestown, we could respond accordingly. But why should he not proceed up the York? He could disembark at your cousin's easily enough, and swoop down on us from the north, taking Middle Plantation and reclaiming Green Spring."

"Yes, but really, don't you think he'll come here? He must reclaim the capital ... it's symbolic, it will catch at the people's hearts ... I think you should prepare for an invasion here."

"It is your decision, General, but I've already sent half of the two hundred men you entrusted to me to guard the banks of the James and the York and it will take several days to call them back again."

"Well, you must do so. We have all the Dragon Swamp men to work with now, and that will help. I'll give Tony some fifty foot and fifty horse and George the same; Jamie will return to Middle Plantation with his hundred and my twenty fusileers. They will be responsible for guarding the rivers so that you can bring your men back here to protect Jamestown. I'd like you to send out the orders this afternoon."

Hansford's face was expressionless. "Yes, sir, it shall be done."

"That doesn't make sense, Nat," said Crewes, the only man present who could speak to the General so bluntly without repercussions. "If you really think Berkeley is sailing here with five hundred men, what does it matter if Tom has one hundred or two hundred ... either way it's not enough."

Nat flushed. "My mind is made up. I cannot leave Green Spring and Middle Plantation undefended." He rose from the table and the others stood as well. "I am going to catch a nap if Dicken can lend me a bed. Tom ... send out your orders."

"Yes, sir," answered Hansford as the men dispersed. It was true that with his naval force Berkeley could invade at will ... perhaps this was as good a plan as any.

Nat paced idly through Lady Frances' suite, now twitching aside a drapery to gaze at the late summer landscape, now eyeing the flattering portraits of her father, Thomas Culpeper, and her mother, Katherine St. Leger. The General thought that the Kentish couple bore the same peevish and haughty expression which distinguished their daughter, but perhaps it was his imagination. He was certainly not one to assess Lady Berkeley objectively. Nat peeked into the bedchamber and then quickly withdrew, wondering what he was doing. He had come here to find Tony Arnold; why did he linger when it was clear that his Captain was elsewhere? The truth was that for the past week he had been on pins and needles, unable to settle to anything. He was gnawed with uncertainty concerning the disposition of his forces. In essence, he had scattered them about the great neck of land which lay between the James and the York, with a slight concentration in favor of Jamestown, but was that wise? Perhaps they were so diluted that wherever Berkeley struck he would have the advantage. Really, what did he, Nat Bacon, know of warfare? He had somehow become a general in a civil war just because he had led a few men south to deal with the savages when

Errol Burland

nobody else had stepped forward to fill the void. If the people knew the truth of the Roanoke campaign they would quickly learn that he had stumbled to victory there through luck, not acumen. And now? Now it was a matter of rebellion ... and high treason. When, oh when, was Berkeley going to show his hand?

Nat turned in relief as Anthony Arnold strode through the door. "There you are, General."

"There *you* are, Tony. Wherever have you been?"

"Why, seeing to my men and my prisoners ... both the savages and the knight."

"Fair enough. Has Tom's messenger reported in yet? Is there anything new?"

"We've heard from both Middle Plantation and Jamestown, regular as clockwork. Nothing is new ... all is as it has been this past week. But Green Spring has produced a surprise!"

"What do you mean?"

"It was your Pamunkeys that turned the trick. They're in the Governor's hay and grain barn, as you know. Well, today I thought I would look the place over with particular care as the savages are kin to the Devil and doubtless have devised a dozen ways to escape since they've been here. Sure enough, I found a place at the back where they were burrowing under the hay, hoping eventually to breach the wall and catch my guards asleep, I daresay. Well, in making their tunnel they uncovered two canon, would you believe? For some reason the Governor had hidden them away ... can you think why?"

"Canon? Damn my blood, the old fox. He always swore that the King never gave him any arms ... We can ask Drummond, but my guess is that they were meant for the new Jamestown fort, the one that never got built. In all probability Berkeley did not want them on public display, a constant reminder of his failure to properly defend the colony. What is their condition?"

"I have no knowledge of great guns, but they look fit enough. There's a whole store of canon ball on the mainland, near Sandy Bay, you know. Do you think we could drag them to Jamestown and set them up to defend against the Governor's ships?"

"Two canon against thirty-two great guns, or more? The odds are hardly impressive, but it would not hurt to try. Certainly it will give the men something to do, put some heart into them. But we need Farlow for this task ... he's the only one who's ever touched such a thing."

Two days later saw Nat and George Farlow exchanging grins as Berkeley's fat brass canon were positioned where the isthmus met the mainland, one pointed at Sandy Bay and the other at the Back River. Each had a gun crew and each had successfully thrown six balls into the water, though

360

the distances of the shot varied wildly. The odds were slim that the metal mastiffs would be able to bite the Governor's army, but it was possible ... and the men loved them, were heartened by the deafening noise and the smell of gunpowder. Sometimes a battle turned on just such a small thing as this. Nat waved good-bye to Farlow at the crossroads and made his way back to Green Spring. Now he could do nothing but wait. The tide had just started to flow as he left the capital. Would this be the afternoon that the white wings of the Governor's fleet would appear in the east?

General Bacon and Captain Arnold sat down to an early supper in the Governor's dining hall. Nat had half a mind to invite Sir Henry Chicheley to join them and begin to set the stage for his exchange with Giles Bland, but he was still somewhat on edge from the morning's canon exercise and he decided to let the knight languish another day in Green Spring jail. Now that he had completed the disposition of his forces Nat felt somewhat more relaxed and he had a good appetite. They had roasted a side of beef yesterday and tonight the cook had provided a cold joint with a whole array of vegetables, hot and cold, and fresh baked bread. Jake stood at the sideboard uncorking red wine and white, pleased with his General's show of spirits. So far there had been nothing but bad news since they came to Green Spring ... perhaps the tide would turn today.

"What's that noise, Jake?" queried Nat as he downed his first glass of claret.

"Noise, sir? You have sharp ears ... there *are* some horsemen. I'll run and find out."

Before the boy had left the room Bacon and Arnold heard the great front doors of Green Spring slam against the walls and a hurricane of men swept down the hall.

"Berkeley?" gasped Arnold, seizing the swordbelt which he had just shed.

"Yes and no," cried William Drummond as he pounded into the dining hall, a haggard Lawrence at his heels and Hansford's cornsilk hair streaming behind them.

"What is it?" cried Nat.

"Berkeley's landed ... this very afternoon," Hansford choked out. "Somehow my warning system failed ... we were taken wholly by surprise. Oh, God! I fault myself." The young man started to sob.

"It's not your fault, Tommy," soothed Arnold. "We didn't have enough men posted ... how could you guard the whole James basin?"

Nat heard the jibe, but this was no time to riposte. It was true – he had reduced Hansford's warning system by ordering the youth to increase his Jamestown force, but who would ever know if this had made a difference? Five ships and ten sloops would outgun his army any way you looked at it.

"Have we lost any men?" asked Nat.

"Not that I saw or heard of," answered Lawrence cooly as Arnold took

Hansford to one side and supplied him with a glass of wine. "They overran *The Unicorn* as easy as kiss-your-hand. Thank God Joanna is in Kecoughtan. I myself escaped with only the shirt on my back ... had to ride bareback on the first nag that came to hand." His voice thickened. "The inn be damned ... my only concern is that I do not know what happened to Clarissa."

Nat looked at his friend with deep concern, but did not press the issue. It was not something which could be discussed in this company. He turned to Drummond.

"And you, Will? What of your family?"

"Sarah and the girls have been at the Blackwater property for weeks and Billy and Johnny know how to look after themselves, so I am not overly worried. But my house ... I wonder if it will survive? Sarah will die a thousand deaths if they torch her beloved home."

Hansford had composed himself and now he and Arnold approached Nat.

"What are your orders, sir?"

"How many of your men followed you here?"

"I cannot say, sir. Probably half. The other half may have gone to Middle Plantation or ... in truth, I am sure that many of them slipped into the woods and are on their way home."

"Well, a head count is your first order of business. We still have an hour of daylight. Go outside and pull your troops together. They'll have to stay here tonight ... they'll need food and a place to sleep. Tony, send a messenger forthwith to Farlow and Crewes. Word may have reached them already, but we cannot know that. Wait ... I must write them some orders. I want them to leave a small force at Middle Plantation, but they should bring most of their men to Paspahegh Field. They'll have to march tonight. Let's see. Some two hundred from Middle Plantation; another one hundred and fifty from Jamestown and Green Spring ... say three hundred and fifty. That's not bad. We'll muster at dawn at Paspahegh Field and decide our plan of defense ... or attack, as the case may be."

"Attack?" queried Drummond. "I fear the Governor outnumbers you, laddie."

"I doubt it," said Lawrence in a level tone. "It was a brave show of ships but I did not see nearly the force that they said Berkeley would bring. I suspect the Eastern Shore failed to provide him with what he had hoped for."

"Interesting," mused Nat. "Well, tomorrow will show us the truth of it."

Chapter 25

September 1676

The September morning dawned fair and the retreating sun shone mildly on Paspahegh Fields. Nat cupped his hand for Folly to lip his breakfast corn, and thought back to the June day when his army had first gathered here to march on the Governor and wrest the commission from his reluctant hand. Now the two foes faced one another again, but this time the stakes were higher: this was a duel to the death and the fate of Virginia itself was the prize.

General Bacon looked around, satisfied. Tom Hansford had regained his composure and was once more in charge of Bacon's cavalry, which was even now gathering about their leader, yellow ribbons dancing in the breeze like butterflies. Tony Arnold had shown his new-found maturity by volunteering to stay behind, moving back and forth between Green Spring and Middle Plantation, securing the prisoners and watching his General's back. Steady George Farlow had brought the men to order after the panic of Berkeley's arrival and now they looked like a proper army, grouped so orderly against the green lawn, each man with his orange badge and bright steel. And Jamie Crewes – stout Jamie – he would never change. Even now Nat could hear his great laugh as he exchanged some bawdy joke with Bacon's fusileers who flocked around him, a blood red band on every sleeve.

Nat glanced south, at Jamestown. Whatever the size of the Governor's force, not a man had stirred from behind the palisade, although Nat thought that he could discern some repairs to the fortifications. More likely than not Berkeley's marksmen were just behind the wooden fence, ready to strike. Bacon was surprised that the Governor had not moved one of his ships into Sandy Bay; a well-positioned three-master could give a devastating broadside to the isthmus. Well, it was only dawn. Doubtless the Governor would deploy his navy ... his strong suit ... later.

It was time for action. In a sense this had boiled down to a contest between the two men, between old blood and young. The last time Nat had faced Berkeley the Governor had offered him a duel, and he had refused. Now he would take up the challenge. He had decided to ride out, alone ... ride the whole length of the isthmus, taunt his foe like a knight of old. His men deserved it; they had borne much and seen little, so far. They needed to be inspired; they needed a champion. He wore body armor, (Farlow had insisted on it), but that was neither here nor there. If fate had engraved his name and today's date on a ball, then so be it. It was in the lap of the gods. Nat gave a fleeting thought to those who waited for him at Curles Neck and then put them out of his mind. He nodded at Jake and the boy rushed forward, cupping his hands. Nat thrust his left boot into the fleshy hoist and flew onto Folly's back like a bird as his whole army cheered. Jake tossed him a slouch hat, black with red and white plumes, and he set it on his curls, laughing. Gathering Folly's reins in his left hand, he waved his right and began a stately progress across the isthmus towards Jamestown.

Pitts huddled behind the palisade, pistol in hand. It was insane. He had no business here. If he had to choose between Berkeley and Bacon, it would be Bacon every time, though he would be hard put to it to say who was the most arrogant. He was not here as a soldier, but because he simply had to see this thing out. How could he tell his grandchildren that he had been in Jamestown on the most exciting day of its history if he did not look about him? *If* he lived to have grandchildren. Pitts heard a great hiss rise from the line of soldiers which stretched to his right, all the way to the Back River. A messenger had just arrived from town ... the men must have been given some orders. He nudged the fellow who stood next to him.

"What's happening?"

The youngster stared at him, obviously confused. "Berkeley's just ordered us not to shoot. Said we are not to make a martyr of General Bacon. What a fool. I'm going to get out of this ... this is not my fight."

"How are you going to leave? There's only one road out of town."

"Not when they're as many boats lying about as I have seen. I'll be over the river in an hour and back on the Eastern Shore in days. Will you come with me?"

"I live here ... I have nowhere to go. Better go now, while there are still boats. Good luck."

Nat slipped from Folly into Jamie's arms, the *huzzahs* of his men ringing in his ears.

"God is on your side, Nat. They didn't fire a shot. It is a sign."

"I hope you are right. Now, let's bring the battle to Berkeley."

Bacon strode to his tent and called for his captains and Drummond and Lawrence. It seemed that the Governor's bark was going to prove worse than his bite. They needed to attack before the Greens moved their

364

ships into a more advantageous position. Nat turned to the most experienced fighter.

"George, what do you suggest that we do now?"

"I am less concerned about the navy than I was before. My men have plumbed Back River and it is too low for any but the smallest craft to venture into; our little canon can dispatch anything they send that way, God willing. As for Sandy Bay, it would be a devilish proposition to position a ship there without our doing some damage, though it could be done. Perhaps they will try, but there is no sign of it yet. Now, why they did not fire on you from the palisade is a mystery. Are they setting some kind of trap? I suggest that we dig a French works in front of our great guns so that they cannot capture our canon with a sally. That done, the Governor will be nicely sewn up for as long as it takes us to determine his strategy."

"And how shall you do that?" asked Lawrence, who, with Drummond, had been admitted to General Bacon's council.

"Oh, spies of course. We'll send some men over tonight in canoes. By tomorrow we should know much more than we do now."

"And what is a French works?" asked the innkeeper, always eager to learn and never afraid to show his ignorance.

"Why, a big trench, of course, an *abatis*. We'll put brush and trees in front of it to give the men even more protection, and spike the trees against an attack by horse. Our gunners will shoot from the trench. The line of sight is perfect: they should be able to pick off the Governor's men and not suffer a scratch themselves."

"But will they not be killed as they dig the trench?" asked Drummond. "They didn't fire on Nat, but that does not mean that everybody will be safe."

"Why, the men will have to take their chances ... this is a war."

"Wait," said Nat. "I want to take as few casualties as possible. The men have given us a great deal ... if they see their friends dying, who knows how long they will remain loyal. Can this *abatis* wait until tomorrow?"

"Yes, but not longer."

"Then we'll bring the savages from Green Spring and put them between the trench and the palisade ... perhaps that will dissuade the enemy from shooting."

Farlow looked puzzled. "They are not going to scruple at killing savages ... I don't take your point."

"Look ... the Pamunkeys will remind them of how this all came to pass. *I* have slain and captured Indians while Berkeley has left his flock to the mercy of the wolves."

"You have a point, General. Do it if you like ... but bring them here this afternoon for I should like to start the trench no later than tomorrow at dawn, perhaps even tonight if the moon will shine for us."

A great clap of thunder rent the air and the men looked up, askance. Farlow groaned. "God in Heaven above, wouldn't you know that it would rain? Well, we'll just have to make the best of it. Let me know when your savages are here. We must press forward."

Nat drew his left foot up by main force and it came right out of his boot which remained enmired in Virginia mud.

"Jake ... get me out of this. The trench is all but finished ... I need a change of clothes."

"Indeed, sir, and a good rest too. Begging your pardon, but you should not have slaved away with the men ... I am sure you are running a fever and all this rain has not helped matters, though it has stopped them from shooting. Nobody can see more than five feet."

"Why, I've explained it a dozen times – I have to show the men that I am willing to do anything I ask them to do; it is only fair. Besides, the rain is letting up. See the blue sky?"

"Well sir, but you are born and bred a gentleman. I think you have pushed yourself too far. Come ... I'll find you a hot bath somehow and then you must rest this afternoon."

Leaning on Jake, Nat started towards his tent, but then turned to look at the *abatis*.

It stretched across the isthmus, ending just in front of the two canons. The bottom was filled with rocks to provide some primitive drainage, though the whole thing looked like a muck hole after three days of downpour. A dense pile of brush, saplings and tree limbs stretched in front of the trench on the Jamestown side, many of the stakes sharpened to wicked points. It was not much to look at, but Farlow assured Nat that it would more than repay the effort used to build it when Berkeley sent out a force against them, which surely he must. The clouds had finally cleared and the September sun burned hot on Paspahegh Field, but Nat shivered constantly. Jake was right ... he had caught some kind of fever; perhaps an afternoon in his tent would set him right.

Nat dozed fitfully, still gripped with ague. He had no appetite, but a raging thirst consumed him. Jake would not let him drink the water for fear it was contaminated, but the men raided the nearby plantations for cider and perry and wine and they kept him well supplied, made it a point of honor to provide General Bacon with what he needed. As always when he was unwell he thought of Lyn's cool hands. How he wished he were in his bed at Curles with his wife at his side and the river breeze on his cheek. When they had dispatched Berkeley – *if* they dispatched Berkeley – he would go home for a spell; nothing would stop him. Comforted by these thoughts, Nat drifted off to sleep and when he woke it was dusk.

"General, General!" called Jake, creeping into the tent. "Are you awake? The Governor sent out a sally and was beaten back! We have won the day!"

Nat sat up, dizzy with fever and stunned with the news. Farlow and Crewes pushed in behind Jake, grinning. "Jamie, George ... what has happened? Have I missed a battle?"

"Aye, but you were not needed, begging your pardon," answered Crewes. "The fusileers in that nasty trench took care of Berkeley's army ... and what an army! A few foot cowering in the van and a line of mangy horses, the riders looking as though they would rather be anywhere than here. Twelve dead and two captured, and not a scratch on our men!"

Nat looked at Farlow. "This is your victory, George. Your French works turned the trick. Congratulations."

Farlow's sunburned face turned darker yet with the compliment. "No thanks to me, General. It's what anyone would have done. But the best thing is that we have two captives, one black and one white, and they have given us something more precious than gold – news from the heart of Berkeley's camp."

Nat rose and adjusted his nightshirt as Jake threw a dressing gown over his shoulders.

"Sit down on those stools, gentlemen. Tell me what you found out."

"Well, the two men are from the Eastern Shore, the white one a servant and the black one a slave. They joined the Governor's army because they were promised their freedom and a piece of land here on the Western Shore when the rebellion was stamped out. Now they are wholly disillusioned, claim they were lied to. They say the army numbers only two hundred or so, and few of them are volunteers – the rest were either pressed or given false promises. The reason Berkeley has not used his ships is that the sailors refuse to fire on us, their countrymen. The camp is rife with dissension; many of the Governor's men have already slipped away and after today's debacle there may be a wholesale revolt."

Nat's head swam, but this time not from fever. He clasped Farlow and Crewes to his bosom and then dropped to his knees and offered a prayer of thanks. It was going to happen ... they were going to oust the Governor from Virginia ... the people were going to write their own destiny.

"And our men are safe? No one harmed?"

"Nary a one," boomed Crewes. "All we have to do now is take care of the true Greens – there are probably fifty men who will stand by the Governor to the end; they could still do some damage."

"We'll hold a council of war tomorrow. Tonight we celebrate. Jake, find Hansford and send to Green Spring for Tony Arnold. Oh, and find me some decent clothes. I want to speak to the men tonight, and I want my captains around me."

The day following the victory dawned bright and fair. Nat's fever had abated and he was out and about among his men, congratulating them on their efforts and urging them to be patient for a few more days when, with God's grace, the Governor's ships would sail east, never to return. Jamie Crewes had drawn the duty of foraging for provisions and he had just set off for Ballard's plantation, curious to know if the planter would remain true to the oath of loyalty he had sworn to General Bacon six weeks ago at Middle Plantation. If so, Crewes could likely garner all his provisions at Ballard's without casting a wider net; if Ballard could not be trusted, Nat would need to know that he should watch his back.

Crewes and twenty swift riders made their way through a forest which was now, in mid-September, touched with scarlet and gold. The summer's humidity seemed to have passed with the series of thunderstorms which had recently caused such misery and the riders were in tearing good spirits. Who knew? With a change in government, they might all find their names inscribed in Virginia's history book as heroes.

Within two hours Crewes' troop was pounding up Ballard's drive. The Captain noted that Nat's old acquaintance had not planted this year: his fields held only tobacco stubble from the previous season and rank weeds which were turning from green to brown as the summer gave way to autumn. Perhaps he had abandoned the place, situated as it was so close to Middle Plantation and Jamestown, a target for strife. However when the riders reached the wooden house wreathed by its circle of mighty oaks, they noted three curricles in the drive, and a small group of blood horses in a nearby pasture. Clearly someone was at home.

Captain Crewes mounted the steps with ten of his men, the others having remained in the drive, pistols at the ready, in case of trouble. He banged on the door with his fist and stepped back expecting a house slave to answer. Nothing happened. Crewes glanced around, but saw nothing. He pounded on the door again. There was no response. His men behind him, he shoved the door wide and heard it crash against the wall. He stepped into a central hall redolent with the scent of roses; fresh flowers stood everywhere, but not a soul appeared. He gestured five of his men to the left, into the parlor, while the rest followed him to the right, into the dining room. As he entered the elegant chamber with its silk clad walls and polished furniture a flurry of white met his eyes as though a flock of geese had taken flight. Astonishment was written equally on Jamie Crewes' strong features and on the soft faces of Betty Bacon, Alice Page, Tabitha Bray and Ann Ballard. There was a moment of complete silence and then Captain Crewes burst into one of his inimitable laughs.

"Ladies, ladies ... how do you do?"

Mistress Ballard straightened her shoulders and pursed her thin lips. "Who are you and what is the meaning of this?"

The rest of Crewes' men crowded in from across the hall and the ladies rustled their white aprons, for all the world like indignant geese.

Crewes sketched a rude bow. "Captain James Crewes, of General Bacon's army, at your service."

Three of the women turned towards Elizabeth Bacon and stared at her. "General Bacon?" cried Alice Page. "You mean the rebel?"

"Why, I would not call him a rebel ... rather, a patriot. But if you mean that he and Governor Berkeley are at daggers drawn, then you have got it right."

The women hissed and moved closer to one another.

"What do you want?"

"Why, I'm looking for one of General Bacon's staunchest allies, Mister Ballard. Is he home?"

Ann Ballard's friends stared at her when they heard the words 'staunch ally,' and she looked away. "No, there is nobody here but us. Tom had to leave on urgent business ... he rode off this morning at dawn."

Crewes smiled. "Urgent business, is it? Could that mean that he got a message last night to the effect that General Bacon won the day at Jamestown?"

Mistress Ballard sniffed. "I know nothing of that. I don't question my husband. He went north with six servants ... said he would be back in two weeks."

"And to what do I owe the honor of meeting all these lovely ladies?"

Alice Page looked down her nose at Crewes. "We meet once a month, have done for years. This month it was Ann's turn to play hostess. If we had known that the rebel was on the loose we would have stayed home."

Crewes smiled and stroked his beard. "Well, perhaps it is all for the best. I have a thought. How would you like to visit the Governor at Jamestown?"

"Whatever can you mean?" cried Elizabeth Bacon, who had been silent until now.

"Ah ... you shall know when General Bacon chooses to tell you. For now please ready yourselves for a journey. You all have a chaise, how charming. I'll have one of my stout fellows drive each of you, with a few outriders to keep you company, and we'll be at Paspahegh Field by tea time."

The women bristled, but an hour later they found themselves on the familiar road to Jamestown. Normally they made the trip full of plans for visiting and shopping, but this day they were wondering about their honor and their very lives.

General Bacon sat on his cot and Captain Crewes stood before him like an abashed child.

"How could you have done this to me, Jamie? My own cousin!"

"I am sorry she was there, Nat, but I could hardly let her go home and bring the others. That Page woman is a bitch ... I'm beginning to regret this whole escapade."

"Regret! Regret! We'll never live this down! Even as we speak the men are questioning my sanity, my honor."

"But Nat, how else are we to smoke out the gentry? Only one lucky canon ball has struck the palisade ... all the rest have missed, it's just too far. And our muskets are only good against men, not logs. If we are to send the Governor packing we must strip him of his supporters, both the high born and the low. The commoners are fleeing like rats but the gentry will stick with him ... it's a point of honor. If you parade the ladies on the isthmus together with the savages you'll send a double message: you've crushed the savages, once again; and should any dispute your authority, their wives will answer for it."

"But Jamie, we know that Ballard and my cousin are not in Jamestown, and I very much doubt that Page or Bray are either."

"That's of no consequence, Nat. Do you think for one minute that Berkeley or Ludwell or Beverley would allow any harm to come to those white aprons? Never in the world."

Nat sighed. "I suppose you are right. Tom and Tony seem to think yours is a good plan, and even George has said that it might turn the tide. What o'clock is it?"

"Going on for noon."

"Well, damn my blood, let's do it. You arrange for the savages to be put on display; I'll turn the ladies over to Tom Hansford. They'll swoon at his beauty."

"I'm so glad you see it my way, General. It shall be done inside an hour."

The sun was still strong on their backs as Nat and his captains rode east along the river road, a solicitous Jake on Blue watching his General with a careful eye.

"Now we'll see if those white aprons have turned the trick," said Nat hopefully. "Are you sure they have been sent home safely?"

"You have my word on it," Hansford answered. "I sent them away under the care of my nicest men. They are probably all home by now. What a diary entry they shall make today!"

Nat smiled wanly. He still felt ill ... the fever lingered, waiting to flare up again. Using the four gentle ladies as hostages sat badly with him. Still, not a shot had been fired since they, and the Pamunkeys, had walked on the isthmus and Jamestown was strangely quiet, as though struck by the plague. They could send spies over tonight, when dark fell, to see whether the ruse had worked, but with luck they would know much sooner. The tide was on the ebb and if the Governor had decided to abandon Jamestown, he and his five proud ships would be on the James now, visible from the river road, sailing east.

Jake had spurred Blue forward and now the five men saw him racing back, his slim body pressed to the roan's neck.

"They're leaving! They're leaving! Five great ships and twice that many sloops! Hoorah, we've done it!"

Nat tried to compose his face, but he could not. He, Nathaniel Bacon of Friston Hall, had just routed one of the King's Royal Governor's from his capital. He turned to look at his captains and, to a man, they threw their right fists in the air in salute and their cheers rent the skies.

"'Tis a fine victory, gentlemen. And all due to you."

"No, sir," said George Farlow. "You are the one who showed the men what a leader is. This is your victory."

Nat flushed with joy and the horsemen turned west to bring the glad tidings back to camp. Crewes guided his horse next to Folly and spoke softly. "*Now* you can go to Curles," he said. He had read his General's heart.

"And I shall, Jamie, as soon as ever I can. But I have one task before me."

"What is that?"

"Jamestown must burn."

Nat slept late in Lawrence's loft and woke to the sound of the ocean. For a long minute he kept his eyes closed, lost in memories. Was he at Hazelwood with the North Sea beating on the cliffs? Was he on the *Adam and Eve*, curled in his bunk with Lyn's hand on his brow? Was he at Curles with the muddy James at flood stage, gnawing at the bluff, with Lyn's step on the staircase as she brought him his breakfast on a tray? Wherever he was, Lyn was there. Nat opened his eyes and sat up. His wife was nowhere to be seen and his heart stopped beating.

Nat tossed his head and cleared his eyes. Of course ... yesterday the Governor had fled downriver and Bacon's army had poured into Jamestown and spent the night in celebration. His fever had returned and Lawrence had vacated his attic chamber and slept in Joanna's bed, since the mistress of *The Unicorn* was away in Kecoughtan. Yes, and Clarissa had been found. Gallant Clarissa, schooled in deceit, had remained in Jamestown, undetected, for the whole ten days that the Governor's force had occupied the capital, living from hand to mouth among the humble cottages where she had friends, and even venturing into the inn from time to time to save what she could of the Lawrences' valuables. The faithful woman had preserved two silver goblets from *The Unicorn's* impressive display of plate, but Berkeley had made off with the rest, laughing bitterly as he did so. Dicken's face never showed much of what he was thinking or feeling, but when Clarissa appeared he had showed everything. Nat wondered how it would all turn out for his friend ... Joanna would be a bitter enemy.

Nat rose and stretched. He felt better this morning. Why had he dreamed of the ocean? Ah, that was it: his men were out and about, roaming the streets of Jamestown, and their voices sounded through the capital in a steady roar which rose and fell periodically, like the surf.

There was a tapping at the door and Lawrence thrust his head into the room, smiling.

"Are you up, Nat? Feeling better?"

"Much better, Dicken. I love this room ... it is like a home to me."

"Excellent. Clarissa is right behind me with a breakfast tray. When you've had time to compose yourself they are waiting downstairs to hear your orders."

"Who is there?"

"Everyone. Crewes, Hansford, Arnold, Farlow. Your boy Jake and Will Drummond and Billy and Johnny. They want to see what comes next, after that cryptic remark you dropped yesterday."

"Very well. Give me time to put myself to rights and the mystery will be revealed."

An hour later General Bacon, in black breeches and white shirt, appeared below. Jake and the Drummond boys had fashioned a ball from some rags which Clarissa had given them and were playing catch in the yard. Crewes was working on his third pot of ale and the other three captains were using cups and saucers to work out some kind of military maneuver on the trestle table. Drummond and Lawrence had disappeared into the little room which Nat always thought of as "Clarissa's." Whatever they were discussing, he would likely know soon.

"Good morning, gentlemen. Or rather, good afternoon, for the sun is high. Let's let the boys play outside, but we'll need Drummond and Lawrence. Jamie, you look hungry. Shall I ask Clarissa to begin preparing a meal?"

"If you would, sir. I'll call the other gentlemen."

With his advisors around him, Nat laid out his plan. He reasoned as follows. Though Berkeley's first sally to the Western Shore had been a disaster, with his five ships and countless small craft, he still owned the Bay and the rivers, and doubtless he would be back soon, more relentless than ever after his defeat. Bacon's army could not continue to hold Jamestown ... it was too much of a drain on their resources. They needed to bring the fight to the Eastern Shore, complete the job that Captain Carver and Giles Bland had so signally failed. Nat and his closest allies were now irretrievably tarred with the brush of treason. The only way they could survive this civil war was to send the Governor back to London with a brief charging him and his Greens with a complete dereliction of duty. If the case ever got to Whitehall, they would prevail.

"A governor has been ousted before," muttered Lawrence.

"You speak of Governor Harvey," said Drummond. "We've had this conversation many times, Dicken. Those were different times with a different sovereign. Besides ... Harvey came back."

"Yes, but to no avail. In my view, the Council prevailed."

"There are few parallels. Berkeley has ruled here for years and he has friends in high places. Who knows how the King will view things? But it is the only possible course. Ultimately London will decide these issues, and it is better to arrive there with the Greens in irons than ourselves. If we do not do as Nat says we will see an English fleet sailing between the capes and will be looking down the muzzles of English guns. We have an army, and a good one. Now we must raise enough of a navy to get our army across the Bay while the Governor is still smarting from his wounds."

There was a chorus of approval; all were in agreement.

"And what steps shall we take to achieve this goal?" asked practical George Farlow.

"I plan to be in Gloucester in two weeks. I will swear the men there to fealty and then I will form a navy. It is there, if anywhere, that we are going to find enough boats to get us across to Accomac. While we're in Gloucester I'll send a proclamation across the Bay to discourage the citizens of the Eastern Shore from following the Governor. But before I do that, there are some critical tasks before us.

"Tom, I want you to review your cavalry and make sure it is fit and strong and loyal. Then use your discretion and let as many of the men go home for a few days as you think reasonable. We'll continue to use Middle Plantation as our headquarters until we move to Gloucester, so put that in your planning.

"George and Jamie, I would like you to follow suit with your men. Assess who is hot for us, who is merely lukewarm and who, perhaps, is cold and will break his oath and cross over to Berkeley. Reward the men with leave as you see fit. Make yourselves comfortable at Middle Plantation, whether at Thorpe's or elsewhere.

"Tony, you have proved yourself at Green Spring, so I'll ask you to continue there for a while. Keep guarding Chicheley ... he's a key player in this game of chess. You might want to move him to the main house, I leave that up to you. As for the Pamunkeys, they are back in that barn are they not?"

"Yes, sir. If they haven't escaped. It's the devil's own work to keep them penned up."

"Well, stop trying. I think their teeth are drawn. Let the women and those men who seem harmless go. Keep only the dangerous ones in custody. Byrd and John Grey send me regular bulletins and they say that the frontier is quiet. God willing, we have put the Indian menace to rest."

"Amen," underscored Crewes as he finished his ale.

"Ah, here's Clarissa with a feast fit for the gods. Go ahead ... I've just had breakfast. I'll talk while you eat."

All but Nat had risen at dawn or had not slept at all, so the company set to with a keen appetite. Nat drank deeply of Lawrence's Rhenish and wondered how many bottles still lay in the cellar ... there would be none after tonight. Nat let a quarter of an hour pass and then he continued.

"Now for it. In my estimation, as the capital, Jamestown will always draw Berkeley. If we leave it standing, he will be back here as soon as he has persuaded a few miserable wretches to join his army. The town has a huge symbolic significance. It must vanish. I know you don't want to hear this, but I am going to raze Jamestown as surely as the Grecians razed Ilium. Tonight it will burn."

Bacon's captains glanced at one another with more interest than dismay. The General had sketched out his plan yesterday; now he was only confirming it. But what of Drummond and Lawrence? Jamestown was their home. Each had a fine house, full of memories. True, Drummond had plantations in Westmoreland County and on the Blackwater, but no place meant as much to him as the fine brick house which looked out upon the broad James. As for Lawrence, the destruction of *The Unicorn* would mean the destruction of his livelihood, his entire life. He would have to start anew, with almost nothing. And what of Joanna? The inn was hers. What would she do when it was gone? Would Nat's oldest friends make the sacrifice?

"Tell me when, Nat," said Lawrence calmly. "Clarissa is safe and it is all I care about." He laughed. "Berkeley took all my silver ... what do I have left, anyway? But here, let me draw another cork. If we don't finish the wine it will perish, and that would be a hanging offense."

Nat looked his appreciation at the innkeeper. "It is a terrible decision, Dicken. I think of your attic chamber as my own. In a sense, it all started there. And then there is your wife ... but stop. If you are willing to make the sacrifice, why should I make it harder for you?"

Nat glanced at Drummond who had walked to the casement and was looking out on Back Street. The big Scot turned and all could see that his eyes glistened with tears. "It will go hard with Sarah," he admitted, "but I hope that the Drummond family is up to the task."

"My heart grieves for you, Will. I am truly sorry."

"It's part of life, laddie. I'm responsible for all this, in a sense. We can bear the burden. Who knows, by the time I get to the Blackwater Sarah will have organized the whole county and she'll probably never want to leave!"

"Spoken like a man, Will. So ... there you have it. Tony, Tom, George, Jamie ... begin moving your men out as soon as you have dined. Jamie, tell my fusileers to report to me here. They'll be in charge of arranging for the townspeople to leave and then they'll help us fire the town. Will and Dicken and I will direct the conflagration. We start at dusk."

The sky was velvet and the moon on the wane. Jamestown lay quiet, holding its breath. A poorwill cried from the fields behind Drummond's house and Nat thought of Lyn. God willing at this very moment she was kissing Mary good night, moving into the parlor to read or sew. She did not need to know what he was about to do.

The clock in *The Unicorn's* common room chimed eight. It was time. Nat strode from the inn and walked steadily down Back Street towards Drummond's. As he walked strange lights flickered fitfully from the humble cottages which lined the road. There! A thatch roof burst into flame, showering the yard with sparks. A sapling had caught ... no, perhaps it was too green to burn. And there! Another cottage went up in flames. The thick glass casements popped with heat and the windows looked like they were weeping. His fusileers had done well ... every hut in Jamestown was aflame.

Nat reached Drummond's. His friend was standing in the street, hands on hips, staring at his brick house. He turned at the sound of Nat's footsteps. "Any minute now, laddie. I just put the match to it. Ahhhh ... see in Sarah's parlor ... and my library ... come. I cannot bear it."

Nat and Drummond returned down Back Street, their faces bright from the flames which soared around them. As they reached *The Unicorn* a great oak burst into flame, and then another. Nat wondered whether the pine forest would burn, or whether it was far enough away to survive.

"Now I'm for the Statehouse, laddie. I won't cry tears there, I assure you."

"Did I give you enough time to save the records?"

"That fellow Pitts and I stored as many as we could find in his jail, of all places. Even if the houses fall in upon themselves when the timbers burn, they may survive in that dank cellar. It was the best I could do. Someone, someday will need the documents."

"It was well thought of, Will. Now off you go. My fusileers should have finished their tasks and you will find them on the green. They have been instructed to help you. Good luck."

"And we're to meet at Green Spring?"

"We should all be there by midnight. Take care."

Nat watched Drummond's back recede into the night and then he turned and reentered the inn. "Are you there, Dicken?"

"Up here, Nat. Saying goodbye to my snuggery. I had a nice little library, didn't I? Well, one can always buy books."

Nat pounded up the stairs; Lawrence had just closed the door to his chamber.

"Did you get Clarissa off?"

"Yes, she crossed to Swann's Point this afternoon and from there she'll go to the Drummonds at the Blackwater plantation. I have no fear for her – the woman is a lioness."

"She is indeed. Did she take the silver cups?"

Lawrence laughed long and loud. "Indeed she did. One for her and one for me. We'll do well enough, whatever happens. Now, Nat, it is time, is it not?"

"If fear so, Dicken. It breaks my heart. *The Unicorn* is almost as much my home as Curles."

"It is time to wipe the slate clean. The whole colony is breaking up ... I should look at it as an opportunity. I have only one thing to do and then I will light the fatal match."

"What is that one thing?"

"Just to say good-bye to Clarissa's room. It has been my Eden. But come, you must hurry to the church. You have saved the greatest and most terrible feat for yourself, and you must start soon."

"I own that I have been avoiding it. The houses of men are one thing, but the house of God is another."

The two men walked downstairs and crossed the common room to the little bedchamber where Lyn had slept on her first night in Virginia. The door hung open and the room was empty of all but bare furniture. Skeptical Richard Lawrence fell to his knees beside the bed and raised his hands in silent prayer. Seconds later Nat joined him. If there were a God, he begged forgiveness for what he was about to do.

Lawrence rose to his feet, expressionless. "Enough, Nat," he said. "Go to the church. Though it may not seem so, we are doing God's work."

"Good bye, Dicken. We meet at Green Spring at midnight." Nat turned and walked into the night.

The stout brick tower rose high above him, strange shadows flickering on its rosy walls. Earlier in the day his men had made all ready. The pews had been reduced to kindling and straw had been heaped along every wall. Nat walked the length of the aisle and knelt before the altar. A simple wooden cross stood on a length of snowy linen and someone had placed bowls of late roses on either side of it. Nat thought that he could smell the roses even through the acrid smoke which now covered all of Jamestown. His heart misgave him. Could he bring himself to commit this sacrilege? Yet the church was the heart of the capital; if he left it standing the town would grow again. All must be destroyed, root and branch. He rose and walked to the baptismal font where he found a flask of oil on a small shelf. Taking the bottle, he returned to the altar and knelt once again. Straw had been heaped around the holy table. All was ready. Nat unstopped the flask and poured the oil on the straw, his throat thick with tension and grief. When there was no more oil he tossed the flask to one side and pulled a flint from his pouch. The whole night was on fire. He struck a spark and the straw caught, greedily. The flames flared up and caught the linen altar cloth and then the cross began to burn. Tears blinding him, Nat turned and ran through the holy building as though the devil were at his heels. When he reached the lawn he turned once to see what he had wrought. He thought that Hell must look like that. Folly was tethered nearby, lathered from fear. Nat threw himself on the great black horse and fled from Jamestown.

CHAPTER 26

SEPTEMBER - OCTOBER 1676

Dusk was falling as Nat and Jake left the trace and, at last, entered the long drive that would take them home. The wind had died and the fields of Curles Neck lay still and peaceful in the soft evening light. Nat had sent home word of his victory at Jamestown, but he had not said that he would follow hard on the heels of the messenger. Would his carelessness make his arrival too great a surprise? The drive curved to the right and Nat saw the copse which protected the summer house from the road and then, outlined against the western sky, his home. Two figures stood on the edge of the bluff, their backs to him, contemplating the river: Lyn and John. Nat's heart turned over and he urged Folly forward, heedless of Jake, heedless of all the world. Lyn turned before John and seconds later she was in his arms.

Mignon looked half Folly's size as the two horses stood idly in the woods nibbling what remained of the summer grass. The gray tossed her head impatiently. It had been a full two hours since she had been abandoned here to shift for herself. Folly was inured to care and he hardly stirred except to rid himself of the biting flies by twitching his sable hide.

Nat and Lyn sat on the rocky promontory under the maple which now blazed scarlet and gold. Nat played with a branch and smiled.

"What is it, love?" asked Lyn softly.

"'Tis the colors. See the green? That's Berkeley. And see how it is succumbing to the red and the gold? That's us. Just as this branch will be wholly crimson within the month, so shall Virginia be ours by October's end."

Lyn leaned against her husband and closed her eyes. "And why is it your fate to make this so?"

"Have you heard nothing I have said this past week? I have some skill, some gift which pushes men to do what they otherwise would never do. Farlow calls it leadership. *I* don't know. It is just that ... finally I have found a place where I *fit*. Does that make sense?"

"Oh, indeed it does Nat, but it breaks my heart. Why is it that you do not fit best here, in my arms? It is all I ask of God."

"I don't know, Lyn, but it is so. We shall have to make the best of the puzzle of our lives, make the pieces fit somehow. Do you think we can do it?"

"We can but try."

Nat held his wife close and turned her face to his and kissed her long and hard. "Now show me how we fit together, sweet. For tomorrow I am off to Bacon's Quarter with John, and then to Gloucester. God knows when we shall be together again."

The day after they had arrived at Curles Neck Nat had sent Jake home, to Byrd's, to visit his mother. With the frontier pacified, Mary Byrd and her little boy had returned home and Byrd's life had resumed its usual course. Of all the English, only he and AbrahamWood kept the trust of some of the savages, and their fur trading flourished even as Virginia lay suffering under the twin blows of an Indian war and a civil war.

Now Nat's treasured week with Lyn had come to an end and his thoughts moved to the Gloucester campaign. First, however, he was going to spend some time with John. The friends were going to ride to Bacon's Quarter and, once there, decide the future of the little farm. Nat had confided to Lyn that, when things were settled with Berkeley and he had returned to Curles, he intended to deed the plantation to John, entice him to stay in Virginia, but he said nothing of this to Grey; much could happen to thwart that happy plan. For now, they were going to enjoy the beauty of a perfect autumn day as they rode west and, on the morrow, collect Jake who would cross the river to join them, and perhaps, with luck, visit Goode at Whitby. With Jake in hand and their business at Bacon's Quarter done, they would return to Curles for one last night and then Nat and the boy would set out for Middle Plantation where the army awaited them, and finally move on to Gloucester to weave and cast the net that would capture the Governor.

Nat sat on Folly in the yard of the brick house, talking with Lyn and waiting for John to collect his things from the wooden house and mount Coke. Grey finally came, apologizing for the slight delay, and swung his pack onto the red horse which danced with anticipation.

"Ready, John?" cried Nat as he turned Folly towards the drive.

"Right as rain, Nat," answered the attorney.

Lyn watched them disappear down the road and returned to the house, pierced with sadness. She would see her husband again in two days, but after that the future was dark to her and she could not read the pattern.

Summer's torpor had fled and the autumn day sparkled as Nat and John traced the familiar road to Bacon's Quarter. They were in no hurry and they rode companionably, side by side, letting their conversation take its own course like the river which lay to their left. Nat heard John's report concerning Curles Neck, its slaves, its servants and its beasts, and he laughed at his friend's endearing stories about Mary who now chattered constantly and ran about like a spring lamb. Nonetheless it was clear to Nat that John touched only the surface of life and revealed nothing of his own hopes and dreams, did not indicate one way or another whether he planned to return to England.

For his part, John quizzed Nat intensely about the burning of Jamestown and the proposed Gloucester campaign. The attorney told his friend that razing the capital had sealed his fate: England would now count him a rebel and, whatever happened to Berkeley, Nat would be a marked man. Nat did not argue, but calmly agreed. Of the two, it was John who was by far the most distressed.

"I can but try and persuade the King that I have acted in his interests," Nat said briefly. "If my argument fails, so be it. This is a big country. Dying a traitor's death is not a foregone conclusion."

John did not challenge Nat's last enigmatic statement. He would reserve his most exacting cross-examination and his most impassioned pleading for a later time.

The sun was setting as the riders crested a ridge and saw Bacon's Quarter before them. They had expected to find the plantation desolate, but instead saw immediately that some unknown hand had, at a minimum, tended John's cabin and the surrounding yard. Curious, they pressed forward. If an enterprising trespasser had already put his mark on Nat's farm, they must dislodge him and send him on his way. When they reached the south-facing front porch of the cabin they noted that it was neatly swept and that a good supply of firewood had been stacked on either side of the door. Nat slipped his pistols from their saddle holsters and, keeping one for himself, handed the other one to John.

"Do you have knife?" he whispered as they mounted the steps and approached the front door.

"Always," replied John beneath his breath.

With a strong thrust, Nat pushed the door open and it swung wide, revealing the one-room dwelling. There was no one inside, but the simple furniture showed signs of care, John's rag rug was spotless, and various bottles of spirits and boxes of foodstuffs stood on the shelves as though they had been placed there that day. The friends walked inside and John examined his things carefully, but there was nothing out of place. While he was looking, Nat climbed the steep ladder-stair to the sleeping loft and determined that it too was empty and it too was immaculately clean.

"I wonder if Lyn wanted to surprise us and sent someone ahead to ready the place?" wondered Nat.

"It would be like her, but I can account for every man, woman and child at Curles and I would be most surprised if one of them had been absent for a couple of days, and I not know it," replied John.

"Well, in any event, it is most welcome. We won't have to do a thing but shoot a turkey for the pot to be completely comfortable tonight," said Nat cheerfully.

"Yes, but it's still odd. We had better keep our eyes open. It was not a good fairy who made these preparations. Why don't you see what is in those parcels and I'll put the horses in the barn, if there is hay, or in the pasture if there is enough grass. I hope my fences are still intact, otherwise we'll have to tether them."

"Keep my pistol handy. Who knows what may be lurking in the out-buildings."

John led Folly and Coke to the barn, his nerves on edge. Neither of the horses gave any indication of alarm and he felt somewhat easier as he entered the building which was redolent of sweet-smelling hay.

"Sure enough, Coke," he said to his horse. "The stalls have been cleaned and there is hay enough for six beasts. You two are as lucky as Nat and I."

"Had I been a savage, you would have been a dead man," said a voice from the loft and John Goode descended the ladder, smiling, as Grey brought his heartbeat back to normal.

"Goode, you *were* almost the death of me. Don't do that again, ever."

"You city folk ... you're easy prey. Welcome home, John. It's good to see you."

"And you. How neighborly of you to have looked after the Quarter. Nat will want to thank you ... he's in the cabin."

"Well, I've finished here. I'll help you put the horses up and then we'll go see Nat. What a hero he is! Between us, I never would have expected it."

"Did you know that we were coming?"

"Of course I did. That boy, Jake, told me that he's to meet you here tomorrow, so of course I knew you would arrive today and spend the night. My horse is in the far pasture where there is more grass – that's why you didn't winkle me out. I have been keeping my eye on the plantation since January, when you left. A few vagabonds have tried to make the place their own, but I scared them off. I've kept things in decent repair. It won't take long to bring it back again. I hope that is in General Bacon's plans."

"You will have to ask him. There ... the horses are comfortable. Let's find Nat – won't he be surprised!"

Two hours later, having supped well, Nat and John and Goode sat by a fire which was most welcome now that the nights were chill. After thanking the old planter profusely for looking after Bacon's Quarter, Nat regaled him with tales of the Occaneechee campaign, the foray into the Dragon Swamp, and Berkeley's defeat at Jamestown. Goode said little, but looked at Bacon intently.

"And what shall you do now?" he asked.

Nat glanced at John's sad face and told the master of Whitby his plans to take the fight to Gloucester County, raise additional men, and assemble some kind of transport to take the army across the Bay to Accomac and bring Berkeley down.

"'Tis treason, General Bacon," said Goode bluntly.

"I know it well, Goode. And if I did not, John would remind me of it every hour on the hour. I can only say that it is my fate ... whatever happens happens. The people deserve to have their voice heard."

"They do, sir, they do. But at what cost?"

"My life is a grain of sand when you consider what is balanced in these scales," replied Nat calmly. "My mind is made up. I am easy."

"And if the Governor has sent to the King for troops and arms?"

"I would be amazed if he has not."

"And do you not think that the great men will declare for the King when the redcoats land?"

"Some will. But many will stay with me, as sure as the sun rises. I shall swear them to a great oath in Gloucester, an oath which encompasses opposing the King. Other princes have lost their dominions ... why not the second Charles Stuart? And if we should not prevail, why there are lands to the south where the rivers run like crystal and one could vanish in the wilderness and be, oneself, a king."

"I fear for you. I would not put my hand to the promoting of such a design."

"Every man must decide for himself, Goode. Your youth was filled with turmoil ... perhaps it is now time for you to rest. But I must go forward."

"Then God bless you, General Bacon. It is time for me to take my leave. I pray that I see you again."

"And I, you, Goode. Good night. Ride carefully, for the moon is but a sliver."

The next day dawned as fair as the last and noon brought Jake and, to Nat's pleasure, Byrd.

"Didn't you trust Jake to find his own way? He's a man now ... he could lead an army."

"I know it. I'm most impressed, as is his mother. No, I am not here as Jake's shepherd – I want to make you an offer."

"Oh? Any offer of yours is sure to be interesting."

"Well, this one might be. Jake told me as much as he knew of your plans for Gloucester. If you are willing, I should like to hear more. If I hear what I expect I should like to offer you my sword or, to put it less dramatically, my services. My family is safe and my business is in good train. Abraham Wood has offered to come up from Fort Henry and tend my trading post for as long as I need him. It is time to bolster my words with actions. Can you use me in Gloucester?"

Nat was surprised and deeply gratified at Byrd's offer. He thought highly of the trader's intelligence and judgment; to have him by his side over the next month or two would be a coup.

"Need you ask, Byrd? I can use you in a thousand ways. One comes to mind immediately. Jamie and my other captains are quartered at Middle Plantation and Green Spring keeping the men in order and patrolling the rivers for any signs of the Governor. I have sent nobody to Gloucester to prepare my headquarters. In truth, I am ignorant of the county and I have not even thought where to settle. The only place I know is Tindall's Point – is the fort fit for habitation?"

"From what I have heard the fort is not fit for a dog. There is only one place in Gloucester for you – Warner Hall."

"Augustine Warner's place? Why, he's as Green as they come."

"Then it will be doubly beneficial to seize his plantation. They'll be one fewer Berkeley supporter and you shall have headquarters fit for a prince."

"Would you do this for me, Byrd?"

"This and many other things, Nat. You have proved your worth. Remember, I have spies everywhere. Do not think that Henrico is insensible of what you have accomplished this summer."

"Then I shall write some orders and have you report to Jamie at Middle Plantation. He will give you the men you need to get the job done. Are you returning home first?"

"I came prepared to leave from here. I can be off this very afternoon."

"Not without me," said a third voice.

Startled, Nat looked at John who had been sitting idly by, whittling sticks to pass the time.

"What are you talking about, John?"

"Like Byrd, I am tired of sitting on my hands. Ever since we came here, Nat, I've done your bidding: cared for Bacon's Quarter, kept Lyn and Mary safe, tended Curles as though it were a lady's bower. Now I want something for myself. We've differed strongly over the past year, but the lines have been drawn and there is only one course now for a right thinking man: to bring the Governor to justice and convince the King to replace him with a man of our choosing."

Nat was silent. It was one thing to risk his own life, but never John's. What if they both should perish? What would Lyn do then? He looked at his friend's face and saw that in this John would have his way. The conversation was conducted without words. He nodded. Grey was right. All kindred spirits should gather together now for the last push. Some would survive, and some would not.

"I am overwhelmed. Overwhelmed by both of you. You honor me; I don't have the words for it. Very well then, I'll write my orders for the two of you. Shall you go together?"

Byrd and Grey looked at one another and both nodded "yes" simultaneously.

"And indeed, why not? And let it be now. We'll sleep at Curles tonight and break the news to Lyn tomorrow. Jake! Jake! Where are you? We're off to war!"

When Nat and Jake arrived at Middle Plantation on the tenth of October it was with a sense of disappointment, even foreboding. They had first stopped at Green Spring to review Arnold's troops and consider Sir Henry Chicheley's situation. Nat expected the plantation to be in good order and the men to be sharp and anxious to proceed to Gloucester. Instead they found an anxious Arnold whose days were filled with dissension and challenges to his authority. At one point, the young captain said, he had been ready to leave it all behind and return to his father's little farm and let Virginia's future take care of itself, but Tom Hansford had talked him out of it.

As for Chicheley, the old knight had been given a chamber in the Governor's mansion. He thanked Arnold for that favor, but otherwise he said not a word, passing his days playing cards against himself and reading the Bible. The heart of the matter, confided Arnold, was that the men longed to be home for the harvest, but more ... they were convinced that the redcoats were on the way and in each mind lurked the fear of being branded a traitor to King and country and dying an ugly death.

"Then we shall have to press forward without delay," cried General Bacon. "Choose a detail to remain guarding Green Spring and Chicheley and let's be off to Middle Plantation. I shall swear all the men to a great oath ... we can only succeed if we are united, heart and mind."

The next day saw Bacon's army muster at Middle Plantation. Farlow, Crewes and Hansford reported the same unrest that Arnold had related. The rumor was rife that Lady Frances Berkeley had reached England and caused the King to raise a force to put down the Virginia rebels. Although the men had been told time and time again that the Governor's wife had left Jamestown before the June Assembly and therefore could report nothing more alarming than General Bacon's disobedience in pursuing the Occaneechee campaign without authority, those arguments were bootless. The army "was sure" that Lady Frances would arrange to send English ships coursing across the Atlantic like so many deer hounds and nothing would shake its conviction. Nat decided to gather the men immediately and swear them to a new oath. If he did not bind them quickly he would lose them.

On the twelfth of October he called a general muster in Otho Thorpe's fields. The sky was a brilliant blue and the forest blazed with Bacon's colors: yellow and gold and orange and scarlet. Nat sat on his great black horse in the middle of the field, the army, now numbering about four hundred men, gathered about him in quadrants, each with its own captain at the alert. General Bacon decided to keep his remarks brief and to the point. More than anything the men needed action; the more time they had to think the more perilous his cause would be.

"Virginians!" he cried. "We are about to embark on our last and most perilous campaign. No one wishes to be home with his dear ones more than I, but duty calls. We have one opportunity, and one opportunity only, to bring down the Governor. Governor? Why do I honor him with that title? He has betrayed his office and is not deserving of the title."

The first cheers rose from the ranks.

"When the ships arrive from England, as we know they must," (groans), "we must have Berkeley in irons, ready to be sent home for trial." (Cheers.) "We can do this in two weeks. Are you with me?" (Loud cheers.) "Those who are not should leave now! Show me your backs!" (Muttering.) "If I do not see them I shall know you are with me." (Tumultuous cheers.)

"Ahh! I see no man's back. It is a good sign. Come then, take the oath which your captains are about to give you and then, brave hearts, follow me to Gloucester!" (Wild cheers.)

Within ten minutes Bacon's army bound itself to follow their General, come what may; never to betray his secrets; and to fight his foes, up to and including King Charles' redcoats.

Within an hour the march to Gloucester had begun.

Warner Hall stood proudly on its broad lawns, a great drive sweeping from the north and the gentle Severn gracing the aspect to the south. General Bacon thundered down the drive, Jake at his side and his army marching smartly behind him. The Hall reminded him of his own new house and, indeed, it had been built at the same time. The two-storied building shone rosy in the October sun and his heart smote him as he thought of Curles. The plantation's owner, Augustine Warner, Junior, was Nat's contemporary and was as highly bred. But similarities in age, family, education and property did not necessarily make a friendship: Nat and Warner had met on several occasions and each had developed an aversion to the other. Nat thought Warner prim and rule-bound; Warner knew Nat to be overbearing and atheistical. To the extent that the two men had rubbed shoulders, they agreed to disagree.

Now General Bacon was going to seize his acquaintance's home. Had John and Byrd succeeded in ousting Warner and his new bride, or would there be a struggle? He had the answer before Folly reached the mansion's front door: John's fair head appeared in an upper casement and a broad swathe of crimson was unrolled until, almost, it reached the ground. Warner Hall was under Bacon colors; young Augustine must have decamped.

"John! How good to see you!"

Grey saluted playfully and left the window embrasure. A minute later he and William Byrd opened the front door and bowed exaggeratedly as Nat slipped from Folly and handed Jake the reins.

"Please enter your headquarters, General Bacon. We expected you on the twelfth. You are two days late, but it gave us time to polish the silver and change the linen. We trust that you will find everything to your liking."

Nat grinned at his friends' nonsense and walked into the house, hugging each of them to him in greeting. As he closed the door he called to Jake.

"Jake, stable the horses and then find me inside, wherever I am. The captains know where to camp: Hansford to the southeast, on the river, so the horses have water; Crewes to the southwest; Farlow to the northwest; and Arnold to the northeast. Tell them to report to me when they have settled the men."

"Yes, sir," called the boy and rode off smartly on Blue, Folly marching obediently behind.

"Now you two," cried Nat. "What wonders have you worked? This is a glorious place. I am almost jealous. In truth, I believe it is better situated than Curles, though we do have its advantage in height. Did Warner give you any trouble?"

"Fortunately he and his lady were away at their Chieskake property. All we had to do was send them a message to stay there until further notice. We got no reply, but no one has come to bother us, so clearly they are obeying our request."

"Will Warner declare for Berkeley?"

"I doubt it. His father stood high in the Governor's favor, but young Warner has never spoken well of the old man. I suspect he will lie low until the storm blows over."

"Well, I'm relieved that it was all so simple. Did he leave any staff or have you had to do the housekeeping yourselves?"

"Warner's overseer, John Townley, is still here. He's been cooperative enough, but he's a tiger concerning Warner's possessions. We've had a few arguments about the family silver and some other issues. We're drinking the cellar dry and Townley acts as though every glass of wine is a cup of blood from his own body."

"Well, I daresay we can get along with the man. I have no desire to despoil the place, but we do have to eat and drink and have beds to sleep on. Is there room for me and my captains?"

John spoke. "Come upstairs. We've given you the master's suite, which overlooks the river to the south. You can use it as both an office and a bedroom.

Byrd and I share a room and if your captains double up as well there are chambers enough. It's a handsome place ... couldn't be better for your purposes."

"Excellent. Let's take a tour and then you can give me your news over dinner. Do we have a cook?"

"Yes, an able one. We dine at one o'clock. I'll tell them to prepare a meal for eight."

Replete, Bacon and his staff sat back and enjoyed the view over Warner Hall's south lawn to the river.

"I could get used to living like this," said Arnold.

"Well, who knows what the future holds?" replied Nat. "Now, if we can stay awake after the sturgeon and the woodcock, let's hear from John and Byrd."

The Indian trader and the attorney looked at one another, and John spoke first.

"Have you heard any news concerning your old ally, Giles Brent?"

"The half-breed from Stafford? No. Does he want to join us again?"

"He may now, but he did not a month ago. Apparently while you were burning Jamestown he was marching south with a sizeable force, having declared for Berkeley. When they learned of the Governor's defeat his men fled and he disappeared in the north."

"Damn my blood, the turncoat!" hissed Nat. "I never liked the man, but I must say he acquitted himself well in that fruitless chase against the savages we endured in New Kent. I wonder what made him cross over to the Governor."

"God only knows. There seem to be many who are blowing with the wind. Even here in Gloucester it is hard to know where their hearts really are. We have suffered no overt hostility, but I doubt that you are going to find the folk flocking to your colors. There's a fear on the land ... most people are sitting on the fence, unwilling to jump until there is a clear winner."

"I don't like the sound of that," muttered Nat.

"It's true though," said Byrd thoughtfully. "Both John and I have scoured the countryside and we've only met a handful of men who are honest enough to say what they think – some can't wait to join your army and some say that they will remain Green come hell or high water. Most, however, won't commit themselves."

"It appears that we have our work cut out for us then. I'm going to send Jamie, Tom and George out to swear men to our service. They'll start tomorrow. Tony is going to stay here to guard Warner Hall. My first task is to draft a declaration and oath for the people of Accomac and to find a way to get it across the Bay; and then I'm going to scour the land for any water craft seaworthy enough to get to the Eastern Shore. I want to take the fight to Berkeley by the end of the month. Any later than that and we run into foul weather."

"Does Brent pose any further threat?" asked Farlow.

"Not based on our sources. It sounds like the northerners have disappeared into the woods to wait and see what happens here. It's the same old story," answered Byrd.

"What about troops from England?" asked Crewes.

"We've not heard a thing. It's possible that the King has learned of the June Assembly, but he can't know about Nat's victory at Jamestown yet. Who can say? Clearly we should post as many lookouts as possible to watch the shipping, but otherwise ..."

"We've left the Peninsula well guarded," said Nat. "It's Tony's job to protect the shores of Gloucester, to the extent that he can. I have to assume that the King will send a force ... that's why we must wrap this up in early November."

"Well, it's a tall order, General," said Byrd, rising. "I wish you the best of luck. Unfortunately I must be off to Henrico in the next couple of days. Mary wrote that Wood is obliged to return to Fort Henry as soon as possible, so my duty is now to my family."

"I'm sorry to hear it, Byrd, but you have done your usual outstanding job in securing Warner Hall for us, so we must let you go. Please give my best to Mary and kiss that little boy of yours for me. How old is he now?"

"Just a year older than yours, Nat ... two years and some months. He's a clever chap and I miss him. With your permission, then, I'll be off tomorrow. With Jake and John and your four captains, how can things go wrong?"

Nat turned to John. "You'll stay, won't you John?"

"You could not tear me away, Nat. It is now or never. This is where I belong."

Tears came to Nat's eyes and he hoped they were unnoticed. He thought a touch of that lingering fever had returned; otherwise John's loyalty would not have moved him so deeply.

Virginia had never looked as fair as it did during the next golden week. The air was mild and the trees burned with all the colors of fire. John and Nat drafted a plea to the people of Accomac to support the popular cause and they were lucky enough to find a fisherman visiting relatives in Gloucester to take the document back home with him and try to have it read to as many as possible. Securing water craft was not as easy, but gradually they built a little fleet which promised to assemble at Tindall's Point no later than the twenty-first of October when, God willing, Bacon's army would be ferried across the Bay to strike its last blow. Crewes and Farlow and Hansford recruited some men from Gloucester, but any way you looked at it, the response was disappointing. Nat would be lucky to have three hundred men and fifty horse when he arrived in Accomac. Still, it was unlikely that Berkeley would have more, so spirits remained high.

As they rode out early every day and returned late every evening Nat was more and more grateful that he had John at his side. Only Grey and Jake knew how disordered he felt. The fever had come back with a vengeance. He could not retain food and he felt as though he was wasting away. The disease came and went and, generally, he could cover his weakness, but lately his captains had been looking at one another askance and he thought they talked among themselves more often than they used to, and seemed agitated. Everything rode on his Accomac campaign. If God struck him down with disease now, the result could only be disaster.

The morning of October twenty-first dawned fair. It was the day that General Bacon and his army were to march to Tindall's Point and begin embarking for the Eastern Shore. Nat woke to find himself soaked in sweat, his linen clinging to him like grave clothes. He burned with fever and he felt as though a thousand insects were piercing his skin. Jake stepped into the General's chamber with his breakfast tray and he looked appalled. Shoving the tray onto the nearest table, he ran to Nat's bed.

"Sir, sir. Are you alright? Shall I call Mister John?"

"Yes, call John."

Grey was at his side in a minute. "Nat, you are burning. You are not going to Tindall's Point today. I shall find an excuse, tell Jamie to explain something to the men. I know – John Pate is the only Gloucester landowner you've not visited since you arrived. He has that house upstream, right on the river and, reputedly, two fine sloops. Let Crewes order the army to sail tomorrow, as scheduled, and tell them that you will follow when you have acquired Pate's vessels."

"It is as good as anything," muttered Nat. "Go, John. And thank you. Oh, my God!"

"My dear friend, what is it?"

"I am burning to death and little unseen devils are devouring me. John! John! Am I dying?"

"Never in the world, Nat. It's just a fever. Jake and I will see you right. Now try and drink something and go back to sleep."

"Yes, yes. I love you, John. Now go."

That evening Nat's fever had abated and he felt almost a new man. He sat in Warner's dining room and looked over the lawn to the Severn. John and Jake sat near him, silent.

"So there is no physician in all of Gloucester?"

"None who owns any skill. Warner himself has a working knowledge of physic, but I doubt the wisdom of asking his help. Townley gave me his whole supply of Peruvian bark and it is that, I think, which has made you feel better."

"Perhaps. Yet this thing has come and gone since the battle of Jamestown. It was foolish of me to get so damp in that wretched trench. I fear that there is more here than Peruvian bark will cure, but tonight I feel much better. I shall set out for Pate's tomorrow. I may as well turn our fable into the truth, as we need transport so badly."

"Never, Nat!" cried John, leaping up. "Lyn would never forgive me if I let you go."

"Ah, Lyn. She'll never know, John. Swear it. Whatever happens, never let her know ... the bad parts."

"Do you mean that?"

"You have protected her well, like a brother. Can you not continue to do so?"

"Yes. Yes, I can do so. Like a brother."

"Thank you. It eases my heart. Now, let us sup. I think I can keep something down. Tomorrow I shall ride to Pate's. It might make all the difference."

"When shall I have Folly and Blue ready, sir?" asked Jake tenderly.

"Have Folly at the front door by eight o'clock. But I ride alone. No! Not a word from either of you. I am going to ride alone to Pate's. If you should not hear from me after several days ... why then I suppose you must come looking for me."

CHAPTER 27

OCTOBER 1676

Pate's simple clapboard house was only one of his many holdings and was more modest than Nat expected. The approach, from the north, was undistinguished, crowded with thick, gloomy cedars which had been neither pruned nor cleared. The trees circled the dwelling like squat, menacing dwarves. What lawn there was grew sparse and rank; indeed, the entire homestead looked uncared for, abandoned.

Eaten with fever and barely able to stay in the saddle, Nat guided Folly to the left of the house and found the stables. Blackberries and wild grape and scarlet creepers were aggressively attacking the little building and its doors hung askew, open wide. A thrush flew up from the underbrush, startled at a human presence. Nat slid to the ground and rested his forehead against Folly's neck as though to draw strength from the great beast. The stallion dropped his head to nibble some weed and then turned a sympathetic, liquid eye towards his master. After a moment Nat looked around, trying to decide what to do next. His mind was not working clearly and he staggered slightly and gripped Folly's saddle. Pate's place was empty ... whoever lived here must have left a month ago, at least. He supposed that he should go back to Warner's but he was drained of energy, sucked dry like a mollusk shell with the meat ripped from it. It was almost dusk ... perhaps he could spend the night here and return to his headquarters tomorrow. He always felt better in the morning ... it was at this time of day, when the sun was dying, that his life force was at its ebb.

Nat and Folly entered the stable together and the cool dimness came to life with the scamper of small, clawed feet. Pate, or his servants, had left a goodly supply of hay in one of the stalls and in a manger lay a scattering of oats, though the mice had made off with most of them.

Nat loosened Folly's girth and the saddle and lynx skin saddle cloth slipped to the ground. Stooping, Nat realized that he lacked the strength to store the horse's harness properly; it would have to remain as it was. He stroked the lynx skin and thought of Jake and Byrd and Rossechy. Perhaps he should simply leave all this behind and strike out for the Roanoke River. Lyn would love the crystal streams and the untouched forest. Lyn ...

Nat snapped his head up. Had he really been dreaming? He must finish here and explore the house. Could Pate have left a caretaker? It seemed unlikely. He hoped he could find a way in ... perhaps he could break a casement, but did he have enough strength? Nat burned with thirst. Before anything, he must find the well. He pulled himself to his feet and stripped Folly of his bridle, tossing it onto the straw next to the saddle. The horse could shift well enough for himself, and he was too faithful to leave. He would be safe enough for one night.

A spasm twisted Nat's abdomen. It was as if some savage creature lived inside him and was wringing him dry. He must find something to drink.... He left the stable and wandered south, towards the river. The well house stood on the south lawn, its cedar-shingled roof glinting silver in the sun's last rays. Nat did not have the strength to winch the bucket up, but luckily it had been left on the lip of the well and there was still some water in the bottom. Careless of what he was drinking, Nat raised the clumsy vessel to his lips and sluiced his face with tepid water, imbibing as much as he could as it fell to the ground.

Somewhat refreshed, he looked around. A nightjar called and he managed a smile. Some part of Lyn was with him here. He gazed south across the lawn to the river. Now he understood Pate's plan: the dwelling's northern aspect was merely functional. Here, to the south, was all the beauty. The York unrolled before his eyes like a carpet woven in subtle shades of brown and green. On each side of the lawn the forest rose in all the hues of autumn: the piercing scarlet of the black gum, the brilliant red and orange starbursts of the maples, the subtle and aristocratic bronze of the oaks, and, spun gold, the tender leaves of the tulip poplar, beckoning, beckoning.... Virginia was calling to him. What secrets would she share if he walked into the golden forest?

John rose before dawn, anxious and restless. He never should have let Nat go yesterday. His friend was clearly ill and God knew what kind of reception Pate would give him. No one in Bacon's army actually knew the planter nor had they given him any warning of Nat's visit. The venture was based solely on a rumor that Pate was sympathetic to the people's cause and on the fact that he had two sloops at his disposal. But what if he was not home? Pate had more than one property in Gloucester and land elsewhere as well ... he could be anywhere. And if he was at home, would he leave his harvest to come to General Bacon's aid when, to be honest, a rational man would concede that the scales were evenly balanced between the forces of the Western Shore and the Eastern Shore? And what of the redcoats?

Anyone but a fool would think twice before taking up arms against the King, even in the King's name. Nat had looked so well ... and had been so forceful, but that damnable fever came and went. During the week at Curles Bacon had taken to his bed twice, for a whole day at a time. A true friend would have stopped him ... or would follow him now.

John dressed by candlelight and made his way downstairs and across the yard to the kitchen. He startled a slave boy whose job was to tend the fire and who slept curled up by the hearth. Joking with the lad, John brought a kettle to the boil and made himself a strong *café filtre* while the slave found some bread and butter and poured some hot milk into yesterday's corn meal to make a palatable mush. The tall Englishman and the little Virginian ate together as the first rays of sun peeked over the eastern horizon. John thanked the boy and told him to go back to bed and made his way to the stable where Coke snorted his pleasure at seeing his master. Fifteen minutes later John had the horse saddled and bridled and led him into the yard where he tied him to the back porch railing while he crept upstairs. The whole house was still wrapped in sleep. Noiselessly, John shoved some linen and other items into a bag and slipped downstairs quietly. The morning glowed as he urged Coke up the drive at a smart trot and, when he reached the main road, pushed the horse to a canter. It would take him the better part of a day to reach Pate's and he felt, somehow, that he had no time to lose.

Jake stirred in his sleep, awakened by footsteps in the hall. He slept on a little cot in General Bacon's bedchamber and he felt embarrassed that he had the whole suite to himself, now that the General had gone to Pate's for the sloops. But John had told him to go on sleeping there, that it was proper. He liked Mister Grey. The attorney was quiet, but there was something reassuring about him. You felt that you could depend on him ... and certainly General Bacon did. Jake guessed that they were old friends ... they talked as though they had known one another a long time. The boy yawned. He must have imagined the footsteps. The house was empty except for John and him and Mister Townley. He turned over and sank back into sleep.

An hour later the hall door opened with a crash and this time Jake leaped to his feet, sleep banished. He did not even stop for his breeches and shoes and socks, but tossed on General Bacon's robe and rushed to the landing, snaphaunce in hand. It was now light enough to see and it took him only seconds to discern the familiar forms of William Drummond and Richard Lawrence in the hall below. Jake's heart slowed: what if it had been Berkeley's men?

"Mister Drummond! Mister Lawrence! Up here! It's me, Jake."

"There you are, laddie. Fetch your master, will you? It's important."

"General Bacon's ridden west, to John Pate's."

"How far?"

"A day's ride."

"Well, who is here?"

"Just Mister Grey and Mister Townley. The army's at Tindall's Point."

"I know – we've just come from there, riding through the night. Call John Grey, will you? And is there any way we could have some breakfast before we push on?"

"Of course. I'll fetch Mister Grey and then I'll see about breakfast. Go into the dining room and help yourselves to whatever you need. Or, if you need a wash, come upstairs and they'll heat some water for you."

Jake returned his fusil to General Bacon's bedroom and rushed down the hall to John's room. He was amazed that Grey had not heard the commotion ... normally he rose with the dawn. He knocked on Grey's door briefly and then stepped inside. To his astonishment the attorney was gone and so was his bag and the few clothes he had brought from Curles. Those footsteps ... could Grey have left early this morning, without telling anyone?

An hour later Drummond and Lawrence pushed their egg-smeared plates aside and drained Warner's silver coffee pot to the dregs. Townley paced anxiously back and forth, wiping the mahogany and making sure that neither of his unwanted guests slipped a knife or a spoon into his pockets.

"Thank you for your hospitality, Mister Townley," said Lawrence. "*The Unicorn* could have done no better. Jake can take care of us now. Would you be kind enough to draw up that little map we talked about, the one which will guide us to John Pate's?"

Warner's overseer withdrew, his brow furrowed. If he could get rid of these two rebels and that damned boy, then he would finally have the Hall to himself. He would have the slaves clean every room and he himself would take a complete inventory. He owed it to Mister Warner and the new mistress. When, if ever, was this turmoil going to end?

"Now, Jake," continued Lawrence as Townley closed the door behind him. "Sit down and we'll tell you what is going on. Until a few days ago Mister Drummond and I were at his Blackwater plantation settling his family and my servant, Clarissa. Don't say a word! I can see the question on your face ... Billy and Johnny Drummond are fine, and they send you their greetings. Well, when all was in good train on the Blackwater we turned north to join the General. When we got to Green Spring they told us that the army had a rendezvous at Tindall's Point – that the General planned to sail from there with as many men as he could find transport for. We pushed on and crossed the York last night at dusk, and made our way to the fort. We expected to find everything in order, the men excited, Farlow, Crewes and the others whipping them up, and the boats being organized and so forth. Not so! Some quarter of the men had slunk away, fearful to face Berkeley and even more fearful of the redcoats. Only a handful of the transports had come as promised ... perhaps enough for half of the remaining men. Hansford was wild ... only one boat was fit to carry horses, twenty at most ... what was he going to do with his cavalry? Clearly General Bacon was needed.

"They told us we would find him here or at this man Pate's, and they told us to hurry, for if he did not appear and take charge they would not answer for the army staying together. We felt that we had to act immediately, so late yesterday evening we pushed on, glad that we had at least half a moon to light our way. We had to ride slowly, so dawn was breaking when we saw Warner's Hall. And now we learn that the General is still a day's ride away. I am grieved that we missed John Grey ... he could have borne our news ... our bodies cry out for rest."

"But I don't know that Mister Grey is going to Pate's, I only guess so. Perhaps he is off to Tindall's Point."

"No, I don't think so. His duty is to General Bacon. If, as you said, the General was ill, Grey will have gone to him. Probably is sorry that he let him ride off alone."

"Didn't you say that he took the Peruvian bark and some other physic?" asked Drummond.

"Yes, sir, he did," responded Jake. "I'm sure you are right, but I would hate to mislead you."

"Well, I don't see anything for it but to ride on to Pate's. Unless, Will, one of us goes there and the other returns to the army?"

"No, Dicken, let's find Nat. This is all about him. He will either pull his army together now or it will fall apart. But there is not a moment to lose. Let's look at what horseflesh you have here, Jake. We should change horses if we can – ours are as weary as we are."

"Yes, sir, follow me," said the boy and the three rose from the dining table and walked out into the yard on as beautiful an October morning as Jake could remember.

An hour later Drummond and Lawrence, on new horses, and Jake, on Blue, rode west to Pate's.

It was midafternoon when John turned into the cedar-shrouded drive and made his way to the clapboard house. It stood derelict, wholly abandoned. John left Coke to crop what little grass he could find and walked up the gravel walk to the front door. It was firmly locked and no one responded to his knock, though a linnet darted from her nest in the ivy over the doorway and crows screamed from the cedars. Leading Coke, John returned to the drive and followed it to the stable. The building's double doors hung open but nothing stirred. The sun hot on his back, John entered the stable's cool darkness; it took a good minute for his eyes to adjust and then he looked about, seeing nothing but empty stalls and an empty loft. One stall appeared to have some hay in it, so at least he could feed Coke before leaving. After having missed Pate, John supposed that a disappointed Nat must have pushed on to Tindall's Point. He would not have done so unless his fever had abated ... perhaps everything was well. John's heart lifted.

He moved forward to see how much fodder there was and whether it would be worth while to let his horse feed, when he stumbled on something and almost fell. It was Folly's saddle. Under it, crushed in the straw, lay the noble lynx skin, the twin of which Coke wore, even now. A foot or so away John saw Folly's bridle, carelessly heaped on the ground. His heart thudded so that he was amazed that the stable did not ring with its beat. Had Nat been taken by surprise and attacked? But if so, why had the attacker left the horse's harness and, yes, Nat's pistols which still rested in their saddle holsters? Nat would never have left his saddle and bridle and cloth and firearms so carelessly ... unless he had been taken ill. John stood, lost in thought. It might be. His friend might have been stricken down ... perhaps had barely made it into the house and was lying there now, waiting for help. And Folly? He had doubtless wandered away ... but it was Nat that he had to think of.

John looped Coke's reins around a post and left the chestnut in the stable. He walked around the house to the south and reached the lawn which stretched graciously to the beckoning river. It was a noble prospect, one that Nat would love. Could he be here, warming himself in the sun? John scanned the landscape and saw nothing but a blue heron which pushed off from the river bank and slowly gathered speed until it disappeared across the river. He climbed the steps to the back porch and tried the door. It was locked, but the catch was flimsy and would doubtless give way to any significant pressure. All the casements were closed ... would Nat have locked himself in the house without letting in some air? There was only one way to find out. John forced the door, which gave way easily, and entered Pate's parlor. Dust lay thick on every surface and John could discern no sign of life and no sign that any human had been here recently. He strode rapidly through the house, checking the dining room and office in the front, and the bedrooms upstairs. All was quiet. The house was tidy and some furniture was even covered with dust cloths, so Pate's departure had not been hasty, but planned.

His heart on fire, John hurried from the house to the kitchen, which lay to the west. The silent room told the same story. Everything was neatly put away, and dust lay thick everywhere. Mouse droppings showed that some creatures, at least, had ventured into the dependency, but there was no sign of recent human occupancy. John emerged and looked across the lawn to the river. It was a glorious afternoon. Could Nat have ridden Folly, bareback, to the river to bathe? But if so, where had he slept last night or eaten today? And why had he left the horse's gear huddled as it had fallen from the great black beast? His heart misgave him and he felt a chill even as the October sun shed its beneficent rays on the banks of the York.

The woods on either side of the lawn glowed with gold and a slight breeze fluttered the soft leaves of the tulip poplar so that they looked like primitive hands. John's care laden heart skipped a beat as Coke shattered the peace of the afternoon with a shrill neigh. It was answered from the eastern woods. Folly! It must be Folly! For some reason Nat had ridden the black into the forest ... well, he loved this season best of all, perhaps he wanted to see it in all its glory. Folly could not be far away ... John would not take Coke, but simply walk ... or run. He raced across the lawn, calling as he went. He plunged into the forest and soon found a faint path – it must be how one reached the river through the trees. Within minutes he saw the black stallion's bulk and was upon him.

"Folly, how glad I am to see you. Where is your master? Nat! Nat!"

The great horse snorted and lipped John's hand and stood silent.

"Is he by the river? Well, stay here and I shall see."

John pushed on in a blaze of red and gold and yellow. One poplar reached higher than the rest; it had a girth of six feet or more, must have been standing sentinel here for well over a century. There was a clearing at its base, as nothing dared grow too close to this noble tree. But there was something odd there, on the mossy forest floor. Something black, like a shadow. Something. It was Nat, supine, his hawk eyes fixed on the canopy of gold which stretched above him, his black curls spread about him, a band of braided gold on his right hand and a gold wedding band on his left, and not a breath left in his poor body.

John fell to his knees and took his friend in his arms and let his tears flow like the river.

A chipmunk peered around the end of a fallen log, its eyes bright as coal. It jerked its tail and scurried back into the forest, disturbed that the clearing under the big golden tree was so changed. Two unknown creatures crowded the mossy lawn; one was still, but one moved about alarmingly.

The chipmunk's motion caught John's eye and he stopped pacing and remembered where he was. How long had he been talking to Nat, talking as though his friend was still with him? It was almost dark. He must have been here two hours or more, communing with the dead. He had reminded Nat of how they met at Gray's Inn; of the days they shared at study and the nights they shared in London's dens; of the knock on the door that told them of Lyn's plight; of Nat's wedding day.... The tears started again. How was Lyn going to bear this? Did she have a premonition of Nat's death when he left Curles? John did not think so ... they had discussed his illness, of course, but everyone in Virginia had the fever now and again, it was simply part of life. No, it would come as a great shock ... a body blow.

But there were more pressing needs. He could not leave Nat's body here in the forest to be soaked by the dew and discovered by the creatures of the night. His poor friend weighed so little now that he probably could hoist him onto Folly one last time and take him up to the house. He would sit with him tonight and return to Warner's tomorrow and arrange the funeral. But first he must get some kind of cover, a winding sheet, for he could not bear to look on Nat's mortal shell any longer, not when his friend's spirit had flown. John remembered the dust covers in Pate's house – one of them would do. He had better go now or it would be too dark to see. John sadly retraced his steps through the woods and the great black stallion walked at his heels like a dog.

As John reached the south lawn Folly began trotting, on his own accord, to the stable. The poor beast had likely scented Coke or remembered that there was hay in one of the stalls. John watched the animal's large form recede when suddenly he heard shouts and the hoof beats of many horses. Could Pate have returned? Had Berkeley's men tracked him down? Or was Jake searching for his master? As these thoughts raced through his mind the familiar form of William Drummond loomed out of the gloaming.

"There you are Grey! Why have you lighted no fires or candles? 'Tis damnably dark. Where's Nat? ... I have news that cannot wait."

"As have I," said John somberly. "Nat's in the forest ... dead."

Drummond sat on his horse as though pole axed. "Never in the world," he said finally.

"It happened before I came ... this morning perhaps, or even last night. I would never have found him but for Folly. The horse was standing guard over him ... I swear it."

"Oh, my laddie, my laddie. This is sore news." Drummond slipped from his saddle and walked to John's side and clasped him tight. "My God ... now what will the army do?"

"For me, I care not. I am still ... I don't know ... in disbelief. I have been with him all afternoon and I still can't believe it is true." John broke down and burst into great sobs. When he looked up he saw Lawrence and Jake peering at him from their horses.

Lawrence looked startled and perturbed, but Jake knew instantly what had happened.

"He's dead, isn't he? General Bacon is dead." The boy started to weep.

"No!" cried Lawrence.

"It is so, Dicken," said Drummond softly. "Grey found him in the forest, alone but for the black horse. He probably died sometime yesterday."

"And I wasn't here!" howled Jake. "I wasn't here to care for him."

"It's not your fault, laddie. It's nobody's fault. It's God's will. And the army ... I wonder if this is a sign."

Lawrence looked stricken. "You are right, Will. This is a blow ... I doubt the army can recover. Well, that's not today's issue. John – where is ... the body?"

John waved his hand vaguely in the direction of the east woods. "There ... I was just coming to get a cloth, a winding sheet. I was going to put him in the house and then bring him to Warner's tomorrow ... arrange some kind of funeral."

"Well, we're here to help you. Come on, it's getting dark. Will – help Jake break into the house and get that cloth for John. Build some fires and light the candles and put the house to rights. And see what's in the kitchen. We'll spend the night here and honor our friend and then decide what to do next."

Two hours later the four friends sat in Pate's parlor where a fire burned briskly. They had raided the kitchen and found a well-stocked larder of staples and had helped themselves to the planter's ham and Dutch cheese and dried fruit. Now Will Drummond was making toddies at the fireside, a jug of rum, a loaf of sugar, and two lemons at his side.

"Here John, this one is for you. You were his oldest friend."

"Thank you. And thank God you came. I could not have done it without you. Now he is laid out properly, clean and orderly. I dreaded having to take his body back to Warner's ... I cannot tell you."

"We can imagine," replied Drummond, handing two cups to Lawrence. "Here, Dicken ... the small one's for Jake ... he's already overcome and he should not have too much rum."

The Scot mixed his own drink and then the friends offered a silent toast to Nat. When they washed him John had taken the gold rings from his hands. He held both of them up to the light.

"Nat wrote a will, you know, and I am his executor. 'Everything is Lyn's,' he said. 'Make it simple, but make it binding. Everything is Lyn's.' He meant the land and the slaves and the cattle, of course, and what gold and silver remained. As for his personal property, he told me to use my own judgment. 'John,' he said. 'John ... you are like a brother to me, so I know that you will do the right thing. Give my things away as you see fit.' Like a brother, he said." John put his face in his hands and sobbed as though his heart would break.

"I'll take the wedding ring and Folly back to Curles. Ah, Lyn, poor little thing! I wonder how she will bear it!"

John paused and composed himself. "Dicken, I would like you to have the braided ring. You taught him well ... he would want you to have it."

Lawrence held out his hand and turned his face to one side so that the others could not see his tears. "Thank you, John. I am honored."

"Will, I want you to have his sword. He mentioned it once. He considered you another father."

"And he was like a son to me," the Scot said gently. "I will keep it – but only if his real father does not wish it sent back to England."

"Jake, I want you to have something to remember the Occaneechee campaign."

"As if I would ever forget it, Mister Grey. He taught me to be a man. Everybody says so."

"It is true. And to remember that for the rest of your life, take the lynx skin saddle cloth you love so much and keep it always. Every time you ride you will think of General Bacon."

Now Jake hid his face in his hands and sobbed.

"And you, John?" queried Lawrence. "He always said you were one who gave all and took nothing. Do you want nothing now?"

"Nothing but my memories and the continued care of Lyn and Mary. He entrusted them to me many times and now they shall be my charge until ... until the future unveils itself."

Lawrence stirred the logs and the friends sat in silence. After some time the innkeeper spoke.

"The night grows old and I fear that Will and I must rest. We have been awake two days running and if we do not sleep tonight I will not answer for the consequences. Will you and Jake sit with Nat?"

"We will do well enough here, by the fire. If we sleep from time to time, Nat will not begrudge us the rest. But what of the funeral? It will take some time to arrange to take him to Curles. Should we make some kind of temporary arrangement at Warner's? What do you suggest?"

Lawrence looked at Drummond and Drummond looked at Lawrence. The Scot spoke.

"You would do well to forget any plan to take him to Curles, John, at least at this point. And to bury him at Warner's might be just as perilous, if not more so."

"Whatever do you mean?"

Drummond sighed. "I hate to burden you with this tonight, of all nights, but necessity compels it. We pushed on here, to Pate's, for a reason ... not just to see Nat again and ask him how best we could serve the people's cause, but to bring him news from Tindall's Point. Lawrence and I were there not forty-eight hours ago and, not to put too fine a point on it, the army is a disaster. The men are falling away like autumn leaves. Crewes and the others told us that if Nat did not bring his troops to order immediately that the whole Accomac campaign would have to be abandoned. As if that were not enough, as we left Warner's this morning to bring Nat this news Jamie intercepted us on the main road and ..."

"I can guess it," groaned John. "Told you that it had all fallen apart."

"Why beat about the bush? The answer is 'yes.' The camp is in chaos. Most of the men have left. What few boats came have already returned home. Panic has struck. There are wild rumors of the King's fleet having been sighted, redcoats having landed in Accomac ... the thing is over, at least for now."

"My God," said John. "Well, at least Nat did not know that. Then I must bring his body home to Curles."

"No, laddie, I think not," said Drummond sadly. "Dicken ... why don't you explain."

"It's like this, John," said Lawrence wearily. "Whatever made the army panic, only Nat could have cured it. When the men hear of his death they will take it as an omen, believe that he was struck down because he espoused the wrong cause. It is a fatal blow ... I doubt the Ring can survive it. We may be able to pull something together, I have not wholly given up hope, but it is doubtful. Once Berkeley hears this news nothing will stop him from reclaiming the Western Shore. And there is no doubt in my mind that King Charles' fleet is even now on the Atlantic, anxious to put down another Cromwell, as it were. Well, much of the King's work has been done for him: that cruel captain, Death, has taken up the Stuart banner. I fear that our cause has died with Nat. And if that is so, what do you think Berkeley's men would do to his body if they found it? What was Cromwell's fate? Charles Stuart pulled him from his tomb and hung his poor bones from Tyburn gallows and then put his skull on a pole at Westminster Hall for all the world to gawk and gape at and learn a rebel's fate. We cannot bury our friend where our foes might find him. Better to leave him in the forest – the wild creatures would be kinder than William Berkeley and Charles Stuart."

John put his elbows on his knees and his face in his hands. This was the final blow. Nat could not even rest at his beloved Curles where Lyn and Mary could bring him flowers and talk to his spirit. Would his ghost have to walk the earth, unhoused? It was too much to bear.

Jake spoke, quietly. "Why should we not bury him in the forest, then? He loved it – especially in the fall. We could bury him where he fell, under the golden tree. Mistress Lyn and Mary could visit him there ... you cannot mistake that great tree, it is like a monument."

"A fitting and gentle solution from a gentle soul," smiled Drummond. "Why should we not honor Virginia's soil by placing him there? God knows, he coursed the forest bravely on the people's business. There could not be a better tomb. And later, perhaps, depending on what happens, Lyn could bring him back to Curles or even to Suffolk, if she decides to return home."

"It is the right thing to do," cried John. "Thank you, Jake. You have served Nat well, even after death."

"Let me add the final piece to the puzzle," said Lawrence. "There is a common area near Warner Hall, a pretty little piece of land on the Severn. We can hold a mock funeral there tomorrow, bury an empty casket ... put some rocks in it, or the like. Make a show of it, and throw them off the trace. With luck Berkeley will be so busy that he will take it at face value and let the coffin lie ... if he digs it up, so be it. He will never be able to find Nat's true resting place."

Their plan made, the four friends raised a last glass in honor of their dead comrade. Drummond and Lawrence climbed the stairs wearily and threw themselves on the nearest beds while John and Jake sat in the parlor and watched the fire burn low. The next day at dawn Nat's body was taken to its final resting place. As John smoothed the moss back into place over the grave he looked up and saw nothing but a crown of gold.

Townley frowned at the south lawn as the rain poured down the casement, almost obscuring his vision. There was something peculiar – almost underhanded – about the way the rebels had brought Bacon's body back from John Pate's. He had offered them the use of the grand *salon* to lay the man out but they had refused brusquely and, curiously, had carried the corpse to the workshop where they let it lie among the piles of lumber while they huddled up a simple wooden coffin. One would have thought they would have offered their general a little more respect, but then most of them were rabble, and God alone knew what went on in their minds and souls. In any event, the *corpus* was probably not fit to be seen.

And then, to cap things off, the rain started, (and wasn't *that* a blessing, it was so dry), and now there they were, a sodden mass down by the river, laying their leader in that strip of common area near the water. He had offered them a nice piece of Mister Warner's woodland, sure that his master would not object, but they had not taken kindly to the suggestion at all. What had the Scot said? "General Bacon belonged to the people and he shall lie in the people's ground." Well, so be it.

Ah! They must have finished. They were all trooping back to the house ... the four who had brought the body back from Pate's and the four captains. Good that he had put down the canvas floor cloth in the dining room where he had set out some glasses and several bottles of Mister Warner's second best sherry. When the little gathering was over he would be rid of them for good. It seemed that Bacon's death had caused as much confusion as a sharp stick in a wasp's nest – at least he had heard the four captains saying they were on their way home, and the other four had packed up too, and had their horses waiting in the stable, saddled and bridled. Another half an hour and Warner Hall would be his once again. And not a moment too soon. He would count the silver again as soon as they had left.

CHAPTER 28

OCTOBER - NOVEMBER 1676

Lawrence paid the ferryman in silver and he and Drummond and Jake and John Grey guided their weary mounts across the mud flats on the York's south bank as the river ebbed. General Bacon's four captains, who had crossed first, waited for them. The eight men were about to part and if and when they would meet again was the question in every mind.

Drummond's strong voice broke the quiet of the late afternoon. The rain had lifted at midday and the whole landscape steamed in the sun, though soon the chill of late October would arrive and remind the horsemen that fall was already far advanced.

"Tom! Dicken! Are you ready to push on to the Blackwater?"

"Yes and no," answered Hansford. "I'll be glad to see my farm, but I still feel that my work lies here. I'll be back."

"As will we all, when we know better how the land lies," affirmed Lawrence. "But first let's look to our families and our fortunes. The day is Berkeley's, if he does not let it slip through his fingers, but the whole story has not yet been written. I suggest that we arrange to meet in exactly a month, for good or for ill."

"An excellent idea," agreed Farlow. "Tony and I will be at my niece's in New Kent. Will you join us there?"

"Better come to Turkey Island," boomed Jamie Crewes. "It's far enough from Jamestown and Green Spring to be safe and it's the most convenient for the most of us."

"I second that," said Lawrence. "When Berkeley returns to the Western Shore he will almost certainly make Green Spring his capital, with Jamestown burned. We should stay well away from the lower James. And what if the King sends a navy? It will almost certainly anchor at Kecoughtan or Jamestown. Henrico is indeed safest and most convenient."

"Then I'll expect you all on the last day of November," Crewes said. "Remember, keep your ears open. Bring whatever information you've gathered and we'll plan our future."

"Agreed," the eight men cried.

Waving their hands in farewell, Lawrence and Drummond rode south, with Tom Hansford right behind them and George Farlow and Tony Arnold turned right, headed west for New Kent. John and Jake and Jamie Crewes rested where they were for a moment, still stunned by the events of the last few days and now sad at seeing yet more friends depart.

"I hope we see them all in November," muttered John. "My heart is so sore; everything looks black."

"Oh, I wouldn't give up yet, Grey," said Crewes. "The Accomac campaign was always ill-fated and it is no surprise that it died with Nat. But many still believe in the cause. It's one thing to balk at crossing the water to an unknown shore to fight; it's quite another to protect your own land and your own family on familiar ground. I think the Governor will have his work cut out for him."

"But there's no leadership, Jamie. Who's going to pull the men together? There is talk of that fellow Ingram, but nobody knows anything about him. He's just over from England – why would Virginians follow him?"

"Well, perhaps they won't, Grey, but after all, they did follow Nat, and he hadn't been here two years when we marched to the Roanoke. Right, Jake?"

"Yes sir. But General Bacon was special. Do you think this Ingram could ever take his place?"

"I know nothing about him, boy. Let's wait and see what happens. God knows my plantation needs all the care I can give it, and I won't be sorry to have a bit of a rest. I don't envy you, Grey, carrying the news to Lyn. I wouldn't be in your shoes for anything in the world."

"I dread it, Jamie. But it is my duty and I like to think that Nat would have wanted me to be the one ..."

"Of course he would," cried Jake. "Well, shall we start? I hope we find someone to take us in tonight, for we won't be at Curles until late tomorrow."

Lyn knew the moment that she saw Folly's empty saddle. It was midday and she was walking along the bluff, before dinner, as was her wont. The day was fine, with a brisk wind from the river, and she was pacing, wondering when she would hear from Nat again. His last note from Warner Hall had been hasty, but positive. Would this great coil, which now everyone called a rebellion, end happily? She supposed that it was possible, but deep down she saw nothing ahead but heartbreak. A horse trumpeted: it could only be Folly. She turned and saw the black charger coming towards her, riderless, between Coke and Blue. A hundred reasons for Nat's absence raced through her mind, but in her heart she knew that her husband was dead. John sprang from Coke and reached for her and before he could say a word she collapsed in his arms.

Late that night she and John were still in the parlor, reminiscing. John told her every detail of the Accomac campaign, glossing over the ugly parts. He stressed Nat's energy, his capacity for leadership, his vision ... he took her through the frustrations of raising transport, the vagaries of command, but always, always came back to how the army loved Nat, would have done anything for him. When Lyn berated herself for letting her husband, so clearly ill, go forth again to fight, John told her, truly, that nobody could have held him back. As the evening wore on they talked of Suffolk ... of Hazelwood and Friston Hall ... of Nat's father and sister and Lyn wept without cessation.

"And I cannot bring him here, John?"

"Not now, Lyn. It is far too dangerous. But later ... certainly later. If you are still here ... depending on what happens with Berkeley. There are many pieces to the puzzle. Can you be patient? I can surely take you there ... it would not be too difficult."

"I hate to think of him lying in the forest."

"It is a beautiful place ... just such a place as Nat would have chosen."

"Oh, John, I don't know how I can go on ... and what of Mary?"

"What, indeed, Lyn? That is why you must take your time, do nothing hastily. May I make a suggestion?"

"Of course."

"Why don't you pay a visit to Mary Byrd? You need a woman's touch and she is your closest friend. Little Mary could play with William, and it would be a change for you. There will be fewer things to remind you of Nat at the trading post, whereas here, wherever you turn, you will think of him. Jake and I could take you there. The boy plans on visiting his mother, in any event. Abraham and Hannah can surely handle things here for a week or two."

"Perhaps you are right, John. I cannot even think now. We'll talk about it in the morning. I shall go up to bed and see if I can sleep. Will you be alright in the wooden house?"

"Of course: it is my home."

The next day saw the mistress of Curles Neck and her daughter on their way to Byrd's trading post, attended by John and Jake. Lyn rode Mignon and Jake rode Blue, while John, on Coke, held Mary in front of him as tenderly as if she were made of glass. They passed the night at Bacon's Quarter and were at the ferry slip by midmorning. They were relieved to find the boat in good order, able to take both passengers and horses. In Henrico, one never knew whether there would *be* a ferry, let alone what condition it would be in. Young Sudbury, the ferryman, told the riders that, to the best of his knowledge, Mister and Mistress Byrd were home and that all was well at the trading post. The crossing was uneventful and by noon they were well on their way to Byrd's.

It was almost two o'clock when Lyn glimpsed the rough logs and cedar shingles of the trading post through the glory of the autumn foliage. She was still dazed. Nothing had felt real to her since she saw Nat's empty saddle. But now she realized that she was about to impose herself upon Mary Byrd, unannounced, at what was likely her friend's dinner hour, and daily life pressed in upon her again.

"John, is this really a good idea?"

"Everybody on the frontier visits the Byrds, no matter what the hour of the day or night. They are used to it. Mary would want you to come, knowing that you would do the same for her."

Lyn nodded, silently. As the three horses crossed the yard the rustic wooden door burst open and Byrd appeared, smiling and waving. John handed Mary to Lyn and urged Coke forward, signaling the Indian trader to one side. He quickly told Byrd the bad news while Jake helped Lyn and Mary dismount, and Byrd now turned a different face to his guest, one marked with sadness and sympathy.

"It grieves me sorely, Lyn," Byrd said quietly. "When I left Nat at Warner's Hall all looked so promising ... and now the whole thing has fallen apart. Come in, come in. Mary has just put William down for a nap and we are about to dine. Please join us; there is enough for twenty."

Two weeks of cosseting in the quiet Virginia forest restored Lyn somewhat. At least now she could think about the future, although when she did it seemed that she was only exchanging the blow of Nat's death for an almost equally overwhelming set of woes. John told her bluntly that, under the circumstances, probating Nat's will would be well-nigh impossible. Rumor had it that Governor Berkeley had returned, or was about to return, to the Western Shore and that he had branded the leaders of the Ring as rebels and vowed that he would attaint them as traitors and seize their estates. Every traitor, the Governor proclaimed, must pay for his crimes not only with his life, but with his property. *If*, John, explained, *if* the Governor prevailed, it was likely, even quite possible, that Nat's lands and goods would be confiscated and that she would lose her home.

Lyn's head reeled as John reluctantly unrolled the future for her. Nat dead, and now, perhaps, she would be stripped bare, left to find her way in Virginia with nothing but the clothes on her back. She would have neither food nor a table to put it on; neither a bed nor a roof to cover it. How would she care for Mary, a helpless child who had not even reached her second year? What would happen to her slaves and servants? Would Mignon be seized? And Folly, the only thing she had left of Nat's? Doubtless the Byrds and the Drummonds would aid her, but she was not going to live on the charity of others. She *did* have property. Hazelwood was hers, outright. Nat, dear heart, had given it to her. That was one answer: she and Mary could return to England, to her little farm. But she had no passage money and no means to raise it....

These thoughts, and others, filled Lyn's head day and night as she paced the forest paths near the trading post, grateful at least that her little girl was safely cared for while she wrestled with her demons. John urged her not to make any hasty decisions. There was still a chance, he claimed, that Berkeley would be brought to justice and the rebels would emerge as heroes, not traitors. Lyn was not convinced. She was sure that the rebellion had died with General Bacon. Things were only going to get worse.

Lyn had not been at Byrd's for ten days when John received an unexpected message summoning him to their friends on the Blackwater. He rode east, promising to be back in a week to escort Lyn and Mary back to Curles. Within a day of his departure Mistress Hartwell was called away to the lying-in of a friend and Jake went with her, for protection and company. William Byrd was rarely home. He was away for days at a time with his pack trains and when he was not trading he was on the north side of the river developing the land he owned there. Lyn and Mary and the two children were left to themselves in the care of Byrd's people. With so little company, the restorative quiet of the frontier, which had been such a blessing at first, became a burden. Ever since the news of Nat's death Lyn's normally balanced personality had suffered a sea change and she was now devoured with restlessness, moving about aimlessly like a rudderless ship. She craved news. She had to know whether Berkeley had returned, whether an English fleet was sailing up the James, whether Curles was still hers or whether it had been confiscated by the Greens. Knowing full well that it was irrational not to wait quietly for John, she could not bring herself to do so and she impulsively decided to rush home, on a lightning journey, and then return as quickly.

It was only ten miles to the ferry and some twenty miles farther to Curles, a day's ride coming and going. If she left early on the first day and slept at Curles, she could be back at the trading post by supper of the second day. Mary Byrd would be alarmed, of course, but Lyn would leave a note and by the time her friend worked herself up into a good case of anxiety, the rebel's widow would be back. In fact, the moon was full and the nights were not much darker than the days. If she left Byrd's at midnight or thereabouts she would be at the ferry by dawn and home by midafternoon. There she would devour all the news which had found its way to Henrico County.

The night after the Hartwells' departure Lyn pleaded a headache and told Mary Byrd that she would put little Mary to bed and then lie down herself, to rest or sleep as the case may be. As usual, her daughter fell asleep quickly. Lyn lay, fully clothed, listening to her soft breathing. The moon shone into the sleeping loft, casting a silver light everywhere. It was so still that Lyn could hear her own heart beat. Two hours later she discerned the familiar sounds of Mary Byrd's nighttime rituals: her friend's footsteps as she secured every window and door; her soft voice as she told William a bedtime story; evening prayers; and the creak of the narrow staircase as Mary and the little boy climbed to the Byrds' half of the sleeping loft, divided from the Bacons' by a thin wall covered with deerskins. When an hour had passed and she heard nothing from the other room, she cautiously rose, her boots and cloak and satchel in hand. She leaned over Mary and kissed her soft cheek. The child's curls were just like Nat's, just such a mixture of black and brown, and she held back a tear. She crept downstairs and set her bag on the floor and removed the note she had written earlier that day, telling Mary to expect her at dusk two days hence. Mary Byrd always set the breakfast table the night before, so she left the note lying on her friend's plate, sure that it would be seen as soon as the household stirred.

Lyn reached the stable without incident. The slaves were sound asleep and the dogs knew her too well to bark. She saddled and bridled Mignon, put on her boots, wrapped herself in her cloak and entered the moonstruck forest. Whatever spirit possessed her, she gave it full rein. "In over shoes, in over boots." She had to know the news, had to know, had to know, had to know.... Mignon's hoofs beat out the rhythm of Lyn's obsessive thoughts as the mistress of Curles passed through the wild woods like a phantom.

Curles Neck lay before Lyn, bare and clean in the late November sun, stripped of its secrets by the fall of the leaves. Her heart turned over as she guided the gray mare from the highroad onto the familiar drive. She had not known how much she loved her plantation until she learned that she might lose it. A weary Mignon walked slowly forward, stumbling slightly with fatigue. Soon the horse scented the familiar odors of home and she pricked up her ears like a hare. As they emerged from a clump of cedars Lyn looked up expectantly, knowing that she would soon see the stately brick house on the bluff with the old wooden house behind it like an aged parent, and the clutch of outbuildings to the west with the simple geometry of the tobacco barns and the long reach of the stable. Startled, she pulled the mare to a halt. The horizon was bare. The familiar outlines of the new house and the old were missing. The mass of the barns was absent. The cabins of the slaves and servants had vanished like smoke. Quite literally, Lyn pinched herself. Had she overtired herself to the extent that her senses were betraying her? Then she saw it: clear against the sheet of gold which was the western sky spirals of blue smoke rose heavenward, as though from a sacrifice. Her home was no more. Curles Neck plantation lay in ashes.

Lyn huddled over Mignon's neck, in physical agony. This was more than she could bear. God had taken first her husband and now her home. What had she done to deserve this fate? The mare trembled, frightened by the smoke, but Lyn pushed her forward. Could Abraham and Hannah have been so careless as to leave a fire untended, a fire which greedily consumed her beloved home? But even so, would the blaze have spread to John's house and to the barns and stables and cabins? Everything was gone ... the conflagration must have been planned. As she proceeded down the drive to the bluff she thought of the day last May when the Governor had appeared, right here, right where Mignon walked. It must be he ... Governor Berkeley was back on the Western Shore and he was taking his revenge.

Lyn tethered Mignon to the redbuds, now bare of flowers, leaves and pods, their iron gray branches spiked against the darkening sky. She descended the path to her little summer house, the summer house which had never been built, but existed only in her mind. Perhaps it was just as well, for if it had been built doubtless it would be a smoldering ruin now. The James coiled around the foot of the bluff, disdainful of her pain. But wait – there was a sloop tied to the wharf. A sloop, and three figures climbing the path. Lyn shrank back, fearful that her enemies were still here. A moment later she rushed down the path and fell into Hannah's welcoming arms.

"Mistress Bacon, whatever are you doing here? You should be at Mister Byrd's. Surely you didn't get a message? It only happened yesterday."

"I didn't get a message, Hannah, but something told me to come. Who is that with Abraham?"

"Why, 'tis Mister Crewes, child. Can't you see? We fled to Turkey Island last night and he took us in and today, when the tide turned, he brought us back to see whether anything was saved."

"Oh Jamie, how glad I am to see you," cried Lyn as she rushed from Hannah's arms to Crewes'.

The big planter blushed and patted her on the head. "It's as bad as Job, isn't it Mistress Lyn? Boils and plagues and all. First Nat and now this. You could have knocked me down with a feather when your servants and slaves showed up at Turkey Island last night – those of them who had not already marched off to New Kent to join Nat's old army."

"Tell me what happened."

"When we get to the top and have found you a place to sit. You are trembling like a leaf and are as pale as a ghost. What are you doing here alone? Is John well ... and your little maid?"

"Oh yes, Jamie, they are both fine. I was fool enough to rush off by myself ... I had some kind of premonition. I *had* to return to Curles. Isn't it strange?"

"Why, 'tis the kind of sense that dogs have, Mistress Lynn, begging your pardon. You must have known that something was wrong. Here, let's sit on your benches. Bless me, many's the day I have sat here drinking with Nat and now ... It makes me want to weep."

Lyn and Jamie and Hannah seated themselves while Abraham tended to Mignon, loosing her saddle and removing her bridle and finding some scraps of grass for her to eat.

"Now, tell me everything," exclaimed Lyn. "Don't spare me."

Jamie Crewes nodded at Hannah, who cleared her throat as she organized her thoughts, and then began.

"All was well after you left, Mistress Lyn. Abraham and I stayed in the big house and kept it tidy, along with Mister John's house. They were beginning to put the little tobacco that there was into the hogsheads, hoping that at least one ship would come this far to take our crop to England. Life was easy for the men. They looked after the cattle and swine and otherwise did not have much else to do. It is always a grateful time of year, after the harvest and before the cold of winter. We got your note about when you and Mister John would be coming back and we were starting to turn out the rooms and make everything ready. Then just yesterday ... were it yesterday, Mister Crewes?"

"Yesterday as ever it were, Hannah. You came at dusk."

"Yesterday at dinner time we were all eating outside, the day was so mild, and we were giving the men a treat, sort of a harvest feast. Up runs Dilsey's Jim and says there were four horsemen on the drive, riding as though the devil were after them. We jumps up and before we can turn around four stout men dressed in green, all on white horses, race towards us. They was clearly not going to stop — we ran like hares with a fox after us. They all had their faces covered with green stuff, so we couldn't see who they were. After they destroyed our feast they lit their torches and circled and circled all the buildings, burning every one. Fearless, they was, for they did not care what we saw. They only left when they were sure that all was ablaze. As they rode off they said something about it being like Jamestown." Hannah paused. "But I know very well who one of them was, for I've seen him at Jamestown myself, many times."

Lyn caught her breath. "Who?"

"Mister Ludwell. The younger one, with the foxy hair. Without a doubt. Abraham says so too, don't you Abraham?" she shouted.

"About Mister Ludwell?" called the black man. "It was him. I would swear it on the Good Book."

"I was right," breathed Lyn to herself. "The Governor is taking his vengeance. I felt it as far as Byrd's."

"There's not a doubt in my mind," agreed Crewes. "But you know you can never prove it."

"Not prove it?" cried Lyn. "All the slaves saw him!"

"But they can't testify," muttered Crewes. "You know that Mistress Lynn. A slave's word is worthless."

Lyn felt as though God had struck her another blow. If she had been more persistent with Nat about freeing Ballard's slaves when they bought Curles, perhaps she would have had a case. But then, probably not. The Governor sat on the General Court, the tribunal which would hear a serious felony like arson. And the Governor was the one who had set this in motion. Berkeley had, at some level, controlled the Bacons' every action since the day they set foot on Virginia soil, and he was still the puppet master. She felt an overwhelming sense of fatigue. If only John were here ... what was she going to do next?

"You must come home with me, Mistress Lynn," said Crewes as softly as his big frame allowed him. "All your people fled there, bringing what cattle they could. Most of them have left already when I told them Nat's army was regrouping at West's Point, but I'll take care of the rest of them, and of your animals. Turkey Island is in a sad way, I've let it go so long. Perhaps it is a blessing in disguise. Abraham and Hannah and all the rest have volunteered to help me put the place to rights. You can stay there as long as you like. I'll take you back in the sloop with Hannah and Abraham can ride your mare. Tomorrow I'll send my fastest man to Byrd's and tell them the news. You'll have your little girl at your side in a day or two. And Mister John."

Lyn could hardly speak. "Thank you, Jamie. I'll do just what you say."

Soon after, Crewes' sloop caught the ebb tide and he and Lyn and Hannah sailed east at dusk, into the gathering night.

Lyn sat on the end of Crewes' wharf, legs dangling, idly watching the flow of the river. Autumn's fire had disappeared leaving only ashes behind. The landscape was a dreary mixture of gray trees, brown water and touches of subdued green where the rushes edged the flow of the James. Nature mirrored her mind, thought Lyn absently, as she watched a widgeon scurry up the bank and disappear into the foliage. The deaths of Nat and Curles Neck had dulled her to near insensibility. She merely existed ... nothing else. Then she thought of Mary. How she longed to have the child's soft limbs in her arms, pressed close to her heart, the gold-flecked eyes turned to hers so trustingly. Her daughter had a scent all her own – like sunlight. If things went badly with the rebellion Mary might be all she had left in the world. If that was God's will she would make a good life for her child, whether it be here or in England. Nat lived on in Mary. To cherish the little one would be to honor his memory.

The sound of hooves woke Lyn from her reverie. Her heart beat fast and she realized that now, wherever she was, she expected danger. She leaped to her feet, turned, and then smiled for the first time in days as Coke's fiery red coat appeared outlined against the silver forest and she saw John's gentle face with Mary's just below it, as the attorney rode to meet her, the child pressed close to his chest.

"John, John! How glad I am to see you. Here, let me take her. Mary, dearest, how well you look. Did Mister John take good care of you? What a brave girl to ride so far!"

Mary clung to Lyn and looked somewhat confused, but not frightened. Lyn silently blessed the Byrds and John for having brought the child through the storms of the last month with so little seeming effect. John dismounted and approached Lyn, almost with trepidation, as if she might break if he moved suddenly.

"You look well, Lyn, despite ... I didn't stop at Curles for fear that the child ... you know."

"Bless you for that, John. I don't know what she would have thought, but better not to take a chance. How confusing this must be for her! But she loved it at Byrd's, did she not?"

"She did indeed. And the little boy loved playing king to her courtier ... 'twas most amusing. It was a happy suggestion of mine, but it did take you away from Curles when ..."

"Surely you don't think that Ludwell would have been deterred by our presence? They came at noon, in broad day ... it was a brazen statement of triumph and authority. I fear for the rebellion if Berkeley's hounds have been given such license. It must mean that the Greens own the Western Shore. Had we been at Curles the result would have been the same ... no, worse, for Mary might have seen things that no child should ever see."

"You are right Lyn, as always." John paused. "I have much news. News that you should hear alone, or at least ..."

"Very well, John. Let's walk back to the house and I'll give Mary her supper and put her to bed. She must be exhausted. Can your news wait?"

"I wish it could wait forever. Listen, how does this sound to you? You know that Nat's four captains and Drummond and Lawrence and I have a rendezvous tonight."

"Of course, it is the thirtieth of November. Jake will be here too, will he not?"

"Well, that's part of my news. Jake has been persuaded, thank God, to remain at Byrd's. William needs him, and his mother is loathe to let him go. But the rest of us are sworn to meet no later than midnight tonight. Can you wait until then to hear my news ... and that of the others?"

"*I* willing? Of course. But what about them? They won't want a woman sitting in their councils."

"Did I say you are always right? There, you are wrong. You will be perfectly welcome. They love you both as Nat's widow and for yourself as well. They know you are trying to find the best course for yourself and for Mary ... be assured that you will be welcome."

"Well then, let me tend to Mary and then you and I can help Jamie put some kind of supper together, something cold that will be ready for them whenever they come. It's almost dark. It must be six o'clock or more already and no one but you has come. Do you really think they will all be here?"

"We shall see. Here, let me take the child, she is quite a weight. Can you lead Coke? Thank God that Jamie was able to take you in ... it almost feels like being home at Curles. I am so pleased to find you more composed, more yourself."

And, to her surprise, Lyn realized that John's observation was true. She felt more tranquil and centered than she had since she saw Nat's empty saddle. Mary and John were her elixir.

Eight o'clock saw Jamie Crewes sitting at the head of his own table with Lyn to his right and John to his left and Drummond and Lawrence next to them. They had partaken heartily of the corn chowder and the cold turkey and rabbit and had complimented Lyn on her venison pie, and now they were playing with dishes of preserved peaches and bowls of walnuts and hazelnuts as Lyn walked around the table and refilled each glass with Crewes' claret. A huge fire kept the cold at bay and a careless observer would have thought that the friends were gathered in mirth to usher in the Christmas season until he saw their faces, which were haggard with fatigue and anxiety.

"Who's going to begin?" asked their host.

"I will," said Lawrence, his voice hoarse with a lingering cold. He looked directly across the table at Lyn and his face softened. "I have some bad news. Are you sure you want to hear it, coming so soon after what you have suffered?"

"For me, it is always better to know the worst than to let my fancy run away with my thoughts. With Mary safe in bed upstairs, there is nothing I can hear that would be worse than what the last month has brought to me."

"Ah, how sad, but how true. Well then, first I'll tell you some things which everyone else here knows. Later perhaps we can digest the news and decide how it affects our several lives. Do you know why we called John to the Blackwater?"

"He has not had time to tell me."

"It happened this way. After we left Warner Hall Farlow and Arnold went to stay with Farlow's niece, Mistress Cheeseman, in New Kent. A week or so after they arrived, Farlow heard that a substantial part of Nat's army was regrouping near West's Point. Some of them reported to this new fellow, Ingram, who calls himself General, but most of them were followers of Major Thomas Whaley, one of Nat's stoutest soldiers. Farlow was enthused, thought our men were well on their way to reconstituting a real fighting force. He sent one messenger to John at Curles, who was then supposed to let Jamie know what was happening; and another to the three of us who were staying on the Blackwater – Will and Tom Hansford and me. John didn't get the message, for you all had gone on to Byrd's and the messenger was either too lazy or too afraid ... whatever ... to get directions from your slaves and find you there. And of course he was not charged with stopping at Turkey Island, so Jamie was left uninformed as well. But the Blackwater messenger arrived promptly and you can imagine how we felt when we heard his news. Within weeks of Nat's death our cause seemed to be righting itself, finding its way again. Will and Tom and I were hot to ride north with the messenger but Sarah put a spoke in Will's wheel and Clarissa in mine, for we had sworn to stay with the ladies for at least a month and they held us to our vow."

Lawrence stopped and drank some wine and wiped his brow, which was steaming. Lyn thought he must have a fever. She thought of Nat, shuddered, and watched him anxiously.

"Well, young Tom Hansford was unattached, as you know. As soon as he heard the good news he pricked up his ears like a war horse. Gone were his careful plans for putting his plantation to rights and enjoying the winter months at home. He threw some clothes in his saddle bags, polished his sword, primed his pistols and was off the next day. Will and I would have given anything to ride with him."

"Aye, lass, it's true," said Drummond sadly. "And if we had ... who knows?"

Lyn knew she was going to hear something terrible. She folded her hands in front of her and concentrated on holding them just so, so that she would not tremble and she would have some place to fix her gaze.

Lawrence looked around the room as though for an escape and then continued his tale. "John missed Hansford by a day. For by then we had sent for John. Now you understand why he left you so suddenly at the trading post. We told him everything and he was as hot as we to join Nat's army, but he too had more pressing duties and could not go."

Lyn looked at John who was staring at the fire, his mind seemingly a thousand miles away. Dear John. He probably never would have said a word about his own desires. Nat had trusted him to care for her and Mary and to place that duty above all other things. This terrible rebellion was pulling him away from his family, like the others, but he would put family first. Family? Had she used that term? But then, she and Mary *were* John's family, as much as he had one. And, unlike Nat, he *would* put them first. She felt a pain in her chest as though her heart was being torn. Please God let her survive these coming months ... and bear whatever Richard Lawrence was about to tell her.

"Well, it seems that Tom Hansford met his old friend Tony Arnold and George Farlow at West's Point. They say that two or three hundred men were gathered there, a goodly number. For reasons that we do not yet know Hansford and Farlow rode east, to Yorktown, and Arnold stayed behind. It may be that they were going to try and organize a navy, as Nat and John did at Tindall's Point. I daresay that we shall find out, some day." Lawrence drank again, as though looking for an excuse not to go on. "But, what happened was ... those who went to Yorktown fell into the hands of Major Robert Beverley."

"I don't think I know that name," said Lyn stoically.

"Then thank the Lord that you do not. He and Phil Ludwell are Berkeley's mastiffs, and I pity the man who falls into the clutches of either of them. You know what Ludwell is capable of by bitter experience. Beverley is the same, or worse. From what I hear, Hansford and Farlow were drinking at a tavern, expecting no trouble, when Beverley's force landed from the Eastern Shore, overran the town and wholly routed our men. I suppose the guards were careless ... who knows? But I should finish. The fact is, Lyn, that Beverley took our friends, together with Farlow's nephew Cheeseman, to the Eastern Shore where Berkeley was still headquartered and ... and he hanged all three of them from one of Arlington's oaks."

Lyn could not restrain a cry. "Hanged! All three! They're all dead?"

"All dead. They died a felon's death." Lawrence cleared his throat. "They say that Hansford asked to be shot like a soldier, but Berkeley denied it. Said he could hang like a dog and strung him up."

"And they had no trial," said John softly, his face twisted with pain. "It was like Carver all over again. Berkeley acted as judge, jury and executioner. He sentenced them and hanged them in a day."

"Is that the law?" breathed Lyn.

"No," said John stolidly. "The prisoners were in custody. Berkeley was in no danger from them. He should have locked them up and tried them under the laws of England. Giles Bland still awaits trial ... as does Sir Henry Chicheley, on our side. It was an act of pure revenge. The destruction of Curles and this thing ... it gives us a taste of what to expect if we do not prevail."

The room fell silent, the men thinking of Hansford's angelic beauty and sweet nature and George Farlow's intelligence and utter dependability. Even now their bodies might be hanging from Berkeley's gallows, a warning for the rebels. Lyn looked at John and Crewes and Lawrence and Drummond and her heart misgave her. Even if they did not rejoin Nat's army each was a marked man ... each might find himself dangling from a tree with a hempen collar. She was overwhelmed with despair.

CHAPTER 29
NOVEMBER 1676 - JANUARY 1677

A large oak log gave way in Jamie Crewes' capacious fireplace and spat embers onto the hearth and onto the heart pine floor. John jumped up and swept the coals back where they belonged and mended the fire, adding more oak and some seasoned hickory. The comfortable blaze mesmerized Crewes and his guests and they sat in silence for some time, drinking claret and staring at the flames. Images of their fallen friends filled every heart: Nat Bacon, Billy Carver, Tom Hansford, George Farlow ... how long would the list grow before one side or the other claimed victory?

The company was roused by the banging of the front door and the rush of footsteps. Each man's hand automatically went to his hip, reaching for his sword and then, not finding that weapon, went to his belt for his dagger. Sharp steel gleamed in four hands. Drummond, who was sitting at Lyn's right, drew her close to his left side. Tony Arnold rushed into the room, his face harrowed with care and his hair and clothing soaked with rain. A storm had arrived, unnoticed.

"Tony!" cried four voices.

Lyn's heart beat fast. So that was Anthony Arnold. He had so much the look of Nat that for one minute ... but no. He was small and slim and dark, but his features were coarser and, above all, he did not have her husband's distinctive hawk eyes.

"Thank God you are still in the land of the living, laddie," said Drummond, taking Arnold's cloak. "Sit down ... take off your boots ... dry yourself. Jamie, is there another cup for Tony?"

When the young man was comfortable he was introduced to Lyn and she was pleased to see the pain on his face when he learned that she was Nat's widow. He had loved General Bacon as much as the rest of them.

"Well, you are a man of your word," said Lawrence as the company composed itself, anxious to hear Arnold's story. "It's still the thirtieth of November, unless midnight has struck without our noticing."

"Aye, it's the thirtieth," answered Arnold. "But I would have come anyway. Things are moving fast. I've come to recruit as many of you as I can."

Lyn's heart sank. Not a man of them would resist Arnold's siren song. They would all be off by daybreak, to cast the dice one more time and hope that Dame Fortune's wheel would raise them up to victory. And what would she and Mary do then?

"First," said Drummond quietly, "do you have any word of Tom and George ... of the bodies?"

"Nay, Will. They are likely still hanging there, exposed to the wind and rain and food for the kites and gulls. Poor Tom. I am almost glad his mother passed on last year so that she did not know what happened to her boy. He was the light of her life."

Lyn thought of Nat and of Mary and once again felt the pain in her chest, like a knife. It was almost easier for the soldiers than for those they left behind.

"Are there any good tidings?" asked John in a measured tone.

Arnold brightened. "Yes, Grey, there are. Apart from some roving forces, Nat's army is pretty much split into three. Lawrence Ingram has gathered a couple of hundred men at West's Point; Tom Whaley has the cream of the crop at King's Creek; and William Rookings has taken Allen's fine house in Surry County and is giving the Southside something to think about."

Lyn could not restrain herself. "King's Creek?" she cried. "Has Colonel Bacon's plantation been taken?"

Arnold looked at her kindly. "Yes, ma'am. 'Tis a pity that the Colonel is your relative, but the fact is that Tom Whaley has overrun the place and made it headquarters for some hundred men."

"And the Colonel and Mistress Bacon?"

"Are fine, ma'am. They were taken in by John Page. I have seen them both, with my own eyes. They are fine, though they grieve the loss of their plantation, of course."

Lyn's head spun. King's Creek! Where she and Nat had been so kindly entertained; where she first got a glimpse of plantation life in Virginia and how enchanting it could be. Colonel Bacon had wanted to make Nat his heir and now the young man lay under the ground and the old man had lost everything he had built in twenty-five years of unremitting toil. War was a terrible thing, even if it was justified. And she had not made up her own mind about the justification for this one. She wondered if she should leave the five men to their business but then she decided to stay. What was said tonight would likely decide her own fate, and Mary's.

Lawrence had come alive since Arnold's appearance. He seemed to shed his fatigue and depression and he pressed for more news.

"What do you know of Ingram?"

416

"Nothing good. Everybody says that he is an ape to Nat's lion. The only men who follow him are the slaves and servants who have left their masters within the past few weeks and have seen the cause as a road to freedom. They are ill-bred, ill-educated, ill-armed ... they are rabble and I, for one, will have nothing to do with them."

There was a long pause as the listeners pondered Arnold's statement.

"Where does our best hope lie?" queried Lawrence bluntly.

"With Whaley, no doubt. All the veterans are at King's Creek. That is where the action will be, for Berkeley's plan is to fight from his ships and so far he has sent them, alternately, up the York or up the James. We would do well to make King's Creek our headquarters and send out troops from there as the fight develops."

"And Rookings?"

"To the extent that the Southside can be raised from its torpor, they will declare for the Governor. I think that Rookings is fighting a losing battle. I wish he would join us on the Peninsula, but he will not – many have asked him, and he has refused."

"He always was hard-headed," grumbled Drummond. "A brave soul, but hard-headed. What does he hope to achieve by dividing our force?"

"You would have to ask him, Will. He's a Southsider and I suppose he thinks he can persuade his countrymen to cross over to our side. But it is not going to happen. The best thing to do is to leave him alone. Perhaps he'll come around on his own."

"I agree," said John. "Nat and I had the devil of a time working with him in Gloucester. But if he ever does come around, he'll fight to the death."

"Aye, that's Rookings," agreed Arnold, taking a great gulp of claret. "Is there more wine, Jamie? I'm beginning to feel like I might survive the night."

Crewes opened another bottle of wine and Lyn took it around the room, filling each cup. Now, she thought, they are going to decide what to do.

"How many ships does Berkeley have?" asked Lawrence.

"The *Adam and Eve*, Captain Gardiner. By the way, Berkeley's named him Admiral. The *Loyall Rebecca*, Captain Larrimore. The *Young Prince*, Captain Morris. The *Richard and Elizabeth*, Captain Prinne. And the newest arrival, the *Concord*, Captain Grantham."

The men looked at one another, grim-faced.

"How many guns?" John queried.

"As many as eighty ... it could be more."

"God in Heaven above!" burst out Jamie Crewes. "Are we supposed to fight that? And what of the King? Has he sent a fleet?"

"It's all rumor right now, but we've captured a handful of Berkeley's men and they say a fleet is on its way."

The five men groaned and Lyn's heart sank. Surely the outcome was clear. By continuing the fight, Nat's friends would simply be throwing themselves on a funeral pyre ... one that was already ablaze.

"It doesn't look good, does it Tony?" asked Lawrence, rhetorically.

"No, Dicken. It's a lost cause. But it's still *my* cause. Tom and I swore to each other that if one of us died the other one would go on to the bitter end. I intend to keep that vow."

"Well said!" cried Drummond. "There's a man of honor. Here's to you Anthony Arnold!"

Bacon's veterans raised their wine cups in salute and Lyn joined them, her heart riven with the thought that within the next months these men were going to die ... all of them, including John.

"Well, I know what I'm going to do," continued the Scot almost placidly.

"And I know what you're going to do, too," interjected Lawrence. "The same as I. You're led by the heart and I'm led by the head and we're both going to make fools of ourselves and make our women rue the day they met us. We're both going to King's Creek to join Tom Whaley."

"You always have to have the last word, Dicken," laughed Drummond, "but tonight I won't argue. You are absolutely right. I have that comfortable feeling inside. I *know* it's the right thing to do. How pleased I am that you will be by my side."

The two friends smiled at one another and fell silent. Arnold looked like a new man and Jamie Crewes had come to life, but John kept his head down and kept staring into the fire.

"Well Jamie," Arnold laughed, "Are we going to let the old men outshine us? Will you come with me tomorrow?"

"Aye, Tony, you know I will. I have been waiting for a sign ... and you have given it to us tonight. We'll see who can get to King's Creek faster, you and me or an old Scot and an innkeeper."

"And who will take care of Turkey Island?" protested Drummond. "Sarah and Clarissa will tend Blackwater for us until the cows come home, but you, Jamie? Shouldn't you look out for yourself? Surely you've given enough ... think of the future."

"There's no future for me if Berkeley's still Governor," replied Crewes. "Besides, I was hoping that John Grey might stay behind ... somebody has to look after Lyn and Nat's little maid."

John looked up, his face expressionless. "You're right that I have a duty even greater than that I owe the cause," he said, looking at Lyn. "Nat swore me to protect his wife and child before all else, and I shall. But I hope to honor that vow and not sit out the fight." He turned to Drummond. "Will, don't you have a friend in Kecoughtan with a town house that is going begging for a tenant?"

The Scot looked surprised, but answered readily. "Aye, laddie, Captain Jervis. He's a man of about Dicken's age. I've known him for years. He owns at least one ship, the *Swallow*, and by now he may have more. I haven't seen him since these troubles began. The poor fellow lost his wife about ... oh, maybe five years ago. He has a splendid plantation, Fairview, not ten miles from Kecoughtan, and the little town house as well. Mistress Jervis loved the town and spent most of her time there. She watched the shipping and was first with all the news from England. But when he's not on the sea Tom Jervis loves the country ... he's quite a gardener, so he has spent most of his time at Fairview since his lady died. He leaves the town house in the hands of a French housekeeper ... what a cook she is! And yes, as I told you at Blackwater, Tom would like to find a tenant for the place. He's not quite ready to sell, as it is so handy for business. He rides in from Fairview perhaps three or four times a month and it makes things easy for him to have a bedroom waiting and to know where his next meal is coming from ... and what a meal! But where is all this leading? I'm not quite sure ..."

"If Captain Jervis would accept a reasonable rent, I have enough set aside to secure bed and board for Lyn and Mary through the winter. And if I knew that they were safe and well-cared for, don't you see, I would feel free to follow my heart and join you at King's Creek."

Lyn felt the strangest mixture of emotions as John spoke. On the one hand, it was the perfect solution for her. She was far from ready to sail for England at this point. How could she leave Nat behind? Her heart would not let her do it. Moreover, if, somehow, the rebels prevailed, Curles Neck might still be hers. If there was any possibility of success, she vowed that she would rebuild her home and laugh in Philip Ludwell's face. Yet, what had John said? That if he "followed his heart" he would fight with the rebels. So caring for her was the path of duty, not the path of choice. She could not name the bitter feeling that she felt inside, where her poor torn heart fluttered. But if she had been a little more honest, she could have a found a name for it: jealousy.

"Lyn. Are you dreaming? Did you hear me? What do you think of John's plan?"

"Why, Mister Drummond, I ... it is a good plan ... a very good plan. Mary and I will be in the center of things, can catch all the news. And we won't be a burden on anyone. Except ... the money..."

"Nonsense, lass. John would spend his last penny on you, you know that. I shall pen a letter to Tom Jervis this very night asking him to take you and the little maid at a nominal fee until the world rights itself and we know which end is up. You'll love Tom ... he's quite a lady's man, got the manners of a gentleman. And then John can join us with a clear conscience and an unburdened heart. Of course you'll miss him, but Kecoughtan is full of fine folk ... you'll have a passel of friends within a month. So, that's settled."

"Why yes, I suppose it is." Lyn looked at John. "Thank you, John." Grey looked perturbed, but said nothing.

Crewes rose and swallowed the last of his wine. "It's late and time for bed. So, Tony, Dicken, Will and I will be off after breakfast. John, use my sloop to take Lyn and the child to Kecoughtan. It doesn't look like much, but it is serviceable. Just keep it there until I send for it, or come myself. Now, Mistress Lyn, will you lend me Abraham and Hannah to manage Turkey Island until we are back from the wars? Please say 'yes.' I couldn't leave it in better hands."

Lyn looked a question at John, who nodded, and then she smiled at Jamie. "Of course you may have them. They will be relieved to know they have a home. And may we leave our cattle here? And Coke and Mignon and Folly?"

"It goes without saying. Well then, one more toast."

The five men and one woman raised their wine cups in unison and called out "Nat Bacon!" Their voices were lost in the forest air as the rain poured down relentlessly and the James gathered force and speed and rushed to the sea.

The rebellion might not have existed as far as Kecoughtan was concerned. The little town on the bay sparkled under a bright winter sky and the distant sun seemed to shine more brightly there than it did at the falls of the James. Each of the village's dozen or so brick houses wore a holly wreath on its brightly painted door and the casements shone like ice crystals.

Mary was enchanted with the town and it gladdened Lyn's heart to take her walking every day after dinner to see the pretty houses and watch the sloops and ketches dance in the harbor. Lyn had not yet met her host, Captain Jervis, as he was away on business at the very top of the Bay, in Delaware, but Marie told her at breakfast that he was due any day so the rebel's widow strolled by the harbor with the thought that she and the child might be the first to see him arrive. She watched for a smart sloop named the *Kestrel*. All of Captain Jervis' vessels were named for birds, as his late wife had wished.

As she stood on the shore Lyn adjusted Mary's hood to protect her from the stiffening breeze and then she pulled her own cloak closer. The child was busy with a pile of oyster shells and Lyn had a few minutes to herself, to think and dream. As usual, the image of John Grey swam into her mind's eye. John had changed. To the extent that he could, given their close quarters in Captain Jervis' neat, but small, brick house, John had grown increasingly distant in the two weeks since they had made their weary way from Turkey Island. Horseless, he wandered the countryside every morning for exercise, whatever the weather, and every day after dinner he secreted himself in Captain Jervis' surprisingly capacious library. Lyn was so used to confiding in John and receiving his advice that now that their conversations remained wholly superficial she felt as though she had lost a limb. She knew that he burned to join the rebels and that his promise to wait for Captain Jervis chaffed terribly, but there must be more. Whether he was here, looking after

420

her, or in the field, following Nat's fallen star, he was still bound to the Bacons. Perhaps he yearned to cut himself loose from the ties of friendship and swim by himself, unencumbered. God knows he had earned his freedom. Whatever he chose to do, she would not begrudge it ... it was just that she could no longer read his mind; she had no idea what he wanted in life. Well, it could not be much longer now. She did not really doubt that some arrangement would be made with Captain Jervis and then John would be free. Free to join the rebels or, perhaps, free to return to England and salvage what he could of a career in the law that had begun with such promise.

Lyn glanced at Mary who was still happily occupied with her shells and then scanned the horizon, gratefully breathing in the sharp, salt air of the port town. She squinted against the brightness of the water and then, sure enough, saw a dainty vessel dancing on the waves. It was the only sloop sailing free; she felt sure that it was the *Kestrel*. A spanking breeze brought the sloop to the wharf and five minutes later it spilled its human cargo on the shore as a dozen or more rough, bearded men bound the vessel tight to the dock and then streamed to Kecoughtan's only ordinary, *The King's Arms*. A minute or two later the sailors were followed by a slim, gentlemanly fellow with ginger whiskers whom Lyn took to be the sailing master. No captain appeared. Her curiosity aroused, Lyn decided to ask the ginger man whether the sloop was the *Kestrel* and, if so, whether Captain Jervis was still aboard. As the man strode up the wharf she signaled slightly with her hand and caught his attention. He looked her way, saw Mary, stared quite markedly at her, smiled and stopped, doffing his rough cap.

"Excuse me, sir," said Lyn tentatively. "Pardon the intrusion, but can you tell me whether that sloop is the *Kestrel*?"

"It is, as sure as my name is Tom Jervis. Are you waiting for some of our furs? I have some of the best-cured beaver I have ever seen from St. Mary's City. They would make you a noble cloak."

Lyn blushed. "In fact, sir, if you are Captain Jervis, it is you I am waiting for! I am Elizabeth Bacon and I hope to be your tenant. This *is* awkward. I wonder if you have any idea what I am talking about. Did Mister Drummond's letter reach you?"

The ginger man's bright blue eyes opened wide with surprise and a look of delight crossed his wind burned face as he reappraised Lyn and Mary.

"You are the rebel's widow? Such a lady? Oh!" Captain Jervis brought his broad hand to his mouth as though he would have stuffed his words right back between his rosy lips. "God bless my soul, I *do* apologize. It's just that ... I had formed a very different picture of you from Will's note."

Lyn was both pained and confused but she decided to make the best of it.

"Well, I mistook you for your sailing master, so we are even! So you *did* hear from Mister Drummond. Then I trust that you will not be too shocked to find your house full of strangers."

"Marie forwarded Will's letter to Smith Island with a bulletin of her own; she knows I always stop there. In principle, I should be glad for you to have the use of my town house." Jervis paused a moment and looked into Lyn's eyes. "No, let me rephrase that. You *certainly* may have the house, under any terms you are comfortable with, for as long as you and the child. desire."

Lyn curtseyed. "You are very kind, Captain Jervis, but I am sure that you will want to consider such an important matter a little further. My man of business, John Grey, is with us, awaiting your arrival. Perhaps, at your convenience, you could talk things over with him."

"There is no time like the present. Let me step into *The King's Arms* to give my men some orders and then we will walk to the house together and settle everything. Grey, did you say? What kind of fellow is he?"

"Oh ... John is an attorney. He came with us from England ..." Lyn's voice trailed off as she followed Captain Jervis onto the porch of *The King's Arms* and watched him disappear inside. What kind of man was John? It was the theme of her waking and sleeping thoughts.

John gave up and laid Gervase Markham's *Way to Get Wealth* on Jervis' little round mahogany table. He must have read the treatise on soil enrichment three times and he had not retained a word of it. If the *Kestrel* did not arrive soon he did not know what he would do. Living with Lyn in these close quarters was a daily torture. It was like being her husband, and Mary's father, in the abstract. The three of them rose together, ate together, sometimes took the air together, played cards and read together, just as though they were wed, yet ever since Turkey Island there had been a stronger, thicker wall between them than had existed since the day he first touched her hand in the dining room at Friston Hall. John supposed that Lyn was preoccupied with planning her voyage back to Suffolk – a voyage she would doubtless undertake as soon as she knew the fate of Curles Neck and Bacon's Quarter. And he? What would he do next? For him, the heart had gone out of the rebellion with Nat's death. Despite Arnold's and Crewes' protestations to the contrary, he knew that the Ring's cause, like Nat, was fated to die young. He feared for his friends. Many of them would perish with their cause.

John sighed and paced the room. Ideas of justice and equity seemed as hollow now as hickory nuts stripped of their meat by squirrels. Let Berkeley eke out his last years here... if he were removed would Charles Stuart send the colony a better governor? It was not likely. After two years in Virginia John had ceased to care for abstractions; only human beings seemed significant, and foremost among them, Lyn. He crossed Jervis' study and stared at the harbor. He would do his duty, as he understood it, to those he loved, and then he would go home. Unless, of course, Lyn decided to stay. Lyn:

the keystone to the arch of his life. Well, he would take things one step at a time. First, settle the rebel's widow and daughter; second, look to his friends; third ... third lay too far in the future for him to see.

The study door was flung open and John whirled, surprise registered on his face. He faced a slim man of middling height, with ginger whiskers, a high color, and bright blue eyes. Who was this?

"Mister Grey? Allow me to introduce myself. Tom Jervis."

John gathered his wits. For God's sake, of course, it was Jervis. The sloop must have come in while he was sitting here, gathering wool. Well, it was what he had wanted, was it not?

"Captain Jervis! What a pleasant surprise. Not a surprise, really, for Marie has been telling us for days that the *Kestrel* was due. I trust you had a pleasant trip."

"Not pleasant, but certainly profitable."

"You were in St. Mary's City?"

"Yes ... and many points in between. It is the *Kestrel's* usual route. I send the *Swallow* up the coast, as far as New Amsterdam, (or, I should say, New York), but we keep the sloop in the Bay."

"I beg your pardon for usurping your library. It has been a great resource to me while Lyn and I ... while Mistress Bacon and I ... awaited your arrival. Allow me to find Mistress Bacon. She has been on pins and needles, using your house in your absence these two weeks as we have so shamefully done."

"Oh, never mind that. We met on the wharf and everything is settled. Of course she and the little girl may have the house ... it would be heartless of me to say otherwise."

John was stunned. Lyn had already met this quick, ginger fellow and everything was settled? They must have accomplished their business in half an hour. Why, he and Lyn had not even decided what rent to offer Captain Jervis, as she was so reluctant to borrow anything from him and their conversations on the issue had been fruitless. He was still at a loss for words when Lyn and Mary entered the room, rosy from their walk and smiling broadly. John's heart sank.

"There you are, John! I knew we should find you here. Mary and I were so blown about by the wind that we went upstairs to put ourselves to rights. Marie says tea is ready – will you come?"

An hour later Captain Jervis and his guests were still seated in the parlor, although the tea things and Mary Bacon had been removed, the former to the basement kitchen and the latter to the upstairs guestroom. Marie was moving Lyn's things from the best bedroom, which Captain Jervis was about to reclaim, and Lyn and Mary were going to occupy the second bedroom, which John had been using. Where John was going to sleep was a question which was vexing Lyn, but she did not know how to raise the subject. She looked at the two men who were sitting somewhat stiffly on walnut chairs which were better designed for the female form than for the male. It was uncomfortably clear that for some reason Captain Jervis and John Grey had not hit it off. Had the Captain been offended by the way she and John had taken over his house even before they had been properly invited? It was not likely. The Captain had an open, airy way about him ... didn't seem in the least bit stuffy. Perhaps, like many men of business, he did not like attorneys. Merchants and planters liked to get things done despite the law, while lawyers were always throwing up fences and hedges and impeding progress. Whatever it was, the past hour had not gone as smoothly as she could have wished.

"Well, it is most generous of you," John was saying, "but if you should change your mind please be assured that I have a little purse set aside for Mistress Bacon's needs despite the fire at Curles Neck. Fortunately I was carrying it on my person when the fire occurred."

"She would be doing me a favor by staying here, I assure you. Marie is an excellent housekeeper, but there is nothing like having a place actually lived in. It could not have fallen out better. I don't stay here but once a month ... I consider Fairview my home."

"I am somewhat surprised you have not sold the place then."

"Oh, I have thought of it a dozen times since Agatha died, but something always kept me from doing so." Jervis turned to Lyn and smiled. "And now I know that fate was guiding my hand."

Lyn blushed. Captain Jervis was charming in a certain breezy way, but she had only known the man for two hours and already he was treating her like an old friend. She peeped at John and saw that grim, expressionless look that she hated so. When he wore that face, you simply could not tell what he was thinking. Probably that he would leave Kecoughtan at the earliest possible opportunity.

"Well if I cannot spend my coins on Mistress Bacon, perhaps I can persuade you to take some on my own account. You don't happen to have a horse that you are looking to sell, do you? I must be off to New Kent tomorrow and we left our riding horses – a fine black, my own chestnut, and Mistress Bacon's gray mare – in Henrico County."

Before Jervis could reply the words flew out of Lyn's mouth. "Tomorrow John? New Kent?"

John looked at Lyn coolly as though surprised at her surprise. "Why everything is settled here, is it not?" he asked stolidly, as though he had been obtaining her a room at an ordinary. "Our business is done and nothing else keeps me. I shall stay at *The King's Arms* tonight and be off tomorrow, if I can find a horse."

Lyn sat silently, looking at her hands. Jervis obviously felt the tension between his two guests, but did not know what to do with it. "I keep a little bay with my neighbor, Smith, not having a stable here. I use him to get to Fairview and back, and Smith has the use of him otherwise, which pays for his bed and board. I am not attached to the creature, as I keep my blood horses at Fairview, and you are more than welcome to have him. Why don't we walk over now while there is still a little light, and you can take a look at him?"

"It is most generous of you, but how will you get to Fairview?"

"Oh, one of my neighbors will lend me a beast, that's no problem." Jervis looked pointedly at Lyn. "In any event, I have decided to stay in Kecoughtan a little longer than I had originally planned. Something has come up which demands my attention."

The innuendo was too obvious. Lyn continued to study her hands while John, his face blank, rose and stepped into the hall for his hat and cloak. Captain Jervis leaned down and peered into Lyn's face. "Something has just come up," he chuckled. "Good evening, my dear. I'll be back shortly. Don't worry about Grey – I'll see that he is well mounted and comfortably settled at the ordinary. Why don't you ask Marie to pack up his things and take them over to *The King's Arms*? I look forward to supping with you tonight and learning a little of your history. From what Mister Grey says, you have had quite a few adventures here in Virginia."

Captain Jervis' plan to have Lyn and Mary as his guests at Fairview for Christmas was accomplished. Initially Lyn had demurred, claiming that she and the child would prefer to spend the time quietly in Kecoughtan by themselves, but when the Captain indicated that he needed Marie to help him host the Twelve Days of Christmas and indicated that Lyn's help would also be invaluable, she felt obliged to accept his invitation. She reminded him that the day after Christmas would be the second month's anniversary of her husband's death and that on the second of January she would mourn the fact that Nat was not present to celebrate his thirtieth birthday. He was forced to agree that under the circumstances she could stay as much in the background as she liked, but in fact he felt quite certain that once she was at Fairview, with Mary involved in all the festivities, that she would come out of her shell and that soon Virginia would begin to look at them as a couple. Had not Lady Frances Berkeley wed Sir William when Sam Stephens' body was hardly cold in the grave? It was the custom of the country. More often than not the most doting widow or widower found him or herself wed to another within six months of the death of the former spouse. Nature must take its course. Who could doubt that Tom Jervis and Lyn Bacon were meant for one another?

Part of the Captain's plan unfolded as anticipated: Mary was in ecstasy. She loved the roomy, comfortable plantation with its open fields and distant sea view and she was quickly adopted by Jervis' staff and spent her days with the cooks and the maids, as happy as a lamb. Lyn's transformation was slower to come. She gratefully accepted the dress lengths of dark cloth which Captain Jervis gave her on Boxing Day and used the excuse of her limited wardrobe, (all but the three gowns she had taken to Mary Byrd's were consumed in the Curles Neck fire), to spend most of the time in her bedroom, sewing. The Captain had given her the best guestroom, the one which looked southeast over the garden and meadows, to the sea. But her conscience nagged her and as the days passed she spent more and more time with the staff, planning dinners and suppers and dances, and somehow Tom Jervis always felt obliged to sit in on the conferences.

By the first of January the servants were treating her as the mistress of Fairview. Her heart sank. She must return to Kecoughtan as soon as possible, but even then the rumors would persist. Should she throw herself on the mercies of Sarah Drummond or Mary Byrd? She, the mistress of Hazelwood and Curles Neck, could not bear the thought. She began to think that she must find a way to return to Suffolk regardless of the fact that her Virginia property was in a kind of legal purgatory. But how could she leave Nat, without having once visited his grave? And what would she do for her passage money? She was almost penniless and John Grey seemed to have disappeared from the face of the earth. Surely nobody would lend her money with Curles as security; apart from her English farm, Folly and Mignon constituted her only significant property and they were at Turkey Island. Perhaps she could ask Captain Jervis one last favor without unduly compromising herself: beg him to arrange that the horses be brought from Henrico and sold for as much gold as possible.

Lyn was sitting at supper with the Captain on the first of January when she broached the subject.

"My dear, the beasts are already here!" laughed Captain Jervis. "The big black, your mare and Mister Grey's chestnut. Did you think I would leave you without a horse? The day after the *Kestrel* made port I sent three of my men up the James on that old sloop that you and Grey came in with orders to find Turkey Island, return the sloop, and reclaim your horses. They arrived this very afternoon. I was going to surprise you with them tomorrow, for today they must rest. They were quite a sight, with their winter coats, and no one having cared for them. But they are fine beasts. Somebody had an eye for horseflesh."

"Nat did," burst out Lyn and began to weep.

Captain Jervis looked sympathetic but also somewhat annoyed. He understood Bacon to have been an impetuous and arrogant hothead – how long was the little widow going to mourn him? On the other hand, her grief spoke well of heart. It was a heart worth winning. The Captain composed himself as did Lyn, who was mortified at her own behavior.

"Well, well they remind you of home, is that it? It is a sad story. Lost your husband and lost your home in a few short months, and it is still upsetting. Of course it is ... how could it not be? But tomorrow you shall see the pretty horses and then you'll feel better. We'll let Mary ride my little pony. How will that be?"

Lyn wanted to remind her host that tomorrow would have been Nat's birthday and that he could not have chosen a worse day to give her yet another gift, another surprise, but she bit her tongue. The man meant well ... he was just woefully insensitive. Had he forgotten what it was like to lose a spouse? Did he not miss his wife? Her hand was everywhere here at Fairview; her taste most refined ... she must have been uncommonly elegant. But, strangely, Lyn did not even know what she looked like for there was not a picture of her in the entire place. Perhaps, for Captain Jervis, one woman was as good as another as long as they could run a household and ... Lyn shut her eyes on the picture of the other duties which would be expected of her. Instead, to her amazement and chagrin, John's image appeared, his face remote and sad. God forbid that John too would perish in the rebellion. That she really could not bear.... Lyn cut off her thoughts which were racing down unexpected avenues. She rose and turned to Captain Jervis.

"As always, you have been most kind. Thank you for bringing the horses. Mary will be thrilled ... they are all great friends of hers. And I, too, am deeply appreciative. Now I can not only ride, I have the means of raising a little money ..."

Captain Jervis looked truly perturbed. "You are not serious about selling the beasts, I hope. Don't you know that you can rely on me to supply all your wants? Lyn ..."

Lyn conveniently dropped her napkin and stooped to pick it up. "My goodness!" she cried. "Look what o'clock it is! Mary will not go to sleep without a story and it is an hour past her bedtime! I am sure you will excuse me, Captain Jervis. I look forward to seeing you tomorrow and visiting my dear horses." With that she fled upstairs, her face red and tears in her eyes.

CHAPTER 30

JANUARY 1677

The *Swallow* was not expected in Kecoughtan for several weeks but its master had traded her beef and hides and pelts and tobacco for good English broadcloth, woolens and spices in record time, and had flitted down the coast as though the devil were after him and snugged up to her home wharf on the first of January. The message announcing her arrival was delivered to Captain Jervis just as he was guiding Lyn across Fairview's snowy stable yard, his hand comfortably on her elbow. Lyn almost laughed at his consternation. On the one hand, his flagship had made a record journey and record profits, which should have brought joy to his heart; on the other hand he had to leave for Kecoughtan forthwith to talk with the master, scrutinize the ship, review the books and arrange for her next voyage. It was a chagrined Captain Jervis who left his guest, with the most profound apologies, and rode off smartly, promising to return as soon as possible. As he was going to take Marie and reopen the town house, Lyn should have offered to return with him, but she could not bring herself to do so. The thought of being alone with Mary for a few days seemed priceless; she would have paid for her solitude in gold if she had any coins. It was Nat's birthday. Now she could honor his memory in peace.

Lyn spent the day with her daughter, playing games and cutting out some frocks for her, and helping the staff at Fairview plan the Twelfth Night festivities. The child had caught a slight cold so the next day, the third of January, she kept Mary in bed and spent the morning reading stories to her and sewing her new garments. After dinner the little girl slept deeply and when she awoke she was well enough to be up and about and the housemaids asked if they could have her company until bedtime. Lyn accepted their offer gratefully. After several days of inactivity she was starved for exercise and she was anxious to ride Mignon and determine whether the mare was still sound. There had been a slight snowfall during the night and there must have been six inches of the white stuff on the ground, nicely crisped over with an icy crust. Lyn kissed Mary and sent her off to the maids' common room where the girls were sewing and gossiping and then she dressed warmly and wrapped herself in her old woolen cloak. Captain Jervis had given her a beaver cloak for Christmas, but she had returned it to him with thanks, telling him that it was worth a fortune and that she could not possibly accept such a gift. She thought of the furs that the Byrds had given her on her first Christmas in Virginia: they had perished in the fire at Curles, as had almost everything she owned.

When she got to the stables she roused the boy, who was drowsing by a brazier, and asked him to saddle Mignon. While he did so she visited Coke and Folly, thinking longingly of both John and Nat as she stroked their sleek flanks and necks. They seemed none the worse for their stay at Turkey Island, but they acted glad to see her and she felt comforted as they nibbled her shoulder and kissed her hand and rolled their liquid eyes in greeting. The slave grinned as he brought the mare outside into the winter sunshine. Indeed, she looked a beauty, her coat gleaming and her hoofs oiled to a neat black sheen. The boy gave Lyn a hand up and she settled on the familiar saddle and felt almost at home ... she, who had no home.

Waving, she rode east across Fairview's dormant fields in the direction of the inlet where the plantation's sloops berthed, the winter sun setting behind her. A snowy blanket stretched around her and in the far distance the sea stretched gray and cold. On her left a copse ran almost to the sea but on her right the fields stretched as far as she could see. Fairview was large and prosperous. She shied away from the thought, but she knew that she could be its mistress on any day that she chose.

Lyn guided the mare to the left where a farm track ran along the woods; unless it was too icy it would be easier going than across the rutted fields. As she neared the point where the inlet met the copse a flock of crows burst from the tree tops as though they had been tossed in the air by an idle boy. They screamed and circled and fled west where the woods thickened beyond the plantation house. Something must have frightened the birds – she would not be surprised to see the fiery brush of a fox or perhaps the hunched shape of a hawk or even a sea eagle. Curious, she kept her eye on the woods, hoping to discern what had caused the crows to flee. Suddenly she pulled Mignon up so abruptly that the mare half-reared. The birds had not been frightened by a wild creature; there was a man in the copse, clearly visible through the naked trees. Lyn turned the horse towards Fairview. She had been a fool to ride out alone; Captain Jervis never would have allowed it. If she was molested by some vagrant she would have only herself to blame. As she got the mare headed towards the house she heard a voice which caused her heart to thud so that she thought it would burst from her breast.

"Lyn! Lyn!" It was John.

In a flash she was off the mare and running through the snow towards him. Her skirts became entangled in some blackberry brambles and she fell to her knees. She did not even feel the ice cutting her flesh nor the cold dampness which soaked her habit. Strong hands gripped her shoulders and she rose to find her lips seeking his. They embraced for a full minute before they both stepped back, aghast at what they had done. John drew Lyn into the shelter of the copse as the mare stood placidly on the farm road, nodding her head as though in affirmation. She knew these two people. She would wait for them to finish their business.

Lyn was the first to speak. "John! I have never been so surprised in my life! But you are so thin and so ragged. You have suffered."

"I and Nat's army. It is all over Lyn. But it's a long story and I am well nigh frozen. Is there anywhere that I could find a bit of shelter, warm my bones, maybe have something to eat and drink? But I don't want Jervis to know ... I'm likely a marked man and I wouldn't want to bring him any trouble, especially ..."

"Oh, fie on Jervis," retorted Lyn, and John's cracked lips smiled, bringing red beads of blood to the surface, as bright as holly berries. "Besides, he's in Kecoughtan. I'm here alone with Mary ... and a staff of twelve. I tell you what. If you can wait a while longer in this bitter weather I'll take Mignon back to the stable and tell the boy that I was too cold to ride farther, that I will rub her down, as I want her to get used to me again, and that he is excused for the day. I will linger in the stable. When it is dark enough that you will not be seen, come to me and I will lodge you in the loft or in one of the stalls. After the household is in bed I'll bring you some food. Oh, John, how can I wait to hear your news? It will almost kill me! But wait we must."

"It's a fine plan, Lyn, now run along. But first, I must apologize for ..."

"Nonsense, John. Clearly we both forgot ourselves. Don't say another word. I'm off – I'll see you soon."

Fairview was so solidly built that Lyn did not have to worry about a tell-tale stair or a creaking door as she crept from her bedroom and descended to the ground floor. Wrapping her cloak about her, she crossed the yard to the kitchen and then hurried to the stable, a bottle of wine and a fat mincemeat pie in her hands. The plantation lay wrapped in slumber. Even the guard dog merely raised his head, thumped his tail, and went back to his dreams. Lyn had left the stable door cracked open so she had no difficulty in entering the dark building. The moon shed just enough light for her to find her way without difficulty to the farthest stall, where John lay snug in the straw, the lad's brazier glowing softly in one corner.

"It's me, John. Are you warm? I've brought enough food for twenty and a full bottle of wine."

"Bless you, Lyn. Yes, my blood is running again and I can feel my hands and feet. You must excuse me – I've stripped to my shirt, as I wanted to hang my things up to dry. Is that the bottle? Ahhh ... I've never tasted anything so good. Here, I made a seat in this corner – sit there while we talk. Will you have some pie?"

"Lord no, I've done nothing but eat since we got here. These people talk of nothing but food and what they are going to wear. I don't know why Jervis has all those books, for he never reads them."

John smiled secretly, but not so secretly that Lyn did not see him. She was glad that he understood her hidden message. Jervis was nothing to her, and never would be. Just a convenience to use, albeit not ruthlessly, until she got on her feet. She felt better than she had in a long time. As for the kiss in the woods ... well, she would have time enough to ponder that later.

"Now, what is the bad news? For it must be bad ..."

John swallowed, took another pull at the bottle, and passed it to Lyn who toasted him with it and then took a swallow and passed it back.

"You know that the bulk of Nat's army and the newcomers – the slaves and servants – decided to follow Ingram and had gathered at West's Point."

"Yes, Arnold said as much at Turkey Island."

"Well, I joined Drummond and Lawrence at King's Creek and we were planning how to pull the good men away from Ingram and put them under Tom Whaley's command and leave the dregs behind, when the worst happened."

"Before you go on ... what of Drummond and Lawrence and Arnold?"

"Will and Dicken are still at King's Creek with Whaley; I don't know what's happened to Tony."

"God keep him. Now go on."

"Do you recall our mentioning that one of Berkeley's ships was called the *Concord*?"

"Yes, because the name was so unfitting."

"Well, it seems that the *Concord's* captain, Captain Grantham, actually knew this Ingram somehow and had a hold on him. Learning that, Berkeley sent Grantham up the York, almost to West's Point, where he called for truce talks. Ingram came out gladly ... thinks highly of Grantham, I gather ... and within a day the fool had surrendered his entire force. The slaves and servants went wild when they heard they were betrayed, but Grantham convinced them that if they put down their arms that no harm would come to them, and they followed him like lambs to the slaughter."

"What will Berkeley do to them?"

"Who knows? He could well pardon them, if they promise to go home and behave themselves. He doesn't want anything to do with the rabble, as he calls them. He's interested in the leaders – especially Will and Dicken."

"My God," Lyn groaned. "So all that is left is Tom Whaley's force at King's Creek. How many are there?"

"Not fifty, Lyn. It is all over."

"And those men on the Southside?"

"All fled ... all gone. Berkeley sent ships up the James, and the rebels surrendered to them just like the men at West's Point."

"Ah. Poor Nat. You know ... perhaps it is just as well that he does not know ..."

"I have thought the same thing, my dear. Ingram surrendered yesterday, on Nat's thirtieth birthday."

Tears crept down Lyn's cheeks and she wiped them with her sleeve. John looked the other way. He dared not touch her ... not after that kiss.

"John – what kind of trouble are you in?"

John sighed. "It is difficult to say. It could go hard for me if Berkeley learns about my efforts at Warner Hall and King's Creek, but I have not actually taken up arms, just helped them organize. The real problem will be if the Governor unearths the full extent of the Ring, for I was as active and keen as Nat in all of that. Time will tell. But Dicken and Will and Tom Whaley are in serious trouble. If Berkeley catches them, they'll hang, no doubt about it."

Lyn brought her hand to her mouth. Kind Will Drummond, like a father to her; and clever Dicken Lawrence, with that active, relentless mind always ahead of everybody else. Well, the charming Tom Hansford had been strung up, as had reliable George Farlow. It was unlikely that Berkeley would show leniency now. But John....

"John, we must find a way to get you back to England ... or to Maryland or Carolina."

"Never in the world, Lyn. I'm not going to run. I only returned here to bring you the news. Tomorrow I'm off to New Kent. I must do everything I can to get Will and Dicken out of this. We have a rendezvous at Gooch's house. If we can get that far, they have a good chance of escaping. As for me ... I may go with them, I may not. I simply have not decided yet."

"You must go with them! Take both Coke and Folly. I'll explain it to Jervis somehow."

"Well, my dear, I'll gladly take the horses, for the little bay I bought in Kecoughtan died under me, poor thing, and I had to walk the last five miles to Fairview. But as for fleeing the colony? There is something here which is holding me back. Do you know what it is?"

Lyn looked directly into John's eyes. "Yes, John, I do. But that thing will be here next month, and next year, and the year after that. It will always be here, wherever you are."

Now he had to hold her. As he stretched his arms for her Lyn rose and settled in his embrace like a bird in its nest. The two of them fit well together. Better even, thought Lyn, as she put her head on his shoulder, than she and Nat.

The snow was melting fast as John made his way through Warwick and James City Counties, taking back roads whenever he could to avoid observation. He stayed well back from the James and the York where Berkeley's ships coursed like wolfhounds, seeking the rebels. Despite the thaw the weather was bitter and most householders remained indoors, so he felt relatively safe, though there was no way to hide Folly's black bulk and Coke's shining coat. John shrugged, literally and figuratively. If it was his fate to be caught, then so be it. He had not figured largely in the rebellion and Berkeley would probably have little interest in him. On the other hand, he was known as Nat's close friend and man of business, and that fact carried a substantial risk. Whatever happened, happened. He must aid Lawrence and Drummond and Whaley to the best of his ability. After that he could think of himself ... and Lyn.

Lyn. The kiss in the woods remained with him and he smiled as he bent low over Folly's neck, trying to avoid the chill wind. He remembered how she had lain in his arms in the stable at Fairview, as though she had finally come to rest after a long, weary journey. They had said nothing ... had simply clung together and then quietly parted. True, she was deeply wounded by her losses and that was part of it ... but there was something more, he would stake his life on it. Take Jervis. If all she needed was solace and protection, the Captain was available; he could give her far more than John ever could. But it was clear that she thought little of the wealthy planter, whereas her feelings for John ran true and clear. He dared not call it love, but it was something he could build on ... something he could dream about ... something that warmed his heart in the stark winter woods as he moved forward on his bleak errand.

It took John two days to reach Gooch's place, which lay on the Pamunkey River, some five or six miles above West's Point. Without his two high bred horses he might not have made it at all. He rode each one for several hours, and then switched to the other, and even so when they reached Gooch's they were exhausted from the bitter weather and the wet clay roads. He thought of Jervis' little bay, which had died under him after those two frantic weeks before Ingram's surrender, when they strove, fruitlessly, to reconstruct Bacon's army. The horse had been gallant and he grieved its death.

It was twilight when he reached Gooch's ramshackle plantation. The place seemed deserted, but he reined in Coke while he was still sheltered by the trees and waited quietly, alert for any sign of the Governor's men. He was about to dismount and proceed on foot, leaving the horses well back in the woods, when he saw a figure walk across the yard from the house to the barn. The man's large stature and silver hair were unmistakable: it was Will Drummond. John stepped into the clearing and waved his hat. Drummond saw him immediately and came towards him, picking up his pace.

"Grey! I never thought to see you. Nat said you were a steady one, and so you have proven. Are you well?"

"I am. But you look worn ... ill."

"I fear that I have a fever. Lawrence had a touch of it too, but he is better now. He's inside, fixing supper, such as it is. Let me help you with your beasts. I was just about to dose my own horse ... we have only one between us and I believe she is dying."

"I see that things are not going well. Is Whaley here?"

"He was the only sound man with a sound beast. We sent him off yesterday, though he offered to stay. Neither Lawrence nor I would leave without the chance of meeting you. Tomorrow is the date for our rendezvous, is it not?"

"Yes, but I am glad I came early, and with two stout horses. If we can get you and Lawrence up and about, I'll send you both packing for Maryland like Tom Whaley."

"Well, we'll see. Is that Folly? And your own red beast? Excellent. Bring them in the barn. Perhaps they'll put some heart into my poor steed, but I doubt it. She has a terrible cough and nothing I do can make it right."

The two men collected Folly and Coke and led them to the barn. "Any sign of the Governor?" asked John as they made their way through the mud.

"No, but they could be here any minute. We're only a few miles from West's Point and our friends knew that we were headed in this direction. Anyone who has been interrogated will surely talk."

"Then we should make a diversion ... go south, hide in the woods, something."

"We have been too ill, laddie. We'd have to go on foot, and neither one of us had the energy to do it. It's only today that Dicken has begun to feel like himself and I have a cough as bad as my mare's, can't seem to shake it."

"I'm glad I've come, then. I'll do my best to take as good care of you as Nat would have."

Drummond smiled wanly and they entered the barn where the mare lay pathetically on her side, trying to lift her head. Drummond knelt down beside her and stroked her neck. John's heart sank as he removed saddle and bridle from Folly and Coke and curried them to the best of his ability with handfuls of hay. At least there was corn for the horses ... he housed his two charges, filled their buckets with water, and fed them generously. The mare was not going to survive. There were three men and two horses. It was up to him to determine how to balance the equation.

Lawrence shoveled the eggs from the greasy skillet onto John's and Drummond's plates and then turned to the hearth to rescue the kettle of mush which, by its odor, was beginning to burn.

"If you have to be on the losing side, always do so with an innkeeper," wheezed Drummond, trying to smile.

"I refuse to admit that we are on the 'losing side,'" retorted Lawrence, as he spooned out the mush and added butter and syrup to each portion. "By the way, that's the last of the butter. No milk, no cheese, no butter. We're down to corn meal and side meat. And eggs, of course, as long as that hen keeps laying. I put some of Gooch's beans and peas to soak but, God willing, we will not be here long enough to use them."

The men ate in silence. Berkeley's shade seemed to hover over them, ever threatening. When they had finished John helped Lawrence clean up while Drummond rested at the table, his head in hands. John wished they had some brandy; he had never seen the Scot so low. He put the last dish back on the shelf of Gooch's hutch, dried his hands with the dishcloth, and hung it over the back of a chair. Now they must plan ... they had no time to wait.

"I think it's going to snow tonight," John began, "but that shouldn't stop you from leaving tomorrow at dawn. Both Folly and Coke are fit. After a night's rest they will be wholly mended ... I daresay they could take you fifty miles tomorrow. A crust of snow will be nothing to them; in fact it will be easier going than in this damnable mud."

"Nothing to them, laddie," groaned the Scot, "but what of me? Snow, mud ... it makes no matter. I am not riding anywhere."

"Yes you are, Will. I have it all worked out. Folly is big enough to take both you and Lawrence. If Lawrence rides, you can hang on somehow. I'll go with you part of the way, on Coke. We'll stop somewhere on the frontier, where nobody would think of looking for us. If you're still unfit, you can rest there for a few days. That's where I'll leave you. One of you will take Folly and one of you will take Coke and I'll work my way south along the fall line until I reach Byrd's. Once at Byrd's I'll be safe. He can help me send messages to ... wherever I need to send them. And he'll find me a horse or a ship, as the case may be, to get me where I need to go. Please don't argue; it's the only way."

Lawrence puffed on his pipe as John spoke, and nodded at what he heard. He had lost flesh and looked utterly weary. "It's a sound plan, John. Have I thanked you for your loyalty? If this plan works, we'll owe our lives to you. Nat always said you were sound as a bell. He spoke truly."

John's heart warmed. It was not the first time that he had heard Nat's praise through the mouths of others. What a pity that he would never hear it directly.

"I'll try, laddie. But now I must sleep, if I can. I've made a bed here, by the fire, but you and Dicken can sleep in Gooch's room ... there are blankets enough. Who will wake us?"

"I will," said Lawrence. "In fact, I doubt that I will sleep. John – take Gooch's bed. I'm going to pack up the few rags that we have left and make all ready and then I'll doze in this chair. It's a pity there is no moon, or we could leave now."

Drummond groaned at the thought, coughed deeply, and rolled himself in his blankets. Before long his breathing indicated that he was asleep. John helped Lawrence pack and then found Gooch's sleeping chamber. He removed only his boots, belt, and dagger and then buried himself in the bed-clothes and was soon asleep as well. The innkeeper sat by the fire and tended it throughout the night. Drummond needed the warmth, and Lawrence would not let down his friend. Grey's plan just might work, he thought; but they had better leave at first light, for Berkeley's men surely would.

John felt someone grip his shoulder and he sprang up, his body taut even as his mind was still clogged with sleep.

"It's only me, Grey. Come on, dawn is breaking. I have a sort of break-fast in the other room, but it is cold comfort. No coffee, no tea ... but I did heat the water."

John shook himself awake. "My God, I slept deeply. Who would have thought it? Two minutes and I am with you. How is Will?"

"Still sound asleep. It is the best thing for him. Between you and me, I fear for him, but there's nothing for it now but to execute your plan. I'll rouse him. I want to be away within the half hour; there is a chill on my heart."

Fifteen minutes later all three men had laved with the boiled rags Lawrence gave them, had huddled on their clothes, and had gathered their possessions. Drummond looked worse than he did yesterday, his breathing raucous and labored. There must be some grave infection in the lungs, thought John, as Lawrence smothered the fire. Each of them had swallowed some warm water which Lawrence had flavored with dried mint, but they left the food untouched. They had one task and one task only, before them: to leave the great rivers behind and reach the frontier. They pulled the door to and stepped out into the yard in the grim light of a winter dawn. There was a thin crust of snow on the ground, its top glazed with ice, and they slipped somewhat as they made their way to the barn. Folly and Coke snort-ed in greeting but Drummond's mare lay still on the straw. The Scot knelt by her and laid a hand on her neck. She was cold.

"She's dead, Dicken," Drummond said sadly. "The little mare is dead."

"It's a pity, Will, but we hadn't counted on her anyway. Watch the yard while Grey and I saddle the black and the chestnut. I have a fear on me such as I have not felt since we left King's Creek with Berkeley's hounds on our heels."

Within five minutes Lawrence had led Folly to the open barn door, with John just behind, talking quietly to Coke, who had resisted being roused so early. Lawrence spoke quietly.

"John. Ride out into the yard and take a look around. If you see them, give a yell, and then save yourself. It is going to take me a minute to get Will settled on this black beast. Hurry, man ... I fear for our lives."

Wordlessly, John stepped onto an upturned bucket, mounted Coke and edged the red horse out into the snow. He heard Lawrence's voice behind him, in the dark cavern of the barn, urging Drummond to climb onto Folly, in whatever way he could mange. Then the silence was rent by pounding hooves and hoarse yells and the dark was riven by the false dawn of blazing torches as a troop of riders poured from the woods into Gooch's yard, their swords glinting like quicksilver. John instinctively touched his heels to Coke's sides, but the signal was unnecessary as the gelding sprang like a deer into the winter woods, terrified by Berkeley's band. John could do nothing but cling to Coke's back as the skeletal branches of oaks and hickories reached for him and the dark cedars loomed up to bring him down. The chestnut tore west through the woods, away from the river, and soon John heard nothing but the horse's muffled hoofbeats on the forest floor and the sound of his own harsh breathing. Five minutes passed and Coke responded to John's hand and eased his pace. Miraculously, they seemed to have left Berkeley's men behind. John reduced Coke's canter to a walk, and finally, as he reached a large clump of cedars, he pulled the horse up altogether.

Horse and rider were in a trackless forest, somewhere between the Pamunkey and the Chickahominy Rivers. Although the hardwoods and the underbrush were leafless, the trees and bushes grew so thickly, and the evergreens were so dense, the two were shielded from sight almost as completely as though it were midsummer. The sun had now risen fully, though it was shrouded in a layer of high clouds, and its light was thin and weak. For the first time since he felt Lawrence's hand on his shoulder not an hour ago John's mind cleared; and when it did he longed for oblivion. His friends must have been taken – there could be no other outcome. Fate had given him a sixty second lead and that had made all the difference ... would probably *be* the difference between life and death. For surely Drummond and Lawrence would hang, would follow in the footsteps of Carver and Hansford and Farlow, there could be no doubt. Coke pricked up his ears and John froze in the saddle. Fool that he was, perhaps fate had not been as kind to him as he thought. There, behind him, rolled the thunder of hooves. Of course: they could track him in the snow. He might cut a fine figure in the Inns of Court, but he was a novice in Virginia's battle fields. Was it here, in the winter forest, that the bud of his relationship with Lyn would die, unblooming? He looked behind him and kneed Coke forward cautiously. Perhaps it would be wiser to stay hidden among the cedars ... but the snow would give him away. As John pondered whether to flee or stay he listened again, his senses strained to the breaking point. That thunder ... it was not the sound of many, but of one. Perhaps one of Berkeley's hounds was keener than the rest and had ventured into the forest alone. In that case, John had a dagger at his side and as fleet a horse as any in Virginia. He pulled Coke up and sat behind his screen of cedar, waiting.

There was only one horse that moved like that, like Zeus, bearer of thunder. Could it be? Had mighty Folly plowed through the spume of Berkeley's men, breasted the terrible wave, and won victory? Would he see Drummond and Lawrence in the flesh, not as sad shades? Nat's black charger pushed through the snowy woods and stopped at Coke's side, his great ribs heaving and his flanks quivering. But Folly had only one rider.

"Dicken! Praise be to God! I had given you up for dead."

"Fate is fickle, Grey. I have always hated the goddess and I always shall. She has chosen me, rather than Will, and why she chose the worse man rather than the better, only the devil knows."

John felt almost sick, faint. "Drummond! Has he been taken or ...?"

Tears ran down Lawrence's stern face. A part of John registered that he had never seen the innkeeper weep before.

"Will was kneeling by the dead mare, struggling to his feet when you yelled. I turned to pull him up behind me ... Oh, God in heaven above, I can hardly say it. Instead of giving me his hand he took that bucket, the one you had stood on, and smashed it on Folly's flank with all his strength. The horse shot after you like a canon ball ... ploughed through the van of Berkeley's troops and was off in the woods before I knew what was happening. William Drummond, God save the mark, gave his life for mine, and it is a sign of these decadent times that whatever force controls the universe accepted the bargain. He's a dead man, Grey. Whether they spitted him there on the snow or whether they'll drag him before the Governor, Will Drummond is a dead man. A dead man, and a better man than I, by any measure."

John did not argue. In his humble scales, as well as in the celestial ones, William Drummond had outweighed Richard Lawrence.

"Come, Dicken. Let's ride for the Chickahominy. The sun is gathering strength and if it melts the snow, we have a good chance of reaching the frontier without leaving a trace."

CHAPTER 31

JANUARY - MARCH 1677

The fourteenth of January dawned cold and bitter but Sir William Berkeley's heart was warm as he stepped from the gangplank of the *Young Prince* onto Colonel Bacon's wharf at King's Creek. They said that Whaley had all but razed the plantation, but the wharf was intact, nice and solid beneath his feet. He wrapped his cloak more tightly around him and walked forward, careful of the silver rime which covered the splintered planks. The Governor looked around for Philip Ludwell, signaled him forward, and took his arm. He was going to step onto the Western Shore for the first time since his ignominious flight from Jamestown last September, and he had no intention of falling or otherwise making a fool of himself. Captains Gardiner, Larrimore, Morris and Grantham assured him that the rivers were once again his; and Beverley and Ludwell told him that Ingram's surrender had shattered the rebels' army. Most of the rabble had leapt at his offer of pardon, the faithless dogs. Now it only remained to mop up those of the leaders who were not already dead, like that blond fellow he had hanged in Accomac; or in irons, like the pernicious Giles Bland. Berkeley's mouth turned down as he silently listed those whom he intended to hunt down and bring to justice. First and foremost, his old enemies, Richard Lawrence and William Drummond. After them, Tom Whaley and Anthony Arnold and James Crewes. Sir William's hand clenched Ludwell's arm. He wanted the rebels so badly that he could taste it. What a great pity that Bacon had not survived to see this day. They said he was buried in Gloucester, not far from Warner's place. When this was all over he would dig the fellow's body up and scatter it to the four winds. The Governor sighed with pleasure and stepped forward onto the soil of the Western Shore.

"Is there enough of Natty's house left to spend the night in, Phil?" Berkeley asked.

"Oh yes, sir. We've fitted up the house well enough. Some of the outbuildings were burned to the ground, but the house was only ransacked. It doesn't look like much, but it will do for one night. If I may inquire, when is Colonel Bacon returning?"

"They say he is at Page's, ill. I suppose he'll return when he feels better. He'll have his work cut out for him."

"That he will. He had a good crop of tobacco and it was wholly destroyed, and his barns burned. His lady will not be happy, either. The rebels ruined most of her fripperies ... china and furniture and such like, and they wrote rude things on the walls. You'd better tell him to leave her at Page's until he's cleaned the place up."

The Governor ground his teeth. "It's what I'll find at Green Spring, won't I?"

Ludwell sighed as he thought of Lady Frances' rose colored suite. "I fear so. We'll know soon. But we have some things to do before you return to Green Spring."

"That we do, Phil, that we do. Where are they keeping Drummond?"

"In the smokehouse." Ludwell laughed. "He was ill and they decided it might cure him to put him there. Do you catch my meaning?"

Berkeley smiled grimly and permitted himself a chuckle. "He's going to be 'cured'? I like it Phil ... tell the fellow who thought of that, that he did well." The smile disappeared. "Ill? I am not going to be cheated of hanging him, am I?"

"I don't think so. If his condition is too bad, we can try him today and hang him tomorrow. Will the execution be at Bray's?"

"Yes, they've set up a gallows there and three have been turned off already. Soon it will be Drummond's turn. I shall enjoy every moment of it. Short of hanging Lawrence, there is no man in Virginia whose death I crave more."

"Ah," interjected Ludwell. "There's the coach. Shall we proceed to the house?"

"You've saved Natty's coach? That's a good thing. But look at the horses ... they're mismatched. What a disgrace."

"We had to use what horses we could, sir. To be frank, we were lucky to find four. When the rebels fled they took every beast they could lay hands on."

"But Phil, there's a dirty white, a skinny bay, a black that looks fitter for a plough than a coach .... This is no way to resume command."

Ludwell clenched his teeth in annoyance, but put on a bland face. "I'm afraid that you have to choose between the coach and riding one of the brutes. Would you rather that we find you a saddle?"

Berkeley scowled. "No, there's no help for it. Climb in and let's get to King's Creek. Faugh ... it smells of mold. What a reception. Someone is going to pay for this."

Ludwell helped the Governor into the coach, took a seat beside him, pushed the leather hanging aside, and gazed out at the snowy landscape. He had forgotten how trying the old man could be. Berkeley looked frail. Perhaps he would not live much longer, in which case.... Fanny was returning with the King's fleet, with Lieutenant Governor Jeffries himself. It would not be too much longer before they arrived and when they did, her recent letter promised, they would bring the King's pardon for most of the rebels together with instructions for Sir William to return to England and explain how it was that Virginia had gone up in flames under his governance. When he sailed, Fanny would doubtless remain at Green Spring. Counting two months for the voyage there, six months of to-ing and fro-ing in Whitehall, and two months for the voyage back, (if the old man was even allowed to keep his post), he would be away for at least a year. A year in which he, Philip Ludwell, would be *de facto* governor and would, doubtless, need to consult with Lady Frances Berkeley on a regular basis. Of course that fellow Jeffries would be the nominal governor, but he knew nothing of Virginia. There was no doubt about it: with Berkeley away, Tom and Phil Ludwell would be in charge. The chestnut-haired man sighed deeply. All he had to do was survive the weeks until Fanny arrived ... it would be difficult, but he could do it. The prize was a noble one: Fanny and Virginia. Ludwell covered a cough with his lace handkerchief and glanced at Berkeley. The old man was pouting. The Deputy Secretary smiled at him and began a light chatter about the various rebels, dead and alive. The Governor soon perked up and by the time the coach reached the plantation house he was in a sparkling mood.

Drummond was hauled from the smokehouse without even the chance to wash and put himself to rights. He knew he was filthy ... probably stank as well. It was almost the worst part. He glanced at his left hand. His ring finger was marked with a deep groove and the flesh showed white where his wedding band had been. He was glad that he had given the token to Dicken the night before he was captured. He had a premonition that things would not go well and he had persuaded Lawrence to put the pretty gold thing in his pocket to take to Sarah if the worst happened. And, of course, it had. How Nat's black horse had leaped into action when he slammed the bucket into those big haunches! Dicken was almost thrown off, but he clung to the beast's neck like a good 'un and the two of them were across the yard and into the woods before Berkeley's men knew what was happening. The fools were so pleased to find him that they had just let John and Dicken go. Probably wanted to get warm and eat breakfast rather than tramp through the white woods. It would have been easy to track his friends through the snow, but they hadn't even tried. It was a good thing. He had lived his life to the full, but Dicken had a good twenty years before him and young John had thirty or more ... he was just getting started in life. Drummond was fairly certain that Grey had a penchant for little Lyn. He wondered if that would work out. The girl had been smitten with Nat, no doubt about it, but John was a fine fellow, really more to his own taste, if the truth be told, than Bacon. Lawrence was the one who loved Nat ... they both had that core of fire which could blaze up and carry all before it. There was only one person that Dicken cared for more than he did for Nat ... the black woman. She had a certain nobility, no doubt about it, but still.... He could not love a blackamoor; they seemed alien to him, as though their thoughts were somewhere else, perhaps back in the jungles where they came from. Drummond shook his head slightly. His thoughts were wandering. Here they were at the house. He should pull himself together. Berkeley could do what he wanted with his body, but Drummond's soul was his own.

The Scot was led into what remained of Colonel Bacon's sitting room. There, on the settee, sat the Governor and Philip Ludwell. Drummond was given a wooden chair, facing the two men, and his escort was told to leave. The rebel sat quietly. Truly, he cared for nothing now, not his appearance, not his life ... only his honor. He had already said good-bye, in his soul, to Sarah and the children. Let the play end ... he welcomed a quick death.

Berkeley smiled. "Mister Drummond! You are very welcome. I am more glad to see you than any man in Virginia. You shall be hanged in half an hour!"

Drummond was silent. There was really nothing to say. Lawrence and Grey would take care of his family; nothing else mattered.

"You say nothing, sir! Now is the time to speak."

The Scot sat in his wooden chair. He smiled. How upset Betty Bacon would be to see her parlor looking like this. She was more house-proud than Sarah, if such a thing was possible. A charming woman, but without Sarah's strength of character.

Ludwell frowned and spoke. "Have you nothing to say for yourself? If not, you shall be taken to James Bray's forthwith and tried tomorrow. You had better speak now or things will go badly for you."

Drummond thought fondly of the dead mare. She had been a gallant little thing, had tried her best until the very last. She had not felt the need to justify her life; why should he?

Berkeley's mouth turned down like a fish. Drummond thought of all the times he had seen that expression. Nothing good had ever come of it.

"This is a farce. Phil, have him taken away. He must be at Bray's tomorrow for the court-martial. We'll leave now, in the coach. I cannot bear this place."

Ludwell rose, stepped into the other room, and summoned the escort. He instructed the men to bind Drummond's arms and take him to Bray's, right away. It was immaterial whether he walked or rode, it was only five miles. He must be ready for his trial at dawn tomorrow. Leaving Drummond sitting in his wooden chair, the Governor and the Deputy Secretary left the house and crossed the muddy yard to the coach. Within minutes they were on their way to James Bray's plantation.

Berkeley's men brought Drummond a cup of water and then lifted him to his feet. The youngest one, who seemed like an earnest fellow, spoke.

"We have horses, sir, and can likely find you another. Will you ride with us?"

"Five miles? My feet will get me there soon enough. I'll walk."

"As you will, sir. Now I must bind your hands. Thank you, sir. Do you give us your parole not to run?"

"Aye, laddie, I give you my word. Shall we go?"

The Governor looked at Philip Ludwell and Robert Beverley and Thomas Ballard. He brought a hand up to his face to hide a smile. Tom Ballard ... the fool's arse must look like a gridiron from sitting on the fence for so long. No, that was not quite right. Ballard had not sat on the fence; he had leaped from one side to the other so often that you couldn't keep track of his gymnastics. His arse would be spotless, but his legs must be tired. The Governor emitted a chuckle. Well, he had Ballard's attention now. The man was firmly in the Green Spring camp and would remain there. All his sins had been pardoned in exchange for his agreeing to sit on this court-martial. He had promised to find Will Drummond guilty, and that was all that mattered. They hadn't even bothered with sworn testimony, except for the affidavit of that fellow Townley. They had to have some kind of record, and Townley's statement put Drummond at Warner's Hall at the very time that Bacon was trying to raise a navy to sail to the Eastern Shore. That was sufficient proof of guilt, in and of itself. The other reports were not sworn, but they were damning. It appeared that the Scot had been plotting for years to destroy Green Spring, no doubt about it. Also, word had just come in that they had taken Bacon's parasite, James Crewes. He would doubtless implicate Drummond if they needed further evidence ... but they did not. A pity that Lawrence and Arnold and Whaley had so far avoided capture, but their day would come as well. Philip Ludwell coughed diplomatically.

"Are we ready, gentlemen?"

"Aye," responded the three other members of the court.

"Bring in the prisoner."

Drummond was brought in from Bray's dining room. He looked no different than he had yesterday, at King's Creek, except that his face was a little thinner and, if anything, he seemed more detached from his surroundings.

"Have you anything to say, Drummond?" asked the Governor brusquely. The Scot was silent.

"This court has met and considered the evidence. We find you guilty of treason. Hear your sentence. You shall hang by your neck until you are dead. Be thankful that we spare you the full rites of a traitor."

Drummond gazed through Bray's casement at the winter sky. The clouds had cleared and the sun shone brightly. He caught the flight of a cardinal from the corner of his eye. It was brilliant red: Nat's color. He smiled.

Sir William Berkeley rose, disappointed. "Take him away and hang him."

The Governor left the room followed by Ludwell and Beverley and Ballard. The two former held their heads high, but Ballard looked at the floor. Drummond's guard of yesterday entered the room and assisted him to rise, for his legs felt strangely weak. The polite young man unbound his wrists and then rebound them, behind his back. They escorted him onto Bray's front porch and down into the yard where he noted that a thin layer of snow still covered the ground.

A great oak grew next to the barn and a rope depended from one of its limbs. Under the rope stood a farm cart with a shaggy brown horse between the shafts. Drummond saw how it was going to be. He would mount the cart and then they would drive it out from under his feet and let his body fall until his neck snapped. He hoped the rope was high enough, for he had heard that sometimes tall men like himself found their feet on the ground before their fall had its full effect, and they died horribly ... or had to be hung again. He measured the rope idly with his eye and decided that it was certainly high enough. He felt sorry for the brown horse. They probably would prod it with something sharp to make it go forward quickly ... just like Folly with Dicken clinging to him like a burr.

The polite young man whipped out a handkerchief and bound it around Drummond's eyes. How strange, thought the Scot. As though that would make any difference. He was helped to mount the cart, just as Billy and Johnny had often helped him up the steps at home after a hard day's labor in the fields or on the river. The rope was prickly and he instinctively moved his neck to avoid the hempen spines until he realized how ludicrous his response was, and that it might be taken for cowardice. He stood stock still and thought of Sarah. Lowering his eyes, he realized that he could see his muddy boots and the rough wood of the cart quite well. The humble objects were the last things that he would see on earth and he took some comfort from the fact. The brown horse gave a scream and lunged forward and William Drummond was no more.

John put down his axe and wiped his brow. He looked at the pile of wood and decided that he had done enough for one day. It was mid-March and Drummond's Blackwater plantation was coming to life. A haze of green covered the rich fields and the songbirds were courting in the hedges. He saw Coke in the pasture, glowing like fire, and he summoned a smile as he thought back on his adventure with Lawrence. After they met in the snowy woods the black horse and the chestnut had eaten up the miles to the frontier as though they were winged. When they reached New Kent's western-most border they found a friendly settler who gave them a place to sleep and provisioned Lawrence for his long journey north along the fall line. The innkeeper had not decided on his ultimate destination. Perhaps Maryland, perhaps the colony which they now called New York, after King Charles' younger brother, James. Wherever he went, he would thrive; Dicken Lawrence was a man of iron.

John walked to the well and drew up the bucket. He drank deeply and then turned as he heard the front door of the plantation house slam. He smiled again. Clarissa. He had gotten to know the African woman well since his arrival, had told her every detail he could remember of Lawrence's escape, and she had shown her appreciation daily. Now she was crossing the yard with a paper in her hand. John's heart skipped a beat. It could be another letter from Lyn. As soon as he had arrived at the Blackwater two months ago he had found a lad who was tough enough to make the long ride to Kecoughtan one day and return on the next; and smart enough to fade into the wood-work so that he did not arouse the Green's suspicions that he carried rebel letters. He and Lyn had exchanged two letters by this means, and he thus kept as current with Virginia affairs as any man in the colony.

Clarissa approached the well, waving the paper. "It's from Lyn, John. Harry came by way of the back lane … that's why you didn't see him."

"He's a sharp lad. Shall we go in? I must read this instantly."

John sat in Sarah Drummond's dining room with a mug of ale at his elbow and his feet stretched out to the fire. He was vaguely aware that Sarah and her four children and Clarissa were all keeping well clear of him, but he hardly gave it a thought as he ripped open Lyn's third letter. It was neatly dated the fifth of March and below the date a dense text unrolled in her dainty hand. This was the one he had been waiting for. It would tell him the progress made by the Royal Commissioners, the King's board of inquiry into the rebellion. It would tell him what action the Grand Assembly had taken at its February session. It might tell him whether Lyn had any hope of preserving an interest in Curles Neck and Bacon's Quarter. And it might tell him the state of her heart.

John summoned the discipline he had learned at Gray's Inn. Instead of plunging into the letter he strode to the sideboard and opened the right-hand cupboard. There, in a cherry box, he kept Lyn's letters. He would reread them from the beginning, so that he missed nothing. When he had assembled all the facts he would know whether it was time to ride north to Kecoughtan or whether he must wait still longer.

The first letter had come in late January. It was written with uncharac-teristic haste and it was hard to read. The first paragraphs were devoted to Lyn's joy at hearing that John was safe at Sarah Drummond's Blackwater property and that Lawrence had escaped north. Then came the sad part. In a cramped, hurried hand Lyn imparted the news that William Drummond had been hanged at James Bray's following a mockery of a trial. The ecstatic Governor, she continued, had then repaired to Green Spring and the colony had felt his wrath as he looked upon his ruined plantation. Two of those who suffered the Governor's rage forthwith were James Crewes and Anthony Arnold. Like Drummond, both had been hanged after summary hearings. The rebels had been scotched like a den of snakes. John looked out the window at the greening fields and thought of Sarah Drummond when he told her the news about her husband and folded her hand around the wedding ring which Lawrence had entrusted to him. She had aged ten years in a minute. And the children, even Billy and Johnny, who were strapping young men, had wept like infants. Clarissa had left the house for a full day, knowing that every time Sarah looked at her that she would think of Drummond, hanged, and Lawrence, alive and free. It had been a terrible time. And then the news about Jamie and Tony. All Bacon's captains had followed their general in death. First Hansford and Farlow on the Eastern Shore, and now Crewes and Arnold. Of those closest to Nat only Jake and Byrd and Lawrence and he remained. And Lyn ... Lyn, the rebel's widow.

John looked back at the letter. He held it to his lips and kissed it for there, in the last paragraph, she had confided that she had not forgotten the embrace they had shared at Fairview and that when it was safe she longed to see him again.

The next letter was dated mid-February and it, too, both pained and heartened him. Lyn told him first of the arrival, right there in Kecoughtan, of two of King Charles' Commissioners, Captain Sir John Berry, who led the fleet, and politic Francis Moryson, an old Virginia hand. Berkeley had been forced to come all the way from Green Spring to wait on them and he had been spitting-mad. After all, the Royal Commission was charged with looking into the causes and the course of the late rebellion, and it was clear to all that the Governor feared for his reputation and even for his position. If things went badly, the King might remove him from office and his later years would be spent in disgrace. In a hurried post script Lyn added that Jervis had just told her, as she was sealing her letter, that the third Commissioner, Lieutenant Governor Herbert Jeffries, had arrived and that with him was Lady Frances Berkeley. The King's fleet had brought a thousand redcoats and Governor Berkeley was expected to house and feed them. Green Spring was in turmoil. The rebellion had been put down and now these grandees were going to pass judgment on the whole coil, from the death of that fellow Hen to the hanging of Jamie Crewes. The Governor and Ludwell and Beverley and the others writhed in anger.

John paced the dining room. Nat's reputation and Lyn's fate, (and thus his own), would depend on these Commissioners. If they were fair and unbiased might they not commend the Ring for its actions and excoriate Berkeley rather than the opposite? Green Spring had failed at its most basic tasks: protecting Virginia from its enemies and governing it wisely. A reasonable assessment of the evidence *must* show that General Bacon was a hero, not a traitor. Herbert Jeffries, John Berry and Francis Moryson. Everything would depend on them.

John leafed through the pages of the February letter until he found the private news. It still grieved him. Captain Jervis had asked for Lyn's hand in marriage and, although she had turned him down, she had told him that she would defer a final answer until October 26th, the anniversary of Nat's death. In his heart John knew that she had given Jervis a gleam of hope only out of pity, but still, might she not change her mind? The colony saw the match as a perfect one and, objectively, public opinion was absolutely right. Jervis's offer solved all Lyn's problems. All, that is, but the state of her heart. Did he have reason to hope that when the wound of Nat's death had healed that she would turn to him, not Jervis? That bitter night at Fairview when he had taken her into his arms …they had declared their true feelings and they both knew it. Time and again he had urged her to come to the Blackwater but she insisted on staying at Kecoughtan until the Royal Commission produced its report and she knew the fate of her Virginia property. True, now that Jamestown was gone the little seaside town was *the* place for news. But he wondered if there was not a second, and more interesting, reason for Lyn's declining Sarah Drummond's charity. Was it not possible that she was indifferent to the linkage of her name with Captain Jervis, whereas the linkage of her name with John Grey carried far more weight? It must be so. He would swear it. John sighed and smoothed the pages of the third letter. Would it signal him to come to her or to wait?

Ah! Here was the news about the Assembly, pages of it. Had any of the Ring been pardoned, or were they all attainted? He could hardly read her tremulous script. Here it was. Jesu! Though Nat Bacon had long lain cold in his grave under the golden tree they had nonetheless attainted him as a traitor and stripped him of all his property. Oh Lyn, sweet Lyn! This would kill her. Nat Bacon would go down in history as a rebel and a traitor. And Curles Neck? Where was it? He had lost his place. There! She said that as a result of the attainder Nat's property had gone to the crown, but only until the King's pleasure was known. The King's pleasure. Then there was some hope … Charles Stuart was notoriously soft towards women. If Lyn petitioned the King directly he might restore her property. It was unlikely, but possible. It would depend on the Royal Commissioners. Jeffries, Berry and Moryson. It was back to them.

John read on. The King had issued a general pardon which forgave all the rebels save fifty-five men, who were excepted. What was it that Lyn had underlined? He, John Grey, was not among the fifty-five. Ah, he was safe.

Whatever Berkeley and Lady Frances and Ludwell might think of him, he was safe. He was free to go anywhere in Virginia, free to go to Kecoughtan. John rose and paced the room, letter in hand, reading as he moved about. Well, *that* was good news, perhaps there was more. Yes, there it was. Although Berkeley had sought to pack the February Assembly with his own men, there were enough honest Burgesses left to have restored many of the June reform laws which had previously been obliterated by order of the King. John smiled. So, Lawrence was vindicated and it was a fitting memorial for Will Drummond. Virginia could and would speak for itself and even Charles Stuart would have to listen.

John turned the page. Lyn had done a calculation, and it was a sad one. After the tide turned against the Ring following Nat's death, Berkeley had killed fourteen rebels, essentially without a trial. Nine more had died since the arrival of the Royal Commissioners. Although the nine received more justice than the fourteen, they had been hanged nonetheless and were just as dead. Twenty-three in all ... and he had known most of them. And among them was Giles Bland. Poor hot-headed Giles. His Virginia adventure had been a disaster and now he lay in the cold ground, nevermore to walk the green fields of Westover. Tears came to John's eyes as he thought of his fallen friends. He would ride soon ... ride to Kecoughtan and take Lyn to see Nat's grave. The first tender leaves would be opening on the golden tree. She could say good-bye and then? Then, perhaps, he could coax her to think of England. Truly, was anything left for them here?

John turned back to the letter and read the final page. What was this? Lyn was taking Mary to visit Sarah Swann at Swann's Point? Ah, *that* was her reasoning. With Jamestown burned and Green Spring unavailable to them because of Berkeley's enmity, the Royal Commissioners had set up their headquarters at Swann's Point. Lyn had no sooner hinted to Sarah Swann that an invitation would be welcome than it had quickly followed. Brave Sarah to take in General Bacon's widow! And clever Lyn! She intended to meet the Commissioners and plead the case for Curles Neck and Bacon's Quarter. John frowned. He wished that Lyn were not so attached to the Virginia property ... it was almost certainly a lost cause. And if she intended to remain in the colony until that story played itself out, England would not see her for many months. Musing, he returned to the letter.

While the Commissioners had been at Kecoughtan, Lyn wrote, she had gotten to know their secretary, Samuel Wiseman, very well indeed. Captain Jervis was off up the Bay in the *Kestrel* and, as he would be gone for a month, he had leaped at the opportunity of making a pretty profit by renting out one of the bedrooms in the townhouse. Wiseman had been her housemate for a week; he was a clever fellow and a kind one. He told her that his masters were going to take evidence from all the counties on the rights and wrongs of the rebellion. King Charles wanted to know the truth about the unrest in his oldest dominion, and it was the Commissioners' duty to provide it to him. Each county was going to be invited to send a list of grievances and they were going to take as much oral and written testimony as the inquiry required. Wiseman had asked her if she knew of any Virginians who might be of assistance in this formidable task. No sooner had the question been asked than John Grey's name had been on her lips every minute of every day until the Commissioners sailed for Swann's Point. As he said good-bye Wiseman told her that if Grey was interested in working for the Royal Commission that he should stop by for an interview and he, Wiseman, would put in a good word for him. John had to smile. You would never know to look at her, but Lyn had a will of iron. There she was, at Swann's Point, not only advocating her own cause, but his. Well, that decided it. He and Coke would be off for Swann's Point tomorrow. He could make the journey in one day, but he would take two so that he would arrive fresh and make a good impression. In two days he would hold Lyn's white hand in his own and, God willing, he would begin the work of rehabilitating the Ring and the legacy of General Nathaniel Bacon.

The mockingbird darted down the green path, leading John on with its joyous song. As he and Coke emerged from the trees he saw the familiar, handsome façade of the plantation house at Swann's Point and his heart beat faster. He tossed his reins to a boy who was idling in the yard and raised his hand to knock on the front door when it opened before him. Sarah Swann burst through the doorway and clasped him in her arms.

"Mister Grey! Lyn said you would come. How I hope you have some news from the family."

"Of course I do, Sarah. I have a whole sheaf of letters in my saddlebag, one from your mother and four more from your brothers and sisters. Here, let me fetch them."

John returned to his horse as the big woman followed him, half tearful and half joyous. She was the image of her mother; the likeness was uncanny. As he retrieved the letters his eye caught a movement from an upstairs window. It was Lyn, leaning from the casement, all smiles.

"John, how wonderful. You're earlier than I expected."

"You were expecting me?"

Lyn's brow creased. "Didn't you get my letter?"

"Of course, but why did you think I would come?"

Lyn's laughter did John's heart good. It had been long since October. "Why, for the job, of course."

He grinned. "Of course. Is Mister Wiseman about?"

"He's in the dining room, where he sits for eighteen hours a day. How he does it, I cannot say. The job is overwhelming. Mister Jeffries spends most of his time at Green Spring, Captain Berry has returned to the flagship at Kecoughtan, and Mister Moryson is riding from one plantation to the next, listening to what the colonists have to say, so it all falls upon Sam."

"Sam, is it? Well, perhaps we should not continue this conversation by shouting for all Swann's Point to hear. Shall I meet you inside?"

"Bless you, John. Mary and I will be right down."

An hour later Samuel Wiseman had hired John Grey to assist him in hearing Virginia's grievances and understanding the history of Bacon's rebellion. John was as impressed with the secretary as Lyn had told him he would be. The young man was slight of stature and ordinary of countenance, but his huge dark eyes radiated intelligence and his quick wit was apparent in every word and gesture. Wiseman was a Londoner who had used a remote connection to Herbert Jeffries' family to obtain a post as one of Jeffries' secretaries. Once his foot was in the door, he had risen to the top fast. When King Charles appointed his master Lieutenant Governor of Virginia and head of the Royal Commission, no one questioned that Wiseman should be the one to accompany the board of inquiry to Virginia and to be responsible for organizing the investigation. Already the grievances were pouring in from the various counties and Wiseman had organized the material, single-handedly, in as workmanlike a way as John Grey had ever seen.

The two men were seated at Swann's dining table, glasses of sherry in hand.

"Now, you are sure that my friendship with Bacon will not cause your masters to reject me for the post?" John asked.

"Between us, they trust me absolutely. I will explain it to them as you have explained it to me. Due to your legal training, you look at things objectively and rationally ... it is the cast of your mind. Moreover, although sympathetic with Bacon's cause, you were at all times moderate in your actions and, in fact, participated very little in the rebellion itself until the end when your efforts went more to saving your friends than savaging your enemies."

"It is true. But you may well hear a different story from the Greens."

"Oh, the Greens! Believe me, there is no love lost between Green Spring and my masters. No, all three of them will be glad to hear from Bacon's side, I assure you. They have heard enough from the others. Between you and me, although I am part of Mister Jeffries' household and should not say it, the key to this Commission is Mister Moryson and I know that he will like you well. You think alike."

"I am deeply indebted to you. As all I own in the world is in my saddlebags and as you have given me the use of a bedroom, I can start work tomorrow, though I know that the job is provisional until approved by the Commission. How long do you suppose that will take?"

"It will take exactly one day. Mister Moryson returns tomorrow and once he approves you, (which he will), the approval of the others is a for-mality. Be assured, Mister Grey, that you have a job as my assistant. The real question is, how long will you want to keep it?"

That evening Lyn and John walked on the banks of the James, staring at the opposite bank where ruined Jamestown lay. They were solemn as they thought of the September night, just six months ago, when Nat Bacon had committed the capital to the flames.

John tucked Lyn's hand under his arm and continued their conversation. "So you have given Mister Moryson your petition to the King and he promised to deliver it when they submit their report on the whole matter?"

"Yes. He was kind, but I sensed that he thought I had no chance. Still, I will wait at Kecoughtan until the outcome is certain."

"But Lyn, that will be months ... perhaps a year."

"My heart will not let me leave Virginia yet, John. It is not the property, although I would love to save Curles. No, I must wait until I know how history will treat Nat. His honor was everything to him and I must do what I can to salvage it."

"I understand Lyn. It is my goal as well. But how will you live? I can exist on what Wiseman promised me, but it is little more than bed and board and I can't cover your expenses. The purse I gave you must be running low. Even you can't live on air."

"Mary and I don't need much. I will write Squire Thomas and ask him to lease Hazelwood and forward the rents to me. In the meantime Captain Jervis will let me use the townhouse for nothing."

"Ah, Lyn, I hate to see you live on his charity. Won't you go to the Blackwater? They want you there."

"It is too remote, John. I must be where I can get news and influence events in my favor."

"But you know what they say about you and Captain Jervis."

"I know and don't care. Jervis is a good man, but he is nothing to me. Surely you, of all people, know that."

John was silent. There were no words for what he felt. "Well, so be it. We'll try it for a while ... you in Kecoughtan, I at Swann's Point. One good thing is that we will be only a day's sail apart. And when we have a chance, when you are ready, we'll visit Nat and you can say good-bye, properly."

Lyn pressed John's arm and when he leaned down to look at her face she kissed his cheek.

CHAPTER 32

APRIL - MAY 1677

Lady Frances wept real tears as she looked at the ruins of her rose-colored suite. The silk wall hangings lay on the floor in tatters like storm-tossed blossoms. The draperies were altogether gone, probably decorating the backs of the rebels' drabs. Most of her dainty furniture had been reduced to kindling. And the heart of the room – her treasured bed – lay exposed, the sheets smeared with mud and filth as though the rebels had fallen into it, booted and spurred, directly from the field of battle.

"Oh, Billy, I had no idea," she said to Governor Berkeley who stood next to her, his pendulous cheeks trembling with rage.

"No, love, how could you imagine the horror? I hardly know how I lived through it. Thank God you were spared all but this."

"There I was, in London, feeling sorry for myself, and here you were, poor thing, in a living hell thanks to Bacon. Well, you know that I advocated your cause to all who mattered, to some effect I believe. Someday I'll tell you the story of how I managed to return on the same ship with Herbert Jeffries. They didn't want me to sail at all, and certainly not with the Lieutenant Governor. I spent the whole wretched passage bending his ear, I assure you. And you, Billy! What a triumph! Bacon dead and the rebels crushed! Now that you are back in power we can mend Green Spring at our leisure. We will just have to make the best of it in the mean time."

"Thank God Phil was able to house you at Rich Neck after landing, instead of coming here. I knew it would be too much for you. I would have done more to the place, but there was simply no time. It was all we could do to patch up my rooms and the great hall, where the Assembly sat in February. Nobody has touched these chambers since the rebels fled in January. Forgive me, love. I simply couldn't do it, what with everything else."

"My dear, what is there to forgive? You had neither time nor energy to lift a finger. No, it is best this way. I already have some ideas about redecorating.

We'll just have to be patient. But, Billy, the grounds! Phil showed me the orchard and the gardens! Not a mulberry standing ... my roses hacked to bits ... what a recompense for the sacrifices we have made for the colony!"

"It hardly bears thinking about. By the way, where is Phil? He handed you down from the carriage and then disappeared. How kind of him to have spent so much time with you, at Rich Neck, when, like me, he has a million matters on his plate."

"Why, I have no idea where he is." Lady Frances took her husband's arm and kissed his cheek. "Does it matter? He is a big fellow and can take care of himself."

"Fanny, perhaps you don't realize it, but I never could have survived without him. He and Beverley and Grantham ... they made all the difference."

"Pooh. You are the one who beat Bacon down. I'll never believe differently."

Sir William smiled and escorted his wife downstairs to his office which, together with the great hall, had been restored to some semblance of order.

"Well, between Tom in London and Phil here, we're in good hands. And we'll need all the help we can get with Jeffries and the others, I promise you."

"Just leave things to me, my dear," said Lady Frances, and rang for tea.

That evening the Governor and his wife and Philip Ludwell pushed their chairs back from Lady Frances' scarred mahogany, replete with a fine supper. The cattle were still missing, but the servants had found some swine in the woods and cook had prepared one of them beautifully. Finally things were getting back to normal. Lady Frances rose as though to leave the gentlemen to their wine and Ludwell laughed.

"Billy, do you think we could forego etiquette for one evening? Your lady has nowhere to retire, unless to your office, which is hardly fitting, and there are only the three of us. It's like family. Cannot she stay?"

The Governor looked up from his claret, somewhat surprised. "Why, of course, Phil." He straightened his shoulders which had been locked with tension, it seemed, for months. "In fact I may leave the two of you to your cards. I am unutterably weary." Berkeley turned to his wife. "My dear, will you excuse me if I seek my bed? I'm afraid you have nowhere to play but here, in our poor dining room. Can you make do?"

Lady Frances rose and helped the Governor from his chair. "Stop fussing, Billy, you dear thing. I am not made of porcelain. I crossed the Atlantic twice in the past year and if I can survive that, I can survive anything. Phil and I have played cards so often in the past six weeks that I believe we could do it on horseback ... or in the dark. You run along and I'll be up later."

"Where will Phil sleep?"

"Billy, go! I've had the blue room prepared. It is far from perfect, but I daresay it will seem like a palace compared to what he had to endure while campaigning. We'll be fine. You'll see. Green Spring will be whole by this summer, or my name is not Frances Culpeper Berkeley."

Ludwell and Lady Frances watched Sir William Berkeley leave the room. He shuffled a bit now. The rebellion had aged him ten years or more. When they could no longer hear his footsteps, Ludwell spoke.

"The blue room, Fanny? Not the rose room?"

"Hush, Phil. The servants ..."

Ludwell ignored her and moved around the table to where she sat. He approached her from behind and swept his hands around her until one lay on each formidable breast. "It was better at Rich Neck, love, but Green Spring has its points ..."

Lady Frances raised both arms and, blindly, stroked the face behind her. "Wherever, Phil. Wherever. Come, let's go upstairs. The servants be damned."

Two hours later Philip Ludwell and his lady lay among the sheets, still entwined. Light from a single candelabrum danced across the walls, the candles stirred by a mild April breeze. The weather had been fine enough to crack the casements and the taste of spring was delicious.

Lady Frances stretched, luxuriously. "I want only two things, Phil. Shall I tell you what they are?"

"Just two?" he smiled, slipping his hand between her thighs. "I can play more tunes than that. I haven't yet taught you all of them."

Reluctantly, Lady Frances moved his arms to his sides and pinned them there. "Now you are my captive. Hush! Listen! I am serious."

Ludwell sat up, cross-legged, and listened. "Very well, Fanny, what are your two things?"

"The first is Elizabeth Bacon, the little widow. I want her to suffer as I have. Nay, more."

"Well, haven't I made a pretty start, burning down that raw house and all the other buildings with it? Even f she gets her land back it will still be years before Curles Neck will be productive."

"And we'll never forget what you and friends did. Never. I wish I had been there to see it."

"I wish you had, sweet. There was something quite rousing about that fire ... very rousing indeed ... like this ..."

"Stop it, Phil. I am really serious."

"I can see that you are. Very well, what do you want me to do to little Lyn, as they call her?"

"Now that Giles Bland is dead, (good riddance), and you are the Commissioner of Customs, you have free access to the mail, do you not?"

"Not officially. But in general I control everything that passes in and out of the colony, so, yes, it would not be difficult to regulate anybody's correspondence."

"Ah, I thought so! Well, I know the little witch is quite a scribe. I believe she writes Bacon's father and others in England who might help her with her property, and I know that she writes that fellow Grey, the one who did Bacon's business."

"Did Bacon's business? So when the rebel was away, Grey warmed little Lyn's bed?"

Lady Frances laughed. "You are terrible, Phil. Don't you ever think of anything else?"

"Why should I? What greater pleasure is there? Here, let me show you ..."

"No, not until I'm finished, then you shall get your reward. Listen. I want you to put somebody trustworthy on the Bacon woman's trail ...follow her every move ... and get a hold of as much of her correspondence as you can. I want to know everything about her. Knowledge is power, as they say. When I know what I am dealing with, I shall know how to exact my revenge."

Ludwell looked sideways at his bed partner. It was a good thing he had her in thrall. If he ever crossed her, she would be a formidable enemy.

"That should not be difficult. In fact, I already have someone in mind to help us. Let me think upon it a little, and then I'll let you into the plot."

Lady Frances stroked Ludwell's cheek. "Thank you, Phil. I knew I could count on you. Now may I tell you my second request?"

"Proceed."

"You know how Jeffries and Berry and Moryson have been persecuting Billy."

"Who could possibly know better than I? Although Berry just looks after the ships ... it is Jeffries and Moryson who are the problem."

"Well, they all work together, so one must treat them together. You know that they brought Billy an order from the King to return to England when it is 'convenient' to explain his part in the rebellion?"

"It has been the largest thorn in our side these two months."

"And you know that all three Commissioners will be here tomorrow to pressure Billy to sail? They want him to take ship no later than the first of May; I have it on good authority."

"It is why we are here, is it not? Billy wanted you at his side to oppose their insolence."

"Yes, of course. But really, Billy has delayed as long as he can. The Assembly has met and done its business. He's spent hours with the Commissioners ... given them all his papers ... explained the whole thing. He really has no good reason to stay in Virginia any longer. Repairing Green Spring is not something which concerns them ... they know that Billy's personal presence is not required for that."

"I fear you are right, sweet. Your husband will likely sail next month; I can think of no other result."

"Well, fearing that we would hear our sentence tomorrow and would have no grounds for appeal, I arranged a little surprise for the Commissioners, and I need your help in executing it."

"A surprise? How exciting!"

"Yes. You know Grimsby, do you not?"

"Grimsby! The hangman! Why, of course." Ludwell laughed. "He's been quite a popular fellow recently."

"Well, he owes me a favor. I won't tell you why, but suffice it to say that he had engaged in some *unorthodox* conduct and I covered for him, to Billy. In return he has agreed to be here tomorrow and to help me with my little plot. You must know that we have agreed to send our coach to pick up the Commissioners tomorrow at Jamestown wharf, when they arrive from Swann's Point, and to return them to the same spot in the evening. Our usual fellows will attend them on the first leg of the journey, but when they return Grimsby will replace Luke as postilion. The Commissioners know him well. They will have to return to their headquarters attended by Virginia's hangman, and there will be very little they can do about it!"

Philip Ludwell sprawled on the sheets and laughed so loudly that Lady Frances had to cover his mouth with both her hands for fear that the servants, or even Billy, would awaken at the noise. As this entailed leaning over his supine body, one thing led to another and quickly the two lovers were busily engaged. Before they became completely distracted, however, Ludwell managed to gasp a few words.

"I believe I can help you, Fanny. It will be my pleasure to take care of Grimsby and make sure he is in the right place at the right time. It will lighten what promises to be a gloomy tomorrow."

John took Lyn's hand to steady her as she stepped from the tiny sloop onto the natural lawn which swept from Pate's house to the riverbank. The bark was so small that he had been able to sail it alone. The ferryman had demanded a whole silver coin for the use of the vessel but he and Lyn, though hard pressed for cash, had decided not to argue, as they thus purchased not only transportation but solitude.

John had it on good authority that Pate was, once again, absent from his home on the York, but he left Lyn in the shade of some sassafras bushes while he encircled the place to make sure that the plantation was unpeopled. The passage of time was curious. So much had happened since Nat's death last October that it seemed years ago, not merely months, that he had crossed this very lawn and found the black horse keeping watch over the friend of his heart who lay dead under the golden tree. Memories flooded back as John walked quietly around the house and then explored each dependency and finally the stables. The place was as deserted and silent as it had been in the fall, as though it lay under a spell. When he was certain that

456

he and Lyn were alone he returned to the back of the house and gazed across the lawn to the river before joining her. It was a noble prospect, as he had remembered it. He feared that she would find her husband's grave mean and undeserving, but she would not. The April woods glowed golden-green as the new growth thrust towards the sun. The birds were silent in the peace of the spring afternoon, but the river played a pretty tune as the natural flow from the fall line met the tidal surge from the Bay and the cross-currents sparkled in the afternoon light. They could not have chosen a fairer day to bid Nat *adieu*.

John strode towards the riverbank, signaling Lyn that all was well. She stepped out from behind the sassafras, small and solemn in her purple silk gown, her face pale and her eyes huge.

"'Tis lovely, John, just as you promised," she said quietly.

"Ah, Lyn, my heart is sore. It was lovely in October as well, but that made no difference."

"We cannot turn back the hands of time. Nat is dead and nothing can bring him back. The greatest honor we can do him is to remember him, always. And remember him as he wanted to be, not necessarily as he was. You and I knew his flaws, John, better than anyone, but we can forget them, can we not? Forget them, and remember the passionate dreamer ...?"

"I shall remember him as I first saw him at Gray's Inn, flame like. He made the other students look like dross. All eyes were on him. And he chose me, poor John Grey, the scholarship boy, to be his special friend. The image is engraved on my heart."

"I too have a special image which always comes to me when I think of him. Someday I will tell you the story, but I doubt I could get the words out today. We were near the water then, too, just as we are now, although it was not a river, but the sea. And the sun was shining as it is today ... the light was golden ... the road ran east, into the sea." Lyn dropped to her knees and cried out. "Ah, my God, it pains me so. I made a promise to him that I would always be there for him ... always. And I have kept my word. I have kept it, but he is gone."

Lyn wept as though her heart would break and John left her so and walked to very edge of the river where he stared mindlessly at the play of the water. She had loved Nat deeply ... would she ever find another man to share her soul? His burden, today, was twice hers. He would say good bye, once again, to his friend. But perhaps he would say good-bye to his dream as well.

When Lyn had composed herself John led her into the forest, along the slight trace which he had followed in October. Then the trees had glowed fiercely, ablaze with scarlet and gold. Now the vernal light was a tender mix of gold and green which welcomed the walkers and uplifted their spirits. All the wild things were at rest and the only sounds were the counterpoint of

457

the river and the breeze and the soft hiss of the leaves underfoot. Before long, the couple reached the glade where the mighty tulip poplar stood, its tender four-pointed leaves moving gracefully like a dancer's hands.

"Is it here?" whispered Lyn.

John's throat closed and he could barely speak. "No, just beyond. We thought this place too obvious for our secret. Do you see where that maple leans over the rock? He lies there, with the stone at his head and the river at his feet."

Lyn encircled John's right arm with both her own and, leaning her whole weight on him, tremulously approached the small clearing where her husband lay buried. The leaves lay thick and undisturbed and there was no way to tell that the small opening in the forest contained a grave. John quietly disengaged Lyn's hands and urged her forward while he stepped back and leaned against the mighty trunk of the golden tree. He had had his moment with Nat and now it was her turn. She needed to be alone.

Mesmerized, spellbound, Lyn approached the graceful maple which shaded Nat's resting place. She dropped to her knees and caressed the stone which was tender with lichen. Bless John Grey. He had chosen this place well. She drew a chain from her bodice and raised the golden wedding ring which was strung upon it to her lips. She then replaced the chain and its burden and bowed her head and raised her hands in prayer. Now, finally, she could let Nat's spirit go. As she did so, she felt him release her as well. She had kept her vow and now she could walk her own path, remembering him always but owing him nothing. It was time to turn the next page in the story of her life.

When Lyn returned to John's side he saw that her eyes were dry and that she was at peace. He had thought that this sojourn might bring her comfort, and he had been right. He waited for her to speak.

"Everything about it is right, John. Thank you, from the bottom of my heart."

"And thank you for those words. My sore heart feels some relief."

"It's true for both of us, isn't it? We have really said good-bye. Now Nat may rest in peace and we must be about the business of life. He would have wanted it so. It is a pity ..."

"What is a pity, Lyn?"

"That there is no memento ... something we could take to Curles, if we ever return there, or even to Suffolk if fate takes us back to England..."

"I know what you mean. But wait. Look at the young saplings rooted around this great tree. Do you suppose ...?"

"John! Once again you have found the solution! Why shouldn't we take one of the young trees with us ... wrap it in my cloak ... and then, wherever we settle we will have a part of the golden tree and we will never forget ..."

And so it was that the two returned to the grassy sward where Lyn waited while John found a stout stick and carefully uprooted a small tulip poplar sapling and wrapped it, earth and all, in Lyn's cloak. The sun was low when they, and the little tree, settled in the ferryman's sloop and glided quietly down the York to the slip where the ferryman, and their horses, waited. They said little as they sailed, but they both felt at peace. Nestled in John's heart were the words Lyn had used when she spoke of the sapling's destination: *they* could take the little tree to Curles ... or *they* could take it to England .... In discussing her future she had joined her name with his as naturally as the York flowed to the Bay on this fair spring day.

John ran a dust cloth over Swann's dining table and stepped outside to shake it. A blue jay scolded him sharply and he smiled. When he returned to the dining room he looked around and gave a huge sigh of satisfaction. The room was paper-free and spotless. Last week he and Sam Wiseman had taken the last evidence concerning the recent turmoil which everybody now called "Bacon's Rebellion." For the next several days the secretary and he had worked long hours pulling together an outline of the events – an outline which the Commissioners had approved just this morning. To his joy, the thrust of the argument was quite favorable to Nat – far more so than he had ever imagined. In the event, the Commissioners had been harsh, but scrupulously fair. Most of the key players were savaged, but that included the Greens as well as the rebels. King Charles would hear that Sir William Berkeley's failings had contributed as much to the upheaval as General Nathaniel Bacon's leveling tendencies. It was as though Virginia had suffered from an acute fever and only now was coming to its senses.

John woke from his reverie and tossed the dust rag onto the sideboard. True, King Charles would hear the failings of both Berkeley and Bacon, but only if he stirred himself and ran upstairs to help Sam pack the huge volume of documents which constituted the evidence supporting the outline. He flushed as he thought of the instructions Francis Moryson had given them just an hour ago: Wiseman and Grey were to take the first ship to London and bring the outline and the evidence with them; they were to establish themselves in Moryson's townhouse in St. James Square; and they were to begin writing the final report concerning Virginia's troubles, a report which would be presented to the King himself and to his Privy Council. Sir John Berry and Francis Moryson would return sometime during the summer, together with that part of the King's fleet and the King's army which was deemed no longer to be needed in Virginia. When the report was finished Moryson alone, astute politician that he was, would guide its progress in the corridors of Whitehall. John Berry was a soldier and, once his duties concerning the army and the navy were discharged, doubtless would be otherwise occupied. Herbert Jeffries, of course, would remain in the colony and would, at long last, take up the reins of Lieutenant Governor. He would do so as Sir William Berkeley had been ordered, much against his will, to board the same ship as Wiseman and Grey and to accompany the two secretaries to London to answer directly to King Charles for his acts and omissions during his tenure in Virginia. The Royal Commissioners had given Sir William until the first of May to relinquish his post, and today was the deadline.

John leapt upstairs, taking the steps two at a time. He found Sam Wiseman in an empty back room, stuffing documents into the last of four stout chests. Sam's liquid eyes gleamed and he smiled at his fellow secretary.

"Is our office empty and ready for Mister Swann?"

"He'll dine there tonight, I'm sure, and be glad of it. But you've finished everything ... I've nothing to do!"

"Nonsense. Your broad back will be useful in lugging these things downstairs and to the wharf. The sloop is ready to go ... chafing like a blood horse."

"I can't believe this has happened so fast. We'll be in Kecoughtan tonight; tomorrow we must get everything organized, past customs, and stowed on board; and the *Rose* will sail on the third!"

"So they tell me, though, as they also say, there's many a slip twixt cup and lip. Are your own things on the sloop?"

"Yes, your trunk and mine are safely loaded. The outline is in your trunk, wrapped in oilcloth and then in deerskin. Our part of the house is clean enough ... Swann's people can do the rest. We've just these four trunks to take care of and then we can sail."

"Well, I hope you find your little friend in Kecoughtan. A pity that she does not know about your journey ... I'm sure she will be distressed to see you go."

"I'll find her tomorrow, even if she's at Fairview. She'll certainly be *surprised* to hear my news ... I do not know about *distressed*. You won't tell anyone that I, as well as Mister Moryson, will be taking her petition concerning Curles with me, will you?"

"Of course not, John. Our masters don't need to know such things. Bacon's widow is perfectly entitled to make a claim on His Majesty's mercy. And good luck to her, too. Just keep it separate from our business, and there will be no problem."

"Thank you, Sam. You've been a good friend."

"Well, in that case, hoist one of these chests onto your shoulders and let's go!"

Lyn sat in the parlor of Captain Jervis' townhouse and dangled the silver bracelet with its charm, depicting a singing bird, from her hand. She watched the pretty object sway back and forth and frowned. Her host was presently at Fairview, but he would be here tomorrow to celebrate Mary's second birthday; the silver bauble was his gift to the little girl. It was too much ... far, far too much. No two-year old child should have such a thing; how could she appreciate it? The cost must have been enormous. In truth, Jervis was trying to entangle her in a web of obligations until she was as helpless as a fly in spider-silk. Then he would put the question to her again and try and force an early answer and the whole colony would expect her to say "yes." If she said "no," she would be a pariah. Tongues were wagging. All Virginia anticipated that Mistress Bacon would be Mistress Jervis before the summer was out.

Once again Lyn thought of the alternatives to staying at Kecoughtan. Sarah Drummond and her family had left the Blackwater plantation for their Westmoreland property and Lyn had no idea how to reach them, or whether she would be welcome if she did. Despite what John said, she had always doubted the sincerity of Sarah's offer to take her and Mary in. Will's death had struck deep and, Lyn thought, in her heart the older woman blamed Nat for the wound. No, the Widow Bacon would have to find another refuge. For the same reason, Swann's Point, where the younger Sarah lived, held nothing for her. Doubtless Clarissa would have offered her aid and solace, but the black woman had disappeared when Sarah Drummond closed down her Blackwater home, and nobody knew where she was. Who else was there? All the rebels she knew were dead, and such family as they had were too hard pressed to succor refugees. Colonel Bacon and his wife were so well bred that they might give her a roof, but she would die rather than ask them for help, they were so aligned with Berkeley. No, living at King's Creek would be impossible. Really, that left only the Byrds. William and Mary Byrd would certainly give her a home, as they had just after Nat died, but they lived at the back of beyond and, unless all else failed, she would not desert her post in the shipping lanes where she received the news from England almost first among the colonists. No, let the vicious tongues wag ... she would continue to rent a room from Captain Jervis until she knew whether Nat's reputation, and her Virginia property, would be restored, either partially or wholly. If nothing was left for her here then she and Mary would find the money somehow and take the first ship home. Despite his dislike of Captain Jervis, she was sure that John agreed ... they had discussed the issue many times.

Lyn started and dropped the silver bracelet. Surely that was a knock on the door? Pray God Captain Jervis had not come a day early! The maid was out shopping with the child and she was alone in the house, so she hurried through the hall and flung the front door open to a sparkling day.

"John! Oh, John. You were in my thoughts, I swear it. Come in, come in. Why did you not tell me you were coming? Is it for Mary's birthday?"

"Mary's birthday! Why, it's tomorrow. I confess, I quite forgot."

Lyn looked crestfallen. "Forgot her birthday? Why, John, that is not like you. Surely you remember her first ...?"

John lowered his voice. "How could I forget? It was the day Sir William rode to Curles with his soldiers and frightened you so. What an irony. He is here, in Kecoughtan, this very day."

461

Lyn paled. "Sir William is here? Is he coming to see me?"

"No, no. God forgive me, I have alarmed you unnecessarily. No, today the shoe is on the other foot. He is here against his will as he is to board the *Rose* tomorrow and sail to London to answer for his sins."

"Sail to London! Then the Commissioners have finally convinced him."

"He had no choice. It was a direct order from the King and he has already delayed far too long. I doubt his reception will be a kind one."

"I hope it is a hot one! Very hot indeed!"

"Well, you may get your wish. May I join you in the parlor? I have a great deal to tell you."

An hour later Lyn had learned that John, as well as Sir William Berkeley, was going to sail on the *Rose* tomorrow, her daughter's birthday. Although she was pleased that the Commissioners' report was going to be more favorable to Nat than could have been expected, and that thus her petition for the restoration of Curles Neck and Bacon's Quarter might not fall on deaf ears, the thought that John was leaving hurt her badly. He had a weighty task ahead of him, a task which might open important doors and permit him to commence his long-delayed career in the practice of law. The fact was, once in London, John might choose never to return to Virginia, she had better admit it. She toyed with the silver bracelet, lost in thought.

"Lyn, have you heard a word that I have been saying for the last ten minutes?"

Lyn's hand went to her neck. When confused or distressed, she used to seize her golden chain and hold it tight for comfort. But since that day in the forest at Pate's she had removed the chain and the gold ring and stored them in her jewelry box as mementos of a past which was fast-receding, like the banks of the York as she and John slipped down the silver river to the ferry.

"In truth, I have not," she stammered.

"You look distressed, Lyn. What is it? Is it Nat? Or Jervis? What, are you looking for the chain you usually wear? Did you lose your chain?"

Lyn kept a hand at her throat and a tear slipped down her cheek.

"Dear heart," cried John. "Tell me, what is the matter?"

"Dear heart, John?"

John stood, aghast. "Forget that I said it. The words should never have left my lips."

"*Must* I forget it, John?" Lyn asked softly.

His heart stopped. This was all wrong. Today of all days ... he had never meant to ask, to say, to utter ....

"Should you like to remember it?"

"I should like to keep the words in *my* heart, if you mean them."

"If I mean them, Lyn?" John seized both her white hands in his brown ones. "You know that you have owned my soul since the day I first set eyes on you. Confess it ... you know!"

Lyn cast down her eyes, but did not remove her hands from his strong grip. "I know it, John. And never has a knight been set more tasks than the Bacons set for you. But it was never my intent ... I never led you on."

"No, you did not, sweet. It was fate that brought us together. You were ever true to Nat, God and all his angels know. But now?"

The violet eyes looked unabashedly into the gray ones. "That part of my life is gone. I have said good-bye to my young love and now ..." Lyn's voice trembled. "Now I am a woman and I am ready to claim a new love, a richer and deeper and riper one. Is that what you meant when you said 'dear heart,' John?"

John pulled Lyn to him and encircled her with his arms. She rested there as though it were her home. "That is what I meant. Will you take the love that I offer you?"

"Yes, John, I will. All that I am, is yours. I will wait here in Kecoughtan until you return and then, God willing, whether in the new world or in the old, we will walk down the years together, arm in arm, until we both grow weary of this earth."

It was fortunate that Captain Jervis was in Fairview, overseeing the planting of his tobacco. He would never know what trick fate had played him in his very own front parlor, the one which looked out over the sparkling bay where the white ships danced, ready to spread their wings for England.

CHAPTER 33

MAY - SEPTEMBER 1677

Mary's second birthday was a brilliant May day with a spanking breeze which spangled the harbor with white-topped wavelets. The *Rose* chafed at her hawsers, anxious to race across the Bay to the vast expanse of the sea. Marie had arrived from Fairview the previous evening in order to prepare Mary's two o'clock birthday dinner and Lyn had left the child playing happily in the kitchen under the watchful eye of both the cook and the housemaid while she mingled with the wharfside throng, anxious to seize a few last private moments with John. Captain Jervis would not arrive from Fairview until just before dinner, so the morning was hers.

As she stood near the gangplank, with one eye on the crowd and the other on *The King's Arms*, waiting for John and Sam Wiseman and Governor Berkeley to emerge and board the *Rose*, she thought of all that had happened on the previous afternoon. It was inevitable that she and John should come together ... they both knew it. It was only a matter of when and how. Silently, she blessed the fates which had caused John to utter the endearment which clarified their feelings and compelled an honest recognition of their mutual love. *Dear heart!* Some would say it was too soon after Nat's death ... that she could not know her heart until more time had passed ... but it was not true. There had always been something between John and her and, in all honesty, Nat's death had simply let that something blossom, where if he had lived it would have died a quiet death. Thank God that they had spoken before John sailed, for if he had left for England with no resolution of their feelings, he might never have returned.

As it was, he had promised to take the first ship back to Virginia once the Royal Commissioners had presented their report to the King and once he had obtained a response to her petition to be restored to her properties at Curles Neck and Bacon's Quarter. What happened then was an open question, the answer to which depended on the royal will. But whatever the King decided, their future would be determined by the two of them together, not by one alone. In the meantime she had a slender purse which would allow her to continue as she was, at Captain Jervis' townhouse, until the first anniversary of Nat's death when, with good fortune, John would have returned. The six months that they would be apart stretched out before them drearily, but each had promised to keep a diary and to send a full bulletin of news as often as a ship sailed from Kecoughtan to London or from London to Kecoughtan. Lyn's heart turned over. Virginia had wounded her deeply, but perhaps it would now come right.

A flash of red on the deck of the *Rose* caught her eye; it was a sailor's cap. Curious, she gazed at the bronzed, muscular fellow, wondering what last-minute task he was performing as the ship neared departure. Then she smiled broadly. The sailor hefted a wooden tub in his brawny arms and headed for a hatch to stow the object below. She recognized the tub: it was the one in which she had planted the tulip poplar when she and John had returned from Nat's grave. So, just as he had promised, John had managed to get the little tree on board yesterday evening. It would sail to England with august company: with Governor William Berkeley and with the two secretaries to the Royal Commission whose duty was to Charles II himself. God willing, the Virginia sapling would find a home in Squire Thomas' garden at Friston Hall. Lyn said a silent prayer for the tree, asking that it be allowed to arrive safely in Suffolk so that Nat would always have a presence at the place where he was born.

A stout woman jostled Lyn and her gaze shifted back to *The King's Arms*. Her face froze. There, on the front steps, dressed in brilliant green, his hair glowing in the spring sunshine stood Philip Ludwell. Lyn's eyes were riveted on the man who had torched her home and who, in her mind, had murdered Tom Hansford and George Farlow. Her whole body felt cold yet her heart quickened in her breast. The chestnut-haired man boded evil; it was a bad omen to see him standing there, smiling and gesticulating as though he were at a court function. And the woman he was talking to had a familiar cast. My God! It was Joanna Lawrence, of all people. Lyn knew that Dicken's wife was staying at Kecoughtan, had been since Jamestown burned, and she had seen her once or twice from a distance, but the two had not met since Lyn last stayed at *The Unicorn*. What on earth did Philip Ludwell and Joanna Lawrence have in common? It was exceedingly odd. One would have expected that Richard Lawrence's wife, (or perhaps widow?), would be the last person who would find favor with the Green party. It was true that Joanna hated the Ring and would have nothing to do with Dicken's cause, but few knew that and she supposed that Richard Lawrence's wife would be tarred with the same brush which blackened his name. Apparently not. Lyn composed herself and covered her head and face with her shawl. She feared Ludwell and did not want him to see her. He would hurt her if he could ... of that she was sure.

Both cheers and jeers rose simultaneously from the crowd. It was Sir William Berkeley. The Governor stepped out onto the porch of the ordinary, blinking in the sun like a mole. Lyn gasped. He had aged greatly since she had last seen him. He was old and frail. She hardened her heart. Age did not excuse his cruelty; nothing did. She pulled her shawl more closely around her face and drifted to the edge of the crowd where nobody would notice her. Some at least, must hate the old man as much as she, for the crowd continued to hiss. Joanna Lawrence retreated into the ordinary and Philip Ludwell took Berkeley's arm and looked around him, fiercely. The crowd quieted. Nobody wanted to be in Ludwell's black book. The Deputy Secretary escorted the Governor down the steps of the ordinary and the crowd parted, opening a path for the grandees to reach the gangplank. Lyn made her way to the corner of *The King's Arms,* both to distance herself from the Governor and to be near the door when John and Sam emerged. The man in green helped Berkeley up the gangplank and both of them disappeared below. Lyn wondered if Sir William would share the captain's cabin or whether he was already in disgrace and would be treated like a prisoner. John was sure that he was going to face the King's wrath and that he probably would never set foot in Virginia again. Lyn could not find it in her heart to mourn Berkeley's disgrace, if that was his fate.

The inn door opened and Sam Wiseman stepped out, talking to somebody behind him. Wiseman saw her and his great brown eyes rolled as he smiled and pointed over his shoulder. Within seconds John was with Lyn and she was in his arms.

"Cruel fate, to part us now," murmured John as he slipped back her shawl and stroked her hair.

"Only six months, dear heart. We are stout enough to bear it," returned Lyn.

"Dear heart. Address all your letters that way, sweet, and I will know that you are still mine."

"I always keep my vows, John. I am yours forever."

Lyn was crushed to her lover's breast and wished that she could nest there, always. She caught Wiseman's signal. It was time for John to go.

"Remember, John, you must write with every ship that sails and you must return by the end of October or I shall be very angry with you."

"And you must be as faithful a correspondent. I want to know all Mary's new words, what the Drummonds are doing, how the Byrds are faring … and how peeved Captain Jervis is that his suit does not prosper."

"You know that I shall think of you every day and write as often as I can. Now you must really go … Sam looks anxious and they are fussing about the gangplank as though they are about to raise it. Oh, John, may God be with you. Be faithful to your little Lyn and Mary, and come back to me when the leaves fall."

John kissed her full on the lips and slipped into the crowd, speechless. A quarter of an hour later the *Rose* blossomed with sail, caught the fresh breeze, and moved out into the Bay on her way to England.

Francis Moryson must have done very well in the tobacco trade, John decided as he gazed out his garret window at the Commissioner's neat little back garden. St. James Square was a prestigious address. True, the bedroom which he shared with Sam Wiseman was small, but it was as clean as a whistle and, thankfully, away from the constant clamor of the square. John could not believe the London noise. He and Nat hadn't complained, that he remembered, when they roomed together at Gray's Inn, though their chambers opened onto a busy alley; perhaps what one could ignore at twenty-two was no longer tolerable at the great age of twenty-eight. He laughed to think that he was already growing old and set in his ways. The truth was that he had become accustomed to the large silences of Virginia and he badly missed the expansive quiet of the frontier, the sense that one could move west forever and not disturb the order of things more than the fall of a single leaf disturbed a forest. As John pondered Moryson's neatly paved yard with its espaliered pears and orderly flower beds he was amazed at how much he missed his little cabin at Bacon's Quarter and the old ramshackle house at Curles; missed William Byrd's questing intelligence, John Goode's steadfastness, Dicken Lawrence's hatred of autocracy... Lyn's sensitive beauty. Dear heart, he thought, keep safe for me. I will return as soon as ever I can and perhaps ... perhaps we shall make our life in the green fastnesses of the colony and lay our bones in Virginia's red clay to rest with Nat Bacon's.

John's reverie was broken by a steady thudding from the bedroom next door where the butler and his wife, Moryson's housekeeper, slept. He smiled again. He and Sam might be preserved from the bustle of St. James Square, but not from the afternoon activities of these two. The man was a stallion. Not a day went by but he and she shook the bedstead like thunder, as soon as the dinner service had been put away. How it was that they had no children was a puzzle. John collected himself. What had he been thinking of? That was it: that his bedchamber might be small, but that his office was beyond cavil. He and Sam had been given the run of Moryson's own library which ran the whole width of the house and looked onto the garden. The whole arrangement - living on the premises, their food and clothing being taken care of, the huge library – had made their task incalculably simpler. Here it was mid-July and they were half-way through the report. When Moryson arrived in August with Sir John Berry they would be finished. Sam said, and John agreed, that the Commissioners would make very few changes to what they had written. The matter of Bacon's Rebellion would be ready for the King's attention in late August or early

September, whenever His Majesty chose to consider it. He knew that they had done an excellent job and, as far as his work went, he was deeply satisfied.

But there was one thing about which he was deeply dissatisfied. It had been ten weeks since he left Virginia and he had not heard from Lyn. The *Rose* had made a sluggish and unpleasant passage and had not arrived in London until late June so that John was quite certain that a letter would be waiting for him, wafted across the sea by a speedier, more fortunate ship. His hopes were soon dashed: there was no correspondence at Moryson's addressed to him. He knew that Lyn had the right address, as he had written it on three separate pieces of paper so that if, by chance, she lost one she would have two more. And he knew that several ships from Virginia which had sailed later than the *Rose* had arrived in London before her. The butler's nephew served as errand boy and jack-of-all-trades and, as Moryson's house held only Sam and himself, the boy had time on his hands and happily haunted the wharfs for John and kept him apprised of all the shipping news. No, something was wrong. In his worst moments he was plagued by thoughts of smallpox and ague … feared that she had died … but he managed to beat those nightmares down. There had to be a more reasonable explanation, but thus far it had avoided him. Perhaps she was waiting to hear from him. Well, he had certainly kept his part of the pact. In the three weeks since they had landed he had sent off as many letters to Virginia. Surely he would hear from her soon.

John started to find Sam Wiseman peering in the bedroom door.

"John, are you deaf? I've called you three times. There's a messenger below from Twickenham. Come, let's see what the old man wants."

Twickenham. That was where Sir William Berkeley awaited his fate, spinning out his days at the gracious home of his brother, Baron Stratton. Sam's "old man:" Governor Berkeley.

"I'm sorry, I was lost in thought. I suppose he wants to know the state of the report. He sends every week, even though he is not entitled to know a thing. Are you surprised that he has not been received at court? I thought he would be beating his own drum the day after we landed and never stop until the King forgave him."

"My sense is that, despite his brother's high standing, Sir William's day is over. Charles is going to treat him harshly … they all say so."

"Well, you have excellent sources. Here we are – where have they put the messenger?"

"In the library."

John and Sam entered the light-filled room with its wall-to-wall bookcases and soft Turkey carpets. A thin fellow with a poor skin stood near the fireplace, twisting his cap in his hands. He looked distressed. Sam and John exchanged glances, each raising his eyebrows. What was this about? Sam, as the senior secretary, took charge.

"Now then, what have you to say for yourself? Do you have a letter?"

"No sir. Sir John told me to ride as fast as I could and just tell you ... no special words were needed, he said. He will pay you a visit later."

"Well then, out with it. What's the message?"

"Oh sir, Sir William ... well, he died last night."

"Died!" cried John and Sam together.

"Yes sir," muttered the man, looking fearfully from one secretary to the other. "He was in bed with a fever for only one day, no one thinking too much about it, and then he up and died. Just after supper it were. Sir John went up to visit him, as was his wont, and there he were ... dead. The Baron is quite cut up about it. Says that you ... well, not you exactly, but the Commissioners ... says that the whole thing killed Sir William, the shame of it."

John could not help but feel moved at the news. He gave the messenger a chair and poured him a glass of Madeira and told him to rest for a few minutes while he and Sam talked. The two friends retired to a corner and spoke *sotto voce*, quickly agreeing that they should write a note of sympathy to Sir John Berkeley and tell him that they were at his disposal when he cared to visit them and share more of the details of Sir William's demise. Other than that, there was not much that they could do. The news would be all over town like wildfire, London-fashion, without their lifting a finger. They would write Herbert Jeffries immediately, but there was no point in trying to reach Berry and Moryson as they were undoubtedly on the high seas, making their way to London. Sam Wiseman, with his sharp intelligence, immediately saw that Berkeley's death would work to the Commissioners' advantage. Now their evidence could be presented impartially, objectively, undisturbed by the sight of a faithful servant tottering about, weeping crocodile tears, stirring the heart of a King who, on a personal level, was known for his magnanimity. Really, it was a good thing, though one should not say it. Sam pressed a coin into the messenger's hand and dismissed him, and he and John decided to take the rest of the day off to ponder the matter. Any death, even that of an enemy, casts a pall on the living and they had no spirit for work.

The *Bristol* arrived on the sixteenth of August, in a heat-wave. The butler's nephew advised John and Sam that Sir John Berry and Mister Moryson would disembark at the Tower steps from a lighter, though he could not say when. The two secretaries, now good friends, arrived at the Tower at ten in the morning and soon learned that their masters were expected at noon. They idled about for a while, but the sun chased them into a nearby inn where they drank lemonade until it was time to return to the quayside. At noon exactly a stately barge deposited the two Royal Commissioners at the steps and John and Sam soon joined them. After a minute of small talk about the passage, which had been swift, Sam broached the news of Berkeley's death, but it fell out that Berry and Moryson had already heard it, for a messenger from Whitehall had boarded the *Bristol* far down the river and delivered the news, among other important matters. Five minutes later Sir John Berry was in the welcoming arms of his wife and five minutes after that his carriage disappeared west; he would stay with his sister who had a London home. Francis Moryson said he would be glad of a long walk and, despite the heat, he was soon striding towards St. James Square, with Sam on one side and John on the other.

Two hours later Moryson pushed his chair back from his own mahogany and circled the table to press more wine upon his secretaries, pouring it with his own hand.

"I cannot tell you how glad I am to be under my own roof. I am no seaman. The voyage always fills me with horror. This time, however, it went smoothly. I've never had better weather. And now to find that the report is finished! I own that I am deeply impressed. I knew Sam never slept, but you, Grey? You look like an athlete and generally they eat and sleep with the best of them."

John laughed. "And I have sir, I confess it. Your staff has spoiled us. It is all Sam's doing ... his gift for organization is nothing short of miraculous."

"Nonsense, Grey," cried Sam, somewhat wine-flushed. "You have the most orderly mind of anyone I've ever met. Did you start out that way, or was it Gray's Inn?"

"Mother says I've always been that way ... made lists from the cradle, as it were. Should you like her affidavit?"

"Oh, I think I've seen enough affidavits to last a lifetime." Sam rose, tossed off his wine, and turned to Moryson. "Now, sir, as I understand it, Sir John Berry will be with us tomorrow at ten for a final review of the report. Is there anything you would like me to do before then?"

"No, Sam, take the afternoon off. I'm going to start on that pile of correspondence which waits in my library. Oh, speaking of correspondence, I nearly forgot." Moryson reached into his coat pocket and pulled out a letter. "John, this is for you."

The blood rushed to John's face and his heart turned over. It must be a letter from Lyn ... it simply had to be. Heedless of Sam's and Moryson's quizzical looks, he ripped open the seal without even scrutinizing the handwriting and quickly saw, not Lyn's neat hand, but a sprawl which he knew to be that of Sarah Drummond. Sarah! Why would Francis Moryson be carrying a letter from her? Would she tell him that Lyn was ill, had died, had wed Jervis ... that Mary had perished of the fever? A thousand thoughts rushed through his brain and he turned pale and had to sit down.

Moryson put a comforting hand on his shoulder. "I am so sorry, John. I had no idea that you were anxious about matters in Virginia. This is no more than a note from one of my fellow passengers, asking you to visit her when you get a chance. Sarah Drummond ... that fellow Will Drummond's widow. Did you not know that she sailed with us to petition the King to give her back her Westmoreland and Blackwater lands? It seems that Jeffries has claimed them for the crown, as Drummond was a known rebel. She contends that her husband, though hanged by Berkeley, was never attainted as a traitor and therefore the lands should come to her, under his will. I don't know the rights and wrongs of it all, but I think that she hopes that you will help her plead her cause."

John had regained his color and his composure. He was embarrassed that he had shown such emotion and sought to downplay the whole episode. "Why, thank you, sir. I mistook the note for a wholly different matter. I know Mistress Drummond well, have even spent some time at her Blackwater plantation. So, she is in danger of losing her property. No wonder she's in London. She's quite a character ... she'll fight like a tiger for her family. I'm sorry you were bothered with this. I see that she is staying at Threadneedle Street. I'll drop her a line and perhaps pay her a visit when I have the time, but I doubt that I'll go any farther than that. My apologies, again."

"Nonsense, lad, it was no trouble at all. I know you had friends among Bacon's followers and I think none the worse of you for it. Who knows better than I that there were two sides to the rebellion ... perhaps more than two. If you would like to help this lady, do so. Your work here is almost finished and you may take as much time off as you like, as long as you are within reach. A little bird told me that the King is most anxious to see our report. My guess is that all my waking hours will be spent at Whitehall for the next fortnight. Now, you and Sam are both excused until tomorrow at ten. Off you go ... I'll see you in the morning."

John's brain seethed. Sarah Drummond! The *Bristol* had sailed from Kecoughtan on the first of July. Sarah must have seen Lyn ... or at least have news of her. He would go to her instantly. John pawed at the note to find the direction. There it was ... Threadneedle Street. She was lodging above a stationer's. It was a good distance away, but he felt as though his feet were winged. After telling Sam that he might be late in returning home, he sped away, oblivious of the punishing sun.

Sarah insisted on pouring John hot tea, though it was the last thing he wanted. He listened politely to the interminable story of Herbert Jeffries' incompetence and the pertness and heartlessness of every official in Virginia. The fact that Jeffries was still using Swann's Point incensed his hostess even farther. He scanned the petition she had written the King and was impressed with its strength and clarity. Sarah might have a temper, but she also had a brain. As she wound down, he thought of a way to inquire about Lyn which would not immediately tip his hand as to his real feelings.

"I shall be more than happy to get your petition to the right official, Sarah. I think I know just the man. However, I can guarantee nothing, I hope you understand."

"Well, of course, John. If things are bad in Virginia I am sure they are worse here. But any help you can give me would be most welcome."

"As it falls out, I have a similar errand to run for Lyn Bacon. She is trying to save her property at Curles and Bacon's Quarter."

"Lyn Bacon! But Nat was attainted, no question about it. The King excepted him, above all others, from his general pardon. Will, on the other hand, was never attainted and should receive the benefit of the pardon. After all, it was extended before Berkeley murdered Will, though we did not know it. Don't you see the difference between my situation and Lyn's?"

"Of course I do, Sarah. I am, after all, trained in the law. In fact I think you have an excellent chance of prevailing, while Lyn does not. But the poor thing wanted to try to save her property and I promised that I would help, as I would be here, on the spot, as it were."

"Well, in that case …. But why does she care about Curles? Fairview is as fine a plantation as anyone could want. And that dear little house in Kecoughtan … what more could she ask for?"

"I don't follow you."

"Well, John, you of all people should understand … you settled her there and met Captain Jervis. The whole colony knows they will wed by the end of the year … it is as sure as the sunrise."

"Knows that they will wed?"

"My goodness, John, where are your wits today? Lyn Bacon and Captain Jervis. They are practically man and wife. All that remains is going to church."

John ground his teeth. He would not believe it. It was just idle gossip, the kind that he and Lyn had discussed when they talked about the pros and cons of her staying in Kecoughtan. But still … he had not received a letter. The asp of jealousy moved in his breast.

"And have you confirmed this with Lyn herself, Sarah?"

"Confirmed? I am not quite sure what you mean. I saw a good bit of her before the *Bristol* sailed and she looked like Mistress Jervis to me. The Captain and she were both in and out of the townhouse as though they had been married for ten years or more. And Mary? What a fuss the Captain makes over the child. I own that she is a darling, but he treats her like a princess … nothing is good enough for her."

"Hmmm, that's interesting," muttered John. "Speaking of Lyn Bacon, did she happen to ask you to carry a letter for me? I was rather expecting that she would write about her property and some other matters … ask about Nat's father, and so forth. I promised to write her if I found the time."

"No, no letter. And she certainly had the opportunity. I stayed at *The King's Arms* for two days and she invited me for tea one day and dinner the next, so we spent some hours together. No, I cannot recall that she mentioned your name."

John rose and walked to the casement which he opened wide and then closed against the noise. The heat and the clamor were relentless and he felt a headache coming on. "Well then, Sarah, thank you for the news from Virginia. If you give me your petition I'll see that it gets in the right hands, along with that of Nat's widow. I'll be at Moryson's for some weeks; come by anytime and I'll tell you what I know. Now I must leave; Mister Wiseman and I still have a good bit of work to do."

"You look overworked, John. I'm worried about you. I don't think London agrees with you. Do you ever think of returning to Virginia?"

"I considered it, but I am losing interest in the idea. Still, one never knows. Good-bye, Sarah. I hope to see you soon."

John sat in the caleche and looked at the black tails and brown backs of the matched bays. He thought of Lyn's fat pony, Lark, and he thought of Lyn. The first of September had come and gone and still no letter. It must be Jervis … what other answer could there be? The front door slammed and Francis Moryson descended the steps of his townhouse and approached the vehicle.

"Ready to go then, John?" the Commissioner asked. "Are you sure you will not take my riding horse and let my boy drive your hired rig and its strange passenger to Suffolk?"

"Thank you again for the kind offer, sir, but I think not. The bays are not blood horses, but they will get me to mother's. And thank you for the week's vacation. I hope the King will have taken some action by the time I return."

"And so do I, John, so do I. My sources tell me that it is very likely. Now who, again, is going to get that sapling from Virginia? It has done splendidly in my conservatory and if nobody else wants it I should love to keep it and raise it. I daresay nobody else in England has a tulip poplar … we could be famous!"

John smiled. Moryson was such a gentleman, so truly kind. It had been a pleasure to work for him and he would continue to do so, dutifully, until the King and the Privy Council decided whether Nat Bacon and William Berkeley would go down in history as villains or heroes.

"It's going to a friend of my mother's, sir. A fellow who has an abiding interest in botany. If he doesn't want it I shall bring it back to you, you can be sure."

Moryson was so honest that John felt badly about his white lie. He had told the Commissioner that he was going to spend a week with his mother near Ipswich, whereas in truth he was going to spend one night in her cottage and continue on to Friston Hall, with the tulip poplar, the next day. He had written Squire Thomas immediately upon arriving and Nat's father had issued an open invitation to him to visit whenever the spirit moved him, with or without notice. John owed the Squire the whole history of Nat's Virginia adventure and he had every intention of seeing Nat's little tree planted at Friston Hall but, given his position with the Royal Commission, these were things which he felt were better kept to himself than shared with the world. Hence the white lie.

"Well, then," continued Moryson, "off you go. I shall keep my eye on Brooke and when he knows anything about the petitions of your two rebel widows, I shall know it as well. With luck, all will be revealed by the time you return."

"You have been kindness itself, sir. Good-bye. I'll see you this day, week." With that, John touched the bays with his whip and began his journey to Friston Hall.

Squire Thomas Bacon wrapped his arms around John Grey as though he were embracing his son. Nat's father had aged considerably in three years; his hair was more silver than brown and his cheeks were clawed with care. Still, the light blue eyes shone as mildly as they had before, and his hospitality was as generous.

"Come in, my boy, come in. Preston will put your bags in Natty's room. You cannot imagine how overjoyed I am to see you ... but sad, too, I own."

Tears came to John's eyes. "Of course sir, how could you not be sad? It is a long, sad story that I have to tell, but one in which Nat was the hero. Of that, there is no doubt."

"Oh John, I long to hear it, but at the same time I dread it. My poor boy, still in Virginia, never to see Friston again." And now the blue eyes were aflood with tears which fell like spring rain.

"But there is a time for everything. Go upstairs and get settled and then we'll have dinner and you can tell me as much of the story as we both can bear. And you must give me Lyn's news, and Mary's. I have not heard from the girl for months."

The tranquil late summer afternoon wore on but Squire Thomas Bacon and John Grey did not stir from the dining room, the dining room where John had first seen Lyn and taken her soft hand in his. John unrolled the tale of Bacon's Rebellion for Nat's father like a tapestry and, with the Squire, he relived the terrible past. They touched on Will Drummond's honesty and Dicken Lawrence's intelligence; on Tom Hansford's bravery and Tony Arnold's keenness; on William Byrd's canniness and Jamie Crewes' wildness; on William Berkeley's cruelty and Philip Ludwell's selfishness; and, at the Squire's insistence, on John Grey's fidelity and Lyn Bacon's loving kindness.

As dark fell the two men pushed their chairs from the table and in mutual accord walked out on the terrace. The Squire's lawn glowed like an emerald in the fading light and John noted the lemon and orange trees in their tubs, exactly as they had been three years before. In another month Preston would take the trees in and house them in the conservatory against the cold weather. It was already September, with October on its heels. October, when John was to return to Virginia. Or would he? What would he return to? Lyn might have disappeared from the face of the earth for all he knew.

"I'm sorry, sir," John said. "I wasn't listening. What was your question?"

"Ah, you're lost in the past as I am, John. I asked you when you had last heard from Lyn. I'm sure she has written me but the letters must have gone astray. The Suffolk mail is notorious ... I swear that I have lost as much correspondence as I have received."

"Well, I sailed from Kecoughtan where she and Mary are staying with Captain Jervis, as you know. We left on the third of May. She saw me off and we promised to write regularly, but to speak the truth, I have not heard a single word from her in the past four months."

"You too! That is most odd. But have you written?"

"Oh yes, sir. Many times. I assume she has gotten my letters, but how would I know?"

"Well, I cannot explain it. She is a faithful correspondent ... used to write more regularly than Natty, which won't surprise you. John ... this Jervis ... do you suppose?"

John felt as though the Squire had plunged a knife directly into his heart. "Do I suppose that Lyn has formed an attachment to Captain Jervis? I saw no evidence of it, sir, but it is the only reasonable explanation .... I could inquire of someone in Virginia, but unfortunately I cannot think of a soul to write. All my friends are either dead or scattered to the four winds. I suppose you could ask Colonel Bacon ..."

"Oh no, John. No, I have not been able to bring myself to correspond with my cousin. How could I? He was so kind to Nat and then ... King's Creek was plundered, you know ... devastated. Well, four months is not so very long. I daresay we shall both hear from Lyn soon."

"I daresay you are right, sir," lied John.

"Well, let us take a turn about the garden and then have supper. After hearing your story I imagine we will both want an early bed. In the morning I'll show you the place I have in mind for the little tree. Will it be alright in the conservatory?"

"It spent the summer in Francis Moryson's and I believe it grew six inches. It is the picture of health and I'm sure one night in your glasshouse will do it no harm. I look forward to helping you plant it tomorrow."

"Very well. May I take your arm? I think I have aged ten years in the last three and I am not as steady on my feet as I used to be."

The next day was as fair as the one on which John had arrived and soon after breakfast he and the Squire donned stout walking shoes and headed northeast, across the emerald lawn and past the stables.

"Nat was not much of a one for church, as you know," puffed the Squire as they climbed the hill which was crowned by the market town of Saxmundham. "But I attend Friston St. Mary's regularly and all my branch of the family is buried there, including my dear wife. I'm planning a memorial plaque for Natty but I shan't put it up until I hear what the King has to say about the rebellion. It's a thorny matter, as you can imagine. Just below the church there is the prettiest natural lawn which is part of my land. It has a view of the Alde and on a clear day you can see the ocean. If you know where to look, you can see the copse at Hazelwood. The lawn has a southern exposure and I think it would be a splendid place for the tree. That way Natty can have a kind of memorial near the church, but not of it, if you take my meaning. And every Sunday I will pass it and think of him. Do you like the idea?"

"I like it well. There ... is that the lawn?"

"Yes, just above us. Another five minutes and we'll be there."

Moments later John and the Squire sat peacefully on the grass and looked south. To the left was the line of the sea and one could indeed see the trees which marked Lyn's farmhouse at Hazelwood; directly south the river glinted through the autumnal foliage; and just to the right Friston Hall lay displayed like a child's conceit of the perfect country house. To the far right the hill blocked any view of the Duke lands which, John thought, was just as well. The Squire had chosen wisely; it was the perfect place for Nat's living memorial.

"You could not have picked a better spot. Nat's spirit shall live here as well as in Virginia."

Silently, the Squire gripped John's hand with his own. He was too moved to speak. Finally he said, "I'm glad you like it. I'll have Preston plant the sapling tomorrow. Perhaps you can give him a hand, as you know the ways of the tulip poplar."

"It will be my pleasure. And now, sir, may I ask you a few questions about the neighborhood? I shall be writing Lyn at least one more letter and I have a whole list of items which she wanted me to ask you when I had the opportunity."

"Ask away, John."

"First, were you able to lease Hazelwood and send her and the child the rent money?"

"Lease Hazelwood? Did she request that I do so?"

"She did indeed. She wrote you in March. I know she did, because I helped her pen the letter."

"Why, it must be one I never received, for I never heard of such a thing. Do she and the child need the cash?"

"I believe so, but don't fret yourself about it. Someday we'll solve the mystery of the letters, if there is a mystery. Now I am to find out what you know about her brother and sisters ... including Alathea."

"I know nothing of Jane Wyatt and suppose her to continue happily at Boxley Abbey. John relinquished his position at court when he fell in with a wealthy widow and soon made her his bride. He and Dorothy Duke have been living at Benhall Lodge this past year and they are the parents of a little boy. I understand that the village is far happier with the son than they were with the father. Rose has returned as their housekeeper ... I know Lyn will want to know that."

"And Rosie?"

"Still thrives at her cottage at Benhall. She visits from time to time ... always brings me something good to eat."

"And now for Alathea."

"The tragedy continued. Offley Jenney never really recovered from the scandal of the baronet's death, though it was hushed up so thoroughly. You and I know that the whole neighborhood knew ... no doubt about it. In any event, he moved in with his mother, leaving Alathea at Red House Farm. He died in his mother's arms the winter after you left ... the winter of seventy-four. They say he had a lung ailment, but I believe the scandal killed him."

"And Alathea?"

"After Jenney died she went to London to stay with her sister for a few months and there she met a cloth merchant from Lincolnshire who had acquired quite a fortune. The two of them hit it off and within months they were married and moved north, to his home. She took the two children with her, of course, and may have had more by now, I cannot say. My only source of news is John Duke and I sense that he has cut his ties with Alathea, although he remains friendly with Jane."

"So, she landed on her feet. That's no surprise, I suppose. And Red House Farm?"

"She sold it to a London family who only uses it for a few months in the fall. I haven't gotten to know them yet, but I hear that they are pleasant enough."

"So that if Lyn should ever return to Hazelwood ...?"

The Squire looked surprised. "Return to Hazelwood? Do you think ...? And bring my granddaughter?"

"Well, it is possible, is it not? And if she does, the specter of Sir Edward Duke will be gone."

"Why, I never thought about it, John, but you speak truly. Yes, if Lyn returns she will find the neighborhood to her liking. But that fellow Jervis ..."

"I know sir, I know. When I return to London I will make it my business to find out why Lyn has stopped writing the two people on earth whom, above all others, she promised to keep in touch with."

477

CHAPTER 34

SEPTEMBER - OCTOBER 1677

John returned to London on the fourteenth of September, riding Prince Rupert, with Preston in the caleche, behind the bays. Squire Thomas insisted that he did not know what to do with the black horse ... said that it reminded him so much of Nat that he preferred to be rid of the animal, though he did not have the heart to sell it to a stranger. John refused to accept the proud creature as a gift, but agreed to borrow him indefinitely. As he left Friston Hall on one shining black he thought of the other one in Virginia and wondered again if Dicken Lawrence, on Folly, had escaped the King's wrath.

John preceded Preston to the stable where he had rented the bays and bid him good-bye. The man was going to do some shopping for his master in London and return on the led horse which had been tied behind the caleche. The mild and beautiful September, which followed a searing August, continued and John sat comfortably astride Prince as the black picked his way daintily through the busy London streets. He arrived at St. James Square late in the afternoon to find both Francis Moryson and Sam Wiseman absent. After advising the butler of his return and determining that no letters awaited him, he made his way to the mews behind the house and spent half an hour with Moryson's groom, settling Prince. When the horse was comfortable, John crossed the back garden and entered the library, planning to go upstairs to his bedroom and unpack his valise. As he stepped through the door Moryson and Wiseman entered from the hall.

"John!" cried the Commissioner. "Your timing is impeccable ... almost theatrical. We have just come from Whitehall where the King's decision was announced."

John paled. If the King in Council adopted the recommendations of the Royal Commission Nathaniel Bacon would, regrettably, be attainted with treason, but Governor Berkeley would be savaged as well. The onus of history would fall on both equally. It was the best that he could hope for his fallen friend and his heart beat fast.

"What a triumph. They accepted everything ... didn't change a word. We have you and Sam to thank for that. You did a masterful job."

John breathed more easily. The confirmation of Nat's attainder would pain Lyn deeply, but she knew it was coming ... there was no other possibility. As for her property, it had gone to the crown and only the crown could restore it to her. What of the other members of the Ring?

"So the general pardon was confirmed, with General Bacon excepted. Were there any other exceptions?"

"Ten in all," interjected Sam Wiseman as Moryson busied himself with the sherry decanter. "Of those whom you know, the unforgiven include Giles Bland, Anthony Arnold and Richard Lawrence."

"Dicken! Then if he is still alive, he remains in jeopardy."

"Very much so."

"And William Drummond?"

"No, he was included in the pardon. Much good it will do him, poor fellow."

"So Sarah's petition must have been granted?"

"Brooke told me so not an hour ago," chimed in Moryson. "Drummond's property will pass according to his will; the widow takes everything." The Commissioner laughed. "You don't need to take the news to her... she was there in person to hear the announcement."

"Why, that's a good thing," John said, his heart lightening. "That's as it should be. But what of Elizabeth Bacon?"

"I know you have a soft spot for her, John, so it grieves me to tell you that the King did not grant her relief. Really, it was not in the cards. The widow of General Bacon, the arch-rebel, could hardly be rewarded with his land ... it would have made the government look soft and weakened Jeffries' position incalculably."

"I expected it, but still ..."

"I wonder what she will do now?" mused Moryson as he handed around glasses of sherry. "Marry the next available fortune, I expect."

John winced visibly and Wiseman patted his shoulder, whispering, "Forgive him ... he knows you handled the Bacons' business but he doesn't know how close you were to them."

Moryson proposed a toast to the success of the Royal Commission and the three raised their glasses high, though John's heart was not in it.

"You have not told me about Berkeley," he said as Sam replenished their glasses.

"I saved the best for last," replied Moryson. "The Council made it clear that, had he lived, Sir William would have been stripped of his post and put out to pasture, with his reputation in rags. This is for your ears alone. I have it on the best authority that, in private, King Charles said of the Governor that the old fool hanged more men 'in that naked country' than the King himself did for the murder of his father. Is that strong enough?"

John shook his head. Bacon ruined, Berkeley ruined, good men slain and good women widowed, Virginia still picking up the pieces. Had any good come of the rebellion? At the moment, he could think of nothing. Thanking Francis Moryson for the news, he asked to be excused and walked wearily upstairs. What would he do next?

The next day brought rain and John slept late as the morning light was dimmed by the thick clouds which covered the city and he did not wake at his usual hour. When he had breakfasted and determined that Francis Moryson would not need him until five o'clock that afternoon he decided to give Prince some exercise and visit Sarah Drummond to congratulate her on the success of her petition. Sure that she would take the next available ship, he decided to ask her to carry a letter to Lyn ... perhaps his last. If the others had miscarried, this one would reach her, for Sarah was a woman of her word and would never let it go astray. Francis Moryson was using the library, so John kept to his room and spent the morning detailing his visit to Friston Hall, the news from Suffolk and, above all, the King's assessment of Bacon's Rebellion and what the royal decision would mean for Nat's reputation and Lyn's wellbeing. He closed with the unfortunate news about Curles Neck and Bacon's Quarter and then, before sealing the letter, sat lost in thought. Should he advise Lyn that he would sail soon and join her in Virginia, as they had planned? Or should he finally admit the inevitable, that by her silence she had told him to stay in England and leave her free to follow her own path?

John sighed deeply and walked to the window. The rain pounded down on the paved yard, muddying the flower beds and drowning the pocket handkerchief of lawn. Summer must be over and now the year would die. Silently he relived his moments with Lyn in the stable at Fairview when she had comforted him and held him close; he recalled how she had enticed him to Swann's Point, leaned on his arm in Pate's forest, and how she had flown to his breast in Jervis' parlor when he had called her "dear heart." Those were moments of truth, engraved on his heart. Surely he had not misread Lyn so badly ... there was nothing fickle about her. Yet, yet ... what explained the awful silence of the past months which stretched between them like a desert? Was it not possible that she was so deeply wounded by her experiences in Virginia that, in his absence, she had been drawn inexorably to shelter under Jervis' protective wing? Yes ... it was possible. Assume that one or two of his letters had miscarried ... she might have come to believe that he had forgotten her and therefore turned to her natural protector. It was altogether possible, really quite natural. He had his answer. He would remain in London unless and until she called for him. Before he could change his mind he dashed out a closing paragraph advising her that he would return to Virginia if she summoned him, but otherwise he would stay in England. The choice was hers. John sealed the letter and stared out at the rain. The weather was fitting ... his mood was as dreary as the day.

By noon the rain had lifted somewhat and John mounted Prince and made his way to Threadneedle Street through the muddy roads. By the time he arrived at the stationer's the sun was peeking through the clouds and the neighborhood children had come out to play. He gave Prince's reins to a likely looking lad, together with a penny, and knocked on the shop door. The stationer himself answered, doubtless anxious for a customer. The man recognized John, whom he had seen once or twice, and his face lighted up.

"Mister Grey, sir! You have saved me a trip to St. James Square. Mistress Drummond left at four this morning to catch the *Swallow*. She wanted badly to say good-bye to you and she entrusted me with a letter which I was to deliver this very day. Come in, come in. I have it here behind the counter."

John's depression deepened. Could nothing go his way? With Sarah Drummond gone he would have to rely on the regular post to take Lyn's letter to Kecoughtan and history suggested that the regular post had played him false ever since he arrived. Besides, he regarded Sarah highly and he had hoped to share with her the King's magnanimity and send her off with greetings for young Sarah and Sam Swann and Billy and Johnny.

"That was quick!" he said. "The announcement was made just yesterday afternoon. How did she get a passage so soon?"

"She's a lucky one. The *Swallow* is a Virginia ship. It has been here two weeks, loading, and she got to know the crew very well. She expected His Majesty's decision daily, so she arranged with the sailing master that if she finished her business here before the fifteenth of September that she could have a berth. She cut it close, but she made it! Her only regret was not being able to say good-bye to her friends, and you were first on that list."

"The *Swallow*. It has a familiar ring. I thought I knew all the Virginia ships ... who owns this one?"

"Why, Captain Jervis of Kecoughtan, I understand. Mistress Drummond said you would know the vessel well ... there is some connection you have with the owner."

John paled. "Yes, I know Captain Jervis," he said softly. "It is a most amazing coincidence." John shook himself. "Well, do you have that letter? I certainly appreciate your consideration for Mistress Drummond and her business."

"Here it is, sir. To tell you the truth, the lady was quite liberal ... can't remember when I've had a guest I've enjoyed more. Her chambers are just as she left them. Why don't you go on upstairs and make a cup of tea and peruse what she wrote. If you have any questions, perhaps I can answer them."

"Thank you, Mister Clarke, I'll do that. And this is for you ..."

John wondered when Sarah Drummond could have found the time to write such a fat letter as that which he held fast in his hand. She must have been up all night ... it would be like her. He settled himself at the little table under the window and opened the packet, which was in two parts. The first was a single page on which Sarah had dashed a note saying how happy she was to be confirmed in her property and that she regretted not being able to share the news with John personally, but she had a berth on the *Swallow* and "time and tide waited for no man." She closed by saying that she had just received a letter from her daughter, Sarah Swann, and rather than reca-pitulate the Virginia news for John he was welcome to read the letter itself, and then discard it.

The twofold contents of the packet explained, John opened Sarah Swann's long missive and read it curiously. It was dated early in August ... this letter, at least, had made a swift journey over the Atlantic for Sarah Drummond to have received it in mid-September. John read quickly through the news about Sam Swann and Swann's Point ... Herbert Jeffries was hardly ever there, but he still paid the rent ... the tobacco was coming along nicely ... they had had a sturgeon for Sunday dinner and she could not remember a tastier one. Then the word "Bacon" caught his eye and he slowed down and took in every word. Sarah Swann wrote that "of all things" she had had a visit from Joanna Lawrence. Joanna had been in Jamestown assessing whether to try and rebuild *The Unicorn* and start her business up again. Being so close, she had "felt compelled" to sail across the river and pay the Swanns a visit. They had had a good gossip, (Joanna "had no idea" whether her husband was alive or dead ... didn't seem to care much), and among other things her visitor had told her that "all Kecoughtan" was talking about Elizabeth Bacon's coming marriage to Captain Thomas Jervis. Apparently Joanna thought it was "a good thing, too" for "everybody knew" that the couple had been consorting as man and wife for months, and it was about time that they made it legal. Joanna described Lyn as "a cat who always fell on her feet" and "wished she had suffered more for what Bacon did to the colony." Sarah Swann had no opin-ion on the matter, and only noted that "General Bacon and Captain Jervis were as different as chalk and cheese, so there was no accounting for taste." With that, the voluble Sarah passed on to other matters.

John let the letter drop to the floor and buried his face in his hands. There it was, then. In early August the whole country was talking about Lyn's approaching marriage to Tom Jervis. Joanna Lawrence lived in Kecoughtan and had no motive to lie or misrepresent the facts. It must be true. Good thing that he had not booked a passage for Virginia. All that remained for him to do was send his last letter to Lyn and that would be the end of it … the end of his hopes. What a fool he had been. He must have been living in a dream since he first took Lyn's hand in his own. He thought he was a good judge of character, but it appeared that he was not. The most important thing in his life, his friendship with the Bacons, had turned to dust. Nat had followed the path of glory to his death and Lyn … Lyn's heart must have died with her husband, leaving only a simulacrum which responded to the nearest protector, like a flower to the sun. So this was what maturity brought: the bright world of his childhood and youth had turned to dust and the whole world was as colorless as his own name.

Francis Moryson's clock chimed five and he, himself, poured tea for Sam Wiseman and John Grey as the three men sat in his library, where the first fire of the season danced merrily on the hearth. Sam eagerly accepted a buttery scone, but John apparently had no appetite. Young Grey had not looked like himself since he returned from Suffolk. Perhaps his old mother was ailing. Well, he, Commissioner Moryson, had some good news for him, news which should put some color in that fresh face and a sparkle in those sea-gray eyes.

"Now, my faithful duo, I've called this meeting to discuss your futures. You can expect to be employed by the Commission through September, for there are still bits and pieces to take care of despite the clarity and finality of the King's decision."

"Sir John Berkeley," muttered Sam, his mouth full of crumb.

"He, among others. It was not a happy moment when he cornered me at Whitehall and named me his brother's murderer. Not a happy moment at all. But his appeals will go for naught, and the others matters are as bootless. No, all will be over by the end of the month. So the question remains, what will you two do next? I know about Sam, but what about John?"

Sam swallowed some tea and smiled. "Yes, I'm off to the Jeffries' on the first of October. I would return to Virginia like a shot if Mister Herbert needed me, but he writes that I can serve him better by remaining here and helping the family with its business. Between you and me, he does not expect to be Lieutenant Governor long. He thinks the King will name someone soon, (I will not say who), and that he will be back in England within the year. I cannot say that I am sorry. I found the colony interesting, but this is home and I hope to make my fortune here."

"And doubtless you will," responded Moryson warmly. "The Jeffries think highly of you … they tell me as much whenever I see them. I will see you rise to the top of the tree, Sam … there's no doubt in my mind."

"Thank you, sir," said Wiseman. "But what of John? Can we keep him here in England?"

"That's the question," replied Moryson. "We'll soon find out." He turned to John who was sitting quietly, his tea untouched. "I have something

483

to tell you, John, but first let me ask you, have you made any plans that I should know about?"

John looked at Moryson's kind face and smiled slightly. "I have made an important decision, sir ... and I made it only today. I shall not return to Virginia ... there is nothing for me there."

"Ah, my boy, I confess it is what I hoped to hear! I always thought you had some kind of attachment in the colony, and I am glad to find that I was wrong."

John grimaced. "No, I've finished my Virginia business. Like Sam, I shall try and make my fortune here, but how, I do not know."

"Well, that is where I may be able to help you. Robert Brooke was very taken with you ... thought you handled the matter of the widows' petitions and so forth like a master. He didn't believe me when I said you were only three years out of Gray's Inn and had never really practiced law at all, having some kind of moral obligation to assist the Bacons. Now that his own duties to the Commission are over he will return to his law practice, and a very nice one it is, too. Brooke is quiet, but there is far more there than meets the eye. He is extraordinarily well connected ... knows everybody of influence in London. He's looking to take on a partner and, before I could say a word on your behalf, he told me he would like to speak to you."

John looked up, astonished. True, he had spent a few hours with Brooke going over the Drummond and Bacon petitions and many other details concerning the rebellion, but he had no idea that the man even remembered him, let alone had developed a high opinion of him. The offer to speak with Brooke was too good to pass up. Besides, what else did he have in his life?

"Why, sir, that is very good of you. Of course I should like to speak with Mister Brooke. What do you suggest?"

"I *suggest* that he is going to sup with me tonight at eight o'clock. Since you are interested, I'll ask you two to join us. After supper Sam and I will retire to the parlor and you and Brooke may have the library. I expect you'll have an offer by the time the evening is over."

And so it was that John Grey contracted to join the law offices of Robert Brooke for one year, commencing October 1, 1677. If the probationary period was satisfactory, by October of 1678 John could expect to see "Brooke and Grey" in gilt letters over the office door. It all happened so naturally that John felt that Francis Moryson must be a magician who had brought things to pass with the wave of a wand. With such good fortune, he wondered why his heart still felt like stone.

It was the 26th of October and the *Swallow* was due at Kecoughtan any day. Lyn mused as she paced Captain Jervis' parlor. What if the ship actually arrived on the first anniversary of Nat's death? It was the date on which

John had promised to return to Virginia, but of course one could not expect him to keep his promise quite so faithfully. Doubtless he would come as close to the day as possible. She had expected to wake this morning with a heavy heart, but to be perfectly honest she felt little or nothing on this sad anniversary. She had said good-bye to her husband last April. Most people would not believe it, or want to believe it, but she had purged her heart on the banks of the York and left it free to make another attachment. And so it had. No sooner had John Grey let slip those sweet words in this very parlor last May than she had known the extent of her love. She would look forward, not back. She knew, somehow, that he would be on the *Swallow* and that soon she would be in his arms.

Which did not, of course, explain why he had failed to write her! Not at all! May, June, July, August, September ... and now it was the end of October. Not one single letter. He was horribly pressed with business, she knew, but still .... At first she had assumed that his silence was due to the dreadful state of the mail, but when July came and still no word .... These last two months had been agony. But there was only one explanation, and that was benign: he simply was too busy to write; he would arrive in person and explain everything. Still, there *was* another explanation. London was a big place, full of important people. Staying at Mister Moryson's, as he was, doubtless John would have met many of the elite. He was so comely, so kind ... wasn't it possible that he had caught the eye of a London heiress and ... and what? Well, forgotten her. John was as true as a die, but he was a man. Three thousand miles of water lay between them. Perhaps the distant image of poor, needy Lyn Bacon did not look so enticing measured against the living presence of a pretty, vivacious London girl. She would know soon ... when the *Swallow* arrived.

Captain Jervis strode into the parlor, grinning broadly. "Still sure you'll see my ship today, and Mister Grey on it, my dear? Still sure that he'll bring you word that Curles is yours or, if not that, secure you a passage home to your little farm at Hazelwood? I'll lay money that neither will happen. Remember, your year is up and I shall expect an answer tonight."

Lyn forced a smile and spoke vivaciously. "I believe I have until midnight, do I not, Captain Jervis?"

"That you do, my dear, that you do! But I hope it does not come to that." He lowered his voice and spoke with greater sincerity. "You know I will not hold you to the letter of your promise, Lyn, but I need an answer soon. Virginia is talking."

Lyn sighed. "I know it well. You'll have an answer today, sir. I always keep my promises."

Lyn's tone did not bode well for Captain Jervis and he sighed. The whole colony knew that it was a good match, but the lady herself did not see it. But if she refused him, she would have to leave. He knew better than she that their names were being dragged through the mud, and his reputation was everything to him. Even bewitching Lyn Bacon was not going to sully his honor.

"I'll leave you alone then. I have business at *The King's Arms*. If you have made up your mind, tell me tonight when I return and we'll see where we go from there."

Lyn had turned to the window again. "Captain!" she cried. "There ... it's a ship ... could it be the *Swallow?*"

Jervis strode to the window and brushed her aside. "Jesu, it is. You're really a witch ... there's my ship, on the very day you said it would arrive. You're uncanny, Lyn. A little frightening."

But he was talking to air. Lyn had rushed to the hall, pulled her cloak from its peg, thrust her feet in her outdoor boots, and dashed across the street to the quayside. Within fifteen minutes half of Kecoughtan was standing beside her as the *Swallow* settled into its berth. Voices swirled around her. "Six weeks they say ... it set a record ... never had such a fast passage ... Jervis has all the luck." She knew John would be there ... she knew it.

Lyn retreated to the corner of *The King's Arms*, the very corner where she had said good-bye to John Grey. She watched like a lynx as the passengers disembarked, unsteady on their sea legs. There was no John among them. Her heart dropped. She had been so sure .... But there! There was a familiar figure! It was Sarah Drummond! Sarah would have all the news from London. Instinctively Lyn shrank back in her dark corner. Sarah was coming to *The King's Arms*. Perhaps she intended to stay the night ... certainly Lyn did not see the Swanns or any of her other children here to meet her. The *Swallow* had flown so swiftly that doubtless nobody expected her. In that case, it would not be impolite for Lyn to visit her once she got settled in the ordinary. She would give Sarah an hour and then seek her out. In the meantime she would go on board and ask the sailing master if the ship had brought her any letters.

Lyn Bacon was well known to the crew of the *Swallow* and she was the recipient of many knowing smiles as she climbed the gangplank and was given free access to the ship. As she descended to the cabin she heard Captain Jervis' voice. Of course he was on board ... she must have missed him in the dark. She thought of the sailors' chuckles and shuddered. Well, in for a penny, in for a pound. As long as she was here she might as well ask about the mail. Lyn tapped on the cabin door and Jervis answered it and grinned.

"I thought it might be you. Come in and have a seat. You were right about the *Swallow*, but not about your friend. No John Grey on this ship. Do you want Dick to confirm it?"

Lyn blushed. "Oh, no sir. I saw that Mister Grey was not among the passengers, but I wondered if I had any letters?"

Captain Jervis looked the question at his sailing master. "No ma'am," answered Dick, gruffly. "I know the addressee of every letter in the pouch and you are not among them. Sorry I am, if you were expecting something."

"Oh, not really. I am more curious than anything. Well, I am sorry to have disturbed you. Captain Jervis, I saw a lady I know disembark and enter *The King's Arms*. I should like to speak with her. If you need me I'll be at the ordinary for an hour and then I'll return to the house." Lyn realized what Dick must have inferred from her words and she blushed deeply. "Good-bye then; I'll see you later."

Within the next half-hour she and Sarah had embraced and were sharing a pot of ale. Lyn almost never drank beer, but tonight she was heedless of small things, wanting only the news of John Grey. Her mind wandered as Sarah unrolled the interminable saga of her quest for justice at Whitehall and she only paid attention when she heard John's name, and learned how kind and helpful he had been to Mistress Drummond. It was the clue she had been waiting for.

"And how is Mister Grey?" she asked in what she hoped was a cool tone. "I have not heard from him since he left in May."

Sarah looked surprised. She had supposed that Lyn Bacon and John Grey corresponded regularly. She bridled inwardly. The widow must have lost interest in her old friends; apparently Captain Jervis was the new lodestar of her life.

"Why he is quite the coming man. Francis Moryson cannot say enough good things about him. And Sam Wiseman told me that some influential attorney was going to offer him a partnership. I cannot recall the fellow's name, but it is somebody well known at court." Sarah laughed loudly. "I would not be surprised if the man had a daughter he wanted to marry off, John is so comely, don't you think?"

Lyn's heart burned, but she tamped down the flames. "Do you happen to know if he went to Suffolk?"

"Suffolk? Why should he do that? Not that I ever heard. No, I doubt it. You have no idea how busy he was, he and Mister Wiseman. Mister Moryson kept them both occupied, I can tell you that. Why, we are old friends, but even I didn't get much of his time. No, John is doing well, you can be sure of that."

"So he is not returning to Virginia?"

"Returning here? I cannot imagine why he would. He never said so. His life is mapped out for him in London. I doubt you'll see him on this side of the ocean soon."

Her mind reeling, Lyn turned the conversation in another direction, and at the end of an hour both she and Sarah Drummond were glad to part, the one with a sore heart and the other with the impression that the Widow Bacon was shallow and cold and that she and coarse Tom Jervis deserved one another.

Philip Ludwell stood in the stairwell of *The King's Arms* and laughed silently as he watched the bewitching little widow leave, her face clouded with care. Another ship without a letter for her! It was the story of her life, and he was the author of that story. Well, not he, but Fanny. When he returned to Green Spring how happy Lady Berkeley would be … so happy that she would certainly reward him in all the ways he loved best. He had taught her some new tricks and he had never had a more apt scholar. Really, it was questionable who the master was now! Generally speaking, he liked to be in charge. Come to think of it, he wouldn't mind teaching the Bacon widow those same tricks, she was such a delicious morsel. Sometimes those pious-seeming women could surprise you between the sheets. But right now he must visit another woman, one who did not speak to his loins but who had nonetheless served him well these past six months.

Ludwell mounted the staircase and tapped on Joanna Lawrence's door. She was expecting him.

"Did the *Swallow* bring anything for the widow?" Ludwell asked.

"No, there was nothing for her, so we didn't have to approach Dick and, for obvious reasons, I'm mightily glad. I don't think we could have bribed Jervis' sailing master to hold back letters for Jervis' mistress."

"I agree. A higher power has taken care of the matter … good. I think we are coming to the end of the road, Joanna. The *Swallow* brought word that Bacon remains attainted and that the crown will keep his property. Mistress Bacon has nothing now. She'll either marry Jervis, which we cannot prevent, or she'll return to England and we'll be shut of her. I think we have managed to sever whatever tie there was between her and Grey and that is what Fanny … Lady Berkeley … wanted, most of all. And all thanks to your diligence. You met every ship, coming and going, did you not, and purloined every letter?"

"I doubt that any escaped me. I have watched her closely and seen her depression deepen as she has seen Grey grow faithless, as she thinks."

"Were they attached?"

"Oh, I think so. She has suffered and, I daresay, he has too. The plan has worked very well indeed. Please thank Lady Berkeley for letting me be a part of it."

"I shall do so. Well, I've come to get the letters and to give you your last purse. Do you have them there?"

"Yes, ten from each of them, and not a single one delivered. There are a handful from her father-in-law as well, and some from her to him."

Money changed hands. "What will you do now?" asked Ludwell, not really caring.

"I shall rebuild *The Unicorn*. It was mine when I made the mistake of marrying Richard Lawrence and it will be mine again. It is all that I have every cared about. Thank you, Mister Ludwell. Have a safe journey to Green Spring."

Lyn helped Mary say her prayers, tucked her in bed, and then went downstairs to lay the table for supper. She felt cold and empty. Nat lay buried under the golden tree and John Grey was lost to her and, as Sarah Drummond had so exhaustively explained, the King had denied her petition and Curles Neck and Bacon's Quarter were lost to her. There was only one reasonable thing for her to do to protect her daughter's future: become the mistress of Fairview. She would give Captain Jervis his answer within the hour. She wandered to the mirror and arranged her hair and then wondered why she was doing it and stopped while it was still in disarray. She was not Jervis' mistress, whatever Virginia thought. There was no need to pretty herself.

The front door slammed and the Captain entered in a gust of cold air. "The day dawned fair, but it's cold now," he said. "Fall is really here."

Lyn tried to smile. "It is indeed. Please sit down. There is cold pheasant and salad and I'll ring for Marie to bring the soup. I think it is oyster."

"Ah, splendid," said Jervis, rubbing his hands. "It is my favorite and she makes it with a quantity of butter."

Lyn knew he was trying to keep the tone cheerful and silently thanked him for it. Captain Jervis was not the most sensitive man in the world, but he was good at heart. Lyn took a bowl of soup and the Captain worked his way happily through all the courses and then the cover was removed.

"Do you mind if I smoke, my dear?" he asked.

"Of course not, sir. Your pipe and tobacco are right here and the port as well."

"I love a glass of good port. Can I persuade you to have one?"

"Perhaps tonight, just one."

"Need a little Dutch courage, my dear?"

"To be honest, yes."

"I don't know whether that bodes well or ill for me, Lyn, but I see that you have an answer for me."

"I do, sir. It is not fair to keep you hanging. Both of us need the relationship resolved, given what people are saying. I saw the sailors laugh ... I know how it is, and it is my fault for letting so much time pass."

"Well, I understand that you needed to hear about your property .... Now, don't keep me on pins and needles. Have you made up your mind to be my little wife? You would make me the happiest man in the world if you did so."

The color rose in Lyn's cheeks and she could hardly get the words out. "Captain Jervis, sir, you have been as good to Mary and me as a man could be, but I shall never wed where my heart is not engaged, and I fear that is the case here. I cannot do it, sir. It would not be fair to you."

"Don't worry about fair, Lyn. Do you think you could come to love me? Or has someone else stolen your heart?"

Lyn hated herself for lying, but she wanted to lessen the pain she saw in Jervis' face. "Nobody has stolen my heart, sir. It is buried with General Bacon."

"Ah, that is the way of it then. Well, my dear, I am not surprised. You think me a crusty old thing, but I knew what your answer would be. My only hope is that you will stay in Virginia, though not in my house, and perhaps you will change your mind."

Jervis' honesty brought tears to Lyn's eyes. "I fear that I shall disappoint you in that as well, sir. I have decided to take Mary back to Hazelwood and live there, in a small way. Her grandfather is nearby and he has never seen her. I think I owe it to him and to her. The truth is, Mary is the image of my dead husband. How can I keep her from her family?"

"You should not, Lyn, you should not. I see how deeply you feel about this. You have made the right choice. And when the *Swallow* has loaded her tobacco you and the child shall have the best cabin on her, and a free passage to London."

Now the tears ran freely down Lyn's cheeks. Impulsively, she left her chair, approached Jervis, and leaned down and kissed his cheek. That was when she saw that his eyes, too, were wet.

CHAPTER 35

NOVEMBER 1677 - JUNE 1678

The *Swallow* left Kecoughtan on a November afternoon of such mildness that you would have thought it late summer, not fall. Lyn looked west at the gathering blue mist behind which the setting sun cast a rosy glow and thought of the bluebird which had greeted her three years ago, and more, as the *Adam and Eve* passed the capes, headed for Jamestown. She had believed the feathered creature to be a good omen, but history had proved otherwise. Her life below the fall line had been one of strife, not repose, and she left Virginia, defeated.

She pulled Mary close to her side and held her tightly. She might have lost everything else, but she had her daughter, and now the child would be the focus of her life. Thanks to Captain Jervis' generosity her purse was big enough to take the two of them first to London, and then to Suffolk. After that she knew that she had the strength to perfect Hazelwood so that the little farm would produce a sufficiency, and more. She expected nothing from Squire Thomas, but she could not help but think that when the old gentleman saw Nat reincarnated in Mary that he would offer her some assistance. Whether she would accept it or not remained to be seen. If Mary had his love, that was all that she asked.

Captain Jervis.... He had returned to Fairview on the 27th of October and since then had communicated with her by message only, until this morning when he had brought himself to return to Kecoughtan to see her comfortably settled on board his ship. He had been deeply wounded by her refusal, more deeply than she first thought, but they parted friends and when the *Swallow* pulled away from the quay he had smiled bravely as he waved his white handkerchief. She knew that the sailors thought her the Captain's whore, but she regretted no part of the commerce between them. Each had acted honorably, he consistently with his character, and she with hers. There was nothing to be ashamed of. And he, dear man, had not only given Mignon and Coke a permanent home at Fairview, but had promised

to make inquiries concerning Abraham and Hannah. Jamie Crewes' plantation belonged to the crown now and her people would not be left there in
peace for long. Applying the ugly logic of the slave laws, she supposed that
Abraham and Hannah, like Curles and Turkey Island, now belonged to the
crown as well, but what did that really mean? If Captain Jervis offered to
take them, surely nobody would stop him. He had promised to write her at
Hazelwood and already she found herself looking forward to his letters. She
hoped that he would remain her friend and a source of Virginia news for
years to come.

The *Swallow* dipped and rose and Mary shrieked with delight. The little girl was not a fearful child. In personality, as in appearance, she was very
like her father. Lyn turned her back on the new world and took her daughter below. Night would soon fall and by then they would have traversed the
capes and reached the open sea. She took one last look over her shoulder
and thought it probable that she would never see Virginia again.

Dick, the sailing master, recommended *The Mermaid* and that is where
Lyn and Mary stayed on their first night in London. They arrived at midday on the twenty-second of December after a quick, painless passage. The
landlady helped Lyn find a messenger and she sent him ahead to Friston
Hall, to let Squire Thomas know that they would soon be arriving. After dis-
patching the messenger, Lyn hired a carriage from the same establishment
and arranged to leave for Suffolk at eight in the morning on the twenty-
third. Snow threatened, but the conveyance was snug and warm and they
would travel slowly, taking two days and spending a night on the road, so
she felt sure that they would arrive safely at Friston on Christmas Eve.
Before it grew too dark she and Mary explored some shops near *The
Mermaid* and bought some simple gifts for the Squire and then some more
for Bess and Henry Hovener, on the off chance that Nat's sister might be
visiting Friston for the holidays. Mary was so excited by the streets of
London that Lyn had a hard time getting her settled for the night, but when
the carriage arrived in the morning both mother and daughter were dressed
and breakfasted and ready to travel. The snow still held off, but Lyn knew
that soon London and Suffolk would lie under a soft white blanket. She
thought of her first Christmas at Curles and then wiped the memory out, so
vivid was the pain of seeing both Nat and John in her mind's eye.

The lime avenue was skeletal and Lyn could see the rosy bricks of
Friston Hall from as far away as the bridge over the Alde. Suffolk had
received almost a foot of snow and the white stuff lay thick over all the famil-
iar places she had learned as a child. To the left, the geometry of Snape
Priory Barn caught her eye and she thought fleetingly of her brother John.
She had not had a letter from the Squire for almost a year, so although she

knew that John Duke was married, that was all she knew. Here they were! Time enough to learn all the news.

Squire Thomas Bacon stepped onto the drive as the carriage stopped and the first thing he saw was Natty's face looking at him. His son! Living again in the child, Mary! From that moment he surrendered wholly to Lyn and her daughter. His life had stopped when Nat died and now, like a watch being wound up, it started again. Soon Lyn was in his arms and Jemmy was leading the horses to the stable to give them a breather before they turned around for London and Preston was sweeping the company inside to have tea because supper, (and it was a good one), was still hours away. Mary acted as though she had come home. She wandered happily through the rooms with the Squire as though she had grown up at Friston Hall and had just returned from a holiday abroad. Lyn and Mary were to stay in Bess' room, of course, and soon after tea grandfather and mother put the child to bed and Lyn whispered that she thought the little girl would sleep through until the morning, so that perhaps she and the Squire could sup alone and exchange their news.

All the fires had burned low and midnight had struck before Lyn and Squire Thomas stopped talking, exhausted. It had been an evening of revelations. They had not conversed long when it became clear that for some reason, beginning in March or April, each had stopped receiving the letters of the other. Thus, Squire Thomas had never learned that Lyn was hard-pressed for cash and had asked him to lease Hazelwood; Lyn had never learned that John Grey had visited Friston in September and had related the entire story of Bacon's Rebellion and, moreover, brought the Squire the little tulip poplar which, even now, was braving the snow on the hillside between the Hall and Friston St. Mary's.

"But surely John told you that he came, child. He is not such a poor correspondent as to have omitted telling you about the week he spent with me, is he?"

"John was an excellent correspondent until this past May. It was only through him that I learned the fate of all Nat's friends after ... after Nat died. He managed to get letters through to me under the most difficult of circumstances. Yet when the *Rose* left it might as well have sailed to the ends of the earth and fallen off, for after I waved good-bye to him at Kecoughtan I never heard another word from him. It is quite a mystery, but I daresay the key is that John simply forgot Virginia in the whirl of London."

"My dear, I don't like to contradict you, but you are quite wrong. John was grieving when he spent that week with me in September and when I pressed him I learned that he was distressed that you had not kept your promise to write him. He had not had a single letter since he sailed. He supposed ... well, to be blunt, he supposed that your attentions were engaged by the fellow you were staying with ...."

493

"Captain Jervis! Of course. Now let me make sure I understand. Beginning last March or April, *you* never received a letter from *me*, though I can recall three at least that I sent. And beginning last June, *John* never received a letter from *me*, though it is burned in my brain that I sent ten. And beginning last spring *I* never received a letter from *you*, though you remember writing at least twice. And beginning in June, when John should have arrived in England, *I* never received a letter from *him*, though you say that he claims to have written ten or twelve. What do you deduce from those facts, Father?"

"Ah, my dear, how happy I am that you call me Father. Deduce? You sound like a scholar. I *deduce* that there are too many letters for it all to be a mistake or a coincidence and I *deduce* that you may have an enemy."

"You are right. I do. And I am such a fool not to have seen it. It all comes together now. Do you remember the name Philip Ludwell?"

"The villain who burned your home?"

"The same. And I told you that he and Lady Frances Berkeley ... well, you know."

"You can put a name to it, child. They were lovers while Berkeley lived and doubtless they are lovers still."

"You have it. Few Virginians had greater cause than Ludwell and Lady Frances to hate your son and my husband. I *know* Ludwell burned Curles, because my people saw him do it. And now I am sure he stole my letters as well, to cause me grief. Did I tell you that he was made Commissioner of Customs after poor Giles Bland was hanged? He could have used his position to get at the mail, and I am convinced that he did so."

"It is likely, my dear. But he must have had help?"

"I know that he did. Now I understand why Joanna Lawrence, who used to avoid me, began dogging my footsteps last spring. Of course. Lady Frances and her lover paid Joanna to keep track of me and then they would know which ships to search for letters. I don't suppose I could take the case to court, but I know in my heart that I was persecuted by the vicious pair, and that you and John suffered as a consequence. Ah, how my heart burns!"

"Neither you nor I know whether you have a case for court, Lyn, but a friend of ours would be able to tell us."

"John?"

"Of course, my dear. I shall write him tomorrow and ask him to visit as soon as he is able. I do hope that he is not tied up with the Christmas holiday, now that he has that fine position with Mister Brooke."

Lyn paled. Would the Squire think she had been fishing for an invitation for John? "Do you really think ...?"

"Of course I think. Nat's best friend ... a staunch friend to you and Mary ... a cool head and a kind heart. Of course he must learn that he was victimized by the Berkeley faction as you and I were. Court is neither here nor there, but he must have an explanation for why he did not hear from you, and he will long to see you, I am sure. Can you doubt it?"

"Not when you put it that way." Lyn rose, weary but buoyed by hope. "Shall we discuss it again over breakfast? If you still think it best you can send a note in the morning and, why my goodness, we may see John Grey shortly."

The Squire rose and kissed Lyn soundly on the forehead. "What a day it has been. I shan't forget it soon. Sleep well, child, and tomorrow we'll send for Grey. Good gracious me, I forgot: tomorrow is Christmas. Indeed, midnight has struck, so it is already Christmas day! We'll walk to church after breakfast and I'll show you the tulip poplar. It doesn't look like much now, but come spring I have great hopes."

Neither love nor money could persuade a soul to leave Suffolk for London on Christmas day, but early on the twenty-sixth of December Jemmy mounted the Squire's riding horse at dawn and promised to be in London by noon of the twenty-eighth or die trying. Lyn told herself that John was sure to be unavailable … perhaps he had gone out of town for the holidays … perhaps Mister Brooke, the one with the marriageable daughter, had a country house and John was there enjoying the Christmas spirit and basking in the attention of the lively and attractive girl. Angry with herself, she shook her head briskly and busied herself with Mary's clothes. She was brushing one of the little girl's frocks when Squire Thomas knocked.

"Are you busy, my dear?"

"Not really. I'm just brushing our clothes and tidying Bess' room. Is there something I can do for you?"

"I wanted to know what you would like me to do about Hazelwood now that Jemmy's gone to London. There are the fires to keep up and Lark to feed and what if there is some food which is going bad? Shall I send Preston and my housekeeper to look after things?"

"Oh no, Father! Why, who would take care of you? May I make a suggestion? It is a beautiful day, and the snow is melting fast. Would you let me ride Fancy to Hazelwood and do the housekeeping myself? There is nothing I would love more."

"Why, it is an excellent idea. I know you are anxious to see your home, and why not today? It won't make you too sad, will it?"

"I'm sure I'll shed some tears, but I must go there sooner or later, and perhaps it would be best to be there alone at first and get used to the place without Nat."

"You are right, I am sure. Will you take Mary?"

"If you could keep her here today I think it would be best."

"My dear, Mary is welcome to stay at Friston Hall forever. Nothing would make me happier than to have the child at my side while you do what you have to do. Don't stay too long, though ... I would not like to have you riding in the dark."

"Don't worry, Father. I'll leave this minute and return while the sun is still shining. Thank you for this ... and for everything."

Hazelwood's bricks glowed as rosy as those of Friston Hall against the snowy backdrop and Lyn's heart beat quickly as she studied Jemmy's tower and her beloved cottage. The garden was buried in snow, but she noted that it was now enclosed with a strong new fence and, to the right, the old stable had been completely torn down and rebuilt handsomely. Squire Thomas had written her of these improvements and both of them exceeded her expectations. Hazelwood was no longer a humble farm, but as neat a little country house as any in Suffolk.

Lyn urged Fancy towards the stable and the mare walked eagerly forward as though she were familiar with the place. She nickered as she walked and another horse called from inside. Lyn smiled. It must be Lark, the fat little pony who now was getting to be great age. Dismounting, Lyn led Fancy through an archway into a corridor bordered by stalls on both sides. There, in a loose box, stood Lark, his thick winter coat making him appear even stouter than he really was. As Lyn approached he became quite agitated and she knew that he recognized her. Her tears fell fast as she knelt in the straw and held him close. All her memories of Benhall Lodge flooded back and overwhelmed her and she was glad that she had made this journey alone.

Lyn spent a quiet morning exploring every corner of Hazelwood. Jemmy had kept the place up well, but his housekeeping was rough, and she took pleasure in airing the linen, turning the mattresses and dusting the furniture until her house shone the way it used to when she was mistress here. When everything was as she liked it she settled at Nat's desk and turned to her hardest task. As she explored each drawer and pigeonhole it was as she feared: she found some of his writings and the tears came again. Here was a note that he had paid "too much" for some shirts which had just come from London. Here was a scribble "to apologize to Lyn for overstaying my time in the city." Here were some figures which were angrily crossed out ... Lyn knew they must show his losses to Bokenham. When she had gathered every scrap, she crossed the room to the fireplace and committed them to the flames. Nat's desk was now hers and it would reflect her new life, one of frugality, prudence and planning, one centered on Mary's wellbeing. As the ashes rose up the chimney, Lyn said good-bye to Nat once more and claimed Hazelwood for herself.

Jemmy returned on the thirtieth of December with the news that John Grey followed close on his heels. He had found John at Brooke's establishment where he lodged in rooms above the law offices. Mister Brooke was in the country, but John was hard at work; business did not stop in London, even for Christmas. As soon as he read the Squire's note, Jemmy related, Mister John's face turned pale and then turned red and he had never seen him so flustered. He told Jemmy to tell the Squire that he couldn't get away until the thirtieth, that he would stay that night with his mother, and, God willing he would be at Friston Hall on the afternoon of the last day of the month.

Squire Thomas' blue eyes danced when he heard the news, but Lyn forced herself to wear a wooden face and she knew her father-in-law was puzzled by her coldness. As John was not expected until tea time on the thirty-first, Lyn decided to spend that morning at Hazelwood hanging some new curtains and arranging Mary's clothes in the chamber which would be her bedroom. Lyn and Mary planned to move to the farm permanently on the first of January, and she wanted everything to be perfect for the child.

Jemmy saddled Fancy for her and helped her mount. "Are you sure you don't need me there today, Mistress Lyn?" he asked for the tenth time.

"Quite sure, Jemmy. You can drive the cart tomorrow, with us and the rest of our things, and take up residence in your tower again, but today I will be fine by myself. Now hand me up that basket with the curtains and clothes … I'll balance it here, in front of me, and be as right as rain. Tell the Squire that I'll be back well before Mister John is expected. Good-bye, now."

The sun shone bright and there was still enough snow on the ground to make it a perfect winter day. Lyn settled Fancy in her stall, gave Lark a kiss and entered Hazelwood. The cottage glowed and she smiled as she looked about her. She thought of Benhall Lodge, of Curles Neck … of all her homes, this was the one which she felt was truly hers. She carried the basket upstairs and entered Mary's room, which looked east toward the sea. The white and yellow room was perfectly simple and, Lyn thought, perfect for a child. Within minutes she had placed her daughter's clothes in the presses. Now everything was as it should be; she could not wait to see her daughter's face when she learned that the room would be hers.

Lyn crossed the landing to her own bedchamber to hang the curtains. This much larger room spanned the cottage and looked both east and west. Climbing on a stool, she began with the east casements, admiring how the white linen panels, edged in blue, fell in neat folds. The Squire's housekeeper had done an admirable job … the whole room would look different, much lighter and brighter and different from when Nat …. She would not think of him. She crossed to the west casements and looked at the shadows of the trees to see what o'clock it was. The shadows were small … it was later than she thought …it must be noon. As she climbed on the stool a movement caught her eye. There, at the garden gate, stood a high-bred black horse. And there, dismounting, was a man whom she would have known among a million. The horse was Prince and the man was John Grey. Lyn's heart stopped. John was well before his time … but no matter, he was here.

She became so weak that the curtains fell from her hands to the floor and she had to sit on the stool and lean her head between her knees to bring the blood back, lest she faint. She heard a knock on the door and could not summon the strength to answer it.

A moment later she heard footsteps on the staircase.

"Lyn? Lyn? Where are you? The Squire said you were here, doing something with curtains."

John Grey stood in the doorway and looked at the small figure which crouched below the western casement, its face pale and its eyes huge.

"Lyn! Are you alright? You look ill."

She was speechless. John came to her and took her by the shoulders and walked her to the bed. He lifted her up as one would a child and settled her against the bolster.

"Did you fall ill?" he asked softly. "Shall I get you some water ... or some wine?"

Still speechless, Lyn nodded. John soon returned with a tray, a bottle of claret, and two glasses. Wordlessly, he put the tray on the bedside table, poured her a glass of wine, and made her drink it all. Her color came back and she smiled weakly. He refilled her glass and poured one for himself.

"My God, you gave me a scare. Now you look well enough, but when I first saw you I thought I was seeing a ghost. Are you really alright?"

"I am now, John," Lyn said, her tone almost normal. "It was the shock of seeing you. It was so quiet here, and I was lost in the past ...."

A look of disappointment crossed John's face. "Of course, you were thinking of Nat. How selfish of me."

Lyn sat up straight, her voice strong and clear. "No, I was not thinking of Nat. I was thinking of John Grey and how he broke his solemn vow and failed to write me a single letter these past eight months."

Now John smiled. "Truly, Lyn? But the Squire has told me your theory about Green Spring and the letters, so you know that I did not break my vow at all."

Lyn smiled with her whole being. "I know you did not, John. Nor did I. I wrote you ten wonderful letters. I suppose they are ashes now ... or perhaps Lady Frances still reads them and laughs over them."

"I was more faithful than you. I wrote you twelve fat missives which, I fear, will never enlighten posterity. Let Ludwell and his lady laugh ... I care not, as long as you are well and safe and ... and here in Suffolk."

"So you think I am right? All things considered, it explains everything."

"I know you are right. It was Green Spring's last drop of venom. But they can't hurt us now, can they?"

"No. No, they cannot. It is really very simple, isn't it?"

"I hope it is simple. Did I read you right? That night at Fairview ... calling me to Swann's Point ... emptying your heart of Nat's memory in the golden forest ... the afternoon in Captain Jervis' parlor ... your embrace when the *Rose* was about to sail. Tell me I have not been a fool."

"You are perhaps a fool to love me, but I know you do, John ... as I love you."

"Dear heart!"

The blue and white curtains remained on the floor as the afternoon wore on and they were soon joined by the bedcover, by Lyn's gown and petticoats and by John's hose, trousers, vest and coat. Prince and Fancy and Lark grew restive and called for their luncheon and called for their tea, but it was dusk before they were attended to and quite dark before the black and the chestnut retraced the path to Friston Hall. It was as well that the horses knew the way, for the riders were paying no attention to anything but each other.

Squire Thomas wished that Lyn had chosen any color but blue for her wedding, but he did not tell her so. It was not her ice-blue gown ... that was lovely and appropriate, for of course she could not wear white again. It was not Mary's dark-blue frock ... that set off her golden eyes and rich dark hair in a way which twisted his heart. It was not Bess' blue ribbons. As maid-of-honor his daughter must look her best and though the world thought her homely, to the Squire she always looked blooming and the ribbons were most becoming. No, it was his garden. After the crocuses bloomed in March and the daffodils in April and the tulips in May his June flower beds were normally a riot of pinks and reds. Had not his illustrious ancestor named pinks, roses and cherry-trees in fruit as most appropriate for the sweet month? How could he create a blue garden in June?

Lyn told him not to worry as the ceremony would be at Friston St. Mary's and by the time the guests came to the reception at Friston Hall they would not know one color from another. Still, it was a care. But it was his only care. The match itself was clearly made in heaven. Wasn't he himself responsible for it? Had he not sent John on to Hazelwood on that cold day last December when the fellow arrived so early, so haggard, so eager? It was clear which way the wind blew. The couple hadn't returned to Friston Hall until it was pitch black, but when they did come back, the bargain had been sealed. He was surprised that they wanted to wait until June to marry, but John had to keep his nose to the grindstone for that fellow Brooke and it had taken them a while to find a proper leasehold in London, one which was close enough for Grey to walk to his office. Well, they had found one. Now they would have a town house and a country house and who could ask for more? All in all it was a good thing that they had waited. After all, June was the month for weddings. Lyn had said "no" to May ... May was for Mary, who had turned three on the third of the month; and for Nat, for May was the month in which the girl had married his poor boy, right here in the parlor, where he was sitting, wool-gathering.

499

The Squire rose and stretched. After all the years of worry he thought he could see peace ahead. Bess and Henry would be coming today for tomorrow's ceremony. Bess was still childless, but sometimes babies did not come right away ... they could wait. John Duke and his wife Dorothy were going to attend. Lyn had seen her brother several times now, though she still refused to visit Benhall Lodge. The little Duke boy was almost Mary's age and the two of them played quite nicely together, though Mary seemed to have the whip-hand. If young Duke and Lyn could mend some fences, then, with Alathea gone, the dark shadow which Sir Edward had cast would finally disappear and Benhall and Friston could live in harmony. And that fellow Wiseman ... he was up in Nat's room reading the boy's diary of his grand tour, that wonderful trip he had made with John Ray so long ago. Wiseman had a brain ... couldn't sit still for a single minute ... always had to have something to do. He was a good friend to John, and well-connected. He had already sent Brooke and Grey a few clients and doubtless more would follow. John ... his star shone bright. If the Squire lived long enough he would see Grey on the woolsack and Lyn could write "Lady" before her name.

Speaking of John and Lyn, there they were, coming up the lime alley. They must have gone down to the river for a walk. Ah, here they were ... they had found him in the parlor.

"Good afternoon, sir," said John. "Are we all ready?"

"Not a thing to be done now, John, until Lyn puts on that pretty dress tomorrow and the church bells ring. I like a morning wedding. Elizabeth and I were married at ten o'clock and we had our wedding breakfast here, just like you."

Lyn kissed the Squire's cheek. "Thank you for all you have done. Left to ourselves I think we would have settled for something much simpler."

"Why, it's still a small affair, Lyn. It could have been much grander if you had wished it. And Rose and Rosie have done half the work ... nay, more. I have hardly had to lift a finger."

"Well then, we'll leave you to rest. John and I are going to visit the tulip poplar. He's brought some letters from London and I would like to read them."

The Virginia tree made a brave showing on the hillside, its tender leaves fluttering in the wind and its cup-like flowers glowing orange and green against the bright sky. John and Lyn settled beneath it and Lyn stroked the silver trunk.

"It's doing well, isn't it, love? One day it will be as mighty as the one which stands guard over Nat."

"To be truthful, I am somewhat surprised, but it looks to have taken hold and be thriving." He kissed Lyn's cheek. "Everything does well at Friston."

"Now then, where are the letters from Virginia? I am anxious to know about our friends."

"Let's start with Sarah's."

"She must have written a dozen pages. Will you give me a summary?"

"Gladly. She herself continues well ... spends half the year in Westmoreland with Billy and half the year on the Blackwater with Johnny. She has decided not to rebuild in Jamestown ... the memories are too bitter. Sarah Swann has given her another grandchild, so she spends a good deal of time at Swann's Point.

"You will be interested in the next item. When she last visited her daughter William Byrd was there, deep in discussions with Herbert Jeffries. He had sailed down with Mary and guess who else was with them?"

"It must have been Jake."

"Right you are, little witch. Jake it was ... almost a man now, and William Byrd's right hand."

"Nat would be so happy. He loved the boy, as who could not?"

The pair paused for a moment, lost in thought, and then John returned to Sarah Drummond's letter and laughed wryly. "You will be delighted to know that Lady Frances Culpeper Stephens Berkeley is going to take a third husband, and his name is Philip Ludwell."

"Well, at least he'll make an honest woman of her."

"And I will make an honest woman of you ... tomorrow."

Lyn laughed. "Go on."

John paused, uncertain how to proceed. "Colonel Bacon and his lady are also well and King's Creek is almost restored."

"Are you worried that I will be upset, John. Why should I be? The Bacons were kind to us and I understand why they followed the Governor's cause ... I wish them well."

John breathed more easily. "I am glad to hear it, sweet. Here's an item of interest. Remember Sir Henry Chicheley, who spent so long in jail at Green Spring?"

"Of course. I never met him, but Nat told me all about him."

"He's as spry as ever and back on the Council. I'm glad of it ... there was something about the old knight that I admired. That's most of what Sarah had to say ... her letters are like lists, wordy but somewhat shallow."

"That looks like Tom's writing on the blue envelope."

" 'Tom' is it? Are you trying to make me jealous? When did 'Captain Jervis' become 'Tom'?"

Lyn stroked John's cheek. "How you ever could have been jealous of Tom is beyond me. Do you really think he is my type? He became 'Tom' as soon as I realized that the kind fellow was really going to write me monthly, with a full news bulletin of all the goings-on in Kecoughtan. He has not missed a month. It appears that Lady Frances and her new husband have other things to think about than absconding with our mail."

"He is a good fellow, at heart. I really started to admire him when I heard that he had brought Abraham and Hannah to Fairview. This letter covers the same ground that Sarah did, but it does add a personal note. You remember that he was engaged to the Turney woman? Well, he has broken off the engagement. I don't think he'll ever find a woman to match you, Lyn."

Lyn blushed. "He'll find somebody. Tom Jervis was not made for the single life. Well, if he writes nothing new, I'll read his letter later. Now what's the third one which you have been so mysterious about?"

John stretched luxuriously and looked up at the sky through the lace of the tulip poplar's leaves. "I won't say a word about this one. You need to read it yourself."

Lyn took the creamy paper and looked at the inscription. It was in a bold, flowing hand which she did not recognize. Curious, she unfolded it and let her eye drop to the signature.

"John!" she cried. "It's from Lawrence! Dicken Lawrence is alive! Oh, what wonderful news."

John sat up and hugged her close. "I knew you would be thrilled. Go ahead, read it. It is very short."

"Why he is in Barbados ... overseer of a sugar plantation ... keeping well ... has a lovely big house, airy, with large porches against the heat. Oh, John! He brought Folly all the way to Barbados ... says he could not bring himself to sell the horse. Oh, Nat would be so glad! And what's this ... he's living with ... can it be? Clarissa?"

"Yes, love, Lawrence rode south to Carolina, not north as I thought. And Clarissa joined him there. They had it all planned. They took ship together to Barbados and have lived as man and wife since. Of course he has suffered for it, but you know Dicken Lawrence. What the world thinks matters not to him ... he follows his own conscience."

"Does he send an address? Yes. Then we can write to him, and to her. John, this is the best surprise."

Lyn lay back on the grass and sought John's hand. Then, turning to one another, they embraced in the shade of Nat's tree.

"Dear heart," said John, and held her to his breast.

"Dear heart," responded Lyn. "Come, let us walk on to Friston St. Mary's and see the place where, tomorrow, we shall be joined before God."

THE END

AUTHOR'S NOTE

When, in the year 2000, circumstances brought me to Virginia from the West Coast, I decided to study the history of my new home beginning with Elizabeth I's original land grant, moving forward in time as the inclination struck me. Now, five years later, I am still stuck in the 17th Century. The reason? The drama and human interest of that turbulent period cast a fatal spell. I was, of course, generally familiar with the Pocahontas story and the import of the creation of the House of Burgesses in our nation's legal history, but I had never heard of Bacon's Rebellion and did not know that such people as Nathaniel Bacon and Sir William Berkeley had ever cast their shadows on Virginia soil.

It was an act of considerable hubris to think that I could add anything to the substantial body of writing about Bacon's Rebellion, but, as Nat Bacon would say, the charm was wound up and I had no choice. If *The Fall Line* introduces a few new readers to early Colonial Virginia I will be most gratified.

It goes without saying that I owe a huge debt to many scholars and institutions. The following is a very brief list.

My thanks to the Arlington Public Library; I have spent many happy hours in its Virginia Room. The Library of Congress and the University of Virginia libraries, including their rare book rooms, have provided treasures.

These historians, among others, have made this book possible: Charles Andrews, Robert Beverley, Warren Billings, Philip Bruce, Jane Carson, Wesley Craven, Richard Morton, Michael Oberg, Helen Rountree, Robert Ryece, Mary Stanard, Wilcomb Washburn, Stephen Webb, Thomas Wertenbaker and Louis B. Wright.

Three contemporary (or near-contemporary) sources were inspirational: the famous Burwell manuscript with its wicked humor; the stately report of the Royal Commissioners, sent by Charles II to investigate the Rebellion; and the recollections of Thomas Mathew, a planter who was intimately involved in the turmoil of 1676/1677. All of these accounts can be found in Charles Andrews' *Narratives of the Insurrections, 1676-1690*.

I have been at all the sites mentioned in *The Fall Line* and, in this regard, must commend the reader to visit Jamestown, where the founding of our nation comes alive; and Colonial Williamsburg, where the imaginative tourist can see Middle Plantation behind the veil of the 18th Century town.

A note about the calendar. In the 17th Century England used the Julian calendar in which the new year began on March 25th. Accordingly, events which, in modern terms, would be dated January, 1677 were then dated January 1676/77. In *The Fall Line* I have used the modern system.

Finally, I must interject a personal note. Three people know that I owe them an incalculable debt: my mother, part of whom lives in Lyn Duke; my husband, like John Grey, truly "the wind beneath my wings;" and my son, who will always be to me what little Mary Bacon was to Lyn.

Errol Burland
December, 2005